FLYING THE COOP

BOOKS BY LUCINDA ROY

FICTION

Lady Moses

The Hotel Alleluia

The Freedom Race

Flying the Coop

POETRY

Wailing the Dead to Sleep

The Humming Birds

Fabric

NONFICTION

No Right to Remain Silent: What We've Learned from the Tragedy at Virginia Tech

FLYING THE COOP
LUCINDA ROY

TOR

A TOM DOHERTY ASSOCIATES BOOK
NEW YORK

FLYING THE COOP

Copyright © 2022 Lucinda Roy

All rights reserved.

Maps on pages xi and xii created by Lucinda Roy
Map on page xiii by Jon Lansberg and Lucinda Roy

A Tor Book
Published by Tom Doherty Associates
120 Broadway
New York, NY 10271

www.tor-forge.com

Tor® is a registered trademark of Macmillan Publishing Group, LLC.

The Library of Congress Cataloging-in-Publication Data is available upon request.

ISBN 978-1-250-80982-7 (hardcover)
ISBN 978-1-250-25891-5 (ebook)

Our books may be purchased in bulk for promotional, educational, or business use. Please contact your local bookseller or the Macmillan Corporate and Premium Sales Department at 1-800-221-7945, extension 5442, or by email at MacmillanSpecialMarkets@macmillan.com.

First Edition: 2022

Printed in the United States of America

0 9 8 7 6 5 4 3 2 1

For girls and women everywhere who are enslaved, silenced, or abused and for Larry, Joseph, Paula, and Tamba, who believed in this story

AUTHOR'S NOTE

Flying the Coop is a story about both the endurance of the human spirit and the horrors of slavery.

It is about where we could end up in the near future, and about the stories that have sustained us in the past.

Because the most deep-rooted hope is honed by suffering, and because oppressive systems premised on prejudice demand an honest depiction, this book contains difficult subject matter, including but not limited to violence, abuse, suicide, rape, and lynching.

Please read this survival narrative when you feel ready to enter the challenging world it depicts.

CONTENTS

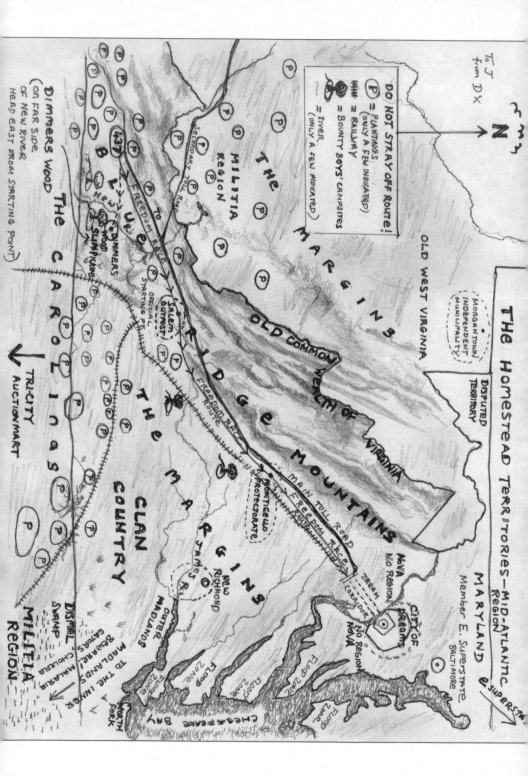

PART ONE
DREAM CITY
BLUES

Wings are what our arms would be
if they were musical instruments

—L.H.J.R.

For Black blooms and it is Purple.
For Purple works off to Brown which is of ten thousand acceptable
    shades.

—Christopher Smart
Jubilate Agno, **fragment B,4**

Out of the corner of her scrunched-up eyes, Afarra sees the tribe of Dimmer-dead clustered around her. She'd assumed the dead would be afraid of heights and that she would be safe up in the nest. Evidently, she was mistaken.

In the nest in the dome of the abandoned flying coop in the city's flood zone, where the stench of mold permeates the dark, ghosts of the worst kind are paying her another visit. The Jim Crow's Nest is a woven basket the size of a big round table, with barely enough room for Afarra, Elly, and Elly's unlike-anything-else-in-the-world, bunched-up Secret Hopefuls. Yet somehow, dozens of Dimmers have planted themselves in the nest where Afarra lies with Ji-ji—her Elly. They've come to rip Afarra apart—bone from bone, flesh from flesh. She's seen *angryangryANGRY!* before, but never like this. Tonight, the tribe of Dimmer-dead want to murder the world.

Only the Dimmers who are freshly dead are recognizable to Afarra as male or female. A few wear tattered clothing with seed symbols over their hearts to designate them as enslaved botanicals from the Homestead Territories. But most of her tormentors are long dead: flaps of rotting flesh dangle from their bones. The freshly dead, the ones who still have eyes, scare her the most. Their fluorescent white irises pulse with rage. Missy Silapu used to say Dimmers' white-ringed pupils could blind you. But so far, even though she's stolen glances at them during this horrifying visitation (and during visitations she's had before as well), Afarra has not been blinded.

More and more Dimmers are lugging their sorrowfulness into the nest. Just in case Missy Silapu was right, Afarra squints at them through half-closed eyelids in hopes that blindness isn't inevitable if Dimmers don't know they're being watched. Once in a while, a Dimmer, clawing its way into the nest, loses its grip and tumbles into the center ring below. Its unearthly shrieks swirl around the flying coop like a swarm of razor blades. Afarra doesn't know if the fall re-kills them or if they simply collect the shatterings and re-form themselves. If they survive, Afarra supposes they must use rage to glue themselves back together cos Dimmer-dead have got a bunch of rage to spare.

Try as she might, Afarra can't figure it out. It should be impossible to squeeze a company this large into a space this small, yet dozens of dead are crammed inside the nest. Then she hears Uncle Dreg's voice (or is it her own?) explaining it to her: "Dimmers don't occupy space the way we do. You cannot reach *out* to touch them. You have to reach *in*. We, the Living, make room for space, but the tribe of Dimmer-dead force space to make room for them."

Afarra hadn't understood this when he'd said it. But tonight she sees it's true. If Dimmers had weight, the nest would detach from its moorings. The whole lot of them would plummet down to the sawdust center ring below. But the dead weigh less than nothing in this world. That is one of their torments: to be without substance in a world that ignores those who don't have any. Yet in spite of this, Afarra feels their weight pulling on her like Sleepybud—a juvi on Planting 437, who crept into her sleep-shed and pulled on her tits with his grabby hands and fire-mouth.

An outcast herself, Afarra knows what it means to be less than nothing, which is why she is tempted to sweep the pitiful tribe into her arms and rock them past grieving, past resentment, past memory itself. But they have returned angrier than ever this time, and she is too scared to reach out. She cowers in the nest instead and pretends to be fast asleep like Elly.

The wizard's voice comes to her again. It is so close and his voice is so deep that she feels her own chest vibrate when he talks: "You cannot reach *out* to touch them. You have to reach *in*." Uncle Dreg's words give her hope. Maybe the old Toteppi wizard has come with them to visit her? Careful not to let them see, Afarra scans the multitude in hopes of finding Uncle Dreg's beautiful old-person face. Even if he looks as bad as he did when she saw him for the last time (his brains spilling down the side of his shot-to-pieces head—*Don't look! Don't look!*), she will love him still.

She searches for her oldest friend without success. It makes sense. The tribe of Dimmer-dead aren't like other ghosts—that's what Toteppi say anyway. They're on a mission to correct a terrible injustice done to them, which explains why the Tribal wizard isn't in their company. Uncle Dreg didn't fret over personal injustice. His only quest was seeking justice for others.

Not wishing to be rude, Afarra tries not to notice the crescent moons of soil embedded in the fingernails of those who still have fingers—proof of their frantic scramble up from the grave. A few (pyred, she suspects) have re-formed themselves from ash, as if no execution, however thorough, can extinguish a Dimmer's burning desire for vengeance.

All at once, Afarra's visitors notice her eyes are open. They zip in closer and extend their arms in undulating supplication. The Dimmers *NEED!NEED!NEED!* and they need it *NOW!*

Experience has taught her the dead are delicate. In the drafty flying coop, the Dimmers move like ebony candle flames. She tries to convince herself that these creatures who occupy the Nearly-There and the In-Between can't really harm her. It doesn't work. Snuggled next to the person she loves most in all the world, Afarra considers waking Elly so she won't be forced to face their fury alone.

—*No!* the spirits tell her, wordlessly. *Do not wake! Just us! No one else! We KILL you if you do it!*

Afarra is accustomed to keeping secrets. No one understands silence-as-survival more than outcasts do. Countless times, the Dead and the Living have demanded she remain silent. Uncle Dreg used to tell her, "Dimmer-dead are not very different from the rest of us. Most of us lose bits of ourselves along the way—a toe lost here, a heart there, a mother, an eye, a tongue, faith, hope, a friend, a mind of our own." The only person Afarra has known who managed to travel through life without losing anything important was Uncle Dreg himself. Apart from his Death Day, of course, when Cropmaster Herring shot half the wizard's skull off. But that was the only exception.

The Dimmers screech at her again. Maybe the shrieks were words once, but they left the alphabet behind a long time ago. What remains is a tornado of bone-shattering suffering. It blasts her in the face. She wants to cry out but her tongue—well-suited to cow- and horse-talkings, bird-word and tree-chat—isn't designed for human or Dimmer speech. Afarra can *thinkthinkthink* but she struggles to *saysaysay*—a bridge too far. Although words are coming more easily than they used to, the distance between thought and utterance is still a chasm.

On Planting 437, the hell they left behind three months ago, Afarra had mastered how to fly away in her head and become *Not Here, Not Now* instead of Cloth-33h/437. But even if a Dimmer decides to plow her here in the nest she can't pull off that magic trick tonight. Can the dead plow a Serverseed in the City of Dreams? *The dead can do anything,* the Dimmers' white eyes tell her.

Afarra forces herself to find refuge. If she closes her eyes and thinks about something else, maybe the Dimmers will vanish like they did before? She thinks of Uncle Dreg again, who knew how to make fear disappear. She pictures his beautiful hair. Like a wiry dandelion too strong to blow away, it crowns his head.

Sometimes, Uncle Dreg's wizardy voice takes root in her mouth and blossoms there, which is very disconcerting and inconvenient, especially when he leaves behind words like *disconcerting* and *inconvenient*, words Afarra would never utter herself. But the Tribal wizard's *usurpation* (his word again, not hers) is nothing like the violations she's endured from others. Uncle Dreg was never about taking, only about giving something back. No male has ever been as kind to her as he was. Every gesture he made, every word he spoke told her how much she mattered.

Missy Ji-Jellybean-Ji-jiSilapu-Elly moans. Afarra's best friend in the world lies under the blackbird quilt, sleeping peacefully. Elly isn't as whole as the wizard yet, but Afarra knows that her beloved Elly is gathering up lost things and grafting them onto her body on her journey back from broken.

And Tiro, the other one of Uncle Dreg's Necessaries? What about him?

Afarra's not sure about Tiro. Often, when she looks at the fly-boy, she sees someone trying to scratch his way out of a cage. Though she loves him like a brother, his *rashness* (another wizard word) alarms her. Unlike Afarra herself— and the Dimmer-dead of course, always on the alert for the next ambush— Tiro hates playing defense. He acts first and thinks second when it should be the other way round. If her speech was more cooperative, Afarra would tell Elly it's very dangerous to love the fly-boy in his present state. He needs more time to gather up the bits of himself he left behind when they escaped from the planting.

Afarra peeks at the Dimmers through her left eye. The rabid dead gyrate around her. One has a sliver of leftover tongue hanging like a worm from its rotting mouth. When the scrap of flesh unbodies itself and darts down to lick her cheek, a maggoty chill burrows into her bones.

She shuts her eyes tight, thinks about how different Dimmers look when she encounters them in her dreams. There, under the cover of sleep, they emerge from the strings of a harp as light-filled spirits. Afarra hadn't known a harp was birthing them till she described her dreams to Elly.

"The instrument you saw sounds like a harp," Elly told her. "Angels play it in paintings, perched up in the clouds. Or could be it's a lyre. Can't remember."

"Angels are not playing a liar. Liars take and smash."

"It's not spelled that way, Afarra. It's a different word."

"They are not playing *lies*!"

"Okay, okay! Keep your hair on."

Afarra had her hair on; she patted her head to check. Elly's laughter, sweet as angel-music.

The Dimmers silent-speak as one: *We cannot stay for long up here in the air! We've slipped out from beneath the underneath. Agony to crawl under a thick blanket of soil and play dead till we rise again!*

From her position on the floor of the nest next to Elly, Afarra does the only thing she can think of to do in response. In spite of the risk, she opens her eyes wide and smiles up at the Dimmers in an effort to let them know she sees their pain. She suspects some of them smile back, though she can't say for sure because many are lipless, some are jawless, and a few have shown up without their heads.

She remembers something else Uncle Dreg told her about Dimmers: "They are in a state of Flux," he said. At the time, she'd assumed Flux was a state like the old Commonwealth of Virginia, Tex-Mex, or the Carolinas, or like one of the many states that make up the Eastern and Western SuperStates. She was mistaken. It was much worse. The state of Flux was a desolate region in the In-Between. A place filled with despair, rage, and a murderous desire for vengeance.

It occurs to Afarra that all the Dimmers she's ever seen have been seeds. It's not their darker skin color that tells her this, or their hair, or lips, or noses, most of which they don't have anymore. It's their desperation, their liberty hunger. She's pretty sure there are others among them, but most will be transplants like her and Elly, with roots stretching back to the Cradle. She wonders whether any fairskins, apart from the ones steaders demonize (Deviants, witches, scientists, and heretics) are among the tribe of the dead. Here in Dream City, where she and Elly have lived for more than three months, the fairskin Districters don't usually treat outcasts like dirt, or single out duskies for torment the way fairskins do in the Territories. Fairskin steaders, on the other hand, would be as dangerous in the afterlife as they are in this one. If steaders joined the Dimmers, they would snatch up all the room in the graves for themselves and make Dimmers' afterlives even more of a living hell.

Afarra nods when her visitors abruptly stop shrieking and ask her if she can help the Dimmer tribe rise for real. She can't understand how they've mistaken her for the Tribal wizard, especially when their rotting faces tell her they know all about her—about the things male steaders and male seeds have left behind for her to deal with, about the beatings Elly's mam gave her, one of which knocked out two of her teeth. Her own mam never beat her. Not once. At least, that's what she remembers, though she was a small seedling when they were snatched and parted from each other. Afarra *missesmissesmisses* her own mam, who hasn't ever visitationed her, which means she may not be dead after all, or, if she is dead, she may not be a Dimmer. Afarra is almost certain her mother isn't breathing anymore cos she hasn't sensed her mam's aliveness in the world for years. If her mam is dead, could be she doesn't visitation her cos she knows her offspring would be tempted to trail after her on her journey back to the grave and lie down beside her. Could be her mam is saving her life by not coming to visit. It's a consolation to Afarra to think of it that way, so she settles on that interpretation.

When she shifts position, Afarra's hand grazes the clunky wooden beads around her neck, which prompts her to figure out why the Dimmers have mistaken her for the famous wizard. Of course! She's wearing Uncle Dreg's necklace of wooden beads, his Seeing Eyes! The painted, wide-open eyes on the beads that enabled the Tribal wizard to see through the Window-of-What's-to-Come must have confused them. She's about to explain that the necklace isn't hers, that it was left by some miracle in her sleep-shed on the planting, when a Dimmer-boy—so much of him still intact she's certain he's male—swooshes himself to the front of the crowd. Apart from the areas of decaying flesh and the rope around his broken neck which makes his head loll onto his rotting shoulder, he looks alive.

The Dimmer-boy tears at something furry in his hands. At first, Afarra thinks the boy's nervousness makes the nest shiver. Then she sees it's not his nerves. It's his rage. His silent accusations pummel her. She clutches at the floor of the nest to steady herself.

—*It's hell down there where seeds rot!* the lynched boy screams, wordlessly. *Save us, Oz!*

—*But I am not knowing how to save,* Afarra doesn't need to say out loud.

—*COWARD! You promised, Angel! With your eyes! At Sylvie Mothertree an' the other live one!*

Solemnly, the Dimmer-boy places the thing in his hands on his head—a pair of furry animule's ears attached to a crown of barbed wire. The furry ears writhe like chunky serpents. The dead boy presses the crown deeper into his skull. Something akin to blood trickles down his forehead and seeps into his eyes, darkening his blaring white irises to black.

The Dimmer-boy's mouth is up against her ear. Was he the one with the raggedy tongue before? She doesn't know. His face is next to hers . . . yet still he hovers there in front of her. How can he be in two places at once? A blast of frigid air infiltrates her skull, gives her an agonizing headache. The other Dimmers start to sway. In spite of the walkway that anchors it to the cage, and the cables that hold it steady, the nest sways with them. The Dimmer-boy holds something in his other hand. A *noose!* He slips it over her head. Afarra wants to cry out but the rope is choking her!

Back and forth the nest swings. Something screams, "*Caw-caw! Weel a-bout an' jump, Jimmy!*"

It's the nest! The nest is shrieking too!

—*COWARD!* the dead boy shrieks without sound. *You promised! With your eyes! At Sylvie Mothertree and the other live one! You promised!*

The nest convulses. She will be thrown out with Elly! They will fall a hundred feet and smash onto the flying coop's center ring below! Afarra wants to die. To rush to the rim of the nest and leap into the dark! The lynch rope stops her. . . . Or is it Uncle Dreg?

With a wizard's certainty, Afarra shouts above the din: "YES! I WILL HELP! I PROMISE!"

The dead hear her vow and gasp. An acreage of air hurricanes around the coop.

Afarra clamps a hand over her mouth. *Too late!* Her six words have set themselves Free!

With the force of a Liberty Train, the words hurtle toward the visitors. Desperate Dimmers jostle each other overboard as they attempt to grab the *YES!* and the *I,* the *WILL,* the *HELP,* the second *I,* and—most of all—the *PROMISE!* But the wizard's words won't be caged. They change into giant butterflies and soak the coop with color! As the butterflies paint the Dimmer tribe with light, Afarra sheds her fear and cries out in wonder.

In the blink of an eye, the nest quiets itself. The tribe melts into the dark.

Her beloved wakes, grabs her gun from under her pillow. "Has the bastard found us?"

"No, not Lotter. Not the steaders neither. Dimmers. In the nest. They come for a visit."

Her beloved puts the gun down and levers herself up as best she can. She rests on her elbow and says wearily, "S'okay, Afarra. I won't let 'em hurt you."

"They are gone now. See? They are thinking I was Someone. That is the reason why they ask me for it."

"For what?"

"For everything, Elly. . . . I promise I will do it."

"Do what?"

"Save 'em. Save 'em all."

"Guess that's one way to get rid of 'em. . . . Go to sleep, Afarra. Only a couple of hours till dawn."

Ji-ji tries to lie down again but her back refuses to cooperate. She groans in frustration, drapes one of her Secret Hopefuls awkwardly over the rim of the nest again, and lies awkwardly on her side. "Don't know why you convinced me to do this. It's nuts sleeping way up here in this wobbly nest. We're not doing it again, that's for sure." Within seconds, she's fast asleep.

Afarra's eyes are wide open; she won't sleep any more tonight. When they discover she's lied, that she's not the great wizard and therefore powerless to help them, the Dimmer-dead will make her pay. But at least they've gone for now. She is alone with her Elly. Her favorite place to be.

Elly isn't the only one living inside a strange new body. Last week, in the mirror in the bathroom she and Elly share—a real toilet with a handle-flush that works on and off (they use a bucket to flush when it doesn't), a genuine shower large enough for two, fed by rain collectors on the roof, and a sink (who cares if it's cracked?)—Afarra saw the wizard's wild hair and old-person eyes staring back at her. Ever since, she's been afraid to look at her reflection.

Coach Mackie will march in soon and shout at them both cos that's what coaches do. How many times has she told them the wonky old Jimmy Crow's Nest is off-limits when she's not there to supervise? Which is why, by the time Coach Mackie arrives for Elly's flying lesson, they'll have climbed down from the nest. She'll find them sitting at the small round table in the kitchen they don't share with anyone else except a few mice, roaches, and rats too clever for the traps they set.

After Elly's lesson, Afarra will tell her about the lying mirror in their bathroom—try to anyway, if she can corral her thoughts into words.

Afarra's heart is beating so fast it makes her chest hurt. It's a certainty. The Dimmer-dead will come back to kill her for lying to them. But at least she didn't have to make the journey back into the grave with them tonight. Tonight, she's sleeping in the nest beside her Elly in the City of Dreams. There's nowhere she would rather be—except perched on Elly's shoulders in the mural Elly drew on the wall of her bedroom just for her. Apart from the wizard's Seeing Eyes, the painting is the best gift she's ever been given. Better than the orange peel from the orange Lucky-Matty gave her. Better than the big red bow Elly kept and put in the forget-me-not box Tiro made for her and Elly painted. She left her treasure box behind on the planting in the rush to escape, but that was not being the end. Elly and Tiro made her a new one. She doesn't have the original orange peel or the red bow, but Elly gave her replicas—the same only newer.

"In the dark, I forget you not, Elly," Afarra whispers, as if her beloved isn't sleeping next to her but is instead a long way away.

Afarra touches the wizard's Seeing Eyes and sees something out of the corner of her eye. The Dimmer-boy? No. Someone else. With a lynch rope in his hand and something small under his arm. Afarra snatches her hand away from the wooden eye beads. She has to be careful. The wizard warned her that seeing too much too soon could make you afraid to go to the Next Place.

Accustomed to contenting yourself with very little is a trick outcasts have to master. Afarra contents herself with the feel of Elly's back—a little sweat, a lot of heat, and the deep, abiding scent of purpleness. She delights in their impossible shimmer. Like joy. No . . . better than joy. Like hope. Better than that as well. Like . . . salvation. (The wizard's word and hers too.)

Afarra buries her head in the gap between her beloved's impossible wings, and searches for a path back to sleep.

1 FIREWORKS

Ji-ji woke to a serious, potentially insurmountable problem. After Afarra had gone to sleep in her own bed in her own room at 9:30 P.M., Ji-ji had lain down for a minute. Exhausted by her flying lesson that morning, when Coach Mackie had pushed her to the limit, she'd fallen into a deep sleep. Afarra must have snuck in while she slept, and now she was snuggled up against her.

Afarra had given many names to the wonders that had blossomed on her Elly's back, including Shimmershines, Secret Hopefuls, Freedom Twins, and Purple Tears. In their retracted position—a position they'd adopted four days ago and refused to budge from—their massive size remained a secret. The ridges created by their intricate root system ran along either side of Ji-ji's spine and arched around her shoulder blades. The two craterlike formations, like eye sockets on a giant's skull, were where her wings, if she could even call them that, nested.

Ji-ji raised her wrist as noiselessly as she could and squinted to make out the mouse's white-gloved hands in the dark. 10:45 P.M.! She'd never make it in time. A quarter mile from their hideout, so as not to be detected by the bodyguards the Friends of Freedom had assigned to protect them, Tiro was waiting in a van behind an old warehouse. Trouble was, when it came to monitoring Ji-ji's movements, the bodyguards were a breeze compared to Afarra, and ever since they'd slept up in the Jim Crow nest a couple of weeks ago, Afarra had been having nightmares. Ji-ji cursed herself for agreeing to Afarra's absurd request. Neither of them were fond of heights, but Afarra's constant pleading had worn her down. Having experienced a terrifying visitation herself when Lua-Dim and Silas, her deadborn, paid her a visit in Father-Man Brine's confessional on the planting, Ji-ji sympathized with Afarra. As the saying went, "Most ghosts only boast but Dimmers always simmer," meaning a Dimmer's thirst for vengeance far exceeded that of ordinary ghosts. Ji-ji still wasn't sure if the visitation by Lua-Dim was a product of her fevered imagination. But she did know that a visitation by the tribe of Dimmer-dead, real or imagined, could put the fear of god into you.

None of this altered the fact that Ji-ji had to get out tonight. She didn't know if her strange new body triggered the yearning she had to look up and see an unobstructed sky, but she did know that her desire to be in the open air was overwhelming. They'd been stuck inside for close to four months. Their first summer in the city was coming to a close and she'd seen nothing. Venturing out into D.C. in the dead of night when she was supposed to be dead herself was beyond reckless. But tonight—for her sake and for Tiro's—it was a risk she *had* to take.

Slowly, she eased herself away from Afarra. The single bed with its lumpy mattress and squeaky frame threatened to betray her. Slowly . . . slowly. . . . She looked behind her. Afarra was still fast asleep. The painted eyes on the wizard's wooden necklace might be permanently open, but they hadn't seen a thing. Slowly, Ji-ji stood up.

"*Elly!*" Afarra cried. "We see you wake!" The "we" referred to Afarra's eyes and the wizard's.

Damn! Ji-ji tried to persuade Afarra to go back to her room. Hopeless. She tried to bribe her with the last square of chocolate from Tiro's latest gift box. That didn't work either.

"You are wearing day clothes," Afarra stated, in a prosecutorial tone. "I think you are being a cheater, a sneaking." Her self-taught language could be confusing, but Ji-ji had no trouble understanding her tonight.

Ji-ji proceeded to make her case. She told Afarra that Tiro was waiting to take her to the Dream Coop so she could see him fly. He was in a van nearby. Knowing how attached Afarra was to her Shimmershines, she said her back was desperate. "They can't stay all cooped up in here, Afarra. Just one night. One night of outside, then I can put up with the inside. Do you understand?"

Afarra relented. "Okay, Elly," she said. "I understand."

"You do? Great! I'll be back before you know—"

"We go together. If not, I rat on you to Bodyguard Large." She meant the large bodyguard Ji-ji had nicknamed Large Bodyguard-at-Large, LBL for short, one of the night-duty bodyguards.

Ji-ji knew Afarra wasn't bluffing. She glanced at her wristwatch again. Almost eleven. "Okay, okay," she said. "But you gotta do exactly what we say."

Taking advantage of the extra pair of hands, Ji-ji asked Afarra to bind her up tight. Her appendages had been known to play up; the last thing she needed was for them to unfurl spontaneously tonight.

Thrilled at the prospect of going outside, Afarra leapt into action. Within two minutes they were ready. In another minute, they were running as quietly as they could, past the desalination plant the city stopped working on years ago, and past waterlogged warehouses. As usual, apart from a few stray cats and one or two street people, who paid them no mind, the flood zone was deserted.

They tore round a corner and there it was, exactly where Tiro had promised. A white van with its headlights off. It purred in readiness. Ji-ji rushed to the van, leapt in, and flung her arms around Tiro's neck. Shocked, she pulled away from the man in the black skullcap.

Marcus, Tiro's flying partner, had puckered up his lips in readiness. When she pulled away, he'd given his usual I-don't-give-a-crap laugh. His mood underwent a tectonic shift, however, when Afarra climbed into the van and plopped herself down in the second row of seats. With an angry jab of his index finger, Marcus killed the engine. In that lazy-river voice of his, tinged with an irritation Ji-ji hadn't heard from him before, he asked what the hell Afarra thought she was doing.

"I am being with Elly," Afarra declared, defiantly.

"Tiro won't like it," Marcus warned. "The deal was I bring *her* to the Dream Coop, not you."

He glared at Afarra in his rearview mirror; she glared right back and poked out her tongue. Normally, Marcus would have shrugged off the insult. Not this time. Tiro's fly partner, who'd often boasted that the only thing he cared about was getting off Planting 437 with a tasty bag of prime weed, lost his temper. Said naïve idiots like the two of them—and Tiro too—went round with blinders on, trusting that the good Lord or a Tribal wizard would intercede to save their sorry asses.

"Listen up, kiddos," he cautioned. "Seeds may call this place the City of Dreams, but D.C.'s a teeter-totterer. It can't be trusted. Too many secessionist sympathizers itching to get their hands on seeds they can export back to the Territories."

In the pause that followed, the best Ji-ji could come up with was "I thought Tiro was coming to pick me up."

"If that fly-boy could drive worth a damn he would have."

"He got his license," Ji-ji asserted.

"So? Licenses are automatically issued to flyers. One of the perks. Don't mean the fly-boy knows how to drive. Dreamfleeters get licenses as easy as we get pus—" The syllable hung in the van like a stone from a slingshot. The turn the conversation had taken seemed to embarrass him even more than it did her. "That shit don't mean a thing," he added. "You know that, Ji-ji, right?"

Marcus glanced in the rearview again and shook his head. Tapping his fingers to his collarbone to indicate the painted eye beads around Afarra's neck, he said, "That freaky wizard necklace'll spook the locals. His Death Day speech is being spouted from here to Kingdom Come. The Reverend Dreamer stepped clean out of his mountain when he heard it."

In her excitement, Afarra nearly stood up. "The Dreamer can *walk*?" she exclaimed.

Marcus couldn't help smiling. His voice softened and he played along. "Course he can walk. Knows Dreg's Death Day speech by heart too. Recites it to the other monuments. Black, White, and Brown, all rising up together. Very kumbaya."

Afarra muttered something Ji-ji didn't catch. She looked real pretty sitting there in the second row of seats, her rich, dark skin glowing, her face filled with joy as she thought about the two dead Black men she trusted. Ji-ji scooted out of the passenger seat and clambered into the second row. She put her arm around Afarra, as if she could protect her from anything the world threw at her. The gesture seemed to touch Marcus, though he was still insistent about the necklace.

"Sorry, Afarra. If you're tagging along, you gotta take that thing off an' leave it in the van."

"The Eyes is *mineminemine!*"

"Never takes 'em off," Ji-ji explained. "Only when she showers so the soap doesn't sting."

A jacket lay on the floor in front of the passenger seat. Marcus grabbed hold of it and flung it behind him into Afarra's lap. "Here. Wear this. An' keep it zipped way up."

Afarra began to argue: "It is too hot for—"

Marcus lost it again: "Think I give a crap? Patrollers are out in force tonight picking up undocumenteds. If they see you with that thing round your neck they'll—"

Afarra pulled a folded paper from her pocket: "I am documented. I have the paper."

"You think a piece of paper'll protect you if a patroller's got a mind to have some fun? Besides, outcasts don't get the same privileges as—" Marcus caught sight of Ji-ji's face. He sighed. "Just take the damn necklace off, or wear the jacket zipped all the way up. Shouldn't be anyone at the Dream Coop when we get there, late as it is, but there's no point risking it. An' zip up your mouth too. Patrollers don't take kindly to weird. If they pull us over you'll get us all lynched."

"They are not lynching people in the Dream," Afarra told him.

"Is that right?" Marcus said, swiveling his head around to face her. "Try telling that to the twelve poor seeds got strung up in Montrose Park last month."

Ji-ji hadn't believed him at first. Zyla had never mentioned it. "You saying they *hung* botanicals? Who?" she asked, not knowing herself if she was referring to the victims or the perpetrators.

"It's *hanged* not *hung* when you're talking about people. Folks always get that shit wrong. . . . Listen to me. This is a Liberty Independent, but it's not nearly as progressive as Atlanta or Austin or Chicago. Free's not Free for ex-botanicals in D.C. Bastards make us pay for it. Zyla clue you in about that? Thought not. Your fairskin fairy godmother sanitizes the menu before she serves it up."

His anger against Zyla Clobershay, Ji-ji's mentor and friend, had come out of nowhere. Ji-ji was reminded of what Lucky Dyce had said about Zyla—how he blamed his father's death on her recklessness. At least Lucky had a legitimate reason to be angry. Ji-ji rose to her teacher's defense.

"What have you got against Zyla? She was nice to everyone at the legacy school."

"Yep, Jellybean, she was. Cute too. Guess I don't believe in fairies . . . or God . . . or mothers, come to think of it. Put the jacket on, Afarra, or I throw you both out an' drive back alone to the Dream Coop to a fly-boy with a broken heart."

Afarra poked out her tongue at Marcus one more time for good measure. Then, with Ji-ji's help, she slipped into the light jacket, at least five sizes too big. It reached past her knees. She had to bunch up the sleeves to see her hands.

Satisfied, Marcus went over the schedule. They'd drive around the Mall once only, then head to the Dream Revival District. "Yeah, I know. You gotta see the Dreamer's statue. We'll pass by the monument. Don't blink else you'll miss him." Not far from the statue was their ultimate destination, the Dream Coop. "Where you kids'll watch me an' Tiro the Pterodactyl fly the Dream."

Marcus pressed the ignition button again; the engine shunted to life. Excited by the novelty of riding in the van, the passengers fell quiet as it shuddered forward. Afarra could count the times she'd ridden in a vehicle on one hand. Ji-ji's vehicular experience was limited too.

They exited the flood zone without incident. As soon as they reached the other side of the river, however, traffic picked up. The steady stream of pedestrians and bicyclists struck them first. Streets were often busy in the late evening when undocumented refugees surfaced to claim a sleeping spot on the Mall, but tonight it looked like the entire city had turned out.

Marcus smacked his hand on the steering wheel, then placed his forehead on his hands. "Oh crap," he groaned, not looking up. "They must've rescheduled the fireworks."

"How come you didn't know that?" Ji-ji asked.

Her question sounded more accusatory than she'd intended, but he didn't take offense.

"The owners censor notifications we get on fleet-issued callers. Don't want their fly-boys out partying." He took out his caller and scrolled through the messages. "Yeah. Here it is. An announcement about the Independence Day celebration. Sent this afternoon to the rest of D.C., but we get it thirty minutes ago. Well that's just great. It's eleven twenty-five now. Fireworks go off at midnight."

Ji-ji remembered what Zyla had told them. After a storm ruined the Independence Day celebration, flooding the Mall and many of the low-lying areas, the mayor had rescheduled the fireworks for last week. He'd been thwarted again when more torrential rain flooded the area.

In a last-ditch effort to escape the hordes of pedestrians heading to the Mall, Marcus headed north, hoping he could bypass the congestion, circle round, and make it to the Dream Revival District. The street he took was blocked off. They turned back only to find the access road jammed with traffic. The van wasn't going anywhere till the fireworks were over.

For Marcus, the plan was simple: wait in the van then head to the Dream Coop soon as the crowd thinned.

Ji-ji pleaded with him to let them get out and walk around the Mall: "We're a stone's throw from the museum. We can walk to the Steps of Abraham too. Stand where the Dreamer stood." With no real hope it would work, Ji-ji made one last plea: "I *gotta* see the Mall, Marcus. Tonight especially. It's like these things on my back can't do what they need to do if we don't go there. I know you're mad at us, but please, I *gotta* see it." She knew it was hopeless. Tiro would have bought into something as crazy-sounding as that, but Marcus, a skeptic, never would.

Afarra didn't go for it either. "No walking!" she asserted. "Very stupid in the dark."

"Out of the mouths of babes," Marcus said, before swiveling around in the driver's seat and looking at Ji-ji in a way she'd never seen him look at anything or anyone before, without irony or irritation, as though he was pondering something that troubled him deeply. His tone was wistful as he said, "Tiro's never been right in the head after he saw those things on your back unfurl. Says they make men believe in God. Makes sense in a world as screwed up as this one they'd have needs too. If we assign each of those things a full vote, it's three votes to two."

"You mean . . . ?" Ji-ji asked, barely daring to believe him.

"Yep. You win. Let's hope those miracles on your back are smarter'n the rest of us. Though I guess that wouldn't be saying much after tonight's fiasco. Stay close. I'm talking to you, Afarra."

"Stupid, *stupid!*" Afarra muttered, furiously. "They are all the time weeping." As proof, she held up the wizard's necklace. Ji-ji stared at the wooden eye beads. Dry as a bone.

Marcus was speaking. Fast. "We head straight there and straight back. It's dark so your—what does she call 'em?"

"I am saying Shimmershines and Secret Hopefuls, Freedom Twins and Purple Tears."

"Very creative," Marcus said, dryly. "Those Shimmershines'll likely see as much as those eye beads of yours, so don't get your hopes up. We're not seeing Lincoln either. Free the slaves my ass."

Ji-ji interrupted: "But he did Free the—"

"Yeah," Marcus replied. "Thing is, a father-man's a father-man. Sooner you realize that the better off you'll be. We steer clear of the west end of the Mall. It's rough down by the pool. We see the outside of the museum, that's it. After our little field trip, it's straight back to the van and on to the Dream Coop. If it's too late, I take you back to the Aerie. Last thing we want is the Friends putting out an APB on you two. Ji-ji, keep your cape on. Afarra, if you take that jacket off I'll stuff you back into it myself. An' don't say a word about Toteppi. They picked some up the other day. No one's seen 'em since. I'll let Tiro know we'll be late." Marcus took up his caller then looked back at Ji-ji. "Can't believe I'm doing this! I'm crazier'n those crazyass eyes she's wearing."

"No you're not," Ji-ji told him. "You're a good person."

"I swear, kid, whatever angle you've got, I still haven't figured out what it is."

Having typed out a message saying they'd be late, Marcus reached into the glove compartment and pulled out a gun. Afarra didn't see him do it but Ji-ji did. She gave him a look that said, "What the hell are you doing?"

"Can't be too careful," Marcus told her, raising his dashiki and stuffing it into his belt. Afarra seemed occupied with the necklace. Marcus lowered his voice and leaned in to Ji-ji. "I hear tell you pack heat yourself. Petrus' gun, right?" She didn't like the way he said that.

"Yeah, I got his gun. I keep it nearby in case the steaders find us. But I don't carry it around with me. Not that I go out . . . much . . ." She forced herself to stop blathering.

"Look," Marcus said, "not all the folks in Dream City are as saintly as I am. Bet Zyla the Fairy Godmother forgot to mention that too. If I'm going down, it won't be without a fight." He handed each of them a face mask. "Keep these contagion masks on at all times. We go incognito."

Afarra, who often found rhymes amusing, burst out laughing. Afarra's laugh didn't let you hold out for long. Ji-ji joined in next, followed by Marcus.

|||||||||||||||

Sometimes a place takes root inside you before you've even seen it. That's the way it was for Ji-ji when she stepped onto the Mall at last and felt D.C.'s contours bind with her own. The oddities on her back stirred in their sockets of bone. Energy rippled out in gentle circles from her spine, as if her back were a body of water and someone had lobbed a stone into its center.

Three things tempered Ji-ji's enthusiasm: the fear she'd be spotted; the knowledge that she'd put Afarra and Marcus in danger by venturing out tonight; and the semiautomatic handgun Marcus had stuffed into the belt of his jeans under his colorful dashiki.

Yet even those concerns, stomach-churning though they were, couldn't smother the excitement Ji-ji felt as she maneuvered through the crowd on the Mall. For the first time since she'd stepped through the walled city's forty-foot gates as one of the winners of the Freedom Race, she was roaming Free. A friend on either side, her torso bound tight so no one who brushed up against her would be alarmed by her mutancy, she made her way toward the one place on the Mall she *had* to see. If anyone had asked her if she could actually hear the voices of the Passengers coming to her from the museum where their stories were enshrined she would have said no. It wasn't a sound exactly. It was more a *sense* that something large was opening up inside her and refusing to close again. An affirmation of Things Lost, a pulsing elegy.

Behind her on her right, Tiro's fly partner remained glued to her back. Every once in a while, he urged her forward. Marcus wasn't the only one eager to get out of there. Whenever Ji-ji paused at one of the stalls or watched an acrobat or mime, Afarra half dragged her away.

The Mall was notoriously dangerous after dark, but tonight the usual residents—the so-called Maulers who slept under stalls, cardboard, sheet metal, or whatever else they could lay their hands on—had been replaced by Districters, who'd come to the Mall to do what Free people did in a Liberty Independent on the Fourth of July—to see the fireworks.

Only it wasn't the Fourth of July. Ji-ji couldn't believe her luck. It was like Independence Day had been postponed twice just for her. They'd be able to walk right up to the museum that paid tribute to the First Seeds and Civil Righters. She looked up ahead and a little to the east. On Capitol Hill, lit up like a birthday cake, lay the most famous white dome in the world. She wanted to see the mayor's pride and joy—the gigantic moat that encircled the Capitol Building. Zyla had told her it was an extravagance the bankrupt city could ill afford, but Ji-ji still wished she could see the moat and walk around in the fountain garden that fronted it. She didn't care that the sweltering humidity made this section of the Mall, lined with porta johns, more pungent than ever; she didn't care that the mud churned up by storms and hardened into stiff waves by a merciless summer sun made walking treacherous. She was roaming around in the city that hadn't slept since Mayor Yardley's Grand Reconstruction had been initiated. As work on the new levees rumbled on in the background, the flood-ravaged city that refused to bend to nature celebrated its faith in its own independence, and the independent spirit of its forebears.

Earlier, when Marcus had handed contagion masks to Ji-ji and Afarra, he'd been adamant that they keep them on. Jellybean Lottermule was meant to be dead and buried, he'd said. *In a way,* Ji-ji thought, *I am.* Ji-ji Silapu bore little resemblance to Father-Man Lotter's Muleseed on Planting 437. Yet staying hidden in the abandoned practice coop and the adjacent three-story building where she and Afarra shared an apartment had been a much harder trial than she'd expected. Christening the apartment the Aerie had been unwise. She hadn't foreseen how often the name would mock her. Her confinement was for her protection, but protection without liberty is a form of torture for someone whose spirit is nourished by trees and grass and an unimpeded sky. What was the point of escaping the Homestead Territories if you wound up caged in an aerie?

A powdered-sugary line reeled her in: a stall where funnel cakes were made to order.

"Uh-uh," Marcus said. "No stopping. We see the museum. It'll be closed so we'll see the doors. Those'll be closed too. That's it."

As he steered her along by her right elbow and Afarra yanked on her left hand with the tenacity of the drowning, Ji-ji clutched a bag to her chest. Inside the small canvas bag with the image of the Capitol dome stamped on the front were her official residency papers, a flashlight, three painkillers in case her back played up, a bottle of water, and a small gift for Tiro.

At that moment, as if to mock her, the churned-up earth sent her flying. If Marcus hadn't caught her she would have fallen flat on her face, brought low by the Mall's undulating sea of crud.

"You are falling," Afarra scolded, stating the obvious once again. "I am telling you the out-and-about is dangerous, Elly. They are saying you will regret." Those beady eyes were getting on Ji-ji's last nerve. Afarra pulled Ji-ji in closer and whispered, "They are saying you are a secret to keep." Ji-ji loved Afarra, but there were times when she was as cheerful as a Doomsday prophet.

Ji-ji pulled away and turned instead to Marcus. She thanked him for saving her.

"Thank me when we've made it outta here," he muttered, as if he doubted it would happen.

His concern fueled Ji-ji's. In the dark, it was hard to read his expression, especially in a contagion mask, something many residents wore after metaflu pandemics wreaked havoc in the city. But his body told her how tense he was.

After a rocky start, Marcus Shadowbrookseed had lived a charmed life. Emmeline Shadowbrook, Planting 437's diviner and the most powerful fairskin female on the planting, had imported Marcus to the 437th when he was eight, after his mother died and he'd been left to fend for himself on the streets of some city. Marcus had never fessed up about which city it was, not even to Tiro. "Only fools look back," he liked to say. "I keep my eyes on the road ahead." The good looks and sandy complexion that had given him advantages on the segregated, viciously hierarchical planting came into play in different ways in the city. Everything about him, from the snazzy way he dressed to the smooth way he spoke, told you he'd hitched his wagon to his own star, which was on a steep upward trajectory. No one was surprised when he was selected to be the planting's flyer rep in the Freedom Race after Tiro was forced to run from the planting. His good fortune could have spoiled him. It hadn't, though it had left him with something Ji-ji couldn't put her finger on. An untouchableness, as if he stayed at a distance from everyone, including himself.

The throng of Districters gathered on the Mall to celebrate the end of tyranny was mostly made up of White residents, but Ji-ji also spotted a fair number of black and brown faces among them. She was relieved. With any luck, the three of them wouldn't attract attention.

They'd approached the National Mall from Seventeenth Street. Moving through the crowd, they passed a fenced-in pit where the Washington Monument once stood. The Civil War Sequel, repeated secessionist incursions, and terrorist attacks hadn't triumphed over Washington, but floodwater had. The obelisk, along with the Jefferson Memorial, had been moved to Founding Fathers Hill, a mile or two away in the Mount Vernon Triangle neighborhood. Soon, when the mayor could find a way to pay for it, Lincoln would follow.

The Dreamer, along with the so-called Mother Lode (monuments to Harriet, Rosa, and Fannie Lou), had been moved to a constructed mound called Fourth Hill in the Dream Revival District. Ji-ji knew exactly where it was on the map in her head. They'd drive by that next. Amazing.

Enchanted by the stalls' bobbing lanterns and makeshift electric lights hooked up to spewing generators, Ji-ji took everything in—the sweet aroma of grilled fish and jerk chicken, the Independence Day flags, the balloons. The stunning variety of food on the Mall made Planting 437's Last Supper of the Spring seem like a modest family picnic. Marcus bought each of them a chocolate ice cream. Still mad at him for agreeing to let Ji-ji walk around, Afarra snatched it from his hand.

"She can be a little bitch when she wants to be," Marcus said.

"She's protective of me, that's all," Ji-ji told him.

Ji-ji looked over at the museum: a crown of upside-down flattened pyramids stacked against a midnight sky. The raucous hectoring of stallkeepers slid off

her. She didn't want to marvel at the live gator on a leash "declawed an' tame as
a puppy," or taste the cicada shishkebabs "tastier'n beef," or the snakes "sweet
as eels" roasted on spits. No way did she want to listen to the bearded steader
on a soapbox preaching about the secessionists' Found Cause. The guns, ropes,
and knives on a stall nearby only made her tired. . . . The thing that called to
her was the white pavilion set up not far from there. Those with lucre to spare
could enter the lit-up tent and dance the night away. She saw the silhouettes of
the dancers flung up against the white canvas.

"See?" Afarra said as she looked over at the large white pavilion where shadows danced. "Dimmer ghosts is everywhere. Following. The Mall adventure
is a bad idea."

Ji-ji squeezed her friend's hand. "It's okay, Afarra," she said. "We're not gonna
stay long."

"We are if you two don't get a move on," Marcus said, propelling them forward.

Ji-ji imprinted the scene on her memory so she could return to it later. Who
knows how long it would be before she'd be outside again? Weeks? Months?
God, she hoped it wasn't that long.

They kept moving forward, closer and closer to the museum. Gamblers
sat at one of dozens of players' booths, betting with ration cards and the fickle
currencies of the Disunited States, District dollars mostly. A few well-dressed
White Districters placed bets with the king of currencies, SuperStates, backed
by central banks in the Eastern and Western SuperStates Alliance.

Ji-ji recalled Tiro's repeated warnings that the city didn't take seedchips, as
if he suspected she kept a stash of the crude wooden chips as cherished souvenirs
of planting life. Tiro stressed how risky it was to offer planting currency to anyone, especially currency from the 437th—what with Uncle Dreg's reputation
on the rise, and the coverage the three of them got as Wild Seed winners when
they'd entered the city. As a fly-boy in the Dreamfleet, he figured he'd be
safe, but Ji-ji and Afarra would be easy prey for secessionist sympathizers. Ji-ji
had assured Tiro that though she and Afarra might look like dumbasses they
were almost as smart as he was. Assured him they knew that planting stores in
the Territories and currency exchanges along Dream Corridor were the only
places you could trade seedchips. Stamped with the planting logo on one side
and the face of the planting cropmaster on the other, the shoddily made seedchips could leave you with a crop of splinters in your fingers. Her father-man's
callously handsome profile would be stamped onto every one of the wooden
"coins" from the 437th now he'd succeeded Herring as cropmaster. Arundale Duke Lotter would despise that type of recognition. He'd want his image
stamped on silver. Or, better still, gold.

"How come no one's betting with rebel dollars?" Ji-ji asked, when she spied another players' booth.

"Rebels dollars're known as *yellers* here," Marcus told her. "Ain't worth crap. Need a bucketful of yellers to place a bet."

Without warning, a volley blasted into the night. All three of them jumped.

A glittering red shower cascaded over the Mall as all eyes turned upward. A waterfall of brilliant white came next. When loudspeakers blasted "The Star-Spangled Banner" in time with the fireworks, Afarra screamed in delight. People oohed and aahed, clapped and shouted.

Marcus urged them to keep making their way through the crowd to the museum. "This is only a prelude," he said. "The real show's about to begin."

Afarra pointed to a tent. "In there!" she cried.

"No stopping," Marcus ordered. "We gotta beat the crowd an' get out before the fireworks are over and the stampede starts. You itching to wind up in God's Furrow?"

"No," Ji-ji muttered. "She's not itching to hear more patronizing rhetorical questions either."

Marcus grunted out a laugh. "You better learn some manners, Lottermule, else you'll rub some steader sympathizer the wrong way an' find yourself shipped back to Lotterboy in a crate."

Ji-ji didn't admit she'd hoped to get a peek of the infamous furrow, see if it was as big as people said. Zyla had told her how the park on the Mall had been bifurcated last year when a tornado had made landfall in the center of the city. The monster carved a deep trough down the center of the park before veering south and shearing off the side of the war-damaged Air and Space Museum. Capriciously, it turned back, only to wimp out three yards from the Capitol Moat. The mayor called it divine intervention. The Washington Monument had been relocated a month before, and nothing in or near the Capitol building had been damaged. Zyla, who detested Mayor Yardley, said the divine should have intervened earlier, before dozens of refugees got killed.

To discourage the homeless from camping on the Mall, the grassy area—already a swampy mess—had not been restored. The mayor's critics swore that a large section of furrow they did opt to fill in immediately after the tornado hit was a mass grave. The gash became known as God's Furrow after a scathing editorial in the *D.C. Independent* when editors claimed it looked as if God Himself had plowed it. Because it separated those on the north side from those on the south, and because circumventing it added miles to your journey, God's Furrow soon took on another nickname: the Great Divide. Tonight, the three of them were on the north side of the furrow, too far away to see it—difficult to see it in the dark anyway. Perversely, thinking about the scar running down the middle of the Mall gave Ji-ji comfort. God's Furrow told her there was a destructive force more powerful in the Disunited States than the one that oppressed botanicals in the Territories. A natural force that father-men and inquisitors, however ruthless they were, could never equal.

The sky lit up again. One firework after another turned the horizon in quick succession from showers of red, to white, to blue. Ji-ji had never seen anything like it. It looked as if the museum were a vase holding a spectacular fireworks bouquet to Freedom.

Ji-ji happened to notice that her left hand was empty. Her left hand was *empty*! She looked around wildly. "Where is she?" she cried over the explosions. "Where's Afarra?"

"She was right here!" Marcus exclaimed. "Right here!"

The two rushed around calling out Afarra's name. *Pop-pop-pop* all around. *Boom, boom, boom!* "Please, God," Ji-ji whispered, "*please* don't snatch her from me!" No one had explained to Afarra what rights that piece of paper gave her. Marcus would have disclosed it earlier, but Ji-ji had stopped him. As a former outcast, Afarra's status was provisional and limited. Her residency could be challenged by any D.C. patroller eager to rid the city of another seed. The Friends were working furiously to get the law overturned, but for now, till the paper Afarra carried was officially ratified (a process that could take years for former outcasts), it was more of a liability than a guarantee. But how do you tell that to someone like Afarra, who'd been through hell as an outcast Serverseed? How do you let her know that outcasts don't perch on the lowest rung of the ladder, they're chained to it?

The rising tide of panic in Ji-ji's chest made it hard for her to breathe. Her friend, her adopted little sister, had disappeared! She tried to remember when they'd relinquished their hold on each other's hands and stopped so abruptly that Marcus trod on her foot.

"What? You spotted her?"

"No. But I think I know where she went. Follow me!"

Ji-ji tore off in the direction of the tent Afarra had pointed to. A lightning-fast runner, she reached it in a few seconds. But before she could push back the flap and step inside, a man shoved himself in front of her. Clean-shaven, he wore a polka-dot bandana. His gun was visible on a holster slung around his hips and secured at his thigh. He carried what looked like an antique revolver. Ji-ji had seen guns like that before. Chances were good it was a convertible. Its owner could slip a mag up inside it to make the conversion. The weapon paid tribute to the old world but massacred like the new one.

Marcus joined them. "Evenin', sir," he said, shifting his voice into a different gear.

"Five Districts or two SuperStates, boy. Per person," the man demanded. He held out his non-shooting hand. Ji-ji's heart fell. Afarra didn't have any money. She couldn't have gotten inside.

Out of options, Ji-ji still had to try. "We're searching for our friend. Can we poke our heads inside? See if she's there?"

The man mimicked her: "'Can we poke our heads inside?' Yeah. I can arrange for you to do some head poking round my crotch if you want. How come you speak like a fuckin fairskin, dusky?"

Marcus eased Ji-ji to the side and stepped forward. Moving slowly so as not to trigger anything, he removed his mask. "She lost her sister is the thing. An' her sister's a bit . . . you know the way some of 'em are, sir. Damaged. Not all there in the head."

The man took a step backward and slapped his thigh as recognition spread across his face.

"*Hey!* You're that rookie flyer! Philosopher Phil, right? I seen you on the billboards! *Damn!*"

"Flying name's Marcus Aurelius. Folks get that wrong."

"Marcus Aurelius, Philosopher Phil, who gives a fuck when you fly the Dream? You an' that partner of yours. That wizard's boy. Got money on you both to take the Most Valuable Partners prize this season. MVP's in the bag. My, but you're cute as a button. Bet those flyer groupies is all over you." The man looked over at Ji-ji: "Ugly ones too, looks like. What you messing around with a dungskin like her for when you got fairskin fillies chomping at the bit for some fly-boy action?"

Marcus chortled. The sound was hollow and full of revulsion, but the man didn't notice. "Ain't that the truth, man," Marcus said. "So can we take a peek inside? I got five Districts for each of us." Marcus attempted to hand him the cash but the man held up his hands like it was a holdup.

"Kipper Cantle's not about to jinx himself by taking lucre from his golden goose! Bad karma. Swore to the missus soon as I saw you two fly in that Freedom Race battle with that mountain of a Tribal—that Tree Laugh fella—I swore you'd take the title. Go on in an' take a look, Phil. On the house. Stay long as you want. Tent was packed 'fore all this fireworks crap started." Kipper looked up at the fireworks. "Yardley's gone overboard—sending our hard-earned taxes up in smoke. Won't be no one else stopping by till this commotion's done." He leaned in and grasped Marcus' forearm. "Trust me, this one's a doozy. Fully functioning too. If you want, I can activate his functions for a small fee. I tell you, boy, a horse ain't got nothin on—"

"Thanks, man," Marcus said. "I'll let you know."

Just then, another staller called out to Kipper to get his ass over there and share a single malt on Independence Day. "It's not Independence Day, you old fool!" Kipper shouted back, but he set out for the shot anyway. "Take all the time you want," he sang over his shoulder as he picked his way over the crud to join his neighbor. "Best rookies I've ever seen. My money's on you, boy!"

Marcus and Ji-ji stepped inside. The tent wasn't very large but it was very dark. Kipper had dotted a few smoky kerosene lamps around. The place stank. At first, Ji-ji thought the tent was empty except for a tall cylindrical cage in the center. Then she spotted a figure swamped by a huge jacket. Afarra rested her forehead against the bars of a cage. Brimming with relief, Ji-ji would have called out, but Marcus put a hand on her arm and a finger to his lips. Ji-ji soon understood why.

Afarra was talking to the occupant of the cage. Most of her words were incomprehensible—a strange, Afarra-type mix of English and other languages. Ji-ji didn't speak Totepp—neither did Afarra, as far as she knew—but she recognized a word or two from her mother's tongue. She heard a few clicks and deep-throated clucks too. But it wasn't the language that took them aback, it was something else. The hulking shadow on the stool in the center of the cage was riveted by what Afarra was saying.

"What is that thing?" Marcus whispered.

It was the only prompt Ji-ji needed. She rushed up to Afarra and pulled her away from the cage. "Afarra! It's not safe!" Ji-ji flung her arms around her and hung on. "Why did you run off like that? I can't lose another sister! Please don't ever do that again. Scared us half to death!"

Marcus came up then. "How'd you get in here anyway? You buy a ticket?"

"No. The Eyes they hear him calling. I come in by the underneath. Under the flap."

"Are you insane?" Marcus said. "Kipper out there wouldn't think twice about handing you off to patrollers! Or pairing you up with this one for jollies. What is that thing anyway?"

Ji-ji looked into the cage. "Is that . . . Oh my god! Afarra, is that Drol?"

"No, Elly!" Afarra cried. "You are being very stupid tonight. This is another one. So I am the one telling him about Drol. I am saying he is not alone. He is very interested. See?"

It was hard to see much of anything when the shadow was sitting in shadow, but it seemed to Ji-ji that the extremely large, extremely furry figure on the stool bore an uncanny resemblance to the poor mutant they'd first run into in the Doom Dell on Uncle Dreg's Death Day.

"Drol is with Man Cryday in Memoria near Dimmers Wood," Afarra reminded her. "He is not being here with us cos he is there with her."

"Cryday's ant, you mean?" Marcus said. "That ape mutant Tiro told me about?"

Afarra was furious. "Drol is not a ape mutant! He is a *man*!"

"Keep your voice down!" Marcus said. "Sure as hell looks like an ant to me. How tall is it anyway? *Whoa!*"

The cage's occupant had stood up. His head hit the top of the cage and the rusty contraption shuddered. At close to eight feet, the prisoner towered over the six-four fly-boy.

"He is very tall," Afarra said, as if her friends were blind. "He is wanted to be Free. Like us. I am telling Muckmock we Free him in a flash tonight. With your gun you do it."

Of course she saw his gun, Ji-ji said to herself. *Since when has Afarra missed anything important?*

"You're telling him *what*?" Marcus said, incredulously.

Ji-ji attempted to reason with her: "We can't Free him, Afarra. I wish we could, I really do. But we can't. He'll get killed if we try it. People are scared of big. Scared of mutants too."

Afarra made a passionate plea: "No cages in the Dream! They are saying to be Free. All of us can live Free together like Uncle Dreg promised for the Rising. The Eyes are saying it to me. I promise already! I tell him you are like him. I swear on your wings to do it!"

"Okay, that's it," Marcus said. He looked back at the entrance. "All we need is for her to say some stupid shit like that in public an' they'll string us up. You're coming with me, kid. Now."

As he moved to grab her, the captive's clawed, hairy arm shot out so fast that Marcus, in spite of his flyer's reflexes, barely dodged injury.

Marcus swore, picked Afarra up, and slung her over his shoulder. He grabbed Ji-ji's hand and pulled her from the tent. Behind them, Ji-ji heard sobs and howls coming from the cage. The sound of suffering, as tenacious as her own shadow, clung to her back and refused to let go.

2 INSIDE THE DREAM INSIDE THE DREAM

Tiro the Pterodactyl sat on his favorite Rosa Parks Perch. From this particular ledge midway up the enormous cage, he had a bird's-eye view of the Dream Coop. The arena lights were on night mode, which meant that the spectator sections where some thirty thousand fans cheered on the Dreamfleet flyer-battlers were mostly in shadow. Coopmaster Nelson kept the lights on in the flying cage in case flyers wanted to practice late at night. Even gave them limited access to the outer control booth so they could activate the high-tech safety harnesses and other equipment.

As a former seed—a Serverseed outcast at that—Amadeus Nelson knew how tough it was to make the transition from seed to Freeman. The plantings were locked cages and all the seeds knew exactly where the bars were. Here in D.C., it was like one day you're walking along happy as Zip-A-Dee-Doo-Dah and then you run into some bastard who's mad as hell the city didn't team up with the Territories, mad as hell to see you strutting around in the Dream Free as a bird, your hair all uppity, your face intact. And then it comes flooding back—what it used to be like on the planting where your family's still held, the avalanche of insults and lashings. The insidious stuff they use to humiliate you too—the Color Wheel, the Great Ladder, Crow Man. . . . Those things get lodged inside a person's head. Got to pry that crap out with a crowbar.

Tiro was grateful to have some extra time before the others arrived. He was way too jumpy. Needed to get a grip. Hadn't expected Marcus to say Afarra was coming too.

Ever since he'd brought that surgeon along to excise the growths on Ji's back, Afarra hadn't trusted him. In a voice that sounded eerily like his uncle's—he still hadn't figured out how she did that—she'd accused him of trying to murder "her Elly." Only he'd been trying to *save* her. He'd tried to explain it, but Afarra had already made up her mind and there was no way he could redeem himself. It was like it was with Ji-ji's mam. Silapu decided early he was bad news. Didn't matter what he did, she never changed her mind.

Afarra's Uncle Dreg impersonation still haunted him. How'd she get her voice all growly and deep like that? Like it was Dreg the Dimmer speaking. Like she was old as the hills, watching you with every beady eye on that necklace. Trouble was, he could see her point. If the surgeon had removed those growths on Ji's back like he'd asked, he and Afarra would never have woken up one day to witness her glorious transformation—her "late-spring metamorphosis," Ji called it. Tiro had to live with the fact that, if he'd gotten his way, he would've ruined everything. It made him second-guess himself. And everyone knew that second-guessing in the fly cage could kill you.

Tiro shifted his position on the Parks Perch, made himself more comfortable, leaned back so he could feel the cold bars of the cage behind him. He hadn't swung over to the perch on a hope-rope this time; he'd taken the conventional route, ascending via the Harriet's Stairs and Jacob's Ladders. He liked to mix things up, keep things fresh and unexpected. It was after midnight on the fake Fourth of July. He'd heard the fireworks, spied a few of them through the coop's gigantic glass dome above the Jimmy Crow Nest. With no one else in the arena, it was like the show was just for him. Now it was over, what he needed was some way to float above it all and not give a damn.

Christ! He was sick of Marcus nagging him, always telling him to open his eyes and smell the roses. Hated those barbs Marcus inserted into his sentences. Fly-boy was lethal when it came to verbalizing. Enjoyed rubbing things in. He didn't need Marcus to remind him he'd made a fool of himself at yesterday morning's practice. Remind him how he'd bragged about a new move then blown it in front of everyone, including Commander Corcoran *and* Coopmaster Nelson. His timing had been off by a mile. He'd flown like a goddam rookie! Granted, he was a rookie, but that wasn't the point. He didn't just want to fly the Dream, he wanted to erase the bars and make the fans, the former seeds most of all, make them believe Freedom was more than a dream.

He'd been desperate to impress Amadeus Nelson—not only cos the coopmaster was a former outcast who'd broken every goddam barrier there was, but for another reason. Something that would sound stupid to anyone but Ji. The coopmaster's first name reminded him of his twin—almost like Amadeus Nelson was the reincarnation of Amadee all grown up. The rainbow top hat with its glitter brim and the bright red tailcoat the coopmaster wore during battles should've looked corny, but on Amadeus Nelson the costume looked *right*. Like he'd always deserved to conduct the most famous fly-coop in the Disunited States, and no one could ever snatch it away from him 'less he decided to let 'em. Amadee knew how to wear his clothes too. Didn't have the fancy shit Nelson had of course. But if Amadee had, say, a neckerchief, he'd wind it round his throat and make it look real fancy. He wore his wide-brimmed hat at an angle too, till Tiro pointed out to him one day that was how their father-man wore his. Tiro still regretted that. He could tell as soon as he said it how much he'd hurt his brother. No one in his right mind wanted to look like Drexler Williams.

Tiro shook his head, tried to clear it. He'd let Williams in again. You couldn't do that. Certain things you had to keep locked shut so you could focus. He looked down into the center of the coop where Amadeus "I'm-a-God" Nelson stood and controlled the action. *Think about him instead,* he told himself. *Think about how much he reminds you of Amadee.* Not that the coopmaster looked anything like his brother. Tiro and Amadee were on the relatively light-skinned, Sand-Tan arc of the steaders' shitty wheel, while Coopmaster Nelson was on one of the outcast arcs, the Coal or Midnight one—a skin tone that could turn you into a Serverseed outcast in the Territories. Coopmaster Nelson proved every day what a load of crap the steaders spouted. Like Jesse Owens in those Olympics they had before World War II, I'm-a-God Nelson blasted a hole in everything the secessionists stood for.

Not for the first time, Tiro wished his skin was as dark as Coopmaster Nelson's, Coach Billy's, or Afarra's—or at least a deep, earthy brown like his uncle Dreg's or Silapu's. Ji's skin tone, even though hers wasn't quite as dark as her mam's or his uncle's, would be okay too. Ji was a lot darker than he was, which made her complexion closer to where he wanted to be. If he was darker, people wouldn't be surprised when he claimed Toteppi blood from the Cradle. His hair was real curly and stand-uppish but not nappy enough for his taste. He loved the feel of nappy and frizzy and wiry. His hair was a tad too soft. Too tamable. It yielded to the pick too easy. Black hair should tell the comb who's boss. As a seedling, he'd sit on his great-uncle's lap and plunge his chubby little fingers into the wizard's hair and love the soft, tangled feel of it. Felt like unsticky cotton candy in his hands. How could anyone not love that to pieces?

Tiro jerked back so hard he banged his head on the bars behind him. It had happened again. He'd felt himself falling. Like in those falling dreams where you tumble off something high and wake up mid-fall. Fly-boys had a name for it: plummet syndrome—PS for short, same initials you use for the added part at the bottom of a note. If it didn't let up, his flying career was over. The sports docs had a bigass name for it he could never remember. Some type of vertigo. To do with the inner ear and balance. Other team docs—the psychiatric contingent—said it was a phobia that therapy and medications could cure. But Tiro, who hadn't told a soul he was suffering from PS, suspected that, like everything else in his life, it was linked to Amadee.

Tiro wished Amadee were here with him to chew things over. The twins knew how the other one was feeling from the expression on each other's faces, by how they walked and held their heads. *Shoulda been me got tractor-pulled, not him,* the little voice in his head told him. He, not Amadee, was the one who always goaded their father-man, half daring Williams to come after him. So Williams lit on the one thing he knew could slice his prideful Muleseed in half.

He took a blade to him like steaders did when they formalized an execution. The scarecrow Crow Man, meant to represent the condemned, was carried in on a litter. To ratify the condemned man's Death Spiral, a father-man would slice the straw man right down the middle, from the top of his straw skull to the balls he didn't have. Tiro felt like that's what Williams did to him that day. Turned him into Crow Man and cleaved him in two.

His mother always told him not to replay that day in his head, to remember Amadee like he was before. But how do you un-see something like that? He hadn't listened to her when she'd begged him not to go back to the field that night, to where Amadee had been hitched to the penal tractor and dragged like a sack of potatoes, pantless—*pantless!*—with his hands tied behind his back so he couldn't protect his face or anything else. Williams obliterated his own good seed to punish the bad seed he hated. Zaini, tearing at her hair, screaming at him. Scared Bromadu and Eeyatho half to death cos his little brothers had never seen her that way before. His mother was scared Williams would catch him out at night without a permission slip and fling him in PenPen. She'd never begged him for anything, but she'd begged that night. And he'd stared at her like he was made of stone. Stared at his great-uncle too, who was speaking in Toteppi and rocking his niece in his arms like she'd rocked her mashed-up son's leftovers earlier that same day. In that moment, Tiro hated the bauble-eyed necklace his great-uncle wore. How could a Toteppi wizard who used the Eyes to see through the Window-of-What's-to-Come fail to foresee the danger Amadee was in?

When Dregulahmo intercepted him on his vengeance quest to kill Williams on that same terrible day, he'd snatched the butchery knife Tiro had in his hand and shoved him to the ground. The old Tribal wizard stood over him and demanded to know if he wanted to scoop the heart out of his mother's chest cos attacking Williams was the best way to go about it. Tiro wanted to tell him he was wrong. But it felt like a grenade had been lodged inside his chest cavity under his Muleseed symbol and over his heart, and all he wanted to do was pull the pin.

So he took off for the flying coop on Stinky Brine's shithole of a homestead, climbed up into the nest, and been ready to fly the hurt out. Been ready to jump. Cos he didn't know how to breathe without Amadee. Cos his brother was the best of the two, the bravest of the two, the funniest of the two, who felt things more than he did and looked at things from all sides and tried to understand why their father-man was a motherfuckin bastard cos that's how good he was. All Amadee did was kiss a boy in a barn. One of Williams' parrot spies saw them and told. Williams must've been gleeful cos he'd found a way to bury his wayward seed so deep underground he'd never be able to climb out. So the evilest person Tiro knew tractor-pulled the best one.

Most days Tiro was grateful Ji-ji stopped him from killing himself; some days he wasn't. She'd told him he'd have to take her with him. He realized then he couldn't expect his mother, the bravest woman he knew, or Silapu either, to gather up their offsprings' broken bodies from the floor of Brine's rusted-out, rat-infested coop. So instead of trying to kill himself, Tiro decided to go back to the field the night of Amadee's murder and search for the parts left behind. Hadn't found much—a fingertip (he wasn't even sure if it belonged to Amadee), a strip of sandy-colored flesh he had to fight off ants to claim that could've come from his brother's arm or his leg or his torso; strips of the shirt his brother had been wearing; and one of his blood-soaked shoes. Which was crazy when you thought about it cos where was the rest of him? Drove him nuts thinking Williams had stashed parts away somewhere so he could gloat over them like a serial killer, till Ji said the rats and buzzards surely got to them first. Another reason why he felt so close to her. Cos she was only thirteen and a half at that time, but she hadn't thrown up or gone all fainty when he'd described how he'd searched for pieces of his brother in the dark. Ji knew he'd feel better if he thought something natural had taken what was left of Amadee and not something as unnatural as Drexler Williams.

That morning of the day it happened, Tiro got this weird feeling things weren't right. He'd been practicing in Brine's rotting fly-coop, mapping out a maneuver he wanted to try with Amadee, who hadn't shown up for practice, which wasn't like him. All of a sudden, he takes off without saying why, while Coach Billy hurls cuss words at his back. He runs faster than he's ever run, then hitches a ride with Silent Pete. Rides the old soldier's wagon hearse (which just appeared out of nowhere like that pumpkin carriage in *Cinderella*) back to Williams' homestead. Tiro still didn't know how he knew he had to get back to Homestead 2, or how he knew where to head when he did. But his uncle always said twins had a special connection that could prevail over distance, and that day it turned out they did.

He came upon his mam by the field they called the cornfield, even though corn hadn't been planted there in years. Williams used it for punishment pulling and other kinds of evil. And there his mother was, in front of the slaughter field, rocking his twin brother's mashed-up body in her arms.

Tiro had seen an image once of a statue. He hadn't found out who made it cos he didn't know how to ask without getting emotional. The statue was marble, looked like, and Mary had Jesus on her lap. A full-grown Jesus, not a baby. And you could tell from the way her head was tilted and the way she held out her hands how ruined she was. That's how his mother looked as she held what was left of Amadee, more damaged than anything he'd ever seen before or hoped to see again.

Williams had taken off by then. Unhitched what was left of the Proclaimed Deviant from the tractor, threw the body to one side (his own seed, his own *son*), and strode off in the direction of his father-house. The bastard was so fuckin dumb he didn't even know he'd just trashed the best thing he'd ever made. Tiro could still see his father-man's iron back way off in the distance—that dark green father-man jacket he wore, his unnaturally square shoulders that made him look like some machine, some robot, like he was all squares and rectangles and triangles instead of flesh and blood. He'd covered his bald head with the floppy-brimmed hat he liked to wear. Always wore it tilted cos he liked the way it made him look. Even from the back you could tell that's what he'd done—set his hat down carefully on his head and tilted it after he'd butchered his own son.

Tiro would have run after him and slit his throat only he didn't have a knife, and he was fifteen (two minutes younger than his twin, as Amadee always reminded him) and scrawny as hell, so he needed a weapon. He went to the dining hall, broke into the kitchen, and grabbed himself the biggest butchery knife he could find. But then his uncle stopped him from killing, and Ji stopped him from dying, and here he was. Flying the Dream on the anniversary of his brother's execution.

He hadn't told Ji why he'd been so keen on her breakout plan after he realized what day it would fall on. Hadn't told her how hard the first and second anniversaries had been there on the planting, how he'd punched a hole in the side of a barn on the first one, and swum into the middle of Blueglass Lake on the second to debate with himself about whether he should return to dry land. Each murder anniversary, he hung on by his fingernails and tried to will himself to bear it. But he'd been grateful when Ji had named it as the day she wanted to visit the Dream, cos Ji kept him steady by making him think he was worth saving. Which sounded pretty pitiful after he said it to himself, so he rethought it. Kept him thinking it was worth seeing what was on the horizon. And she'd been right. Cos here he was in the Dream inside the Dream getting ready to fly his heart out so his best friend could see how hard he was trying to believe in the future.

"You'd like it in here, Amadee," he murmured. Not that he needed to say things out loud, but it had become an anniversary ritual to speak to his dead twin, and it felt like a comfort to utter the words, made it feel like actual conversation. "You'd never think looking at this place the city's pretty much bankrupt. D.C. took on a mountain of debt to build it. We got everything here.

Simple things we had in Stinky Brine's coop on the planting—trapezes, trampolines, King-spins, an' Douglass Pipes. But we also got Biles Trials, Ali Stingers, Baldwin Beams, DuBois Toys (we call em 'Two-Boys' cos the projections
make it look like you're two people—crazy, huh?), an' a bunch of other stuff
too. Crazy stuff." (Why he assumed Amadee had ears but no eyes in the afterlife he couldn't figure out. But when it came to dialoguing with the afterlife,
Tiro had concluded it was better just to do what felt right. "We got an Ellison
Wheel big as a building, largest wheel of its kind. It's got these paddles function
as landing platforms an' springboards. With a touch of a button, Coopmaster
Nelson can expand and contract it, spin it fast, or spin it slow. Can make the
whole goddam wheel invisible, pretty much, if he wants. Uses some techno-
lighting trick the fleet filched from the E.S.S. They say they got technology in
the SuperStates like you wouldn't believe. Makes most things in D.C.—apart
from the Dream Coop of course—look like antiques. Marcus says D.C. owes
so much money to the Eastern SuperState the Dream's more Serverseed than
city-state. Though I guarantee a few Serverseed outcasts would disagree with
that assessment. Anyhow, this place cost more than the forty-foot wall they
built to keep out the undesirables. Insurmountable they call it, the wall. You'd
hate it. Cameras, barbed wire, armed patrollers in towers. . . . Seeds on the
wrong side weeping. Insurmountable would drive you crazy. You'd be joining
Coach Mackie on her soup runs, fussing over the homeless refugees. They call
'em Papers and Maulers round here. But don't worry—I don't call 'em that.
Figure you'd give me a tongue-lashing if I did. If you were here, I swear you'd
blow your whole entire salary on strangers. Hand over your ration cards to anyone who asked. Guess I'd have to hold on to 'em for you cos you couldn't be
trusted to look out for yourself."

Tiro looked down at the center ring again. Amadee may not love parts of
the City of Dreams, but he would've been head over heels for the Dream Coop.
His brother always loved hearing about its history—how the game found its
roots in the yearning of seeds, then incorporated elements from the circus, video
games, ancient colosseums, and fight cages. Coach Billy used to call it a memorial to the struggle for Freedom, one that needed to be respected. Which was
probably why, now Tiro thought about it, there were only a handful of White
flyer-battlers on most pro teams.

The exclusively fairskin team from the Father-City of Armistice tried to
make up for that imbalance. They'd even messed with the names of equipment
in their fly cage, which was why, after that type of disrespect, hardly any teams
from the Liberty Independents would fly in Armistice anymore. This coming
season, the Armistice Yells' schedule consisted almost entirely of away battles.
Tiro liked to think of how pissed off Grand Inquisitor Worthy, right-hand

ass-licker to Lord-Father of Lord-Fathers Sessill Morson, must be. Spend all that money on a high-tech fly-coop to compete with D.C.'s Dream Coop and hardly anyone gets to see it! Amadee would appreciate the irony in that. "So this is what I think, Amadee. I think the whole flyer-battler experience is like one of those multi-tiered, three-dimensional chess games. Only you don't have chess pieces, you use *real* bodies instead of—" He cut himself off. Thinking about it like that made him feel like he was a body part. Made him remember how tore up Amadee was. He shook his head to clear it.

"See that bigass console on the platform down there beside the center ring? They call that the hutch. Only it's not a hutch, it's more of a stage, so go figure. During battles, Coopmaster Amadeus Nelson orchestrates the action like a fuck— Sorry. I know you don't like it when I swear. Orchestrates it like a goddam maestro. In this City of Dreams, you can rise from the bottom rung an' become a star, as long as Marcus hasn't convinced you the whole entire enterprise is crap."

Tiro breathed in. If magic had a smell, it would smell like D.C.'s Dream Coop. Several stories above him sat the coop's Jim Crow, built on a scale that dwarfed other nests he'd seen. "Can fit two dozen grown flyers in there, easy," he said. "More if they breathe in. Coop's full of secrets, but the nest's got the most. Only I'm-a-God Nelson knows 'em all.

"It's risky, but I gotta keep flying. Gotta get Mother an' the boys off the 437th. An' here's the main reason why I come up here. I got something to tell you, something real sweet. The bastard's agreed to a figure in writing, Can't go back on it now, the lawyer says, cos it's in a written contract signed by all parties. Mother an' the boys'll be granted their Freedom, long as I hand over an eye-watering petition price to Drexler Williams, the bastard who murdered you an' agitated for the execution of Uncle Dreg. Bastard's got me over a barrel. Fleet's giving me an advance on my salary. Be indentured to this coop for years after this, but what else can I do? What would you do? I gotta get 'em out, Amadee. He'll kill 'em if I don't. . . .

"Anyhow, there's more good news. A sponsorship's on the horizon. Me an' Marcus been approached by a pharma company wants to feature us in an ad for killers—those over-the-counter pain meds in itsy-bitsy red-white-and-blue packets. The ones you gotta shovel in a dozen at a time to make a dent in a headache. Marcus says we're on the cusp of celebrity."

Tiro smiled to himself. His fly partner had been proven right last week when four White girls ran into the fly-boys in Upper Georgetown and pleaded with them to sign autographs on their arms. Tiro had been scared someone would report them, even though he knew interracial anything was okay in D.C. But still. . . . When the girls held out their pale forearms and giggled as Marcus signed them, it felt like a sting operation. Any minute, a D.C. patroller would show up and lead them off to PenPen, even though penitence penitentiaries only existed in the Territories. Marcus had signed his name with a flourish and let one of the girls—the one with the blond streaks in her hair—kiss him on the cheek. "Don't worry, bro. I didn't sign a thing. Ain't about to get suckered into something I can't get out of. Ben—the Born Freeman who's a Friend of Freedom—says Marcus has slipped into liberty like it was a zoot suit he was born to wear. Yeah, I didn't know what a zoot suit was either, but Ben showed me a picture an' it's Marcus all right. . . ."

Amadee was sitting next to him now on the perch. Felt like it anyway. Not that it was a bona fide Dimmer visitation, but it was the next best thing. Amadee wasn't in pieces either. He was put back together. Not like Frankenstein's monster. Whole. Like he was before the tractor pulling.

"They'll be here soon. Wish you'd seen it, bro. When I woke up and I seen her there by the window all unfurled . . . I swear I thought I'd died an' gone to heaven. She can't do that no more . . . *anymore*. Fuck it—sorry! What's wrong with *no more*? Nothing. Lotter's got this gavel in my head. Brings it down every time I get a word wrong. Funny how a bastard like him takes offense when it comes to grammar an' cussing but couldn't give a damn if he brands or lops or lashes. It's like all the outrage he's got he pours into that one obsession. To hell with the rest. Guess you can't whip or rape a seed ungrammatically, so he was cool about participating in that shit. Hope things ain't as messed up where you are, bro. I really do.

"Thing is, her wings—we still don't know if that's exactly what they are—they've gotten cranky. Won't come out to play when she asks 'em to, she says. She makes a joke of it—you know how she is. But you can tell it gets to her when she can't control 'em. . . . When I saw her that morning after her metamorphosis, I was like swept away by those alleluia wings of hers. They shimmered so bright you needed sunglasses almost! They got these tiny flaps on them caught the sun like mirrors. I seen her make the flaps move in sequence—like wind through a field of—" (*No, not a field—something else. . . .*) "Like the keys on a piano when you swipe your hand across 'em, or the strings on a harp. Looks like she's playing her own body! Only it's getting harder for her to do it. Been weeks since she done that trick. Coach Mackie says she's gotta practice. Doc Riff says it's way too early to write 'em off. But this whole flying business is an iffy proposition. Yeah, I know. Tell me about it. . . . Purple Tears, Afarra calls 'em cos they got that same purple sheen the metal death tags got on Sylvie. Same color as Sylvie's blossoms in the spring. Sounded like a poem when Afarra said it, but now . . . It's like it's made 'em into a mournful thing.

"Know what I did? I chose one of the flaps near the tip of her left wing an' wrote your initials on it. Ji didn't laugh when I asked if I could do it. She's not one to laugh at you if it's important. Don't get me wrong. Didn't do it cos of the purple tear they hung on Sylvie after the tractor pulling. I did it so you'd become something . . . different. Like how Uncle Dreg used to say about translating purple pain into something good, remember? So I wrote 'A.D.' Ji didn't ask how come I chose Dregulahmo instead of Williams cos she knew already. She chose Silapu for her Freedom name. Figured if those things on her back start working, you could fly one day.

"You'd know exactly what to say to make Ji feel better. You were always great at that, bro. I'm lousy. But I thought if I, like, flew for her tonight it would be my way of saying all the shit I can't say out loud. Not the corny, romantic crap—I don't mean that. Don't even know how I feel about that anymore. It's like Williams beat the man outta the boy an' now I can't remember what it feels like to be a man. Deep, huh? Don't expect another nugget like that one. Churning out that beauty was like passing a kidney stone." Tiro knew he was making light of things to hide his embarrassment. He told himself this was Amadee he was talking to. If he couldn't trust his dead twin, who could he trust? He began again.

"Used to be horny all the time but it's died down. . . . Okay, I'll give it to you straight. When I get horny it's going along okay till I remember what you looked like in that field. Everything all tore off. . . . Then—*poof!* Gone. Deflation to the max. Snails are more impressive than what I got down there. . . . Scares me sometimes. I'm way too young for that crap, right? Should be horny as hell all the time. Like Marcus. Man, that boy eats more pussy than a— Sorry. . . . How come you were always strict 'bout not saying shit like that? Oh, Amadee. . . . You shoulda told me, been up front. I woulda stood guard that day. Warned you and Juan. Think I gave a damn who you kissed? Think I bought into that Deviant crap they fed us? You coulda trusted me, bro. I would never betray you."

Tiro noticed his hands were shaking. He shoved them under his butt and sat on them. Nerves. "Like Amadeus says in his opening spiel, the Dream Coop's where dreams rise up. One day, could be the White House'll be all fixed up. Who knows? Maybe another person like us'll be in the Oval Office, an' the country'll be all put back together. Like Uncle Dreg said, the Rising can't be stopped. Just gotta believe in it."

His brother wasn't sitting on the perch beside him anymore. Never had been. He'd just wanted it so bad he'd imagined it for a while. He called out to the shadows: "Hey, Amadee, I been meaning to tell you. You can Dimmer me if you want. . . . Never been afraid of ghosts. People is way more scary. . . . Hey, bro? You there?"

3 A RISK WORTH TAKING

Y ou are liars and cheatings! Sneakers too!"
Afarra wasn't intimidated by their location. Appalled that they'd left Muckmock caged on the Mall, she'd marched into the Dream Coop, unimpressed by how spectacular it was, and proceeded to yell at everyone. They couldn't shut her up at first. But at last Ji-ji persuaded her that yelling in the empty arena could alert security to the fact they were there.

Tiro was clearly disappointed in Afarra's reaction to the spectacular coop. Ji-ji tried to make up for it by assuring him the place was even grander than she'd imagined, hoping he wouldn't notice that she, too, had trouble focusing after what had occurred on the Mall.

After Tiro had guided the two visitors up dimly lit back stairwells to the upper levels of spectator seating, a place he called "the gods," Ji-ji gave him the gift she'd made for him. A sketch she'd drawn of Amadee's favorite tree, the one on the west side of Williams' planting close to the boundary between Lotter's Homestead 1 and Williams' Homestead 2. She'd done sketches of it before and knew its shape by heart. She'd taken a risk and drawn a figure in the tree. A male, lounging on a tree limb a few feet up, reading a book. The sketch was small (Ji-ji didn't have any large sketch pads), so you couldn't say exactly who it was. But she hoped Tiro would see what she was trying to do and not think it was insensitive.

Tiro trained his flashlight on her sketch. Almost imperceptibly, his breath caught in his throat. He tried to thank her but wound up simply nodding. Ji-ji covered for him—told him she couldn't wait to see him fly. His face told her she'd been right to draw the sketch. It made her feel that venturing out tonight hadn't been a totally selfish act after all.

Afarra, who hadn't been gifted to Silapu back when Amadee was killed and who therefore had no idea about the significance of the day, started up again, though she wasn't yelling this time. "Liars and cheatings! Zyla will be very disappointed when she hears."

Tiro looked at Afarra in surprise. "Since when did you give a crap what Zyla thinks?"

"You are very stupid, Flight Boy!" Afarra folded her arms in disgust and flung herself down into the seat behind her. "It is not safe. That is why I do it."

Tiro turned to Ji-ji for a translation.

"She means she didn't think it was safe for me to come to the Dream Coop tonight. S'why she followed me out to the van an' jumped in before I could stop her."

Tiro tried to place his hand on Afarra's shoulder. She slapped it away.

"Do not touch me, Flight Boy!"

The insult was deliberate. Afarra knew how much it grated on Tiro to hear the nickname his great-aunt Cryday had come up with.

"If pickers take her it is *your* fault. I will be blaming you all the days in your life!"

"I bet you will. But Ji—your Elly—she's safe here."

Afarra made a face. "Man Cryday is saying you are very stupid. Like me. I am saying it too."

She'd finally gone too far. Tiro's patience had run out. "It's two in the morning, for fuck's sake! Who's gonna know you're here?"

"*Huh!* I tell Zyla you are saying 'fuck' like the Cellists in Monticello. Always very rude in the miscegenations with the not-Free nakeds. I have seen them say this offending word all the time. I am telling Zyla this myself."

"What the hell's she talking about, Ji? Who are the not-Free nakeds?" Before Ji-ji could respond, Tiro added, "What's wrong with you, Afarra? You used to be real sweet."

"And you used to be a moron," Afarra shot back. "At least you are being consistent."

Tiro and Ji-ji looked at each other. Since when did the former outcast, who'd mostly taught herself how to speak English, use phrases like "at least you are being consistent"?

"The pickers is here an' now," Afarra mumbled. "I am *seeing* them."

Ji-ji looked around uneasily. Though the cage was partially lit, the seating, which encircled the fly cage and rose up in tiers around it, was mostly in shadow.

Afarra wrapped her arms around herself and rocked back and forth in her seat. "Pickers *pickpickpick* till the bones is clean. Buzzards. They pick runners in the Freedom Race. We rescue. Some . . . too late. They die."

Ji-ji's heart went out to her. Of course. Afarra was thinking about the picker attack during the Freedom Race. The terror they'd lived through when they rescued the runners haunted her too. "I promise," Ji-ji said, easing herself down beside her friend and putting her arm around her, "there's no pickers in the Dream. Only in the Territories. They got laws against it here. You seen any pickers or Bounty Boys searching for runaway seeds in this liberty city, Tiro?"

"Ain't seen a one," Tiro replied.

"There. See? We're safe in the—" Ji-ji broke off suddenly and pulled away.

Afarra's body had stiffened. Her eyes were focused on something they couldn't see. Her voice took on a haunting quality, as if she'd jumped down into a grave and was calling up to them. "If they find out Elly is breathing, they will gouge them! Leave two big holes like this." Afarra formed her hands into a circle as big as a dinner plate. "Blood gluggling out of holes. *Gluggle, gluggle.*"

Horrified, Ji-ji leapt from her seat.

"*Jesus!*" Tiro cried. "What the hell's wrong with her?"

Ji-ji felt sick. In her recurring nightmare, she'd seen that butchery herself but never told Afarra about it. Maybe Afarra was haunted by Tiro's attempt to excise her sproutings. That would explain it. Whatever the reason, Tiro needed a clear head to fly safely. She had to calm things down.

Ji-ji came up with a compromise: "How 'bout we don't stay as long as we planned? We arrived late, so we'll see a few maneuvers then leave."

She looked over at Tiro, who nodded in agreement.

Tiro tried again: "Pickers got no authority in a liberty city. You're safe here."

Afarra snapped out of her daze and shot up from her seat. She poked his chest with her finger, said, "You think this city is *safe? Huh!* Think Lotter is not looking *all the time?*"

"Keep your voice down," Tiro ordered. He flicked his fingers against his thigh anxiously. Ji-ji noticed him staring at the necklace. The moment they entered the coop, Afarra had unzipped the jacket. Said his Eyes were getting "claustrophobinized in the dark."

Visibly flustered, Tiro turned to Ji-ji, grasped her elbow exactly where Marcus had earlier, and led her a few feet away from Afarra, who sat back down in her seat and muttered to the necklace in a language only she understood.

"Think she could be right?" Tiro said, too softly for Afarra to hear. "She's been right other times in the past. Think it was a mistake to let you come here?"

"It wasn't a mistake. An' I didn't need your permission. Coming here was my idea." He didn't look convinced, so she kept going. "The steaders think I'm dead. Or even if they suspect I'm not, they think I'm damaged." A flame of fear leapt inside her. "Could be they're right."

"Your wings're shy, that's all. Like a tortoise. Like to hide away in their shells."

"I'm not worried," she lied. "Coach Mackie says they're ornery. Like me."

"Hey, you two lovebirds. You think you got all the time in the world? Think again."

Ji-ji jumped. She'd forgotten all about Marcus. Though he'd kept his voice low, it echoed in the cavernous arena. Tiro's fly partner lounged on an upper-level Parks Perch near the top of the cage, which meant he was at roughly the same level as they were. Ji-ji was struck again by how much he looked like Tiro. No wonder people often mistook them for brothers.

Marcus let out a theatrical sigh and said, "How long's it take to find a seat in an empty thirty-thousand-seat arena, folks?"

Tiro looked at Ji-ji. "You sure you're still okay to watch us fly the Dream?"

He smiled down at her with that smile of his that melted seeds and infuriated steaders. God, he was good to look at in his black-and-gold, figure-hugging fly suit. His hair was styled like Marcus'. During their trip to the Mall, Marcus had worn a skullcap, so Ji-ji didn't see his hair till he removed his cap after he entered the coop. They wore their hair short on the sides. Wings had been shaved into it above each ear. The hair on top and down the back was longer. Someone had taken pains to intricately braid the longer hair. It looked good—regal. Made Ji-ji think of Egypt, the Cradle, and the braided manes of stallions. Tiny gold and silver charms had been woven into their braids for luck—more pairs of wings, crescent moons, stars. On the planting, they'd be slapped with dandification fines, a lashing, or worse if they'd dared to appear like that.

"Go on then," Ji-ji urged. "Marcus is waiting. I came here to see you fly."

"Copy that," Tiro said and nodded over at Afarra, who crossed her arms disapprovingly and looked away. Ji-ji could tell he was hurt by the snub. He bounded up the stairs to the exit.

Ji-ji took a seat beside Afarra. She felt terrible. Muckmock's agonized cries echoed in her head. "I know it's risky," she admitted, "but I had to come here tonight. I'll die if I stay cooped up."

"We are still being cooped up," Afarra grumbled. "In a coop."

Ji-ji smiled. "It's not the same. The Dream Coop's about choice. Okay. I know the choice is limited. But it's not like the fly-coop on the planting or our practice coop in the flood zone. . . . I'm sick of the rats an' roaches . . . scared I'm a freak. What if these things decide not to retract one day? What if they unfurl an' I can't get 'em back in their . . ." Her voice trailed off.

"Nests," Afarra said. It was the same word Ji-ji herself sometimes used to describe the strange hollows in her back.

"You think they look like nests?"

Afarra nodded. "They are saying it."

"They say anything else? They tell you if I'll ever be able to . . ."

Her voice trailed off again. She didn't want to jinx herself by using the word *fly*. She settled for "They say if I'll ever be able to use 'em?"

"Oh yes," Afarra said, enthusiastically. "They are saying it in Dimmers Wood with Man Cryday when they are sprouting."

"Yeah, I know. You told me. But what about now? They still saying it?"

Afarra shrugged as if the question were incidental. "Sometimes."

"Well, I guess sometimes is better than no times. . . . I try, I really do. Mam said I was a Try-Again. But something's shifted. I'm not making headway any-more. It's like I'm going downhill."

Afarra slipped her hand in Ji-ji's. "No downhill," she said, so sweetly that Ji-ji got choked up. "We go *uphill*. To the moon, remember? Okay. We see Tiro fly then we go 'fore they pick us. Then we go look for Muckmock tomorrow to save. Then we find Charra. Then Bonbon."

Ji-ji was touched by how firmly Afarra stuck to the plan of searching for her sister and brother. Finding them was what Ji-ji dreamed about as often as she dreamed about flying. But Afarra's dogged certainty scared her. Too much faith could wound you as much as too little could.

"Afarra, listen to me. We can't save everyone. You told me you had to save the Dimmer-dead too, remember?"

"It is not being easy to save the dead. They are dead already. That is the prob-lem. Muckmock is for being alive an' Free. He is telling me this."

Afarra looked up at the dome. Though they were high up in the arena, the dome was still several stories above them. "When Tiro is in the nest, how much more to the moon?" The dim light inside the coop allowed them to see the pale silver disc of the moon through the glass dome. Afarra attempted to measure the distance with her fingers. "Not far, I think, isn't it?"

"Doesn't look like it's far away, but it's a long, long way from here."

"A long, long way," Afarra repeated, wistfully.

"You still mad at us?" Ji-ji asked. "You know we couldn't Free him, right?" Afarra gave her a look that said she should have tried harder. It wasn't an accep-tance, but it was better than her earlier hostility. "Be nice to Tiro, okay. He's having a hard time tonight. It's the anniversary of—"

"He is being very stupid," Afarra said. "Okay, okay. I am nice if no pickers is coming."

"Fair enough," Ji-ji said. Probably good not to mention Amadee to Afarra. Tiro valued his privacy and Afarra could blurt out something that could upset him.

Ji-ji leaned back in her seat. Not even a hawk could spot them up here in the gods, the highest and darkest tiers of the arena. She turned to Afarra and reassured her once again: "We watch Tiro an' Marcus fly the Dream for a few minutes, then we leave."

Tiro had impressed upon her that people didn't say "fly *in* the Dream." Granted, the slipup wasn't as bad as calling the pre-Sequel nation the "States United," like secessionists did, but it was pretty close. If you said fly *in* the Dream, Districters knew you were from the boonies. "May as well sew a seed symbol to your chest," Tiro told her, "hitch yourself to a wagon, an' proclaim yourself a goddam Mule!"

After her discouraging flying lessons and tonight's close call with Afarra, sitting up there in the gods began to feel like a victory. One day, maybe she would fly the Dream too, without the aid of a harness or a trapeze, hope-ropes, pulleys, trampolines, fly-wheels, or zip lines. The first human—mutant?—ever to fly unaided. Elevation, a right denied to females in the Territories, would be hers to claim. She knew she could never fly in public; it would be a death wish. But she could sneak in again one night so she and Tiro could fly side by side, like he used to with Amadee.

She leaned forward to see what the flyers' first move would be. Tiro had joked when he'd led them up there that the gods section was so high "you could get a nosebleed if you stood up too quick." High up though the seats were, sitting in the gods didn't give them an unobstructed view. Ji-ji and Afarra had to peer past struts and pillars to see the action. Ji-ji wished for better seats.

When they'd entered the Dream Coop, Afarra had pointed to the spacious VIP balcony on the opposite side from where they now sat. Located midway up the stands in the fancy stadium seating on that side of the arena, the plush seats in the balcony looked more like thrones. Afarra had demanded to sit up there and had sworn at Tiro and Marcus when they'd said no. Midway up the tiered seats on the north side of the arena, the wide balcony jutted out several feet and afforded its occupants a clear view of every part of the cage. A wide banner in the Dreamfleet flyers' black and gold colors hung from the underside of the balcony. The gold lettering shone with the city's motto: JUSTITIA OMNIBUS—"Justice for All." Ji-ji would opt for that hopeful motto any day. It put the Territories' insidious motto *Growing the Territories One Seed at a Time!* to shame. But sitting in the well-lit balcony would have left them totally exposed. Ji-ji had tried to explain this to Afarra earlier, but her friend was no more receptive to this than she had been to leaving Muckmock behind.

Ji-ji scanned the cage again. Directly ahead, the multistory Ellison Wheel loomed, the largest wheel of its kind. It made Ji-ji think about something she'd read in the *D.C.Independent*. Last season, a veteran flyer and former Commonseed named Catapult Clyde leapt from the wheel to a hope-rope and missed. The safety net over the center section of the cage had caught him, but he'd landed awkwardly on his neck, a fall that had left the thirty-seven-year-old father of seven, a former Commonseed, paralyzed from the neck down. (*Don't think about Catapult Clyde. A freak accident. Tiro's wearing his safety harness.*) Ji-ji could make out the high trapezes and glittering X Boxes that dangled from the cage's ceiling. (*Easy to fall from those.*) A complicated series of movable Harriet's Stairs spiraled up inside the cage to take flyer-battlers to ever-more-reckless staging platforms. (*Please guide him like you did the others, Harriet.*)

At the highest point of all, the oversize Jim Crow's Nest hung from its thick cables. Unlike other nests, this one wasn't attached to the cage by a walkway.

Looked as if the only way to reach it was to swing there on a hope-rope. Tiro had told her that Coopmaster Nelson could push a button and make the great nest tilt and sway. Rumor had it, he could even make it rain or snow up there, as if it had its own special climate zone.

By this time, Tiro had joined Marcus in the cage. He waved to them. Ji-ji waved back, though she doubted he could see her do it. Afarra didn't wave. "Be nice," Ji-ji reminded her.

Soon the fly-boys were leaping from one piece of equipment to another, battling each other, using their martial arts skills and wooden practice weapons as they worked their way up higher and higher up inside the cage.

"I feel like an ant in more ways than one," Ji-ji joked. When Afarra didn't react, she added, "Get it? Ant. The other name for mutants." Ji-ji regretted her joke as soon as it left her mouth.

"Like Muckmock," Afarra said, "who is not being saved by us." She saw Ji-ji's pained face and added, "Marcus is the bad one. He is the one who picks us. He is very bad."

Ji-ji was tempted to argue with her, but she didn't have the energy. Besides, it was a relief not to be the target of Afarra's hostility. Tomorrow, she would explain why they couldn't save Muckmock. For tonight, she'd watch Tiro and Marcus fly.

Tiro wasn't one of those cautious flyer-battlers who keep mainly to the apparatus on the ground level—the King-spins, Colvin Coils, Douglass Pipes, and Lincoln Logs. Tiro *had* to climb. Showing off even more than usual to entertain the only two fans in the building (having put on a safety harness so he didn't give them heart attacks), Tiro rode the Ellison Wheel up past the midlevel staging ring they called the donut and leapt onto a 'Bama's Drama—a cantilevered trampoline attached to the side of the cage. From there, he bounced onto Dredful Scotty, an elevator-type affair with a narrow, wobbly platform. The Dred carried him to Good Trouble, an upper-level staging dais. He climbed a Jacob's Ladder and two of Harriet's Stairs to the top of the coop, where he grabbed a hope-rope and swung in the direction of the nest way up in the dome. Having fought off an ambush by Marcus, who'd leapt down from a dangling X Box and nearly dislodged him from the hope-rope, he planted himself in the Jim Crow. When he doffed an invisible cap and bowed in their direction, even Afarra cheered.

Silapu used to warn her daughter that Tiro was reckless. But watching him propel himself from one piece of equipment to the other, Ji-ji knew her mam was only half right. Tiro was reckless, for sure, but his recklessness wasn't rooted in carelessness; it was rooted in yearning. In a city filled with thousands of former seeds, Tiro's yearning was contagious.

As she watched Tiro and Marcus, Ji-ji understood why flyers never said they flew *in* the Dream. For the Black and Brown ex-seeds who made up the vast majority of the flyer-battler teams throughout the Territories and the Independents, D.C.'s spectacular new Dream Coop wasn't a place. It was an unquenchable idea devised by seeds who housed flight, struggle, and history inside a cage because there was nowhere else to put it. A flying coop conceived of by a people who refused to let Freedom perish. The way Tiro flew confirmed to Ji-ji that Man Cryday had been right all along. The race wasn't a competition you entered. The countless seeds and former seeds *were* the Freedom Race. Here in D.C., the city that pledged fealty to a dream, all you had to do was look up to discover who you were meant to be.

Afarra had fallen silent. Ji-ji looked over and saw her friend's rapt expression. Despite its flaws, and they were many, the Dream Coop sang its hymns to everyone who remembered what it cost to fly a way home. This was what you did as a former seed when you lived in the City of Dreams: you ventured out in the dead of night to pray.

Afarra grabbed Ji-ji's arm and dragged her down between the seats.

On the way down, Ji-ji banged her knee. "*Ow!* What are you doing?" Ji-ji hissed.

"*Steaders!*" Afarra hissed back. "In the V-P-I!"

As soon as she dared, Ji-ji peeked over the tiered seats in front and looked across the arena to the VIP balcony. A group of six or seven men were clustered inside it. Though she was too far away to say for sure, Ji-ji thought she recognized one of them: Mayor Adolphus Yardley, the man Zyla referred to as a "pompous-looking toad," and someone the Friends suspected of being a secessionist sympathizer. Of all nights, why did the mayor choose this one? And what the hell were he and his cronies doing in the Dream Coop at two in the morning?

Tiro and Marcus had stopped flying. Looked like they were talking to the unexpected visitors. Yes! They were giving them time to escape!

"Stay down low else they'll see us!" Ji-ji whispered. "We head for the exit up there." She pointed back behind them. "See it?" Afarra nodded. "Don't forget, stay low."

They were about to start their ascent up the stairs to the exit when Ji-ji hissed, "*Wait!*" She reached over and zipped up the ill-fitting jacket Afarra wore so the wizard's necklace remained hidden. "Keep it zipped up. Don't forget." Afarra, a look of sheer terror on her face, nodded again. "It's okay. They can't see us. It's too dark up here. But don't stand up, for god's sake!"

They weren't far from the exit when Ji-ji remembered something. Her proof of residency papers! She'd almost left them behind! How could a dead person leave proof of residency papers in the Dream Coop! Quickly, she told Afarra to wait there while she grabbed her bag. She duckwalked back and snatched it off the seat, slipped it over her head, and threaded her arm through the long strap. She made her way back to where Afarra, whimpering softly and crouched on her haunches, waited.

"It's okay," Ji-ji told her. "They're not here for us."

As the two females duckwalked toward the exit, quick-thinking Marcus launched into his Uncle Tom spiel. "Good evening, Mr. Mayor, sir. Excuse our presence, sir. Only time rookie fly-boys like me an' him get to practice our secret moves is late at night when the veterans is sleeping. Gotta take any advantage we can get."

The mayor, sounding flustered, asked what move they were practicing.

"We got this new Ellison move down pat," Marcus added. "We love the E., right, Tiro? Lifts you up an' slams you down. Never know what's comin'. Can hide inside the nooks an' crannies, be invisible an' leap out—Ta-da! Gotta be careful, though. If seeds like us get concertina'ed in them metal spokes it's seedchips all around!"

The men on the balcony roared with laughter.

Marcus again: "Want us to show you round, Mr. Mayor, sir?"

Too busy working her way up to the exit at the rear of the gods, Ji-ji didn't hear the mayor's response. They'd reached the exit doors! Soft as a whisper, the two females pushed down on the safety bar. As quietly as they could, they pushed one of the doors open. Out in the dark corridor—Gently! Gently!—they eased the door shut behind them.

Made it! All they needed to do was find the back stairwell and—

An ambush from behind!

"Pickers!" Afarra cried, just before hands the size of dinner plates thrust out from the darkness and hauled them off into the gloom.

4 WITH THE RIOT ON YOUR BACK

J i-ji's thoughts crash into each other. She tries to scream for help. The giant clamps down harder on her mouth. She kicks him. No reaction. Kicks him again. Doesn't flinch. *I'm right up against him. He'll feel my back!* The picker smells of weed. Ji-ji thinks fast: *If he's high, he's slow. Bite down on his fingers! Bite down hard as you can!* The pig merely tightens his grip. *When did pickers get this big?*

A barrage of realizations—*Afarra an' me are Pickers' Picks now—four breasts, two vaginas, a back that says freak! But I'm fast an' Afarra's slippery. We're not dead yet. . . .*

The giants sprint down a black hallway clutching their fear-choked, tear-choked victims. Other men's voices behind them, getting closer. Yardley's men? Tiro and Marcus? No. Can't be. Takes too long to make it to the gods from the cage.

Picker One turns left. Afarra's picker follows. They come to a halt. *Is that a door? Too dark to know for sure. Yes, it's a door.* The pickers open it, shove them inside to an even deeper darkness.

For one blissful moment, Ji-ji thinks they'll be on their own in there . . . before the giants barge inside and lock the door behind them, order them not to scream. Hot as hell in the small room. The door is sturdy. The pickers can do whatever they want to them in there.

Darkness is fear is a raping room is darkness is fear is a raping room . . .

Will they kill us if we scream? Yes. From now on, every word the pickers utter will strip them of themselves and each other. The room—a storeroom?—smells of disaster, of big things hacked to smallness. *How will I bear it if they sample Afarra, the friend who came to me after Lua died, the one who's seen me as I am and loved me for it?*

Then Ji-ji remembers the just-in-case-of-ambush knife strapped to her thigh. Friends Ben and Germaine have taught her how to plant her body like a man behind the upward thrusts. *You'll get one chance. Make it count. Slice off any piece of picker pork you can get your hands on!* But how do I slice pickers the size of trees? She knows what awaits them if she doesn't try. She and Afarra will be wrenched from each other. A dismembering. Afarra shipped to a Serverseed camp to be processed for re-servitude. Her caged like Muckmock and made to perform for gawkers. Faster than sound, faster than light, Ji-ji threads her options onto a rope in her head.

Option 1: Gut Picker One. Option 2: Gut Picker Two. Option 3: Slice either one.

Problem: How do we escape through a wall of pigs?

A voice—Afarra's? the wizard's?—says, *"With the riot on your back!"* Afarra silent-says it with the whites of her wide-open eyes. In the pitiless gloom, Ji-ji imagines Afarra's pretty mouth twitching with fear like Soapsud's did—the pup Ji-ji kept a secret from her mam for three days after her brother Clay was auctionmarted, till Silapu (roaring drunk and rage-grieving) found Soapsud under Ji-ji's bed and hurled him across the room like something un-alive. Her sister Charra rocking her, telling her not to cry. *How will I find Charra in the Madlands if I've been picked by giants?* A tiny wound of a yelp is what Ji-ji remembers when Soapsud hit the wall.

If she and Afarra have to die tonight, let the killing be like that. Fast. Pre-memory.

"With the riot on your back!" Afarra's eyes say, in unison with the homicidal necklace.

Can I do it? Can I unfurl so fast I knock 'em out? Yes, I can. I've done it before.

Quick as a heartbeat, Ji-ji visits the cabin in The Margins where Rudy the Picker held the female runners. Her new sproutings (no more than seedlings back then) nudged out from under her T-shirt like two blind snakes while she pushed the broken bottle into Rudy's jugular. The most up-close, violent thing she's ever done.

Do what Afarra an' the Eyes tell you! Unfurl a riot!

No! Wait! Since when can I unfurl at will? An' how can I rip through the bindings Afarra wrapped me in? My T-shirt an' cape—could be they'll yield . . . Gotta shed the bag! Can't unfurl with a canvas strap holding me in. How do I maneuver 'fore they beat me up, break me? The futility of it all a knife in the gut: *Unfurling won't work as a distraction, fool. There's a larger problem. Afarra will never run without you. . . .*

In the storeroom, too dark for silhouettes, the men are invisible. But they are there.

Time plays tricks, feeds her through a grinder. Ten minutes must've passed. Twenty? No. Only a few seconds. Faster than sound, faster than light, Picker Two flicks on his flashlight before he shines it on their tits. Afarra takes this as her cue, flings off her jacket to reveal her only weapon!

The wizard's strange Seeing Eyes are visible for all to see.

If they think we're witches, the pickers won't rape us, they'll slit our throats instead!

Inside a second that's splitting like an atom, Afarra resurrects the out-loud, outsized, worm-filled wizard's voice: "You touch her, I *kill* you! Their Eyes—watching!"

Picker One doesn't get it. "Whose eyes?" he asks.

"God's," Afarra tells him. "Watching!"

Picker Two: "Everyone shut the fuck up!"

Ji-ji tilts her head in the dark to listen louder. Something familiar grabs her attention. The room screeches to a halt as stars align. A merciful circle of light clicks on in her head.

They aren't . . . these men aren't . . .

A saucer-sized hand thrusts itself inside the waistband of her sweatpants, gropes for the knife. "I use the peeler," Afarra whispers, "to *slice!*"

Ji-ji grabs hold of her hand. "Listen to me, Afarra! *Listen!*"

"*Ssh!*" again from the pair by the door.

"They're not pickers!" Ji-ji says, half laughing, half crying. "They're not fair-skins! They're *flyers,* Afarra! They're *friends!*"

Friend Two whispers, "No offense meant but shut the fuck up! Place is swarming with Yardley's men." He chuckles nervously, adds, "Hear that, Tree? Pickers! Not even a blind man would mistake you an' me for them bastards." To prove his point, Friend Two trains his flashlight on the other man's face. Because he's nervous, the flashlight trembles. The other giant groans under his breath, shields his eyes.

"Put that thing down, Georgie! You're blinding me, man!"

Georgie-Porge trains the light onto the floor. "Sorry, man."

Georgie-Porge Snellingseed, Tiro's friend and fellow flyer-battler from the 437th, stands at the door with Laughing Tree, the seven-foot flyer-battler, the one fans claim can uproot a sapling with his bare hands. Laughing Tree, the famous Tribalseed from the Freedom Race, who felled a boy by accident in the Monticello flying coop and carries him around on his back cos his legs don't work anymore, towers over Georgie. Next to Laughing Tree, Georgie-Porge looks like a younger brother in need of a growth spurt.

"I hear 'em," Georgie says again, jumpy as a flea. "Everyone . . . quiet!"

He flicks off his flashlight and plunges the storeroom and its contents into blackness.

|||||||||||||

"They've gone," Tree said. "Turn on your flashlight so they won't be scared." By "they," he seemed to be including Georgie too, whose rapid breathing told Ji-ji how fast his heart was racing.

Tree apologized: "Didn't mean to scare you ladies." (The word "ladies" pulses with tenderness. Ji-ji can hardly bear it.) "Had to whisk you off before we could explain the plan. Heard men heading in our direction. Needed a cover story. Our plan was to say you were groupies who'd snuck into the coop. Not sure if they would have fallen for it, of course. But we was hoping they'd let us escort you off the premises. Hope we didn't hurt you, us being big and you being small, and Georgie here being clumsy—foulmouthed, too, when he's jumpy."

"Figured if we ran into those effheads," Georgie said, in deference to their guests, "they'd think twice 'bout confronting us. Figured you'd play along. Glad we didn't test that theory."

All this time, Afarra had stood frozen. Now, she let out a gasp of joy and vaulted toward the men. In her excitement, she forgot to pull her hand out from the waistband of Ji-ji's sweatpants. Just before her pants were yanked to her knees, Ji-ji managed to extricate it.

Georgie, who'd picked Afarra earlier, picked her up again and hugged her. He put her down quickly, as if he didn't have a clue why he'd done something as sentimental as that.

Tree must've sensed what the one thing people who've been traumatized need above everything else: to know what's coming next. "Here's the plan," he said, keeping his voice low. "We stay quiet as mice in this stockroom till they've gone. Georgie an' me, we're here cos Tiro asked us to guardian-angel over you. Us being Friends ourselves, like you. Sorry it's a squeeze. Georgie sweats like a pig when he's nervous."

Georgie ordered Tree to damn well leave him out of it.

"Cool it, man," Tree said. "Let's behave like gentlemen. . . . Anyone fancy a bite of a candy bar? Got squashed in the melee but it's edible."

"For god's sake, Tree," Georgie muttered. "You're worser'n Marcus. Everyone from the islands talk like you? If so, I ain't about to visit. Had enough fancy Lottery lingo on the 437th to last me a lifetime an' then some. What the hell's a maylay?"

"Hand-to-hand mischief. What these two did to us when they mistook us for pickers. My nahna was from the islands but I'm from all over—Ole Mississip, the Caribbean, the Cradle, Europe, New Zealand. . . . Steaders like the idea of a giant Tribalseed from the Cradle, so that's the story they settled on. Not s'posed to be seed-picking in the Caribbean after the last global treaty, but pickers don't play by the rules. Was visiting my nahna when they—"

Georgie butted in: "No one gives a crap, Tree. Honest they don't."

A loud bang. Everyone jumped at the same time. "Y'hear that?" Georgie asked. In a panic, he thrust the flashlight under his T-shirt as if that were the only way to turn it off.

"Sounds like a door slammed," Laughing Tree whispered. "Everyone stay quiet. Don't worry. Georgie and me can take 'em if we got to, but if we don't got to we won't."

"We take 'em too," Afarra whispered.

Laughing Tree chuckled softly. "I bet you could. . . . Georgie, that thing's got a switch on it. Don't need to smother it like that, man. It's not some candle you gotta snuff out."

Without removing the flashlight, Georgie switched it off. His torso fled to the dark side.

After a while Tree said, "It's nothing."

"Sure sounded like something," Georgie argued.

"Sounded like a door slamming," Tree said. "Whoever slammed it moved off."

They listened for a while longer before Tree tried again: "It's real chocolate. From Europe. Imported. From Belgium or somewhere. Fleeters our size get extra rations cos we're big guys. Fleet beefs us up to keep us battle ready. Want some?"

Ji-ji couldn't figure out how Afarra saw Tree's hand in the pitch-dark. But a second later it sounded like she'd stuffed the entire candy bar into her mouth. Ji-ji figured out that Afarra was trying to thank Laughing Tree, but her mouth was full of chocolate. Ji-ji thanked him for her.

"No thanks needed," Tree said. "Hearing her chomp away is thanks enough."

For the second time that evening, Ji-ji had narrowly escaped catastrophe. It felt like someone was trying to tell her something—something she didn't want to hear.

Then, without any warning to anyone, not even herself, Ji-ji burst into tears.

||||||||||||||

After waiting in limbo for more than an hour to make sure none of Yardley's men were roaming the corridors, Tree and Georgie got the all-clear message on their callers from Marcus.

Cautiously, they exited the storeroom and led the visitors down the Dream Coop's shadowy stairwells all the way to the basement, where a maze of dimly lit corridors greeted them. Double doors led to a cavernous space the size of the Gathering Place on a planting. A maintenance and staging facility, Tree said, filled with coop equipment—King-spins, Douglass Pipes, Lincoln Logs, X Boxes, Colvin Coils, and the like. The place felt sinister to Ji-ji, as if pickers could leap out from the shadows any moment and haul them off. In the dark, it took her a while to make out what the huge contraption was in the center of the space. At last she figured it out. A half-assembled Ellison Wheel lay on its side like a felled giant.

Tree worked hard to lighten the mood: "They say there's a ton of new stuff being shipped in under wraps almost every day. The coopmaster himself isn't privy to all the secrets this place has to offer." Tree stopped talking. Details like that wouldn't make them feel easier about being there.

The first cavernous space led to a second, more cavernous one that Tree identified as the Pit. A gaping round hole in the center, with a shaft like an elevator above it, puzzled Ji-ji. She asked what it was.

"Center ring's directly above the hole, where the shaft leads. Down there in the hole there's a circular tank. Can't see it now, too dark. Take my word for it. They can fill that huge tank with water an' turn it into a pool. The center ring in the arena above bifurcates—slides open right down the middle, smooth as peanut butter. Then I'm-a-God Nelson elevates the entire thing. Whole contraption comes up so the center ring turns into a see-through pool. It's an engineering marvel. Never seen anything like it in a Liberty Independent or the Territories either. Not since the Age of Plenty. Course, the SuperStates've got a ton of techno-wizardry so they've got things we can't dream of yet."

"SuperStates don't got fly-coops," Georgie stated.

"True," Tree agreed. "I tease Ink when we come down here to get away for a while an' ponder things. Poor kid needs to ponder. I tell him they plan to put gators in the pool. Makes him laugh. I tell him our rivals'll have a fit when—" Tree caught sight of Afarra's horrified expression. "I'm only teasing! Whole contraption's vegetarian—right, Georgie?"

"You giving 'em a tour?" Georgie snapped. "Or are we headed out to find the others?"

Afarra grabbed Ji-ji's hand. "We go now," she urged.

"It's okay," Tree said. "We're safe down here. Place is deserted late at night."

"We go!" Afarra insisted. "We go *now*!"

"Get her to shut the hell up!" Georgie said.

"She's scared," Tree told him.

"Who gives a—?" Georgie stifled the word he was about to use. "Voices carry down here. For all we know, some of Yardley's men is still around."

Tree nodded, turned to Afarra, and spoke to her as gently as a father: "You want me to ferry you the rest of the way, Afarra? S'no trouble."

The big man was a lot older than the rest of them—nudging forty, Ji-ji estimated. When he held out his powerful arms to Afarra, she calmed down immediately.

"I can carry you too, Ji-ji, easy as pie. Got a tree limb available," he joked.

Ji-ji shook her head, told him she was fine. Snuggled up against the battler, Afarra looked like a child; and although Ji-ji had become convinced that she and Afarra were much closer in age than she used to think they were, right now, in Tree's enormous arms, Afarra looked very small.

They hurried on through the basement, went down a number of echoing tunnels, took a few flights of stairs, and emerged in a secluded area some distance from the arena.

Parked next to a long one-story building, a familiar van. Tiro and Marcus emerged from it to greet them. Having ushered the girls into the vehicle, they lingered out of earshot to confer with Tree and Georgie. Ji-ji grew nervous. An evening assembly of four adult males would never have been permitted on the 437th. Every so often, Tiro glanced back at the van and waved, as if he wanted to assure her all was well.

After a minute or two, Tiro and Marcus hurried back to the van and climbed in. As the vehicle lumbered off, Afarra waved goodbye to Laughing Tree. She kept doing so long after he was out of sight. "He is saying Ink is not being heavy either," she said. "He is saying he is happy in the ferry-nest. Ink. Ink is the happy one in his ferry-nest. Not Tree. What is a tree to do in a nest?" Afarra giggled at her own joke. Ji-ji, overwhelmed with relief that they were safe at last, joined in.

Tiro, sitting in the front passenger seat, pulled up a box that lay at his feet. Ji-ji knew what it was—one of his famous gift boxes. Every two weeks or so, he either delivered one himself or handed it off to Ben, Germaine or Zyla to give to them. Everything, especially food, was hard to come by in the city, ration cards only going so far. They'd come to rely on his generosity.

Tiro pulled out a fancy box with a bow on it. He held it out to the second row, where Ji-ji and Afarra sat: "Fleet owners flew 'em in from somewhere in Europe. Real chocolate like they used to have in the Age of Plenty. Wanna try—"

Before he'd finished his question, Afarra had snatched them up. Within seconds, she'd ripped into them with the same steady concentration Ji-ji had seen in veteran coach Billy Brineseed when he'd smoked a nervous cigarette on what was destined to be his last day in Planting 437's fly-coop. (Was Coach B still in exile in the Rad Region, or had his friend Pheebs—all four foot six of her—defied the odds and rescued him? Ji-ji chose to believe the latter. The only stories she could bear tonight were ones with happy endings.)

Humming contentedly to herself, Afarra appeared to have recovered from their ordeal, but Ji-ji wasn't fooled. People dealt with stress in different ways. Smoking had taken the edge off for Coach Billy, drinking and drugging were how her mam used to cope. Looked as if eating was Afarra's way of consoling herself. Ji-ji knew what her own stress suppressant was—drawing. Her fingers felt twitchy without a pencil or pen in them. She still had her bag with her notebook and pen in it, but even if she'd felt calm enough to sketch, the old van's suspension would ruin it.

If she could have sketched something right now, it would have been the fireworks. She'd call it "Not on the Fourth of July." The viewer would be standing behind Afarra as she gazed up at a sky blazing with fireworks. Muckmock would be standing next to his new friend, holding her hand. You'd see them from the back—an enormous hairy figure next to a small skinny one. You could tell from their backs how happy they were to be in each other's company.

As they drove through D.C.'s backstreets in the wee hours of the morning, Tiro and Marcus filled them in on what happened. Ji-ji wished they'd stop talking; she wanted nothing more than to enjoy a quiet ride home. But the fly partners got a rise out of needling each other. She hadn't realized till tonight how differently they saw things. On a planting, seeds were all on the same side. She was beginning to understand how different things were in the City of Dreams, for all of them.

Marcus described how Wing Commander Corcoran had rushed onto the VIP balcony not long after the mayor showed up. "Looked terrible," he said. "Bed hair, tie half knotted. Corcoran reports directly to the mayor. Tells you all you need to know about how messed up this city is. Yardley's amassing power again. Suckers won't know what hit 'em if he gets his way this time."

"Those suckers is us, Ji," Tiro explained, "the Friends of Freedom. The Gospel according to Marcus is pretty long-winded."

Marcus wasn't deterred. "I'm not only talking about the Friends. Those kumbaya reunionists in the SuperStates are just as bad."

"Buckle up, Ji. Here it comes."

"Mock all you want, T. Name me one time when diplomacy an' reason ousted tyranny? You can't cos it's never happened. The fleet's not a military enterprise. It's ceremonial. A holdover from the air and naval fleets the city had during the Sequel. Yardley co-opts the fleet for propaganda purposes. His surprise visit floored ol' Corker. Feeling was mutual. Yardley nearly pissed himself when Corcoran appeared on the scene."

Ji-ji asked how the wing commander knew the mayor was in the Dream Coop.

"Tree made a quick call to Corcoran," Tiro replied. "Told him he'd joined me an' Marcus for a late-night practice when he heard trespassers in the coop. Said he didn't know who they were."

Marcus launched into an impersonation of Tree, mimicking his deep bass to a tee: "Evening, sir. This is Tree, sir. Wanted to notify you about an irregularity, Commander Corcoran, sir. I'm going out on a limb here, but believe me, this is no laughing matter." Tiro tried and failed to keep a straight face.

Adopting his own voice again, Marcus got serious: "When things get dicey, Ji-ji, never give away more info than is necessary. Being sneaky is what keeps seeds alive."

"Sneakiness didn't pay off this time around though, did it?" Tiro pointed out. "Plan backfired. Corcoran sends a goddam army of security personnel to search the place. S'why Tree an' Georgie had to grab you. The Friends know for a fact some of those fleet's security guys are secessionist sympathizers. Corcoran fired a couple dozen after that business in the spring."

Ji-ji didn't need Tiro to explain to her what "that business in the spring" meant. The attempt to oust Corcoran from office and push D.C. further toward the Territories had put the fear of god into her and everyone else. But the Friends seemed confident the worst had been averted.

"I'm sorry 'bout that mess back there," Tiro said. "Tree said they didn't have time to explain 'fore they shoved you in a storeroom. Said you broke down in tears back there."

Embarrassed, Ji-ji said, "It was nothing. Doc Riff says my hormones are going crazy. Probably explains it."

Marcus grinned in the rearview and raised an eyebrow.

Hormones! Ji-ji thought, mortified. Desperate to change the subject, she said, "How come Yardley was in the coop tonight?"

Marcus looked over at Tiro, said, "Think we can trust these two, seeing as how they've been officially inducted into the Friends of Freedom?"

"Which is more than you have," Tiro reminded him.

"You know I'm not a team player, T. Like to rely on my own sources. So, Ji-ji and Afarra—a choc-sop if ever I saw one—this is what we know. Adolphus Yardley's cozied up to members of the Supreme Council. Looks like this includes—drumroll, please—the grand inquisitor himself. Fightgood Worthy was Lotter's guest at the Last Supper on the planting, Ji-ji, remember? That time I laid down my life for my friend so he could become a Wild Seed. A favor he still needs to repay."

Oh, yes. She remembered Fightgood Worthy all right. . . . Watching in the doorway, that inscrutable look on his face as Inquisitor Tryton assaulted her. She remembered every detail. . . .

Marcus addressed Tiro: "You see Corker's face when he saw Redipp there in Yardley's entourage?"

"Who's Redipp?" Ji-ji asked.

"Drayborn Redipp," Marcus replied. "Yeah, I know. Sounds like a sinus infection. Redipp's the biggest asshole in the fleet. An assistant coach for the reservists."

Tiro corrected him: "*Assistant* to the assistant coach."

"Redipp's been sucking up to Yardley for months," Marcus said. "Bastard's up to something. Corker's days are numbered. Our noble wing commander's way too friendly with the Friends. There's rumors he was secretly inducted into the organization. But if that's true, his membership must've lapsed, along with a desire for equity. Treats flyers like seeds. Even the few fairskin flyers he's got."

"No way they'll get rid of Corcoran," Tiro said. "Fans'd go crazy."

"Fans always go crazy. S'why they're called fanatics. But fortunately for the mayor, most fans' heads are as empty as a seed's pocket. Soon as the owners dangle something pretty an' shiny in front of 'em—that's where you an' I come in, T—they'll forget about poor Corker. . . . By the way, Ji-ji, I never thanked you for saving the city from catastrophe."

Thrown by his comment, all she could find to say was "That was Lucky mostly."

"Yeah, so I heard," Marcus said. The way he said it made her uneasy. "Been meaning to ask—what you doing messing with that lily-white mercenary when you got a stud like T chomping at the bit? Know how long he's been practicing that move he did for you tonight?"

Tiro told him to shut his mouth. "Why you always gotta go too far, Marcus?"

Marcus took his hands off the wheel in mock consternation. "Well *ex-cuuse* me! Didn't know you were as sensitive as Ink. All I'm saying, Ji-ji, is you got us to look out for you now. Got a lot riding on you. All of us. Friends . . . reunionists. No need to cozy up to some fake steader anymore—assuming there is such a thing. Like my man Ralphie said, can't be Free till you know who you are. We gotta stick together in this crazy circus of mirrors. Trust our own."

"Last thing Ji needs is you lecturing her tonight."

"It's not a lecture, T, it's a sermon. If you were a tad bit smarter you'd know the difference. She's got a special purpose. Proved it when she offed those Bounty Boys an' found Worthy's letter. Proved it again when she sprouted a pair an' metamorphosed herself with you, my boy, as witness. *Metamorphosed* is a real word, by the way, pardner. Look it up."

"Me too," Afarra said. "I am being there for the pair. We are all seeing it. With the Eyes."

"Yeah," Marcus said. "You were there too, hon." His anger toward Afarra had apparently been snuffed out by their brush with disaster. Or maybe he felt guilty? No. Ji-ji sensed that guilt wasn't an emotion Marcus indulged in very much. She listened as he continued talking.

"Just want you to know I'm a fan, Ji-ji. When you pick your Dream Team, forget about Tiro Dregulahmo, great-nephew of a wizard. Marcus Aurelius, fearless stoic, will be your wingman."

To Ji-ji's relief, Tiro changed the subject this time: "So, to make a long story short, Redipp's in cahoots with Yardley. But don't worry. Corcoran's an ally. Treats flyers with respect."

Marcus' laughter was laced with mockery: "How many times I gotta tell you? Corker's no better than the rest. Only difference is morons like Redipp are worse at hiding their true colors."

Tiro refused to rise to the bait and returned instead to his earlier line of conversation. The wing commander's arrival had given him and Marcus an excuse to bolt, he said. Just before they did, they'd overheard Yardley tell Corcoran he'd stopped by with a team of engineers to assess the new equipment in the coop. Claimed he would have stopped by earlier only he was delayed by the Fourth of July post-fireworks fund-raisers. "Final battle of the season's against the Hell's Yells from Armistice, our archrivals," Tiro explained. "Hell's Yells is one of only three teams stand a chance of beating us, so everyone's focused on that matchup. The Atlanta Tricksters and Chicago Campaigners are powerhouse teams, but not good enough to beat us this season. Don't worry, Ji. Corker's on our side. Ask Amadeus."

Marcus shook his head. "An' who says I'm-a-God can be trusted? I know you worship the ground I'm-Not-Mozart walks on, but did you ever wonder why he's the longest-serving coopmaster the fleet's ever had? Trust me. If he hadn't done a whole heap of compromising over the years, he wouldn't be perched on one of the Dream's highest rungs. Think about it. He was an outcast, on the lowest rung of the steaders' Great Ladder—no offense meant, Afarra." Afarra, still feasting on the box of chocolates in her lap, didn't appear to be listening. Marcus kept talking.

"Nelson's a former Serverseed in a city that's not exactly keen on coloring outside the lines. Outcasts—especially ones who have the audacity to rename themselves after a Black savior like Mandela—don't rise to the top 'less someone's wheel's been thoroughly and repeatedly greased. Could be the one person we should all be wary of is our noble coopmaster. As I've always said, T, any arc on the Color Wheel is Uncle Tom capable."

"What the hell are you rattling on about, man? Nelson's ten times the—"

Marcus covered his right ear with his hand to indicate to Tiro that he'd stopped listening. "I refuse to listen to a moral reprobate like yourself. I have it on good authority you're a sneaker and a cheating. Ask the choc-sop." Marcus removed his hand from his ear. "Listen an' learn, T. Last time I looked, this was still the *Dis*united States. Dream's been festering here for centuries. Don't matter how spiffy a Serverseed looks in a top hat an' tails."

Before Tiro could argue with him again, Marcus slowed down. He pulled into the same spot where he'd parked earlier that evening, about a quarter mile from the abandoned practice coop behind a flood-damaged warehouse. Tiro insisted on accompanying their visitors back to the Aerie. Marcus told him to make it quick. Said he was in desperate need of his beauty sleep.

They covered the area quickly, dodging the many puddles and potholes that characterized one of D.C.'s worst flood zones, and they snuck in via a side door.

"You okay?" Ji-ji asked, having checked no guards were nearby.

"Yeah. Thanks for the sketch, an' for—you know—remembering. Sorry it was a bust."

"It wasn't. We got to see the Mall an' the fireworks. An' we got to see you fly the Dream."

Afarra bounded up the three flights of stairs to the small apartment. Softly, she called back down and begged Ji-ji to come to bed.

Tiro still had the box in his hand. He went over the contents: cookies, bread flour, sugar, fresh fruit and vegetables, candles, three pairs of socks for each of them, five cans of salmon, a notepad and pen for Ji, bottles of genuine spring water, disinfectant, a tiny bottle of perfume, and a bar of soap that smelled like roses for Afarra, who'd never got over her love of sweet-smelling soap after her stay at Sally's House in Monticello. His gift was grander than hers had been, but she knew things like that didn't matter to him.

Awkwardly, with the box between them, they hugged each other. Although he was much taller and more muscular than she was, he felt fragile, brittle almost.

"You okay?" she asked again.

"Sure. Just tired. S'been a long day. Didn't fly so good at practice."

Afarra leaned over the banisters and called down again for Ji-ji to come up to bed.

"I gotta go," Ji-ji said, reaching for the gift box.

"You want I should carry the box upstairs? It's pretty heavy."

"It's fine, I got it." She turned back and said, "You flew like a bird tonight, Tiro. Zaini, Bromadu, Eeyatho, Uncle Dreg an' Amadee—those two most of all—they would've been real proud."

Hoping she'd said the right thing, she hurried up the stairs, more grateful to be home than she'd ever dreamed she would be when she'd set out that evening.

|||||||||||||||

Safe in the Aerie, Ji-ji lay next to Afarra, who'd insisted they sleep together on Afarra's narrow bed so they could "watch the painting rise." Ji-ji figured she meant watch the sun's rays rise on the mural she'd painted, but she preferred Afarra's version to her own. It paid tribute to the wizard's Death Day prophecy and the Rising he predicted. The candle, one of Tiro's gifts, sputtered out. It didn't matter. Dawn had arrived.

Ji-ji heard a bodyguard pull up and another pull away in the car that spent more time in the repair shop than it did on the road. The guard she'd nick-named Large Bodyguard-at-Large was being relieved of duty by his replacement, ignorant of the fact that his two charges had snuck out and back in again under his nose.

Afarra mumbled something unintelligible and hugged Ji-ji tighter. The whiff she got of chocolate on Afarra's breath made Ji-ji smile. She wouldn't get much sleep. Coach Mackie would arrive in a couple of hours to give her another flying lesson. For once, the thought of failure didn't dishearten her. For a few precious hours, she'd lived the life she'd dreamed about on the planting. She could milk that memory for weeks—months, if she had to.

A gash of sunlight shone on the mural through a crack in the drapes. Enough light for her to see the entire painting, which didn't look as romanticized to her as it sometimes did. On the lower right side, there Ji-ji was with Afarra, who rode on her shoulders. On the upper left of the mural was the moon. "Ladyest Moon," Afarra called her. Claimed she was "the most girliest, most moonish moon of all," whatever that meant. Ji-ji decided the moon was One Being's One Eye, the Cradle God from Uncle Dreg's First Story. In her mural, against all reason, her unfurled wings (yes, she had a right to call them that) retained their purple shimmer in the darkness. She and Afarra smiled ecstatically. Two loons being loony together, flapping their way to Luna, the Ladyest Moon. Afarra sat perched on her shoulders so she wouldn't get in the way of the giant wings, "the riot on her back." Afarra hadn't actually said those words, yet Ji-ji had heard them loud and clear, as if the two of them were so close they could hear each other's thoughts.

As usual, Afarra slept with the wizard's Seeing Eyes around her neck, her mouth open in a small *o* as if a favorite story had delighted her again. Fearful though she was that Afarra would choke, Ji-ji had given up trying to ease the necklace off her at night. Invariably, if she tried to remove it, Afarra woke in a frenzy and demanded to know what she was doing. Ji-ji had asked to try on the necklace the other day, but Afarra had shaken her head emphatically. "His Eyes is *mine* to carry," she'd said. "He is giving them to *me*." "You said they were lying on your mat in your sleep-shed. Said you didn't know who left 'em there." "He is *telling* me" was all Afarra would reveal.

The necklace's wildest, wide-open eye—the one painted on the fat wooden bead in the center—gazed at something. Ji-ji followed its gaze over to the moon on the mural. The stark white eye, a perfect circle, stared right back.

Tonight, Ji-ji's impossible dreams seemed possible. She'd learn to use these unruly Freedom Twins on her back if it killed her. She'd find her sister Charra in the Madlands. Together, they'd search for Bonbon, their little brother. Impossible things could happen, *did* happen. You had to be ready to play your part.

In the uncanny way she had of knowing what Ji-ji was thinking, Afarra woke and mumbled, "We go find her like you said. Charra in the Madlands. Bonbon too. His Eye is watching, Elly."

"So is hers," Ji-ji replied, looking at the painted moon.

Then, without any sense of letting go, Ji-ji floated down on the sweet, soothing drafts of sleep.

Ji-ji and Afarra sat cross-legged around the scratched-up coffee table with the mismatched legs. Furniture, like everything else in D.C., was hard to come by. But Zyla and the Friends had nevertheless managed to cobble together sufficient used and salvaged items to furnish the apartment. In the center of the coffee table was a metal wastebasket. Next to it lay a box of matches. Next to that lay two sheets of white paper—one with a lot of writing on it, the other with very little. A small gap between the drapes allowed a sliver of September afternoon sun to enter, which revealed that the ink on both sheets of paper was purple. Ji-ji didn't need to explain the significance of the color to Afarra. Former seeds knew that the metal death tags hung from penal trees were called purple tears. Seedlings throughout the Territories sang the purple pain rhyme while they mimed the playing of fake guitars as if they were extensions of their own bodies.

> Purple pain is prince again
> Rain tears and wince again

"You ready?" Ji-ji asked. Afarra nodded.

Ji-ji took a deep breath. Coach Billy had told her that establishing a group below regular seeds was the steaders' masterstroke cos it gave everyone a punching bag. She liked to think of today's ceremony as a way of punching back. After the terrifying incidents at the Mall and Dream Coop, Ji-ji felt the need to grab hold of life and claim it as theirs. The ceremony she'd planned for today wouldn't mean much to anyone except the two of them, of course, but that was the point. The friends who were as close as sisters were the only people who mattered. Today, they would rewrite the world in their own image.

Ji-ji had already explained to Afarra that "whereas," as far as she could tell, didn't mean much of anything, even though, like "resolved," it was in capital letters for emphasis. Those words simply provided context and made the resolution more official. Legal language had to be formal and unclear, Ji-ji explained, otherwise people didn't think it counted. She read the words slowly:

"WHEREAS Serverseed outcasts in the Territories are named after boycloths or girl-cloths, the steader term for underwear;

"And WHEREAS all Serverseeds are assigned to the lowest rung of the steaders' Great Ladder, beasts—i.e., animals, mutants and traitors—being the only group on the only rung below them;

"And WHEREAS Armistice, the Father-City of the Homestead Territories, does not require plantings to keep records of Serverseed births and deaths, having decreed that outcasts don't officially exist. . . ."

Ji-ji paused. She'd lifted the next part straight from *An Abbreviated History of These Disunited States,* the history textbook Zyla had given her on the planting. Historian Maeve Exra's words carried more weight than hers did. They'd helped Ji-ji maintain her sanity on the 437th. She slowed down even more to signal her reverence for them.

"And WHEREAS Serverseeds' extreme subjugation reinforces the steaders' heinous Purity Doctrine and the colorist malignancy at the core of steader ideology;

"Therefore, let it be RESOLVED from now on that the former Serverseed outcast formerly known as Cloth-33h/437 will be known throughout the Disunited States and the entire world as Afarra;

"And let it be RESOLVED that she is entitled to the same rights as every other Freeman and Freewoman."

"A door with a lock for privacy—like here, isn't it?"

"Exactly," Ji-ji said. "Privacy is a right for sure."

The next resolution had been one of the hardest cos she'd had to explain to Afarra how tenuous her residency status was.

"And let it be RESOLVED that her friends Ji-ji an' Tiro, together with Zyla and the Friends of Freedom, will work tirelessly to upgrade her status from provisional residency to regular residency;

"And let it be RESOLVED that, from now on, Afarra's official birthday will be on October—"

"Cos I like the *O* cos it comes quick after September. With the cake."

"Exactly," Ji-ji agreed. She started over with the birthday resolution.

"And let it be RESOLVED that, from now on, Afarra's official birthday will be on October 12th cos she is snatching that symbolic number back from the father-men an' using it entirely for her own delight."

Ji-ji picked up a cardboard folder from the floor by her feet. She'd decorated it with the city's Justitia Omnibus seal, though she'd taken a few liberties with it. Instead of Lady Justice placing a wreath on a statue of George Washington, she'd drawn Afarra placing a wreath on the Dreamer's statue. She wished she'd done a better job with it, but it would have to do. She'd kept the Capitol in the background, and the *Justice for All* saying in Latin was still there in a banner at the bottom. But she'd added an exclamation point for emphasis to counter the ones steaders' used on their hateful motto *Growing the Territories One Seed at a Time!*

Ji-ji wasn't sure if D.C. allowed people to mess with the state seal. For all she knew, she'd broken a law by doing so. But then it wasn't like she hadn't done something similar before. You could be killed on a planting for imaging something, and she'd drawn a map of the 437th and hidden it under her bed. Redesigning the city-state's seal wasn't nearly as reckless as that had been. Besides, the folder didn't belong to anyone except them, and they weren't living on a planting in the Territories anymore, having made it to the City of Dreams.

With care, making sure not to crease it, she placed what she called Afarra's Resolutions in the folder and handed it to her friend.

"Mine?" Afarra said. "I put it in my new Forget-Me-Not Treasure Box."

"It won't fit 'less you fold it up. How 'bout we use the gift box Tiro brought last time? I'll draw forget-me-nots on that box too."

"Okay," Afarra said. "We burn the other paper now?"

"Yeah. This is the other part, the Immolation Ritual. It makes these resolutions an' the bond between us unbreakable. Afarra, please read out the letters an' numbers like we practiced."

Afarra read out each letter and number: "C-L-O-T-H 3–3-h." She struggled with the slash, then remembered what it was called. "Forward slash 4–3–7."

"Perfect," Ji-ji said. "Now we set fire to it to extinguish the name forever. If someone says it in the future, it can't hurt you cos it's not really you."

Afarra took a match from the box and struck it. It flared a bluish purple in the semidarkness. Ji-ji held the paper with Afarra's planting designation on it while Afarra put a match to the corner. It didn't catch at first, as if the steaders were holding on to their claim. Suddenly, an orange tongue flared and engulfed one side of the sheet. Ji-ji held the flaming paper for as long as she could before dropping it into the wastebasket on the coffee table. They watched the flame peter out. It was done.

Ji-ji's heart was pounding. She told her beloved friend the truth: "Afarra, I want you to know you're the best goddam human I've ever met. Tied with Uncle Dreg. I love you so much."

"I love you more, Elly," Afarra said, and smiled.

Ji-ji caught a glimpse of the gap in her mouth where Silapu, in a drunken rage, had knocked out two of her teeth. One day, she'd take Afarra to a dentist and buy her two new ones.

"Cloth-33h exists no longer," Ji-ji said. "Long live Afarra."

Just when Ji-ji was starting to suspect that the whole ceremony had meant more to her than it had to Afarra, her friend reached over and took her hand. Her grip was firm, determined, *old*.

"Cloth-33h exists no longer," Afarra repeated, in a voice her own and not her own at the same time. "Long live the Dreamers. Long live the Dream."

6 ON PURPLE TEARS

Ordered to remain in her room, Ji-ji heard Zyla with Afarra in the kitchen. It was October twelfth, Afarra's official birthday, and they were making a birthday cake to celebrate. After five months in the city, Afarra had become close to Ji-ji's former teacher. Their easy laughter echoed through the apartment. Ji-ji had offered to make the cake, but Afarra had told Zyla she wanted to make it "as a surprise." Zyla had pointed out it wouldn't be a surprise if she made it herself. "Yes it will surprise," Afarra had told her. "Elly will say, 'Oh!' like this." She placed her hand over her mouth, "Like the *O* in 'October.'" Zyla, still thinking Afarra had misunderstood birthday surprises, had tried one more time: "It's *your* official birthday, not Ji-ji's. That's why you're the one who gets the surprise." As it turned out, Afarra hadn't misunderstood anything. "Elly is the one needing a surprise," she'd said. "To make her happy again, isn't it? To eat a double-chocolate fudge cake with chocolate frosting an' chocolate insides."

That evening, the three of them sat down to a birthday feast of salad, spaghetti primavera, homemade bread, and birthday cake. Tiro and the other flyboys were on the road, battling the Campaigners in Chicago, but they'd sent gifts to mark the auspicious occasion. Zyla had borrowed a camera so Afarra would have a memento of her first official birthday.

Ji-ji was struck, as always, by Zyla Clobershay's thoughtfulness. The petite blond Friend of Freedom visited daily unless she was on a mission. Sometimes she came with Germaine and Ben, but mostly alone on her moped. Much tougher than she looked, as her daring missions with the Friends demonstrated, Zyla was in her midthirties—roughly the same age as Ji-ji's mam had been when she was murdered. Although the White woman differed in many ways from Silapu, they both had an agile intelligence, a quick wit, and a fierce protectiveness of children and young people. Zyla was born in Colorado in the Unaligned Territories, but her parents were deeply committed to the cause of reunification. According to Germaine, Zyla was being groomed to take over when Alice retired as one of the co-leaders of the Friends of Freedom. Ji-ji could see why. The woman was fearless. Fearless to the point of recklessness, Lucky claimed. But Ji-ji hadn't seen the reckless side of Zyla. All she'd seen was her uncanny empathy, which had made the two years when Zyla Clobershay taught at 437's legacy school some of the few planting experiences Ji-ji treasured. As a Serverseed outcast, Afarra hadn't been eligible to attend school. In between training for the Freedom Race and her work as the chief kitchen-seed, Ji-ji had tried to teach her a few basic things for safety's sake. Numbers, for example, and words on labels and signs. Zyla was making up for lost time by teaching Afarra to read.

Zyla took a photo of the two girls seated at the kitchen table with their arms around each other. She'd purchased a frame so Afarra could keep the photo on the small side table by her bed. In front of Ji-ji and Afarra were two huge hunks of chocolate cake with mounds of chocolate frosting piled on top. Truffles, sent in another gift box from Tiro, were arranged in the shape of a heart on top of the cake. There were other gifts too: Large Bodyguard-at-Large had presented Afarra with a pack of cards; Tree and Ink had sent a set of colorful cloth napkins, which Afarra could surely use right now; Ben and Germaine had sent a cookbook filled with chocolate recipes and mouthwatering photos; and Marcus had sent Afarra the fanciest gift of all—a jacket in the black and gold colors of the fleet. He'd had the Dreamfleet tailors make it to his specifications and it fit like a glove. Ji-ji decided that Marcus was more thoughtful than she'd given him credit for.

Ji-ji's gift came from both her and Tiro. He'd made a much larger wooden treasure box than the ones he'd made for her in the past, and Ji-ji had painted bunches of forget-me-nots all over it. The box with its slide-to-open lid measured nine by eleven. Lined with purple velvet, the box could hold Afarra's Resolutions and some of her other larger treasures. Afarra was over the moon.

How could Ji-ji tell her she was as terrified of the future as she'd ever been in her life?

||||||||||||||||

The next evening, Ji-ji sat at the small writing desk Tiro had made for her. He'd learned carpentry on the planting, and the compact oak desk testified to his skill. She'd placed the snow globe he'd given her on the table alongside Lucas Dyson's lucky dice. A blanket lay across her shoulders. The sweltering heat had suddenly retreated, replaced by an unfamiliar chill. The flood-damaged Aerie would be miserably cold during their first winter in the city, but Zyla and the Friends of Freedom had anticipated this and provided them with a mountain of blankets and two portable oil heaters. Obtaining oil wasn't easy, however. They'd need to use the heaters sparingly.

Ji-ji was supposed to be working on her survival narrative—the memoir Zyla and the Friends had urged her to write ever since she'd arrived in the city. But the words wouldn't come; or if they did, they sounded like someone else had written them.

She picked up her pen again. Father-Man Lotter had tried to cure her of left-handedness, which he'd taken as a personal affront. Said it was the "trait of cretins." Fortunately, he'd lost interest in her again soon after that and forgotten all about it. Years later, when he happened to ask her to write down some instructions for him, he'd snorted in disgust. "Thought I'd cured you of that left-leaning nonsense," he'd said, before his focus shifted back to his sole obsession—her mam, who wanted, more than anything, to kill him. Would she include that explosive detail in her memoir, or would the Friends excise her mam's murderous yearning from the story?

She put the notebook aside, considered taking out her sketch pad, then changed her mind.

In the kitchen, Large Bodyguard-at-Large sat with Afarra playing Go Fish. She could hear them laughing together.

Ji-ji opened her notebook again and dug a line with her pen through every page of the memoir she'd written so far. What was the matter with her? Why couldn't she write the damn thing?

And then, a flash of inspiration. A journal! Why hadn't she thought of that before?

Journals weren't illegal in City of Dreams. She could write whatever she wanted and no one else would have the right to read it or punish her for it. More important, she could write in her *own* voice, be as honest as she wanted and mine the pages later for her survival narrative. If she could look back and review the entries, maybe she'd discover she was making more progress than she thought. At this stage, anything was worth a try. With trepidation, Ji-ji began.

|||||||||||||||

October 13: My first entry. It's like this notebook will be a friend I can speak to. Thing is, it's like they're not even <u>there</u> anymore. Like Afarra's Freedom Twins have decided to hibernate. How does a pair of wings with a span larger than twenty feet retreat so far into someone's back they virtually disappear? I feel like someone's pried em out & left me with nothing but sorrow. It's like they've abandoned me & a part of me knows none of it was real. Sometimes I half-expect to wake up on Stinky Brine's homestead & discover I'm his seedmate after all cos Lucky never showed up to let me out of Brine's confessional. Or he did, but we got caught & I'm locked in the confessional again staring at Truffie the skeleton. No one comes to visit me. Not even Lua-Dim

with her sifting-down braids & her dead deadborn. Lucky never leaves me a light to find. This purple pain—it's killing me. Why can't I shake it off?—LBL's leaving. Afarra'll be in soon. I gotta find a way to climb out into daylight. All I do is sink down deeper. Help me. Someone. <u>PLEASE!!</u>

October 22: I still can't believe it! Two days ago all of a sudden they wake up! I can do it again! Furl, unfurl, furl, unfurl! It's like something clicked in my back—some switch that was stuck before. <u>THA-WUMPH!</u> The sound they make as they flare open! Like the sound laundry makes on a clothesline when it flaps in the wind. <u>THA-WUMPH!THA-WUMPH!</u> Zyla called Doc Riff & told him my back had sprung to life again. I could hear his voice loud & clear cos he was almost as excited as Afarra. Says it proves they're still viable. Viable just became the best word in the entire goddam dictionary! LBL heard about it. He shows up this evening to play cards with Afarra & knocks on my bedroom door. I open it. LBL is standing there with this bouquet of daisies, applauding. I lost it. Not sure who was more embarrassed, LBL or me.

November 30: Need to do a better job keeping up with this journal. Too much good stuff going on to sit still & write. It's all SO good I get scared. Scared it won't last. Terrified I'll wake up one day & be back where I was in mid-Oct. But then I stop myself from going there. If you can't enjoy the present cos you're always dreading the future what's the point? Thanksgiving was the way I'd dreamed it would be. They all came by at different times to avoid arousing suspicion in case the steaders find out I didn't die & think I could be an existential threat to the Territories after all. Tiro, Zyla, Ben & Germaine, they all stopped by. We gotta tread carefully. "No more jaunts to the Mall for you, Missy"—Zyla says. Still don't know how she found out. Afarra swears she didn't tell her but A's been as crazy excited bout my sudden viability as I am so—who knows?—it could've slipped out. Doesn't matter. What's Z gonna do? Ground us? (Ha-ha) I'm working on controlling em. Most of the time I can. But they're strong as my thighs when I used to run miles every day—stronger even. Two great big muscles that look like they're made of??? Closest analogy I can think of is water. Or mirrors made of shards in a thousand shades of purple & silver. More & more I see why Afarra calls em Purple Tears. I'm not freaked out by that anymore cos of what the doc said. Riff saw me flinch when Afarra called em that when he was examining me. The doc said it was a fine name for them. Said names for many indigenous people were about connection, whereas names for other people in the Disunited States were an expression of individuality. Afarra perked right up when he said 'whereas.' She looks over at me & nods, like whatever the doc says from now on is an official resolution. Then Riff said it could be I was carrying those we'd lost. That my wings (he always calls em that now) honored the ones the steaders killed. I said it certainly felt like it at times when they got heavy as lead. The doc laughed at that. He's got a good sense of humor & a nice smile. Female seeds used to make up excuses to go see him at the clinic. Could be his sense of humor helped keep him sane tending to seeds in the Territories for all those years. Uncle Dreg always said humor was underestimated as a preservative. (meaning a preservative of human life not a preservative you put in food.) Doc Riff's sense of humor prompted me to show him Amadee's initials. Only they'd almost worn off. Weren't sposed to wear off at all, but I guess the ink wasn't as permanent as Tiro an I thought. Or maybe cos I keep em on the move now with furling & unfurling the friction took its toll. Riff said he could tattoo the initials onto that same flap if I wanted. I said yeah, sure. T's birthday's in December. That'll be my gift to him. Along with another sketch. Once in a while, they unfurl spontaneously. <u>THA-WUMPH!</u>—all on their own. The left one knocked Mackie over yesterday but all she did was laugh. Seems like everyone is laughing these days including me. Coach has been in a good mood ever since my back "revivified"—that's what she calls it, only she rolls her *r*'s so it sounds a lot more impressive when she says it. Scots have the best accents. Afarra tries to do it, too, but she can't. Says her tongue isn't flighty enough. Hilarious. Zyla says the way Scots pronounce their *r*'s is called an alveolar trill. I told her that's kinda how my wings feel when they unfold. As if they're trilling superfast. I unfurled for Tiro, Ben an Germaine. They'd seen me do this already of course, after I blossomed in the spring. But it seems like my wings have grown since then. These days, when Doc Riff examines me he smiles more than I've ever seen him smile. If this is the extent of what I can do, it's enough. The pain has all but disappeared. Sometimes you can be too happy. I'm not a freak. I'm brand new. Afarra swears I'm an angel, same thing Lua-Dim said in the confessional. I remember everything you told me, Lua. I swear I do. Wish you were alive to see this. Wish Uncle Dreg and Mam could see it too. Charra will see it soon. I'll never doubt the wizard again.

December 8: Been too excited to write. Nearly a week ago, another miracle. Usually my wings unfurl so they look like two gigantic semitransparent sails. (<u>Note to self</u>: Do a sketch of the different shapes they take.) Usually, they're these ludicrously outsized sail-like things, curved out from my shoulders and shaped like you'd expect wings to be—like the ones on angels in old paintings only bigger than that—heftier. But light too & see-thru, almost like the wings on cicadas. But recently, I get this strange sensation in my back, as if someone is giving me one of those deep tissue massages flyer-battlers get. & lo and behold, I find I can alter their morphology (if that's the right way to use that word) so it's more expressive. I can <u>CHANGE</u> the shape!!! Sometimes I can make em look more like eagle's wings, sometimes I keep most of the wings retracted so they resemble the wings of smaller birds. Still no feathers, but who cares? It's not just wings either. Once, I formed them into what Zyla swore was a double helix!!! But it only lasted for a split second & without a big mirror it was hard to see if she was right. & what would they be doing that for anyway? is a good question. Whatever shape they take, they've always got the same, small, semitransparent flaps all over em that look like fish scales. Afarra says the flaps are closed eyelids. Tiro has always called em mini wing flaps. I can move the flaps synchronously again, just like I could when I first blossomed. Feels like I imagine the ocean tides feel on your body. Rhythmic. Powerful. The Friends want to take me to the Eastern SuperState even if all I can do is what I can do now. Alice, the leader of the Friends, stopped by to see why everyone was going nuts. She wept when I unfurled for her & morphed em every which way. Zyla said she'd known Alice for years & has never seen her overcome like that. Alice seems like the type of White woman who keeps a lot inside. Used to be married to a cropmaster who tried to kill her, Zyla says, when she asked for a divorce. Had to run like hell to the Eastern SuperState to be rid of him & even then the bastard comes looking for her. Alice told me I could help "turn the tide" of reunification and rid the country of the scourge of plantings for good. Said dozens of Liberty Independents could be persuaded to link arms with the SuperStates. All they needed was a symbol to rally round & I could be the greatest symbol the Friends had ever had. 1st thing came to mind was the Dreamfleet mascot. The man in the eagle costume who jumps around like a clown & makes fans laugh. That's not what she meant but that's what I saw. Alice didn't actually say I had an obligation to serve but you could tell that's what she would've said if she didn't think it would sound coercive. Zyla was pissed. Called Alice out on it. Told me choice was sacred for Friends of Freedom, so I never had to do anything I didn't want to do. Said I was Free now. She's right. I am. Free as a bird! If I live to be a hundred, I'll never be able to say what it means to have my body back. . . . Tiro's doing okay. I was worried it could be hard for him, but he & Marcus & Tree too had the best rookie season in Dreamfleet history. Won every single battle—home & away. They've gotten pretty famous. Tiro wears a disguise when he stops by. Poor Tree can't go incognito, but Tiro says he's very patient with the fans. Personalizes his autographs & never gets irritated. I figure it must be the weed mellows him out. So the flyer-battler season is almost done for the Dreamfleet while my flying season is about to begin. . . .

December 25: Z's gift—two capes for me to wear—one plum-colored, the other navy blue. I can retract my wings completely now. It doesn't even look like I suffer from a curvature of the spine. T's Xmas gift was another gift box filled with treats, even better than the ones he's given us before. A's gift—a poem she wrote herself and read aloud. She's improving fast after Z figured out dyslexia was the culprit. Z's learned a few tricks to make it easier for A to recognize words & not jumble em up. A is over the moon. The other day she says, 'WHEREAS you can fly, let it be RESOLVED we will rise together.' Could be the best sentence anyone's ever said to anyone. Her poem was excellent, though there were some lines I'll ask her to explain. I've pasted it below:

Afarra's Poem
We are flying to the ladymoon on Purple Tears
She appears to be asleep it's a lie
If i die i will not cry like the moon eye am seeing her weeping
With the roar of wide mouths O i am seeing him too
The stone moves. Who moves it. We do. Who speaks to me.
i hear the creatures with my thousand eyes.

No one sees me thru the window of what's to come

After she read it aloud and the applause died down, she said she's writing her *i*'s small & that's all there is to it. Z tried to make her write *I* with a capital & she was very offended. She was more offended when Ben suggested she change 'eye' in line 3 to *I* & add a few periods. Told him to go to hell. But after she saw she'd hurt his feelings she was real nice to him. She knows we owe our lives to Ben & Germaine for getting us safely to Monticello. Think she surprised herself by how passionate she was about capitals. The other night, I heard these far-off voices moaning out in pain & I thought of Muckmock. I look around thinking someone must be nearby. But no one is. Then it went away. Mostly everything is wonderful. I'm filled with so much anticipation I feel like I'm levitating. Gotta look down at my feet to check they're still on the ground!

January 1: Here are some of the names Afarra has given them: Shimmershines, Secret Hopefuls, High-Flys, Gifts-To-Give-Them, Hand-Me-Downs, Freedom Twins, and of course Purple Tears. As far as we can tell, their dominant shape usually favors passive rather than active soaring. I dream of riding the thermals the way eagles do. Sometimes they look more like the elliptical wings of ravens, perfect for aerial acrobatics and bursts of speed.

January 3: Yesterday Z and A said I was beautiful. We were standing in the living room—the only room large enough to accommodate my unfurled self. My wings took on their original shape. About 80% of the time that's the shape they take. I've never been beautiful in the way men, steaders especially, use that word. 'Plain as whole wheat' Mam used to call me when she was drunk or high. Said it to Lotter once. Beauty to them had to be a certain way & I wasn't it. Charra was. Mam was. Luvlydoll too. Even though Luvlydoll never got to be more than a toddler before metaflu took her you could tell her prettiness would last. So here's my new resolution:

> WHEREAS people often use beauty to tell someone they're not enough, let it be RESOLVED that beauty is the wearer's to possess not the viewer's to determine.

Yes. I like that. I, Ji-ji Silapu, am in possession of my own unique beauty. I am at peace with the incomprehensibility of who I will become.

January 4: What's weird about them is this. (It's not the only thing that's weird, but this particular weirdness is freaking me out today.) Sometimes they're light as air, then the very next moment they're heavy as a pair of wet sails. Sometimes I imagine they exist in another dimension, a place where the rules of physics & evolution don't apply. I asked Doc Riff to explain why they defy science & reason. He'd been stumped too, at first. Then he'd thought about it for a while and said our rush to define things sometimes worked against us. 'Too many men make the world smaller,' he said, 'so they can swallow it whole.' His people, who'd been in this country for centuries before the Europeans arrived, weren't afraid of mystery so they didn't feel a need to conquer it. Instead they embraced the unknowable. Lived with it as a neighbor. Unknowables. One of the few names for the things on my back that does justice to their strangeness.

January 6: It's natural the doc says. They're probably strained with all the furling & unfurling. But then I get terrified cos they don't look like any wings anyone's ever seen. I've looked into it. Spent dozens of hours leafing through books Z brought me. Gone online too, whenever the Friends verify the network's secure. Too many things from the Age of Plenty have been lost, Z says, so books, if you can find em, are still the best bet.

January 8: This is what my research tells me. I got no primary, secondary or tertiary feathers, no vanes, or hamuli, no rachis—the hollow centers barbs protrude from. I told Tiro what I'd discovered. 'Planes got feathers?' he says. 'No. Planes fly without flapping, right? You know how fans call me Tiro the Pterodactyl when I fly the Dream?' (He tells me Marcus showed him an image of a pterodactyl.) 'Not a feather to be seen on them dino wings.' I tell him 'Pterodactyls aren't dinosaurs or birds either. They're flying reptiles.' He's dubious. 'Look pretty dinosaur-y to me. Anyway, point is, you don't need feathers.' Then he says the only flyer who wears feathers in the coop is X-Clamation, '& that peacock ditches his rainbow dandification cloak soon as he starts to fly. Struts around bare-chested & gives the fans a thrill. Not that X can fly for real. None of us can . . .'cept maybe you one day. . . . Guess you'll leave us poor fly-boys in the dust.' He laughs then, but I suddenly understand how painful it is for him not to have the potential to defy gravity like I may be able to do one day. It hits me again that I've been given this amazing gift, yet here I am getting crazy anxious. 'So it seems to me,' Tiro says (he stretches out his arms & runs in circles in the kitchen to imitate a plane) 'feathers is optional.' Then he stops & looks at me & says, 'Seems to me you only need one more ingredient to fly like a bird.' I ask him what that is & he says, 'Speed, Ji. Speed.' & all I can say is 'I hope to god you're right.'

<u>January 10:</u> It's natural, Riff says. Nothing to be alarmed about.

<u>January 26:</u> Doc says my hormones are totally out of whack—that's what he meant anyway, only he used medical terminology. His kindness scalds even more than his pity. Something isn't right & it's not just hormones—though god knows they're screwed up too. My whole biology's nuts. Don't even feel like myself anymore. About half the time I can't unfurl properly. They come out twisted or get stuck halfway out. Other times they unfurl & stay that way stiff as boards. Doc Riff called in Dr. Narayanan cos he's a board-certified surgeon & backs are his specialty. (Not backs like mine, backs in general.) Dr. N didn't have the answer either. I'm trying not to panic. Germaine stopped by. Says it's like childbirth. If you tense up too much you can't deliver. I screamed at her. 'What do *you* know about it?' Then after G's gone, Z tells me Ben & Germaine have lost two womblings and suffered two deadborn births. That's how she knows what childbirth is like. I run out to apologize only I forget my wings are unfurled & slam up against the door frame & Z & A hold me till I stop weeping. I guess Riff may be right bout my hormones.

<u>January 30:</u> Got stuck in the unfurled pose again. Another spontaneous unfurling. The goddam things are stiff as boards. T stopped by. Called it my 'rigor mortis pose' which confirmed every fear I've got. They collapsed soon as he left. The collapse was accompanied by this weird sound. Like cascading water or glass shattering. I could hardly bear to look behind me. When I did, all I see is a floppy train. Couldn't furl em up again for the life of me or get em to stiffen either. Had to go to bed like that. Dragging the things behind me like twin corpses.

<u>February—all of it:</u> The worst is happening. I got A to bring me alcohol. I got T to bring me weed. I drank it, smoked it. Didn't help.

<u>March 1:</u> Haven't been able to furl the things up in weeks. They're permanently droopy. I drag em behind me like some ugly train. If I can bear it, I'll do a sketch. If I can't I won't. I can't do this much longer. Fuck.

March 3: From what I can tell my back and shoulder muscles are starting to atrophy. I've lost the ability to open and close my wing flaps. Paralysis is setting in. Doc doesn't say that. Doesn't need to. They've changed color. Turned from a shimmery silvery purple to a dull gray. Like ash that's left in a fireplace after the fire's gone out. A few days ago, they itched like the worst case of poison ivy. I've scratched em so often—in my sleep mostly—I've gouged out some of the flaps. Would've gouged out a bunch more if Afarra didn't watch me like a hawk.

March 6: The pain set in this morning. Relentless. Can't write much. Only lets up a few seconds at a time. When I open my eyes to another day of torment all I want to do is SCREAM!!!!!

March 12: The things on my back are dragging me into a black hole. I'm a Try-Again Mam said. I'm a Try-Again who's done with trying. T visited today. The pity in his eyes, the way he avoided looking at me. . . . JesusJesusJesus! WHY??!!

March 16: These are my names for the infestation on my back—Ugly Sisters, Locked Doors, Purple Torments, Sick Jokes, Stink Spans, Lotter's Legacies. I need to know what role my father-man played in my freakish engineering. When I was in Dimmers, Man Cryday said it didn't matter how I came to be like this it mattered what I became. The tree witch was WRONG! I need to know why I'm a monster. The wizard was WRONG too. Im not some miracle . . . Im Jellybean Lottermule . . . Arundale Lotter's stinking mutant . . . O god o god o god help me!!! At night when Afarra's asleep I imagine holding a gun to Lotter's head as he begs for mercy. . . . After he's shit his pants I pull the trigger. . . . Free of him at last I'm as numb as the withered monstrosities I drag behind me. . . . These days even in my fantasies I can't feel anything at all.

April—all of it. The news has SHATTERED me. last hope-rope gnawed through. Should've known this would happen during the month of dread. In the godforsaken Territories, Propitious Gleanings. Juvi males shipped off to auctionmarts. Mothers weeping. i hear them all the time.

Seeds dream of the Freedom Race, hope they make it to the fabled City of Dreams. i was a dreamer too once. Pain ricochets through my body i grub around inside it. A monster Roots digging trenches in my back 'Some pain is alone to carry'—Afarra said that to me once. she was right.

||||||||||||||

Ji-ji flipped through the pages of her diary. From the end of January onward, it was filled with purple tears. Which is why, late one night when Afarra was fast asleep, she tore out the pages from those purple days, cut them into small strips, boiled them in tea, and put the sodden mess in the trash bag Large Bodyguard-at-Large collected and took to the dump.

She'd erased the words for pain. Pain itself was the only thing left to obliterate.

7 EPIPHANIES

Sunlight blazed through partially shuttered skylights and striped Ji-ji's face. Half-asleep, she searched for oblivion again, gave up, opened her eyes. The intensity and angle of the sun reminded her that spring had begun. Yet, apart from that one trip on the fake Fourth of July, she'd remained in hiding. And now, she'd woken up to face another day in the Dream.

Damn.

For the second time, they'd slept up in the nest again, at Ji-ji's insistence this time. The climb up had been perilous without Coach Mackie's assistance. When Ji-ji had made the climb last month in hopes that a ride on the zip line would "revivify" her appendages (an idea born of desperation), Coach Mackie had shouldered one of her deformities and Afarra had carried the other as Ji-ji made her arduous ascent up Harriet's Stairs. The zip line exercise was a bust. Her flying lessons had become flying in name only. She remained on ground level doing strengthening exercises Mackie claimed would build stamina. Strange thing was, although Ji-ji had never flown, she felt as if she'd been able to do that once upon a time. That was the hardest part. The agonizing loss of a gift she'd never really possessed.

Yesterday, Ji-ji had finally convinced Mackie to let her try the zip line again. Mackie would never have acquiesced if she'd known Ji-ji planned to spend the night up in the nest too. Ji-ji had taken the advice Marcus gave her to heart: only give out as much info as you have to. Keep the rest of yourself a secret.

Afarra lay in a deep sleep beside her, her beautiful dark skin so lovely in the gathering light that Ji-ji leaned over and kissed her forehead. Who would tell her how beautiful she looked asleep if her Elly didn't? Zyla maybe? Yes. Zyla would tell her.

Ji-ji reached back and ran her hand over her deformities. Force of habit. Months ago, she'd abandoned the idea that feathers were in her future, but she still yearned to feel something—anything—that would suggest the deformities had sprung to life again. With her fingers, Ji-ji pried one of her wing flaps open. Immediately, she was hit with a sour stench like moldy yogurt. A crusty substance had formed underneath, as if Afarra was right. The flaps were a thousand sleep-filled eyes. Ji-ji fought to stop herself from gagging.

It was now or never. Ji-ji pushed back her mam's blackbird quilt and attempted to rise without waking Afarra. Her back spasmed. Agony! She hoped Afarra would stay asleep for a while. Her friend's unflagging optimism depressed the hell out of her.

As gently as she could, Ji-ji rolled onto all fours and arched her back to get the kinks out. Another spasm down her spine! The metallic taste in her mouth told her she'd bitten her tongue. She spat out blood and swore under her breath. Grasping the side of the nest, she hauled herself up. The pain intensified. She refused to scream. . . . One more Herculean effort and she was on her feet!

For a moment, she felt powerful—like an animule must feel when it rears up on its hind legs and throws off its burdens. Her triumph was short-lived. She almost toppled backward from the weight, even though, most of the time, her deformities weren't heavy in the usual sense of the word. If she'd stumbled a little more she would have toppled out of the nest like one of those baby birds. The thought didn't alarm her. Doc Riff was fond of telling her that the growths on her back were "incomprehensibly light, almost weightless." Whenever he said this, Ji-ji wanted to yell, "Weightless my ass! You try dragging these two shits behind you day in an' day out, then tell me how weightless they are!" She didn't say any of that out loud of course. Didn't speak much anymore.

When her appendages used to spontaneously unfurl as if a sadist in possession of a remote control had decided to mess with them, Afarra used to swear they were "being vicious." Took Ji-ji a while to figure out she meant "vivacious," a word Man Cryday had used to describe them. But now Ji-ji decided her initial interpretation was correct. The enormous malformations hanging from her back were as vicious as life itself.

The knowledge that there was another Wingchild in the world had been Ji-ji's greatest consolation. Charra, her beautiful, courageous sister, would understand what it felt like to mutate into some freakish bird-girl. She would celebrate and grieve with her like she used to on the planting. Charra would know exactly what to say to inspire her to keep going. But last Wednesday, on the first day of spring, Tiro and Zyla had shown up at the same time to sever the only hope-rope she still clung to. Must've thought the news of Charra's death would be easier (for her? for them?) if they delivered it together. It wasn't.

Dengue hemorrhagic fever had killed her elder sister down in the Madlands. Ji-ji wouldn't have believed it if it hadn't been for the gift Charra's followers had enclosed, along with a note saying dengue fever had taken her. The dog-eared book of nursery rhymes Charra used to read to her to help her fall asleep brought Ji-ji to her knees.

Still wincing from the pain in her back, Ji-ji shuffled forward and tripped. She kicked her pitiful train out from underfoot. Gingerly, she grasped her left appendage and raised it to her nose. Not good. She and Afarra struggled to maintain Doc Riff's rigorous hygiene routine. The cleaning ritual took all day. They had to stretch out each bulky appendage (like a supersized version of Uncle Dreg's story-cloths) and expose the underside of hundreds of tiny overlapping flaps to scour them. The tiny flaps, which used to be soft and pliable, had calcified. A few were as sharp as glass and could inflict painful paper cuts. Doc Riff liked to point out that had she been able to fly, the rushing air would likely scrub them clean. Was he deliberately trying to hurt her? Didn't he realize that trying harder was grinding her to dust?

An arthritic stiffness had spread throughout her body. Ji-ji hadn't told anyone, not even Afarra, how excruciating the pain was or how many killers she was taking to counter it. Nor had she told anyone how she'd begged Doc Riff to perform a wexcision. The doc had told her a double wing amputation was "out of the question." When Ji-ji kept insisting he try it whatever the risk, he'd shown her the results of tests he'd conducted when he'd snuck her into the St.-Francis-the-Radical Charity Clinic in Adams Morgan in early March. The roots had wrapped themselves around some organs and fused with others, snaking through her body till it was impossible to tell where they ended and the rest of her began. Appalled, she'd thrown up all over the doc's sneakers.

Dragging them behind her and inching forward, bent over like an old woman, Ji-ji crossed the narrow walkway connecting the nest to the circular welkin, a metal platform twice as high off the ground as the midlevel donut platform. Dizzy, she paused to steady herself, tried not to look down into the well of the coop. Suicides must have felt the same urge on the 437th when they leapt from the Shot Tower before the steaders boarded it up. The bird-girl who couldn't fly imprisoned inside a flying cage. Sloppy Delilah Moon would've chuckled at that. Where was Sloppy now? Living somewhere in the city with Chaff Man the Executioner and his little dog Circus? Had she found happiness at last or was she as bitter as she used to be . . . as bitter as Ji-ji herself was now?

Ji-ji surveyed her prison. The cage that took up almost the entire volume of the practice coop was a fraction the size of the one Tiro flew in. The Friends had done their best to improve the place, but you needed a ton of money and a large crew to repair and maintain it. A couple of part-time handymen Friends, both as old as Methuselah, did the best they could. During heavy rains, the skylights in the dome leaked. Planks were missing from the walkways, the wood that hadn't rotted had been chewed on by rats, and rust made most of the equipment unusable. Ji-ji stared down again into the well of the coop. One small step and she would plunge a hundred feet or more.

Afarra sat up abruptly, wide awake. As usual, half her head was covered in messy braids and the other half was undone. She looked around wildly for Ji-ji and soon found her.

"You are waking!" she exclaimed. "I am overslept by the Dimmers again, but I am waking now."

Unsure if she could speak without bursting into tears or saying something she'd regret, Ji-ji opted not to reply. Instead, she shuffled farther along the welkin platform to gaze out of one of the dome's grubby skylights. Afarra was less likely to bother her if she thought she was content to look at the view.

The huge skylights in the dome were one of the few attractive features that remained in the old building. The practice coop, hastily erected years ago, had been constructed out of salvaged scraps from three other practice coops. They'd crowned the edifice with a dome so it would look more purpose-built than it actually was.

Ji-ji stared at the scene below. Some distance away lay the Anacostia River. Like the Potomac, the Anacostia had flooded the city more times than residents could count. Her view was blocked by abandoned warehouses and dilapidated office buildings built after D.C. finally repealed the 1899 Height of Buildings Act and before flooding became chronic.

After her visit to the Mall and the Dream Coop on the fake Fourth of July, Ji-ji had drawn a map of the City of Dreams, highlighting some of the areas she'd seen and the areas she most wanted to visit. The cheerful map, with its foreshortened buildings and cute monuments, seemed ludicrously optimistic to her now. The naïve fool who'd drawn it had died months ago.

A vivid green flash darted over her feet! Ji-ji leapt back in surprise. "What the——? Oh, it's you." Ji-ji glared at the intruder. An iguana the size of a large cat glared back. His zigzag beard and mottled green skin turned her stomach. "You think *I'm* ugly?" he seemed to say. "Take a look in the mirror!"

In his weekly broadcast, delivered in a smug monotone, Mayor Yardley reiterated his desire to rid the city of its iguana infestation, as if it would come to pass automatically if he repeated it enough. Checking to see that Afarra was occupied, she hissed at the iguana: "Get lost. I got nothing." The lizard blinked once, twice. "Get out of here, you filthy——" Her realization almost made her laugh. When it came to filth, she didn't have a leg to stand on. The iguana eyed her with the disdain of an inquisitor. At last, he seemed to have an epiphany: he'd approached the wrong girl! He shot off in the direction of the nest.

"Na-na!" Afarra cried in delight. "I am being sad you are not here to greet us this morning!"

Domesticate the bastard, Ji-ji thought. *Perfect.*

Desperate for fresh air, Ji-ji cranked open the window a couple of inches before it got stuck. Flakes of paint like yellowed dandruff slid off the skylight's grilles onto the welkin platform. The discordant sounds of a city waking up came to her over the breeze.

From across the Anacostia came the banging of construction and the drone of giant sump pumps. The levee system wouldn't fail this time, Adolphus Yardley promised. But they were waging a losing battle. As a result of the Long Warming, the city had migrated to another climate zone. During D.C.'s sweltering, humid summers, congregations of gators sunned themselves on the steps of the Capitol. Zyla joked that they were city senators taking a break from legislating. At one point last summer, Tiro had brought along a copy of the *D.C. Independent* that featured photos of a half dozen gators, one of them said to be more than twenty-two feet long. Enterprising refugees had wrangled them out of the Mall's Reflecting Pool. That night, the refugees celebrated their windfall by roasting the gators over open fires. The feasting had lasted for days. For weeks afterward, the Mall area stank of burnt gator.

Ji-ji looked at her wristwatch. The grinning mouse's white-gloved hands pointed to the time: 7:25. Coach Mackie would be here between 8:00 and 8:30. They could pretend they hadn't slept up in the nest but what would be the point? She couldn't decide if she believed the story Lucky had told her that the cute little mouse in blackface was a rodent god Americans used to worship in the Age of Plenty. Lucky was a Brit, and Germaine said Brits liked to get a rise out of people. Ji-ji still couldn't figure out why Lucky had never come to see her. After her condition started to deteriorate, she'd written to him letting him know things weren't going as planned, yet she'd never received a reply, not even a cryptic note and a pair of dice like the ones he'd sent her before.

A woman's voice, originating from the coop's center ring directly below them, startled her. Mackie had arrived early. "What are you doing up there on the welkin? Is Afarra up there too?"

Afarra left off feeding scraps to Na-na and scrambled out of the nest. She ran across the walkway, joined Ji-ji on the welkin platform, and stood sheepishly beside her.

"*Ha!*" the woman crowed. "Caught you red-handed!" The coach rolled her r's more than ever when she was on the rampage. "How many times have I told you not to come into the coop at night? Place is swarming with rats. Want to have your ears chewed off, is that what you're after?"

Ji-ji and Afarra shook their heads. No, they didn't want to have their ears chewed off.

"So why are you up there when—" Coach Mack broke off. In a fit of speed, Na-na scurried across the rope walkway.

"Afarra! Are you feeding that wee creature again? You think the Friends of

Freedom have rations to spare? A wild animal isn't some kind of *pet*! When they turn the poor wretch into a pair of shoes, whose fault will it be?"

Afarra took offense. "I will not let them turn Na-na into shoes! If they try, I attack!"

The coach waved a dismissive hand in the air and began pacing around the center ring. Dressed in her customary fatigues and army boots, Coach Mary Jonah Macdonald wore her favorite tartan baseball cap. Like Coach Billy, the only other flying coach Ji-ji had met, Coach Mackie was a fan of rhetorical questions. Among the things that drove her to distraction were pencils. ("Pencil users suffer from a lack of character—always second-guessing themselves and erasing things.") Even more offensive to her were the English, wishy-washy males, and sandals. ("Wear shoes, damnit! Protects the toes from shrapnel.") Ji-ji could never figure out why Mackie had volunteered to give her flying lessons. Teaching would-be pilots to fly planes and coaching flyer-battlers bore no resemblance to the type of flying lessons she needed. Ji-ji had come to the conclusion that an eagle or pigeon would be a more suitable instructor.

Every morning before her lesson began, Ji-ji wished Coach Mack were less resolute. Her main trait was perseverance to the point of un-swervability. Ji-ji once told Zyla that even if Mackie were about to pilot her plane into a mountain, she wouldn't swerve in case it indicated a lack of character. Ji-ji tried to hate her, but Mackie thwarted that too. Unfortunately, Mary Jonah Macdonald couldn't completely conceal the fact that she was a very generous person. She'd made room in her two-room apartment for six stray cats, three rescue dogs, and a python called Monty she'd retrieved from a dumpster. She had an adopted son too, also called Monty—a coincidence that did not indicate a lack of imagination on her part, she said, as he was already christened. Monty (the son, not the python) went on soup runs in Kingdom Come with his mother at night and did on-the-job training as a nurse by day. The indomitable Scottish coach had the kind of Try-Again spirit that would have inspired the old Ji-ji to try harder. As it was, it exacerbated Ji-ji's sense of failure.

"You ready for your lesson?" Coach Mack called up. "Ready to zip down from the Crow?"

"Sure," Ji-ji called back, surprised they hadn't been treated to a lecture. Then she figured it out. Zyla must've told her about Charra. Coach Mackie's uncharacteristic reticence was pity.

"Have you got your safety harness up there?"

"Yeah. Got it right here, Coach." Ji-ji held it up.

"Afarra, help her climb into it."

"Don't need help," Ji-ji shouted back. She turned to Afarra and told her to climb down and get two killers from the side table in her bedroom.

"You are needing the killers now?" Afarra asked, as her fingers rotated the large wooden beads on the wizard's Seeing Eyes. "The pain it is very bad? You must not fly if the pain is bad."

"Pain's not bad right now. I'm warding it off is all."

She didn't need to ask again. Her loyal friend was already jogging toward a Jacob's Ladder. Just before she began to descend, she turned and smiled. The smile would have defeated Ji-ji's resolve if Afarra hadn't continued down the ladder.

She had only a few minutes before Afarra would come running back. As fast as she could, gritting her teeth against the pain, Ji-ji removed her shirt to reveal one of the flight bras Zyla and Germaine had made for her. She tottered to the nest, grabbed the harness she'd secretly worked on last night, and strapped herself into it. It wasn't easy to leave her deformities unrestrained without Afarra's help, but her coach wouldn't let her ride unless the pair was—as Mackie put it—"liberated." Speed could help her "motivate them to function," her coach theorized, concurring, unbeknownst to her, with Tiro's hypothesis. But Ji-ji guessed the main reason why her coach had okayed the zip line exercise was simple: to fool her into believing all hope wasn't lost.

As usual, Mackie reminded her to keep her head up. "Birds don't look down" was one of her coach's favorite sayings. Ji-ji always looked down.

The zip line was old, but handyman Shin Dartmouth checked it regularly and so did Coach Mackie. The weak point was the old-fashioned harness, with its frayed straps and moth-eaten fabric. They'd patched it often. Ji-ji and Afarra were tasked with checking it for rips and tears after practice. The leather and fabric on the harness were worn. Yesterday, with a little wheedling from Ji-ji's knife, it had ripped almost in two. She'd made the tear look natural, as if the material had frayed.

She was dawdling, procrastinating. Afarra would be back in a few minutes. She had to act fast. Should she take off her god-mouse watch so it wouldn't get broken and leave it for Afarra who'd always admired it? No. No time to leave time behind. *Ha! You're real witty, Ji-ji.*

"You ready?" Coach called up.

"Yeah, I'm rrrready." She'd mimicked her coach's accent. God knows why. Nerves.

"Are you mocking me, girl?"

"Who? Me?"

Awkwardly, Ji-ji clambered up onto the rim of the nest, reached up, and attached the harness to the zip line cable that ran all the way from the dome to the far end of the cage. "Charra, wait up," she murmured. "I'll be joining you real soon."

She was about to grasp the handles to the zip line when Coach Mackie called up to her again: "Remember, Ji-ji, my pet, don't look down!"

The world switches to *NOW!NOW!NOW!* Her grumpy coach has never used a term of endearment to address her. "My pet." Two words snatch away her concentration. Her balance follows. She lunges at the zip line's handles! Got them! No! She hasn't!

She falls forward. Is jerked back by a harness designed to fail! A ripping sound.

NO! I've changed my mind! The harness doesn't know this. She feels it slip from her body!

A scream. Hers? Afarra's! Returning with the killers! *Too soon! Go back! GO BACK!*

Then the deadly rush *downdowndown* and tumble-down some more! The center ring below a giant sawdust fist eager to smash her face in. *Regret! REGRET!*

She falls through space into the mouth of Afarra's scream. Her friend. Someone she's chosen to leave behind to fend for herself. Unforgivable.

A crazy-sonuvabitch somersault of faces—TiroAfarraBonbon LuckyZyla-ManCryday GermaineBenMarcusTulipPikeTreeDipGeorgie dozensmore. . . . Their living loveliness crucifies her.

Too late, Ji-ji has a realization: only a damn fool would abandon faces as lovely as these.

8 BREAKING NEWS

elluva long way down, Tiro thought, as he stood on Sojourner's Sill, the highest trapeze staging platform in the Dream Coop, and looked down into the center ring. If plummet syndrome ambushed him way up here, he could plunge to his death, easy. But he was doing the sensible thing for once and wearing a high-tech safety harness. Ji would be proud of him.

He used to feel invincible in the coop, believed he could beat anyone. Though Laughing Tree was the strongest battler by far, his size limited his movements inside the cage. As Tree himself said, he had one primary tactic: root himself to a staging platform and fell opponents. Usually, the twelve judges awarded more marks to battling, but they made exceptions if flying maneuvers were spectacular. Marcus flew with impressive speed and agility, and his battle moves were almost as sneaky as the stunts X-Clamation and Re-Router pulled off. But if he was in the zone, Tiro could fly and battle like no one else in the fleet. A once-in-a-generation athlete, Coopmaster Nelson said, after he saw him fly for the first time.

Flying had always come naturally to Tiro. Once he'd told Ji that flying for him was scripture—first time Ji said he had a way with words. He didn't, of course. Which was why he'd done a terrible job last week when he'd gone over to the Aerie with Zyla and broken Ji's heart.

In the days following, his flying had been terrible. Yesterday, he'd messed up again during practice in front of the coopmaster and the wing commander. The two of them didn't always watch practice together. Commander Corcoran was the money man, the director who kept the wheels of the Dreamfleet turning and liaised with the owners. Coopmaster Nelson was the coach, the hands-on side of the organization. But both men had been in the coop yesterday, in heated conversation with each other most of the time. They'd seen him fly like a clay pigeon, head spinning so bad he couldn't see straight. Felt like the entire fly cage had been plopped into the ocean. Everything swaying and bucking. Wave after wave of nausea. . . .

This morning, in an effort to shake off yesterday's abysmal performance, Tiro had arrived early for the practice session. Alone in the Dream as he waited for Marcus, he thought about how Ji's face had caved in when they'd broken the news to her about Charra. Zyla had done a better job of it than he had, though even she couldn't make it bearable. *Felt like we were scooping Ji's heart right out of her chest,* he thought, addressing his late brother. *After we told her the news, Ji kept flipping through the book of nursery rhymes Charra's followers had sent her, like she was searching for clues or something. Her dead wings trailing behind her. Sweet Jesus! Doesn't she have enough shit to deal with without the news about Charra too?*

Tiro's hands and knees were shaking. He slapped his fists against his thighs and kneaded his fingers to get the worry out. Nerves.

"Hey, fly-boy! You asleep or what?"

The greeting startled him. Directly ahead toward the center of the cage, Marcus sat on the trapeze that reigned supreme in the Dream. The high trapezes were the highest in any coop in the Disunited States. Its twin, lashed to a post near where Tiro stood, was equally high. Wasn't easy to get up to trapezes as high as that. So how come he hadn't seen Marcus work his way up the cage? His inattentiveness spooked him. Miss something like that during a battle and you could get Inked. Tiro scrubbed that dumb word from his brain, fearful of blurting it out to Ink by accident. No doubt about it. Marcus was a bad influence.

"Where you come from, man?" Tiro asked.

"Where you think? I rode the invisible side of the Ellison up to the donut, climbed a Jacob's Ladder or two, leapt onto a Robinson Plate, an' voilà! Here I am."

"Don't make sense. Can't get there that way."

"You may be right. Could be I took the Williams Smash, jumped onto a Hughes Pod an—"

"Okay, man, I get it. Shoulda seen you coming."

"Damn right you should have, kiddo."

"Don't kiddo me. We're almost the same age."

"Physically perhaps, but not intellectually. How many times has Uncle Marcus gotta remind you daydreaming's dangerous in the Dream? Some Armistice fly-boy'll toss your skinny ass into ancient history. Gotta keep you healthy so you can perform your tricks for the owners."

Sick of his partner's biting criticism of the one place where he felt at home, Tiro asked, "How come you enlisted, O Great One, if all this is crap?"

"You will recall, O Dim One, I didn't enlist initially. Then I reasoned you'd never make it without me. The fans—god bless 'em—want to see a Mule fly. And the Mules is us, Dumbo. By the way, who were you talking to?"

Shit. He must've been talking out loud to Amadee. "How long you been spying on me?"

Marcus laughed. "Better watch out, fly-boy. Talking to yourself is the first sign of madness. Remember Mad Ma Hennypen on the 437th?" Marcus did one of his famous impersonations: "'The Tribe-Dim revealed to me the truth the Passengers know!' You got a duty to keep yourself physically an' mentally fit, T. The whole athletic-commercial complex is banking on gullible fly-boys like you to distract the masses."

The only way to shut Marcus up was to give as good as he got. "Seems to me, Mr. Shadowbrookseed . . ." Marcus clutched at his heart like someone who'd just been shot, lolled his head to one side and pretended to expire. Tiro refused to let his partner's antics distract him. "Seems to me, Philosopher Phil . . ." Marcus groaned again. Tiro ignored him. "Seems to me we don't got much choice but to fly our hearts out. I need lucre an' you need . . . What do you need anyway?"

Marcus shrugged: "A sunset'd be peachy. You got one o' them sassy little red-eye blots?"

"How many times I gotta tell you? I don't do red-eyes or flukes. None o' the hard stuff. Promised Ji I'd lay off that crap. S'a sucker's game."

Marcus cocked his head like a puppy and started to whimper: "Suckers is humans too."

Tiro had to laugh. Marcus swung back and forth lazily, propelling the trapeze with his long, muscled legs. "You plan on telling me why you keep messing up?"

"That flamingo maneuver's tricky as hell," Tiro replied.

"So? You've landed on one foot before. You chicken?"

Tiro didn't rise to the bait. "Could be, I guess."

In an instant, Marcus had looped his legs over the bar of the trapeze and turned upside down. He hung from the bar by his knees in a catcher's position and continued to swing back and forth. It always irritated Tiro when Marcus did this. For one thing, it was harder to read his expressions when he was upside down; for another, he was even more inclined to preach the Gospel of Saint Marcus when the world looked as topsy-turvy as he said it was.

"Careful," Tiro continued. "You don't got a harness on."

Marcus feigned surprise. "Hey! You're right, Sherlock! But I got me a net way down below. See that little eye down there? Can catch a whole lot o' nothing in that. Long as I don't bounce off it like Ink did. Lucky for me, I ain't prone to bouncing. Once I alight on a thing, I don't let go."

Ain't that the truth, Tiro thought.

"So how's about we play catch again?" Marcus offered. "I got the best hands in the business. Keep that harness nice an' snug, fly-boy. Your timing's off by a millisecond an' you'll be Inked."

"It's not *my* timin' I'm worried about. An' that's not funny."

"Course it's funny. Everything's funny if you think about it long enough.

Corker'll have our hides for breakfast if we don't pull off this new move. What's up with you anyway, man? You high?"

"Fuck no! . . . Been a tough few days I guess."

Marcus righted himself and sat on the swinging trapeze with the ease of a practiced flyer. Tiro envied his partner's brash confidence, which extended far beyond his attitude in the coop. Marcus had slept with a ton of women since they'd arrived in the city. All one-night stands, as far as Tiro knew. White girls exclusively. Marcus claimed he was out to prove miscegenation was legal in the Dream.

"Truth is, man." Marcus paused to look around. The coop was empty but he still lowered his voice. "Truth is, that thing with Ji-ji's back was a sweet dream. Got caught up in it myself, an' you know me—I never get caught up in anything. But that's all it was, a dream. Was never gonna come true." He paused. Lowering his voice still further, he added, "You found that surgeon, right?" Tiro nodded. "Okay then. I set some lucre aside for emergencies. I can help you out."

Tiro couldn't believe his ears. "You mean it? You'd help out? You serious?"

"Don't sound so surprised. I have it on the best authority I'm a good man. 'Sides, if we don't help out our own, who will? An' you already got a shitload of lucre you gotta fork over to Williams."

Marcus' generosity had ambushed him. "Thanks, man," he said. "I'll never forget this."

"Believe me, man, I'll make sure you don't." Marcus laughed, then got serious. "We both know you could be the best flyer-battler who's ever lived. Faster than Tree, better than"—Marcus looked around the cage to check it was still empty before proceeding—"better than that flaunty peacock X-Clamation. You fly like a bird even though you're big for a flyer—double cutaways, birdies, backend straddle whips, shooting stars. Don't matter which move it is, you can execute. Your battler skills are so damn good they're scary. If you were more ruthless, you'd be invincible. As I keep telling you, your fondness for mercy is your only flaw. You're almost as pretty as me, so the cameras love you. Play your cards right an' you write your own ticket at season's end."

"Thanks, partner," Tiro said, genuinely moved. "Didn't know you gave a damn."

"I don't generally. But in your case, especially when my success is linked to yours, I make an exception. But you were an embarrassment at practice. After yesterday's fiasco, Nelson could've yanked us from the pregame lineup in the fall instead of giving us extra practice time."

"Yeah, I know," Tiro admitted. "Sorry, man. Okay, let's go for it." Marcus looked doubtful.

"I mean it," Tiro added. "Had to get some crap outta my system. I'll nail it this time."

"Attaboy!" Marcus revved up his swing. As soon as he was satisfied with his speed and velocity, he turned upside down into the catcher's "lock" position, wrapping his legs around the cables so his thighs were up tight against the fly bar to cope with the centripetal force that was about to hit him. The timing had to be perfect for a smooth catch.

Tiro picked up his grips then discarded them. He'd fly bare-handed. Nothing would come between him and the bar. With his back to Marcus, Tiro slipped his hand into the tiny pocket he'd sewn inside his leotard. He retrieved a red pill and popped it in his mouth. It fizzed on his tongue then disappeared.

An I-don't-give-a-crap-about-anything confidence flooded his brain, the spark he needed. Yeah, one little sunset had done the trick—or helped him do it. He grinned at his own wit as he turned back to face Marcus. His limbs weren't shaking anymore but his heart was doing a backflip. Suns could do that—make your heart a liability. He applied chalk to his hands and smacked them together. In the coop's floodlights, the fine white powder sifted down like ash.

He grabbed the trapeze bar, watched Marcus swing, and counted the beats. He trusted his catcher, trusted the aerial riggers. All he needed to do now was trust himself.

On cue, Tiro launched himself from Sojourner's Sill, counting in his head the way Billy taught him. He kept his eyes on Marcus, extended his swing. Couldn't let go yet. Timing wasn't right. . . . And then it was! He let go, somersaulted through the air, and was caught, cleanly, by Marcus.

They swung once, twice. "*Hup!*" Marcus cried and flung his partner in the direction of the largest 'Bama's Drama trampoline in the coop. The routine was crazy hard—a degree of difficulty so extreme the Jury of Judges would award them a slew of bonus points if they pulled it off. Tiro had to land clean on the giant trampoline, do a couple of somersaults, steady himself, leap onto an O-Laud-Ah zip line, and hightail it over to the Ellison. From there, he'd have to swing himself onto the rotating Ellison at the exactly right moment, making sure the paddles were aligned correctly so he didn't get his fancy harness tangled up in the wheel like he did yesterday. To thrill the fans, he'd stick the landing on one foot.

He blamed his recklessness on the sunset. Blots made you stupid brave. Which explained why, instead of making a clean leap toward the 'Bama's Drama, he somersaulted again in midair, flipping in the responsive harness like he'd practiced in his head before landing on the 'Bama trampoline. In a single leap, he grabbed hold of O-Laud-Ah's zip line. He was doing whatever the hell he wanted!

Marcus yelled in fury as Tiro zipped to the Ellison, landing cleanly on one of the giant wheel's wide paddles, balancing on one foot like a goddam flamingo! All he had to do was ride the wheel to another 'Bama's Drama trampoline and bounce off it onto the donut platform. If this was a real battle, his opponent would likely be waiting there for him, unaware that the Pterodactyl, a bird of prey, a bird of terror—no, a flying *reptile*—was about to pick him off the platform and fling him into the net. But for now all he had to do was land on the donut.

Yes! He'd made it! *Sweet!*

Tiro felt himself laughing. Amadee's laugh. His brother was laughing uncontrollably cos he'd executed one of the routines they'd talked about doing together years ago.

Marcus, enraged by his partner's antics, worked his way down to ground level, while Tiro slid down a hope-rope and landed gracefully in the center ring.

Marcus caught up with his partner. He cussed him out as he came: "What the *fuck,* T? We're *partners!* You don't try a move like that without telling me first! You get tangled up in that goddam harness an' you break your goddam *neck!*"

Triumphant and high from the sunset, Tiro managed to say, between bouts of laughter, "You . . . *ha-ha!* . . . sound like . . . *ha-ha!* . . . Coach B!"

He struggled to compose himself. He had to at least sound like he wasn't high as a kite. "I made it, didn't I? Can do anything I want in this Thurgood harness. Tiro the Ptero reigns supreme! Damn, I was *good!* Admit it, man!"

You could see the wheels turning as Marcus thought about the points the twelve black-robed judges would give them if they pulled off that move during the heat of battle. His mood softened. "Nearly broke your goddam neck. . . . Though if you keep flying like that we're a shoo-in for the partner trophy this season. . . . Sure would look good alongside our rookie trophies. . . . Knock X an' Router off that perch they been squatting on for way too long." Marcus put his arm round Tiro's shoulders. "Amadee couldn't have executed it better," he said, the finest compliment Marcus had ever given him. Exactly what Ji would've said, after she'd finished cussing him out for recklessness.

Tiro was trying to hold it together when Marcus swore under his breath. Tiro followed his gaze to Orlie and Georgie-Porge, who headed to the cage through the arena's main seating aisle.

"Don't goad him, Marcus. You know how it gets to him."

"Me? Goad our little Orlie Poorly? Never!"

Marcus turned toward the fly-boys and yelled, "Hey there, Fallee Poorly! You see that flamingo move by the Pterodactyl?"

Orlie didn't respond, but Georgie did. "We seen it," the big man called back. "*Sweet!*"

"Talk about an odd couple," Marcus observed, as Georgie-Porge and Orlie opened the door to Dreamblast Corridor, the chicken-wire-covered shaft leading to the main cage, where battlers could be trapped by opponents. (X-Clamation had trapped Tiro there once. Not good.) "It's like a before and after ad for those steroids the team docs're always pushing."

Tiro had to concede that Marcus had a point. Georgie, on one of the duskiest arcs of the steaders' evil Color Wheel, was over fifteen inches taller and a hundred and fifty pounds heavier than the featherweight Orlie, who could pass for a fairskin. Unlikely pairings were something the Dreamfleet was known for. They frequently baffled opponents, who'd trained for more traditional pairings and had trouble adjusting to the vast differences in style between them.

Marcus made a face. "I'll never understand why you petitioned for that pasty little turd."

"They came as a pair," Tiro replied. "Coach B paired 'em up for a reason. Can't have Porge the Forge without Orlie. Be like having pepper without salt, fries without ketchup."

"Ketchup's exactly what that little bitch'll be if he goes up against some of these fly-boys—or Re-Router, for that matter. She'd Ink him in no time."

As Georgie and Orlie emerged from Dreamblast Corridor and stepped into the heart of the fly cage, Marcus didn't hide his annoyance, shouting his next comment at Orlie.

"What you doing here, Poorly? Thought we had the coop to ourselves this morning."

Orlie had a response at the ready, one he'd obviously been rehearsing: "Tiro told us we could practice for an hour. Said you didn't need the cage to yourself."

Marcus gave Tiro the evil eye. Tiro shrugged it off. The sunset had mellowed him.

"Fans'll go nuts, T!" Orlie gushed. "Landing on one leg like that. Knew you'd pull it off."

"He's full o' crap," Georgie-Porge stated. "He swore you'd break your neck."

While Orlie frantically denied he'd ever said that, Marcus gave Tiro an I-told-you-so look. Tiro ignored it. He knew things about Orlie Mallorymule that Marcus didn't, including the fact that Orlie was an attempted suicide, which meant he'd been to places Marcus had never been and was never likely to go. You had to give someone credit for making it back from a trip like that.

"Okay," Marcus said, irritably. "You can practice, but keep away from our side of the cage. And keep away from the upper tiers too. We got a ton of new moves to go through up there."

"Understood," Georgie-Porge replied.

The four were about to head off in two different directions when Tiro spotted Laughing Tree and Ink jogging up Dreamblast Corridor. "Hey, looks like we got more company," Tiro said.

Marcus turned, shook his head. "You give Trink permission to practice with us too?"

"Wasn't me," Tiro said. "An' don't call 'em that."

"What about you, Poorly Fallee?" Marcus demanded. "Been handing out permission slips?"

"I ain't handing out nothing!" Orlie replied, indignantly.

"Hey, Tree!" Tiro called out. "You got permission to practice this morning? My fly partner's in a tizz an' wants to know."

Orlie hooted with laughter. "In a tizz! That's a good one, T!"

Georgie shoved Orlie so hard he nearly fell over.

Marcus called out: "Hey, Trink! You know you got a parrot on your shoulder?"

Tiro told Marcus to zip it. There were some things it wasn't okay to joke about. Sure, it did look weird to see Laughing Tree jogging through Dreamblast with little Ink Wrayseed in a homemade nest strapped to his back. If Tree hadn't been a seven-foot, three-hundred-and-fifty-pound giant, lots of other flyers would have teased him about it too. But Tiro liked to think if Amadee had survived the tractor pulling and been unable to walk, he would have spent weeks designing and building a basket so he could carry his brother around. He understood why the giant strapped the boy-in-the-basket to the acreage on his back. If Ji hadn't been obliged to hide out, Tiro would've done the same for her—wrapped up her pitiful wings and carried her around so she wouldn't miss the world as it happened. Like Uncle Dreg used to say, you take on others' burdens to lighten your own. Tiro wasn't sure why that magic trick worked, but all he had to do was look at the contentment on Tree's face when he and Ink were together to know it did. This morning, however, the expression on Laughing Tree's face wasn't contentment—far from it.

As he reached the group of flyers, Tree struggled to catch his breath. Ink peered over Tree's impressive shoulder and spoke up for them both: "They *fired* him! No notice—nothing!"

"Fired who?" Marcus asked.

"Wing Commander Corcoran!" Ink replied in his high-pitched voice.

Marcus gave Tiro another I-told-you-so look.

"That's crazy!" Tiro said. "Corcoran's got more friends in this city than——"

"Ink's right. Corcoran's out," Laughing Tree, less winded now, affirmed in a voice as low as Ink's was high. "Been replaced by Drayborn Redipp."

Tiro didn't believe it. Through his sunset haze he said, "But Redipp's the assistant to the assistant coach! No one even likes him."

"Could be that's the point," Marcus said, keeping an eye on Orlie, who'd scurried off and was madly texting on his caller. "Could be the City of Dreams has just woken up to a whole new nightmare. Mark Marcus' words. Our flying circus just got converted to a colosseum. You ready for martyrdom, boys?" Marcus nodded in Orlie's direction. "What's that traitorous fucker up to? Think I should go an' smash his caller? Into his face is what I mean."

"Leave Orlie alone, Marcus," Laughing Tree warned. "Think the mayor is behind this?"

Marcus pried his eyes from Orlie. "Course he is. Yardley's as crooked as they come. Could be this has something to do with the surprise visit he paid to the Dream last summer."

Georgie dashed the back of his hand over his sweaty upper lip. Corker had promised to try pairing Georgie up with Annalissa, a formidable new female recruit from the Liberty Independent of Atlanta. With Redipp's appointment, the chances of that happening shifted to zero. Redipp was a colorist through and through. No way he'd take kindly to a former Commonseed like Georgie.

"Corker told me I'd make the lineup. Think Redipp'll honor a promise like that?"

"What do you think?" Marcus told him. "It's Dipshit Drayborn we're talking about."

Georgie looked devastated. "There's talk of kicking out most of the reservists. Voiding our residency papers. Think they can do that?"

Before Marcus could reply, Orlie sprinted back to their circle.

"Redipp trains the reservists," Orlie said. "There's rumors he's a . . ." His voice trailed off.

Ink, who prided himself on being in the know, took up the slack: "Redipp's a secessionist sympathizer. A puppet for the inquisitors in Armistice."

"Everyone knows that," Georgie shot back. "We ain't fuckin idiots."

In spite of the numbing effect of the sunset, Tiro could feel the negative energy radiate off Georgie. Didn't make sense. On the planting, Georgie-Porge Snellingseed was the most easygoing Commonseed you ever saw. Basked in the adoration of his fairskin Liberty Laborer father and his Tribalseed mam. Sure, Georgie would "forget" to catch Orlie occasionally during a routine, but it wasn't like he didn't check first to make sure there was a net underneath. D.C. had worked on Georgie in reverse—made him more stressed out than he'd been on the planting.

"Ink's right," Orlie said. "Redipp's bad news. Freedom don't mean a thing 'less everyone buys into it. But D.C.'s split fifty-fifty. Justice needs a critical mass. She can't protect you otherwise."

Marcus eyed the petite fly-boy suspiciously. Orlie was meant to be a dumbass. Marcus seemed to take personal offense at his sudden switch to philosopher.

Laughing Tree—or rather Laughing Tree frequently interrupted by Ink—informed them that Redipp had called a meeting of all fleeters for eleven A.M. Ink said they'd heard the new commander planned to switch up the roster and "get rid of the fluff."

"What fluff?" Orlie asked, shakily.

Marcus shook his head in phony sympathy. "Guess your days in the fleet are numbered, Poorly. Guess you'll be erecting your little tent at the foot of the Dreamer in Kingdom Come."

"Shut up, Marcus," Tree said. "With your fluffy new haircut, you won't be safe either."

Tiro happened to glance toward the main entrance again. "Hey. Is that Ben an' Germaine?"

He peered toward the pair striding up Dreamblast and spotted Germaine Judd's long, thick braid and lean body. She strode alongside the only Black man Tiro knew who walked with the kind of stocky, weight-lifter confidence Born-Free Bently did. What were Ben and Germaine doing in the coop? As former pros in the Dreamfleet, they had the right to enter the arena, but Germaine avoided it like the plague. Must be urgent for both of them to show up out of the blue like this.

Marcus whistled in surprise, said, "This coop d'état must be a doozy if it brings the Judd back to the Dream. When's the last time the luscious Latinx Minx set foot in this place?"

Orlie couldn't skedaddle fast enough. Georgie watched his fly partner retreat. "Traitorous motherfucker," he mumbled. "Spotted him exiting Redipp's office last week. He nearly fainted when he saw me. Fucker's parroting for certain. . . . Feels like everything's slipping away, y'know?" The big flyer bowed his head. Was he crying? Yeah, he was. Damn.

"Chin up, buddy," Tree said. "Nelson decides who flies in the cage an' who doesn't. Appeal to the coopmaster. You're a strong battler. If you an' me wouldn't be way over the partner weight limit—well, heck, I'd partner with you myself."

Georgie sniffed. "Thanks, Tree," he said. "Guess I'll speak to the coopmaster."

Marcus, who'd never met a bubble he couldn't burst, advised Georgie not to get too excited.

"Since when does I'm-a-God rock the boat?" Marcus asked. "Don't rely on the coopmaster, G. He'll let you down."

Tiro saw that Ben and Germaine were now jogging toward them, fast. Tiro's hands twitched apprehensively.

Marcus sensed his partner's unease. "S'okay, T. Bet they've come with news about Corker."

Filled with dread, Tiro hurried toward the Friends of Freedom. Marcus, Georgie, and Trink weren't far behind. When they approached, however, Tiro could tell the news was for him alone.

Ben grabbed his shoulder—a bad sign; Germaine took his hand—a worse one.

Tiro struggled to clear his head. "Has Williams killed 'em? Am I too late?"

"No, no! It's not your family, T," Ben assured him. Satisfied that all four of the other fly-boys present in the coop were Friends of Freedom, Ben continued. "It's Ji-ji."

Tiro hadn't realized he was swaying till Marcus grabbed his elbow to steady him. He heard a din in his brain—something vicious spinning way too fast.

Germaine said, "She fell. This morning during practice. Riding the zip line. Harness broke."

Tiro stared at them blankly. "Is she . . . ?"

"No. She's badly injured but she's alive," Ben told him. "You've gotta come quick. We've got the truck waiting outside."

Marcus told him he'd tell Redipp Tiro was suffering from a stomach bug or something.

Tree and Ink urged him not to give up hope. "She'll pull through," he said.

"It'll be okay," Ink added. "Ji-ji's got you an' Afarra like I got Tree—right, Tree?"

"No doubt about it, buddy," Tree said.

Dazed, Tiro let Ben and Germaine hurry him down Dreamblast.

Georgie-Porge tore after them. He lifted Tiro off the floor in a bear hug and blubbered into his ear: "Tell the little runner we're all rooting for her, okay?

Tell her we got her back! Tell Afarra that too. Don't forget." Tiro wanted to nod but his head wouldn't agree to it.

Blind with terror, Tiro stumbled forward. A single, horrifying thought slaughtered all the others: *Don't let her be all in pieces like he was! Don't let her look like he did at the end.*

Not even the haze of a sunset could make another sight like that survivable.

9 THE GARDENER OF TEARS

eing dead made her happy. Weightless, suspended in the dark . . . no yearning for lost things, no voices in her head repeating what would never happen. She could barely remember her own name, or the name for suffering, or the name for god. She'd faded like a star fades in the lightening sky. She was a sound-not-there. She was heaven.

Her feet were the first to return. *Cold! Cold!* Next, the sound of her teeth chattering. After that, her heart thumping. She was flung back into semiconsciousness, mutated and cursed.

Someone mumbled through a curtain: "Don't worry, my pet. Doc's on his way." *My pet.* Two words to topple her. Who'd said them? She couldn't remember.

Whispers around her bed. She tried to say, *Speak up! I can't hear you!* before a runaway stallion galloped across her body.

She knew her body was broken.

Another detonation of agony! Someone . . . (Doc Riff—was it him?) said, "This will help." Didn't he know by now nothing could? *Cut 'em off!* she wanted to scream. No point. He would never do it even though it would be a mercy kill. *Coward!*

Afarra lay on the floor beside her bed. Painted eyes squinted in the daylight and winked in the dark. "Uncle Dreg is saying it will be okay." Afarra again. Or the dead wizard, whose hopeful message sickened her. However hard you tried to avoid it, the future caught you in its net. Like an explosion in reverse, shards of her were coming back together. Survival was a terrorist.

Tiro by her bedside. Sometimes she was there with him; other times she couldn't tell where *there* was. Occasionally, he would take her hand and squeeze it, spout things like, "You'll get through this, Ji," and "You're looking way better today." She tolerated his lies and platitudes cos they seemed to make him feel better.

Once—or was it twice?—Uncle Dreg's face in a bloody sky. Wizards should look optimistic. The sun peeking from behind a cloud or something else hopeful. A rainbow maybe? But he glowered, as devastated as she was that dreams didn't come true. To bolts of lightning and claps of thunder, Wizard Dreg-in-the-Sky recited his Death Day sermon:

A blessed awakening!
Black, Brown, and White flocking together!
Heads of midnight, heads of earthlight, heads of moonlight!
Faith and Hope will nourish you, but only Love can dream you Free!
My beautiful birds of paradise, you are destined to fly
the coop and bring together the tribes of the world!

In spite of how hard she tried to resist them, his words moved her.

At one point, Ji-ji saw Tiro in Stinky Brine's coop after Amadee's murder, ready to leap from the Jimmy Crow. She took his hand again. The nest's jutting-out twigs dug into her butt cheeks. If she leapt, the nest could hook her skirt. She'd have to dangle from there and watch Tiro's fall. What she'd made Afarra do. Unforgivable.

If he discovered it was deliberate, would Tiro be mad at her for leaping after her sister died when she'd stopped him from doing the same thing when he lost his brother? Did he suspect she'd cut into the harness herself? Did they have that kind of connection?

Tiro disappeared, replaced by . . . Doc Riff? No. He smelled medicinal. This person smelled earthy. Not earthy like Lua did before she died, not earthy like the grave, earthy like spring.

"Let . . . me . . . go. . . . *Please!*" she begged. A face took shape. Man Cryday, the Gardener of Tears, the Toteppi tree witch who'd wexcisioned Charra but refused to perform the same mercy on her. Without asking for permission, the witch took her hand. Dark finger-roots crept up Ji-ji's arm.

Later—how much later she couldn't tell—Ji-ji was abruptly conscious. Her failed attempt at suicide assaulted her. She'd wound up even worse than where she started. With a rush of clarity, she realized the agonizing truth: she wasn't about to die anytime soon.

|||||||||||||||

Ji-ji looked around. She was lying on the bed in her room in the Aerie. Man Cryday and Afarra were close by. Her body formed a crucifix—deformities spread out on either side, draped over furniture so they didn't touch the floor. She felt exposed. A specimen on an exam table.

Her room looked different. The lumpy mattress and the books on the book-shelves were the same, but someone had shoved an adult's sleep cot up against one wall and cushions lay everywhere. Their happy colors offended her. The room didn't smell the way it used to; it had been cleaned. Pine. Her room smelled of pine. A colorful rug lay on the floor. Someone had tacked pictures to the walls. She couldn't make out what was on them cos the room was fairly dark, though it was a sunny day if the light entering through a gap in the make-shift blackout curtains was anything to go by.

Ji-ji turned her head to her left. Her deformity on that side twitched as it rested on the various props supporting it. She marveled at how clean it was. Every flap shone in the narrow light from the window. The odd little wing flaps looked beautiful—like the pieces inside the kaleidoscope on Lotter's desk in his father-house. On the side table next to her bed, Ji-ji spotted the snow globe Tiro had given her. Beside the snow globe lay the dice Lucky had sent to let her know he'd survived.

She turned her head to the right. The deformity on that side looked like a cumbersome white sail. It took her a moment to figure it out. Someone had bandaged most of it up. Splints too.

"I see you have deigned to join us again. About time."

The Gardener of Tears was wearing one of her green head-ties. Her skirt and blouse looked freshly ironed. She wore large hoop earrings and wooden bangles that clicked against each other when she moved her arm. Her face was old-smooth and as impenetrable as always. *She misses her trees,* Ji-ji thought, before she could stifle her empathy. Nothing good could come of her alliance with the bearer of sorrowful names.

Afarra awoke, saw Ji-ji, and whooped in delight.

"Hush!" Man Cryday said. "She's not out of the woods yet."

Makes sense, Ji-ji thought. *A tree witch would know if someone was still in the woods.*

"How do you feel?" Man Cryday asked. As usual, her Toteppi accent dueled and danced with the English words she spoke.

"Am I broken?" Ji-ji asked.

Man Cryday tilted her head to one side and said, "You want the truth, is it not so?"

"Yes," Ji-ji replied, bracing herself.

Uncle Dreg, brother to the woman they called the Gardener of Tears, used to wrap his words in something soft to avoid hurting her. Man Cryday didn't.

"Your right wing is broken in three places. Multiple compound fractures. Michael—Doc Riff—is not sure it can heal. Neither am I. A battle is being waged between ingrown colonization and extracorporeal liberation. We are consulting with Dr. Narayanan. Your condition could be pathological or simply the result of trauma. In other words, the bone may be diseased, we cannot tell. It is not like other bone. It is not like anything. It changes in front of our eyes—repositions itself in response to being perceived. We are no longer sure if the wings are biological in the usual sense or the result of scientific and technological advancement beyond anything we have seen before. Of course, it could be a combination of those things, yes? It is even possible my brother was right, and your wings are the apotheosis of stories we have told each other for centuries. . . . Or maybe not. Dregulahmo was a storykeeper and therefore a dreamer. All dreamers are prone to flights of fancy—pun intended."

Could the old witch be more annoying if she tried?

Man Cryday continued. "We are relying upon avian biology and Mary Macdonald's experience as a veterinary assistant. We would prefer to consult with specialists, but there are few such people outside of the SuperStates, and it would be dangerous to reveal your survival to others beyond our circle of Friends." She paused. "Frankly, when it comes to an injury as extensive as this, we make it up as we go along. Our inexperience as we try to address your condition means you may or may not recover fully. . . . And no. I cannot amputate. A wexcision would kill you."

"*No killing!*" Afarra cried, twirling the eye beads around her neck. "He says no killing!"

Man Cryday took Afarra's hand in hers. "No killing," she said in a tone much kinder than the one she'd used to address Ji-ji. "Tell my brother I intend to keep the promise I made to him."

Reassured, Afarra calmed down. She drew up a chair and sat in a crouched position, ready to pounce if the need arose, as close to the head of the bed as Ji-ji's wingspan allowed.

"You said I can't heal. What's the point of keeping me alive if—"

"I said we do not know if you will heal. That is not the same thing. Everything in the future is *may* happen not *will* happen. Anyone who does not remember this is a fool."

"You got no idea what it's like dragging these filthy things around."

Man Cryday snorted in disgust. "You are right, Jellybean Silapu. They were indeed filthy. You stank. You think you have the right to disrespect the miracle of your own body?"

Pain flooded her. Ji-ji didn't have the strength to stop it. "I can't do it!" she wailed.

Afarra turned sharply toward Man Cryday and growled at her like a snarlcat.

"She is *trying!*" Afarra roared. "Be *nice!*"

"Ha!" Man Cryday said. "I see you have your bodyguard with you this morning. Once again, my brother is trying to boss me around. You should know that Afarra has never left your side these past two weeks."

"Two weeks?"

"For more than two weeks you have been lying here. We kept you sedated while you healed. It is taking longer than we anticipated to see any improvement. Afarra has helped me clean and . . . redecorate." Man Cryday nodded at the pictures tacked to the wall. Ji-ji realized they were story-cloths. Some were ones she'd seen in Man Cryday's cabin; others she'd never seen before. "These stories will nourish you if you take the time to study them. Some I drew myself. Now he is gone, I am the storykeeper's stand-in. Ironic, yes? Dreg would have laughed until he peed in his pants."

In the face of that irreverent comment, some of the floodwaters receded. Man Cryday made room for herself on the bed. Even when she sat down, the old woman's back was as straight as a knife. Ji-ji envied her. She could hardly remember what it felt like to have a back that didn't try to crush you.

The tree witch softened her voice a little. "We do not know if you will heal in the right way. You are unique, so we must learn as we go. We had to redo the splints due to swelling. We hope to avoid stiffness and synostosis, but we are flying blind. . . . That was a joke."

"It wasn't funny," Ji-ji said.

"If you want to survive, you had better start laughing at the world. What is left without humor? Endurance without joy is bitterness. Look at what happened to Silapu. Bitter till the end."

"No she wasn't," Ji-ji argued, rising to her mam's defense. "You don't know anything."

"Believe me, I know a lot more than you do. So . . . are you going to tell me?"

"Tell you what?" Man Cryday simply looked at her. *She knows,* Ji-ji thought. *The tree witch knows everything.* The last remnants of the wall Ji-ji was hiding behind collapsed.

Afarra was listening, so all Ji-ji said was "You don't know how hard I've tried. It's like dragging corpses. I can't feel 'em at all."

"Even now?" Man Cryday asked. "You cannot feel anything, child?" Ji-ji shook her head.

Man Cryday stood up and walked to the tip of the right wing, which she touched gently.

"You feel that?" Ji-ji shook her head. "What about this?" Man Cryday pinched her wing this time. Ji-ji shook her head again. "It may be too early. Larger birds take longer to heal."

"I'm not a bird."

"No. But your wings are avian in design, though remarkably, they seem capable of re-forming themselves depending on what they are called upon to do."

"What are you talking about? They don't *do* anything."

Man Cryday ignored her and continued with her diagnosis. "You had simple fractures at the metacarpals. The humerus required pinning. If you heal enough to function—"

Exasperated, Ji-ji exclaimed, "You're not listening! I'm *paralyzed*! Why didn't you cut 'em out when they were sproutings like you did for Charra? You've sentenced me to life in prison!" An almost imperceptible tightening around Man Cryday's mouth told Ji-ji her barb had hit home.

Man Cryday sat back down on the bed. "Afarra, tell her," she said.

"Tell me what?"

At that moment, Coach Mack barged into the room. "*She's awake!*" the coach exclaimed. "I knew it! I knew the lass would pull through!"

Germaine Judd and Zyla Clobershay crowded in behind the coach. The five females stared at the sixth. "Does she know yet?" Zyla asked.

Was Charra alive after all? If her sister had survived, she would will herself to recover enough to travel to the Madlands and find her. She would tell her about their little brother Bonbon, how he could be a Wingchild too. Charra being alive—the one thing with the power to change all things. Coach Mackie began to speak but Man Cryday raised a hand to silence her.

"The fall should have killed you," Man Cryday stated. "Obviously, it did not."

That was what I forgot to ask about, Ji-ji thought. *It's not Charra. It's me.*

Man Cryday turned to Afarra. "Tell her what you saw, child. She trusts you."

"I am seeing you fall," Afarra began. "I am seeing—"

Ji-ji interrupted her: "I'm sorry, Afarra. I never meant for you to see me—"

"*Shush!*" Man Cryday scolded. "You must learn to listen. Go on, Afarra."

"I am seeing you fall, an' I cry out 'No,' like this, '*NO!*' Too late for the words to catch. There is no net underneath and you are fallingfalling down. Twirlytwirly like a Harriet Stair. And I am not riding on your back to the moon so it is not the time to do it but still you do it."

"Do what?" Ji-ji whispered, half remembering something she hardly dared believe.

"Fly!" Afarra exclaimed. She threw her arms out wide. "I see you *fly,* Elly! Like a *bird!*"

||||||||||||||||

For a few seconds after hearing the news of her maiden flight, Ji-ji sat perfectly still. At the instant when the thing she yearned for most had occurred, she had almost succeeded in obliterating herself before she'd had a chance to experience it. In an attempt to kill her pain, she might have succeeded in murdering her dream. She laughed hysterically, then stopped laughing as abruptly as she'd started. The females looked at each other. Ji-ji could tell she'd made them uneasy.

When they thought it was safe to do so, they told her Afarra wasn't the only witness. Coach Mackie had seen it too. The only reason Ji-ji's fall hadn't been fatal, her coach said, was "a last-second revival of her extensions." Vaguely, Ji-ji recalled the moment when something surged across her back as if her body had suddenly been plugged in, or like a tree must feel when rain comes after a long drought and every bud opens itself up to the sun.

Man Cryday asked the others to leave, said she needed to speak to Laughing Girl alone.

That's me, Ji-ji thought. *I'm Laughing Girl. Am I laughing again?* She raised a hand to her mouth to check. *No, thank god. Mam used to laugh when she was having one of her breakdowns.*

After Man Cryday had settled herself into a chair and resumed her sewing, Ji-ji felt strong enough to ask her if she'd revealed her suicide attempt to the others. Man Cryday said she hadn't, though Afarra had guessed the truth. "The others think it was an unlucky fall."

Afarra knew. Of course she did. Ji-ji thanked Man Cryday for keeping her secret.

"It is your secret to tell, not mine. Afarra does not complain about the damage you have done to her because she is devoted to you. A thankless occupation, yes? What has that poor soul done that you would treat her with such thoughtlessness? Mary too. She nearly had a heart attack."

Ji-ji pointed out that Afarra wasn't meant to witness it. She'd returned early with the killers.

"A pitiful excuse," Man Cryday said. "Be more careful next time."

Ji-ji's surprise at the fact that the tree witch anticipated there would be a next time must have been evident on her face because the old woman put down her sewing and addressed her again.

"Most suicides are not satisfied with a single attempt. Do you know why, Jellybean? Because they are chronically forgetful. I want you to remember what it felt like when you fell. Burn that moment into your memory. Imagine how Afarra felt when she saw you about to splatter yourself in the cage." Man Cryday leaned forward in her chair and rested her hand on the blackbird quilt on Ji-ji's bed. "I understand the temptation. Believe me, I have had it too. Yet we must resist."

"Why?" Ji-ji asked. She felt as though her life depended on the tree witch's answer.

Man Cryday spread out her arms to encompass her surroundings. "What have my brother and I been trying to tell you? Because of *this,* of course! This magnificent world we live in! Though the fools in it try to savage us daily, we need to actively resist despair. . . . I owe you an apology."

"You do?"

"When I saw the state of your pitiful wings. . . . Well, let's just say I had not realized things had deteriorated to this degree. . . . My mind has been on other things. Did Zyla tell you there was a Toteppi massacre on a planting in the 500s and another in the 300s? Little ones too. Slaughtered." Man Cryday looked distraught. *Why didn't it occur to me before,* Ji-ji thought, *how much pain she has to shoulder as the Gardener of Tears?* "Unfortunately," Man Cryday continued, "radical homesteaders are hell-bent on the idea that the Territories must be cleansed of all Toteppi—most outcasts too."

Ji-ji felt sick. "Why pick on outcasts? What harm can a Serverseed do?"

"Outcasts are vulnerable. Easy targets. Radical steaders are ignoring edicts from Grand Inquisitor Worthy about the need for restraint during the labor shortage."

Ji-ji shifted uncomfortably in the bed. She didn't want to think about the incident in the storeroom with the inquisitors. Ever since Tryton's assault, she'd been haunted by the idea that Grand Inquisitor Worthy was out to destroy her. Somehow she knew he didn't want to do it quickly either; he wanted to do it real slow. Fightgood Worthy wanted to *watch*.

"Don't let Worthy pull you into his orbit," a voice in her head urged. *"Drag the bastard into yours."* At first, Ji-ji assumed it was her own voice or Man Cryday's. Then she realized it was Silapu's. She didn't mention it to Man Cryday. She had few moments of connection with her murdered mam, and the last thing she wanted to hear were more barbed comments about Silapu from the tree witch.

Ji-ji shifted her position again. Man Cryday asked if she was in pain. When Ji-ji said no, not much, Man Cryday lit into her. "I'm glad to hear it. You have been abusing painkillers. Very stupid." She sounded exactly like Afarra. "Why do you think they are called killers, Jellybean?"

Ji-ji was angry too. "How should I know? Maybe cos we like abbreviations?"

"You're on the verge of being a drug-sop like your mam. Is that what you want?" That was the last thing Ji-ji wanted, but she had no intention of admitting that to the tree witch. "Then stop abusing your own body, Jellybean."

"Why should I? My own body's been abusing me."

Man Cryday gave her one of her penetrating looks. "Yes. I see why you would say that. . . . But what if this isn't about you or those wonders on your back. What if it's always been about others . . . about serving others?"

Man Cryday paused for a moment, then said, "After years of struggle, the Friends have liberated only a small fraction of those in captivity. Resettlement of refugees on a massive scale isn't feasible. We must destroy the planting system and redistribute the land to those who have been forced to seed it for decades. A full-scale overthrow of Territorial rule is required. What we lack is an audacious idea to rally around."

Ji-ji knew where Man Cryday was going with this, but she wasn't ready to be audacious. All she wanted were answers to urgent questions.

"Zyla an' Tiro told me Charra's dead. Told me she died of dengue fever. Is it true?"

Man Cryday looked down at her sewing. "Yes, my child, it is. I am very sorry."

Ji-ji had known Charra was gone, but having Man Cryday confirm it gutted her.

"You learned this news of your sister's death recently, yes?" Ji-ji nodded. "It is terrible to lose a sibling. But we women who know the grief of purple tears must also grieve by *doing*. Here"—she handed Ji-ji a cloth—"wipe the snot from your nose. That's better. Do you need a moment to compose yourself?"

"No," Ji-ji said, suddenly aware of how much she needed to spend time in the company of strength right now. She was grateful when Man Cryday kept speaking.

"I intended to come earlier, but . . . we are in a muddle. The Friends are divided amongst themselves, pecking each other to pieces. A faction has broken off, thirsty for all-out war. Others adhere to the nonviolent path espoused by the Dreamer. Some of us argue for a middle way."

"You don't sound confident."

"Confidence is for optimists. Resolve is a better quality. It incorporates hardheadedness."

"Guess I must be pretty resolute then. My hardheadedness helped me survive."

"You made a joke, yes? It was not funny, but it is a good sign."

"I wish you'd visited earlier, Man Cryday. Maybe then I wouldn't . . . ."

"I wish I had too, child. I should have. Germaine and Zyla tried to tell me how bad your condition was. But Zyla Clobershay can be hyperbolic, and I assumed I had time. . . ." The tree witch shook her head. "Never put your faith in Time, child. He is without pity. . . . I always imagined I would have time to argue again with my brother and tell him what a foolish idealist he was. I have waited for Dregulahmo to Dimmer me. But I am a scientist of sorts, so he does not come."

The tree witch looked so sad that Ji-ji said, "Maybe he'll come when you're not looking?"

"Yes, child. Maybe he will."

Ji-ji turned her face away from Man Cryday to ask the next question. Easier to ask it if she didn't have to look into the eyes of the tree witch, who seemed to read her thoughts as easily as she read the rare trees she tended. "Did you find Bonbon? Did Lucky?"

"Sadly, no—though we're almost certain your little brother is not in a server camp. We still think he may have been taken to the Decipula in Armistice."

Not the answer Ji-ji wanted, but there was still a chance Bonbon was alive, which meant there was still a chance she could keep her vow and rescue him. She moved on to another question.

"Think I'll fly again? Think it was speed got 'em working?"

Man Cryday snorted in disapproval. "Speed? Is that what my flighty great-nephew told you?" Her tone was as dismissive as it had been in Memoria.

"No," Ji-ji replied. In an attempt to defend Tiro, she sought refuge in a partial truth. "Coach Mackie thought speed would help."

Man Cryday backtracked. "Oh? Well then . . . yes. It is possible speed had something to do with it."

Ji-ji decided to risk offending the tree witch. At this stage, what did she have to lose? "I don't think Coach Mackie . . . I mean, I'm sure she's a great pilot but . . ."

As usual, Man Cryday didn't beat around the bush. "You want another fly-coach, yes?"

"Yes . . . I guess. Maybe. . . . Can you teach me to fly?"

"Me?" Man Cryday laughed to herself. "I am an unconventional surgeon who tends trees. What on earth do I know about flying, child?"

"Thought you knew everything."

"*Ha!* Dregulahmo used to say my tragic flaw was that I thought I did. Mary Macdonald is a good woman, one of the most generous people you will ever meet. Have you met Monty?"

"Her son?"

"Her python. . . . And her son. Do not underestimate Mary Macdonald. That remarkable woman served as a ranger pilot in her homeland of Scotland, to say nothing of her time as a volunteer pilot in the Eastern SuperState army, and two years as the only female flyer-battler assistant coach in the Dreamfleet. She has served honorably as a spy for the Friends of Freedom."

"I don't underestimate her," Ji-ji contended.

"Yes, you do. It is what people do to eccentric females they assume they know. Eccentricity is not a flaw or a sign of what is lacking. Eccentricity is the hallmark of originality in a mature female. Something society could benefit from cherishing. . . . Some months ago, Mary concluded she was not the right flying coach for you. But the outlook was not promising. Therefore, the question of a fly-coach was moot. Now it may not be."

"So do you think I'll be able to—"

"I do not have a necklace of Seeing Eyes that allows me to peer through the Window-of-What's-to-Come," the tree witch said. "But yes, it is possible. Zyla, the Friends, and I have selected another coach for you. Someone we trust."

"Do I know him?"

"What makes you think your coach is male?"

"Do I know *her* then?"

"What makes you think your coach is female? I can tell you it is someone who refers to himself as *he*. You may know of him, but you do not know him . . . yet."

A whisper of hope. Could her new coach be Tiro's old one? Could Pheebs have rescued Coach Billy from the Rad Region? If so, the practice coop could soon be littered with goddams. She would treasure every one of them. Coach B, Uncle Dreg's close friend, had given her the wizard's map of the Freedom Race route and told her Dimmers were tricksters who could come back as boulders if they wanted. If anyone could teach her it would be him.

"So you think this new coach can teach me how to fly?"

"Perhaps," Man Cryday said, guardedly.

"Will he come soon?" she asked.

"And what is the point of having him come now when your wing is broken and you are splayed out like a starfish? He is a busy man. You want to waste his time? He will come if you heal."

Ji-ji had a million questions. "I can't feel anything. Does it matter?"

"Of course it matters. But we are hopeful this numbness is temporary, particularly because, last night . . ." Man Cryday paused. Ji-ji held her breath. "Last night, you partially furled and unfurled your left, unbroken wing in your sleep."

If she hadn't been splayed out like a starfish, Ji-ji would have hugged her. "I did?"

"No. I am lying."

Ji-ji gasped in disappointment. "You are?"

"Of course not, child! I am not a sadist. As I said, you need to work on your sense of humor. If last night is anything to go by, your left wing is vivacious, which suggests it has the potential to reinvigorate itself. Alas, that news is not altogether good for it suggests my brother may not have been completely wrongheaded after all."

"Was that another joke?"

Man Cryday tilted her head to one side and said, "What do you think, Jellybean?"

"I think it was. . . . But it wasn't funny."

"*Ha!* I see you are stumbling toward humor. I am glad you are listening."

Yes, she was listening. Even when it looked as if she wasn't paying attention, she was listening with her whole soul. The truth was, Uncle Dreg used to make her feel better, but Man Cryday made her feel better prepared.

To extend their conversation, Ji-ji asked another question that had been troubling her: "Did you find anything in the letter Worthy sent to Zeba-diah? You think there are clues we missed?"

"We are human. Life is about missing things and finding our way back to them again—is that not so? Losing and finding. We cannot have one without the other."

"Yes, sure, I know," Ji-ji said, frustrated by the tree witch's vague response. "But do you think Fester—Fightgood Worthy, I mean, the grand inquisitor—do you think Fightgood Worthy an' his brother were planning a coup here in the Dream? Do you think the Friends and those reporters at the *Independent* thwarted it? Think we're safe now?"

Man Cryday blew out her cheeks. "So many questions! All right. Here is what I think. I think that mankind's yearning to oppress is like a brood of cicadas. It goes underground for a period of time where it waits for the next opportunity to emerge. Adolphus Yardley, a nincompoop with a mountain of insecurities and an unquenchable thirst for power, may be that opportu-nity. Two weeks ago, he ousted Sean Corcoran from the Dreamfleet. Yes. You are right to look concerned. The fleet is ceremonial these days, as you know, little more than a team of athletes. But this was not the case during and immediately following the Sequel. If Yardley intends to remilitarize the Dreamfleet, we are in deep trouble. Dream City is a beacon we cannot afford to extinguish."

The news filled Ji-ji with apprehension. "So the letter I found didn't help in the end?"

"Of course it did! It gave us some valuable time. If they were planning a coup, it was put on hold. Zebadiah was running drugs up through The Margins to the E.S.S. and down south to the Madlands. A lucrative source of funds that dried up after you and Lucky killed him." Ji-ji winced and looked away. "No need to be ashamed, Jellybean. There are mercy kills, is it not so? And Zeba-diah was a sadist like his brother. It was therefore a mercy you killed him. I do not believe that even Dregulahmo, pacifist though he was, would disagree with that conclusion. Sometimes we have a duty not to let others continue to abuse us. You found that letter, and now we have time."

"Thought you said Time was without pity."

"*Ha!* You are listening. Yes, I did say he is without pity. Our task, therefore, is to find a way to make Time a friend to the Friends—distract him perhaps with something shiny."

Man Cryday was one of the wisest people Ji-ji knew. A different kind of wise from Uncle Dreg, but wise nevertheless. Fearful she might never get another chance to question her, she pressed her further. "You think the steaders are planning to attack? Remember the part in the letter where Fester said, '*After the city is redeemed, we pick the T from every planting and escort them to their new nests. If we run out of mice, we find more.*' Then he wrote 'DC' in parentheses. What did he mean by new nests?"

It was Man Cryday's turn to look surprised. "Did you memorize the letter, child?"

"No. I don't even have a copy. I only read it a couple times 'fore Germaine took it to Alice, an' Ben took off with a copy for you. We'd been ratified for the Freedom Race as Wild Seeds, an' the Monticello Protectorate—one of the weirdest places I've ever seen—" Ji-ji broke off when she saw Man Cryday's raised eyebrow. "Sorry. Got off track. Thing is, everything was moving super fast. But whole sentences from that letter come back to me. Like it's a warning. . . . They planned to move '*under the cover of plain sight.*' I remember that part too."

"Then we all need to be ready, Jellybean. Which means you need to get strong."

The tree witch smiled down at her. A breathtakingly beautiful, uncharacteristically optimistic smile. The kind of smile only elderly people who have known deep suffering can pull off. Taken aback by how much the Gardener of Tears looked like her wizard brother, Ji-ji thought, *The trees you tend in Dimmers Wood must love you very much.*

Ji-ji happened to look again at the fabric in Man Cryday's strong brown fingers. She asked her what she was making.

"A journey quilt."

"What's a journey quilt?"

"For Toteppi, it is a quilt of symbols that relate to a journey our people have made, are making now, or will make in the future. You have one on your bed."

"This? Mam's blackbird quilt?"

Ji-ji didn't want to remember how the quilt hung from the ceiling to hide her mam's seedingbed, or how inadequately it stifled Lotter's grunts when he plowed her. "Zaini gave it to Mam as a grieving gift," Ji-ji said, "after we lost Luvlydoll."

"Ah. To the last metaflu pandemic, yes? My brother told me you were with your baby sister when she died. A breathing death is a dreadful one to witness. . . . You remember how hard Luvlydoll struggled to breathe?" Of course she did. Why was Man Cryday punishing her like this? "Do you know why little Luvlydoll struggled so long?"

"I guess . . . I guess she wanted to live."

"Correct. But Luvlydoll's little body could not fight for her anymore. Metaflu overpowered it. She was not in possession of options. Do you want to live, Jellybean?"

"Yes . . . I guess I do . . . I think so. . . . But . . ."

"You are terrified you will return to the condition you were in before. You are afraid you will be a freak." Gulping back tears, Ji-ji nodded. Man Cryday continued: "I think we desperate ones—by that I do not mean Toteppi only. I mean all those who bear the greatest burdens in this world—outcasts like Afarra, whose lives are worth less to most people than a pair of shoes or a carry bag, and others across the world whose wailing you hear if you commune with the roots of the earth and listen. . . . Even in the Age of Plenty, they were always here, trying to get the rest of the world to listen. . . . I think we desperate ones living today have a resurgent—what English word am I looking for? A resurgent *talent,* a gift fed by need. . . . Mary says you were only a few feet from the ground when your wings uplifted themselves and flapped you into hovering. Like a hummingbird's wings. You could not break your fall completely, yet your wings saved your life. You remember this?"

"Sort of."

"They flapped so hard and fast, Mary said they looked more like propellers than wings. You were plunging down at a terrible speed. A great force had to be summoned to halt your fall."

"But I didn't summon anything. It just . . . happened. I hardly remember it now."

"Remember what I told you in Memoria the day after your sprouting? Dregulahmo told you the same Origin Story, yes? In Totepp, a language older than memory, *to* means 'bird,' and *teppi* means 'to remember.' Your mother was Toteppi, so these stories are yours. Stories are the wings of dreamers, and that explains why some of the Middle Passengers, even though they were not Toteppi and could not speak Totepp, and could not possibly remember us, found their way back home to the tribe of birds whose songs filled their dreams. Your body, your wings—perhaps they are the Rememberers?"

A lot to think about. Old and young fell quiet for a while. Man Cryday took up her sewing while Ji-ji looked at the story-cloths hung around the room.

Ji-ji dozed. Her mind looped back to the planting. . . .

At the back of one of the basement storerooms in the dining hall on the 437th, an antique pinball machine sat under storage crates and a tarp. Every so often, when Ji-ji and her dozen female kitchen-seeds were convinced Overseer Crabstreet was too high or too drunk to come looking for them, they would plug it in (assuming power was on in the dining hall) and watch its insides spring to life. The colors, lights, and buzzers would go nuts. They found it impossible to believe that, in the Age of Plenty, both fairskins and duskies used to play on machines like this one. Ji-ji and her kitchen-seeds would never be the play-ers who controlled the outcome; they were the little silver balls shoved from one place to the next by flippers—tiny paddles that guided the balls through an elaborate maze. *Flipper* reminded Ji-ji of the word *flippant*. It captured the precariousness and disposability of a female seed's life in the Territories. The detailed diagram in the instruction booklet the kitchen-seeds found taped to the machine's underbelly identified each obstacle. The names for most of its other parts had stuck, too: *plunger, ramps, pop bumpers, drain . . .*

The pinball machine confirmed what Ji-ji already knew, even though she couldn't articulate it at the time: a seed's fate was determined by steaders whose thrusting, plunger-filled hands forced their prey up ramps, round bum-pers, and down drains. It became a source of mockery to Ji-ji. Eventually, she ordered her kitchen-seeds to stop plugging it in. Sloppy Casperseedmate, a.k.a. Delilah Moon, the most vocal of the twelve kitchen-seeds, accused Ji-ji of acting high an' mighty like her father-man. Ji-ji hadn't been able to explain why thrusting the little balls through the maze had felt to her like rape.

Man Cryday once told her she could either make herself or let others make her. And now she realized she didn't have to be some miserable little ball careening around an arbitrary maze, flipped from one torment to another. She'd told Afarra that a so-called Cloth could become her own self on her own terms, so why did she have to keep teaching herself that same lesson? There was a chance she'd ruined everything by leaping from the nest, but two weeks ago, she'd summoned the power of her own body and defied gravity itself. . . .

Ji-ji woke with a start. The tree witch was still there, keeping watch by her bed.

"Thought you'd gone. Will you stay long?"

"Long enough to see you out of the woods."

"Good. I'd like that. Thank you."

Man Cryday laid her strong, earth-brown hand on the blackbird quilt again and said, "Silapu's quilt, made for her by Zaini—my niece, your flight-boy's long-suffering mother—who gathered up her torn-to-pieces son and rocked him in her arms. What do you see when you look at it, Jellybean?"

"I see three birds in a tree—an Immaculate tree, Mam called it. A flock flying away."

"Because something has surprised them. Is it not so?"

"Yes," Ji-ji agreed.

"Why then do the other three stay?"

The simple question baffled her. "I don't know. Guess I never thought about it."

"Yet it is the most interesting question of all. They stay, child, to guard the tree."

"Yes," Ji-ji said. "I see that now."

"Good. Keep looking. If you do, there is a reward."

"There is? What is it?"

"If you are lucky, you will see more."

T he snarlcat is being a Weeping," Afarra said. "Like us on the planting."
Tiro wished she hadn't said that. Weepings—the seeds' name for
themselves, inspired by the snippets of fabric they were forced to sew
onto their clothes—thrust him back to the 437th. He pictured the hideous seed
symbols—half-black, half-white ones for Muleseeds like him, Ji, and Marcus;
solid black ones for Tribalseeds like Uncle Dreg and Silapu; and brown ones
for Commonseeds like Georgie-Porge. All of these symbols had three smaller
seeds falling from the parent seed like tears, hence the seeds' sorrowful nickname. Yeah. Seeds were Weepings all right.

Tiro looked over at Afarra, who had inched closer to the cage again after
he'd warned her not to. As an outcast, her seed symbol had been even more
sickening than symbols worn by regular botanicals. Serverseed outcasts' black
seed symbols were broken in two. No seedling "tears" fell from the large broken seed for one terrible reason: depending on the severity of the labor shortage, outcasts were prevented from procreating.

"He is being a Weeping," Afarra insisted again through her contagion
mask. "We find Muckmock after this. I promise on Elly's you-know-whats
we save him."

Tiro shook his head in frustration. At least Afarra hadn't blurted out Ji's secret, but none of them had been able to convince her they couldn't save the
mutant she'd seen on the Independence Day celebrations. Probably why she'd
been desperate to come to this exhibit. Thought her new friend would be sitting there waiting for her to rescue him.

"C'mon, Afarra," Tiro said, as gently as he could. "We been standing here
for ages. We gotta catch up with Ji, Marcus, an' Georgie, see the museum. You
wanna see that, right? Ji—Elly—she'll miss you if we don't leave soon. She'll
wonder where we've got to. . . . Afarra, you listening?"

Due to the wide-brimmed floppy hat she wore, the contagion mask, and
how much shorter Afarra was than him, Tiro couldn't see hardly anything of
her face. But she made her rebellion patently clear by ignoring him and speaking to the cage instead.

Against his better judgment, Tiro turned his eyes to the cage again. It was
barely large enough for the male snarlcat to stand. His dull coat, matted mane,

and the gray crust around his eyes revealed how badly he'd been cared for. But it was the way he lay there in the cage with his great head on his paws that distressed Tiro the most, as if the only thing he wanted in this world was to be put out of his misery. Seeing something so powerful caged up *disrespectfully* like that made him want to weep. Yeah, he was a Weeping all right.

The crooks operating the exhibit charged an admission fee of either eight or seventeen dollars, depending on whether you paid in SuperStates or local District currency. Territorial dollars—known as *yellers* mostly in D.C., but sometimes called Lousy Lucres or crappies—weren't accepted. A kid who'd attempted to pay for his admission in seedchips had been chased off like a dog. Ration cards could serve as payment too, the crooks said, though Tiro doubted anyone would be dumb enough to part with any. As a flyer-battler, Tiro had the luxury of being paid in Supers, so he'd handed over sixteen of them for two tickets to the shifty-looking bastards who manned the entrance. Soon as he set foot inside he realized he'd been fleeced. He hated being taken for a sucker.

His head was pounding. He wiped his brow with the purple neckerchief he often wore in honor of Amadee. He and Georgie had downed a few too many tequila shots last night, and now he was paying the price. The stench inside the dirty pavilion wasn't helping either. Earlier, a girl—a former seed, looked like, with scars on her legs and a banged-up lip—had tried to hose down the cages. Drove the poor ants crazy, so the White men at the entrance had screamed at her to cut it out. She'd obeyed at once. The terror in her eyes told Tiro the girl had been trained to obey. Another reason why he wanted to punch the men's smirks off.

When they'd first entered the pavilion, Tiro had suggested to Afarra that this could be the same snarlcat they'd shared a boxcar with on the Liberty Train to Monticello. She'd looked at him as if he was the biggest dumbass in the world. Employed her own crazy brand of logic when she said, "This snarlcat is not being *anything like* the snarlcat in the boxcar. That one was *sleeping* and this one is *awake*." He hadn't bothered to argue. What would be the point?

"Time to go," Tiro urged again, and reached for her hand.

Afarra stuck her hand in her jacket pocket and made one of those rude guttural sounds she liked to make these days. Tiro struggled to maintain his patience. He'd been in a good mood when they entered. Had a shitload to be grateful for. Ji had been up and about for a couple of weeks. Her right wing had healed completely. Doc Riff said her recovery was "astounding." He'd actually used that word though he was a pretty low-key guy. Said there was almost no trace of injury. Seemed like the wing had regenerated itself. Ji could furl and unfurl both of them whenever she wanted. And the colors! *Man!* The colors on her wings were spectacular. Mesmerizing. Like what you'd see on a lake at sunset when the sky swings from purple to mauve to maroon, and the silver flecks on the lake make your heart leap in your chest cos the whole expanse is so goddam breathtaking.

Tiro had argued against the trip to the Streetfood Fest-on-the-Mall, said it was too risky. Zyla, Ben, and Germaine said the group should be safe enough in daylight as long as they wore contagion masks and hats. They'd been right so far. In their contagion masks, hats, and sunglasses, even he had trouble picking the girls out in a crowd. Their protection contingent were trained battlers too, so it wasn't like they were vulnerable. If you counted Ink, there were five flyer-battler bodyguards in total. (Ink's bodyguarding skills were understandably limited, but Tree counted for at least two, so Marcus—smartass that he was—argued there would still be five of them even if Ink was "Inked." At least Marcus had the decency to whisper it to Tiro and Georgie-Porge so Ink didn't hear him.)

The Mall, though still a muddy mess, looked less scary during the day than it did at night. A fresh outbreak of metaflu in the Disunited States—down in the Rad Region near the Gulf, mostly—had spooked folks. More than half the people gathered on the Mall wore contagion masks. Paired with baseball caps and sunglasses for the fly-boys, the masks provided great cover. Tree was the exception, of course. Hard to disguise a seven-footer with a bigass basket on his back. But folks were hesitant to ask Tree for his autograph. You could tell they doubted if it was really him under the mask, hat, and sunglasses. Seemed to find it difficult to believe a flyer celebrity like Laughing Tree would cart a boy around, so most steered clear of him and his "damaged son" the way folks do when they're not sure how to react to someone without putting their foot in it.

Tiro had never been able to understand why people acted like idiots around people with physical challenges. Pretended they were invisible or spoke to them like they were morons. Bottom line—Tree was left alone, pretty much. Even so, afraid they'd stick out like a sore thumb, as he put it, Laughing Tree kept his distance, "poised to come to the rescue if called upon to do so." Tree was one of the good guys, for sure. Ink had brought a pair of binoculars. Every so often, he scanned the crowd on the lookout for danger. It cracked Tiro up to see it. Ink, who didn't look like he'd hit thirteen yet, had a crush on Afarra. Ink had been the one to suggest the pair accompany them to the mutant exhibit. Ink promised to keep an eye on things, make sure everything was "copacetic." The kid was nearly as obsessed with vocab as Marcus was.

From the Lincoln Memorial to all the way down past the museum, the Mall was packed. Bands playing—the whole shebang. The zoological exhibit near the Capitol Moat was at the quieter end, where a handful of people were dumb enough to fork over a small fortune to stand in front of cages that stank of shit and piss so they could gawk at creatures less fortunate than themselves. Christ! He would kill for some fresh air.

Tiro tried again: "Time to head out, Afarra."

Afarra shook her head doggedly. "No," she growled.

Tiro bit down on his lip to control his irritation. He pictured Marcus in the museum, showing off his knowledge of history. Bet he was talking Ji's ear off with this date and that date. Not that they had all the stuff they used to have in the museum. Not even close. Place had been looted like crazy during the Sequel and the conflicts that followed. But it was still *their* place and he'd wanted to see it. Saved it till he could see it with Ji. Then Marcus, whose attitude toward Ji had done a one-eighty after he'd seen her unfurl the other day, had shoved himself forward in that slick way of his. Georgie, almost as much in awe of Ji as Marcus was, was touring the museum too. Of all the places in D.C., the African American museum was the one Tiro would've liked to see cos it told him his history mattered. No matter what type of crap people fed you, they couldn't erase you completely. But then Afarra *had* to see the mutants. Like she'd die or something if she didn't.

So here they were, precisely where he didn't want to be. Tree and Ink were over on the other side of the pavilion by the stripers. Tree, who'd been cornered at last by three enthusiastic fans, was signing autographs.

"Hey, Afarra. Want some ice cream? I saw a stall back there. With ice cream. Want some?"

Nothing. How was he going to get her out of here without causing a commotion? He wished they'd never seen that kid with the flyers.

They'd been standing a stone's throw from the museum when a scrawny-looking White kid with greasy hair and an attitude shoved handwritten ads into their hands and yelled something mostly unintelligible about the greatest show on earth. The written ad was equally boastful. At the top of the page in capital letters were the words "SPECTACULA ZOO EXIBIT!!!" After what happened with the ape-man, Ji and the fly-boys did all they could to distract Afarra so she wouldn't learn about it. But she happened to see an ad on the ground and picked it up. Zyla was teaching her to read, and the word *zoo* was one she recognized. And that was that.

When they'd reached the pathetic display, a trip that had taken ages due to how crowded it was at the other end of the Mall, the marquee above the pavilion's entrance promised "A Zoollogical Exibit of Rare Exotica and Savage Mutants!!!" The only satisfaction Tiro had gotten from the exhibit so far was that the White exhibit owners were even lousier at spelling than he was.

As it turned out, the "rare exotica" consisted of a few leashed monkeys cowering on crates, and three annoying parakeets that squawked "hello" at visitors. The "savage mutants" were locked inside four rusty cages. The male snarlcat Afarra was fascinated with lay inside one cage; another cage held a female snarlcat and her cub; the third held four stripers who stared out through the bars like gangsters in a jail cell. The last cage housed a lone striper whose antennae on the top of his bony skull were all bent over. The striper's fur was so mangy his stripes had nearly disappeared. Tiro remembered Man Cryday said a striper's "tiara" responded to stress in much the same way as an orca's dorsal fin: droopy antennae signaled an unhappy striper. Tiro didn't need Man Cryday to tell him these mutants were misery personified.

Tiro had seen a zoological exhibit of a similar caliber before. Peregrine's Peripatetic Petting Zoo visited Planting 437 once a year. In an uncharacteristic move one year, Father-Man Williams had paid the entrance fee for any of his numerous seedlings who wanted to go see it instead of attending school that morning. (Drexler Williams didn't believe in seed education and did everything he could to undermine it.) Tiro and Amadee, along with Williams' other seedlings, had petted a small armadillo, two miniature donkeys, an ostrich with one eye missing, a creature whose name he couldn't remember that looked like a large, buck-toothed rat, and a female wallaby all the way from Australia. Tiro and Amadee had wanted to take the wallaby home after Peregrine's assistant told them the correct term for her was a *flyer,* but they'd had to settle for patting her on the head. Peregrine said the wallaby was "continuously fertile" and therefore an inspiration to female seeds. He'd eased a fake baby wallaby into the female wallaby's pouch so they could see how she carried her young. Fake Baby Wallaby was made from authentic wallaby hide, Peregrine said. He bragged about how he'd sewn the button eyes on it himself—a boast that explained why one eye was higher than the other. "That's what you jills need," Peregrine had advised the females in the group, as he spat out globules of tobacco-laced spittle, "a cute little pouch for your seedlings."

In the following months, the twins had nightmares about that zoo. Too young to know why it had bothered them so much, Tiro and Amadee kept coming back to what Peregrine had said about the pouch as he'd looked at the female seedlings. The wallaby had been lashed to a post to prevent her from escaping. The brothers spent hours making plans to launch a Friends of Freedom–type raid on the zoo next time it stopped at the planting. They would release all the animals into the wild, though one of the details they hadn't worked out yet was how they would accomplish this without first escaping from captivity themselves.

You could say their wish came true. According to Uncle Dreg, a few years later, en route to a planting in the 300s, Peregrine and his assistants were attacked by a pride of snarlcats. Peregrine sent a Mayday on his caller before he was devoured. Rumor had it his menagerie escaped. Tiro and Amadee decided the petting zoo animals were in on the ambush. They must have communicated with the snarlcats, Amadee said. Obviously, the stripers had aided and abetted them too. Even softhearted Amadee didn't have much sympathy for Peregrine. Fairskins rarely got their just deserts in the Territories.

Amadee would have hated seeing wild animals caged up like this. Hated it. Tiro wasn't animal crazy the way Amadee was. Sure, he liked them well enough and would never be cruel to them, but they weren't his kin like they were for his brother or Afarra. Usually, snarlcats scared the crap out of him. With their shaggy manes, terrifying teeth, and daggerlike claws, these supersized lions would terrify anyone. But this creature was too pitiful to be scary.

Afarra chatted away to the cat in that crazy lingo of hers. Tiro told her to keep it down. She glared over at him—at least that's what he thought she probably did, though her mask and floppy hat made it hard to say for sure. Maybe cos she'd been forced to raise herself mostly, Afarra was feral. Tiro wasn't sure if that was a disrespectful way to refer to someone, so he'd never say it out loud, but there was some truth to it. When he thought about how bad her life had been as an outcast, all he wanted to do was protect her. If only she wasn't hell-bent on driving him batshit crazy this afternoon.

Tiro told himself to start looking on the bright side. He had a lot to be thankful for. The speed of Ji's recovery was miraculous. She could retract her wings into hollows on her back and the ridges on either side of her spine. It was like this magic trick you thought you'd be able to figure out if you saw it in slow motion. Today, dressed in the lightweight, plum-colored cape Zyla had made for her, her wings retracted into her back, Ji looked totally normal. You'd never know she had something amazing underneath. All that was left now was to see if she could fly. She hadn't attempted it yet. Too risky till Doc Riff declared she was a hundred percent. Even if they never functioned like a bird's wings, Tiro was confident she'd be okay. It wasn't like before. They weren't a handicap. She could roll them up and look like a regular person. She could keep her wings under wraps for the rest of her life if she wanted.

He felt a pang of guilt. Is that what he wanted? No. He didn't want that. Maybe a part of him used to once, but nearly losing her had changed him. He couldn't put his finger on exactly how he was different but he was. She wasn't in pieces was the thing. She was *whole*. It was like he'd convinced himself good things wouldn't happen to him anymore, like he'd been tied to rail lines for years listening out for the goddam train. But ever since Ji's recovery, he'd been able to take a deep breath. His flying had recovered too. These past two weeks he'd flown unaided. Not even a whisper of that plummet syndrome/vertigo problem. Flown the dream like he owned it. Without sunsets or any illicit drugs at all. Yeah, okay—so he drank too much occasionally. (Last night with Georgie-Porge, for example.) But what fly-boy didn't? And if there were times when the miracle of her back, if he was being real honest, made him feel . . . what? Smaller? Less? He told himself he was a jerk for thinking like that. He smothered his envy cos that's what friends did. And he was Ji's friend—he really was.

The other day when he'd called her late at night, he'd actually said the right thing. Like that time when he'd said flying was his scripture. This time he'd said something that popped into his head. He'd said, "I fly the Dream, Ji, but you *are* the Dream." Afterward, there was about ten seconds of silence cos neither of them knew how to top that. Then she'd asked him to take her and Afarra to the Streetfood Fest, and he'd said yes, confident Man Cryday, who was heading back to Dimmers Wood the next day, would nix it. Only she hadn't.

The snarlcat gave a phlegmy snort and stood up. Its arched back grazed the bars of the cage as the animal struggled to stretch. Positively evil to lock the creature in a cage that small.

Tiro was grateful Ji hadn't opted to come with them. She'd flinched in horror when she'd read the flyer. In spite of how amazing her wings were, she'd confessed to him that sometimes she saw herself as a freak, a mutant. He'd assured her she was nothing like the terrifying creatures steaders were rumored to have crossbred. Snarlcats and stripers looked like biological errors, he told her, while she looked like . . . He'd struggled to find the right words. She looked like "a high-tech angel." Another brilliant word choice. (*Watch out, Marcus. Here comes Tiro the wordsmith!*) Not that he could blame Ji for being sensitive. Her wings were . . . *weird*. Gorgeous but weird. It was like she was on the way to becoming a different species.

At night, he fretted about what would happen if the steaders discovered she was still alive. He reminded himself she was eighteen months younger than he was. He needed to show her he was confident about the future, let her know he would be there to protect her. If the steaders discovered her secret, they'd want to either kill her, lock her up and experiment on her, or parade her around in some cage. People would pay to come see the "freak." That would never happen on his watch. He'd promised Uncle Dreg he'd look out for her, for Afarra too, and that was what he intended to do. He'd gotten there too late to help Amadee. He wouldn't make that mistake again.

He made the mistake of breathing in too deeply. The stench threatened to knock him out. Before he could tell Afarra they had to get out of there, she glared at him. "I am *not* going!" she declared, stubborn as an animule. Kept talking to the snarlcat in that crazyass lingo. Tiro cursed Man Cryday for filling her head with that ant whisperer crap. Mutants weren't the listening type. If Afarra thought she was invincible it could be real dangerous. . . . And while he happened to be thinking about who irritated him, what the hell was Marcus doing treating Ji like royalty? He made a fuss about opening the van door for her, helped her into the front passenger seat like she was breakable or something. Kept asking if her wings were comfortable. He'd actually said, "Are your wings comfortable, Ji-ji?" Dumbest question ever asked by anyone in the history of mankind. When Tiro had joked that the museum looked like an upside-down basket, or like one of those funny hats African American women in the District wore to church, you'd think Marcus had designed the damn thing himself from the way he overreacted. Claimed this was some ancient design called a ziggurat. Tiro had never heard a more ridiculous word in his life. On the spot, he'd made up a little rhyme:

> *Hey, niggers, where you at?*
> *Come to the Dream, see the ziggurat.*

Georgie-Porge was the only one who'd cracked a smile. Marcus, in his role as High Priest of Assholiness, had preached about how the n-word disrespected the entire race, which was why you could get fined in the SuperStates for using it. Blah, blah, blah. You could tell he was showing off in front of Ji, trying to prove how goddam sensitive he was. Yeah, Marcus could be a pain in the ass, but no one got on his nerves more than the tree witch.

Before she left for Dimmers, Man Cryday advised all of them to let Ji "spread her wings," which Tiro took to be the witch's lame effort at a joke. Looked at him with those snooping eyes of hers, called him "flighty-boy," and warned him not to be overprotective. Said "chauvinism isn't confined to steaders," and "no man has the right to stand in the way of a woman flying Free." After he got back to the Dreamfleet compound and Marcus explained what chauvinism meant, Tiro had spent hours coming up with witty comebacks he wished he'd flung at his great-aunt. The witch knew how to slice off a man's balls just cos he didn't relish reading a dictionary from cover to cover. He was coming up on nineteen in a few months. The witch needed to treat him with respect.

And another thing. What kind of screwed-up, masochistic female calls herself Man Cryday? Marcus had this theory that her name was a riff on this Man Friday character in some book, which made Tiro think of those arty-farty literary illusions—or was it allusions? Hell if he knew. The ones Zyla used to spout off about in the Planting legacy school. Seemed like illusions were a way to shame people like him who hadn't read as much as you had cos they'd been living life instead.

Calm down, T, he told himself. *What the hell's wrong with you?*

Afarra cooed and clucked at the snarlcat. Through the open flap in the black-and-gold Dreamfleet fan jacket she wore—the one Marcus had bought her, probably to make him look bad—two of Uncle Dreg's Seeing Eyes glared at him. It was too warm and humid for a jacket, but she'd refused to take the necklace off so they'd all insisted she wear it.

Tiro reached over and zipped the jacket up. Afarra, who hadn't seen that coming, let out a little scream of panic as if he were a homicidal maniac. He hadn't intended to scare her so he felt like crap. He whispered to her that if folks caught sight of the necklace they'd freak out. Under her breath, he heard her say, "Bugger off." It hurt like hell when she said that. He knew their friendship wasn't close like it used to be. But the way she said it . . .

Another phlegmy grunt from the snarlcat jolted Tiro back into the present. He *had* to get out of here. He scanned the pavilion looking for Trink. Not hard to spot them cos there weren't many people there and the pair towered over everyone. They were gaping at a cage of stripers. Tiro tried to get their attention. Hopeless. Through the open side of the pavilion, Tiro had a clear view of the Mall. It would get dark in a couple of hours. The city's homeless flocked to the Mall at night, unless there was some kind of official celebration in which case the mayor filled the place with cops and patrollers and the homeless stayed away. But today the festival finished at five. They needed to be out of there by then.

Thousands of refugees had taken up residence on the Mall after KingTown, the tent city in Kingdom Come in the Dream Revival District, had become so packed with tents and makeshift shelters you could barely walk among them. Tiro felt sorry for all of them. The Maulers who lived on the Mall were even worse off than the nearby Papers in Kingdom Come. At least the Papers who'd staked their tents at the feet of the Dreamer had a few rights grandfathered into the D.C. Constitution to help them escape eviction. Didn't mean they were safe, as the raids on KingTown demonstrated. But for the Maulers who'd snuck into D.C. before Insurmountable was completed only to find KingTown packed to the gills, it was much worse. Last in, first out, some of the politicians were fond of saying. More and more refugees were being turfed out of the city each night. Mayor Yardley spoke about "cleaning up" the Mall, which meant ridding it of Maulers. Tiro stopped himself. Thinking of them as Maulers and Papers was like calling people botanicals. Shit. Did that mean Marcus could be right about the n-word? Tiro decided to think about that mindbender some other time, preferably when someone wasn't pounding a stake into his skull. He shook his head, then regretted it immediately cos it made his headache even worse.

The men who'd taken his lucre at the entrance were staring at them. Not good. They needed to get out of here. Last place you wanted to be on the Mall after dark. Before they set out he'd downed a couple pills the sports docs prescribed for jitters. It hit him that they hadn't worked. They'd done the opposite, made him even more jittery, short-tempered too. He should've stayed with Ji. Suppose she forgot to keep her mask on and some parrot working for the steaders spotted her and realized the "existential threat to the Territories" had risen from the dead? *Calm down, T,* he told himself again. *She's got a mask, a wig, a hat, sunglasses. She'll be fine.* Yet he couldn't rid himself of the pit in his stomach. He had to check she was okay. Uncle Dreg had asked him to protect her, and he wasn't about to let him down.

"Okay, Afarra, we seen enough. Time to get back to Ji an' the others."

"He is a Weeping," Afarra repeated, "like us."

"We're not Weepings anymore, okay?" The sharpness in Tiro's tone startled her. Shit. He was making things worse. He tried again. "All I'm sayin' is, we got out. We're Free. Got the papers to prove it."

Afarra stuffed her hand into her pocket. "I am keeping my paper here. See?"

Tiro grabbed her wrist. She froze. He'd scared her again. "Remember what we told you?"

Hastily, he loosened his grip on her thin wrist and leaned down close to her ear so no one could hear them. "You gotta keep your paper hidden, okay? There's hundreds—*thousands* of folks round here don't got papers like we do. They ain't lucky like us. We gotta hold on to 'em. If we don't, we're in deep sh—" He hesitated. "—we got problems."

Tiro didn't know why it bothered him so much if he swore around Afarra. Didn't make sense, seeing as how he and Ji had come to the conclusion she was probably about the same age as Ji was. After the time she'd spent in the Monticello Protectorate listening to the cussing of Clansmen, militiamen, and Bounty Boys, Afarra had grown fond of swearing herself. Said "Shitshitshit!" and worse whenever she felt like it. Yet in many ways, she was still the most childlike person he'd ever met. The other day Marcus asked if Afarra was "on the spectrum," if she was special. But Tiro hadn't liked the way he'd said it. Sounded patronizing, which was why he'd told Marcus to shut his mouth. She was Afarra, that's all. She didn't need some label pinned to her by people who had no idea who she was. Only he wished to god she weren't so goddam annoying right now. He realized that Afarra was addressing him and not the cat for once. He paid attention.

"So I am speaking to the sorrow cat. I am saying how it used to be for him in The Margins with no cages. An' he is feeling better when I say it. An' I am saying seeds are Weepings too. You, me, Elly. That is our name. I stay with the cat. Who is Lonesome. That is his name. We stay."

Afarra pointed to the pavilion entrance. Soon, the stalls that weren't there permanently would be dismantled, replaced by the topsy-turvy, improvised homes of refugees. The dwellings would be made from scraps they'd salvaged—cardboard, canvas, plastic, corrugated aluminum, bits of clothing and garbage bags. God, it was depressing. "Weepings," Afarra repeated. She stopped pointing and turned back to face the cage.

Tiro didn't want to think about those they'd left behind. It would drive him crazy if he did. He wanted to fly like a bird in the Dream and not be plagued by the idea that he wasn't nearly as gifted as his dead twin or his miraculous best friend. He wanted to Free the ones he loved so Williams wouldn't re-rape his mother and auction off his little brothers. What if Williams had raped her already? What good was a dead wizard's impotency curse when you got right down to it? If Uncle Dreg couldn't save himself, how could he save anyone else? He wanted the world to slam into reverse and travel back to the Age of Plenty before it was all fucked up. Before there were seeds and plantings, before there was a Sequel and a climate out to kill you, before metaflu pandemics meant you had to dig mass graves on plantings till your hands blistered worse than they did when you flew the coop. . . . But he couldn't. He couldn't do a goddam thing about any of that right now. But there was one thing he could do. He could get away from the stench of this sordid place.

He grabbed Afarra's arm roughly and began to drag her away.

Lonesome sprang to life. Tiro didn't see the big cat's paw before it ripped off the sleeve of his T-shirt! Its formidable claws grazed his arm. He yelped in pain. Jesus!

The snarlcat's bone-chilling roar made the gawkers in the tent scream. The shifty-looking men at the entrance came barreling toward them.

Tiro, more shaken than hurt, and more furious than either, shouted at Afarra: "What the *fuck* is wrong with you? You're coming with me, *RIGHT NOW!*"

The fear in Afarra's eyes didn't make him ashamed. It made him stronger than she was.

He grabbed her arm and began to drag her from the pavilion. Suddenly, he came to his senses. What the hell was he doing?

He fell all over himself apologizing. Afarra looked at him like he was the devil himself and took off running toward the center of the Mall, desperate to get away from him. The snarlcat roared after her like a thing gone mad.

"What you do, boy?" the men who'd swindled him demanded. They'd surrounded him. "You goad the cat or what?"

Tiro swore, pushed past them, and tore off after Afarra.

There she was, up ahead, weaving through the crowd. Her hat fell off as she ran. She didn't stop to pick it up and neither did he. Ji must've convinced Afarra to let her braid her hair. He'd never seen her with her hair all neat like that. He wanted to tell her how pretty she looked. He'd make it up to her. She'd forgive him, wouldn't she? Yes, she'd forgive him.

He was gaining ground on her when a small dog ran between his legs and tripped him up. He lost his footing and tumbled into the Great Divide. He righted himself mid-somersault, landing on his feet in a move that delighted two nearby children.

He stared down at his clothes, at his ripped T-shirt. He was covered in muck. *Shit!* What was she doing taking off like that? In a few bounds, moving with the ease of an athlete, he climbed out of the furrow and surveyed the area. After a moment, he spotted Afarra's skinny ass weaving through the crowd. The stupid dog yapped near his feet. Without thinking, he kicked it out of the way and took off again. Furiously, he called out her name. The crowd was too thick for him to make much headway. . . .

He'd lost her!

He forced himself to halt. He needed to calm down and think things through. Then it hit him. He knew exactly where Afarra was headed. Who did she always want to go back to? Her Elly. She'd run off in the direction of the museum to join Ji. Tiro felt a surge of relief. It wasn't far to the museum; she'd be safe there.

He turned to see Trink charging up behind him. Astonished people made way for them.

"What you do to her?" Ink cried.

"Me?" Tiro said. "Nothing! I swear! Cat went nuts. Scared her half to death."

"Poor little thing," Tree said. "We should fan out—look for her."

"Yeah," Tiro agreed. "But I think I know where she's headed."

He explained his theory to them; they both agreed the museum was her likely destination. Tree suggested they take the route on the south side of God's Furrow in case she'd crossed over to the other side. They'd meet up in front of the museum. No. No need to contact Marcus or the others yet, Tiro said, cos he was 99.9 percent certain that's where they'd find her. If they hurried, they could treat her to that bag of the fried chicken livers she'd been eyeing when they'd passed a street vendor near the museum. Trink jogged down to where they could cross over the Great Divide, while Tiro stayed on the north side and headed back through the crowd, scanning it as he went. Afarra was easily distracted. If any tent looked like it could hold a mutant, that's where she'd be.

He was halfway to the museum when he spotted an exchange occurring in the narrow gap between two stalls. He stopped walking, jammed his hand into his pocket, and felt around for cash, part of which he planned to use to treat Ji and Afarra to something special. He approached the men. Neither one wore a mask. The shorter of the two was Black, with a messy fro; the other man was White with one of those funny handlebar moustaches White people wear. From the way they'd been huddling, Tiro knew the White man was the one he wanted.

"Hey!" said the Black man, excitedly, as if he recognized him.

Tiro put his hand up to his face. Goddammit! His mask was hanging from his left ear. The right strap was broken. He'd lost his cap too. *Damn!*

"You that Pterodactyl flyer?" the Black man asked.

"Nope," Tiro replied, curtly. He could tell they didn't buy it, so he added, "The Pterodactyl's my brother. Haven't seen him in years."

"Pity," the White guy said. "Saw him fly the Dream last season. Kid may be a rookie but he sure don't fly like one."

"Tell me about it," Tiro said. "You got anything special, man?"

"Sure do," the White man replied. He turned to the Black man and said, "Get lost, Fish." Fish scurried off as fast as his bum leg would let him.

The White man took Tiro's elbow and steered him behind one of the canvas flaps that partially hid his stall. He was a regular who sold a whole mess of things—from peanuts and gator jerky, to bullets, tobacco, liquor and knives.

"I got the best batch o' suns you ever had. Twenty-five each. Don't accept Lousy Lucres or seedchips. No Independents either. Those District dollars an' Atlanta Greens're dropping like a stone. Gen-you-wine SuperStates is the only ones Lippy Verdi takes. That's me. Lippy. Friends call me Requiem. Bet a smart boy like you knows why too. Cute, eh? Like they say, I got the best suns north of the Great Divide." Beneath his gray handlebar moustache, Requiem rearranged his lips into a smile. The effect was creepy, like watching a spider grin.

Tiro turned away from Lippy and moved in closer to the side of the stall so no one could see how much lucre he had on him. He reached into the front pocket of his jeans, pulled out some cash, and peeled off a one-hundred-dollar SuperState. He pocketed the rest. He'd planned to stop by the bank and deposit his salary after he treated the girls. No sweat. He'd make up for it, easy, soon as he got paid for that pharma ad. He turned and held the note out to Lippy, who snatched it from his hand and held it up to the light, then licked his fingers, touched the note, and licked his fingers again to check it wasn't fake. His grin revealed a set of teeth in urgent need of a dentist. "Four suns it is."

Tiro realized that Lippy Verdi hadn't expected him to cave so easily. He'd been taken for a sucker again. He thought about snatching the note back, but the man had that genial way about him made you think he could fuck you at the drop of a hat. For all he knew, Lippy had a semiautomatic nearby ready to blow the head off difficult customers.

Tiro watched as Lippy counted four little tablets into his hand. Red dots in his palms. What was the name of those things nails left? Stigmata. Yeah. Stigmata with the power to tame the world.

"You need a bag?" he asked.

"Nope," Tiro told him. "I got a mouth."

Lippy laughed then got serious. "Don't take too many at once, okay? Suns ain't for amateurs. Too many an' it'll feel like your eyes is gouged out from the inside. Believe me, I know."

Tiro slipped the pills into his pocket. Before he got more than a few yards away, he dug down into his pocket and drew out one of the small red pills. It had been weeks since he'd had a little pick-me-up. After a day like today, he deserved it. He popped the sun into his mouth. He'd save the rest. No more than one a day. Two tops. . . .

The tiny red pill set his tongue on fire. It was a lot stronger than he was accustomed to. Good. Maybe he wasn't such a sucker after all? His fury fell away. He was mellow now. On track.

God, that feels good, Tiro thought, as he forgave himself for everything.

11 MEMORIALS

The moment she heard the sound surging toward them, although she couldn't put her finger on what it was, Ji-ji knew they were in trouble. Marcus and Georgie-Porge knew it too. In the atrium of the museum, the din became louder. Hundreds of voices, fused into a bludgeon, cried in unison. *"Liberate the Dream!"*

Through the glass front of the museum, they could see the many-limbed monster.

"Oh shit!" Marcus said. He grabbed hold of Ji-ji's arm and led her and Georgie to a spot that afforded them a clearer view of outside. A few feet beyond the glass doors, hundreds of steaders streamed up to the entrance. They'd been in the museum for about thirty minutes and hadn't felt the tidal wave surging toward them.

"They're armed," Marcus said, as he stared out at the crowd beyond the glass doors.

"What they doing coming here?" Georgie asked. "Think they come to wreck the place?"

"Don't know," Marcus replied. "But I do know it's time for us to leave."

They looked around the atrium. Large sections of the museum were cordoned off. Most of the visitors already inside were Black or Brown, but there were also a sizable number of White Districters who, like them, had chosen the wrong day to visit the museum.

A White woman with a lanyard around her neck that held her museum ID hurried over to them. Her glasses had slipped down her nose; she pushed them back into position with fingers that fluttered nervously. "Don't worry," she said. "The staff just learned the steaders obtained last-minute permission to stage a rally outside, but they're *positively prohibited* from coming in."

"Thanks, ma'am." Marcus said, all politeness. After the woman stepped away to reassure the other visitors, Marcus added, bitterly, "An' who'd you think's gonna stop the bastards if they *positively* decide they don't need permission to do whatever the hell they want, lady?"

"We gotta get out," Georgie-Porge said, breathing fast enough to hyperventilate.

A steader armed with a long gun and a bowie knife, joking and laughing, swaggered through the glass doors, held open by a D.C. patroller. Another steader followed, then another.

"So much for not letting the bastards in," Marcus said.

Ji-ji looked over at the woman who'd assured them the steaders weren't permitted to enter. The woman gave her a helpless, frightened shrug.

Soon, the trickle changed to a flood. Bearded steaders strode into the expansive atrium, some masked, some not. On their shirts, they wore the seal of the Father-City of Armistice: a bearded father-man straddled a planting, brandishing a rifle in one upraised hand and an ear of corn in the other. Some carried long guns, others semiautomatic handguns. A few wore *bad kangaroos,* the grenade pouches guards wore in the Territories. Others had simpler weapons—sticks or knives. None were searched, none questioned. Many of the men received warm greetings from the D.C. patrollers at the door. Ji-ji felt sick.

"But . . . but everyone needs a license to carry in D.C.," Georgie muttered, incredulously.

"Yep," Marcus said, scanning the lobby. "Requirements for nonresidents are even stricter. Looks more an' more like this was a coordinated event."

"*Jesus!*" Georgie-Porge whispered. "*Jesus!*"

"Keep it together, Georgie," Marcus ordered. "I got a little something here myself." He patted his side. "If things get dicey, Ji-ji, you head for the nearest exit. Run like the wind an' don't look back. You'll make it. You're the best runner I've ever seen. I'll cover you."

"But they'll kill you if you—"

"No arguing," Marcus said. "Know what these fuckers'd do to you if they find out what's under that cape? For all our sakes, you're the one we gotta protect. If you talk, don't sound too educated. I'd give you the same warning, Georgie, but you sound seedy, so you'll do just fine."

Georgie gave a nervous laugh in response. Ji-ji couldn't believe how cool and collected Marcus was. She couldn't say something funny right now if her life depended on it.

Ji-ji forced herself to do better. "Let's look for another exit," she suggested.

"Sounds like a plan," Marcus agreed.

The three of them hurried through the lobby's atrium, hugging the walls to avoid steaders. They didn't get far. Most of the first floor was cordoned off. Signs that read CONSTRUCTION IN PROGRESS dangled from yellow caution tape. D.C. patrollers were stationed at those areas. Looked like they didn't plan on letting the visitors escape.

Ji-ji happened to look across the lobby. The White museum lady ducked under a caution tape held up for her by a patroller. She looked back once, guiltily, caught Ji-ji's eye, pretended she hadn't, and scurried away. Ji-ji knew the woman would abandon them. In situations like this, the only reasonable option an unarmed female's got is to run. Would she run if Marcus told her to? Probably.

Marcus guided them to a trio of patrollers. All three rested their hands casually on their weapons, as if they couldn't imagine anywhere more comfy to put them. Deferentially, Marcus asked if they could pass. Ji-ji noticed the stark white dome of the restored Capitol building on their navy caps. It had never looked more sinister to her than it did this afternoon.

One of the patrollers addressed the other two: "Now why would I let these three juvis miss all the fun? Can you think of a reason?"

"Nope," one of the other patrollers said. "Can't think of a one."

Marcus didn't push his luck. They retreated back into the lobby.

As more and more steaders entered, other visitors started to panic. Parents with children looked around frantically for a way out.

"How come it's all patrollers an' security?" Georgie asked. "Where are the cops? An' how come there's no Black patrollers or security? Should be some, right? Always a few Black ones."

"Keep it together, man," Marcus said. "We're not completely screwed yet. . . . See the security guard over there by the entrance? The tall blond one with his arms crossed? He's our best bet. None of the steaders've greeted him so far. Let's hope patrollers an' security ain't in cahoots. If they are, an' if things get dicey, we may have to go with plan B an' shoot our way out."

"If we make it out we'll be surrounded by steaders," Ji-ji pointed out.

"True," Marcus said. "But it's a helluva lot better to be outside surrounded than inside surrounded. Trust Uncle Marcus. They got us cornered if we stay in this fish tank."

Marcus instructed Georgie to stay close. Then he grasped Ji-ji's arm more tightly than ever and guided her in the direction of the entrance. His grip was like steel.

They passed by groups of steaders who strolled through the lobby as if they owned it. The men shoved past visitors and shouted to each other in a jovial, aw-shucks manner ripe with menace. A scuffle broke out. The lobby had become too crowded for Ji-ji to see where it was, but the sound of cussing, landed punches, and grunts echoed through the atrium. Ji-ji checked to make sure her mask was in place. If they made her remove her sun hat, she had a wig on. She told herself the chances of anyone recognizing her were slim, then struggled to take her own word for it.

They approached the armed security guard. His blond hair was greasy, his eyes a lot meaner up close than they'd appeared from a distance. Marcus began to plead their case. Asked if they could exit. Said his cousin Maisy here was about to upchuck. *I'm Maisy Here,* Ji-ji thought.

The guard, who was suffering from either a bad cold or severe allergies, called his bluff. Demanded to know if Maisy here was suffering from metaflu. The question was a tough one. Say yes and it might convince the guard to let them leave. But she could also be hauled off to one of the dreaded decontamination centers; say no and they had no excuse to leave, apart from the fact that the museum's most recent visitors were itching to shoot them. With limited options, Marcus played it like he was a bit slower off the mark than most. Repeated that Maisy here was ready to upchuck.

The guard, distracted by a sudden urge to blow his nose and mollified somewhat by Marcus' Uncle Tommyness, seemed ready to let them pass when a second guard ambled up. Wiry thin and shorter than Guard One, he spoke with a northern accent. New York State? New England? In spite of the mask and cap Marcus wore, this second guard recognized him at once.

"You're that fly-boy," Guard Two stated. "The one they call Philosopher Phil."

"Philosopher!" Guard One exclaimed, clearly offended.

Guard Number Two turned to Guard Number One and said, "This fly-boy was one of the seeds won the Freedom Race last year. The wife was glued to the screen. You saved that crop of jills from being eaten by mutants in The Margins, right?" Marcus, bashful as could be, giggled nervously and nodded. "D.C. station covered it. You see it, Vlad?"

Vlad looked at Guard Number Two like he was positively certifiable. "Why would I watch crap like that? Think I give a rat's ass 'bout some Freedom Race?"

"You got a point, Vlad," Number Two said, warming up to his partner's antagonism. "Whole thing was a dud this year. Runners got picked, flyers pathetic—all of 'em."

Vlad shook his congested head, snorted up a load of phlegm, and said, "Last thing this city needs is more Tribals, Mules, an' Commons. Guess he expects to be treated special now. Guess this Philosopher fly-boy thinks he's exceptional."

The steaders, like a wildfire, moved ever closer. Many of them appeared to be drunk or high. Some carried bottles and flasks in their hands. Some yelled across the atrium; one peed against a statue; another ran a stick along the walls, undeterred by the damage he was doing; another posed for a photo while his buddy wrote "Territorial Rule!" on the wall behind him; yet another grabbed yards of yellow caution tape, wrapped it around his body, and waltzed to a tune in his head while patrollers looked on and laughed. Foolishly, a guard tried to prevent a steader from removing a sign. Patrollers swarmed to the rescue, persuaded the guard to desist.

Georgie's height and build caught Number Two's attention next. "Didn't see you last season. You a flyer like your heartthrob buddy here, boy?"

"I'm a reservist," Georgie told him.

"Is that right?" Vlad said, seizing, piranhalike, on this snippet of info.

Ji-ji knew that Georgie had generated a serious inferiority problem among the guards. Where they were flabby, he was muscle. A head taller than either of them, he could take them out easy if the fight was fair, which it wouldn't be.

"Yeah," Vlad admitted, "you got the build for a battler. Must be a lousy flyer if you can't make it into the regulars. Black as coal, ain't you, boy? Could be he's one o' them Serverseeds they didn't snip on account of the labor shortage. Look at those biceps, Yankee Jim! Big as melons." Vlad sneezed, wiped off his snot with the back of his hand, and reached over with the same hand to squeeze Georgie-Porge's biceps. The violation registered as a jolt up and down Ji-ji's back.

The guards ignored her completely. Their battle was with the fly-boys. They were poised at a familiar crossroads. If Georgie told the guard to get his hands off him, they were doomed.

Marcus took control of the situation—played it like Ji-ji would have if she'd had her act together, which she didn't, and if hearing from an uppity female wouldn't have infuriated the guards further, which it would have.

"Sir," Marcus said, addressing Vlad. "Sorry to bring this up again, but when Maisy upchucks it's bad. Real bad. Stink this place out for days if she does it in here. Had some o' them chicken livers from that stall close by. Told her no but this bitch, well, she ain't one to listen."

"Yeah," Vlad said. At last, he removed his hand from Georgie's biceps and turned his eyes on Ji-ji. "Must be tough for bots from the boondocks to adjust to city life."

"You got that right, sir," Marcus agreed.

Now that the pecking order had been confirmed, Guard Jim had a bout of chumminess. While Vlad discharged a sneeze into his biceps-squeezing palm, Yankee Jim wanted to know if fly-boys got free tickets to battles. Said they didn't have flyer battles where he was from and he fancied watching a coop battle in the flesh. "Think you can get tickets for the two of us, boy?"

Marcus nodded enthusiastically. "Sure can, sir."

"Y'hear that, Vlad?" Jim said. "Wanna see a battle in the coop this fall?"

Vlad sucked his mucus back up his nasal passages and played hard to get. "Maybe," he said. "If I ain't busy."

Guard Jim chortled. "Busy with what, Vlad? Self-service?"

And just like that, the mood swung from chumminess to lynching.

Vlad's face reddened; the veins bulged on his temples. Yankee Jim, aware he'd gone too far, bit his lower lip. Guard Two had embarrassed Guard One in an encounter that was supposed to culminate in the fly-boys' humiliation, not Vlad's.

Ji-ji knew what would happen next. Vlad would redirect his anger at Georgie, who sported the largest and blackest biceps by far, which made him the most offensive. Alternatively, Vlad would take it out on the Philosopher cos Marcus was tall, pretty, and perilously light-skinned too. Or if harassing members of the Dreamfleet made Vlad think twice, he might notice the Brown female standing between them and take it out on her as the most viable, least consequential option.

The tableau held for three seconds . . . four . . .

None of them saw the man approach from the side. To defuse the situation in the split second before it exploded, he cried out a hearty greeting and slapped one chunky hand on Marcus' shoulder and the other on Georgie's. "What are you fly-boys doing here? Skipping practice, I bet!"

The guards stood to attention. Vlad sneezed then apologized.

"Commander Corcoran!" Yankee Jim said. "Didn't see you there, sir! Great season last year, sir. Lookin' forward to this one. I've always said—an' Vlad here can vouch for me—you're the best wing commander the fleet's ever seen. Sorry you stepped down, sir. Was a tragedy in my book."

Corcoran addressed the guards: "Why are you boys standing here? Are you deaf? There's a fight breaking out over there. . . . Well?"

The two guards loped off in the direction of the scuffle. Corcoran swore under his breath, then he steered the group down a short corridor that dead-ended in a door. He hurried them into a deserted hallway so they wouldn't be spotted.

After he was sure no one had followed them, Corcoran said, "What the hell do you think you're doing? Place is swarming with steaders!"

"We didn't know nothing about it, Commander Corcoran," Georgie said. "She said this was the museum with the black shit in it." By "she," Georgie meant her, Maisy Here. She didn't look up.

"Only today it looks like it's got some white shit in it," Marcus said.

Ji-ji waited for Corcoran to react. He looked at Marcus and squinted. "You're damn lucky you said that to me. Those guards back there'd shoot your brains out if you spoke to them like that."

"Yep," Marcus said, looking his former commander in the eye. "S'why I never said it to 'em. So what's going on? The steaders come here to trash the place, kill a few seeds?"

"It's that god-awful exhibit," Corcoran replied. "Got co-opted."

"What exhibit?" Georgie asked. "We didn't see no exhibit when we was——"

Corcoran cut him off. "You'll see it soon enough. They've set up the blasted thing so you've got to walk through it to get out. Stay alert. These boys are itching for a fight."

At that moment, Ji-ji looked up. Corcoran's gray eyes widened as he stared at her face. In their haste to get away from the guards, Ji-ji's mask had slipped to her chin. She yanked it up again. Beside himself with fury, Corcoran turned on Marcus and Georgie.

"What's the *hell's* the matter with you? You think she's safe here, of all places?"

Ji-ji froze. Corcoran knew who she was! He must've recognized her from the Freedom Race. Did he know she was meant to be dead? Was that why he was looking at her like that? . . . No, that wasn't it. He knew more . . . much more. . . .

Marcus started to make excuses: "We didn't know anything was going down here."

Corcoran snapped back: "Well now you do. This is the *last* place she should be. *Idiots!*"

Marcus and Georgie-Porge tried to defend themselves. Corcoran waved them quiet. "Shut up and get in line," he ordered. "Don't speak to anyone and keep your heads down." He looked at Ji-ji again and moderated his tone. "I'll follow. Make sure she gets out safely."

Corcoran must have seen how worried she looked. He leaned down and whispered in her ear, "*Alis volat propriis.*" The Latin saying Ji-ji had heard for the first time in Memoria that meant "She flies with her own wings." Ji-ji knew then the rumors were true. Sean Corcoran was indeed a Friend of Freedom. The former wing commander knew who she was, knew *what* she was, and had pledged to ally himself with her and others like her to fight for the cause of Freedom.

There was no time to digest this news before Corcoran shepherded them out of the hallway, down the corridor, and into the throng of visitors being herded through the lobby. He fell back behind them, a dozen or more people between them. Every so often, Ji-ji glanced back to see if he was still there. Once, he nodded in her direction. Some of her terror abated. She suspected others in the crowd were Friends too.

"I think we got Friends here," she whispered to Marcus.

"Should be more," he whispered back. "They got caught flat-footed."

She was tempted to tell him what Corcoran had whispered to her but decided against it. There was no love lost between the two of them. Better to keep a precious thing like that to herself.

Armed security guards funneled the visitors into lines of two or three abreast. Loud groups of steaders shoved past the other visitors in an attempt to provoke a response. Over in another section of the lobby, Ji-ji saw Vlad and Jim drag two visitors (one White, one Black, both bloody) into a side room. Georgie's impressive stature and dark complexion drew stares and comments from the steaders. A couple of them tried to bait him but he ignored them. They got bored and moved on to their next target.

The crowd was packed too tightly for them to see what the exhibit was. But as they shuffled closer to it, Ji-ji noticed that most of the people around them, even the steaders, grew quiet. They'd wound their way through the atrium and entered the new annex that was still under construction. Ahead on either side of them was a walk-through replica laid out in a wagon-wheel design like plantings in the Territories. The replica was so large it took up the entire annex.

Ji-ji came to a dead stop. Marcus urged her to keep moving. His words were echoed by guards nearby: "*Keep moving! Keep moving!*"

Ji-ji forced herself to put one foot in front of the other. The visitors entered through the open gate in the electric fence. Like the one on Planting 437, this one had a lookout tower. The fry-fence reached Ji-ji's waist. A yellow sign warned visitors not to touch the electrified fence. Yes, she knew better than to do that. To make it more realistic, the designers had added the murderous buzzing sound you heard when the fence was live.

Marcus, holding her so tight and so close she could feel his heart beating in his chest, wasn't Philosopher Marcus Aurelius anymore; he was Marcus Shadowbrookseed, a Muleseed from the 437th. George the Forge shrank to Georgie-Porge Snellingseed, a Commonseed whose parents dared to exhibit an "unnatural affiliation" by loving each other without regard to race or prohibitions. She wasn't Ji-ji Silapu, the existential threat whose miraculous back defied logic; she was Jellybean Lottermule, Lotter's Muleseed. "*Keep moving! Keep moving!*"

Alongside White, Black, and Brown Districters, fellow former seeds, lucky Born Freemen and Freewomen, and hundreds of armed steaders, the friends shuffled through the planting. Ji-ji tried not to see the father-houses, factories, and seed cabins, but she couldn't help herself. There was the dining hall where she toiled with her fellow kitchen-seeds, the place where they found the antique pinball machine (*plunger, drain, flipper, little silver ball*). And there was the planting flying coop where males were permitted to fly inside a cage. Two things on the 437th were missing from the replica: the arsenal known as Murder Mouth seemed to be unique to her planting, and a planting school for botanicals. Progressive plantings taught seedlings basic reading, writing, and math. This one, apparently—like the 368th, where Ink and the poor lynched boy in ass's ears were from—didn't bother with luxuries like that. *"Keep moving! Keep moving!"*

The cabins on the seed quarters of the twelve homesteads reached Ji-ji's ankle where her copper seedband would have been if Lucky hadn't saved her in time and she'd been seedmated to Father-Man Brine like Lotter intended. The horse barns reached her buttocks, where Inquisitor Tryton forced himself on her at the Last Supper while Grand Inquisitor Fightgood Worthy looked on before he intervened. The cropmaster's father-house reached her nipples, grabbed too many times by too many hands to count. The large communal structures like the dining hall, the pray center, the penitence penitentiary, and the penal tree reached her neck. *"Keep moving! Keep moving!"*

They made it to the center, the hub of the wheel of fire. Look to the right: Execution Circle, where Uncle Dreg was tree-lynched till Sylvie, the strangest tree in the world, broke her bough and down came the wizard, Cradle and all. That should have been the end of the story, but it was only the beginning. *"Keep moving! Keep moving!"*

Ji-ji didn't want to look at the penal tree in the center of the replica, the tallest thing on the planting. She didn't want to see the noose, which hung down from its sturdiest limb. She tried to block out the tinkling sound made by the metal tags on the tree, each inscribed with the name of a lynched seed. Someone who enjoyed realism must've set up a fan somewhere to make the tears nudge up against each other to produce that sound. Ji-ji couldn't decide whether the designer's attention to detail was impressive or appalling, but she did know the sound wounded her. *Purple earrings,* steaders called them, while seeds like her called them *purple tears.* A sign hung from the tree told visitors this. Ji-ji tried not to stare at the not-to-scale hooded executioner who, in the replica's only fanciful depiction, stood shoulder-to-shoulder with the penal tree. Clever lighting merged the executioner's outsized shadow with the penal tree's so that darkness loomed over the center of the planting. Ji-ji pictured Chaff Man II's curly red hair under the black hood. He was weeping for his beloved Pomeranian, the dog he offered to save by lynching Uncle Dreg. The steaders, missing the irony altogether, cheered when they saw the size of the executioner. *"Keep moving! Keep moving!"*

Finally, after walking through what seemed like the largest planting in the Disunited States, Ji-ji spied the exit. Next to the exit, one more ambush. A large shadow-box display featuring seed symbols sewn onto seedlings' shirts and shifts: a black seed symbol for Tribalseeds, a black-and-white symbol for Muleseeds, and a brown symbol for Commonseeds. All three seed symbols had seedlings falling from the large seed to remind wearers they had a duty to procreate. Next to these garments, a replica of a planting's official Color Wheel with its crude swatches of color that enforced the planting's caste system. Another seedling shift was displayed near the Color Wheel. The broken black seed symbol bereft of tears made Ji-ji want to smash her fist into the shadow box and rip up the ugly shift. *"Keep moving! Keep moving!"*

Ji-ji ferreted out a source of comfort in the here and now. She grabbed it and held on so she wouldn't drown. When Afarra returned from her visit with the mutants, Ji-ji would get her those fried chicken livers she wanted. They'd been in a hurry earlier and nixed Afarra's suggestion that they stop and get some. She wouldn't just get her one bag either. She'd get two—three if Afarra wanted.

They were outside! They'd made it out alive! In the too-bright light of the afternoon, the steaders clustered in groups. The former seeds gave them a wide berth.

A nun made a point of seeking them out. She addressed Georgie-Porge and Ji-ji in particular. Perhaps because Marcus' complexion was lighter than theirs, she assumed they would be more personally affected by the exhibit. "The steaders weren't supposed to be here," the sister said to them, keeping her voice low. She had heavy bags under her eyes; her old-fashioned veil was on crooked. Her eyes darted from Georgie and Ji-ji to the steaders and back again. "This exhibit is meant to be for *you*. A tribute from the SAJ, the Sisters' Alliance for Justice, a way to historicize and acknowledge the suffering so the planting system will be seen for what it is and never be forgotten. The homesteaders came out of nowhere! No one anticipated . . . How could we have known it would attract . . . ? They showed up armed, you see. We couldn't stop them."

Ji-ji felt sorry for her. "It's okay, sister," she said. "It's not your fault."

After the nun had moved off, Marcus said, "Stupid bitch. Who did she imagine would show up to this circus?"

Ji-ji made a halfhearted attempt to defend the nuns before Georgie chimed in to say Districters needed to know what plantings were like so they could take up arms against them.

Marcus scoffed. "Is that what Snelling taught you?"

"Why you keep picking on him?" Georgie said. "He's a good man."

"No such thing as a good steader, G. It's an oxymoron. Not even if he is your pappy an' he's partial to a little brown sugar." Georgie ordered him to shut up. Marcus ignored him.

"Mold's broken," Marcus said. "Don't make good White ones anymore."

"The sisters do good work," Georgie argued. Clearly upset by what he'd experienced in the museum, he sounded like someone about to dissolve into tears. "Snuck antibiotics into the seed clinic that time we had the pneumonia outbreak. Saved my mam's life."

Marcus backed off a little. "You're right. It's not their fault. The good sisters don't know any better. But don't forget, Georgie. There's nothing more dangerous than a well-meaning do-gooder. Look at the mess they've made. Think these steaders'll head back to the Territories without amusing themselves first with a little seed predation?"

"What the hell's seed predation?" Georgie asked.

"Another word for it is *granivory*," Marcus told him. "It explains a lot of things. Thing to remember is this, G. Seeds will always pay for others' charitable works. Always."

Ji-ji looked over at the exit to see if Corcoran had come through yet. She wanted to speak to him, but he must've remained inside.

In raucous groups, steaders fanned out onto the Mall, looking for something to goad, hoping to start a war.

"We should get out of here," Ji-ji said. "Where are the others? We said we'd meet up here."

"Hey? Is that Tree?" Georgie pointed to a group heading toward them. The unmistakable figure of Laughing Tree jogged side by side with Tiro. Ji-ji stood on tiptoe hoping to see Afarra, but the crowd was too dense. The two groups converged.

"What's going on?" Tiro said, looking around uneasily and leaning in so no one would hear him. "Where'd all these beards come from?"

Ji-ji looked around too, panic rising in her again. "Where's Afarra?"

"Snarlcat scared the crap outta her," Tiro said. "She's not with you then?"

Behind them, Ji-ji heard men laughing. Men from the Territories. Men on the lookout for seeds. Seed predation, Marcus said. Ji-ji knew exactly what that meant.

"You *lost* her!" Ji-ji said. "But this city's swarming with . . . You *lost* her! We gotta find her!"

"Don't worry, Ji-ji," Ink said. "I got my binoculars—see?" He held them up as proof.

"She was headed in this direction," Tiro said.

Marcus grabbed Tiro's arm roughly, pulled him in closer. "You seen what's come to the Dream for some fun today? You think a Serverseed's safe? What the fuck, T?"

"It was Lonesome," Tiro protested. "The cat. Name's Lonesome. Went crazy. No warning."

"It's true," Tree said. "That's how Tiro got scratched up on his arm. Snatched her away in the nick of time. Could've been mauled otherwise."

"She'll show up, Ji," Tiro said. "How far could she have gotten? Bet she's by that chicken liver stall. Bet we'll find her right there. I gave her a few bucks. Bet she's there."

Ji-ji couldn't speak, couldn't look at him.

She took off through the crowd and left the fly-boys in the dust.

|||||||||||||||

It took some time for them to catch up with her. When they got Ji-ji to calm down for a moment, they moved off to a quieter part of the Mall to regroup. For her, the worst of it was that Tiro was high. He swore he wasn't when Ji-ji accused him, but he had the same glassy look her mam used to have after she'd downed a couple of Lotter's pills. She knew for a fact he was lying.

"Last time I saw her she was heading in this direction," Tiro said. He sounded defensive and defiant at the same time.

"She wouldn't just run off like that," Ji-ji argued.

"Woulda caught up to her, easy," Tiro continued, "only I got tripped up by some stupid dog. Fell in the goddam furrow. S'why I'm covered in muck."

"Ink and me didn't see the whole thing," Tree said, "but the snarlcat went crazy. Could be Afarra thought he'd break out of his cage. Could be why she took off."

Ji-ji snapped at him: "For god's sake, Tree! This is Afarra we're talking about! If she thought the cat was trying to escape, she'd help it, not run off!"

Her logic was sound. They looked over at Tiro. The sight of so many steaders on the Mall seemed to be hitting home at last. He told Ji-ji not to worry, swore it couldn't be more than forty minutes since she ran off. Definitely less than an hour. . . . Marcus cussed him out.

Tree broke in: "Arguing won't help. We need to focus on finding her," he said.

The fly-boys split into two groups: Marcus, Georgie-Porge, and Ji-ji formed one search party, and Laughing Tree, Ink, and Tiro formed another. The same groups as before, only one was missing. Ji-ji was grateful. If she had to look at Tiro again, she'd say something she'd regret for the rest of her life. The enormity of their task was daunting. The sun was going down. The Mall would soon be filled with the city's poor, desperate to claim their sleeping plots. Some steaders lingered, though most headed away from the area after their trek through the museum.

Ji-ji knew they didn't have long. Zyla and Germaine had told her how, each night, law enforcement played a game of cat and mouse with the Mall dwellers who lacked temporary resting-place permits, TRPs. The trick was to establish your night-shelter as fast as possible and make it look as if it had always been there. Germaine had warned Ji-ji how dangerous this area was after dark. She knew what she was talking about. Before she became the first Latin female flyer-battler in the Dreamfleet, and before she'd been inducted into the Friends of Freedom, Germaine had been homeless for several months in D.C. In her mid-thirties like Zyla, Germaine Judd was worldly-wise. Afarra, on the other hand, knew almost nothing about the city. How would she protect herself?

With every minute that passed, more refugees, many with small children, arrived. For would-be Mall dwellers, a vast flock meant safety in numbers. Vendors abandoned their stalls and booths. Some of these structures were permanent and greatly prized. Anxious parents shoved toddlers under them while older children scavenged for scraps among the garbage left behind from the day's trade. The process was chaotic and often violent, Germaine said. It wasn't unusual for fatal altercations to erupt at dusk as the homeless staked their claim to a grave-sized spot to call their own for the night.

Ji-ji suggested they head to the Lincoln Memorial. From there, they could see the entire Mall. She'd seen the iconic photos from the memorial in Zyla's history books. She knew that the mass of people would make spotting Afarra impossible, but that was all they had left to try.

Maneuvering up the steps to the memorial was tricky. People were packed in like sardines on steps that served as sleeping ledges. Ji-ji had to dodge hands and feet, blankets, and the occasional camping stove. Once, to her dismay, she almost stepped on a swaddled infant!

Ji-ji, Marcus, and Georgie reached the top of the steps, turned, and looked east, across the shallow Reflecting Pool. The flimsy chicken-wire fence around it was trampled in multiple places. Garbage floated in the pool. Without consciously thinking about it, Ji-ji saw what the National Mall must have looked like when the Dreamer gave his speech. Back then, the Washington Monument hadn't been relocated to Founding Fathers Hill. In the photos she'd seen, it used to be straight ahead, its reflection in the pool one of the most enduring images of the city. In 1963 by the old calendar, a quarter million marchers had gathered at this site. "Free at last!" Ji-ji whispered. Georgie-Porge heard her. "Free at last!" he repeated. A smattering of nearby Mall dwellers overheard them and joined in. It wasn't so much a declaration as it was a promise. "Free at last!" they said, softly.

Ji-ji grabbed the fly-boys and pulled them in closer. "*Quick! Get behind me! I'm unfurling!*"

In an instant, the two men were behind her. Ji-ji closed her eyes and focused. If she were to reveal her secret now, on the steps of Lincoln's memorial, with steaders roaming around the city, she'd never find Afarra. She was bound tight. Her Purple Tears would have to rip through the bindings and her clothes to unfurl. But the force at work in her back convinced her they could do anything they wanted. The Dreamer's voice had been a clarion call in her head. She needed to disempower herself. She pictured Lotter holding up the Color

Wheel to little Bonbon's lovely face while he lay in the amazing cradle Uncle Dreg had crafted—the priceless gift she'd smashed to pieces after Bonbon was taken. She pictured Lua on her seedbirth bed, staring up at the cabin's ceiling, her deadborn nearby in a bloody cardboard boot box. She pictured her mam at the fry-fence, felled by Petrus' bullet, being rocked in Lotter's arms. Gradually, her wings became dormant again.

She exhaled and began to relax the muscles in her back. "They've quieted down," she said.

"You sure?" Marcus asked her. He looked as shaken as she felt.

"Yeah, I'm sure."

Breathlessly, they hurried inside the chamber. It was just as packed inside as it was outside—teeming with refugees who'd gathered at the feet of one of the few bearded father-men they trusted.

Ji-ji was taken aback by the size of the statue. Lincoln was seated on what looked to her like a colossal throne. You had to crane your neck to see him. She wished they'd sat him on a simple rocking chair and carved a less adamantine expression into his face. She wanted to see the expression Father Abe must've had when he contemplated the horrors of war. The expression on the statue was relentlessly stoic. Yet maybe that was the point? Here was a man who would not be moved. The D.C. Congress planned to move him anyway, of course. In Phase 3 of the city's Grand Restoration Plan, Lincoln's temple would join Washington's obelisk on Founding Fathers Hill, farther away from the flood zone and those who needed him most.

You could tell by the green mold on the temple pillars how far the floodwaters had come during the last deluge. But none of that bothered Ji-ji. In spite of the statue's lack of softness, a peace descended on her when she entered the memorial chamber. Zyla had told her Lincoln would be twenty-eight feet tall were he to stand. His face was so chiseled and angular, she wasn't sure if he was flesh-made-rock or rock-made-flesh. Maybe the sculptor was right to make him look like that. How could you endure the country's first Civil War unless you'd learned to turn yourself to stone?

And then Ji-ji saw it—the mural on the chamber's south wall. A half-naked woman, hands raised to the sky, surrounded by Freed slaves. But it was her golden, outspread wings that made Ji-ji gasp. She rushed toward the mural, leaping over people as she went. Someone had painted *her*!

Ji-ji soon saw she was mistaken. It wasn't her at all, not even close. Unfurled, her own wings were larger than those of the female in the painting, nor did the wings look anything like hers. They were what you would expect them to be—the romanticized wings of birds, lush with golden feathers, while hers were . . . she had no idea what hers were, but they looked nothing like these did. Only an angel who could defy gravity would be able to stand with wings as heavy as those.

According to the plaque, the female represented the Angel of Truth. She was very pale with what looked, in the failing light, like orange hair. The slaves on either side of her were half naked too. Ji-ji wondered if the angel had partially disrobed herself to make them feel at home. The slaves looked more like her than the angel did. They gazed out from the mural with weary expressions. All of them had one thing in common: inside the drafty temple, they looked very cold.

Georgie-Porge joined her. "Jesus!" he murmured. "She's *naked*! An' she's got *wings*!"

Ji-ji wasn't sure which of these characteristics fascinated Georgie more, though by the way he gazed at the painting, she suspected it was the first one. With Georgie-Porge standing next to her, she didn't feel comfortable looking at the mural anymore.

"She's not here," Ji-ji said.

Marcus called them over. "We should head back," he said.

As they walked back down the steps, Ji-ji tried not to imagine how petrified Afarra must be. The sun was setting behind the memorial. Candles, oil lamps, and cooking fires were turning the Mall into a pulsing river of light. If you didn't take into account the suffering of the thousands of homeless who'd made the long pilgrimage to the City of Dreams only to discover the dream was as elusive as ever, the vista was beautiful.

A woman on the steps played a beat-up old guitar. Shoeless, in a tattered shift, she told you she'd been searching for you high and low, and now, at last, she'd found you. The woman's voice circled over the stone man in the Lincoln Memorial before it laid itself down so deep in God's Furrow it almost buried itself alive.

> *Lost too many, loved too much*
> *Sailin cross the water*
>
> *I got to worry, got to sweat the night away*
> *Dream's about to kill me, s'always the way*
>
> *Found me an angel took me to bed*
> *Messed up my mornin, mussed up my head*
>
> *Lord, the Dreamer's long-time gone*
> *Lord, the Dreamer's long-time gone*

Lord, the Dreamer's long-time gone
Come back for me in the mornin

Angel Mama, take my hand
Cradle me to mournin

By the end of the song, as they headed over to where the van was parked, Ji-ji knew Afarra wouldn't be in the Aerie waiting for her. She wouldn't be in the Jim Crow's Nest in the abandoned practice coop either. Ji-ji knew Afarra was lost. All she could do was what thousands of people like her did every day. Tonight, that one simple thing seemed like the most courageous act in the world:

Keep moving. . . . Keep moving. . . . Keep moving.

12 EXPECTATIONS GREAT AND SMALL

As dawn approached, after another nearly sleepless night, Ji-ji entered Afarra's room. She stood and looked at the mural. Wearily, she sat down in front of it. She stared at the figure of Afarra as if she could will her lost friend off the wall and back into her life if she wished for it hard enough.

It had been five days and still no sign of her. Ji-ji didn't cry—didn't have any tears left. What upset her most was the same thing that had tormented her when her little brother Bonbon was Serverseeded by Lotter—the idea that she was powerless. Given her limited faith in the living, Ji-ji appealed to the dead.

Don't let her be scared, Uncle Dreg. If you can journey from there to here, please comfort her. . . . Mam, you did terrible things to her, but you said you regretted it. Make up for it by protecting her now. Lua-Dim, Afarra is like you—loving, generous. Please give her some armor if Dimmers have any to spare. Charra—no one, not even Uncle Dreg, made me feel as good about myself as you did. It will be hard for Afarra after she's known happiness in the Dream. You were a warrior. Help her, please!

A knock on the door. Zyla Clobershay's voice on the other side. Ji-ji's teacher and mentor from Planting 437's legacy school had moved into the Aerie after Afarra went missing but had opted not to sleep in Afarra's room, sleeping instead on the lumpy sofa in the living room. Zyla must have guessed that Ji-ji would want to spend time in Afarra's room. One of the many things Ji-ji loved about Zyla was that you didn't have to explain things to her. Like Charra, Zyla just *knew.*

"Mind if I join you?" Zyla said.

Though Ji-ji didn't turn around, the company was welcome. "Yeah, that's fine."

Zyla entered quietly and sat down next to Ji-ji in front of the mural. Ji-ji leaned her head on her former teacher's shoulder. The perfume Zyla wore, a floral one, sent to her every Christmas by a friend in Colorado, reminded Ji-ji—like everything else did—of Afarra. It took her back to one evening last summer.

Afarra had leapt up from the table during a dinner Zyla had cooked for them, rushed over to her, and flung her arms around her neck. Afarra, who often smelled things first to check they were safe, had pushed aside Zyla's long blond hair, inhaled her perfume, and said, "I am liking the flower smell. It is very prettyful. Like you, Zyla Clobershay." Touched by the unexpected compliment, Zyla had said, "Not nearly as prettyful as you, Afarra." And just like that, *prettyful* became one of their favorite words. Afarra's embrace of Zyla had been even more surprising, coming as it did after yet another day of fierce wrangling with her over the necessity of removing Uncle Dreg's necklace when she bathed.

Not long afterward, as a result of her improved nutrition and shocking growth spurts, Afarra's periods began. They'd begun several times in the past only to peter out. She confided in Ji-ji and Zyla that her "blood was dribbled out all morning." She had to fix it fast cos all her girlcloths and Ji-ji's too (which, apparently, she'd borrowed) and one of her birthday napkins from Tree and Ink (which she'd stuffed up there to "plug it down") were a mess. Ji-ji didn't have to explain to Zyla why this disclosure was a far greater compliment than the prettyful one had been. In the Homestead Territories, where outcasts who'd reached puberty were in great jeopardy, Ji-ji had repeatedly reminded Afarra only to tell those she trusted most in the world when her bleeding began.

"Germaine's coming over," Zyla said. "She wanted to be here for your first lesson with your new coach. . . . Tiro, Marcus, Tree, and Ink went out to search for Afarra again before dawn this morning. That's every day this week before practice. Ben's with them again, of course. We've got people on the lookout all across the Territories too."

Ji-ji tried to look hopeful, but with every day that went by the chances of finding Afarra diminished. Serverseed outcasts didn't officially exist in the Homestead Territories, which meant no records would be kept of her whereabouts.

"Germaine's got some news," Zyla said, happily.

"She does!" Ji-ji jerked her head off Zyla's shoulder and looked at her.

"Oh I'm sorry, honey. It's not about Afarra."

Ji-ji looked down and muttered, "What then?"

"Well . . . she wanted to tell you herself, but I don't think she'd mind if I told you. . . . She's pregnant. Ben and Germaine are expecting."

Ji-ji tried to gin up some enthusiasm "That's great," she said.

"They lost the other two, you see, so they're—"

Ji-ji interrupted her, desperate not to speak about lost things: "You told me 'bout that already." She stood up and announced she was hungry.

Zyla scrambled quickly to her feet, her body supple from the physical demands of the numerous missions she'd been on for the Friends of Freedom. "I'm hungry too. How about pancakes?" She seemed thrilled to have something she could do for Ji-ji at last.

"Yeah," Ji-ji said. She didn't add, "Afarra's favorite," but she knew they were thinking it.

"Don't eat too many," Zyla warned. "Your new coach has a strenuous work-out planned."

Ji-ji had never told Zyla or anyone else how she'd pinned her hopes on the notion that her new coach would be Billy Brineseed. She knew how unlikely it was he'd been rescued from the Rad Region, yet she couldn't shake the feeling it would be him. He would be disappointed in her weakened state when he saw her. But eating food involved digesting it—not easy to accomplish these days, while sleeping involved waking, a torment. Ji-ji would wake up and reach out for Afarra, expecting her to have crept into her bed as usual, that crazy neck-lace looped around her neck, her braids all messy. She'd reach her hand behind her and be forced to acknowledge that joy had disappeared. Afarra, Finder of Joy, was the name Ji-ji had given the main character in one of the stories she made up to distract them both when the old building in the flood zone creaked and moaned at night.

According to one of Ji-ji's tales, after Joy receded from the world, Afarra, Finder of Joy, went on a quest to locate the source. Joy was a she-river, Ji-ji said, who got diverted when a group of dastardly demons built a goddam dam. So Afarra, Finder of Joy, had to wage war with the dastardly demons and de-stroy the goddam dam so Joy could flood the land again. She needed reinforce-ments, so the she-river called on all the animals, including mutants definitely, and including Muckmock and Drol, and the black stallion in Memoria, and the stripers Man Cryday whispered to, and the snarlcat in the Liberty Train box-car, and the one on the Mall on not-the-Fourth of July. Together, they defeated the dastardly demons and dismantled the goddam dam. When Ji-ji got to the end, Afarra would laugh with her mouth wide open, the two missing teeth Silapu knocked out clearly visible, as happier-ever-after as anyone living in the Dream.

Ji-ji failed at breakfast. She took two bites before it struck her how absurdly ambitious she'd been. Zyla was equally un-hungry, so they gave the pancakes to Large Bodyguard-at-Large, who was devastated about Afarra's disappearance. He sat at the bottom of the flight of stairs leading to the Aerie and dolefully devoured their breakfast.

Neither Zyla nor Ji-ji was in the mood for conversation. With an hour to go before her lesson and forty minutes before Germaine was set to arrive, they retreated to the kitchen to listen to the old radio Ben had purchased at a flea market and repaired for them.

Ji-ji usually enjoyed the songs selected by Rosyrose Glyerson, the host of D.C.'s early morning show, while Zyla liked the dash of gossipy politics Rosyrose threw in, especially the parts when she skewered Mayor Adolphus Yardley, referring to him as Dolphus the Doofus. Afarra loved Rosyrose's name, which the irreverent radio host, a former Commonseed, had given herself, on account of the fact that, as she put it, she rose early and had a rosy disposition. "It is like my own name," Afarra would say. "You are calling me Afarra, Elly, cos I come from afar." Most of the songs Rosyrose played used to be popular during the Age of Plenty. A St. Lucian transplant, Rosyrose liked to play songs from the islands. Singing and dancing without permission on plantings was forbidden, and neither Ji-ji nor Afarra had known what to make of the music at first. It hadn't taken them long to fall in love with it, however. But this morning, when Rosyrose played a sweet island melody by a soulful singer named Marley, about a woman he urged not to cry, all Ji-ji could think about were the words her mam used to say: "round and round seeds go, lashed to the Wheel of Misfortune." The singer's notes of consolation ripped Ji-ji apart.

"Turn it off!" Ji-ji cried, slamming her hands over her ears. "Turn it *off*!"

Zyla flung herself toward the radio like someone trying to save a life. She turned the radio off, then rushed over to Ji-ji, gathered her up in her arms, and rocked her like Charra used to.

"Afarra's never coming home, is she, Zyla?"

"I honestly don't know, hon. But it's been a while, and we've got no leads yet. Man Cryday and her followers are combing The Margins. Friends are on the lookout from the Madlands to the Unaligned Territories. Friends in the Liberty Independents are searching too. The Friends won't give up till they've exhausted every lead. And I'll *never* give up."

Ji-ji wouldn't give up either. "I'm ready for my lesson," she said.

Zyla clasped Ji-ji's face in her hands, tilted her head, and kissed her on the forehead. "Yes, sweet thing," she said, "I believe you are."

||||||||||||||||

An hour later, on the coach's bench in the center ring of the abandoned coop, Ji-ji sat between Zyla and Germaine, grateful for the company of the two women. Roughly two decades her senior, the two Friends of Freedom never treated her with condescension.

Germaine had a look about her Ji-ji had never seen before—a kind of tentative bliss, if such a thing existed. Yet she seemed wound up. She twirled the ends of her signature black braid and tapped her foot nervously. Germaine Judd was the fittest female Ji-ji had ever known. She could bench-press weights most men would struggle to lift. Her biceps were hard as rocks, her shoulders and thighs powerful, her stomach taut from the rigorous routines she put herself through each morning. Easy to imagine her pioneering her way to prominence in the coop as the first Latin female flyer-battler in Dreamfleet history. If she'd stayed in the fleet, Zyla said, Germaine could have become famous. As it was, Germaine liked to boast that she was a footnote in Dreamfleet annals, and footnotes were her favorite place to be. Someone who felt uneasy in crowds, Germaine avoided the spotlight. Another reason why Ji-ji felt close to her. Ever since Germaine and Ben escorted her from Dimmers Wood to the Monticello Protectorate, Ji-ji had felt comfortable around her. Like Zyla, very little intimidated her. But Germaine and Ben had bonded with Tiro—Ben had especially—which explained why Ji-ji felt much more awkward around Germaine these days.

"Sorry, Germ," Zyla said. "I know you wanted to tell her."

"It's fine, Zy," Germaine said. "An' don't call me Germ. . . . Good news is in short supply. I'm glad she told you, Ji-ji. . . . Let's hope this one's a keeper."

Zyla reached across Ji-ji to lay her hand on Germaine's not-yet-showing belly, said, "I've got a good feeling about this one." Ji-ji had never been close to a pregnant woman who had the same rights to her child as a steader male did. She wished Afarra could share in this moment.

"Can't get used to you with that boycut, Zy," Germaine said. "Which is weird cos *I* cut it."

With her hair cut short, Zyla looked like a different person. A couple of days ago, irritated by how long it took for her hair to dry, Zyla had asked Germaine to lop it all off. Said she didn't care if it made her ears stick out like jug handles. Said she'd always thought her ears were her most dramatic feature, and now everyone could enjoy them. Ji-ji was glad Zyla hadn't cut her hair a few years earlier. No way she would have been employed at the Planting legacy school if she'd shown up for the interview with hair as subversive as that. The father-men didn't permit fairskin women to wear their hair "boyish" or "mannish." Not that there were many fairskin women on plantings, apart from one or two teachers and the diviner. Understandably, most Wives-Proper opted not to watch their husbands "grow the Territories one seed at a time."

"Don't forget, Germaine. It's Zyla if it's a girl and Zylar if it's a boy. You told Ben yet?"

"No I did not," Germaine replied. "Ben's a good man but he's got his limits."

It was no secret that Zyla had objected fiercely to Germaine's marriage to Ben. Zyla and Germaine used to be a couple years ago, and though Zyla and Ben were friends now, it seemed to Ji-ji that Ben could never quite forgive Zyla for what she'd said about him when she'd first met him, and Zyla could never quite forgive Germaine for ignoring her sound advice and marrying a male.

Germaine placed her hand on Ji-ji's knee. "You okay?"

"I'd be doing a lot better if you two told me who my new fly-coach is."

"Uh-uh, can't do that," Germaine said. "If you don't know who he is, you can't parrot."

"She's right. If we told you, we'd have to kill you," Zyla joked, "to be on the safe side."

Germaine tried to explain: "Secrecy was one of the terms of the agreement—for security reasons. No one except the two of us, Man Cryday—an' the co-leaders of the Friends, of course—could know his identity ahead of time. 'Sides, for all we know, he won't be able to get away."

Ji-ji hadn't imagined this possibility. "You mean he may not even show today?"

"He'll be here," Zyla said. "He said he would, and he's a man who keeps his word."

"I've guessed who it is," Ji-ji blurted out.

The two women looked at each other. "Who?" they both asked at once.

Ji-ji had gone too far to pull back now. Besides, he'd be here any minute. "Coach B," she said. They looked bewildered. "You remember, Zyla. Billy Brineseed." She almost added "Tiro's coach," then thought better of it. She hadn't uttered Tiro's name since Afarra's disappearance.

"Of course!" Zyla said. "The arborist. The fly-coach. Uncle Dreg's buddy." Zyla addressed Germaine: "Poor man had to hang those revolting metal tags on Sylvie's branches."

"It isn't him then," Ji-ji said, deflated.

"No," the women replied in unison. "It's someone even better," Zyla added. "You'll see."

With difficulty, Ji-ji swallowed her disappointment. Billy would have understood. On that last day in Brine's flying coop, he'd volunteered to look out for Afarra till Ji-ji submitted a kith-n-kin petition. Having lost Uncle Dreg, his best friend, Billy would know what her disappearance meant.

Out of the blue, Germaine started speaking. Her speech sounded rehearsed: "Ben says he's a hundred percent certain Tiro's no drug-sop. T swears he's never had a sunset before in his life. The crook who sold it to him saw him coming. T says the man swore it was a steroidal androgen. The docs in the fleet get kickbacks from pharma for touting those. Tiro had no idea—"

Zyla interrupted her: "What the hell are you doing? Did Benny-Ben ask you to say that?"

Germaine hesitated. "Okay . . . he did ask me to speak to you, Ji-ji. Ben an' Tiro are real close. I said I'd put in a good word. T's devastated. Goes round beating himself up. Literally pounds his own skull like he can knock some clue loose to help us find her."

Zyla gave Germaine a look that said, *Don't go there right now.* Germaine went there anyway.

"So we wondered if you could talk with Tiro. Let him apologize. He feels terrible."

"No," Ji-ji said, emphatically. "I can't. . . . Not yet."

"It's okay," Zyla said. "Tiro has a lot to sort through. Most young men do at his age."

On the rickety bench in the center ring of the abandoned practice coop, Ji-ji leaned forward to rest her forearms on her thighs. Though it was early morning, it was already humid in the coop. Encouraged by how good stretching felt, she leaned down all the way till her palms lay flat on the floor. She let her shawl slide from her shoulders. She didn't need to worry about her companions freaking out over the weird hollows, mounds, and ridges on her back. Zyla and Germaine had made a new set of bras for her they'd dubbed *liberator bras* (*libbies* for short) with a halter neck and wide back and side straps to allow her wings to move unimpeded without leaving her exposed. Earlier that morning, one of the bodyguards the Friends of Freedom had assigned had laid down fresh sawdust in honor of the new fly-coach. The sawdust felt good under Ji-ji's palms. Was this what sand felt like on the beach? She and Afarra had often talked about going to a beach one day. . . .

Ji-ji stopped stretching, sat up again, and pulled her shawl around her shoulders. She had a renewed determination to fly for a reason she hadn't revealed to anyone except Na-na, who'd scurried into Afarra's bedroom looking for his friend the night she disappeared. That first awful night, Ji-ji had slept in Afarra's room, or rather she'd lain there wide awake. The iguana, who wasn't ugly after all, she decided, just different looking, was on a quest for his favorite human. "After I learn to fly," she'd told him, "I'll embark on my first mission." The iguana had cocked his head as if he understood every word. "I'll search for Afarra till I find her. Swoop down, snatch her up, an' fly off with her. The two of us will soar to the moon. See?" Ji-ji had pointed to the mural. Pretty much impossible to make out the details in the dim light, but Ji-ji figured the iguana saw better than she did. "Think it looks like us, Na-na?" Na-na had scurried off to formulate his critique. Or scurried off to rail against the weeping, inconsiderate girl who never fed him.

Ji-ji looked at her windup wristwatch. 7:25.

"Germaine," Zyla said, "been meaning to ask. How come Man didn't ask *you* to coach her? So what if they kicked you out of the fleet. You're still the best female flyer they've ever had. Re-Router's great too, but she has to play second fiddle to that peacock."

Germaine agreed: "Everyone plays second fiddle to X. But he flies the Dream like an angel. You hear the rumors?"

"Which ones?" Zyla said. "X's affairs with every rookie fly-boy he can lay his hands on?"

"No, that's old news. The Friends think he may be in league with the secessionists."

"What are you talking about?" Zyla said. "He's an egotistical, lascivious sonuvabitch, but X's mother was a Commonseed and his father an African Indigenous. He'd never betray——"

"That's what *I* thought," Germaine insisted. "But one thing you can say 'bout X-Clamation is he *always* has an angle. These riots are the excuse Yardley an' his flunkies've been waiting for. They'll shop for allies in unexpected places."

The steader invasion of the city had resulted in numerous brawls and assaults. No one knew how many of the city's poor had been injured or killed, but there were reports in the *Independent* of bodies being loaded onto unmarked trucks in the dead of night.

Distressed by the conversation, Ji-ji popped her knuckles. "Has the trouble died down yet?"

Zyla took hold of her hands to quiet them. "The copies we distributed of her birthday photo should help us find her. . . . She looked so prettyful with her mouth all covered in chocolate."

Ji-ji wished Zyla hadn't said that. *Prettyful* suddenly sounded a lot like *pitiful.*

Not the type to leave questions unanswered, Zyla circled back to her earlier topic. "I still don't get it. Why didn't Man Cryday ask *you* to be her fly-coach?"

Germaine's smile faded. She looked ill.

"You okay?" Zyla asked, full of concern. "You need the bathroom?"

"No," Germaine replied. She flipped her long black braid behind her and looked at Ji-ji.

"Actually, I've been meaning to tell you. . . . Thing is . . . Man Cryday *did* ask me to coach you, Ji-ji. I declined. Sorry. Figured I should confess now cos it occurred to me Cryday could've told your new coach. Wanted you to hear it from the horse's mouth. . . . I hope you can forgive me."

At a loss for words, Ji-ji mumbled something incoherent.

"When I heard who else Man Cryday was thinking could coach you, I knew he'd be a way better choice than me. . . . So it all worked out in the end." The three of them sat in fraught silence for a while before Germaine spoke again: "I promise you, Ji-ji, if I could've said yes, I would have. Please don't be hurt. Have I hurt your feelings?"

After the past five days, Ji-ji was so wrung out she didn't have any part of her body left to hurt. But she was curious. "Why did you say no?" she asked.

"Man Cryday told you about another Wingchild. Someone I knew, right?"

Ji-ji recalled what Man Cryday had told her. Her time in Memoria had been so crazy she hadn't thought about it much till now. "Yeah . . . when she told me about the other Wingchildren—about Charra an' Silas, Lua's deadborn. An' I told her I thought Lotter suspected Bonbon could be a Wingchild too. Man Cryday said you knew a Wingchild who died."

"Yes, he died many years ago," Germaine said, clearly agitated. "But it's still hard for me to talk about it. . . ." Germaine, who rarely lost control of her emotions, was on the verge of tears.

Zyla got up and hurried round the bench to hold her tight. "I'm sorry," Zyla said. "I didn't mean to upset you. I should've kept my big mouth shut."

"No, it's not your fault," Germaine said. "I miss him sometimes, that's all. He was like a brother to me. But his back was nothing like yours, Ji-ji. One day, when the time's right, when I feel stronger, I'll tell you about him. I promise."

They heard the noise at the same moment. "Is that him?" Ji-ji asked. Before she'd finished the sentence, Zyla and Germaine had stood up and drawn their weapons.

"Don't shoot my balls off, ladies!" a man called out. "I'm a totally innocent homo sapien!"

Zyla laughed. "You're lucky we didn't blow your head off, creeping up on us like that."

The women holstered their weapons.

The man must have entered through one of the doors farthest from where they sat. Ji-ji peered into the shadows. A figure in a hooded sweatshirt stood just outside the beams of light that entered the coop through the skylights. His hood was pulled up so she couldn't see his face.

Zyla ran toward him. He did the same. Much larger than she was, he lifted her off her feet and twirled her around. Ji-ji had never seen Zyla react that way to a man before.

"Who is he?" she asked.

"I'll let him introduce himself," Germaine told her. "He's taking a substantial risk coming here. But trust me, Ji-ji, he's the best coach for you. Wasn't easy to persuade him to do it, but our little Zyla could charm the skin off a snake if she set her mind to it."

Zyla led the man back to the others. As he emerged from the shadows, his wrinkled pants and a black contagion mask became visible. He removed his mask and pushed back his hood to reveal graying hair and a dark complexion. Why did his face look familiar? Where had she seen it before? The man surveyed the coop and looked at her with something she had difficulty identifying. Then she understood what it was. Disdain.

The man held out his hand to Germaine, said, "Been a long time. Looking good, Germaine."

"You too," Germaine said. "Let me introduce you to—"

Ji-ji jumped up too fast and tripped over her own feet. Germaine reached out to steady her.

"Her coordination needs work, obviously," the man said.

"It's *you!*" Ji-ji exclaimed. She heard herself and wished she'd come up with something much smarter. She'd seen his face on the Dream Coop's high-tech billboards and on the screen recordings Tiro had shared with her. Her shock amused him. He smiled and bowed his head in greeting.

"Coopmaster Amadeus Nelson, at your service."

His accent was hard to place. Eastern SuperState? The Cradle? The Caribbean? Yes. The Caribbean . . . maybe? Ji-ji got the feeling that he'd worked hard to make his accent untraceable.

"Fans call me I'm-a-God, the Dream Master. You, I presume, are the Existential."

From the way Dream Master I'm-a-God looked at her, Ji-ji knew one thing for certain: he was not impressed. His next words proved her point. "Let's get this over with. I'm a busy man."

|||||||||||||

Zyla and Germaine had planned to stay, but Amadeus Nelson insisted the women leave. Zyla began to argue with him. Still smarting from the coopmaster's disdain, and determined not to seem intimidated, Ji-ji insisted she would be fine. But now, as her friends headed for the exit arm in arm, she wished Zyla had revealed her coach's identity earlier so she could have found out more about him. His casual reference to her as "the Existential" worried her. More worrying than that were comments Marcus had made, which echoed in her head: "The one person we should all be wary of is our noble coopmaster." Did Marcus know something about him the women didn't?

"Zy looks like a boy," the coopmaster said.

"I like it," Ji-ji asserted.

"Makes her ears stick out like a pair of wings." He looked at Ji-ji as if he wanted to see if she got the joke. She didn't laugh. "So, Existential," he said, "I guess we should begin."

"That's not my name. I'm Ji-ji . . . Jellybean . . . Ji-ji . . ." She was going to say she preferred to be called Ji-ji Silapu, but she didn't want to call herself by her chosen name in front of a man she didn't trust. She stuttered out a correction: "It's just Jellybean."

"Just Jellybean. A good, solid name." He sat down on the bench. Amadeus was darker than she was—on the Coal or Midnight arc of the Color Wheel like Bonbon and Afarra. Sometimes he looked strikingly handsome in an arrogant way; at other times, she couldn't say how he looked. Odd as it sounded, it was as though he withheld that info from her. He kept his eyes glued to hers, which made her acutely aware of her own body's shortcomings. Standing before the most famous Black man in D.C., Ji-ji decided to go on the offensive.

"Are you from the Caribbean?" she asked.

He looked surprised by her question, but he went ahead and answered it. "While massacres are in vogue, it's foolhardy to disclose one's origin story."

Was he implying he himself was Toteppi, or was he warning her he knew she was?

It crossed her mind that Tiro would be amazed to see her speaking with his idol. Then she remembered she wasn't speaking to Tiro. What did it matter what he thought?

"So . . . are you going to show me these Extraordinaries on your back?"

"Now, you mean?"

"Of course now. Isn't that why I've been summoned to this condemned coop, which stinks of mold and rat droppings? To see the miracle Wingchild?"

His sarcasm offended her. *Time to sow a little respect,* she thought. She let the shawl she'd wrapped around herself slip from her shoulders. She didn't turn her back to him; she wanted to witness his reaction. She began to reveal herself . . . slowly.

Her Extraordinaries, as he called them, emerged over her shoulders as two nondescript sproutings, no longer than her arms. He assumed she was done.

At that moment, she elongated them the way she'd taught herself to do, unsheathing them till two giant, rolled-up scrolls brushed the ground and twin-towered over her head. Dream Master I'm-a-God wasn't sighing impatiently anymore.

As if opening a rolled-up parchment, Ji-ji unscrolled her wings, inch by inch, till they spanned out on either side of her like glistening panes of water-glass. While I'm-a-God's mouth was slack with astonishment, she made the tiny wing flaps move in waves, as if a relentless breeze were skimming over wet grassland, or invisible fingers were plucking the strings of a harp.

The Dream Master rose from the coach's bench and found his voice.

"They weren't exaggerating," he whispered. He sank back onto the bench and buried his face in his hands. In the blink of an eye, he'd recovered so quickly she wondered if she'd only imagined he'd been overcome.

"Turn around," he ordered. His tone told her not to argue.

Her wingspan was so substantial that she had to take several steps backward to account for its size before she turned. At first, having her back to him didn't bother her, but her uneasiness grew as goose bumps popped up on her flesh. She'd had enough.

She pivoted to face him. Her left wing smacked him in the face. Before she could apologize, he'd grabbed hold of it.

"It's almost as though it isn't there," he murmured. "No obvious network of veins, no clear musculature. Do they feel heavy?" Ji-ji snatched her wing from his hand. "If I'm to teach you," he said, "I need to know what I'm working with."

"Maybe I'll teach myself."

"And how has that gone so far, Just Jellybean?"

She couldn't decide what to make of him. One thing she did know, however, was that they needed to be on a more equal footing.

"If you want to touch them again, you gotta ask my permission."

He hesitated for a moment, then said, "May I touch them again?"

"No." She could tell from his raised eyebrows that she'd surprised him again. Good.

The coopmaster looked to be in his late forties or early fifties—Lotter's age. Ji-ji had rarely spoken to a middle-aged Black man before. Though men of a similar age worked on the planting, male and female seeds were routinely kept apart unless they had permission to procreate, to form a longer-term mating unit, or to work together. Nelson's unapologetic maleness (if that was the correct way to describe it) disarmed her. To counter it, she came up with a bold idea. She voiced it.

"I need to interview you. See if you're suitable."

Amadeus Nelson scrutinized her. "If I submit to an interview, I want something up front."

"What?" she asked, warily.

"To feel your wings again. I won't hurt you. You have my word."

She stepped toward him gingerly and turned around so he could see her back.

Very gently, as if he were scared they would break, he ran his fingers over her wing roots and the strange hollows and ridges on her back. His touch disoriented her initially. Soon, however, it reminded her of the way Doc Riff and Man Cryday touched her when they were making a diagnosis.

"These segments," he said, "they feel . . . strange."

"We call 'em wing flaps," she told him.

"They move independently and synchronously, yes?"

"Yeah."

"And they pivot too?"

She hadn't thought to use that word to describe them. "Yeah . . . I guess."

"And the wings mirror each other."

"What do you mean?"

"When I touch you on these flaps on the right wing, the left wing responds in the same place in exactly the same way, as though I'm running my fingers over that one too. Didn't you know?"

"No."

"Could this be a recent phenomenon?" She had no idea. She shrugged. "You are still learning how to live inside these impossibilities, yes?" he said.

For the first time, he'd said something to make her think Man Cryday might have been right to choose him.

"Do you feel this? When I run my hand across the wing like this?"

"Yeah." She felt it all right.

"Does it feel the same as it would if I were to run my hand across your arm?"

"No. . . . When you touch my wings, there's, like, a gap between the touch and when I feel it."

"A delay?"

"It's not about time. It's about . . . I don't know . . . location maybe. Like my wings are up there in the nest while I'm down here. I feel the touch, but the feeling comes from a different place."

"Go on," he urged.

She tried again: "It's like they're mine and not mine at the same time. There's times they suck up the rest of my body an' they're the only thing I am. Then there's times I don't even know they're back there. Please stop touching them now."

He removed his hands immediately. "Thank you," he said.

She hadn't expected him to thank her. She turned around to face him, careful not to smack him upside the head this time.

"Well? I don't have all day. The interview you requested."

"Oh yeah," she said. Crap. She should have thought this through more carefully.

"How about we sit down?" he suggested. "I interview better when seated, don't you?"

She didn't admit her experience was limited to practice interviews with Coach Billy and Tiro for the Freedom Race's oral exam, and the exam interview itself with the race monitor in Monticello.

He sat down at one end of the bench. Ji-ji furled her wings to sit at the other.

"Do they always rustle and whir when you furl them?"

She hadn't consciously thought about it before. "I think so."

"How fast can you furl and unfurl?"

She shrugged. "Haven't timed it in a while. But it's damn fast. Getting faster too."

"Interesting. Perhaps they can be strengthened like regular muscles. Or at least the muscles around them can be. . . . Well? No time to waste. What's your first question?"

She paused, then said, "Why did you agree to come here? Do you owe Man Cryday a favor?"

"Of course. Who doesn't? I owe Zyla Clobershay a few favors too. Though I didn't agree to come here to repay any debts. I agreed because I was intrigued."

"You didn't believe I was real."

"On the contrary, I believed *you* were real. Though I admit I didn't believe your wings were. Thought you were like some of the blighted tribe I used to hear stories about as a seedling."

She thought it wise not to mention the bird tribe in the Toteppi's First Story. Not till she knew him better anyway. So all she said was "What tribe?"

"The original word for them has been lost. People say it was too sad to utter. The closest thing to it, in another language of course, is the Swahili *malaika aliyeanguka,* which means—"

"—fallen angel," Ji-ji said, remembering the term Man Cryday used to describe Charra. In her excitement (yes, she was getting more and more excited about working with him) she'd forgotten to censor herself.

"You've heard of them. They say that, centuries ago, they used to live Free in the mountains, which could explain how the Flying African story got started way back when."

"Here, you mean?"

"Here and other places. Islands in the Caribbean, in South America. Wherever the kidnapped were taken. But according to some versions, the tribe had deformities on their backs, not wings, as well as other shocking abnormalities that made small-minded people persecute them."

"How come you think you can teach me?"

"Don't know if I can. I'm a fly-coach, stage manager, choreographer, fight instructor, storyteller, and, with the help of my engineers, a magician. This exercise with you would be very different. I need to do more research into initial takeoff velocity, kinetic energy, the relationship between the force exerted by your legs and the force exerted by your wings during takeoff. . . ."

Her curiosity piqued still further, Ji-ji asked, "What's kinetic energy?"

"Something a body needs if it wants to accelerate from rest. You have to make it yourself. It's inside you. In your legs, I hope. The scant research I've done indicates that the first few wingbeats are critical for takeoff, but the legs may play an even greater role. I'm no scientist, no engineer either. Which means—if you'll excuse the pun—we'll be flying blind."

In the face of the coopmaster's honesty, Ji-ji's wavering defenses deserted her.

"I don't know if I can do this. I'm a real fast runner. But apart from that, and cooking and drawing, I'm very ordinary. My coordination is lousy too. Guess that's obvious."

"I see. Well, as we appear to be locked inside a confessional, let me also make a confession."

The Dream Master spoke to her with a directness he hadn't used before: "The fact is, it's more than likely we'll both fail. To be honest, spectacular though those things are on your back, they don't look very functional. Should you decide to hire me, we'll need to discover together whether or not, for the first time in recorded history, unassisted human flight is possible."

Ji-ji's heart sank. "There's been a mistake. A misunderstanding. Man Cryday should've told you. I don't have enough lucre to hire you. I don't have any to speak of. Not even seedchips."

His smile wasn't patronizing this time. "I was speaking figuratively. My services are Free."

"Oh. . . . Okay. . . . Then I should probably let you know I hate heights."

He raised an eyebrow. "That does make things more complicated."

"An' I'm nearsighted in one eye. . . ." She didn't want to add anything, but he'd been honest with her, so she said, "An' I'm scared shitless."

The Dream Master took a deep breath in and let it out slowly. "People say I'm the greatest maestro ever to conduct the coop. When I became the first Serverseed coopmaster, I imagined it would be the greatest challenge I would ever face. I was mistaken. If I ace this grueling interview, *you* will be my greatest challenge. But perhaps, working together, we'll make it work, yes?"

Ji-ji's heart was beating fast. The more he spoke, the more she wanted him to coach her.

"Man Cryday says you may have flown already."

"It was instinct. I was falling. From up there." Ji-ji pointed up to the Jim Crow Nest. "I'm inches off the ground, apparently, when my wings start to whir, an' I hover like a hummingbird, Mackie says. Mary Jonah Macdonald. She was my coach but she gave up. I don't remember much about the hummingbird part. Coach Mack and Afarra, my friend, they both saw it. My wings broke my fall. Sort of. Then it healed like it was never broken. Doc called it a miracle."

"Curious. You don't have the type of wing morphology that will allow you to hover like—"

"I know! I don't have primary, secondary, or tertiary feathers—or vanes, hamuli, rectrices, or rachises. Don't even have hollow bones. Should be way too heavy to fly even if I could get my ass off the ground. My wings change shape spontaneously. Man Cryday says it's a needful thing."

He laughed. "I see I'm not the only person who's been conducting a little research."

"Zyla's been helping me. She was my teacher on the planting. Now she's my friend."

"Yes. Zyla Clobershay's path and mine have crossed in the past. . . ." He looked down at his broad hands and studied them like a palm reader. "Had your wings been similar to a bird's wings, flight would not be feasible. Their scale and accompanying weight would have made it impossible for you to stand, let alone fly. It's as if someone came up with a design lightweight enough to make flight achievable in humans."

"You think the steaders engineered me then?"

He shook his head. "I don't believe they're smart enough. Not sure anyone is. Climate change, the Sequel, pandemics threw this world into chaos. Scientific discovery stalled. Nothing like the choice steaders made to implement the Necessary Reversal in the Territories. Simple necessity. Yet even in the Age of Plenty no one could've pulled off something as sophisticated as this."

Amadeus Nelson's voice changed. He wasn't lecturing to her anymore; he was in a dialogue with himself. "Those wonders on your back are . . . *inexplicable*. Man Cryday shared a few theories—genetic engineering being the obvious one, or the manifestation of a people's Freedom-thirst. . . . But that last theory tramples the rational, the logical, and the reasonable." He seemed to remember she was listening. He looked over at her. "I'm as attached to that particular trinity as Uncle Dreg was to his." She wasn't sure if the Dream Master was referring to Tiro, Afarra, and her, the Trinity Uncle Dreg used to speak of, so she kept quiet. "The rational makes flights of fancy difficult. In the end, the question of what caused you to become this way is a mystery. For now, we'll have to be content to focus on one task only."

"To teach me to fly."

"No. Artists of the body, like artists of the mind, craft their own dreams. The myth that others can make them come true has caused great suffering in this world. A coach's task is to help the artist become as strong as their potential allows and escape the most pernicious enemy of all."

The grand inquisitor's sharp features leapt into Ji-ji's mind. "Which enemy?" she asked.

"Fear, of course."

She decided to lay it on the line. At this point, what did she have to lose? "I gotta learn to fly. I need to find Afarra, my friend. She's a former outcast too.

She's more special than anyone. I need to find my little brother Bonbon next. He was sent to a server camp maybe. If it kills me I gotta learn to fly. If I don't, I can't save anyone."

"Zyla told me about your friend. I'm sorry. . . . Losing people is hard."

"Afarra's not lost. She's just not found yet."

"Yes, that's an important distinction. So, am I hired, figuratively speaking?"

Ji-ji smiled this time. "Yes, you are."

He stood up. "Amadeus Nelson reporting for duty. Now, let's get started. First, show me exactly what you can do with those Unknowables. Next, we decide on a training schedule. You're as puny as a weed, Just Jellybean. Time to craft some muscle."

13 THE RIGHT TO ROAM

By seven in the morning, the few leads the flyers had about Afarra's whereabouts had dried up. "Time to head back," Marcus said, in that preachy voice Tiro hated. "We're late for practice again an' Redipp'll hit the roof." They were entering week two of the search with nothing to show for it. Marcus, who'd been all about finding Afarra in the beginning, had none of the fervor he'd had a week ago. Said the chances of finding her now were "infinitesimally small," like all he wanted to do was show off his fancy vocabulary.

Laughing Tree looked over at Tiro, who was standing next to Marcus. The group had assembled not far from the Lincoln Memorial end of the Mall. "It's okay, Tiro," the big man said. "Ink and me got our warm-up this morning roaming all over the place. We can skip the warm-up and search for another thirty minutes. Right, Ink?"

"Sure," Ink said. "Another thirty. No problemo."

Tiro was grateful. Tree and Ink rarely disagreed, and though there was a quarter-century gap in their ages, and Ink wasn't a flyer anymore, Tree always treated him as an equal. Marcus claimed they were conjoined twins separated by a generation. Ink told anyone who would listen he knew the risk he was taking when he tried to dislodge Tree from the donut ring in the Jefferson Coop. "What do I need legs for," Ink liked to say, "if I can persuade a tree to cart me around?"

Arriving at the search area at the crack of dawn, they'd witnessed the Mall waking up to another day of cat and mouse. In the humid summer heat, Mall dwellers abandoned the stalls they'd slept under, on top of, and in between, before the vendors, cops, and D.C. patrollers arrived. The shelters of those who didn't have temporary resting-place permits were speedily disassembled. A few kids, unafraid of what was lurking in the Reflecting Pool's foul water, stomped over trampled sections in the chicken-wire fence that surrounded it and splash-battled each other.

Marcus repeated his warning about tardiness. Said he'd rather be dead than subject himself to Red Droopy's lecture. When Redipp overheard one of the veteran flyers refer to him by that name, he'd kicked him out of the rotation for the first game of the season. Marcus said it proved that Redipp's wife's complaints were true: droopiness was one of Drayborn Redipp's salient characteristics, whatever *salient* meant.

After nearly two weeks, Tiro still felt like he'd been hit by a truck. Hard to believe Afarra had run off like that. What the hell was she thinking? He half expected her to turn up at the Aerie all smiles and Seeing Eyes, braids a mess. That's what he had to imagine her doing cos if he imagined her doing anything else it plunged a knife so deep into his chest it poked out the other side.

Tiro addressed his fly partner. "If you're scared of a little lecture, Marcus, head on back to Droopy. Trink an' me'll follow."

"We got one van," Marcus pointed out. "An' I'm the only one can drive worth a damn."

Tiro addressed Trink: "Think we can walk back to the Revival?"

Laughing Tree shook his head. "Sorry, Tiro," he said. "Take too long. How about we split the difference? Search for another twenty then head back? How about it, Marcus?"

Marcus looked peeved. "Not much we can accomplish in twenty minutes." He sighed in frustration, shrugged, then nodded in agreement.

"Great," Tiro said. "I'll sprint down to the crook sold me those fake steroids. See if he saw something. I'll meet you back at the van. Be there in ten. Fifteen, tops."

"Fine," Marcus said, in a way that told you it wasn't. "I'll go with you."

"No, man, I got this. Be faster solo."

As he took off, Tiro heard Marcus call after him. Warned him if he didn't get his ass back to the van within twenty minutes he was walking. Tiro glanced back over his shoulder. The three of them were heading off in the direction of the van, parked on a nearby side street. Tree jogged along next to Marcus fresh as a daisy, like he could carry the kid another ten or twenty miles if he wanted. Tiro couldn't figure out how Tree did it. Ink was a lightweight for a fourteen-year-old, but the weight of the boy and the basket was considerable, even for a giant. No surprise that the seven-footer was rumored to have injured eight picker pirates before they managed to truss him up in Martinique (or was it St. Lucia? Jamaica?) and smuggle him onto a cargo plane bound for the Territories. If the picker pirates hadn't been desperate to get their hands on the seed price an undamaged Tree could command at the auctionmart, they would never have taken him alive and un-maimed. Could be they decided on the spur of the moment to pick him. Risky to act in violation of the treaty prohibiting labor exports from the islands. Must've seen the size of him and couldn't resist. Tiro couldn't figure out if it was Tree's worldliness that let him take things in stride or his personality. But it was his relationship with Ink that impressed Tiro most.

Every morning since Afarra's disappearance, Laughing Tree had placed Ink in the homemade carry basket, hoisted the contraption onto his back, fastened the wide straps across his massive chest, and set off with the others before dawn. Tiro had carried Ink a few times. Never wanted to do it again. Corcoran had asked the coop engineers to fashion a sling-type, ergonomic carrier he thought would be a lot easier on the big man's back. Enter Red Droopy, who put an end to projects he called "indulgent and frivolous." Redipp ordered Tree not to carry Ink around anymore, said he could injure himself. Threatened to pull him from the lineup if he disobeyed. Everyone and their mother knew Red Droopy didn't give a shit about Tree getting injured. Enjoyed tormenting him is all. Like he had a thing against dark-skinned flyers, which explained why he gave poor Georgie-Porge hell and treated Orlie with kid gloves. Tree told Tiro he didn't give a damn if he was fired. A friend is a friend, he said. You stick by them through thick and thin. So far, he'd gotten away with it too. Red Droopy seemed more than a little intimidated by Laughing Tree. Tiro didn't like to admit it to himself, but there were times when he was jealous of the friendship between Tree and Ink. He and Marcus were close—sort of. But their friendship had a bunch of caveats. The friendship between Tree and Ink was unconditional. Ink told Tree everything (often, all at once), and Tree told his friend what little news he had to share. Tiro got the impression from Marcus, rightly or wrongly, he was putting up with his fly partner till he found a better option.

This morning, they were one man short. Up till now, Georgie-Porge had accompanied them on these searches, but he and Orlie had been singled out for torture by the new wing commander and ordered to clean the toilets and locker rooms after Orlie's performance in the coop had been even more sub-par than usual. It was all but certain Orlie would drag Georgie-Porge down with him and they'd both be booted out of the reservists. Soon as Tiro had a moment to gather his thoughts, he planned to put in a good word for them with Coopmaster Nelson. Georgie had spoken to Nelson himself, but it hadn't panned out so far. But that was only cos the coopmaster was likely thrown by Corker's firing. Probably deciding which battles to go to the mat for and which to steer clear of. However powerful you were, you couldn't fight every battle all at once. Had to pick and choose. Something the Friends of Freedom would need to do too, looked like.

Tiro was hoping the Friends would side with the Dreamer Coalition in the D.C. Congress. Marcus said the politicians in the Coalition weren't exactly "stalwart advocates for Freedom." But if you waited around for human nature to turn hero, you'd be waiting till doomsday. If these rumors about militarizing the fleet were true, they had to oust Redipp and force the fleet to reappoint Corcoran. The Friends had scheduled a meeting. Maybe they'd have proof by then that Redipp was in league with Armistice? Tiro was satisfied he already knew the answer. The fleet had to get rid of Redipp fast, and Friends and flyers needed to band together with the Coalition to make it happen.

Tiro passed a girl with messed-up braids. He knew it wasn't Afarra, yet his heart skipped a beat anyway. He'd been so deep in thought he'd slackened his pace. He revved it up again, dodging dwellers, vendors, dogs, cats, and a platoon of rats circling a garbage pyramid. He was on the lookout for a gray handlebar moustache. He knew how unlikely it was Lippy Verdi had seen Afarra, but it was the only door left to try. In his pocket, he had a copy of the photo Zyla took on Afarra's official birthday. The Friends had cropped Ji out of course. Thank god he didn't have to rely on a verbal description. There was no one worse than him at describing what someone looked like.

Last night, Germaine had advised Tiro to wait a while longer before he tried to contact Ji again. Said she herself was in the doghouse over something, though she wouldn't say what. What bothered Tiro most was that Ji assumed he'd lied to cover up his own part in Afarra's disappearance. Sure, the sunset he'd taken had been a real mistake. Been too high to know how bad things were. But no way it was his fault Afarra bolted. Since her disappearance—apart from the prescription steroids, anxiety meds, and the odd painkiller the sports docs doled out—he'd had nothing but a few drinks. Hadn't been obliged to reveal his PS affliction to get the anxiety meds either. Simply told the docs he was worried about his family back on the planting, which was true. The docs had loaded him up with pills that made plummet syndrome a thing of the past. As long as he continued to straighten up and fly right, this season's salary would cover the cost of the remaining kith-n-kin petitions. Soon, his mother and little brothers would be living high on the hog in an apartment he'd already put his name down for. Only missing piece of the puzzle—Afarra.

As Tiro ran, he decided to lob up a quick prayer, just in case. Problem was, he didn't pray worth a damn. He'd stopped believing in anything, for the most part, after Amadee's tractor lynching, apart from Uncle Dreg's prophecies, and that was off and on. But he prayed now as he sprinted down the Mall. Promised God he'd never look at another black-market drug in his life if Afarra turned up unharmed. He had a bright future, that's what Nelson said. Best flyer he'd seen. Those were the coopmaster's words. When he'd said them, Amadeus Nelson sounded so much like Amadee it sucked the breath right out of him. I'm-a-God believed in him, which meant he had a duty to believe in himself. Not that he intended to become a long-hauler. A few seasons would be all he'd need to rack up a small fortune. Then he'd coast along on his celebrity for the rest of his life. Do good with it too. Support his family. Help the Friends and their allies reunite this fucked-up country. Fly too long and you paid for it in the end. Most veteran flyer-battlers were a mess: knees shot, hips shot too, broken noses, lost teeth, scars from head to toe. More than a few suffered from tremors and dementia, though some of this was likely on account of drug-sopping not battling. Most of the older flyers were specialists like Mudmudoom Quadroon, Georgie's buddy, whose martial arts expertise made him lethal on the battle platforms. In a team situation when you needed to send in a skilled flyer-battler to take down a few opponents on the welkin platform, Mudmudoom was the one you wanted. The flying didn't do you in but the battling did. After a few concussions, a few falls, a few hits with battling staffs or slashes with coop swords, your body went to hell. The few female flyers usually got out pretty quick cos most females weren't near as dumb as most males.

If Ji could fly someday, maybe he'd sneak her into the Dream Coop and watch her fly from one piece of equipment to the next. He wished Germaine would tell him more about the progress she was making. Like trying to get blood out of a stone. Wouldn't even tell him the name of her new coach. Hadn't even told Ben, Ben said, putting it down to prenatal crabbiness. If Ji didn't manage to fly, Tiro hoped she was okay with being grounded like a regular human. She could tuck her wings away and no one would ever suspect she had all that crazy shit on her back. Be less of a threat to the steaders if they didn't see her as the fulfillment of some stupid prophecy in their stupid *One True Text*. She could live Free in the city they'd daydreamed about since they were seedlings. . . . When his family arrived he'd breathe easy at last. *Please, God, help me find her. I promise I'll stay clean.*

Distracted by his prayer, Tiro ran right past Lippy's stall and had to sprint back. It was Lippy all right. The unmistakable gray handlebar moustache on the White dealer who called himself Requiem, on account of some corny insider joke Tiro still didn't get.

"Hey, Lippy," Tiro called out. "Lippy Verdi . . . Requiem . . . remember me?"

The same Black man who'd been hanging around Lippy last time huddled with him again this morning. Tiro figured the shorter man must work for Lippy in some capacity, not clear what. Lippy handed the man SuperStates and gave him instructions about something.

Lippy greeted Tiro with his in-desperate-need-of-a-dentist smile. "Well," he said, ecstatically, "if it isn't Pterodactyl's twin come to pay me another visit!"

Tiro came to a halt a couple of feet away from Lippy and his associate. He felt compelled to correct him. "Flyer's not my twin," he said.

"Oh yeah," Lippy said. "He's your cousin, right?"

Tiro couldn't remember if he'd said the Pterodactyl was his cousin or his brother, so he settled for ignoring Lippy's question. None of his goddam business.

"Need to ask you something," Tiro said.

The Black man stood there staring at Tiro. Lippy shoved him aside, said, "Get lost, Fish. I got important business to transact with this gentleman here." The way he said it made Tiro uneasy, but there was no time to spare second-guessing himself.

As Fish retreated, Tiro drew the photo out of his pocket and showed it to Lippy. "You seen this girl?" he asked, still breathless from his sprint. (He'd have to go easy on the bourbon and steroids if he wanted to be in good shape in the fall.) Lippy's face fell as he realized this wasn't the transaction he was expecting.

"My friend," Lippy said, "don't waste this unique opportunity. As luck would have it, my man Fish just delivered a new consignment. A very special one. More refined."

"Not interested," Tiro said. "You seen her?" He pointed to the photo again.

"Sorry, kid," Lippy said, coldly. "I don't make a note of every Mauler I see."

"You sure? She had these nice braids in her hair, an' she was wearing a jacket. A fan jacket in fleet colors. Black an' gold. About this tall." Tiro indicated a place at chest level with the flat of his hand. "Could be anywhere from fourteen to seventeen. Not sure." Not a good note to end his description on. Made it sound like he hardly knew her.

"Sorry, boy," Lippy said, not bothering to hide the fact that he didn't give a crap. "They all look alike to me. Know what I mean?" Yeah. Tiro knew exactly what he meant. "Well, if that's all," Lippy said, "I'll let you go. If you ever need a nice pick-me-upper, or a downer, if that's your thing, or a few flukes, y'know where I am. Tell your relative I got special discounts for fly-boys."

Tiro looked at Lippy Verdi, looked down, shuffled his feet, stared at Lippy's gray handlebar moustache. A bribe could loosen Lippy's tongue, but it was just as likely to encourage the dealer to lie, send them off on a wild-goose chase. Tiro's hand slipped into the pocket of his shorts.

The change on Lippy's face was immediate. Tiro knew that Lippy knew he was about to hook another live one. It was like someone had slotted a dime in the dealer's maw to start his spiel.

"You won't believe the quality of this latest batch. Comes in powder too. You a smooth-ash man? Bet you are. Got to have a good tolerance for ash. Ash is for discerning connoisseurs like yourself. Sunset pills is good—don't get me wrong, but powdered suns is a totally new experience. Draws out the high real slow, like the longest, sweetest pussy you ever had. Yessirree. Ash draws the high out slow as molasses. No herky-jerky ups an' downs. Smooth sailing all the way."

Tiro felt the notes in his pocket. He'd slipped them into his shorts for emergencies and to treat Ji and Afarra to something special. Lippy had a firm hand on his shoulder. Tiro glanced at it. Mottled, pale, with coarse gray hairs sprouting from the knuckles. He let the hand steer him behind the stall's dirty canvas flaps. The two were hidden now. Safe.

"Try a small sample," Lippy said. "See for yourself why this batch is a good investment. Nothing like those run-o'-the-mill suns I sold you before, boy. In a class of its own. Here . . . a taster. Gonna light you up good, as my man Fish likes to say. Light you up good an' proper. Requiem's guarantee." Requiem sprinkled a few grains onto Tiro's extended index finger. The finger puzzled Tiro cos he hadn't willingly held it out. He allowed his arm to raise his finger to his mouth, and allowed the tip of his finger to touch his tongue and rub itself along the gum line. *Sweet!*

"See, boy," Requiem boasted. "What did I tell you?"

When Tiro had walked behind the curtain, in his left pocket he'd had his residency papers, in the right he'd had one hundred and fifty SuperStates, along with Afarra's photo. When he exited, his papers were still in his left pocket; in his right, Afarra's photo and a mere twenty-five dollars in SuperStates nudged up against his investment: a packet of fine white powder in a small plastic bag a fraction the size of one of the eye beads on Uncle Dreg's necklace.

Tiro had left the stall behind and was speeding through the mass of humanity on the Mall when he felt a tap on the shoulder. He turned. Requiem's fish man. What did he want?

"I hear you're lookin' for someone," Fish stated.

"Not anymore," Tiro said. "Got what I need."

Tiro began to move off. The man grabbed hold of his elbow.

"The female," the man said. "The one with braids an' a fleet jacket. Heard you say you were looking for her." The man's speaking voice was more educated than Tiro had assumed it would be from his appearance. If he was a former seed as the harvester tattoo on his arm suggested, he likely came from one of the progressive plantings where seeds received an education.

Tiro knew when he was being taken for a sucker. "Get lost," he said.

The man smiled. One of his front teeth was missing; the fanglike one next to it was chipped in half on the diagonal. He wore a shirt that was probably white originally (though it was hard to say for sure) and a pair of baggy, threadbare pants, hitched up with a rope. He had a deep scar over his right eye, and his left ear bloomed like a cauliflower where someone had smashed it with something. . . . A fist? A club? Fish had a poor man's edginess and a greedy man's intensity. Tiro suddenly understood where the man got his name from. He stank of rotting fish. Tiro felt a surge of pity for him. God knows what kind of abuse he had to put up with working for Lippy Verdi. But time

was running out. He needed to get back to the van. He made his excuses and
started to leave.

Fish was nothing if not persistent: "I *seen* you. In the Dream Coop. You're
not his brother like you said last time. You were being modest. You're him.
Been watching out for you ever since you stepped through Insurmountable's
gates. I was a seed myself. In the 800s. I'm your biggest fan."

"Great. Thanks. Gotta go. Got friends waiting."

"I saw her. A female in a fan jacket. With braids."

Tiro wasn't about to fall for the oldest trick in the book. Fish had overheard
his conversation with Lippy and was hoping to extort money for phony info.
Tiro turned to leave. The man grabbed on to his elbow again, more stubbornly
this time, and lowered his voice.

"Wasn't the jacket I remember," he said. "Was the beads she wore. Fuckin
freaky! Eyes painted on 'em peeking out. Staring at me like the devil himself.
She some kinda witch?"

|||||||||||||||

Tiro raced up to the van as Marcus was pulling away. He pounded on it and
screamed: "*Wait! Hold up! I got something!*"

To a torrent of rebukes from Marcus about cutting it fine, Tiro climbed into
the fleet's loaner van and began to recount what he'd learned. After he heard
the details, Marcus was skeptical.

"You sure you didn't mention Uncle Dreg's necklace when you spoke to
Verdi? And are you sure this guy didn't see you earlier with Afarra? Could be
that's how he knew about the necklace."

"I'm sure."

"Absolutely certain?"

"Christ, Marcus! How many times I gotta tell you. He *saw* her being
dragged off."

Laughing Tree was doubtful too. "You have to pay him for that information?"
he asked.

"Cos if you did," Ink added, "it ain't worth crap."

"That's the thing," Tiro said. "He didn't want anything 'cept a free ticket
to the battle against Armistice in the fall. Which was lucky cos I didn't have
much left to give him."

"Thought you had a whole bunch of SuperStates on you," Marcus said.

"Yeah. Must've left 'em back at the dorm."

"Guess it's a good sign if he didn't demand payment for the info," Laughing
Tree said.

Ink looked thoughtful. They all knew the boy had a serious crush on Afarra. Looked to Tiro like Ink was trying to decide whether believing she'd been taken was easier than not knowing what had happened to her. Ink asked Tiro to repeat what the man had told him. Tiro did so.

"The man," Tiro said, "goes by Fish—Can Fish. He told me he'd seen—"

"Canned Fish!" Ink exclaimed. "What kinda name is that?"

Marcus shook his head. "No weirder than a Tree who laughs."

Tiro's frustration was boiling over: "Not *Canned*," He spelled it out: "*Can.* C-A-N."

"Is Can short for something?" Ink asked.

"How should I know? Shut the fuck up, all of you, an' listen!" The conversation with Fish had sobered him up fast. "This guy Can Fish says he saw Afarra with a male and a female. Said she looked scared. Said the man, a fairskin, was leading her off, away from the Mall. West toward the Potomac. Means they could've taken her across to Greater D.C. The female was Black. She was laughing, Fish said. Thought something was real funny. Looked dirt poor. The fairskin didn't look much better, he said. Had a beard."

Ink gasped: "A steader!"

"Steaders aren't the only men with beards," Marcus reminded him. "An' steaders don't usually hang out with Black females who laugh a lot. They like their females quiet."

"You've got a point there, Marcus," Tree agreed. "But there were hundreds of steaders on the Mall that day. Can't say for sure he wasn't one of them."

Ink wedged another question into the conversation: "When did Can Fish see her necklace?"

"When they dragged her off. It poked out of her jacket an' he recognized it."

Tiro hadn't said Fish recognized the necklace before. There was a pause as the three of them digested this additional information.

Marcus was the first to speak: "So you're telling us this Fish character knew it was Uncle Dreg's necklace?"

"No!" Tiro replied, frustrated by how difficult it was to get them to understand the significance of his discovery. "Told me he'd seen a necklace like that on the planting where he grew up. Said it belonged to a Toteppi woman. Said she's dead now. Said the necklace killed her."

Ink gasped again. "It was a *murdering* necklace?"

"Yeah, Ink," Marcus said. "Some necklaces are homicidal. Tree never teach you that?"

"I bet what Fish meant," Tiro continued, "was that the necklace proved to the steaders she was a Tribal witch. S'why she was killed. Fish said Afarra better be careful strutting around in a necklace like that case it rubs people the wrong way. Said if I found her, I should tell her that."

Ink took offense. "Afarra ain't the strutting kind. I never seen her come close to strutting. Not once. The damn Fishfool say anything else?"

"Nope. That was it."

"It's not much to go on, T," Marcus pointed out.

"It's a lot better than nothing," Tiro said. "We know for certain she was snatched. Didn't just run off."

Tiro let the news console him. At least it meant he hadn't been the one to cause her disappearance. Who could have foreseen that some White male and Black female would be scouring the Mall looking for ex-Serverseeds to snatch? Chances were good they took her cos of the necklace. If so, maybe they ripped it off and let her go? Only if that was the case, why hadn't she shown up later at the Aerie? She was out there somewhere, with people who most likely wanted lucre. He would find her if it killed him. Redeem himself in Ji's eyes and his own.

"We need to get this info to Ben an' Germaine," Tiro said. "They'll relay it to the Friends. We can go over it with 'em when we meet in a few days if we haven't found her yet."

"It's after seven thirty," Marcus said. "We gotta get going."

He was pulling out when a sharp rap on the van's back doors took them all by surprise.

"What the hell?" Marcus said.

Out of nowhere, two D.C. patrollers and three cops surrounded the van. All the men except one were White. The windows on the van were already down. The Black cop came around by the van's driver's-side window and peered in at the passengers.

"Is there a problem, Officer?" Marcus asked.

"Where you off to?" the Black cop asked. He looked to be in his late fifties. Bags under his eyes big enough to store groceries.

Tiro began to sweat. His hand rubbed up against the small wad of powder. *Fuck! Oh fuck!* From the look of fury Marcus gave him, his fly partner had guessed why he was freaking out.

The White cop strolled up and stood next to the Black one. The White cop couldn't be more than nineteen, if that. Around Tiro's age, a year or two younger than Marcus. In a voice closer to yelling than speaking, he demanded to know what they were doing roaming around this area.

"We're fly-boys," Tiro said. "We got a right to roam." *Jesus!* Why'd he add that part?

"Is that right?" the kiddie cop said. "You got a right to roam. Since when?"

"You got papers?" the Black cop asked.

The White kid-cop drew his gun before the older Black cop had finished the word "papers." He pointed it at Marcus. "Don't move," Kid-Cop said. "None of you move a muscle, understand?"

The few people who'd still been gawping on the street a moment ago scuttled off.

The barrel of the gun was long, thick, and shiny black. The young cop's hand was steady as a rock. That fact alone told them he was no virgin when it came to murdering.

One of the patrollers sidled up. "Take it easy, Butterball," he said. "No call for that yet. I'm sure these boys'll cooperate. Right, boys? I'm sure they've all got their residency papers handy." The passengers nodded. "Good. Butterball here is spooked. Thinks you look suspicious. So . . . fly-boys, you say? Don't see flyers running around in a beat-up old van. Fly-boys I know ride Cadillacs."

"Or one o' those motherfuckin Mercedes," a gruff voice said. One of the other patrollers? Tiro couldn't tell from where he was seated, and he wasn't about to turn around.

"This van's a piece o' crap," Gruff continued. "What is it anyway? An old Chevy, you think? Bumper's all tore up, one taillight smashed, dents everywhere. The Dreamfleet'd do a better salvage job than this. Hear tell they got their own shop, own mechanics too."

The first patroller said, "Guess ticket sales are underwater now old Corker's out. Never did like that self-satisfied sonuvabitch. Redipp'll whip 'em into shape."

The officers laughed. In addition to the young White Butterball pointing the black barrel of his gun into the van, Tiro could make out all but one of them clearly without turning his head. Their hands rested itchingly on their holsters. A bead of sweat dribbled down Tiro's forehead and into his eye. He didn't move, hardly blinked. The Black cop told them to raise their hands. He poked his head inside the driver's-side window to check they were complying, swiveled his head to check out Tree and Ink in the back. Tiro's hands were shaking; he tried to will them quiet. The other cops seemed content to let the Black cop take the initiative. He was the scout in the group. There would be a lot on the line for him but not near as much as there was for Tiro. Not near as much. . . .

The Black cop left Kid-Cop Butterball standing on the driver's side, walked round the front to the sliding door on the passenger side, and slid it open. He was joined by one of the patrollers.

The patroller laughed: "Since when do fly-boys come in the crippled variety?" he asked.

Tiro couldn't see him do it, but he knew Laughing Tree bristled at that.

"The cripple's called Ink," Marcus said, not missing a beat. "Our mascot. Sits in a Jim Crow Nest, an' this giant here straps it to his back. See it there in the back of the van?"

"A mascot?" Kid-Cop Butterball said, peering inside the van.

The barrel of his gun was inches from Marcus' chin. If Marcus had eased down a little, he could have slid it into his mouth.

"Don't look like much of a mascot to me," one of the officers said. Tiro couldn't tell who.

Marcus agreed. "Yeah, I know. He's not outfitted up. Sometimes we dress him up like a chicken. Gives the kids a kick to see him carted round in the nest with a tuft of feathers stuck on his head. Kids love it. Specially the wheelchair kids."

"I got a nephew in a wheelchair," the Black cop said. "Polio."

"Yeah. Ink goes down great with the polio kids. He got injured in the Jefferson. Shattered his legs. Van's a loaner. We're newbies. I'm Marcus. They call me Marcus Aurelius in the coop."

"Oh yeah," the patrollers on the sliding door side said, pointing at Marcus. "I heard of you."

Marcus introduced the others: "This big buck all hunched over in the back is Laughing Tree, an' this pretty one's my partner, Tiro the Pterodactyl. Flies like a dream in the Dream."

The young White cop looked at Tiro: "You the one they call Dregulahmo? The one related to that Tribal witch doctor? You a rabble-rouser?"

"Believe me, Officer," Marcus said, "my boy here ain't rabble-roused even once his entire life. Can't even rouse hisself when the alarm goes off or when he gets laid either."

All the men chortled, even Kid-Cop Butterball.

"Okay," the first patroller said, "you can put your hands down. Butterball, put that damn semi away, for Christ's sake! The District of Columbia ain't the Wild West."

Slowly, so as not to excite anyone, the riders in the van lowered their hands.

Kid-Cop looked heartbroken. "Guess you flyers are for real then," he said.

"You boys win one for the city," the Black cop said, as he slid the side door shut. He poked his face in Tiro's window, up close enough for Tiro to smell the tobacco on his breath. "Don't want the Dream embarrassed by them secessionist cunts. You can go. Drive careful."

"Will do, Officer," Marcus said. "Thanks, Officers. We 'preciate it."

Marcus set his eyes on the road, thrust the van into gear, and drove off.

They'd almost reached the Dream Revival District before any of the four spoke again.

Marcus was the first to say something: "Those motherfuckers better watch out. If I run into any of them on a more equal footing, I'll slit their fuckin throats."

"No such thing as an equal footing," Tree said. "It's why Ink and me will head up to New York soon as we got enough to make the trip an' scrape by when we get there. The Supers have got real equality, not this half-assed crap. Right, Ink? It's okay. We're safe."

Ink looked like he was about to throw up. The big man patted the boy's shoulder.

"I ain't scared," Ink assured them. "I knew you'd kill 'em, Tree, if they was to touch me."

The boy demanded to know why Marcus made up all that crap about him being a chicken. Took a while for Tree to settle him down. Felt he'd been disrespected. To console himself, Ink came back to Tree's idea about leaving. "Maybe when Tree an' me head to New York we'll take Afarra with us. She'd be safe there. Think she'd like it up there, Tree?"

Tiro smacked his head with the palm of his hand. He'd remembered something. Something he should never have forgotten. "Oh *shit!*" he cried. "I know who snatched her!"

Marcus jerked the wheel hard right, pulled over, and screeched to a halt. "Who?" he cried.

"I got tripped up, remember? I told you. When I ran after her."

"When you fell in God's Furrow, right?" Ink said.

"Seems appropriate," Marcus said. "You were covered in shit when you caught up with—"

"Shut the fuck up, Marcus! For once in your goddam life, stop bein' a smartass an' *listen!*" Tiro was shaking so hard he had to put one hand over the other to calm them. "I fell cos I tripped. I tripped cos a little dog ran in front of me." Tiro looked directly at Marcus and said, "That White man with Afarra. I forgot Fish said he had red hair. *Curly red hair.*"

Marcus looked at Tiro. Both flyers' eyes were wide with fear.

When Marcus spoke, his voice was barely above a whisper: "Jesus, T. You don't mean . . . ?"

Ink was beside himself: "What? What is it? *Who* snatched her?"

Tiro uttered the words that had been swirling around in his head for the past few seconds, ever since he realized he'd seen the little dog before: "Chaff Man II, Planting 437's executioner. That's who took her. Sloppy too, I bet. How the hell do I break it to Ji Afarra's dead?"

14 ELEVATION PROHIBITIONS

The Dream Master was out to kill her. Each day for two weeks straight, he'd shown up at 5:45 A.M. to conduct a training regimen so extreme it brought Ji-ji to her knees by the time he called a halt to it. "No fat, only muscle"—his mantra as he stood in the center ring and led her from one grueling workout to the next. For the rest of the day, her body throbbed, her bones ached, and her palms were so sore she moaned in pain when Zyla applied Man Cryday's healing cream to them. Her wings hurt too. A pulsing pain triggered by the strenuous exercises he put them through: jumps and climbs, furl/unfurl workouts, wing flap agility exercises, flexibility routines. . . . She'd been accustomed to hard labor on the 437th. She'd worked grueling fourteen-hour shifts as chief kitchen-seed, prepared Lotter's meals, and run for miles each morning to train for the Freedom Race. But this backbreaking training routine was as intense as the race itself.

Amadeus Nelson didn't countenance rest periods unless he instituted them himself. The exercise she hated most was bench leaps. Leap up, leap down, up, down, up, down. . . . Her thighs rebelled by cramping up. It became impossible for her to run as fast as she used to. A close second to the staggering slog of bench leaps was the hand-over-hand climb up the hope-rope. All he would say in response to her questions about the validity of the torture was that she needed strength, speed, agility, and fearlessness. "I won't have any of those things if I'm dead," she muttered.

The routines were dishearteningly similar to ones for flyer-battlers. Not once during fourteen days straight of practice had he asked her to leap from one of the lower Rosa Parks Perches and attempt liftoff. "He enjoys inflicting pain," she told Zyla, who offered to speak with him. "No," Ji-ji said, picturing the coopmaster's patronizing smile. "I can handle it." She still didn't know how her implacable coach knew Zyla, who was as tight-lipped as he was about their relationship. She wondered how I'm-a-God would react if she were to drop down dead in the middle of an exercise. Probably command her corpse to be there at the same time the next morning.

As Ji-ji's hopes of flying faded, her hope of finding Afarra—that scrap of it she had left—faded too. Not a single lead had panned out. No one had any idea where she was or if she had been snatched. Tiro stopped leaving messages for her. She worried he'd stopped looking altogether.

At the end of the second week of training, Ji-ji reached her limit. The coopmaster had been barking orders at her for nearly an hour; her worn-out body shrieked in protest.

"Okay, Just Jellybean," he said. (His old joke about her name had worn thin ages ago; these days, she suspected he used it simply to antagonize her.) "Time for planks. Let's hold the position for three minutes. Ten push-ups in between, then another three minutes." It was the "let's hold" that infuriated her, as if there was an "us" in this lopsided relationship.

Ji-ji eased herself down the hope-rope and landed in the center ring, a few feet from where he stood. The bindings on her swollen, blistered palms hadn't helped; her hands smarted. It was already hot as hell in the practice coop, yet she detected not one bead of sweat on his face. Not *one*.

He assumed she hadn't heard him and repeated his previous command. "Planks next. Hold for three minutes, then ten push-ups, then another three minutes."

"I don't think so," she said.

"What?"

"No," she said, more defiantly.

She waited for him to sandblast her with sarcasm. Instead, he simply walked over to the coach's bench and sat down. She eyed him warily.

"You are frustrated," he said, stating the obvious.

She laughed. Her laugh was supposed to be scornful. She messed up and snorted.

"Why?" he asked her.

She steeled herself to follow through. "Cos you're not teaching me to fly."

"Come," he said, indicating a place beside him on the coach's bench. "Let's talk."

What was he doing? "Are you giving up on me?"

"*I'm* not the one giving up. Come. Sit."

Ji-ji dragged herself over to the bench and perched at the other end. She'd expected rebellion to feel like victory. It didn't.

For a while, they sat in silence. Then he said, "Why do you think I'm pushing you so hard?"

"Cos you can. You're the coach, not me." Aware she sounded whiny, she only got angrier.

"You could have said no a week ago. Why now?"

"I'm fuckin exhausted, that's why!" She'd sworn in frustration in his company (when she messed up a routine or pulled something, for example), but she'd never deliberately sworn in direct conversation with him before. She waited for him to explode.

"I'm fuckin exhausted too," he said.

Caught off-guard again, she stumbled toward a response. "How come *you're* exhausted? I do all the work."

He raised his eyes to heaven in frustration. "You know what time I get up to arrive here at the crack of dawn?" She shrugged. "Three forty-five. I make sure I'm not followed, which means driving part of the way, stopping off at a friend's all-night café, changing in a private room in the back so I won't be recognized. Then I board a boat and come partway by river. I walk the rest of the way here."

"How come you don't drive?"

"How many vehicles do you see in this derelict flood zone? An occasional visit wouldn't be noticed, but a regular rendezvous would. Besides, in the past, my car's been monitored, and borrowing another could mean I implicate someone else. So, I stumble over here in the dark and work with you without recompense. I do the same thing in reverse to get back to the Dream Coop. Then I begin my real day. If I'm lucky, I get three or four hours' sleep before I start again. Have you heard me complain?"

Ji-ji shook her head. His bloodshot eyes looked as weary as she felt.

"And while I'm here in this vermin-infested coop, I have to be on my guard." His jacket lay on the bench between them. He reached into it and pulled out a handgun. "I carry insurance in case we get a surprise visit from the Territories." He slipped the gun back under his jacket. "Don't look so worried. As far as we know, even if the steaders have discovered you survived, they don't think you're a threat. But all that can change in a heartbeat."

His honesty triggered hers. She asked a question that had plagued her since Afarra's disappearance: "You think someone's snatched Afarra to get at me cos I'm a threat?"

He shrugged. "I don't know. I'm sure the Friends have some theories about what happened. I try and stay out of their business if I can. Don't get me wrong. The Friends are brave people. Most of them are good people too. Look at Zy. She could be living in relative safety in the E.S.S. or one of the more progressive Independents. But she's committed to reunification. That's her dream. A United States of America."

"It's not yours?" Ji-ji asked.

"I gave up on dreaming outside the coop a long time ago. I'm too much of a pessimist to be a Friend of Freedom. Not that it would make any difference whether I've been inducted into the Friends or not if secessionist sympathizers discover us here."

Lucky Dyce had said something similar to her once when he'd explained why he wasn't a Friend of Freedom. She hadn't understood the risk the coopmaster took to coach her.

He returned to her complaint. He sounded tired, but he didn't sound annoyed. "So you don't like my approach to these sessions?"

She felt bad about complaining now, yet she forced herself to speak up. "I guess it's like you're not teaching me to fly, you're training me to be a flyerbattler."

"And what exactly do you think you'll need to defy gravity?"

How the hell do I know? she thought. Out loud she said, "Feathers? A miracle?"

"Feathers would indeed be a miracle at this stage. And in my experience, an overreliance on divine intervention is foolish. As I see it, you need three things: strength, speed, and endurance, yes? Every single exercise we've done over the past two weeks is meant to strengthen your body so you can cope with the strain flying will exert on it. Your legs are getting stronger by the day, and you're more flexible, agile, and faster than you were when we started."

"I'm not faster. I'm way slower."

"You ran as fast as any flyer I've got in the Dream earlier."

"That's still slower than I used to be."

He jerked his head back in surprise. "Is it? Huh. I didn't know that."

"You never asked. Seems like I'm forfeiting speed in favor of strength is what I'm trying to say. This arrangement isn't working. It's gotta be a . . . I don't know . . ."

"A collaboration?"

"Yeah. You gotta tell me *why* we're doing stuff, an' I have to tell you how it feels. Like there are days when it seems my wings want to be here an' days they don't. An' on the days they don't, doesn't matter what you tell me to do cos they won't obey."

"How obedient do they feel today? Not very, if their owner is any indication."

"They feel like they're on loan. Like the books Zyla gets me from the library."

He seemed intrigued by that. "Hmm. . . . Okay, let's try a liftoff."

He'd called her bluff, a bluff she hadn't intended to make. Panic fluttered in her chest.

"You want me to try an' take off? Now?"

"That's what all this is about, yes? Be careful what you wish for. It can bite you in the ass. Now, climb up to Sojourner's Sill, grab a hope-rope, and try swinging and flapping at the same time. See if you can lessen the velocity of the swing. No need for a harness."

"I'll still be holding on to the hope-rope, right? I don't have to let go?"

"Definitely do *not* let go. Afterward, try sprinting across the floor from one side of the cage to the other. Build up speed and flap at the same time. Like swans and geese do when they take off from a body of water. You've seen them do that, yes?" She nodded. "Remember, the initial upward thrust should come mainly from your legs and feet, understand?"

Ji-ji nodded, then didn't move.

"What's wrong now?" he asked.

"S'pose it doesn't work?"

He chuckled. "I can guarantee it won't. Not at first. Maybe never. We'll need to keep trying."

She hadn't expected him to cave like this. "S'pose I fall?"

"If you fall while sprinting across the floor of the coop you'll survive. Rarely have falls from that modest height been fatal. For the other exercise, you'll be clinging to the rope. You'll be fine."

She sat motionless. If her wings didn't function, how would she ever find Afarra or Bonbon? What was the point of all the pain she'd endured if those freakish appendages on her back didn't do something? She braced herself for a lecture. He despised timidity. He surprised her again.

"Know what they used to call me?" he said, as he straddled the bench so he could look at her without turning his head. "When I first flew in the coop in the Territories? They called me Jolly Golly Gowler. The father-man who purchased me was called Burke Gowler. Originally, my planting designation was Cloth-34m/636. But one day they caught me somersaulting behind the dairy barn. One somersault after another. I attempted a triple double too. Messed it up of course. But it made them salivate when they thought about the lucre the planting would get if I was a winner in the Freedom Race. Father-Man Gowler elevated me to Commonseed so I could compete. I was movin' on up, Jellybean. All the way up to the next rung of their Great Ladder. I was grateful too. Nothing worse than being a Cloth. Treated like dirt by steaders and seeds alike. I went from Cloth-34m to Jolly Golly Gowlerseed. Golly was short for 'golliwog,' a minstrel rag doll from way back. Looked like the cartoon face on your watch. You know that's Mickey, yes?"

"What?" Captivated by the story, his question had come as a surprise. "Oh yeah. My friend Lucky told me about him. He was a rodent deity in the Age of Plenty."

The coopmaster raised an eyebrow but he didn't contradict her. "I guess that's close enough. . . . For a couple of years, I flew the coop like no one had ever flown it. Battled well too. Wasn't always the strongest but I was the wiliest.

Till I was injured showing off without a harness. Fell twenty feet. The planting healer predicted I would be crippled for life. Burke Gowler couldn't profit off me anymore. My injury inspired Burke Gowler to remember I was on one of the duskiest arcs of the Color Wheel. Demoted me back to Serverseed. Gowler must've been torn between gloating and mournfulness at the loss of easy lucre. Said I was a 'flaunty flyer.' Said I flew as if the world belonged to me, so I needed to be taken down a rung or two. One thing he was right about—the flaunty flying. I used to feel omnipotent in the coop. All the best flyers feel that way, as if the bars of the cage can't hold them. It's how X and Tiro feel when they fly. Should be how Tree feels when he battles, except Tree doesn't give a crap about winning. Got his mind on other things."

"I used to feel like that when I ran," Ji-ji said. "Like I could take off, if I wanted."

"Hang on to that feeling. Draw on it. Could be your body was already trying to tell you something, predicting where it wanted to take you. . . . Where was I?"

"You were injured." Ji-ji didn't want the story to end yet. She had to know what happened.

"Oh yes. Soon as I could hobble, Gowler exchanged me for a nanny goat. Shipped me off to serve on Planting 624. That was his big mistake. I recovered. *Made* myself get strong. Vengeance fueled me. Kept thinking the stronger I got the more it would piss off Burke Gowler. . . . You know what it's like to rehabilitate yourself after your body has been broken. I hope you never have to do it again. Imagine doing it day in, day out, without a healer like Man Cryday to tend to you or any hope of success. It hardened me—in good ways and bad. After I recovered, Coach Patton Slovanovichseed, the fly-coach on my new planting, defied the rules about no outcasts flying in the coop. Everyone called him Patty. He trained me in secret like I'm training you. Made me promise to do something for him in return. Said I had to pass the favor along by training a gifted flyer I believed in as much as he believed in me. Said I had to promise to do it, however risky it was.

"During the planting championship battle, Patty put a black executioner's hood over my head, rechristened me the Ebony Executioner, and let me battle incognito."

"What happened?"

"I won. No one could beat me back then. When they unhooded me and saw I was Cloth-34m/624, they didn't punish me. Patty had anticipated that. Knew Cropmaster Ezekiel Etcher was as greedy as they came. Etcher couldn't promote me fast enough from Serverseed to Commonseed so I could compete as Planting 624's flyer-battler rep. I was back on the Commonseed rung I was perched on earlier. He ratified me for the race, and I made it all the way. One of only four flyer-battlers to win their Freedom that year.

"After I won, I spent the next few years improving myself. Spent a hunk of my salary on tutoring. Learned to speak the way educated people do, studied and practiced till I sounded more schooled than they did. Dressed impeccably too." He looked down at his clothes. "These sessions with you being the exception, of course. Don't forget, fairskins are less likely to shoot us if we're well dressed. Most bullies are cowards, and smart clothing signals possible repercussions."

He'd triumphed. A happy ending. She needed that. But he wasn't done yet.

"I wasn't out of the woods. The fleet was still the fleet, and the commander at that time was even more of a bastard than Redipp, which is saying something. Ezekiel Etcher, 624's cropmaster, had outed me as an outcast after he got his paws on the planting's reward. For three years I was forced to clean the coop, cook for my fellow flyers, and wait on Wing Commander Hungerford."

Ji-ji saw how much it cost him to relive this. "At least there was a happy ending," she said.

"Not quite. Story's got a kicker. Someone had to be punished. That's the key to seeding fear in the Territories and making sure it bears fruit. Coach Patton was a good man who made a tragic mistake. Patty assumed it would be *him* they'd come after. He'd been prepared to make the ultimate sacrifice. Had it all planned out. Instead, Etcher snatched the son Patty seeded with Presdy, the African-Indigenous woman he loved. The kid's name was Bomartin, but we called him Bommy. Bonny Bommy. Sweetest child you ever saw. Like a little brother to me. Six years old. The steaders had to teach botanicals a lesson. Bommy became the youngest seed ever lynched in the 600s."

Instinctively, Ji-ji reached out and patted her coach's arm. "I'm sorry, Coach. I really am."

He looked down at her hand, patted it once, and changed position so he wasn't straddling the bench any longer. His stricken profile told her he was reliving the story in agonizing detail.

"Bommy's mother, as I said, was an African American. An A-I, to use the steader terminology. A-Is, as you know, are on a higher rung of the ladder than botanicals, protected by various laws and treaties, as long as they can prove their ancestry. Not always an easy task to produce records, of course, given the mess the world's in. Clever to invent that Great Ladder for us all to perch on. . . . The steaders didn't account for the fact that many A-Is would identify with seeds, of course. Didn't realize that African Americans would fight to the death to Free those who'd been imported, or that they'd fall in love with seeds, like Presdy did when she met Patty.

"By virtue of the maternal line, Bommy had a right to a trial he never got. His mam's A-I status riled up the SuperStates and Independents. Some say Bommy's lynching may have been one reason why the block of western states opted to remain as Unaligned Territories in the end. The murder of a six-year-old boy reminded people how savage the planting system was. Others say it didn't make any difference. Nothing more than another lost seedling in a black sea of losses." The Dream Master swallowed hard, paused.

Ji-ji wanted to find the right words to comfort him, but she only had trite expressions of sympathy to offer.

He spoke again, his voice cracking under the strain. "Bommy wasn't lynched till a few weeks after the Freedom Race. Cropmaster Etcher couldn't risk losing the kickback cropmasters get. He sent me a letter detailing the lynching, done in secret with only a few witnesses. Newspapers like the *Independent* and some of the big ones in the SuperStates hadn't got wind of it yet. Funny how you don't realize a letter is a grenade till you begin reading. . . .

"Patty's grieving wasn't over. Presdy, Bommy's mam, couldn't pry Bommy's Death Day screams out of her head. They fished her from the planting well a week after Bommy's lynching. Patty didn't last long after that. Bommy was his heart and Presdy was his soul. Can't survive without those things. So he leapt to his death from the Jim Crow Nest in the planting fly-coop."

Ji-ji couldn't move; he didn't either. The Dream Master sat as still as stone, unblinking.

"I haven't pushed you too far, Jellybean. I know how far too far is. . . . Man Cryday told me you attempted suicide a couple months ago when things got bad."

Ji-ji's anger resurfaced: "She shouldn't've told you 'bout—"

"Of course she should. I'm your coach. I push you to your limit, not beyond. Every day, those of us who've survived against the odds have a duty to prove that the ones who made the sacrifice were right to put everything on the line. We have to prove we're worth that type of sacrifice. Do you understand?" Like someone coming up for air, the Dream Master took a deep breath: "That's only the second time I've told anyone that story."

"Who did you tell it to the first time?"

"Zyla Clobershay . . . soon after we got engaged. And now, let's find out what kind of story those Unknowables on your back are itching to tell us. You ready?"

||||||||||||

She hadn't flown. Not really. But she had hovered for a moment or two. The Dream Master ran up to her and swung her around.

"How long was I off the ground?" she asked, excitedly, as he put her back down on it.

"Two, three seconds," her coach replied, triumphant. Already later than he'd planned to be, he had to get back to the Dream Revival District in time for a meeting with the new wing commander. "I need to go now. But you made a giant leap today, literally. No doubt about it."

"Thank you," she said.

"Don't thank me. Thank the Indescribables on your back."

She'd never seen him so happy before. The instant her feet left the ground he'd let out a whooping sound. Not a cheer exactly. More like the sound children make when they're too excited to use words. Brimming with triumph, Ji-ji rushed back to the Aerie to tell Zyla the news. She had questions for her former teacher too. Were the two of them really engaged?

He sat at the kitchen table with his back to her. Zyla had her arm around him. He turned—his face wet, his breath catching in his throat. Tiro. Ji-ji halted in the doorway.

"I saw you!" he sputtered. "Saw your feet leave the ground, Ji. It was . . . amazing!"

Puzzled, Ji-ji looked to Zyla, who understood what she was asking.

"That's not why he's upset," Zyla said. "He's got something to tell you."

Ji-ji felt her back contract, as if someone had threaded a rope in a circle just under her skin and now an invisible hand cinched it tight. In little more than a whisper, Ji-ji asked, "Is she dead?"

"No," Zyla told her. She left Tiro at the table and ran to hold Ji-ji.

Distraught, Ji-ji pushed her away. "What's happened?"

Tiro had come bearing gifts. A large box sat on the kitchen table, tied with a big, bloodred bow, like the one Lotter had wound around Afarra's head when he gifted her to Silapu.

Tiro stood up. She wanted to ask, "How come you're bent over like an old man or like someone with a bellyache?" She thought it instead, then wondered if she'd said it too. He'd come bearing gifts. In one hand, a box with a bloodred bow. In the other, poison.

He pointed to the box. "I brought you something," he said.

Zyla guided Ji-ji to a chair. Placed her hands on her shoulders. Ji-ji thought, *Zyla's pressing down on my shoulders cos she's scared I'll fly away.* The noose in her back grew tighter and tighter.

Tiro spoke. Out flew the first poison dart. Out flew the second.

Poison dart one: Chaff Man. Poison dart two: Sloppy.

The executioner who'd lynched dozens, and the ruthless, bitter kitchen-seed.

The face spoke: "Me an' Georgie, we figure maybe it's for ransom . . . why they took her." *If I draw his contorted face,* Ji-ji thought, with shocking clarity, *I'll call it "Guilt Unmasked."*

"They'll torture her," she said. "They'll kill her slowly."

Her voice spiked liked barbed wire, Ji-ji said, "Has anyone sent a ransom note?" He shook his head sheepishly. "Well then. Guess we can rule out that dumbass theory."

He began to apologize, but she rolled right over him, told him to shut the fuck up, demanded to know the truth. "Admit it," she said. "You were high."

He broke down completely then. Wept like a Weeping. Confessed. Blamed it on the meds doled out by the sports docs for anxiety. Stuttered out something about some falling syndrome. She didn't care. He told her he'd been out with Georgie-Porge drinking tequila the night before the trip to the Mall. Told her about his splitting headache.

"A hangover," she said. Her mam, blind drunk, swayed in and out of her peripheral vision.

He described how he'd tried to zip up Afarra's jacket cos the wizard's Seeing Eyes poked out. How he'd grabbed her to get her out of the stinking mutant exhibit. How the snarlcat's paw snagged him—"like it had come to her defense or something." Ji-ji thought of Muckmock, who'd also tried to protect Afarra when Marcus had hauled her away on not-the-Fourth of July. Tiro said Afarra took off before he could stop her. He emphasized how he'd run after her, fallen in God's Furrow.

"So at least that part wasn't a lie," Ji-ji said.

Yes, that part was true. And the part about the little dog tripping him up, the dog he should have recognized.

"Circus," Ji-ji said. *Chaff Man's little pooch,* she thought. *The dog he offered to hang Uncle Dreg to save. The Pomeranian lynched with the wizard and the executioner till Sylvie the Penal Tree unlynched them all. Funny how merciless mercy can turn out to be. . . .*

Tiro's mouth said he would've kept searching but he thought Afarra would head back to the museum for sure. He halted. Started up again. Halted. Eventually he said, "And then there was this dealer. Lippy Verdi. They call him Requiem. Don't know why."

"Verdi," Zyla said. "Verdi's 'Requiem.' It's a piece of music—a mass by Giuseppe Verdi."

"Who cares?" Ji-ji said. "You lost her cos you're a drug-sop like Mam. They've had her for weeks! You know what they'll do to her. He's a killer. Sloppy's his apprentice. Betrayed the runners in the Freedom Race. Led them into a trap. Sees Afarra as a Cloth. I was a fool to trust you."

"I'll make it up to you, Ji."

"How?" she asked, with mockery.

Zyla said they could search for Chaff Man and Sloppy in addition to Afarra now. If they were still in the city, it would be hard for them to hide. "Not many Pomeranians in the Dream," Zyla said. "We've got a meeting of the Friends coming up. The one that was postponed. We'll pool our resources. Work out a strategy."

Ji-ji had another question. A very important one. "When did you find out?"

Tiro didn't answer.

She shouted at him, "WHEN?"

He looked from her to Zyla and back to her. "A few days ago. A week. A bit more," he said.

Ji-ji remained calm, switched off as much of herself as she could. "Who else knows?" she asked.

"Marcus . . . Trink. The three of them were with me when I figured it out. I told Georgie-Porge too cos he was meant to be there only Droopy made him an' Orlie clean the toilets cos they . . . Nothing. Don't matter. Then we told the Friends co-leaders, Alice an' Paul. They ordered us not to tell anyone else for now."

Ji-ji turned to Zyla. "Did you know who'd taken her?" she asked.

"*No!*" Zyla exclaimed. "I would never have kept that from you! Why did Alice and Paul order you not to tell us?"

"They said we should wait cos Ji had a new coach, an' the news could upset her."

Zyla, also furious now, said, "Who gave them the right to make that decision?"

Tiro began to apologize again. Said some of the Friends hadn't wasted any time and had immediately begun to search for Chaff Man, Sloppy, and Circus, in addition to Afarra. Alice and Paul had appointed a special task force, he said. He'd been out too, searching whenever he could.

He was still speaking when Ji-ji got up and exited the kitchen.

She walked back to her room, shut the door, and sank down with her back against it.

I'm-a-God was right. Fear was the real enemy. Tonight, she'd murder the enemy for good.

||||||||||||||

Afraid to allow herself to think about what Afarra was going through (if she was still alive, that is), Ji-ji focused on the task ahead of her. If she'd been in a state of mind to find joy in anything after Tiro's brutal visit, it would have been that she was about to flout every single one of the Territories' Elevation

Prohibitions. On plantings, female seeds were prohibited from exceeding their "divinely decreed stature." Everything from tall hairstyles to heels was taboo. She'd been permitted to ascend to the upper story of Lotter's father-house to clean it, but she had to keep her eyes "cast down demurely." While there, she was prohibited from looking out of windows. The result of this conditioning was self-defeat: steaders had prohibited her from elevating herself; now, *she* was the one prohibiting herself from elevating. She had to break that cycle. It wasn't about her anymore; it was about rescuing the girl who would walk through fire to save her. If she was too late, it was about killing the ones who'd snatched her.

She hurried to the kitchen, careful to tread softly. She made a cheese sandwich and brought it back to Afarra's bedroom. She sat on the edge of the bed and ate with purpose. She drank one of Zyla's beers. It was warm. No problem. She wished she had some of her mam's whiskey or a few of Silapu's happy pills to give herself courage, before she realized how hypocritical that was.

Ji-ji didn't think of herself as superstitious, but she'd been raised by a woman who was. In times of crisis, she looked for signs and relied upon the interpretation of dreams to guide her. She returned to her own bedroom and retrieved her talismans: the map she'd drawn of Planting 437, the snow globe Tiro had given her (yes, she'd include that too), Petrus' gun, and the four dice Lucky sent. Ji-ji shook the globe for luck. Against a whimsical city skyline, the flyer, silhouette-black, swung back and forth on a tiny swing in the blizzard of all blizzards.

She placed the map on the floor, handling it as carefully as Uncle Dreg used to handle his story-cloths. She positioned the snow globe on a bent corner of the map to hold it down, and placed the gun on the other corner. She wouldn't roll one die at a time cos she was superstitious and the word *die* freaked her out. Instead, she rolled all four at once.

And there it was: One, two, three, four pips, all lined up in sequence! A sign if ever there was one. She'd cast her do-it-yourself spell. It would have to do. The other day, Amadeus Nelson had said mathematics revealed today's logical patterns, the ones we can live by till new ones usurp them. He wouldn't think much of the lucky sequence of her dice. No matter. Signs were hard to come by. She'd take this one, grateful that it seemed to indicate she was on the right path.

She looked at herself in the full-length mirror Germaine and Ben had salvaged, repaired, and presented to Ji-ji so she could, as Germaine put it, "marvel at herself," after she'd confessed she still felt like a freak at times. She'd been unfair to Germaine. If all went well, she would apologize.

She sat down at the small desk Tiro had made for her and felt a twinge of sympathy for him which didn't last. She wrote a quick note to Zyla. Explained why she had to try and why she had to do it alone. Said if something went wrong, Zyla must still keep her promise and search for Afarra. It occurred to her this might be her last will and testament.

Ji-ji unfurled her wings, studied them in the mirror—what she could see of them anyway. The Dream Master, who spoke lyrically about her back at times, had said her wings were mathematically and biologically intriguing, light and shadow, formed and conditional. She liked that.

Ji-ji poked her head in Afarra's room and waved goodbye to the Afarra in the mural, who remained silent. She headed for the practice coop.

Once inside the dimly lit coop, the climb up to the Jim Crow's Nest was a long one, via Harriet's Stairs and Jacob's Ladder. Fit as a fiddle, she accomplished it in no time. From the welkin, she crossed the rope bridge to the nest, where Na-na waited for her in the shadows.

"Hey, buddy. You come to see me fly the coop?" She could've sworn the iguana nodded.

She stepped up onto the rim of the basket, looked down into the coop's sunken eye. A long way down. Another catastrophic fall if her back refused to come to her aid. How could she help Afarra then? She couldn't. And there was something else. She wasn't the same person she'd been when her wings were a fetid shadow. This wasn't the way. Too reckless. Too selfish.

All this time, the Dream Master had been trying to tell her something. Her strengths weren't her wings, they were her legs and her speed. Her strength was *her,* as she was before the metamorphosis, when she would run so fast it felt as if her feet barely skimmed the ground as they drummed the skin of the earth. She wouldn't rely on her wings to rescue her from a fatal descent, she would rely on her strength to propel her upward.

She'd tried running across the floor of the cage before but never surrendered herself completely to speed. This morning, she'd come closer than she ever had, but she'd pulled up early, as soon as the ground beneath her feet fell away, scared of crashing into the bars of the cage. She couldn't remember a thing Amadeus Nelson had told her about the takeoff velocity in birds and the transition from the ground to the air, but maybe it didn't matter? Maybe she was overthinking it? Perhaps all she needed to do was let go? If she placed her trust in her own body, maybe it would know instinctively how to act? Perhaps what she needed to do was *become* flight?

She climbed down from the rim of the Jimmy Crow, walked back over the footbridge, stepped onto the welkin platform, and descended the equipment in reverse order—Jacob first, then Harriet.

As soon as she set foot on the floor of the coop, she took off running, unfurling as she went. She had to shed her fear, be defiant in the face of failure.

Faster, faster! Legs pumping the ground. She needed thrust, she needed power. *DO IT!*

She'd reached the center of the center ring. She leapt onto a Lincoln Log and ran up an inclined Douglass Pipe. Boldly, as if defeat was off the table, she leapt onto a King-spin. From there, a Rosa Parks Perch, and from there she launched herself into the air! The pair flapped once . . . twice! And then . . .

She was *airborne!* Aloft! Four feet! Ten feet! Moving faster than she'd ever moved before!

She was *flying!*

She saw him standing there near the open gate to the flying cage . . . watching in his hooded sweatshirt! The Dream Master had come back to witness her first flight!

Awkwardly, she banked to the left and flew toward him. . . . He pushed back his hood.

Fear grabbed her by the throat. Blond hair . . . a steader beard! *Lotter!*

Ji-ji forgot to flap. She entered a wild spiral she couldn't control! Fear, Fear, Fear grabbed her by the throat! Crashing! Descending too fast! *Too fast!*

Father-Man Lotter rushed up to snatch her as she careened toward the bars of the cage. The force of their collision slammed him down with her. They tumbled together over and over, crashed into equipment as they rolled, crashed into the bars of the cage as she tried to scratch out his eyes and he cursed her. Him on top of her looking down in the coop's dim light!

She raised her knee with all the force left in her and jammed it into his balls. He jumped up and clutched his crotch.

"What the hell is *wrong* with you?"

She rose, retracted her wings in an instant, and hurled herself at his neck.

"*Get off me!*" he cried. "You're nuts!" She ignored his request and clung to his neck.

"*Lucky!*" she cried. "You came *back!*"

"More fool me," he said. "And by the way, just so you know, you're the worst bloody pilot I've ever seen."

15 THE FRIEND OF MY FRIEND

As Lucky and Ji-ji made their way from the practice coop to the Aerie, Lucky kept coming back to what he'd witnessed: "Otto said you couldn't fly worth a damn. But you were flying!"

"Who's Otto?" she asked.

Instead of replying, he groaned in pain. Due to his injury, the three flights of stairs proved difficult. "Make cutlery your weapon of choice next time," he said. "It's less lethal."

Halfway up the second flight, Large Bodyguard-at-Large intercepted them. Ji-ji started to introduce them, then realized it was unnecessary.

"*Lucky!*" the bodyguard cried. "What you doing here? Hey, you okay, man? Here, let me." He shouldered Lucky's backpack, looped Lucky's arm over his shoulder, and hoisted him up the remaining stairs. "So what you doing here?" he asked again, his excitement on full display. Ji-ji wondered who'd swapped places with the mournful bodyguard who prowled the practice coop.

"I came to see Jellybean fly the coop," Lucky replied. "Didn't know she'd try to kill me. How come you told me she couldn't fly worth a damn, Otto?"

"Cos it's true," the bodyguard countered. "No offense meant," he added, addressing Ji-ji.

Apparently, Large Bodyguard-at-Large was Otto. How come she didn't know this already? She attempted to make amends by asking Otto where he came from.

"Dad was an African American from Arkansas. Mom was from the Mideast, originally. I go by Otto. Real name's Otter. Dad liked otters. Said they were underestimated. Said under the right circumstances, an otter can kill a croc. Arkansans have a sense of humor when it comes to names."

"So do Toteppi," Lucky said, "right, Jellybean? You always fly like your arse is on fire?"

Otto gasped. "You telling me she *flew*! For real? No way! When?"

"Tonight," Lucky said, "just before she unmanned me."

"At last!" Otto exclaimed. "Her earlier attempts were pitiful."

"Thanks," Ji-ji said. She could see why he and Lucky were friends. "How long you been spying on me?"

"Wasn't spying. Lucky asked me to keep tabs on you. Send him updates."

"Don't look at me," Lucky said to her. "The Friends were the ones assigned Otto to bodyguard duty. When I heard he was a guardian for the angel-to-be, I got in touch and asked him to keep me posted. Otto and me go way back. He told me how bad you were—as an angel, I mean. I therefore arrived here with extremely low expectations. Hence my shock."

"Wish I'd seen it," Otto said. "Your first flight! Bet it was beautiful."

"It wasn't," Lucky asserted. "She's can't steer worth a damn. Almost smashed my skull in when I rescued her from a fatal collision with the bars of the cage. Then she kicks me like some damn . . ." He glanced over at her. He was going to say "mule." In the old days, he would have. He'd changed. "Kicks me like some sodding pillock," he said. She remembered he'd called her that when they'd journeyed through The Margins together. She'd forgotten to look it up, but she got the gist.

Otto roared with laughter. "I would've paid good money to see that," he said.

The commotion woke Zyla, who came running to the door. To Ji-ji's relief, she greeted Lucky cordially enough. Ji-ji soon realized his visit wasn't unexpected.

"He's in distress," Otto said. "Jellybean kicked him in the balls."

Ji-ji tried to explain that she'd mistaken Lucky for Lotter, but no one was listening. Otto said he needed to return to guard duty before any other "steader type" snuck into the coop. He took hold of Lucky and kissed him on each cheek, ruffled his friend's blond mop, and took off.

"Otto's effusive," Lucky said, by way of explanation. "Gets it from his mother."

Zyla fetched a cushion and placed it on the same chair at the kitchen table where Tiro had sat earlier that day. She and Ji-ji eased him into it. Buffeted by too many emotions at once, Ji-ji pulled up a chair and sat beside Lucky so she could study him up close, a death grip on his hand to prevent him from disappearing. If anything, Lucky looked even more like Lotter than he used to when he was masquerading as Lieutenant Matty Longsby on the 437th. But though he had the same wavy, shoulder-length blond hair and a beard much like Lotter's, the shocking blue color of his eyes didn't pierce you the way her fatherman's did. He had a small, deep scar on his left cheek, just above his beard, and a faded scar on his temple, not visible till he pushed back his shaggy blond hair. She couldn't remember if he'd gotten those during the battle with the Bounty Boys. Though he was roughly Tiro's age, he seemed older. She dared not ask him how long he planned to stay in the Dream, afraid he would say it was only for a day or two.

Lucky said he needed something to stop his balls from screaming. Zyla poured him a double brandy from her secret stash.

"Got any ice?" he asked. "For my balls, not the brandy."

There was a smidgen of ice left at the bottom of one of the coolers the Friends resupplied when they could. Zyla scooped it up and wrapped it in a wet cloth, which Lucky slapped on his crotch over his pants. Ji-ji wouldn't put it past him to exaggerate his injuries to get a rise out of her.

"Be better if you slipped off your pants," Zyla suggested. The look Lucky gave Zyla made his lingering antipathy toward her evident. Zyla shrugged. "Your choice," she said.

Gingerly, Lucky repositioned the ice. "Couldn't you see I was trying to save you?" he said. Zyla asked what he meant. "She flew," Lucky said. "Never seen anything like it."

Zyla addressed Ji-ji. "Is this true? Did you actually take off and fly?"

"She was flying all right," Lucky said, "like a drunk albatross. Couldn't steer worth a damn."

Ji-ji explained to Zyla what had happened. She expected her former teacher to tell her how foolish she'd been; instead, Zyla, overcome, rushed over to where she sat and hugged her.

"We must be careful," Zyla said, relinquishing her hold on Ji-ji. "Lucky, don't tell a soul."

"I'm not gormless," he snapped.

Zyla bristled. "Want me to take a look at your testes? Apply some of Cryday's pain cream?"

Lucky glared at her. "Very kind of you, Zyla. But I'm not ready to be eunuched tonight."

Ji-ji had other things to focus on: "Afarra's missing. Did you know?"

"Man Cryday told me," Lucky replied, his flippancy replaced with seriousness. "Said you could use some help with the search."

Ji-ji asked if Zyla knew he was coming. She nodded. Ji-ji felt a surge of gratitude. It couldn't be easy for Zyla to welcome the person who blamed her for the death of his father.

"Chaff Man's got Afarra," Ji-ji said, her throat catching. "An' Sloppy's with him."

Lucky looked as sick as she felt about it. "You sure?" he asked. She nodded. "*Shit!*" he said. "Man Cryday didn't tell me that."

"She didn't know," Zyla said. "I spoke with Alice today. The Friends kept it quiet."

"Why the hell did they do that?" Lucky asked. "I got to know Chaff Man—Cherub—on the 437th. Never met anyone less like his name. What's he doing with Afarra?"

Ji-ji and Zyla relayed to him what Tiro had disclosed that morning.

Lucky, who'd never liked Tiro, railed against him. "Thick as two short planks," he said. "How many Pomeranians does Tiro think there are on the Mall, for god's sake?"

Devastated though she was by Tiro's behavior, Ji-ji felt uncomfortable when Lucky attacked him. She changed the subject. "You should be dead," Ji-ji said. "How did you escape alive from The Margins?" Immediately afterward, she regretted the question. Only part of the ending was happy. She saw fake Muleboy in his fake mule ears swinging from the live oak. She was firing at one of the Bounty Boys who was charging toward her. She heard the shots, smelled the blood, smelled Zebadiah's burning flesh. "*Coward!*" Fake Muleboy mouthed at her, as if he already knew she'd never rescue him in time. She had a confession to make.

"After I left you there under the oak, I found the stallion. I should've gone back for you."

"Don't be daft. What good would that've done? You would've blown my cover in a second and we'd both be goners. Luckily, the Bounty Boys we shot—"

"*You* shot. I missed. Except for Chet. Was aiming for his head an' I hit his chest."

"You're right. I was being modest. It was all me. Let me rephrase it. The Bounty Boys we ran into, the majority of whom *I* shot, were sworn enemies of the Clan that found me. That body we saw floating in the river—Jimbo, Daryl's brother, remember?"

Yes, she remembered everything as if it were happening now. She nodded.

"As luck would have it, Jimbo Bloaty-Floaty and his kid brother, Daryl Bounty Boy, had a feud going for years." Lucky took another swig of brandy. Like it had in The Margins, alcohol made him talkative. "The Clansmen that found me were out to avenge Jimbo's murder. He was their leader, see. Jimbo and Daryl had been trying to kill each other for years. The Clansmen were only too happy to learn I'd killed Chet, Zinc, and the others. Could've knocked me down with a feather when I learned later that our man Zinc was Zebadiah Moss. You know what they'd do to us in the Territories if they found out who we killed?" Ji-ji saw the grand inquisitor's deep-set eyes in the doorway of the storeroom. Yes, she had a pretty good idea of what he was capable of.

"So being the quick thinker I am in a jam," Lucky said, "I told the same story I'd told Chet and the others. Said I was escorting a Mule to her new owner—blah, blah, blah. Said the Boys tried to sample you, chased you to the river, and you were swept away. I lived up to my name that day, and proved the old adage too: 'the enemy of my enemy is my' . . . Come on, Jellybean, stay alert."

Zyla provided the answer: "The enemy of my enemy is my friend."

"Bingo, Madam Clobershay. I guess that makes the friend of my friend my enemy." The dig was directed at Zyla, who didn't react.

"But your body was found under the live oak," Ji-ji said, "half-eaten by snarl-cats."

"Must've been one of the Bounty Boys," Lucky said. "Lucky for me, the Clan wasn't inclined to bury their enemies. I probably would've bled to death if they had been." He asked for another brandy. Zyla slid the bottle toward him. He poured himself a triple, took a couple of swigs.

Ji-ji still couldn't figure out how Lucky had managed to survive, given how badly he'd been wounded. "Did the Clan patch you up?" she asked.

"Clansmen aren't the patching-up type. They only carried me back with them as a favor, seeing as how I'd rid them of Daryl and his men. Never expected me to make it. Turns out, there were a couple of nuns the Clan had waylaid a few months before and taken as 'Wives-Improper.' That's what the Clan leader called them. Wilf, his name was. Wilf Tobinger. A bona fide wit. Would've done well as a Brit. The nuns were trained nurses, but neither of them was witty in the least. They were frightfully earnest—like you, Jellybean. After a few days, I was able to hoist myself up onto the back of a knock-kneed mare and bid adieu to my hosts. Couldn't wait to leave. Sisters Long-Suffering and Holier-than-Thou were killing me with kindness and platitudes."

"So you didn't rescue them?" Zyla asked. "The nuns who saved your ass?"

"Don't like nuns," Lucky said, "not even the ass-saving kind. You're the exception."

"I'm not a nun," Ji-ji told him.

"Oh yes you are," Lucky argued. "Most nunnified person I've ever met."

Ji-ji didn't let herself be distracted: "So the nuns are still there then? With the Clansmen?"

"Oh, for *god's sake*!" Lucky exclaimed. "That's the lesson you take from the story? Yes, the poor little nuns are still there. . . . Oh for *fuck's sake*! Don't look at me like that. What do you want me to say? Okay, I broke into the shed and tore the chains from their ankles with my teeth while—"

Ji-ji gasped. "The sisters were kept in a *shed*? In *chains*?"

"Oh Christ! Wish I'd never brought it up. How many times you expect me to rescue people?"

None of them got to bed till close to three in the morning. Lucky offered to sleep in the kitchen but Ji-ji insisted he take Afarra's room. She showed him where it was, and the two of them stood there for a minute looking at the mural Ji-ji had painted.

"It looks just like her," Lucky said. "I gave her an orange once."

"I know," Ji-ji replied. "She never forgot it. She kept the peel in a box Tiro made for her. It turned brown and shriveled up, but she still loved it."

"Let's hope I feel the same way about my balls," he said, wistfully.

"She's still alive," Ji-ji had insisted. "At least, I think she is."

She waited for him to mock her; he didn't. Instead, he looked at her with his disconcerting, Lotter-blue eyes and said, "Man Cryday thinks she is too. It's why she wanted me to come and help with the search. She'll hit the roof when she hears about Chaff Man. You know Uncle Dreg helped get him and his family un-indentured? And that's how he repays him. Even Dregulahmo, the great pacifist wizard, would want to slit his throat."

One last question hung in the air between them. She forced herself to ask it. "Bonbon. Man Cryday said you never found him."

"Sorry," Lucky said. "It wasn't for lack of trying. If he's alive, and if your suspicions about him being like you are true, they'll probably have him in the Decipula in Armistice."

Ji-ji wanted to ask him to tell her more about it, but she was afraid of what he might say.

Lucky spoke again: "Witnessing you fly like that, Ji-ji, was . . . amazing."

She waited for him to add something to undercut her or himself. He didn't.

|||||||||||||||||

A few days later, Ji-ji, wearing the same disguise she'd worn to the museum, was driven through D.C.'s dodgy backstreets, escorted by Lucky and Otto. Otto's car was an ancient European model about four sizes too small for him. He sat hunched over in the driver's seat.

"The Friends are very PC," Lucky said, "like to divvy up the leadership. Paul's Black, Alice is White, but that's the extent of the difference between them. Two peas in a pod."

"What have you got against Alice and Paul?" Otto asked. "They're over the moon about her progress. Can't wait to see her unfurl. Maybe they'll ask you to flit around for a while, Jellybean."

Zyla had already warned Ji-ji that "flitting around," as Otto put it, could be on the cards. She hadn't taken to the air since she'd crashed into Lucky. Without the Dream Master, embroiled in Dreamfleet business since she'd made her first tentative attempt at getting off the ground, she'd had no success. Yesterday, Zyla joked that her Secret Hopefuls liked to keep their hopefulness a secret.

"You'll have to excuse Otto," Lucky said. "He's a true believer. Don't put pressure on her, Otto. She'll fly away, and then where will the Friends be? Up shit creek without an angel to paddle."

"Lucky's jealous," Otto said, peering through the car's parsimonious windshield. It was drizzling. Apart from the rhythmic squeak and greasy half circles they produced, the wipers didn't appear to be functional. "He's stopped believing in anything. I got a few decades on Lucky, and on you too. Take Otto Knash's word for it, it's a whole lot more satisfying to believe in something than it is trying to persuade your friends *not* to believe in anything. He knows it too. S'why he hangs out with people like us, hoping it'll rub off."

"People like us?" Ji-ji said, puzzled.

"The faithful," Otto replied.

"I'm not one of the faithful," Ji-ji said.

"Course you are," Otto stated. "Couldn't fly otherwise. . . . Hey, we're here."

In the unlit street, the building looked like an abandoned school or a church. They drove around back and exited the vehicle. At a small side entrance, they were met by an armed guard.

"*Alis volat propriis,*" the guard said, to which Otto responded, "She flies with her own wings."

Lucky whispered to Ji-ji, "At least our fanatical Friends got something right."

"They're expecting you," the guard said. "General meeting's still in progress. Take the back staircase and go directly to the large conference room. Special gathering's in there."

Zyla had explained why she, Ji-ji, wouldn't be able to attend the general meeting. It made sense that only a small circle of thoroughly vetted Friends would be permitted to see her, but it also reminded her how little liberty or independence she enjoyed in this Liberty Independent.

"Welcome to All Souls and Sinners Crypt," Otto told Ji-ji. "Was a morgue during one of the early metaflu outbreaks. It's haunted. Seen a ghost here myself. Headless guy with a runny nose."

Lucky and Otto led Ji-ji down wide wooden stairs to the basement. The staircase was almost pitch-dark. Otto switched on a flashlight. At the foot of the stairs and the end of a long, tunnel-like corridor, the area opened up. From the look and smell of things, this place had been flooded as frequently as the practice coop. Voices echoed down the corridor from somewhere nearby. She heard drumming too. In addition to local and regional leaders of the organization, Otto said, Friends came to the meeting from the Unaligned Territories, the SuperStates, the Cradle, and other places around the world. Ji-ji wished she could join them.

Otto opened the door to a large room. In the center sat a huge oval table surrounded by about two dozen chairs. Tiro stood at one end of the table with

Ben and Germaine. He greeted her with a strained smile. Someone must have told him Lucky was visiting—Ben or Germaine probably; he didn't look surprised to see Lotter's former lieutenant. Lucky had visited with Ben and Germaine the day before yesterday. Nevertheless, the couple greeted their young English friend as if they hadn't seen him in years.

Ji-ji tried to see who else she recognized. She spotted Doc Riff and Dr. Narayanan talking with Coach Mackie and a man Ji-ji thought could be Mackie's son, Monty. Three Friends she'd met at the spur-of-the-moment induction ceremony for her and Afarra in Monticello were there too: Otumbo Jehovah, Mad Cleo, and Terence Pham. Zyla was in a heated discussion with the co-leaders—Alice, a striking, white-haired White woman in her late sixties or early seventies Ji-ji had met before, and Paul, a compact, Black man with a kind face, who looked to be in his fifties. The co-leaders acknowledged her with a smile before Zyla began haranguing them again. Whatever Zyla was saying upset all three of them. A moment later, the co-leaders left the room.

Ji-ji headed toward Zyla but Tiro intercepted her. He greeted her awkwardly and asked if he could speak with her. Reluctantly, she agreed. He led her to the other end of the room. He looked so worn out that she was tempted to comfort him. She resisted; she'd done that too often.

Ji-ji had planned to let him begin, but her excitement got the better of her. "I flew. For real this time. Not like what you saw. Didn't hover for a second or two either. I *flew*. Was pretty ugly though. Nearly crashed into the bars of the cage."

"I know. Zyla told Germaine who told Ben who told me. It's great news, Ji, it really is. Anyhow, I know you're sick of hearing me say this, but I wanted to say I'm sorry one more time. It was my fault she ran off. I know I can never make it right, but it won't stop me from trying."

They'd wound up in front of an enormous framed painting. Ji-ji recognized the scene at once: Uncle Dreg's Death Day at Execution Circle. Painted from the point of view of seeds in the viewing coops, it was supposed to be uplifting. The fairskin father-men stood stiffly on the penal platform dressed in their ceremonial robes. None of them looked like the real father-men on the 437th. The rest of the scene wasn't accurate either. Uncle Dreg wasn't stripped down to his underwear, his hair wasn't smeared with muck, and his Seeing Eye necklace hadn't been exchanged for the two huge wooden balls the guards hung around his neck. The steaders looked terrified, as if they'd already been defeated; the seeds were cheering. There was a sort of halo around the wizard. Sylvie, the giant penal tree, loomed over everything like the giant hand of God.

The purple tags etched with the names of the lynched looked more like purple earrings than purple tears. One of Sylvie's boughs was broken, and Chaff Man the executioner was standing a little ways off from Uncle Dreg. Chaff Man had his yappy dog, Circus, under his arm, but you couldn't see his expression due to his executioner's hood. Another inaccurate detail. The artist seemed confused about the executioner's role. In reality, Cropmaster Herring had tried to lynch Chaff Man and Circus alongside Uncle Dreg, but the painting told you nothing about that. Roll the action forward a few seconds and Herring would blast a hole the size of a fist in the wizard's head. Soon, Uncle Dreg's brains would ooze from his skull, Herring's bullet would ricochet off Sylvie, and the cropmaster would be dead too. Those who looked at the sentimental painting would never understand how harrowing the experience had been. The artist, who hadn't witnessed the travesty, had made it palatable. Ji-ji decided it was one of the most dangerous paintings she'd ever seen.

Paradoxically, the painting's deception made her conclude that she needed to be as honest with Tiro as he'd been with her. "I can't forgive you," she said. "Not yet. Maybe one day. I know what they'll do to her, you see." Tiro looked as if she'd struck him and moved to walk away. She reached out to stop him, said, "But I also know what it cost you to tell me the truth. You need help, Tiro."

"I got it under control now," he said.

Ji-ji wanted to argue, then she realized there was no point. He was where he was and she was where she was. Sometimes you can't change something as stubborn as that.

"It's not all on you," she admitted. "I was the one had to see the museum. An' I was the one reached out to Sloppy during the Freedom Race. She an' Dip came as a pair, and Dip was always a friend to me. I guess Lucky was right." Tiro looked puzzled. "The other day he said the friend of my friend is my enemy. Guess it was always true in Sloppy's case."

Tiro looked at Lucky, laughing with Ben and Germaine. "Marcus says he can't be trusted."

"Who? Lucky? What are you talking about? He saved my life."

"So he claims," Tiro said.

Ji-ji's temper flared: "You two are *idiots*! I was *there*. . . ." She happened to glance at the painting again. "That painting's awful," she said.

"Yeah, it is," he said. "Circus looks good though."

They smiled then fell silent. Ji-ji noticed that the artist hadn't included the outcasts' viewing coop up the hill on the rim of Execution Circle's amphitheater. Afarra had watched the execution from there with the other Serverseeds.

She'd escaped the steaders, but the executioner had made his way to the Dream and snatched her anyway.

Just then, Laughing Tree and Ink entered the room. Georgie-Porge trailed behind them. Ji-ji and Tiro were walking over to greet them when Ji-ji happened to catch sight of someone through the door where Otto stood guard. "I'm late for the general meeting," the girl said. "Where is it?" Ji-ji tore past the fly-boys and grabbed the girl's hand. Despite warnings from Otto that this meeting was off-limits, Ji-ji pulled her inside. "It's okay," Ji-ji called back to him, "she's a close friend."

Ji-ji led her into a small alcove. "It's *me*!" Ji-ji said, keeping her voice low and removing her contagion mask. "This is a wig." To prove her point, she lifted it up at the hairline. "Tulip, don't you recognize me? It's Ji-ji!"

Tulip looked as if she were about to faint. She grabbed the wall behind her to steady herself. "They told me you were *dead*!" she whispered. "After the race. You died. We had a service."

Ji-ji explained that she had to lie low, keep herself and her back a secret. Tulip, astonished, touched Ji-ji's cheek then hugged so much breath out of her that Ji-ji, laughing, had to pull away.

Tulip looked much the same. She still braided her hair into a coronet on her head, and still had a strong runner's body, but something had changed.

"I got inducted," Tulip told her. "I'm a Friend of Freedom. Got sworn in. Thought they could help me with something. Can't believe you're alive, Ji-ji! News like that is usually vice in versa for seeds. The ones you thought was alive turn out to be dead."

Tulip looked around for Afarra, asked how she was doing. Ji-ji realized that her fellow runner was one of the few people who would understand why having Sloppy in the mix terrified her.

"Sloppy Delilah took her. Seems like she's still with that executioner—the one we saw during the race in the back of those picker trucks."

"Sloppy!" Tulip hissed. "That bitch? She *hated* Afarra! Said she was a Cloth. Wouldn't run next to her. Betrayed us too, I figure. Ratted on the runners. What's Sloppy doing with Afarra?"

Ji-ji summarized the situation as best she could. Tulip seemed to be listening at times; at other times, she drifted off into her own world. Ji-ji put it down to the shock of seeing her. Gradually, however, she concluded it was something else. "You okay, Tulip?"

"Oh . . . yeah. Sorry. I'll search for Afarra soon as I get Rosemary an' Thyme settled. Looks like the Friends found a fairskin lady agreed to take us in for now. I seen her when you pulled me in here. That one over there with the funny hat an' jacket."

"Her name's Mary Macdonald. Goes by Mackie," Ji told her. She decided against adding the part about Mackie being her first fly-coach. Better to take it a step at a time. "Mackie's real nice."

"That's a relief. Don't get many good fairskins in my experience. . . . Not many good duskies either. . . . Friends is very religious—you know that?" Tulip looked around furtively. "Not me. I'm faking it. But those after-service suppers is *awesome*. Real meat they got. No ration cards required! Little Thyme loves beef more'n fresh eggs, which is saying something. So I sneak a few bites into my pockets. Religious don't care, long as you feed the hungry an' say 'Amen.'"

Tulip went on to say she'd heard from their fellow runner, Big Pike.

"Did she find her father-mate?" Ji-ji asked.

"Yeah, she found him. Charlie Fortinum. Bald as a coot an' ugly as a weasel, Pike said, remember? He was dead. After those steaders sent him to a labor camp in the Delta for Unnatural Affiliation, he didn't last long. Don't hear of fairskins getting punished much, so it's refreshing. Pike's cut up about it, though, so don't tell her I said that. . . . A bunch of fairskins here tonight. Almost as many as us—you noticed? Didn't think they gave a shit about seeds. Guess some do."

"Where's Pike now?"

"In the Dream somewhere. I'm hoping to bump into her if she joins up. Figure she will, seeing as how she ain't scared of nothing, not even snarlcats. Got a favor to ask her. Remember how she carried that little runner Simply Danglefoot—the one lost her foot in that ant trap? Slung her over her shoulder like she weighed less than a liveborn?" Tulip choked back tears.

Ji-ji rubbed her friend's arm to comfort her. "What is it, Tulip? What's happened?"

"My brother, Clown. He's here in the Dream."

Ji-ji's heart went out to her. Clown was to Tulip what Lotter was to her. A monster.

"We don't got much, but it was enough for us an' we were happy. Mam an' me, an' little Rosemary an' Thyme. My kith-n-kins, all together. Remember me telling you 'bout Thyme? The twin that got stuck in Mam's seed canal an' it left an impression? Rosemary's real bright for seven, but Thyme's got a few brain stems missing, so she don't always know which way is up. That Clown . . . he come an' took advantage while Rosemary an' me were out getting food a coupla weeks ago."

Out of the corner of her eye, Ji-ji saw Marcus dash into the room. He pulled Tiro aside and spoke with him. They looked over in her direction, as if they were speaking about her. She couldn't worry about that now. "What happened?" Ji-ji asked.

"We got back an' found Mam lying on the floor. Head bashed to pulp."

"Oh no, Tulip! That's terrible!"

"Neck twisted round so the back was the front. Wouldn't hardly know it was her cos her face was pretty much obliterated, but it was Mam all right, with her apron on like she was baking the bastard a pie. An' she was wearing the skirt I give her. Blood everywhere. Even on little Thyme." Ji-ji held her friend, whose whole body trembled. "Clown wasn't there but I could smell him. Told the cops he did it, but the law never listens to folks like us. I knew it was him cos Thyme keeps saying '*Cown, cown!*' cos she can't say the letter *l* to save her life. Mam's lucre jar was empty. Clown knew where she hid it cos she was always dipping into it on his account. Couldn't figure out how he got off the planting. Then I find out Mam petitioned the planting to let him roam Free! Still don't know how she managed it. She must've forgave him for that poking he did on me when I was a seedling. Poked the twins too. Mam knew."

Ji-ji gave her the only meaningful thing she had to offer: "I lost my mam to murder too. I ever tell you that?"

Tulip frowned. "Can't remember if you told me or not. . . . Everything's a swirl. Murder's the worst thing in the world. Keeps repeating in your head. It's dumb to forgive people. That's what I told Big Pike 'bout her Charlie. He may've been decent, I said, but he was still a steader. A striper never changes his stripes an' a clown don't change his spots either. So I'm thinking it wouldn't take much for Big Pike to put Clown in a choke hold an'——"

Zyla approached then. "I'm sorry to interrupt," she said. "Alice and Paul are about to conclude the general meeting. They want to introduce you to this small circle of Friends. Do you feel up to it?"

Ji-ji nodded and introduced Zyla to Tulip. "Zyla used to teach me at the Planting legacy school. She's more like my big sister now though."

Visibly moved, Zyla thanked Ji-ji. She extended her hand to Tulip.

"Any friend of Ji-ji's is a friend of mine," Tulip said.

With a teacher's instinct, Zyla said, "Are you okay, Tulip?"

"Been a long coupla weeks," Tulip replied.

Ji-ji didn't want to leave Tulip yet. "I'll join you in a moment, Zyla," she said.

Zyla nodded. As she stepped away, she invited Tulip to come and visit them very soon.

Ji-ji looked around the room. She couldn't abandon Tulip. Not only was she in a fragile state, she'd been hit with a resurrected friend. Soon, she'd see Ji-ji's back on display too. She looked for Mackie but couldn't find her. She caught sight of Laughing Tree and Ink and beckoned them over.

"Tulip, this is Laughing Tree, and this is his friend Ink. You can trust 'em both."

Tulip's face lit up. "I remember you! From the Freedom Race an' the Jefferson Coop."

"That's us," Tree said.

Ji-ji wished Tulip hadn't brought up the Jefferson Coop, where Ink had his accident, but it didn't seem to bother them. She asked them to look after Tulip, saying she was new to the Friends and had been through a very rough time recently.

"Sure," Ink said. "Us rough-timers gotta stick together, right Tree?"

As Ji-ji moved off with Zyla, she heard Tulip ask if Tree was available anytime soon. "Cos if you are, there's a favor you could do for me. Won't take long for someone strong as you, an' I'll help. So will Rosemary and Thyme. I'm teaching 'em how to homicide. You scared of clowns?"

||||||||||||||||

As soon as Alice and Paul joined them again in the conference room, the select group of Friends were led through another door, down a tunnel, and into a lofty, barrel-ceilinged space they called the crypt. Alice and Paul asked Ji-ji to step forward into the center of the circle. She'd known the request was coming, but being stared at by about two dozen Friends, some of whom were strangers, made her feel exposed and clumsy. For the first time, she saw Corcoran, the former wing commander, standing next to the co-leaders. He saluted her encouragingly.

Ji-ji removed her cape and shirt, grateful that the wide-banded *libby* bra covered much of her torso. She looked ordinary from the front, so only those standing behind her murmured when they saw her back and shoulders. Even in the fluctuating light from the candles and oil lamps, they could make out the elaborate root system on her back, and the cratered flesh that resembled eye sockets.

When she began to unfurl, a collective gasp went up. She hadn't intended to do more than that. Asked Zyla to tell Alice and Paul that's all she would do— unfurl quickly then furl back up.

To her dismay, her wings mounted a rebellion. They ambushed her with one flap! *Two!* Somehow, they bent her legs and thrust her up into the air. She hovered some twenty feet above them, her wings brushing the ceiling, her feet level with their upturned heads!

Tulip clapped a hand over her mouth in amazement. Ink screamed Ji-ji's name as Laughing Tree roared in delight. Ben and Germaine looked stunned. Tiro and Marcus, standing side by side, stared up at her and clapped and cheered with the rest. Alice and Paul nodded like proud parents. Neither Zyla nor Lucky looked as thrilled as the others did.

Obliged to hover above the Friends for about thirty seconds before she could get her body under control, Ji-ji descended gradually. Friends who'd crowded in to watch her took a step back to accommodate her wingspan.

As soon as Ji-ji's feet touched the ground, Lucky came up beside her. "Quite a show," he said, as wild applause and ecstatic cheering echoed through the crypt.

"Wasn't deliberate," she told him. "They did their own thing."

"Won't be the case much longer," he warned. He sounded genuinely concerned. "You've opened Pandora's box, Jellybean. Can't shove the genie back now."

A chant arose, led by Paul and Alice: "*Alis volat propriis! She flies with her own wings!*"

"See, what did I tell you?" Lucky said. "It's started."

|||||||||||||

The Friends of Freedom sat around the table in the conference room. Having spent the first hour discussing what "this" meant (Ji-ji was the "this," or rather her back was), they'd then spent the next hour discussing the dire situation they were in. The two steader factions Man Cryday had told her about in Memoria were as obsessed with flight as ever. The Literalists believed they needed to cleanse the Territories of Toteppi, Alice said, to avoid the existential threat prophesied in their *One True Text*. The Futurist steaders, on the other hand, wanted to harness flight for their own purposes. Rumors that Sessill Morson, the Lord-Father of Lord-Fathers, had ordered the grand inquisitor to build an army of buzzbuzz drones more advanced than anything in the Disunited States had been substantiated. Meanwhile, Paul added, the SuperStates and Independents, still suffering from the repercussions of the Sequel and plagued by instability brought about by climate change, pandemics, and other calamities, were more reluctant than ever to risk another civil war.

Zyla cut in while Paul was speaking. "We know all this. Tell her what you want her to do. Spit it out so she can make a decision."

"No need for that accusatory tone, Zy," Alice said. "You and I want the same thing."

Alice proceeded to invite Ji-ji to travel with her, Paul, Sean Corcoran, Zyla, and a few others in a delegation to the Eastern SuperState. Ji-ji would reveal herself in New York at a meeting of the Friends of Freedom like she had tonight. Her choice, of course, Alice emphasized.

Ji-ji knew what awaited her. Lucky was right. Pandora's box was unlocked.

And yet wasn't this the fight she'd dreamed of waging, a fight for a cause that formed the core of who she was?

"I don't know," Ji-ji said. "I'll need to think about it."

Paul interceded again: "You can't imagine how important a symbol you could be to—"

Lucky jumped in: "Perhaps she doesn't want to be owned by you lot."

"Who is this guy?" Sean Corcoran asked. "Is he a Friend?"

"Yes," Lucky replied, "I'm Jellybean's friend. Man Cryday's too."

Alice agreed: "Lucas Dyson has a right to be here. He's proven himself worthy, which is why Cryday trusts him. And I trust Man Cryday. With my life." A miffed Corcoran shifted in his seat.

Alice directed her subsequent comments to Ji-ji. "The situation is deteriorating faster than we anticipated. Arundale Lotter is being hailed as the Twelfth. Grand Inquisitor Worthy is grooming him to assume control of the Territorial army. The cult that's forming around Lotter—and, indeed, around the entire planting and its unique penal tree—is gathering strength. More steader pilgrims than ever are making the trip to the 437th to pay homage to Sylvie. Lotter's new position has put your birth planting on the radar as a major power center in the Homestead Territories.

"You have little reason to trust us after we kept things from you. Zyla is right to be upset with us. We should have told you who took Afarra, but we knew you were getting close to being . . . complete. I know what it's like to be owned, Ji-ji. I was a Wife-Proper, married to a steader at fifteen. I lived on a planting. I know it's not the same for Wives-Proper as it is for seeds. But I do know what it's like to be held against my will and abused by the bastard who controls everything I do. I saw with my own eyes the horror of the planting system. I never forget it."

Paul saw Alice's distress and took over: "Right now, the steaders assume you're either dead or disabled. We've fed them both stories to put them off the scent. But the kidnapping of Afarra has changed the calculus. We don't know whether the executioner is working alone or if he was put up to it by Lotter. Lotter is already managing the drug trade for the Supreme Council. His meteoric rise and the steaders' attempt to mythologize the 437th are designed to serve as a counternarrative—an antidote to the stories swirling around Uncle Dreg's Death Day sermon, his great-nephew's success in the Dream Coop, and . . ." Paul paused. ". . . and rumors of a powerful mutancy bred on that same planting and seeded by the Twelfth. We're not sure whether they're referring to you, Ji-ji, or to other hybrids the Supreme Council in Armistice may claim Lotter seeded."

Alice spoke again: "We think the letter Worthy wrote did indeed detail a plan to invade the Dream. We have every reason to believe we were successful in averting an attack last fall. We also suspect, however, that the invasion of the Mall on the day your friend was taken was a dry run. A rehearsal for a more coordinated invasion of the city."

Mackie was doubtful: "Surely the Supreme Council wouldn't flout the non-aggression pact?"

"They never counted on rural resistance," Corcoran pointed out. "Urban rebellions were one thing; they expected those. Rural rebellions are a totally different kettle of fish."

"Sean's right," Ben said. "Rural communities are declaring themselves Seed Sanctuaries. Most are met with aggression and quashed, but some of them are defying Armistice. Urban Independents like Atlanta, Chicago, Salt Lake, and Austin are lending their support to these rural uprisings. But if Armistice perfects these new drones, the dream of a Reunited States will die."

"If they capture D.C.," Paul added, "it will set us back decades. If the E.S.S. sees you, and if we can somehow get word to the plantings that Dreg's prophecies have come to pass, many seeds will be inspired to rise up. We can build on the momentum Dregulahmo's Death Day speech has inspired. . . . So, Ji-ji, when do you think you'll have a decision for us?"

Ji-ji looked around the room. The weight of the role they wanted her to assume pressed down upon her. She didn't know what she was or how she came to be the way she was. And yet . . . She saw Lotter hold the disgusting Color Wheel to Bonbon's beautiful face; she saw the seed symbols like bullet holes in seeds' chests; she heard the obscene steader rhyme in her head: "*The only way for a seed to be Free / Is to swing on high from a penal tree.*"

"The day after tomorrow," Ji-ji said. "I'll have an answer for you then."

"Thank you," Alice said. "Whatever you decide, we will keep searching for your friend."

As the meeting dispersed, Paul rushed up to Ji-ji and took her hand in his. Tears streamed down his face. "My son was killed in a raid. If you make this sacrifice, it will never be forgotten."

After Paul moved off, Marcus came up to her and whispered in her ear that he and Tiro had something very important to tell her. "Trust me, Ji-ji. This is big. Huge."

The urgency in his voice convinced her to agree. If they had news about Afarra, she wanted to be the first to hear it. She checked that Coach Mackie was taking Tulip home, then she told Lucky she would be riding with Marcus. "You sure?" Lucky said. "Yes, I'm sure," she replied. "Suit yourself," he said.

She couldn't tell if she'd hurt his feelings. He'd stay the night with Ben and Germaine, search for Afarra again tomorrow, and be back at the Aerie by early evening. "Just as well," he said. "Zyla's getting a bit fed-up with the British invasion."

A short time later, Ji-ji sat in the front passenger seat of the old Dreamfleet van. Marcus drove and Tiro sat behind him. One of the Friends' vans followed with four newly assigned bodyguards. Otto brought up the rear of the convoy.

"Well?" Ji-ji said to them. "Have you got news about Afarra?"

"No," Tiro replied. Her heart fell; she'd been tricked. "It's *good* news . . . about someone else."

"What we're trying to tell you," Marcus said, "is you've been lied to."

Stressed to the limit, Ji-ji lost her temper. "How is that *good* news? Who lied to me? The Friends? You? Or did you fail to share some other critical detail with me?"

Tiro spoke fast, his excitement palpable: "Ji, you remember how Zyla an' me told you that stuff? Well, we were wrong, only we didn't know it. Didn't find out till after you an' me spoke tonight. By that time, Marcus' friend had called with the truth."

Ji-ji's stomach did a somersault. "What 'stuff'? What are you talking about?"

Tiro took a deep breath and slowed down. "Zyla got word that Charra was dead, right? We came to see you an' broke the news. Only—"

"Only it was a goddam *lie*!" Marcus exclaimed. "T says he doesn't think Zyla knew the truth but we're damn sure Man Cryday did. I did my own investigating. Got friends down in the Madlands. We found her, Ji-ji. We found your sister. She's alive!"

"Charra? Not dead?"

Tiro could barely contain his joy: "Alive an' well an' leading raids in the Madlands!"

"Leading a whole goddam movement, you mean," Marcus added. "An' there's something else. Me an' Tiro, we're taking you to see her, if you wanna go."

Ji-ji could hardly breathe. "You know where she is?"

"She was in Norfolk originally," Tiro said, "only your mam thought it was North Fork, remember? Well now she's deeper inside the Madlands in a community called Turnabout. Marcus an' me can take turns with the driving. A few days there, stay a week or so, a few days back."

"Timing's perfect," Marcus told her. "Fleet's on hiatus while fall season's on hold. The Dreamer Coalition in Congress got their way. Fleet's under investigation for that shit went down last year. They're rooting out secessionists. Out to prove Yardley's a traitor an' reinstate Corker. The Friends are behind it. The

Dream Master's been working with Corker an' the Friends too, from what I hear. Though if I'm-a-God's in on the plan, guess we shouldn't put too much stock in the outcome."

"Don't listen to him," Tiro said. "Marcus has never met a move he liked that he didn't come up with himself. Main thing is, we won't be flying for a while, but they still gotta pay us."

"We must tread carefully," Marcus advised. "Do what we want to do not what they expect us to do. If they find out you've discovered the truth, they'll bundle you off before——"

"But why would Man Cryday lie to me? An' what about Charra's book of nursery rhymes?"

"Couldn't tell you why she did it," Marcus said. "But T's great-aunt is weird as shit, you know that."

"Zyla'll go nuts when she finds out the truth," Tiro said. "Could be the Friends are in on it too."

"Always assuming little Miss Clobershay doesn't know already," Marcus said.

Tiro, irritated, turned on him: "How many times I gotta tell you, man? Zyla doesn't know! You weren't there when we had to break the news. I was. No way she knew the truth."

Ji-ji, reeling from the disclosure, struggled to put the pieces together: "You think Charra could've left the book with Man Cryday when she had the wex-cision?"

"Yeah," Tiro said. "Bet that's what happened. Marcus has been trying to tell me we can't trust the Friends. But they're not all bad. I'd trust Ben an' Germaine with my life. Zyla too."

Marcus cut in: "You gotta see the Friends for what they are, Ji-ji. Asking you to perform like that tonight like some circus animal! I mean, what the hell? They're out to control you, *use* you. Hate to agree with Lucky, but he was right. They wanna *own* you. From what I hear from my friends down in the Madlands, Charra's not exactly the compliant type. The Friends are shit-scared she'll encourage you to have a mind of your own. Charra has her own ideas about how to wage this liberation war. The Friends of Freedom want you to be their little dancing bear."

"What've dancing bears got to do with anything?" Tiro asked.

Marcus sighed, indulgently, said, "Take it easy, bro. S'a metaphor."

"A lousy one. . . ." Tiro looked back at Ji. "You okay?"

"I don't know." The news was starting to sink in. "Charra's *alive*!" she muttered to herself.

"She's alive all right," Marcus assured her. "You ready to escape these bozos an' sneak off to the Madlands tomorrow? Afterward, if you still fancy a trip to New York with Frenemies Inc., it'll be your choice, not theirs. The timing'll be up to you. So . . . what'll it be?"

"Give her time, Marcus. She needs to take it all in."

"Afarra!" Ji-ji cried. How could she have forgotten? "What about the search?"

Marcus shook his head. "Look, Ji-ji. Every goddam Friend is out looking for her. A few less won't make a difference. An' there's no way you can look yourself. Too risky. You honestly think the Friends'll take no for an answer if you decide not to traipse up to the E.S.S.? With people like them, it's *always* about manipulation."

Tiro told him to shut up. "Let her think, man. You sound like the Friends."

"The hell I do!" Marcus declared, hotly. "River's a mile wide between me an' them."

Marcus presented his final argument: "Okay, Ji-ji, last thing to consider. Who better to help us find Afarra than Charra? Could be she'll come herself or send her best men to help in the search."

Ji-ji glanced behind them. The Friends' van, loaded with bodyguards, sat on their tail.

"I don't need time to decide," Ji-ji said. "Charra's my sister. I'm going to the Madlands. And then I'm coming back to search for Afarra an' Bonbon. After that, I'll decide about the E.S.S."

Marcus slapped the wheel and yelled, "Yeah, baby! Bitch is flying with her *own* wings now!" He glanced at his side mirror. "Gotta get rid of a few hangers-on tomorrow. Gotta get rid of Lotter Junior, too. Freaky how much those steader bastards look like each other."

"Lucky's not a steader," Ji-ji said. "He's not a Friend either. He's a merce-nary."

"Is that meant to be reassuring?" Marcus asked. "Sure looks like the Twelfth. You know there were rumors he was Lotter's son? Lotter could be the progenitor of all kinds o' shit."

"Shut up," Tiro said. "You're just talking crazy now."

Ji-ji reflected upon what he'd said. "You really think she could help us find Afarra?"

"Course she could," Marcus said. "She's your sister. She'd do anything for you."

"An' you know how to get there?"

"Sure we do," Tiro said. "I know it's not the same as finding Afarra, Ji. But it's like it's the next best thing. Even their names rhyme—Afarra, Charra. Yeah, that was dumb. I'm excited is all."

"It'll be fun," Marcus told her. "It's what friends do. A vacation to the malaria-ravaged, gator-infested swamps of the Madlands. Only one more thing we need to make it perfect."

"What's that?" Tiro asked.

"A halfway decent map. You got one, bro?"

16 THROUGH A BACK WINDOW

Occasionally, when Black-Hood-Without-the-Hood talks at her, Afarra sees the Dimmer-dead escape from the gash of his mouth. The Dimmers flee from his grave-hole and zip around the shed like buzzbuzz drones. The lynched dead have ropes around their necks; the pyred ones are burned to the bone. Afarra is roped too. Not her neck, her hands and feet. She doesn't know how long they've held her, but she sees the sun go up and down through the shed's warped shutters and tries to count like Elly taught her. Counting isn't something she's good at. She's getting better at other things. Like thinking. Wizard-in-Her-Head is teaching her. Not just words either. She tries to listen, but it's hard to listen when you're scared to death.

Black-Hood-Without-the-Hood and Sloppy-Call-Me-Delilah live in the falling-down house. Afarra lives in the falling-down shed out back. Black-Hood-Without-the-Hood stomps around like a father-man. Sloppy-Call-Me-Delilah stomps around when he's away, creeps around when he's not.

Afarra is tethered by a rope wrapped round her waist so she can ease herself up on a bucket to pee. Can shit in it too, but she can't wipe herself unless her wrists are untied and they've remembered to leave her a wad of paper or water and a cloth, which doesn't happen often. She knocked the bucket over once. Sloppy-Call-Me-Delilah was furious when she slipped on the piss. But she undid Afarra's wrists and let her clean it up, and she gave her a dry shift to wear.

Sloppy-Call-Me-Delilah brings her slop to eat. Gray mush with hunks of gristle in it. Sometimes with flies or ants, sometimes not. Occasionally, a crust of bread. Afarra eats the bread a crumb at a time. Makes it last for hours unless the *rats!rats!rats!* invade. If they do, she stuffs the bread in her mouth and swallows so the rats can't nibble it out of her.

Underneath where they've tied her wrists and ankles—bracelets of raw flesh. "Don't scratch, Cloth," Call-Me-Delilah warns. "You'll get infected an' croak. How come you're so unreasonable? You trying to commit suicide?"

So far, Afarra hasn't said anything to them, apart from Elly's name, which she repeats over and over: "EllyEllyEllyEllyElly" . . . Whole sentences are coming easier in her head than they used to, but she doesn't tell her jailers about this. *Best to keep your thoughts to yourself, child,* his Seeing Eyes say. Apart from the wizard's necklace, Elly's name is her only self-defense.

At night, the Dimmer-boy visits. She looks in the corner of the shed and there he is, neck snapped, head lolling. His mule ears puzzle her before she remembers him from the practice coop when she is lying in the nest next to Elly. The Dimmer tribe is punishing her. She'd promised to save them and they know she lied. The boy with the mule ears and egg-white eyes is their messenger. He is too sad to be afraid of. In the terrifying shed, he is better company than the rats.

Afarra misses her friend tonight. "Elly, can you hear me?" Her voice turns wizard-y as she does what she promised and shares some of her strength. "*Do not overthink things,*" Afarra's wizard voice tells Elly as it leaps over the distance fence. "*Let the Freedom Twins lead the way.*" The wizard values persistence (his word, not hers). Over the wizard's shoulder, Afarra sees Elly rise—*FlapFlap!* Her friends and theirs clap and cheer. So beautiful! Afarra is glad she didn't miss it.

And now, Afarra's captors have come to the shed to torment her again.

"She look younger to you?" Black-Hood-Without-the-Hood asks.

"I guess," Call-Me-Delilah replies.

"*Damn!* How'd she shrink like that? She a witch like Uncle Dreg?"

"He was a wizard," Call-Me-Delilah says, too softly for him to hear.

"That's it. I've had enough of this procrastinating. Take those eyes off her. *Now!*"

"You're big an' strong, Mr. Holleran," Slop-Delilah says. "You'll be better at snatching 'em from her than me." Afarra hears Slop add, under her breath, "An' you're a goddam executioner, for fuck's sake."

"How many times I gotta tell you?" he says. "His beads is powerful. I seen some of the tricks he can do with 'em. You mess with shit like that an' you turn into a frog or something."

"You're right, Mr. Holleran," Call-Me-Delilah says. "That would be a real tragedy."

"You insulting me, bitch?"

"No!" Call-Me-Delilah issues another warning to Afarra: "Mr. Holleran'll poke you again if you don't take 'em off *right now*! Cloth, you listening to me?" Afarra shakes her head. "*Ha!* Got you! See that, Mr. Holleran? She heard me! Her eye-rolling was an act. Told you she's not an epilepsy or a retard. Seen enough of 'em to know when someone's faking it."

Black-Hood-Without-the-Hood cups his hand over his crotch and stares at Afarra, who's seen that look before. Last time he had it, he drove his *gottadoit-now!* up her seed canal. She thinks of Tulip's sister Thyme who left an impression on Tulip's mam with her head. Black-Hood-Without-the-Hood has left a similar impression on Afarra (not with his head). Even when she's alone, she's worried a part of him is still wedged up in there. Has to jab her fingers up inside her soreness to check it isn't. She's lucky. Her bleeding is on the wane again. After they snatched her, as a precaution, Afarra shrunk down and decided not to let her bleeding cycle start. That was Lua's problem. Too much bloodletting. Females got to be careful. Blood can murder them otherwise.

"Time to teach you a lesson," Not-Slop says, sliding a knife from behind her back. "I gotta cut you if you don't spill the beans. Lord knows I don't want to, but you given us no choice."

In the flickering candlelight, Not-Slop's knife is longer than the knife Elly used to slash Matty-now-Lucky's throat. Elly failed cos Matty was Lucky, that's what Elly said. Afarra knows she herself isn't lucky anymore. That's why they snatched her from the Mall while the Mall-man with the flower-blossom ear watched. She's busy being *Not Here, Not Now,* which is why she doesn't think about how ruthless the angry kitchen-seed is with knives. (She's seen her slash the necks of chickens in the planting kitchen. Seen her smile while she does it.)

Not-Slop's not all bad. One time, she crept into the shed, took Afarra in her arms, and rocked her, careful to avoid the necklace. She spoke while Afarra and the Eyes listened.

"See?" Not-Slop said that night. "I can love you too. All you gotta do is take off those freaky eyes, then we can be friends forever an' I can protect you. . . . You smelled nice when we snatched you. Of roses. I was the one saw you. I said to him, 'That's her.' 'Jellybean?' he said, cos that's who we're on the lookout for. 'No, her sidekick,' I said. Then he sent in Circus, who sent Tiro tumbling into that ditch, an' the rest is history. Vengeance is mine—you heard that saying? Very apropos. . . . Jellybean was always spoiled. Needs taking down a peg or two. Bitch Clobershay gave her one book after another. Only gave one to me. A thesaurus. So I could look up other words for murder. Told Casper the bitch was teaching things weren't on the curriculum. Casper tells his boss, Lotter, an' Lotter tells his boss, Herring. Blond bitch had to run. Shame someone warned her 'fore she could get pyred. Would've enjoyed hearing the bitch scream. . . .

"He stole your papers. You're a Paperless now. Even if we let you go, you can't live in a permanent residence in the Dream. You'll be a Paper, or a Mauler even, with nothing to show for all your escaping. I'm official. Mr. Pokeprick's got my papers for now, but I've narrowed it down to three places where he could've hid them.

"You want me to love you, Cloth? All you gotta do is take off the necklace so he won't beat us to a pulp." When Afarra didn't take the necklace off, Not-Slop slapped her around. *Slap!Slap!* Slapped herself into a Weeping. "Look what you made me do!" she blubbered. "Your mouth's bleeding. Why've you gotta be so ornery? All we're saying is take off the necklace an' tell us if Ji-ji's alive an' where she's hiding out. He wants to know for certain she's croaked. Lotter won't give up till then, guaranteed. You'll confess it sooner or later. Chaff Man'll kill you otherwise.

"What's going on with you anyway? Looks like you're shrinking. Look like a goddam seedling. You know what that's called? It's called youthanizing yourself. You can go to prison for that. You aiming go to prison an' rot, Cloth? Pokeprick won't miss a wink of sleep after he kills you cos he's done it a hundred times an' he's a callous sonuvabitch. Not like me. I agonize over everything. When I heard Dip got recaptured by the search hounds, for instance, it almost did me in. I blame your precious Elly. Bet she left Dipthong Spareseed behind cos she was a Tainted an' Jellybean was scared she'd catch Phyllis. Dip's seed canal was clean as a whistle, Doc Riff said, an' I can vouch for that. Pokeprick's poked you, so you could be a Tainted. You could have a cock disease like Phyllis. Dip called it Phyllis. It's an abbreviation cos syphilis scares people. The etymology of Phyllis comes from phallus, which means cock. Phallus, Phyllis—sound almost the same, see? It's like you find the word an' trace it back to its roots an' then the world opens up to you an' you can pass right through to a better one. Me I've always been exceptional, but Dip was the only one who noticed. . . . He doesn't wash except once a week, if that, so I douse myself up afterward with vinegar. Kills the bacteria up inside. Disinfectant does too, only that's hard to come by. If you tell me where she is, I'll get some vinegar for you too. . . .

"An' by the way, Jellybean's grammar's not half as good as mine. Lotter himself complimented me once, after I served him his lunch. Said I was articulate for a Commonseed. His exact words. He's just about the handsomest White man there is, but don't be fooled. He's not sensitive like me. He's the devil in wolf's clothing. Your precious Ji-ji's the same—probably talking shit about you right now, saying how glad she is to be rid of the stinking Cloth. . . . Here's a secret for you. I cut myself sometimes to get the bile out. See?" She'd shown Afarra her arms and legs. Even in the dim light, Afarra could see the desperation scars. "Want to know why I do it? Cos I can. So you gotta obey me, understand? I'm a danger. But not right now. *I'm* your real friend, not her. Jellybean's not even pretty. Not like Silapu or her father-man. Plain as mud. A real disappointment."

And now, Sloppy Delilah is here again. With her cutting knife this time. And with him, who's falling-down drunk like Silapu used to be. They say: "TakeitoffNOW!" and "Whereisshe?"

"I been patient," Black-Hood-Without-the-Hood says. "A man can only wait so long. Cloth's pretty for a Serverseed, ain't she? Much prettier'n you are. Got a few teeth missing like you, but it looks a damn sight better on her. You think she's pretty?"

"How the fuck should I know?" Call-Me-Delilah says. In an instant, he has his hand round her throat. Not *her* throat, Delilah's—who drops the knife.

He shouts way down into her back teeth: "You backtalking me, Common?" He slams her up against the wall of the shed. The shed shudders.

Afarra remembers his shudder. Her on all fours the way he likes it so he can't see the eye lumps of the necklace beneath her shift. The hump-lumpiness of him behind her—*"gruntgruntgrunt."* Don'tbescareddon'tbescared! It wasn't her he did it to. It was *Not Here, Not Now.* So it didn't count.

"Think you're special, Common, cos you can read an' write? All those fancy words! All that fuckin legacy schooling don't change a fuckin thing. You're still a Commonseed. Vanguard Casper's seedmate whore! I spoiled you. Let you out on a daily basis. You're common as muck. Casper's cunt, that's what you are! *Say it!*"

Delilah is choking. "I'm . . . C-Casper's . . . c-c—"

"Okay! I give you his necklace!" The words fall out before Afarra can stop them, though she would rather Black Hood drove up her seed canal again than hand over her remaining treasure. He hears Afarra's promise and removes his hands from Delilah's neck. Gasping, she sinks to the floor.

Afarra unclasps the necklace and lets it fall. He kicks it to the side with his ratty sneaker toe.

"Well, I'll be damned!" he says. "Who knew the Cloth'd give a fuck about what happened to you? Should've tried throttling you before. Fish'll give me a good price for these. Come over here an' pick 'em up. Stuff 'em in a bag or something. Don't want that black voodoo staring at me."

Fear widens Delilah's eyes, but she takes a step toward the necklace. Afarra feels something climb up her throat—a thunderstorm she can't quell. The wizard's voice occupies her mouth.

"Cherub Holleran! You have sown a field of rotting corpses! You will reap what you sow!"

"Hear that?" Holleran cries. "It's the Black wizard! His *voice!* He's found us! He's *here!*"

Cherub turns and runs out of the shed like a chicken with its head cut off.

Delilah pounds the floor with her fist. "Lying bastard! He never gives me a fuckin thing!"

Afarra's voice has returned to her. She uses it to say, "Don't cry, Sloppy."

"Fuck off, C-Cloth!" Sloppy Delilah sobs. "How many times I g-gotta tell you? I'm not Sloppy. I'm Delilah Moon. This is all on you, freak!"

As fast as lightning, Afarra reaches out and grabs the beads. With difficulty cos her wrists are tied together, she slips them back over her head.

"Think that wizard crap'll protect you? Think again. You're doomed, Cloth. Doomed."

Cherub's voice from the house. "I need feeding! Come here, you ugly bitch! *NOW!*"

"*Shit!* Guess I'll have to take a rain check. Don't fret. I'll be back 'fore you know it, bitch."

A minute later, when Afarra hears the door open, she's sure it's Sloppy come to slice her. It's not. It's Circus. He licks her all over, undeterred by the necklace or her stench. He's come to her before when he can sneak away from his master. She tells him not to make a sound. He swears he won't bark or whimper even.

She asks Circus for a favor cos her wrists and ankles are roped, and there's a tether round her waist too. Without hesitation, her new friend pats over to the knife and nudges it with his nose till it's within reach. Hands shaking, Afarra uses it to cut the ropes from her hands and feet. The blade isn't sharp and her feet are easier than her hands. She steadies the knife between her knees as best she can and cuts the rope from her wrists. In her rush to escape, she slices into her thumb. Never mind about that now. She saws through the tether rope around her waist: *sawsawsaw*. Each moment she thinks she hears Sloppy Delilah coming. Or Pokeprick himself.

The last rope falls away. She stands, wobbles, steadies herself. She's *Free!* Almost.

Circus tells her he is sick to death of that ugly bastard Holleran. Can she take him with her?

She hesitates. If he yaps, he'll betray them both. But she's alone and she needs a friend more than anything else in the world and he's asked her to do him a favor after he's done one for her and one good turn deserves another. . . . She tucks the cute little dog under her arm and tiptoes to the door of the shed. She creaks it open.

Sloppy's face in the back window! Afarra ducks before Sloppy sees her. Sloppy's standing at the cracked window washing dishes, singing to herself. The executioner must've gone out or passed out. Who knew Delilah Moon could sing pretty enough to make you forget what a bitch she is?

> *They say he was a dreamer*
> *they say he was a fool*
> *they say he should've took up arms*
> *been cruel, cruel, cruel*

They say the boy, the cotton gin,
the open-lid, the grave
belongs to us who know his tears
who pray an' pray an' live in fear

I'm just a sinner rowin slow
Just a sinner sinkin low

Just a sinner sufferin

In the dark, in possession of two priceless treasures (if you don't count the knife she stole), Afarra tiptoes across the garbage dump of the backyard. As long as Circus doesn't give them away, they will be Free. She catches sight of her reflection in another window. Thinks she sees the wizard's face. "*Please* stay quiet," she whispers to Circus, who promises not to say a word.

|||||||||||||||||

Tiro looked up briefly. He'd only just opened the letter, and he wasn't happy about being interrupted. Marcus entered their bedroom with a cute, limp-haired White girl who clung to his arm with groupie fervor. Tiro wasn't surprised. Marcus always claimed that if pussy was available, he wasn't about to turn it down. Said he figured it was a way to give the Territories the finger. At least it was only one groupie this afternoon.

"Hey, T, you packed?" Marcus asked. "Not long to go 'fore we head out."

Tiro looked down again, kept reading.

"Where you fly-boys going?" the girl asked, in a high, squeaky voice and northern accent.

Marcus ignored her question and addressed Tiro: "Got dibs on the couch for the next few minutes, okay? Hey, you all right, bro? Look like you seen a ghost."

Tiro looked up from the letter. He sat on the bed in their Dreamfleet apartment—a bedroom to share, a functioning bathroom, a tiny sitting room with a used couch Re-Router gave them that had seen heavy use this past year, and a kitchen alcove with a mini refrigerator and two-ring kerosene burner. When Tiro first saw the place, he thought he'd died and gone to heaven. Seemed like years ago now. It was nothing like the swanky apartments the older pros lived in, but it was theirs, and they could come and go as they pleased.

"Not bad news, I hope," Marcus said.

"He won't do it," Tiro said, like someone sleepwalking.

"Who won't do what?"

"What he promised."

Tiro handed the letter to Marcus, who began reading.

"Sonuvabitch!" Marcus said. "When did this arrive?"

"Today," Tiro said, his eyes wild. "The agreement was in writing. A contract. Signed."

"I don't know, man. Seems to me like he'd be liable or something."

"Yeah," Tiro said, as he snatched back the letter. "He's liable for sure. . . . So what can I do?"

Marcus shrugged. "I don't know, man. This is a toughie."

Marcus turned to the young woman and said, "Sorry, darlin'. A friend in need an' all that crap. You know how it is."

The woman put her arm round his neck, tried to coax him into changing his mind: "But you promised we'd spend time together before you left on your trip," she said.

Marcus snapped at her: "Are you deaf? I said I gotta spend time with my fly partner. He's had shitty news, needs comforting." Marcus cupped his hand over her breast and squeezed, pulled her toward him and kissed her hard on the mouth.

When he pulled away she said, "We got time, Aurelius."

Marcus smiled at her. "I guess you're right, baby. Fancy a threesome, T? Take your mind off things. Greta's happy to oblige—right, Greta?"

Greta looked Tiro up and down. "Sure," she said. "He's real cute too."

"Not nearly as cute as me though," Marcus said, as he pushed her hair from her forehead.

"No, babe," she agreed, laughing. "No one's near as cute as you."

"Work on your adverbs, darlin'," Marcus said. "So, T. You want in?" Tiro didn't reply.

"What's wrong with him?" Greta asked.

"He's training to be a monk. Nurturing his celibacy."

"For real?" she asked.

"Of course not," Marcus said, tightly. Tiro was still staring at the sheet of paper in his hand.

"Is he crying?" Greta asked.

"Shut the fuck up," Marcus commanded, his voice a crowbar. "Get out of here. *Now.*"

Greta turned to go and Marcus slapped her butt. "*Ow!*" she said.

"Don't be a baby," Marcus called after her. "You know you like it harder than that."

Tiro listened to the click of Greta's stilettos as she exited through the door and walked down the corridor. Marcus switched to preacher mode.

"I tried to warn you," Marcus said. "Told you he'd never give you the satisfaction of—"

Tiro interrupted him: "I been thinking." His voice was shaking. He dug at his skull where Re-Router had shaved a pair of flyer's wings. "I've come up with a plan. You gotta get a message to Old Shadowy. She's a Friend of Freedom, right? She can persuade Williams. You can twist her round your little finger. An' she loves you like a son."

"Emmeline Shadowbrook sure as hell is *not* my mother."

"But she was real good to you. If you get in touch with her she'll—"

"You crazy? Diviners don't perch on the same rungs as father-men, T. Fairskin females got hardly any power on a planting. Emmeline's an advisor to the cropmaster, an' the cropmaster is Lotter. Think he wants to alienate Williams, his chief henchman? Think he'd listen to an old bat like Emmeline? She hasn't lasted this long cos she takes chances; she's lasted cos she plays it safe."

Tiro rose from the bed and paced around the bedroom. He chewed on the stubby fingernails on his right hand, took a break, then chewed on the left. "You saw what he did to Amadee. Bromadu an' Eeyatho are seedlings. No way they can protect themselves. He's raping her by now. Drexler's superstitious but it's wore off for sure. Think Uncle Dreg's curse'll stop him now he's hanging on to 'em?"

Marcus shook his head. "To be honest, man, I was surprised it stopped him at all. Drex Williams never struck me as the type to be intimidated by a dead Tribalseed's curse."

"I gotta save 'em!" Tiro cried, beating his forehead with his open palm. "He'll hitch the boys up to that . . . he'll . . ." He balled the letter up and threw it on the floor. "He'll tractor-lynch 'em both! Proclaim they're Deviants like Amadee. Like he said I was. Would've made good on his word if you hadn't volunteered to stand in for me that time."

Marcus tried to reason with him: "The news sucks, but you've gotta get a grip, T. Williams likely never intended to grant your petition. Gets a rise out of pulling your chain."

"I'll *kill* him!" Tiro cried, helplessly.

"Get in line. Williams is the meanest motherfucker on the 437th. S'been tried already."

Tiro stopped pacing, stood riveted to the floor. "Other seeds've tried to kill him? Who?" Marcus shrugged like someone who'd given away too much. "*Who?*" Tiro repeated.

"If you must know, one of the would-be murderers was Coach Billy."

"Don't tell me," Tiro said bitterly. "Uncle Dreg stopped him too."

"Like he stopped you? Nope. This time, Uncle Seeing Eyes was in on it."

Tiro took a step backward, said, "That's crazy. Uncle Dreg was a pacifist."

"Guess he had a moment of enlightenment." Marcus studied Tiro with the same penetrating gaze he often wore when he wanted to gauge his fly partner's reactions. "It was after Amadee was tractor-pulled. Emmeline said he didn't let you or Zaini see how mad he was cos he knew he had to keep it together for the family. Emmeline said he lost faith in the dream for a time."

"How did she know all this?"

"She was in on it." Tiro's mouth dropped open. "Yeah, I was amazed too when she told me. Old Shadowy decided to lay it all on the line for once. The plan was to poison Williams' food at the Harvest Festival. Used some toxin that's a bitch to trace."

Stunned, Tiro leaned up against the dresser. "So how come he's still breathing?"

Marcus shrugged. "Apparently, your uncle thought Billy must've changed his mind an' never laced Williams' food after all. Billy believed Emmeline chickened out an' snatched Williams' plate away at the last moment. She's got a pious streak a mile wide. Funny thing is, she didn't chicken out. When Emmeline's high, bitch don't lie." Marcus chuckled. "She swore to me Billy poisoned your father-man's venison stew an' she watched him eat every bite. I believe her."

"An' this was after Uncle caught me heading off to slash the bastard's throat and wrestled the knife from my hand?"

"Yeah, I know. Pot calling the kettle black, for sure. But you gotta admit he saved your ass. Williams would've snatched the knife from your sweaty hands an' carved you up like a Thanksgiving turkey. Anyhow, the old folks' clumsy attempt at homicide didn't work. For all we know, Billy laced the bastard's food with enough poison to kill a rhino an' he still refused to kick the bucket. Evil's got a way of marinating in its own juices. Acts as an antidote. The moral of the story's obvious."

"It is?" Tiro said, obviously baffled.

"Sure. Even a pacifist can grow a pair if the crime's obscene enough. An' that tractor-lynching Williams did to his own son was as obscene as they come."

Tiro paced again. His shock at the murder attempt had receded. "I won't let this stand."

"I hear you, bro. But to come back to the point I was trying to make—we keep a cool head an' think things through. The steaders've got all the aces. We got all the low cards."

Exasperated, Tiro threw his hands up in the air. "So we can't win then?"

"Sure we can. But we need to be strategic."

Tiro let out a grunt of exasperation: "This ain't some fuckin game, man!"

"Hey, calm down, bro! You aiming to put a hole in the floor with all that

pacing? The reason our side loses is cos we forget it's a game. We're always waiting for God, or kindly Whites, or executed wizards to level the playing field.
Luck don't ally itself with people like us. Lucky don't either, if you ask me,
though Ji-ji would fight me on that one. . . . Hey, you paying attention? What
I'm saying is there's a way to rescue Zaini an' your brothers."

"Yeah, there is," Tiro agreed. He strode over to the room's lone dresser and
pulled the top drawer open so hard it leapt out onto the floor and landed upside
down. A 9 mm semi fell out with a thud. Tiro scooped it up and held it in his
shaking hands.

Marcus yelled at him: "*Jesus,* T! That's not some fuckin *toy*! You could've
shot your damn foot off if it was loaded! Or worse, shot me!"

Tiro fell to his knees and rifled through the drawer. "Where's my ammo?"

"Calm down," Marcus said. "What's wrong with you, man? You on something? *Calm the fuck down!* You even listening to me?"

Tiro heard Marcus tell him to calm down, but how could he do that? His
nightmares were bad enough when he was convinced he'd see them all again
soon. What would they be like now?

At night, he saw his mother rocking Bromadu's and Eeyatho's shredded bodies in her arms, one on each side. "Which is which?" she asked him. He looked
to see which of his brothers' corpses was taller, but their little bodies had been
ripped to pieces so he couldn't tell. Failure burned the back of his throat. He
always dry heaved in the nightmare. His mother was as kind and loving as ever.
She reached out to him with bloody hands. "Come, son, let's mourn together,"
she said in Totepp. And he understood her, even though he didn't speak the
language. It was worse than if she'd spat on him. What do you do when someone hands you forgiveness and you know you don't deserve it? He'd wake up
covered in sweat, think it was the blood of his slaughtered brothers. Had to
leap out of bed and check the sheets to make sure it wasn't. The nightmares
were made worse by the sleep aids the sports docs prescribed after he'd told
them he couldn't sleep. But if he didn't take them he never slept at all. Yesterday, he'd been ecstatic. For once, he'd been able to deliver good news. Ji-ji had
been over the moon when they'd told her about Charra. Same way he would
be if she were to come to him and say, "Amadee's not tractor-lynched. Was a
goddam lie. Let's go find your brother in the Madlands." But she would never
be able to say that to him. No one would.

Tiro staggered over to where Marcus was standing and jabbed a finger in his
face. "Where is it? You put it somewhere? What the hell you touch it for? It's *my*
ammo." Before Tiro could stop him, Marcus wrenched the gun from his hand.
"What you doing?" Tiro cried. He felt like a little kid.

"Stopping you from acting like a moron. Why you think I hid your ammo in the first place? Cos most evenings, you're high or drunk enough to blow off my nappy head before you figure out it's not sitting on your own neck, dumbass!" Marcus slid the gun into the waistband of his jeans. "If suicide's your thing, so be it. But stay sober an' don't drag me into it. . . . Now sit your ass down an' listen."

Tiro considered tackling him, but Marcus was as strong as he was, and he was too gutted to do it. He plopped down on his bed and buried his head in his hands.

"You don't get it, Marcus," he groaned through his fingers. "You ain't got no family."

"You're right. Guess I'm the lucky one."

Tiro raised his head and looked at the person he'd now flown with more often that he'd flown with Amadee. Through the haze of his own misery, he said, "I didn't mean it like that."

"I know what you meant," Marcus said. For a second, he sounded hurt. Then he scrubbed the hurt from his voice and preached again. "Calm down an' listen. Maybe you'll learn something."

Tiro took a deep breath. If Marcus delivered another sermon, he'd strangle him.

"That's better," Marcus said. "Now let's go over what we know. We know the Friends of Freedom are as likely to agree to raid the 437th as they are to admit their adherence to nonviolence is why we're in this mess. We also know Charra's got a handy band of raiders. An' we know that, at long last, we've got our own ace in the hole."

Tiro sat up expectantly, "What's that?"

"Not what. *Who*. A bird of prey, T. A magnificent bird of prey. See how she rose last night, bro? You ever seen anything like it, T, cos I ain't. Almost converted there an' then to Friendliness. *Whoo-whee!* No wonder the Friends are chomping at the bit to hitch the former Muleseed up to their Freedom wagon."

"We're not askin' Ji to risk her—"

"She's outgrown you, bro. Makes her own decisions. S'pose we ask Charra to raid the 437th?"

Tiro pulled on his lip nervously, said, "Charra? You serious? Think she'd do it"

"Maybe. A raid on the 437th would be personal. From what I hear, Charra doesn't mess around. Uses methods the Friends disapprove of. S'why they're intent on squelching her. Charra's an existential threat to them like Ji-ji is to the steaders."

Tiro whistled in surprise. "You think she'd help us raid the 437th. Is that what you're saying?"

"No. I'm saying, *we'll* help *her* raid the 437th."

As a glimmer of hope turned into a flame, Tiro stopped shaking. Maybe Marcus was right? "How come I didn't come up with that?" he said.

Marcus patted Tiro on the shoulder. "I could fill the Dream Coop with all the shit you don't come up with. The stars are aligning, bro. For once, for my sake, try not to blow it."

||||||||||||||||||

Ji-ji checked her watch. They would be waiting outside in the van by now, parked in the secluded spot behind the warehouse, out of sight of the guards. She had to be quick. She wished she'd come across the Dream Master's letter earlier. Zyla must've left it on the kitchen table for her. She didn't have time to read it now; she would have to read it later. She stuck it in her pocket.

She wasn't sorry to leave the Aerie behind. She wouldn't miss its moldy stench or its vermin; she wouldn't miss its creepy corridors and damp locker rooms. But she would miss this: the apartment she'd shared with Afarra.

Man Cryday had taken most of her story-cloths with her, but she'd left the ones that told the First Story. Ji-ji wished she hadn't. Looking at them only made her angry. Man Cryday had lied to her about Charra. The betrayal had eradicated every scrap of trust between them. Zyla told her last night they wouldn't be returning to this place if they decided to head up to New York. They'd need a more secure hideout, she said. Ji-ji wanted to tell her she was headed to the Madlands, but she knew Zyla would try to stop her. To avoid having to face her, she'd complained of a headache and gone to bed as soon as Tiro and Marcus had dropped her off last night. By the time she woke, Zyla had already left to meet up with the Friends. She wouldn't be back till after midnight. Three hours to go till then.

Ji-ji grabbed the last of her possessions: the four dice Lucky sent, the snow globe Tiro gave her, her map of Planting 437, and Charra's book of nursery rhymes. She'd already packed a bunch of personal stuff, including her libbies, her drawing pad and pencils, the blackbird quilt, supplies for the road, and her gun. She'd left two letters on her bed—one for Zyla and one for Lucky. Marcus would rail at her for that if he learned she'd done it. She didn't care. You don't abandon your friends without a word.

She grabbed her bag, ran into Afarra's room and looked at the mural one last time. She grabbed a pen and scrawled on the mural. Next to Ji-ji and Afarra, she drew a life-size heart. Inside it were the words *"ELLY LOVES AFARRA."* Afarra couldn't read well, but she would recognize the names, and the heart would tell her the rest.

Ji-ji snuck out into the night. Otto wasn't on duty, and neither were any of the other bodyguards who'd watched over them previously. These guards were younger, inexperienced. Ji-ji had no trouble sneaking out.

When she climbed into the van, she was surprised to find not only Tiro and Marcus in the front but Tree and Ink sitting in the van's third row.

"We invited Tree and Ink to ride with us down to the Madlands," Tiro explained, as she strapped into a seat in the second row.

"Never know when you'll need a tree to give you a hand with something," Marcus added. He started the engine.

"You sure about this?" Ji-ji asked the pair, concerned for Ink in particular.

Tree explained that he'd been summoned to Redipp's office that morning. "Said the fleet was shipping Ink back to the 368th," Tree said.

"Called me a burden," Ink added, indignantly.

The ghastly things Ji-ji had witnessed on that planting when she'd been loaned there as a rental at harvest time still haunted her. "But that's a death sentence!" she said.

Tree concurred. "Lucky for us, the Dream Master had warned me 'bout what was coming down the pike. Advised me to stay calm. So I gave Redipp the impression I was leaning in favor of compliance. Told him it was a pain carting a whiner around all the time."

"He was only kidding," Ink said. "You was only kidding—right, Tree?"

Laughing Tree assured Ink he was kidding.

"But your kith-n-kin petition for Ink was approved," Ji-ji said. "He has a right to live in the Dream."

Marcus told her things had changed: "Some of those new lawyers Red Droopy's hired claim it wasn't a legitimate kith-n-kin cos Tree didn't know Ink before he fell. The long and the short of it is, Tree's resigning from the fleet soon as he can. Staying out of sight for a while seemed like a good idea. It'll come as one helluva surprise for Redipp. He needs big battlers in the lineup to compete with the brawlers from Armistice, an' Tree here's the biggest an' baddest we've got. Redipp'll have to rely on Georgie-Porge, move him out of the reservists."

"Which is good news for Georgie," Tiro added. "Been real low lately."

They were a few miles away from the Aerie when Ji-ji, sitting behind Marcus, caught sight of a skinny figure in the side mirror. She turned to look out through the back window. She couldn't see much cos Tree's head was in the way, but she thought she saw . . .

"*Stop!*" she cried.

Marcus slammed on the brakes. "What is it?" he said.

"I saw her! Back there! Running into that alley!"

"Who?" Tiro asked.

"*Afarra!* Behind us!" Everyone turned to look. "She ducked into that ally on the right."

They peered into the night. Just then, a group of street children emerged from the alley, looked around, then ran back again.

Ji-ji thought she caught a glimpse of the girl she'd mistaken for Afarra. She groaned. "It's kids, that's all," she said.

"You want us to go back an' check?" Tiro asked.

"No," Ji-ji replied. "It wasn't her. The girl was too small. It was just some kid."

Tiro reached back and patted her hand. "Sorry, Ji."

"*Shit!*" Marcus said, as he turned back to the road ahead. "So that's why the kids took off! Patrollers up ahead." A dozen D.C. patrollers were farther down the street, marching in their direction. "We need to get out of here, fast!" Marcus said. He eased his foot down on the gas, and they drove past the patrollers without incident.

"We made it!" Ink cried.

"We're not safe yet," Marcus reminded them. "Still have to get past the border patrol at the southern gate."

"Think the patrollers'll want to search the van?" Ink inquired, anxiously.

"Let's hope not," Marcus replied. "If they do, let me do the talking. I mean it, Ink. Keep your mouth shut, okay?"

Ink took offense: "I always keep my mouth shut. Right, Tree?"

The closer they got to the South Gate, the quieter they became. When they were a few blocks away, Marcus instructed them to put on their contagion masks.

Insurmountable, D.C.'s forty-foot, barbed-wire-topped wall, looked even more intimidating in this part of the city, where the only structures nudging up against it were the makeshift hovels of the poor, and a few sad-looking cinder-block patrol barracks. There were only a handful of patrollers at the southern gate. Almost everyone exited the city along Dream Corridor to the west, or north to the Eastern SuperState.

Not wishing to draw attention to his unusual size, Laughing Tree scooted down in his seat.

"Think they'll search the van?" Ink asked again.

"Not if I can help it," Marcus said. "I do the talking. Everyone else, zip it."

A lone patroller strolled up to the van. The white Capitol dome on his cap glowed in the dark. He was light-skinned, but his Spanish accent made Ji-ji hopeful. The patroller tapped on the driver's-side window and signaled to Marcus to roll it down. He peered into the van. He was about Ji-ji's age—about seventeen. Eighteen, at most. They said you could join the D.C. patrollers as young as fifteen if you could read and write, and if you weren't an obvious drug-sop.

"Where you guys headed?" the patroller asked. He sounded bored.

"South," Marcus said. "Hope we've come to the right gate, Officer."

"You know what it is like down there, right? Scariest place in the Disunited States."

"Yeah, we know," Marcus said.

"Swarming with gators," the patroller continued. "Malaria, dengue fever, mutants too, snarlers and stripers both. Most folks with any sense down south are looking to come up north. Why you heading in the wrong direction?"

"There's a clinic down there," Marcus said. "Our kid sister's real sick."

"What's wrong with her?" the patroller asked.

Marcus shrugged. "Don't know, Officer. But there's a clinic specializes in skin contagions near Jacksonville. The charity clinic here in the city recommended it. Don't know why they told us to take her all the way down there. Thought they had more doctors in the Dream than down south."

The patroller jumped back from the van as if it were ablaze. "She a Jangler?"

"No," Marcus said. "Definitely not. Least, they don't think so. She's in a lot of pain, but she's been real brave. The disease is eating away at her back. God willing, she'll be okay."

"*Jesus!*" the patroller said, taking another step back and making the sign of the cross.

"You wanna see our papers?" Marcus asked through his mask. "We got 'em right here. Gwen, baby, pass me your papers so the officer here can take a look."

The patroller raised his hands defensively. "*No!* I open the gates. You stay in the van."

The patroller gestured at them to move along. "And disinfect that vehicle 'fore you reenter the city," he ordered.

"We surely will, Officer," Marcus said. "Good advice. Thanks."

The patroller yelled back to his partner: "All clear. Open the gates, Fred!"

To Ji-ji, the massive gates seemed to creak open in slow motion. Marcus started to drive through them onto the pitted, deserted road heading south when the young patrolman rushed up to the driver's side again and rapped on the window. Ji-ji's heart stopped.

"Here," he said, "for your sister." He placed what looked like a stone in Marcus' hand, but then Ji-ji realized it was an orange. The gates clanged behind them.

The young patroller shouted, "Dios te bendiga!" as they drove away. Zyla had taught her what that meant. "God bless you, too," she whispered.

As soon as they'd driven a few hundred yards, Tiro slapped Marcus on the back. "You come up with that story on the fly, man? Impressive."

Marcus called back over his shoulder: "Hey, Ji-ji! Your nose dropped off yet?"

The other passengers roared with laughter, but Ji-ji was thinking about the gift, the patroller's small kindness. It reminded her of the orange Lucky had given Afarra.

Exhausted by the range of emotions she'd experienced recently, Ji-ji drifted off to sleep, thinking of her lost-and-found sister. *I'm coming, Charra,* she thought. *Nothing can stop me now.*

||||||||||||||||

Afarra waits in the dark for hours before she dares climb the stairs to the Aerie. She doesn't know the exact time but she thinks it's only an hour or two till midnight.

Earlier, she ran into a group of children who knew where the old practice coop was and helped her find the way in exchange for taking turns holding Circus. They steered her away from a gang of patrollers, helped her hide in an alley. And now, at last, she's home. Only there's a problem. She searches among the men for a face she recognizes, but none of the people she spots are familiar. Could be they're not Friends of Freedom at all. Where is her friend Otto?

Without alerting anyone, having reminded Circus to keep as quiet as a mouse, Afarra creeps up to their apartment with Circus in her arms for comforting. Up the flights of stairs to the Aerie. . . . To Elly's room. Which breaks her.

Elly is gone! Her treasures—the quilt, her clothes, the snow globe, the dice, even Petrus' gun—all *gone!*

And now Afarra knows for certain that the strange men guarding the practice coop and the Aerie are not Friends. Ji-ji has run off to escape them! She and Circus must do the same.

She grabs her few possessions and stuffs them into a garbage bag—her small pile of clothes and girlcloths, her toothbrush, hairbrush, comb, the learn-to-read book Elly and Zyla gave her. Her treasure boxes are too big so she removes the items from them. She isn't sure if she should take the Resolution. What if they discover it? But she's a Paperless now and maybe the Resolution will let her stay in the Dream?

Afarra sees it then. A message from Elly. Inside a heart.

"See?" she whispers to Circus. "She is not forgetting."

Circus licks her face, but even that can't console her.

The empty Aerie screams, "*GET OUT! NOW!*" But where will she go? She has no papers. Without papers, she is nobody, nothing. . . . Tiro? No. The Dream Coop isn't safe. She doesn't want to watch him fall. And if Elly is gone, he would be with her, yes? Elly loves him. She would never leave him behind. . . . Zyla? Ben and Germaine? She doesn't know how to get there from here, doesn't know the address of Zyla's apartment.

Then she remembers what Elly said and remembers his photo in the history book. She tucks Circus more tightly under her arm. She will seek refuge with someone who will never hurt them.

"He will protect us," Afarra tells Circus as she creeps back down the stairs.

Circus stares at the eyes on the necklace. He believes her.

Over in the Dream Revival District, the Dreamer's pale-as-the-moon statue uncrosses its granite arms to welcome them.

PART TWO
MIGRATION

The ride thrilled Ji-ji Silapu, as if she were living in the Age of Plenty in the United States, when people like her made journeys like these. The ride terrified Jellybean Lottermule, who lived in the Age of Paucity in the Disunited States, when former seeds, unless they were mad, didn't make journeys like these into the Madlands. Ji-ji patted the paper in her pocket that certified her as human and as a permanent resident of D.C. Hopefully, it counted for something in this untamed region. The idea that she would soon see Charra again gave her courage. Her warrior sister feared nothing; she mustn't either.

Two hours after Marcus exited the main highway heading south and turned onto one of the secondary roads, the rain began. Little more than a sprinkle at first, it gained in strength then backed off, a process that repeated itself several times. The hot van turned humid.

The ride was jarring. The suspension on the van was a joke—like riding in Silent Pete's horse-drawn wagon on the planting. The wiper on the driver's side was cranky—bent and out of sync with its partner. The one on the passenger side was warped too. In his role as navigator, Tiro complained about the lousy visibility. He peered at a torn map of the old Southeastern United States from the Age of Plenty, one that looked as if it had been gnawed on by rodents or roaches. Every so often, Tiro trained his flashlight onto the ancient map and read out the places they passed, most of which didn't exist as viable communities anymore: Thornburg, Arcadia, Ladysmith.

Marcus, more knowledgeable about the area than the others, explained how, after the Sequel, most of the remaining residents in this area of the Commonwealth of Virginia sought refuge in D.C., the plantings, or the Eastern Super-State. Some of the small "towns" along the way boasted a cluster of stores and residences, and resembled the Salem Outpost where the Freedom Race began, and where Ji-ji, as a seedling, had traveled a few times with Lotter. Richmond was the exception—a struggling Liberty Independent desperate to retain its status but plagued by floods and Clan raids. The city hadn't fared as well as some of the other Independents, Marcus said, so he planned to give it a wide berth. But skirting Richmond altogether meant veering off onto a road that looked as if it hadn't seen a maintenance crew in decades. Tiro told his fly partner he was crazy. The detour would add hours to their journey, more if the road stayed as crappy as this. Marcus wouldn't budge. Everyone knew, he said, you took your life in your hands if you drove through Richmond.

"Thought Richmond was held by us," Tiro said.

"Who's 'us'?" Marcus asked.

"You know, *us*," Tiro replied. "Blacks, Browns, A-Is, mixed, former seeds and the like."

Marcus shook his head: "You saying you never met a bad seed, T? Or a bad A-I?"

"No," Tiro replied, defensively. "But it's not like Richmond's a Clan camp."

"Fairskins don't have a monopoly when it comes to armed robbery," Marcus asserted.

Tiro bristled: "Just sayin' you don't need to act all scaredy-cat 'bout a liberty city."

"You wanna drive," Marcus said, "seeing as how you know so much?"

Tiro's mood shifted in one second flat. "Right now, you mean? In the dark?"

"Yeah," Marcus replied. "Right now. In the dark."

There was a long pause before Tiro responded with a limp "It's raining, man."

Marcus snickered. "Fly-boy's gotta learn to drive in the rain at some point."

"Not when I got a whole bunch of passengers could get killed," Tiro argued.

"My point exactly," Marcus said, smugly. "The driver's got a responsibility as Guardian of the Van. Stop reading out those fuckin place names. Map's prehistoric. All the roads've changed."

Tiro was quiet for a while, but he kept studying the map, as if they'd only make it safely down to Charra if he made a mental note of every community they passed. The guard at the city gate was right: riding south through the scariest place on the east coast was insane. No one knew for sure how many militias and Clans there were; no one knew if the rumors that gators and crocs (they had both) had grown to outlandish sizes were right. But they all knew Tiro wasn't the only scaredy-cat in the van. Driving through the dark added a new layer of terror for former seeds. When the rain began again and didn't let up, the tension in the van rose.

Tiro looked from the wipers to Marcus and back again. "Wipers are 'bout to fall off."

"Don't be a dumbass, T," Marcus told him.

Tempted to suggest they fix the wipers while it wasn't raining hard, Ji-ji kept her mouth shut. What did she know about windshield wipers on salvaged vans? She had to have faith that Marcus knew a helluva lot more about them than either she or Tiro did. It worried her, however, when Tree also said he thought they might want to take a look at them. Marcus, not nearly as dismissive of the big flyer as he was of his fly partner, agreed to check them when they stopped to relieve themselves.

Soon, the rain let up again and conversation turned to other things. Not far from Doswell, they took a wrong turn and drove down what appeared to be an old service road. A short while later, it dead-ended. As they made their way back, Marcus pointed to the ruins of what he said was a theme park. In the night sky, eerie silhouettes of a giant Ferris wheel and what Marcus identified as looping roller coasters brooded over the landscape. The wheel, reminiscent of the Ellison Wheel in the fly-coops, looked like a mechanical version of One Being's One Eye in the Toteppi Origin Story.

Ink was fascinated. "Who used to ride them rides?" he asked.

"Everyone," Marcus told him.

"Seeds too? An' Passengers?" Ink asked.

"No Middle Passengers around in the Age of Plenty," Tiro said. "They were earlier."

Ji-ji enjoyed seeing Tiro interact with Ink. He'd always had a way with young people. Knew what to say so they wouldn't be scared. Ji-ji suddenly realized what a good teacher he would be. He had Zyla's patience and her genuine desire to help young people navigate through a world that often dismissed them. She'd have to tell him that sometime, assuming he got his act together for more than a minute at a time.

"No seeds in the Age of Plenty," Tiro continued. "Back then, everyone was, like, equal."

Marcus laughed derisively, said, "Man, you got a lot to learn. Never a time when everyone was equal. No such thing as an Age of Plenty for folks like us. This region of the U.S. was always the South with a capital *S*, always had its knee jammed up against our necks. Inferior schools, crappy hospitals. Theme parks like these were no exception. Think we were allowed to ride all those rides? Think again. They let duskies in but we had to pay extra. Double or more."

"I woulda paid double," Ink said, as he craned his neck to gaze longingly at the ruins. Hearing Ink talk about the old park, it seemed to Ji-ji that he'd lied about his age. Smart though he was, Ink was almost certainly a lot younger than fourteen. Thirteen, at the most.

"Think they let Damaged ride back then?" Ink asked. "For extra, I mean."

"They let everyone in," Ji-ji said. She had no idea whether or not it was true, but she wanted the boy from the blighted 368th to imagine a time in history when he could just be a boy. "Didn't charge extra either," she added. "Everyone paid the same. You could've afforded it, easy."

Ink turned to his friend and said, "You would've paid for me to get in, right, Tree?"

"No fun riding alone," Tree confirmed. "Gotta have a partner."

When Marcus began to remind them how the world wasn't nearly as perfect as seeds always seemed to imagine, and that prejudice was rampant even then, Ji-ji leaned forward and whispered in his ear. "Don't spoil it for him," she said.

A few seconds later, Marcus surprised her by smacking his hand on the wheel as if he'd remembered something. "Hey, Ink," he said, "Now I think about it, Diviner Shadowbrook told me *everyone* got in an' they all paid the same— duskies, fairskins, Damaged, an' Tainted."

"Yeah," Ink said, cheerfully, "bet that's how it was. Right, Tree?"

"I bet it was, buddy," Tree said.

In the rearview mirror, Ji-ji nodded her thanks. Marcus acknowledged it with a weary smile.

Ink's nervousness made him chatty. He asked one question after another about Planting 437. Said the place sounded a lot better than the 368th. Ji-ji knew from her brief experience on Ink's infamous planting that he was right. Ink described how, on the 368th, you got lashed or worse for not using the approved words on the Seed Vocabulary List. He recounted how awful it was to see all the female seeds in their black modesty hoods—even the littlest ones, who couldn't see where they were going through the slits and often tripped over things. "No modesty hoods on the 437th," he said, enviously, "An' no vocab list either. You all had it easy."

Ji-ji tried to steer the boy away from planting life. Unfortunately, prying Ink off a subject proved difficult. Being an orphan, Ink was drawn to Marcus' story, in particular.

"Hey, Marcus," Ink said, "Old Shadowy was the fairskin female lady raised you, right? She the one tutored you, taught you to read?"

Marcus snapped at him: "No one raised me. I raised my own damn self!"

Ink was startled into silence. Marcus caught Laughing Tree's expression in the rearview mirror and moderated his tone: "But . . . truth is, Emmeline's just about the best-read person I've ever met. So if she says everyone paid the same to get into that theme park, everyone paid the same."

Tiro looked back at Ji-ji and registered his surprise with a bemused grin. Marcus didn't praise Emmeline often, and when he did there was always some backhanded comment to follow.

Encouraged, Ink returned to his favorite subject. "What was the dream park called?"

Marcus, exhibiting superhuman patience, corrected him: "Not a dream park. A *theme* park."

"What's a theme?" Ink asked.

Marcus sighed. "Rescue me, Ji-ji, for god's sake," he muttered.

Ji-ji tried to explain but wound up confusing Ink even more.

Frustrated by Ji-ji's explanation, Ink asked if the park had another name.

"Can't remember," Marcus admitted. "Kings Palace or Queens Domination or something."

Tiro chuckled. "Queen's Domination. Sounds like S an' M."

Ink was fascinated. "What's an S an' M? They have kings back then in the Uniteds?"

"No," Ji-ji said. "No kings. No queens either. Not in the U.S. It was a re-public, so everyone had a vote like they do now in the SuperStates and most of the Liberty Independents."

"Botanicals don't get no vote in the Territories," Ink said. "Or sometimes they get, like, a two-thirds or three-fifths vote in progressive parishes. Think that'll change on account of your wings, Ji-ji?" Ji-ji hesitated. Tree didn't.

"Sure it will," Tree assured his young friend. "After they see what we saw, you think steaders can go back to the old way of thinking? Not possible."

Marcus chimed in. "Tree's right. How's that ol'-timey song go? If a needle can wink its eye and a rubber band can play, a seed in flight will take your breath away. Right, Ji-ji?"

"Marcus," Tiro said, "why you always gotta be so sarcastic, man?"

"You tell me, Dumbo. Could be the company I been keeping."

"Yeah, could be," Tiro said. "Or it could be you're a moody sonuvabitch."

"Well," Marcus said, vindictively, "this moody sonuvabitch wants to take a nap now. You're up, fly-boy. Time to impress the masses with your driving know-how."

The masses weren't too happy to hear that Tiro would be taking over, but Marcus said he was starting to nod off. Unless they wanted to pull over so he could grab some shut-eye, someone else had to drive. Tiro, who'd already told them how much he hated driving in the rain, offered to keep Marcus awake by going over some of their fly-coop routines. To Ji-ji's relief, Marcus agreed.

While Tiro and Marcus argued about which maneuvers they should draw on during their first coop battle of the fall, assuming they had one, Tree and Ink asked Ji-ji what Charra was like.

Ji-ji described her incomparable sister using modifiers like brave, funny, beautiful, and wise, but none of these did justice to her qualities. Ji-ji was tempted to gush—say something like, "Most people fell in love with Charra when they saw her, and fell even more deeply in love with her after they got to know her," but that would make her sound even younger than Ink. Eighteen months younger than Tiro, three years younger than Marcus, and more than two decades younger than Laughing Tree, Ji-ji didn't want them to treat her like some kid.

The truth was, she owed her life to Charra. Like Uncle Dreg, her sister had instilled hope in her during times of despair. The only one of the siblings who could steer their mam away from the precipice, Charra charmed you into believing anything was possible and made you feel like you were the most significant person in the world while she did it. She had an uncanny knack for sensing what you needed. "*Resist, resist, resist!*" was Charra's mantra. Whenever steader propaganda told Ji-ji she was worthless, Charra taught Ji-ji to "scale herself up."

Charra's wicked sense of humor made people gravitate toward her too. She gave steaders nicknames that stuck. Father-Man Lotter became Goddam Plotter—an ironic nod to how much their father-man despised cussing, and how much he enjoyed scheming against his enemies. Charra turned Pastor Cam Gillyman, Planting 437's True Hybrid preacher, into Pastor Sham Gullible. Tryton, with his lustful, roving eye, became Inquisitor Bite-'Em. And Cropmaster Michael Herring became the Archangel Cod. Charra's irreverent nicknames proved dangerously unforgettable. On more than one occasion, seeds uttered them inadvertently in the company of steaders. When Dipthong Spareseed called Cam Gillyman "Pastor Gullible," she'd been forced to spend a scorching-hot afternoon in the planting pillory. If Charra and Ji-ji hadn't snuck her some water, Dip swore she would have "expirated from thirst."

Ji-ji had no idea where Dipthong Spareseed, her friend and fellow kitchen-seed, was now. Dead perhaps, or toiling on the planting. Earlier, Tiro had told Ji-ji about the devastating letter he'd received from Father-Man Williams. Ji-ji agreed they had to get Zaini, Bromadu and Eeyatho off the 437th as soon as possible. Yes, of course she'd help him rescue them, she'd said. Neither of them mentioned that mounting a raid on one of the most powerful plantings in the Territories would be as impossible as Alice has warned them it would be at the Friends' meeting. Dreams made the world bearable, so Ji-ji imagined Dip's joy when the raiding party liberated every seed on the planting. Dip loved Ji-ji and Charra both. What would she say when the sisters turned up out of the blue to rescue her? In D.C., Dip wouldn't be a Tainted anymore (always assuming they could get her inside the city walls). She could rip off the contamination cross that marked her as a former syphilitic, and rip off her brown Commonseed symbol too. Living Free for the first time in her life, Dip could adopt the four children she yearned to care for—reparation for the four womblings she'd done away with so they wouldn't be raised in captivity.

Yes. The raid on the 437th would be sweet. . . . Which brought Ji-ji to another important question. What would Charra say when she saw her little sister could fly? Ji-ji would need to handle the revelation delicately. Not only had Charra undergone a wexcision, she'd also given birth to a deadborn Wing-child. Ji-ji could only imagine what that must be like. Her own successful metamorphosis (*successful*—she'd never actually attached that word to herself before) was likely to conjure up conflicting feelings in Charra. You had to take into account what someone else had gone through before you foisted your own good news onto them. On the other hand, Charra had never been envious of anyone. Her sister forged her own path without dwelling on others' good fortune. Silapu was wrong when she'd said Charra wasn't a Try-Again, wrong to say Charra's temper flared and she burned too hot and fast before she turned bitter in defeat. Their mam couldn't see it, but Charra burned slowest of them all, always had.

Four years older than Ji-ji, Charra, still a child herself, had been the one who'd found ingenious ways to distract Silapu after Luvlydoll died. When Charra had returned from her night shift at the planting furniture factory to find that Luvlydoll had passed, Charra had been the mother their mam would've been if Silapu hadn't been high. After Ji-ji showed her Luvlydoll's corpse, Charra, only about eleven at the time, hadn't railed at her, hadn't demanded to know why she hadn't come and fetched her from her shift. She didn't give herself over to weeping or smash her forehead against the wall like Silapu had. She didn't say, "Why didn't you keep her alive, you little fool! Or try to revive her, or done something, *anything* less stupid than watch her die?" So Ji-ji didn't have to say that the reason why she hadn't tried CPR, even though she'd seen Doc Riff do it, was that she would've had to bring Luvlydoll back to that terrible, raspy breathing that made her throat bleed and made her scream and scream. Instead of making her feel worse, Charra had said how thankful she was Ji-ji had been there to hold their baby sister and make sure she hadn't died alone. She'd reminded her that Doc Riff had told them Luvlydoll didn't have long, so there was nothing else she could've done. "I'm not afraid of dying like Luvlydoll," Charra had said. "You know why? Cos I want to die in your arms. If there's anyone who can send me into the afterlife feeling like I'm loved to pieces, it's you, Beany." Then Charra had rocked Ji-ji to sleep, the way Ji-ji had rocked Luvlydoll.

For weeks afterward, as Clay, their soon-to-be-auctionmarted brother, lay snoring in his bed nearby, Charra had climbed into Ji-ji's narrow bed in their small bedroom and held her close whenever she was beset by nightmares. As they tried not to hear Lotter in the cabin's main room ordering their mam to love him back, Charra would whisper fanciful tales in Ji-ji's ear, some of which were remakes of Uncle Dreg's stories and some of which were uniquely her own. Just when you were certain all hope was lost for seeds in her tales, something came along to save the day. By the time Charra got to "happy ever after," nothing on the planting was as scary as you thought.

One of the cruelest things Lotter had ever done was seedmate Charra to Petrus. Ji-ji still remembered her sister's face when Silapu broke the news. Like the other twelve father-men on the planting, Petrus was a bastard. Perhaps you could argue he wasn't as sadistic as Father-Man Williams or as manipulative as Father-Man Lotter, or as slimy as Father-Man Brine, but life as fourth seed-mate to that ignorant bastard would still be unbearable for anyone with half a brain. For Charra, it was a living hell.

Ji-ji still couldn't figure out why their father-man had settled on Petrus, a man he despised. For years, Lotter had boasted about the exorbitant seed-price he could command when he offered his beautiful Charra up for seedmating. The most light-skinned of all Silapu's offspring, with the type of combable hair steaders favored, a lean, agile body, and a face as lovely as Silapu's, Charra could bring in top dollar from any steader who'd wanted her as a seedmate.

For years, Charra strategized about her future. Either she would run before she was seedmated or get seedmated to someone she could twist around her little finger. She had her eye on Northrup Herring, Cropmaster Herring's youngest Stepson-Proper, a sickly-looking, gangly specimen, who visited the planting for three months out of the year to help with the harvest. Northrup was infatuated with her. A few steaders who didn't owe fealty to the planting took their seedmates back with them to Armistice, a privilege Northrup enjoyed. Charra's plan was to exit the planting as one of his seedmate picks. When they got close to the Great Lakes, she would run off to a Liberty Independent— Chicago, perhaps, or Milwaukee. Charra said Northrup was intimidated by her beauty and by any words that were more than two syllables. "I won't even have to fuck him, Beany," she'd boasted. "After I'm Free, I'll send for you. I got it all worked out. You'll see."

Ji-ji had never been able to erase Danfrith Petrus' expression from her memory as he clasped the copper seedmate band onto Charra's ankle and pocketed the key. Planting 437's Sixth Father-Man had purchased a lockable ankle band so she couldn't remove it without his permission. He'd looked at Charra as if she were a T-bone steak he had every right to chew on. When Pastor Gillyman had recited the words to conclude the ceremony—"As God the Father knows, and as it is written in His *One True Text,* it is a father-man's blessed duty to grow the Territories one seed at a time"—Petrus had exclaimed, "Damn right it is!" An explosion of spittle from his ragged mouth had sprayed her sister's face. Charra had wiped it off with the back of her hand, and Petrus—Ji-ji knew this for a certainty now she was older—had taken note of her sister's obvious repulsion toward him. Petrus had been besotted till then like Lotter was with their mam. But unlike Lotter, Petrus' passion wasn't as deep-rooted. By the end of the first week, his ardor was in retreat and his hatred for uppity seeds had taken over. The man who would later shoot and kill their mam at the fry-fence, the man whose gun Ji-ji carried, the man who'd killed little Lua by spurting his seed into her child-sized belly, had drunk so much during the afternoon of the seedmating ceremony that he'd been unable to perform that night, according to Charra. She'd sworn she would never let a moron like Petrus touch her.

But he had. Repeatedly. Everywhere.

Shocking to see how frail Charra looked when Ji-ji stopped by her seedmate cabin to see her that last time before she disappeared, when Ji-ji hadn't even noticed her sister's belly bump. Petrus had tried to beat the life out of her and he'd failed. Charra escaped. Not Charra Lottermule or Charra Petrusseed-mate, but Charra, her Own True Self-Evident Self, the singular individual who couldn't be cowed by any man for long. Like Uncle Dreg, Charra didn't permit suffering to defeat her; she converted it into fuel and used it to power a rebellion. That's what Ji-ji wanted to do. Who better than the sister who mothered her to help solve the riddle of how powerful she could become?

A flash of lightning forced Ji-ji back into the world of the swaying van flying south. The rain had started up again. A sluggish, distant rumble. Another. . . . "Was that thunder?" Ji-ji asked.

"Yeah," Tiro replied, adding kindly, "It's way off in the distance, Ji. Don't worry."

The toll roads were treacherous, but the back roads were worse. Each time they drove through a section of road that was partially underwater, Ji-ji held her breath. Impossible to say what lay beneath the surface.

"Rain's picked up," Tiro said. "Think we should pull over, man?"

Marcus leaned forward over the steering wheel and peered up into a black sky. "Nope," he said. "Be over 'fore you can say—" Marcus' voice broke off at exactly the same moment as the driver's-side windshield wiper, immediately followed by the one on the passenger side.

"*Shit!*" Marcus cried.

Tiro looked over at him. "Thought the wipers was fine."

"Shut up, T. I mean it."

"So how come these fell off? Can't see a goddam thing on this side. What do we do now?"

Marcus answered by coming to a full stop and then reversing back down the road a ways. "We gotta find 'em an' stick 'em back on," Marcus said. "*Shit!* Anyone see where they went?"

His question struck Tiro as funny. "Oh yeah, we saw 'em, Aurelius. Saw exactly where each one landed on the side of the road. Should be easy as pie to find 'em."

Marcus swore in response. He stopped the van and told Tiro and Tree to get out so the three of them could search.

"Why not me?" Ji-ji said.

"You stay here," Marcus said, in a much gentler voice. "Can't have those wings getting wet."

"For god's sake, man," Tiro said, "she's not some delicate flower. She was raised on a planting. She's tough as nails, right, Ji?"

"I said she stays inside," Marcus insisted. "It's pelting out there. Lightning too. Last thing we need is for her to get struck. This whole trip would be for nothing. C'mon."

"What about traffic?" Tiro asked. "We could get run down in the dark."

"Are you kidding me?" Marcus exclaimed. "When's the last time we saw anyone on this pathetic excuse for a road? An hour ago, that's when. Since we turned off the South Toll, it's—"

Tiro butted in: "An' whose idea was that? Not mine. I said we should stick to the highway."

"We do that an' we'd be stopped by every militiaman who wants to make a quick buck."

"Thought the tolls weren't manned down south?" Tree pointed out.

"Officially they're not," Marcus said. "But militias and Clans've moved in. There's impromptu checkpoints all along the main highway. Trust me."

"That's exactly what we did, bro," Tiro pointed out. "An' look where it got us."

"Shut the fuck up, T, an' help me look for the goddam wipers! It's cats an' dogs out there!" Marcus opened the door, then realized what they were up against. "*Jesus!* Anyone got an umbrella?"

Twenty minutes later, Marcus and Tiro were back in the van, sitting with grim expressions in puddles of rainwater. They dried themselves off with the towels they'd lifted from the Dreamfleet dorm. Due to the density of the foliage on either side of the road, finding the wipers in the dark proved impossible. They debated staying there till dawn so they could look for them in daylight, but none of them fancied the idea of being sitting ducks on a deserted road in the South, especially a new South that looked distressingly like the old one.

"We'll have to get a new set," Marcus said. "Or refurbished ones if we can find 'em."

"Where?" Tiro asked, apprehensively.

"Look at the map," Marcus said. "Could be there's an outpost or a small town nearby. Could be a repair shop or something."

Tiro was dubious. "A repair shop in the heart of Clan country. What could go wrong?"

Contradicting assertions he'd made earlier, Marcus countered with the idea that not everyone in the Madlands was a Clansman, militiaman, or Bounty Boy. "This is disputed territory. They got a few regular people living round here too. Just got to know where to look."

Lightning cracked the sky like an egg, rousing Ink, who'd been in a deep sleep. Waking up to a scene every former seed had nightmares about panicked him. "What's happened? We stuck here in the dark in Clan country? Has the van broke down? How come we're not moving, Tree?"

"We're not moving cos we've stopped," Marcus replied. "Don't be a girl, for god's sake."

"Leave him alone," Tree warned.

"Happy to oblige," Marcus countered. "Long as you keep your conjoined twin quiet."

Ink piped up again: "It's rude to say—"

Marcus shot back before Ink could finish: "Think I give a damn? Tell your little buddy to put a sock in it, Tree. I'm not in the mood. I mean it."

As the fly-boys argued, Ji-ji wondered how lost wipers became a personal affront. Eventually, she'd had enough.

"You're acting like morons," she said. Everyone stopped talking and looked at her in surprise. She had their attention and continued more confidently. "We should pull off the road an' search for the wipers while we wait for the rain to stop. Except Ink, who can guard the van."

"By myself?" Ink asked, fearfully.

Ji-ji knew how terrifying it could be to sit by yourself in the dark. "Or you can go with Tree," she suggested, "if you don't mind getting drenched. Or you can both wait in the van while the three of us search." She expected at least one of them to argue with her. Instead, they proceeded to follow her plan, Ink opting to stay in the van alone as long as he could borrow her gun.

After Ji-ji handed the gun over to Ink, Tiro said, "Don't fire at us by mistake, kiddo."

Ink laid the gun down beside him as if it were a sleeping baby and swore not to shoot them.

A few minutes later, having parked the van behind some bushes and out of sight from the road, Ji-ji and the others scoured the shoulder. Not that there was much of one to scour. Thunder and torrential rain made it tricky for them to hear each other, so they stayed close—Ji-ji and Tiro in one group, Marcus and Tree in another. Ji-ji had thought to bring a poncho Germaine had given her. The others had taken off their T-shirts. They would change into another pair of shorts when they returned. Every so often, Ji-ji ran back to the van to check on Ink.

The rain intensified. Soon, the road turned into a channel of rushing water. Ji-ji felt relieved to have made the right call. No way they could have driven through this in the wonky old van.

Something swirled up against her ankle! Ji-ji yelped, shone her flashlight down into the stream of water coursing along the road. A dead duck's bloated, upturned body floated near her leg. Not far behind the duck, a small flotilla of ducklings, all drowned, all tangled up in something.

Tree and Marcus ran up to her and Tiro. "It is a bad sign," Laughing Tree said, as he made the sign of the cross, "to see a dead mother duck."

"Could be he's the father," Tiro suggested. They looked at him. "Ducks are very paternal."

"Fuck the duck," Marcus said. "It's dead."

Tree shook his head. "Thought ducks could swim." Ji-ji suggested that something could've killed it. "Then it killed its babies too," Tree told her. He dipped his hand down in the water. "Someone strung them together. See the rope?"

"*Christ!*" Tiro said. "What sicko does that?"

"Someone who wanted to keep all his ducks in a row," Marcus quipped. No one laughed.

"We should get out of here," Tiro said. No one disagreed. *There are certain kinds of cruelty a seed learns to steer clear of,* Ji-ji thought. *Anything to do with rope is one of them.*

Upon their return to the van, the group strategized again.

"Can't stay here," Marcus said. "Van could be swept away. Gotta find higher ground."

Tiro was leery of that idea: "It's muddy as hell, an' we got a crappy van with low clearance. Get stuck or washed away 'fore we got a hundred yards down the road."

Tree said he'd seen a small hill a few yards back, not too far from where the van was parked.

"We get the van up there," he suggested, "an' sit out the storm."

"An' how do we do that?" Tiro asked. "Road's underwater an' the ground's muddy as hell."

"You're forgetting something," Marcus said. "We got a tree to help us."

They all turned to look at the big man in the back. Tree laughed, bashfully.

Fifteen minutes later, Ji-ji stepped on the gas while Tiro, Marcus, and Tree pushed the van from behind and Ink issued instructions. The wheels screeched in protest, but eventually they got the vehicle up onto the mound. Once there, they realized how modest their achievement was. The mound was more like the mound of a baseball field than a genuine hillock, with barely enough surface area to hold the van level. They were marooned, however, so it would have to do. They had to hope the water wouldn't rise much more and that it would recede fast.

Exhausted, the three mud-encrusted flyer-battlers climbed back into the van. The fly-boys had stripped themselves down to their underwear so they wouldn't have to wait for hours for their second pair of shorts to dry. They toweled themselves off, slipped on their dry T-shirts and shorts, and did their best not to think about the predicament they were in.

Marcus and Tiro plunged into sleep at once. Laughing Tree soon followed; his sonorous snores echoed over the downpour. Ink wrapped his arm around Tree's great forearm, rested his other arm on Petrus' gun and slept too. Ji-ji hadn't told Ink it wasn't loaded. After a while, she decided she would feel better with protection and risked waking Ink to retrieve it. As quietly as she could, she pulled her gun from his hand. She slipped out the empty mag and inserted a loaded one.

She peered out of the windows to gauge the height of the water and rehearsed how she would react should a hulking gator attack them, or a hungry pack of snarlcats, or militiamen, or a Clan. Uncle Dreg had told her that not all Clans were hostile. As an errander, he should know. Some Clan camps were more like communes, he said, inhabited by those who cherished autonomy and weren't afraid to live outside more protected spaces. But Ji-ji knew she couldn't count on that. Most Clansmen would take one look at the van and its contents and lay claim to the vehicle on the spot—lay claim to its contents, too, especially if they thought they could hold the fly-boys for ransom. She imagined how they would react when they saw her back, wondered if she could fly off before she was exposed then return to mount a rescue. Probably not. She'd be a sitting duck, and they'd already seen what Clansmen (militiamen?) did to ducks for fun. Nor did she think the beat-up old van would offer much protection. They'd locked the doors, but the double doors at the back had an unreliable latch. Hit it just right and the doors popped open—a trick Tree had discovered, apparently, on one of their trips to search for Afarra when Marcus had left the keys in the van and they'd had to break in. Ji-ji wished the fleet had been willing to lend them one of the new vehicles with features like auto start, self-drive, rechargeable batteries, and fancy AC units. But automobile manufacturing wasn't exactly going gangbusters—or going much at all, not even in the SuperStates, and luxuries like new cars were prohibitively expensive. She smiled to herself and shook her head. Here she was wishing for a fancier vehicle when not much more than a year ago she'd only ridden in a car, truck, or van a handful of times.

They had the windows up almost all the way to keep out the rain. It was steamy inside. The scent of rain mingled with the smell of sweat. The odor didn't bother Ji-ji. This was good male sweat, produced by labor they'd decided to do for themselves, not labor steaders forced them to do. It smelled sweeter somehow, cleaner.

Ji-ji had been eager to read the note from Amadeus Nelson. She'd forgotten about a letter once before and it had almost led to disaster; she wasn't about to repeat that mistake. Now seemed like as good a time as any to read it. She retrieved the letter from her bag. It was in a sealed white envelope with her name in confident cursive on the front. Zyla had scribbled the Dream Master's name on the bottom of the envelope too, so Ji-ji would know it was for her. Ji-ji retrieved a pen from her bag and blacked it out, just in case. She opened the envelope and flicked on a small flashlight to read.

Though Amadeus Nelson's ironic voice was evident from the start, he'd referred to events in such a way that, even if the letter was discovered, it wouldn't be a liability.

> ~~Dear Just Jellybean~~ Dear Ji-ji,
>
> I hear you have found your way onto the path you were meant to travel. At the gathering, you astounded your friends, or so a little bird told me. I am glad. My reputation was on the line, and I did not fancy having to explain to the MC why I had failed.
>
> You are now awash in blessings, which is not always a blessing as you will no doubt discover. You will be pulled this way and that. Everyone will want a piece for themselves. Beware. Dreams revived are dangerous in the hands of those with their own agendas.
>
> I will not visit again. You have grown beyond my skills. You are the dream fulfilled and now I am an empty nester. This is as it should be. I will not say I will miss our get-togethers for I have locked them away in a treasure box I intend to open once in a while so I can enjoy your company.
>
> As you journey forth with your friends, keep your eyes on the lies some will spin. Your instincts are good. Rely on them to guide you.
>
> People will disappoint you. There will be times when you will disappoint them. The third kind of disappointment, however, is the worst kind. It occurs when we disappoint ourselves. Concentrate on the last one, and do not worry too much about the other two.
>
> On many occasions, I go on walkabouts around the Dream. I will keep my eyes open for small snatched treasures. I promise. I am glad to hear you are heading North. For us, in the past and today, it is almost always a safer option.
>
> Yours ever,
>
> JGG

It took Ji-ji a moment to realize what the initials stood for. Then she remembered the flyer name he'd been given was Jolly Golly Gowler, a name only she and Zyla would recognize.

The Dream Master's words touched her, but they also made her apprehensive. She wasn't heading north with the Friends; she was heading deep into the South. *Birds fly south in winter,* she thought, *but this is the end of the summer.* She tried not to let it bother her too much. She wasn't a bird; she was a girl who was still learning to fly. Other parts of the letter made her heart soar. "You are the dream fulfilled," he'd written. From the man who'd had so little faith in her at first, the words carried weight. He'd written about a figurative treasure box—she and Tiro had made a literal one for Afarra. And he'd called Afarra a treasure he promised to search for cos he knew how much that would mean to her. The letter marked a turning point: her coach had become her friend. She hoped he would understand why she had to make this journey south. She had a feeling he would.

Ji-ji turned to check on Ink again and saw that Tree was awake, staring at her. She felt guilty.

"The gun wasn't loaded," she said, speaking softly so she wouldn't wake the others.

"I know," he told her. "I checked."

She felt the need to explain: "I was scared he'd shoot himself by accident."

Tree smiled. "That is quite possible. . . . I'm glad it was good news. Your letter."

She'd forgotten it was in her hand. She folded it up quickly. "How do you know?"

"You were smiling while you read it," Tree said, softly.

"Oh," she said, then added, "I'm sorry."

"Sorry for what?" Tree asked.

"For this," Ji-ji said, gesturing to the rain on the roof. "For bringing you to Mount Ararat."

"You didn't. Redipp did. The waters will pass soon. The ark remains intact."

His voice was kind. For the first time it occurred to her how uncomfortable the big battler must have been squidged up in the back.

"I saw you cross yourself," she said timidly, concerned about offending him. "Back there, when we saw the dead ducks."

"Habit. My mother used to cross herself like that. Nuns taught her to love their God. But I don't find anger appealing, and their God is sometimes very angry. Nor am I fond of obedience. Redipp has reminded me of that. I like my gods to have a sense of humor. My faith isn't theirs."

His response piqued her curiosity. "What is it then? If it's not theirs, I mean."

He raised his eyebrows in surprise. "No one has asked me that question in a long time. Give me a moment to think." The big man sat very still and looked down at his lap for several seconds. Then he said, "It is a *doing* thing, my faith. It's not about dreadful things that may come to pass if you do not do this or that. It's about what you can do now. . . . Now, I will ask *you* a question. What is it like to have those magical things on your back?"

Ji-ji took a deep breath and did the best she could. "I forget 'em sometimes. Then I don't, an' they feel like someone—some god with a sense of humor maybe—grafted the things onto my back. At other times, they feel like they're the only thing I could ever be."

"I see," Tree murmured, pensively. "It's the same for me. When I carry Ink I imagine at times he is a weight to carry. But most of the time it's not like that. Instead, *he* is carrying *me*." He chuckled to himself. "You're saying to yourself, 'I'm with a madman in the Madlands.'"

He was wrong. His statement had touched her deeply. She said, "I'm saying to myself I'm glad you and Ink decided to come along. I can't wait for you to meet my sister."

Strange, she thought, *how one friend seemed to know they had to step in for another.* Here was Laughing Tree taking over from where Amadeus Nelson had left off, just like Afarra had helped fill the hole left when Lua died, and Charra would soon help fill the void left by Afarra.

Ji-ji asked Tree something she'd wanted to ask since the Friends' meeting: "Did Tulip ask you to murder her brother?" He nodded. "What did you tell her?"

"I said I would help her do it, if I could. Or that I could maim him instead, if she preferred."

She assumed he was joking, but when she looked at his face, she realized he might be serious. "You were joking, right?" she said. He looked at her: no he wasn't. "S'pose they catch you?"

"Suppose they *don't* catch *him*. What then? They're not even looking, Tulip says. The Dream is fickle. Sometimes it loves us, sometimes not. After we return from this journey, I hope the Friends will carry you to a safer place. For now, we help each other."

Ji-ji wished she'd never introduced Tree to Tulip. "It would be murder."

"Yes. So it should never be done till other options are ruled out. You have killed before?"

Ji-ji felt as if he'd spat on her. The word "Killer" must be tattooed on her forehead.

She launched into a justification for the shooting of Bounty Boy Chet and the murder of Rudy the Picker. She realized too late that he had only heard about Chet and knew nothing about Rudy. She stumbled from one excuse to another till Laughing Tree raised a huge hand to quiet her.

"The world is a violent place," he said, with sympathy. "You were defending yourself."

"Yes . . . Only I . . . well . . . I initiated it. With Chet I had to do it cos they were lynching a fake Muleseed." She lowered her voice still further. "From the 368th." Tree looked surprised, but he didn't say anything. "They made him wear Mule ears to torment him. Only I couldn't cut the boy down in time. An' with Rudy I had to do it cos, if I didn't, all the runners would've been snatched by pickers. Some had been raped already cos I got there too late. It was a rescue mission."

"I see," Laughing Tree stated. She couldn't tell whether he was judging her or not.

"Could be Clown won't bother Tulip an' her sisters now," she offered, hopefully.

"Perhaps. But I'm a lot older than you, so you should listen to me when I tell you that clowns like him never change. My own brother was a clown. It's why I recognize him. Tulip's brother has felt what it's like to rape and kill. He enjoys it. He will be on the hunt now."

Tree's words terrified her: "On the hunt for who?" she said. "For Tulip? Her sisters?"

"Not for who. For *what*. He'll be on the hunt for repetition. . . . Listen. It's stopped."

He was right. The rain had stopped. The threat had receded.

Ink stirred. Tree patted his hand to let him know he was standing guard, and the boy fell asleep again.

Under the spell of the sky's sudden quiet, the two friends kept watch as the other passengers dreamed on in the dark.

18 NO GOING BACK

I t could have been worse.

Ji-ji consoled herself by focusing on the positives. Foremost among them was the fact that the rain had finally let up. In spite of the potholes, the tires were intact. They had a spare tire in the back for emergencies and enough food to last for days. Tree had thought to leave a couple of containers out to catch the rainwater last night, so there was plenty of spare water in case there was nowhere safe to stop along the way and fill the canteens. It was becoming clear to all of them, however, that they weren't nearly as prepared for this trip as they should have been.

It wasn't long past dawn, but already the promise of sweltering heat and humidity hung in the air. The farther south they drove, the worse it would get. Although they'd searched for more than an hour, they hadn't been able to find the windshield wipers. If they couldn't find somewhere to purchase replacements, they had to pray no more storms would hit before they made it to Turnabout. They still had to push the van off the mound, through the mud and onto the road. The engine had been reluctant to start up a couple of times the day before. Tree, who'd worked for a few months as a mechanic, warned them that if it turned out they needed parts they were screwed. Clan camps and militia outposts were not indicated on Tiro's map, so they couldn't predict how hostile an area might be. At the speed they had to drive along these bumpy roads and the roundabout route they had to take, Turnabout was still a couple of days' drive away—longer, perhaps. After last night's storm, it was possible they'd come upon a fallen tree or other debris on the road and be forced to find another route. The fleet callers had stopped working only an hour out of D.C. They'd picked up a signal near Richmond but it had been short-lived. Pitted with potholes prior to the torrential downpour, the road was now filled with large puddles and small ponds. But at least the asphalt was visible again, for the most part—a lean gray line winding south.

"Could be worse," Laughing Tree said.

"Could be *way* worse," Ink agreed.

"Not by much," Marcus said, as he scratched the swollen red lumps on his arms. He'd suffered worse than any of them last night. Tiro joked that all the mosquitoes in the Madlands must be female cos they wanted to suck on Aurelius almost as much as his harem did.

They checked their supplies. Ji-ji was pleasantly surprised to discover that Tiro had packed more carefully than anyone else. Among other things, he'd brought several changes of clothes, a first-aid kit, rope, sunglasses, mosquito netting, toilet paper, a small tent, a couple of sun hats, bug spray, a camping stove, five flashlights (one for each of them), blankets, and two extra pairs of sneakers. He and Marcus wore the same size shoe. Because of Tiro's foresight, Marcus, unlike Tree, didn't have to wear mud-encrusted, sodden sneakers that morning.

Marcus' supplies told Ji-ji a lot about what he anticipated from this trip. In addition to clothes, tarps, rope, food, and cans of gas, he'd brought half a case of whiskey, a couple of lethal-looking knives, four canisters of pepper spray, and what Ji-ji suspected was a cache of weapons in an enormous crate he wouldn't let anyone touch.

Ji-ji and Trink were the weak links when it came to preparedness. Apart from her gun, clothes, food, toiletries, and an extra pair of shoes, Ji-ji had brought her treasures: the snow globe, Lucky's dice, Silapu's blackbird quilt and a few other possessions which were as priceless to her as they were useless to everyone else. She redeemed herself somewhat by producing a flashlight and a knife, though neither was as impressive as Tiro's flashlights or Marcus' lethal-looking blades.

Aside from a duffel bag of clothes and food for him and Ink, Laughing Tree had brought a radio, which so far had produced only static; Ink's medication; a recipe book; and the new canvas carrying contraption Tree had hurriedly completed after Amadeus Nelson had given him a heads-up about Redipp's plans. The design was kinder to Tree's back and far less bulky than the makeshift "nest" they'd used previously.

"What the hell you need a recipe book for?" Marcus asked.

"It's a gift," Tree told him. "From me an' Ink. For Charra. Figure she may not get an opportunity to shop much." They all stared at him. "What?" Tree said. "Didn't anyone teach you to bring a gift when you go visit? My granma was from the Caribbean. Nahna would slap me from here to next week if I showed up as a guest empty-handed."

"S'a nice gesture," Ji-ji assured him.

"A spare wiper would've been nicer," Marcus grumbled.

Ji-ji hadn't thought to bring a gift for her sister. Maybe she could improvise? She certainly couldn't give the gun they'd taken from Petrus. The pretty snow globe Tiro had given her wouldn't work as a gift either. He would be hurt if she gave it away, and in spite of the problems between them, she never wanted to part with it. . . . The *quilt*! That was what she would give her sister. She'd have to do it with care. The last thing she wanted Charra to think about was how the quilt used to hang down from the ceiling in their mam's cabin to hide Lotter's rutting. She needed to give it an alternate history. She would tell Charra what Lua, as a Dimmer, had said about blackbirds, let her know much had come true. She would repeat the words of the lullaby Lua-Dim sang during the harrowing night in Brine's confessional when she'd rocked Silas PrettyBlack, her deadborn, and sang,

> When the bough breaks the cradle will fall
> And up will rise PrettyBlack, Cradle and all.
>
> Blackbird, pretty bird, take to the sky.
> Bye-bye, Blackbird, time to fly . . .

Ji-ji would tell Charra about Uncle Dreg's Death Day sermon too. More likely, Charra and she would recite it together. Surely everyone fighting to Free seeds must've heard it by now and committed the Oziadhee wizard's inspiring words to memory. Her sister had been right all along to believe that Toteppi from the Cradle had a special role to play. One day, as Lua-Dim's lullaby and Uncle Dreg's prophecy foretold, they would take to the sky like the blackbirds on the quilt.

Ji-ji recalled Man Cryday's observation about the three birds that stayed put after something frightened away the rest of the flock. But she didn't trust the tree witch anymore. She had lied to her about Charra. Who knew what else she'd lied about? She would ask Charra to explain what the quilt meant. Her sister had always been able to explain everything. Thinking about the quilt raised Ji-ji's spirits. She wasn't arriving empty-handed. Like Laughing Tree and Ink, she had a gift.

Dislodging the van from Mount Ararat wasn't as bad as they'd feared, but that was almost entirely due to Laughing Tree, who'd never, according to Ink, encountered a strength challenge he couldn't overcome. Before they pushed the van off the mound, they set out some tarp and piled their belongings onto it so the vehicle would be lighter. They pushed the van to within a few feet of the road, still keeping it partially hidden so they could reload it unseen.

As they piled things back into the van, Ink urged everyone to feel Tree's biceps. Said they were "big as melons and deserved respect," as if all of them had been disrespecting his biceps till then. Ink took credit for his friend's superhuman strength, basking in reflected glory and telling anyone who'd listen that Tree got a great workout carting him around.

Marcus approached Ji-ji, who was standing a little way off from the others. "Kid makes it sound like he's doing Tree a favor," he complained.

"Maybe he is," Ji-ji replied.

"Yeah. The kind of favor an owner does for an animule when it loads crap onto its back. . . . These bites're killing me! How come I'm the only one got bitten?"

The derision in Marcus' voice when he spoke about Ink upset Ji-ji. It reminded her of how Lotter used to talk about seeds on the planting who were classified as "Damaged."

"That why Ink irritates you?" Ji-ji asked. "You think he's taking advantage?"

Marcus shrugged. "Could be I don't like seeing a strong Black man bowing and scraping to a little shrimp. As a friend of mine used to say, guilt is an indulgence. Makes you do dumb shit."

"Tree cares for Ink. He loves him."

"I love pizza. Doesn't mean I want to cart around a hundred pizza pies on my back for the rest of my life." Marcus seemed to recognize how callous he sounded. "Don't listen to me," he added. "These goddam mosquitoes are to blame." Marcus' arms hadn't just been bitten, they'd been attacked. Dozens of painful bites from wrist to shoulder. He'd scratched them till they bled.

Ji-ji asked if he'd taken his malaria pill. He said he'd taken a double dose just in case.

"Didn't think you were supposed to double up on a dose," she said, remembering what Doc Riff told her when she used to volunteer at the seed clinic on the planting about the side effects of medications, most of which were unregulated and sold on the black market. "Could be that's why you're in a shitty mood. You shouldn't scratch either. You'll infect 'em."

She was a hypocrite. When her itchy wingsprouts drove her insane, she would have scratched them raw if she could have. "I brought some of Man Cryday's special ointment," she said. "Try some. Soothed my wingsprouts during the race. Bet it'll help with those bites."

Marcus' face relaxed into a smile. "Thanks, Ji-ji. Yeah. . . . I know I've been a pain in the ass. Going south's freaking me out more than I thought it would. Too much history. Too many trees."

Ji-ji wasn't sure if he was making a dark joke about lynching, or if some of his irritability had transferred itself from Ink to Laughing Tree. He sensed what she was thinking.

"Tree's okay," he said. "Got a helluva lot more patience than I do. Soon as we get to Turnabout I'll be a new man. You'll see."

"Thanks for volunteering to find Charra," Ji-ji said. "Nothing means more to me than that."

Marcus seemed embarrassed—not an emotion she usually associated with him. "No thanks necessary," he said. "Got my own reasons for making this trip. An' Tiro over there, he'd do pretty much anything you asked him to. Carry you to the other side of the world on his back if you wanted. Make Tree the Packmule jealous."

"We've been friends since we were seedlings. I'd do anything for him too."

"Yeah, I know. Let's just hope the drug-sop's worth it." Marcus noticed that Tree was loading up his mystery crate. "*Hey!* Hold up, Tree! I got that one." Marcus hurried over to retrieve it.

Ji-ji tried not to think about how Marcus had described Tiro. He had problems, sure. Temporary ones. The term *drug-sop* applied to Marcus, known for indulging in weed as often as Old Shadowy, and to her mam in an even worse way. Not to Tiro . . . she hoped.

Ensconced in their usual places in the van, the four passengers watched as Marcus struggled. The key had gotten bent after it refused to turn in the ignition. Infuriated, Marcus smashed it into the steering wheel. Tiro hadn't helped the situation when he'd made a joke about the key being as bent out of shape as Marcus. Marcus didn't find it funny. He straightened it out as best he could and jammed it into its little slit. Still wouldn't turn. He lost his temper, swore, jerked it out, swore, jammed it in again, yanked it out. "No one uses fuckin keys these days! Van's crap. Absolute *crap!*"

"Hey, man," Tiro said, "calm down! You're making it worse. Let me try."

"You wanna drive? Is that it?" Marcus said.

Tiro kept his cool. "Sure. S'not raining now."

"Fine," Marcus said. He tossed the bent key into Tiro's lap, thrust open the door, tore over to the passenger side of the van, and climbed in. As Tiro scooted over into the driver's side, Ji-ji overheard Ink in the row behind her ask Tree why Marcus was so angry.

"Got a lot on his mind," Tree told him.

"You won't let him hurt me, right, Tree?"

"No one will hurt you. He's letting off steam. Ignore him, son."

It was the first time Ji-ji had heard Tree call Ink "son." It sounded good. Like a real family.

Tiro worked on the key for a while then slid it into the ignition. The engine sputtered to life.

"*He did it!*" Ink cried.

"You stick with me, kiddo," Tiro called back. "Tiro Dregulahmo's got the magic touch."

Tiro turned out to be a much better driver than expected. In fact, he was better at skirting potholes than Marcus had been. Marcus seemed ready to instruct him on the finer points of driving, but as soon as it was clear Tiro had things under control, he slathered some of Man Cryday's ointment onto his arms, sighed with relief, and nodded off.

The passengers relaxed after Marcus started to snore. Ink rattled on about everything he observed along the way—trees, bushes, and more bushes—and warned everyone to be on the lookout for gators, stripers, and snarlcats. "They could be in the road, T. You ready for that?" Tiro patiently fielded every question Ink threw at him.

Apart from a couple of pit stops so people could relieve themselves along the side of the road (or farther back out of sight, in Ji-ji's case), they drove all morning without incident. Midafternoon, when Marcus offered to drive again, Tiro gratefully accepted.

In spite of the intense heat, Marcus woke up in a much better mood. He regaled them with stories he'd heard about the Madlands from Emmeline Shadowbrook and said that liberation squads like the one Charra led were the heart and soul of the Freedom movement. He chastised them for not knowing the Freedom Anthem, saying every liberator worth his salt knew it by heart. He offered to teach it to them so they wouldn't embarrass him when they met up with Charra's veteran Freedom fighters. He was uncharacteristically patient, repeating each verse till they got it right. Ji-ji could hold her own when it came to singing, but Tiro was horribly out of tune, and Laughing Tree, who swore he was tone deaf, growled the words rather than sang them. Marcus, on the other hand, was an impressive tenor, and Ink's singing voice shocked the whole lot of them into silence when they heard it for the first time.

"Where'd you learn to sing like an angel?" Marcus asked him.

"It's how I always sing," Ink replied, guardedly.

They waited for Marcus to take a verbal swipe at the boy who irritated him almost as much as his bites. "Well," Marcus said, "it's fuckin marvelous."

Ink beamed.

Together, Marcus and Ink led the way. The song was rousing, the beat insistent. Stirred by the anthem, Ji-ji felt like a Freedom fighter riding into battle. Marcus told them the last three words had to be shouted at the top of your voice. They yelled till their throats were hoarse.

> No more the seed, no more the plow
> Seeds are the victors now!
> Hear the wind whisper
> the dream's holy name
> "Freedom," it whispers, again and again.

No more the seed, no more the plow
The cause is the only path left for us now
Their laws are a travesty
Their promises lies
We'll fight for our legacy, fight till we die

Defy their oppression! Go forth, unify!
Lord-Father of Armistice, get ready to die!
Justice, sweet justice, get ready to rise!
DEFY! DEFY! DEFY!

A sharp bend in the road.

A Black man jumped out in front of them and waved his arms frantically in the air. His battered truck tilted at a precarious angle in a ditch. Looked like the man had taken the corner way too fast. He screamed at them to stop. The only word Ji-ji caught was "*HELP!*"

Marcus swerved to avoid him. With its high center of gravity, the van almost tipped over.

"*Jesus Christ!*" Marcus yelled. He kept on driving.

"What you doing, man?" Tiro cried.

"Keeping you alive," Marcus replied.

"That wasn't some steader or Clansman," Tiro argued.

"So? Think it's safe to stop for everyone who drives like a goddam fool?"

Tiro banged his hand on the dashboard. "I say we stop," he declared.

"Marcus is right," Ink said. "It's way too dangerous to stop."

"Out of the mouths of babes," Marcus said, as if the matter was settled now Ink had spoken.

Laughing Tree interposed. "We stop. There were little ones in the truck back there."

"There were children in the truck?" Ji-ji asked, anxiously.

"Two, maybe more," Laughing Tree said. "Saw them peek out. Be dark soon. We passed five or six vehicles, two with Territorial flags a few miles back. It's not safe for little children to be stranded on this road. We go back."

Marcus was stunned: "It's not safe for *us* either! Have you forgotten where we land on the Color Wheel? Where *you* land especially?"

Tree didn't rise to the bait. "This is the Madlands," he stated, calmly, "not the Territories."

Marcus was irate. "So? Madlands, Margins, Territories! If you think that makes a fuckin bit of difference, you need to take a break from animuling an' read a few books once in a while!"

Tiro put his hand on the wheel. "We stop an' help 'em, Marcus," he said.

Marcus turned on him next: "Get your goddam hand off the wheel, T!"

Tiro let go of the wheel, but he repeated what he'd said earlier: "We go back an' help."

"Far as I can see," Marcus pointed out, "that makes it two for turning back an' two against. Driver's vote counts double. We keep going."

"There's five of us in this van," Tiro reminded him. "Ji, what's your vote? Think we should go back or drive on?"

"You *insane?*" Marcus asked. "You risk the Existential for the sake of a bunch of strangers?"

Ink was getting frantic. "Say drive on, Ji-ji! It's *dangerous*! The man could be existential!"

"Not *him*," Marcus said. "*Her*. She's the Existential. We gotta get her to her destination."

Ji-ji swiveled round in her seat in the second row to address Tree in the third: "You sure there were kids in the back?"

"I'm sure," Tree confirmed.

"Could be a trap," Marcus pointed out. "Wouldn't be the first time militias used seed bait."

Seed bait. That's what did it. "We go back," Ji-ji said, with conviction.

Ink wailed in consternation: "*No! Please!* It's not safe! If it's a picker trap those bastards'll ship us back to the plantings! Or *lynch* us! I *won't* go back there!"

"Ink, it's okay," Ji-ji said. She reached back to pat his knee. "We got Tree an' we got weapons. We'll be okay. . . . We should have our guns drawn, just in case."

"You think?" Marcus said. His sarcasm reverberated inside the van.

Ji-ji felt Laughing Tree's eyes on her. The word "Killer" must be a blinking neon sign on her forehead. Couldn't be helped. If it hadn't been for what Tree had told them, she wouldn't have felt obligated to turn back. But how would she live with herself if she left little children cowering like sitting ducks in a truck on a side of the road in the Madlands? She pictured them all strung together with a lynch rope. If they didn't go back, who would?

"You sure you want to do this, Ji-ji?" Marcus asked. His voice was doom-laden but he wasn't yelling. "If we keep going we reach Charra's camp by the day after tomorrow. We got no wipers an' a shitty map. The van can be outstripped by a pedal bike. You sure about going back?"

She wasn't sure. Marcus was right; it was risky. They were deep inside Carolina Clan Country. If this was an ambush, the odds were against their escape. Though she hadn't yet got a glimpse of the ocean, Tiro had told them the coast was off to their left. Driving east to escape an ambush, even if there was some trail they could take—not an option. Besides, the low-riding van would be useless off-road. Flat, swampy, gator-friendly land surrounded them. On either side of the road, the foliage was overgrown. Anything (a pack of stripers? a snarlcat?) or anyone (Clansmen, Bounty Boys, pickers) could be hiding in there. She wanted to tell Marcus to drive on, she really did. Her hands were super cold, the way they got when she was petrified.

"They're us," she said. She'd said it too softly for them to hear. She repeated it more forcefully. "They're us. We got no choice. We turn back."

"Okay then," Marcus said, resignedly. He'd capitulated. Part of her wished he hadn't.

"Roll the windows up an' hang on!" Marcus added.

Without missing a beat, he executed a three-point turn on the narrow road. The tires squealed and the van rocked. Things shifted in the back. Ink started to whimper in the seat behind her. "Shut up, Ink," Ji-ji said, sounding like Marcus, who'd known all along how eager inhabitants of the Madlands were to go hunting. In the back of her throat, the sour taste of terror.

Ji-ji drew Danfrith's gun out of her backpack and felt its lethal, Father-Man-Petrus weight in her small brown hands as they embarked on a rescue mission none of them wanted to make.

||||||||||||||||

It seemed to take hours to get back to where they'd seen the truck in the ditch, but in reality it was only a few minutes. They hurtled down the road accompanied by Ink's occasional stifled whimpers, which made him sound more like a small dog than a boy. His fear was contagious.

Marcus told Tree to retrieve the crate from the back and pry it open. There were guns inside, he said, and a few grenades. "Don't touch the fuckin pins or we'll be blown to Kingdom Come. Not the one in the Dream either," he joked. Ji-ji marveled at his ability to joke at a time like this.

By the time they spied the tilted truck in the ditch, everyone was convinced it was a trap. Ji-ji wished she'd voted no; her stomach was churning. She'd remembered too late she was a lousy shot. She'd meant to practice, but how do you do that when you're hiding out in an abandoned coop in the city's flood zone? Marcus slowed the van way down and issued last-minute instructions. Ordered them to keep the doors locked and weapons at the ready.

"You got the grenade handy, Tree?" Marcus asked.

"Got it. Don't intend to use it on children."

"Children can be decoys too," Marcus cautioned. "Okay, Freedom fighters, think of this as a rehearsal for the big raid on the 437th."

Ji-ji realized it wasn't the first time Marcus had been in a situation like this.

Probably why the last thing he wanted to do was repeat the experience. Like Lucky when they were on the run, Marcus was thinking several steps ahead. He had the same practiced ease with weapons Lucky exhibited.

"You see any children?" she asked.

"No," Tiro said, as they slowed down and drew nearer to the truck. "Truck looks empty. Front an' back. Don't see the man flagged us down either."

At that moment, the man stepped out from behind the truck. Ji-ji saw him more clearly this time. A Black man of average height, he wore a pair of glasses duct-taped together, and a threadbare, scruffy jacket (in this heat!) that looked like it must have been expensive originally.

Marcus came to a stop, rolled down his window, and pointed his gun directly at the stranger.

"You came back!" the man cried, helplessly, as he stumbled toward them. He spotted Marcus' gun and flung his hands in the air. He started to back away and beg for mercy.

"Don't shoot! *Please,* man! *Don't hurt us!*"

He said "us," Ji-ji thought. Marcus held his gun steady.

Tiro rolled down his window and levered his upper body up and out so he could peer over the roof of the van. Marcus ordered him to get his ass back in the car. Tiro didn't comply till he'd assured the man they'd returned to help.

"S'okay," Tiro said. "We won't hurt you."

"Not unless you're planning something stupid," Marcus added.

Tree had rolled his window down too. In a calm voice, he asked the man what happened.

"Territorials on my tail. Took the curve too fast. They ran us off the road . . . for the hell of it! You see the steaders' homestead flags on the trucks back there?"

"Yeah," Marcus said. "We saw 'em."

Tree grabbed the door handle and slid it open.

Marcus couldn't believe it. "What the *hell* you think you're doing, man?"

"There are children," Tree stated. He stepped onto the road. "Behind the truck."

Sure enough, a small brown face peered around the side of the vehicle.

The man in the suit rushed over to the child, who couldn't be more than two years old, and swept the toddler up in his arms.

"You got to get through me first!" he cried.

Two other small children rushed out from behind the truck and cowered behind the man.

Laughing Tree said, "We came back to see if you need help. That's all. We took a vote." He yelled over his shoulder: "There's two other little ones, so three altogether. Told you."

"We're not blind," Marcus yelled back.

Tree addressed the children: "Don't be scared. We're fly-boys. Know what fly-boys are?"

The oldest child, a boy in dire need of a haircut, dressed in a soiled shirt that looked as if it had once been his Sunday best, peeked out from behind the man and said, "Fly-boys fly the coop."

Tiro shouted from the van: "What's your name, man?"

"Stamos," the father replied.

"Listen, Stamos," Tree said, "I'm about to come up an' offer you my hand in a handshake cos that's how I was raised, and my Jamaican nahna would have a hissy fit if I wasn't friendly to brothers like you. When I do that, I would prefer it if you didn't pull out that gun you got tucked in the back of your pants. My body looks better with a head on top. I'd like to keep it that way."

Stamos looked as if he was about to have a heart attack.

"Tree's big but he won't hurt you," Ji-ji called out. "I promise." Pathetic she knew, but she couldn't think of anything else to say, and the poor man looked like he was about to pass out.

"She's right," Tree said. "I'm between you and the van, which means I'm trusting you not to blow my head off. My name's Laughing Tree. My little buddy's name is Ink. Ink's in the van, praying I won't get my head blown off, cos if I do, he'll be at the mercy of the irritable bastard who's got a gun aimed at your chest. That wouldn't be good cos the mosquitoes bit him up bad last night and he was short on patience to begin with. The irritable bastard, I mean, not the boy."

Ink, whose confidence in his friend was absolute, waved and threw out a "hi" from the van. The boy peeking out from behind his father waved back. "I ain't a fly-boy," Ink called out. "Used to be. Got crippled in the Jefferson in Monticello. Tree carts me round so I—"

"Where you from?" Marcus demanded. Without anyone noticing, he'd stepped out of the van and moved off to the side. If Stamos pulled a gun on Tree, Marcus would have a clear shot. But if he fired, he'd as likely hit the toddler as the father. Laughing Tree saw what he was doing and again placed himself between Marcus and the stranger. Marcus cussed him out. His curses sawed through the air between them like a chain saw. Tree didn't budge.

"Charlotte," Stamos said, warily. "We're from Charlotte."

"That's a Liberty Independent," Marcus said. "What brings you to the Madlands with a truckload of seedlings?"

The man flinched when Marcus called his children seedlings, but he kept his thoughts to himself. The eldest boy didn't show the same restraint. He leapt out from behind the man and stood before them with his hands on his hips.

"Who you calling *seedlings*?" the boy cried.

Tree laughed. "Guess you're a Born-Free, right?" he said to the boy.

"I sure am!" the boy boasted.

His father told him to shut up. The girl peeked out this time. She couldn't be more than five. The older boy was about eight. Why would anyone drag their small children through the Madlands?

Ji-ji stepped out of the van and walked toward them. She pointed her gun down to the ground so she wouldn't frighten them. Tiro ordered her to get back inside. When she ignored him, he leapt out himself and came up beside her.

The little girl was terrified. "It's okay," Ji-ji said, addressing the girl. "What's your name?"

"Ruthie-Ray," the girl said.

"That's a real nice name," Ji-ji told her. "My name's Jellybean but people call me Ji-ji. I got some candy here. Want some?"

"I asked you a question," Marcus said, walking toward the group, gun still pointed at the man's chest. *Or is it his head?* Ji-ji thought. *Or is he pointing it at the toddler?*

"Where you going?" Marcus demanded.

"Atlanta."

"Keep your hands where I can see 'em," Marcus said. He called back to the car: "Ink, watch the road. Warn us if something's coming." He turned back to Stamos. "You took a roundabout route to get to Atlanta from Charlotte. Why'd you veer so far east?"

"Toll road from Charlotte's swarming with . . ." The man hesitated.

"With what?" Marcus asked.

The eldest boy piped up again: "With Clan bastards," he said.

Stamos told his son to shut up.

"What's in Atlanta?" Tree asked.

The man hesitated. Almost imperceptibly, he looked back at the truck. "A surgeon," the man said. "Not many decent surgeons in Charlotte. Not since the last pandemic and the siege."

"I forget," Marcus said. "How long that siege last?" A trick question. A test.

"Eight months," the man told him. "Ended a few months back. November. But by then the city was . . . crazy. No law enforcement, not much food. Gangs of looters roaming the streets."

Marcus seemed satisfied with that answer. "What you need a surgeon for?"

The little girl couldn't wait any longer. She ran out from behind her father, rushed up to Ji-ji and grabbed the candy. Stamos tried to go for his gun, but Marcus warned him if he moved a goddam muscle he was dead.

The man yelled at the children to run, but they were no match for Tree and

Ji-ji. They only got a few feet before Tree swept up the boy and Ji-ji caught the little girl. Like the rest of her family, the girl was shockingly thin.

Stamos was nearly hysterical: "Don't hurt the children! That's all we ask!" The door of the truck swung open.

Stamos ran to it screaming, "*Don't shoot! Don't shoot!* It's my *wife! Don't shoot!*"

A bald woman, so thin her bones jutted from her flesh, fell out of the truck and onto the ground. She screamed at them not to hurt her babies. Stamos rushed to shield her.

"She's *sick!*" Stamos cried. "Needs surgery." He appealed to Laughing Tree: "Please, man! I'm *begging* you!"

"It's okay," Ji-ji said. "We'll help you. Don't worry, Mr. Stamos. We're your friends."

The man looked from Ji-ji to Tree and back again. He glanced over at Marcus, who'd lowered his gun at last. Finally, Stamos understood they weren't in danger anymore. Fighting back emotion, he helped his wife to her feet and called to his children, who ran to him. The family embraced in a tight circle. "They came back for us," the mother sobbed. Overcome with relief, the man kept shaking his head and saying, "We thought this was it."

After a few moments, the man recovered sufficiently to speak: "Name's Sidney," he said. He extended his hand to Laughing Tree. "Sidney Stamos. My lovely wife here is Olivetta. This is our eldest boy, Reed. Our little girl is Ruthie-Ray. Likes candy, don't you, Ruthie? And our littlest one is Rowdy. In more ways than one. *R* is Olivetta's favorite letter—right, honey?

"We're gonna be okay," Sidney Stamos said to his family, as if he still didn't quite believe it. "These are our people come back to help us. We're gonna be okay."

|||||||||||||

It wasn't as difficult as Ji-ji assumed it would be to get the truck out of the ditch. Working together, they were able to rock it into an upright position. Stamos had wisely brought a shovel. (Ji-ji didn't want to think about the reason for that.) As fast as they could, they dug a small exit ramp and pushed the truck out of the ditch. When Tiro suggested they escort the family down to the turnoff for Atlanta, Sidney Stamos broke down. Said it was the first time in ages strangers had volunteered to help without wanting something in return. He swore he'd never forget it as long as he lived.

As they labored to get the truck back onto the road, Sidney disclosed more about their situation. He was a lawyer in Charlotte. He didn't say exactly what his wife, a former elementary schoolteacher, was suffering from, but cancer seemed like the obvious diagnosis. Atlanta was their last hope for treatment.

Ji-ji knew that the city was a Liberty Independent, one of the first to issue its own Declaration of Urban Independence (colloquially known as a DUI), along with a constitution very similar to the original one for the U.S., except that all people—men and women, Black, Brown and White—were pronounced equal. Atlanta's Declaration hadn't sat well with the Territories, but the city had been too powerful to oppose. Like other urban Liberty Independents that fought for their autonomy after the Sequel, Atlanta was a thorn in the side of the Supreme Council in Armistice. A constant reminder that the secessionist cause had only been a partial success and that many of the largest prizes in the South, the Midwest and the West were lost. Sidney had heard from his cousin who lived in Atlanta. He'd offered to act as their sponsor. The city, though not prosperous by any means, was in recovery mode like D.C. It had food and medicine, a disciplined municipal army, and trade agreements with both the SuperStates. Perennial water wars with neighbors had at last resulted in a viable treaty.

"We'll find a good surgeon in Atlanta," Sidney said, hopefully. "Food too."

"We got plenty of food," Ink said. "Want some?"

"The Lord will reward you all," Olivetta said, her voice so weak they had to strain to hear it.

The children were ravenous. Ji-ji had often been hungry, but she'd never been starving. It pained her to see how grateful they were for such modest offerings. Olivetta promised her husband she would eat later. He carefully put some aside for her and instructed the children not to touch it.

During the rest of the journey, the van led the way, closely followed by the truck. They drove through most of the night, stopping only for a couple of hours so Sidney could nap. Tiro offered to drive the truck so Sidney could rest for a while, but Marcus was wiped too. Eventually, they all agreed it was wise to pull over and let the drivers nap.

Tree and Ji-ji kept watch while the others slept. Ruthie-Ray had pleaded with her father to let her join Ji-ji in the van. He'd been reluctant at first, concerned she would be a nuisance, but Ji-ji promised to take good care of her, and Olivetta told her husband it would be okay. Inside the van, the little girl, chewing furiously on the last of the candy, snuggled up to Ji-ji, who told her about the magical City of Dreams, leaving out the nightmarish parts.

"I want a sister like you," Ruthie-Ray said. "Visit me in Atlanta every day, okay?"

The journey was slower than they'd hoped. The roads were too badly maintained to risk driving much faster than thirty or so. But it could have been worse. The weather stayed dry, and for Ji-ji, at least, it felt good to travel with a family and know they'd done the right thing by helping them. Once, they had to turn back and find another route because part of the road was washed away.

Several times they stopped to let gators cross. On numerous occasions, Ink swore he caught sight of stripers or snarlcats loping off into the undergrowth.

That night, after another shared meal, they exchanged stories about life in Charlotte and Dream City. Marcus had advised the D.C. group not to say where they were headed, but Ink blurted it out anyway. As it turned out, Sidney and Olivetta had heard of Turnabout. Said there were stories about a well-trained force of raiders there. Former seeds, African Americans, Latins and Asians so fierce even the Clansmen and militias avoided them. Tiro looked over at Ji-ji and smiled encouragingly when they said that.

The next evening, after another arduous day of driving on dicey roads, they reached the turnoff to the main East-West Toll Highway that led to Atlanta. Marcus said the road would be guarded by Atlanta patrollers, so they should be okay. They'd driven dozens of miles out of their way to make sure the family reached the road safely but none of them regretted it. As they said goodbye, even Marcus got choked up.

As a parting gift, Marcus presented a 9 mm semi from his stash to Sidney, who only had a .22-caliber. Marcus said a .22 wouldn't do much more than irritate a Clansman even if he managed to hit him between the eyes. Sidney said he didn't know how to thank him.

"Thank us by getting safely to Atlanta," Marcus said. "No more the seed, no more the plow," he added.

Sidney smiled broadly. "From your mouth to God's ears, brother. Reunify!"

Olivetta grabbed hold of Ji-ji and wouldn't let go. "Thank you! Thank you!" she whispered.

The woman drew back in alarm. Ji-ji froze. She'd let down her guard. The woman had felt the strange ridges and bumps on her back!

Ji-ji was inventing stories to explain them when the woman shook her head. "I'm sorry, honey," she said. "You're too young. Cancer is a terrible thing." Ji-ji exhaled. Cancer. She should've thought of that. "I've got a few months, at most," Olivetta added. "Sid thinks I'll have longer with surgery. He's a good Christian man, and he's been through hell. How can I take away his dream?"

As Ji-ji watched the truck's taillights disappear into the evening, something gnawed at her. When Marcus had approached Sidney, his gun drawn and ready to fire, he'd reminded her of someone else. She hadn't been able to put her finger on it till now. Marcus had looked just like Bounty Boy Zebadiah Moss, Fightgood Worthy's twin brother. Menacing. Merciless. It sickened Ji-ji to think she'd been on the terrorizing side of the fence.

She had to let it go. Things had turned out well. Marcus hadn't killed anyone. The situation could be much worse.

She focused on happier things. Increasingly, Ji-ji felt her sister's presence, as if the van was a fish and Charra was reeling them in. Her back felt it too—the pull exerted by family. *Her* family.

They resumed their journey, headed in the right direction again. The others had fallen asleep. Tiro, driving, asked her if she was excited. She said she was.

"What you plan to say when you see Charra, Ji? Been a long time."

Ji-ji thought for a moment. "Guess I'll say thank you."

"For what?"

"For fighting to stay alive so I can love her all over again."

"Yeah," Tiro said. "That'll do just fine."

iro didn't want to believe it. The night before, they'd said goodbye to the Stamos family and set off on the last leg of their journey. Earlier today they'd been singing. That anthem Marcus had taught them. Laughing. Joking with each other. Marcus in a good mood for once. And now, *this*.

Tiro tried to block out Ink's sniveling. It hadn't stopped. He had a hard enough time holding himself together as it was. Ink sat hunched over in the van's third row. Ji sat next to the weeping boy and did her best to comfort him. Marcus drove. He had his eyes fixed on the road. Didn't look at the man beside him in the passenger's seat, the navigator's position. Any of the three masked bastards riding in the van with them could blow their heads off. God only knows what they were doing to Tree. He'd been ready to fight till they'd pointed their guns at Ink and Ji. Tree had gone quietly as a mouse after that. They'd trussed Tree up like a turkey and loaded him into the back of their truck. Took five of them to get him in there. Made sense they'd want to secure him first. Made sense they'd be careful about it. Didn't want their property to sustain damage, not when it was worth a small fortune. Who could command a higher price at auctionmart than a man the size of a tree?

Earlier, before the ambush, Marcus had pulled onto a dirt road out of sight of the main road to wait out the rain. Without wipers, couldn't see a damn thing. Tiro had volunteered to take the first watch. "You awake enough?" Marcus had asked. "Sure," he'd said. But he'd dozed off like everyone else to the sound of rain and the rumble of thunder. Hadn't intended to fall asleep. Hadn't taken a damn thing, apart from a couple of killers he'd swallowed to take the edge off an old ankle injury. He'd been jerked awake in the middle of a dream about Dimmers. The ghouls swarmed round the van, jabbed at him with their long black fingers. Dozens of them. Initially, when he'd seen the shadows shifting outside, he'd thought he was still dreaming. No. These shadows were real! A dozen masked men. Long pants, black shirts (leastwise, they looked that way in the dark), gloves, night goggles. Nothing showing, not even their hands. Their goggles made them look like robots.

These weren't Clansmen, not with equipment like this. These were militia. Could be one or two females among them too, Tiro couldn't say for sure. Well trained. Didn't say a word hardly. Spoke to each other using code and grunts and hand signals. Not being able to see their faces terrified Ink most of all. "Who are they?" he kept repeating, till Tiro wanted to smother him. The worst of it was they were only an hour or two from Turnabout. If they hadn't gotten lost twice, they'd be there already. He told himself none of this was his fault. The roads looked nothing like the ones on his sucky map.

He'd been cradling his gun in his arms when they rapped on the windows. Cradling it like a liveborn. Hadn't even had time to raise it to heart level. Hadn't had time to aim. Their attackers had ordered them to climb out. Marcus had woken up and started cussing at Tiro. Like he knew in his sleep that Tiro, whose only job had been to stay awake, would let them all down.

Lined up outside in the rain with the others, Tiro saw they couldn't fight their way out. Their attackers had guns and rifles—hunting rifles mostly. A couple of scary-looking assault rifles too. At their belts they carried knives, cuffs, rope, and what looked like grenade pouches. One of them took the cuffs from his belt and used them on Tree, fastened them behind his back. Another used his rope to bind Tree's size 23 feet at the ankles.

They'd cuffed the rest of them apart from Marcus. Tiro's hands were cuffed behind him like Tree's, but they cuffed Ji's and Ink's in front. Tiro tried to take that as a positive sign. Could mean they had some mercy in them. No. Probably not. More likely, they didn't see Ji or Ink as a threat.

Tiro was relieved they hadn't killed the boy as soon as they discovered he was damaged before he realized they weren't doing Ink any favors. Probably had a few comrades who liked to spend their leisure time with boys like Ink. Could be they were saving him for something special.

They'd stood in the rain for a few minutes while the masked militiamen rooted through their stuff. Only one of the bastards spoke, his voice gruff and almost unintelligible, like he was disguising it so they'd never know who their assailants were. The militiamen demanded to know who they were and where they were headed.

Marcus had put on his usual Uncle Tom, weaving crap with truth with the ease of an expert liar. Said they'd been heading back to the Dark City from Atlanta. Had friends there they'd been visiting. The wife was real sick.

"What's his name?" the militiaman had asked.

"Stamos," Marcus had replied, smooth as silk. "Sid Stamos. Wife won't live long. Olivetta's her name. Got cancer. My boy ain't real good with a map. Guess we got lost."

Tiro hadn't been able to figure out at first why Marcus hadn't said they were fly-boys. He was taking a gamble that none of them would be recognized. Then he put two and two together. Marcus must've figured they wouldn't take too kindly to fly-boys from a Liberty Independent. They'd want to know what the hell they were doing riding around in the Madlands. Marcus' version was safer for now. The bastards hadn't bothered to ask for their papers. In theory, if they had papers saying they were Free, they couldn't be waylaid in the Madlands. In practice, they were as vulnerable as ever. The Madlands were the Madlands, and papers could be confiscated.

The militia took most of their stuff from the back of the van and reloaded it onto their vehicles. Didn't bother to go through it first. Just loaded it into the backs of two big army-type trucks with oversize wheels and tread as deep as your fist. Cost a pretty penny. Stolen for sure. Tree was their only hope. Maybe the powerful battler would break Free from the ropes, reach into Marcus' weapon crate and save them all? Not a chance. They'd run rope round Tree's middle section, taped his mouth shut, and slipped a goddam hood over his eyes. Laughing Tree, the gentle giant, looked like a goddam executioner.

Was that what they planned to do? Have him lynch some of the others? Ink? Ji? Please god no. He'd persuade them to spare her if it was the last thing he did. He'd reveal her secret if it came right down to it. Tell them how valuable she was. They wouldn't kill her if he did that. They'd keep her alive as a curiosity. . . . No. He couldn't do that to her. Ji would rather be dead. . . . Could be they'd pyre her as a witch soon as they saw her back. One of them (a female?) searched Ji, but they were in a hurry and it wasn't much of a pat down. So far, they knew nothing about her crazy-as-shit wings. Tiro had heard stories about militia commandos who kept a dozen or more Wives-Improper. Could be their commander didn't like any of his men to deep-search the females before he did.

They ordered Marcus to drive, follow the truck in front. The second truck fell in line behind them. Flicked its headlights on full once in a while so it was easy to see what was going on inside the van. The rain had eased up so the wiper deficiency wasn't too bad, especially as Marcus only had to follow the truck in front. Tiro wasn't even sure if the militiamen noticed there were no wipers. Their silence was deliberate. A way to intimidate them. It worked.

Like Marcus, Tiro had a gun pointed at his face. Ji and Ink didn't, though the third militiaman (woman?) kept a close eye on them both, gun at the ready. Tiro suspected Ji had her knife hidden somewhere, but what could she do with a damn pocketknife?

If they tried to separate him from Ji, that's when he'd make his move. She'd know he'd been her friend forever, right up to the moment when death parted them. She'd know he was prepared to risk everything to keep her safe. Didn't matter if it was futile, mattered if it was attempted.

Ink's whimpering went up a notch. "It's okay," Ji said. "Tree'll be okay."

Ink was bawling too much to respond. Could hardly breathe he was so upset.

"He needs his inhaler," Ji said to the men. "He's having an asthma attack. Can I get it for him? It's in his bag. Behind us in the back. Or maybe it's in the back of one of your trucks. Can I check an' see? *Please*. He can't breathe without it."

The militia exchanged looks. The one in the passenger seat was the leader. He nodded. With some difficulty cos she was cuffed, Ji managed to lean over and find Ink's bag. The person guarding her told her to open it real slow. Tiro had guessed right. She was female. Ji might be able to take her. Which left one each for Marcus and Tiro. Both armed to the teeth. Not good.

Ji found the inhaler. Administered it to Ink, whose breath was scary raspy, like a handsaw on a tree limb. After he'd taken two big puffs, Ji made a circle of her cuffed arms and looped them over the boy. Tiro looked away cos it hurt too much to see how hard she was trying to console him. "It'll be okay," Ji repeated. Tiro hated himself for his helplessness. Hated himself worse for falling asleep. Wanted something to take the edge off. Wanted it so bad he thought he'd die if he didn't get it.

One of the men ordered Marcus to pull over onto the side of the road. The truck in front was already slowing down. Had they arrived at their camp?

Tiro knew his fly partner's mind was racing, thinking three, four steps ahead. Marcus was smarter than he was, wilier. If only they had an opportunity to communicate, they could work together. Whatever it was, it wouldn't involve a suicide mission. Marcus wasn't into martyrdom.

After the van came to a stop, the lead bastard in the passenger seat told Marcus to get out of the van real slow. Told him to head on up to the truck in front, same truck they'd loaded Tree onto. The militiaman scooted over from the passenger seat and followed Marcus outside, gun trained on him the entire time.

"Where you taking him?" Tiro cried.

Too late. Marcus was gone. Night swallowed him up.

Another militiaman climbed into the driver's seat.

"Where's Marcus?" Tiro yelled.

The gunman next to Tiro had him in a choke hold before he could utter another word. The gunman in the driver's seat reached back and taped his mouth shut. If he hadn't been cuffed he could've taken them both, easy. The last thing Tiro saw before they slipped a hood over his head was Ji holding Ink and lying to him again. "It'll be okay," she said.

From beneath his hood, Tiro heard them tape and hood the other two. Ji begged them not to tape Ink's mouth, said he needed to breathe. They didn't listen. Tiro cursed himself for not making his move when Marcus was led from the van. Now it was too late.

Sometime later, the van slowed down. Though it was hard to detect the light level under the thick hood, Tiro smelled the early-morning air. There was another sound too. Seagulls. Must be close to the coast. He couldn't say for sure they'd been traveling southeast, but from the angle of the sun on his body he suspected it. He was hauled out of the van, heard Ink's muffled sniffs nearby.

With one militiaman on either side—the one on the left as tall as he was, the one on the right shorter—they marched him forward. He could feel the heat from a low sun directly ahead. Must be marching him east. He tried to listen out for Ji and Ink. Were they behind them? God, he hoped so.

A few seconds later, he was shoved inside. Inside where exactly he couldn't say. They shoved him hard enough to make him lose his balance. He knew how to fall so he didn't hurt himself, but he shouldn't have worried. He fell into a mound of hay.

They put something down beside him. Ink. The boy was half sobbing, half choking underneath the tape and hood.

Was that Ji coming in now? *Yes!* They pushed her in more gently than they'd handled him. She plopped down beside him.

Ink couldn't catch his breath. Tiro and Ji both tried to let them know they had to rip the tape off the boy's mouth else he could die! "*Mmm! Mmm!*" they said as loudly as they could through taped mouths.

A bustling beside him. Ji spoke! They'd removed the tape. "You got to take the tape off," she said. "He can't breathe!"

Voices. Men talking it over. A female too. Someone nearby bending down. A change in Ink's breathing. "Thank you!" Ji's voice! More voices.

Someone ripped off his hood. Tiro's eyes adjusted to the light. They ripped the tape off his mouth, ordered him to stay quiet. If he didn't, they'd gag him again.

There were four militia standing over them—three men and a woman, looked like. They were in a barn. Hay underneath them, horses in stalls around them. Their captors warned them again to keep quiet before walking out. The three of them were left alone.

Ink could barely speak. "Wh-What's was that s-sound?"

They listened. *How can a sound be faint and strong at the same time?* Tiro thought.

"It's the ocean," Ji said.

"I never seen the ocean," Ink confessed.

"Me neither," Ji told him.

"Seen the rivers an' the t-tidal basin," Ink said. Tiro knew why the boy was talking. He wanted to fill the air with sound so his pounding heart wouldn't be the only thing he could hear.

"You okay?" Tiro asked Ji.

She nodded. "You?"

"Yeah."

Their hands were still cuffed. Tiro's behind him, theirs in front. But at least they could see and speak. Ji wanted to know where Marcus and Tree were.

Tiro looked at Ink, said, "I bet they're okay. Just asking 'em questions is all."

"Yeah," Ji replied. "That'll be it."

For the next few minutes, they tried to convince Ink they were okay. But Tiro could tell Ji knew how hopeless things were. In the light of day, the militiamen were, if anything, more intimidating than they'd been last night. Disciplined, well-armed killing machines.

"You still got that knife?" Tiro asked.

Ji shook her head. "Had it round my thigh. Woman who frisked me took it."

"She did? That was quick."

"She knew what she was doing."

"Think they're in cahoots with the Territories?"

"Don't know," Ji said. "Could be. Could be they don't answer to anyone."

Ink asked again if they were going to die.

"No," Ji told him. "If they wanted us dead, we wouldn't be locked in this barn."

Tiro lowered his voice. Two guards were posted just outside the flimsy barn door. "We need to get our stories straight," he told them.

"How?" Ji whispered back. "Without Marcus an' Tree?"

"We do the best we can," Tiro told her. "Take Marcus' lead. Tell 'em we went to Atlanta to visit Sidney an' Olivetta. Could be they'll search you again, feel your back. If they do, say it's—"

She broke in before he could finish. "I'll say it's cancer. If that doesn't work, I'll just have to grab Ink an' fly off."

Ink's face lit up. "You can do that?" he asked.

"*Ssh,*" Ji warned. "Keep it down. Yeah, I think I can do that. You're not very heavy."

"What about Tree?"

"Sorry, Ink. No way I can lift him. But we can fly to Turnabout an' bring back reinforcements."

Tiro didn't think any of it was feasible, but he went along with it to calm the boy down.

"Guess those wings of yours sure do come in handy," Ink whispered. "Guess we're not defenseless. . . . Ji-ji? Don't leave me behind, okay? Or if you gotta do that, maybe T can kill me real quick 'fore I even know it, so it don't hurt."

"What the—? I'm not doing that!" Tiro said, too loudly.

Ji reminded him to keep his voice down. "Tiro won't need to do it," she promised the boy, "cos you'll be with me."

"Can't go back to the 368th," Ink said. "They did . . . terrible things to us seeds . . ."

"I know," Ji said. "You're not going back, I promise. Right, Tiro?"

Tiro nodded. Made him sick to do it cos it was true. Ink would never be sent back to the 368th. Now they knew he couldn't walk, Ink had been moved from the asset to the liability column. As a Damaged, he was disposable. If he was lucky, he wouldn't be raped before they killed him.

"Think we'll get to see it?" Ink asked.

"See what?" Tiro said.

"The ocean," the boy told him.

"Maybe," Ji told him.

Ink got a faraway look in his eyes. "Sounds real big," he said. "Bet them waves're something."

"Yeah," Ji said. "Bet they are."

They heard footsteps outside. A man's voice said there were three of them inside. *Yeah,* Tiro thought. *Two Mules and a Damaged.*

Tiro looked at Ji and shook his head. Shrugged, as if to say it couldn't be helped, as if what he was about to do would put an end to things, but it would be an end *they* made, not an end made for them. Her expression told him he wouldn't be resisting alone. They'd do it together like they used to, and that made it okay. Or not okay but bearable.

"You ready, Ji?" Tiro asked. She nodded.

"Ready for what?" Ink asked.

The door opened. "Here they are, Commander," one of the guards said.

Alongside the masked guards, silhouetted in the doorway, a short man not wearing a mask.

It was hard for Tiro to make him out at first cos dawn was blaring behind him. But he saw the sunglasses and could tell that the man was young and bald. No, not completely bald. His skull was shaved on both sides, and he wore long black braids on top.

The man spoke.

||||||||||||||||

For Ji-ji, the worst part wasn't waking up in the van to find herself surrounded by masked militia, dreadful though that was. It was how much everything else dissolved in the face of the ambush. The things she'd anticipated—her reunion with her sister, the raid on the 437th, fighting for Freedom alongside those she loved—turned to dust, replaced by the familiar drumbeat of dread that accompanied the lives of seeds. Put a foot wrong, and it could be lopped off; say a word wrong and your tongue could be next. Public "pruning" was a savage act, but anticipating it was worse. Dread disempowered you, told you your life was meaningless. Over the years, Ji-ji, like all survivor seeds, had learned to live with it. When explaining the power of Uncle Dreg's Seeing Eyes, Auntie Zaini had told Ji-ji that the difference between botanicals on plantings and humans who lived Free was that botanicals were trained to live in fear of the future while humans were taught to look forward to it. That's why Dregulahmo's gift of prophecy was a powerful one, she said. It upended that relationship and gave seeds access to a new way of thinking, not just about the future but about themselves. "The key is imagination," Zaini used to say. "About what we allow ourselves to see."

Ji-ji saw this: They'd been captured by damaged people with small souls. Having lived Free, she wouldn't be forced back into captivity. She'd grown too large for a cage. She wouldn't be their freak either. She sensed the same determination in Tiro. They would go down together.

Their keepers underestimated them. What if she unfurled, right here in the van? In the confined space, she could smack them down with her powerful wings, turn the tables on them. She felt the pair pulse on her back, urging her to act. Would that work? She needed to think it through.

Her wings would shock them, but within a second or two they'd start shooting and slaughter everyone in the van. Alternatively, if she managed to slap the guns from their hands in time, chaos would ensue. Marcus would lose control and crash the van. Could be they'd have an opportunity to escape, but there was a truck ahead and another behind. They wouldn't get far.

She thought about asking if she could pee. The female would accompany her. Just before she crouched down, she could unfurl super fast and knock her over. After that, she could fly off and find Charra. But she'd only ever flown for a minute or two, and her wings had minds of their own. They could just as easily slap *her* in the face. This second plan was as full of holes as the first.

Ink's despair was catching. Ji-ji was scared they'd shoot him. She'd managed to get them to agree to her giving Ink his inhaler, but his thin body shook in her arms. Without Tree, Ink was lost.

When they ordered Marcus to pull over and they'd led him away, Ji-ji was devastated. Of all of them, Marcus was the best at anticipating what lay ahead, the one who knew the most about militia in the Madlands—how they functioned, what they did with prisoners.

They were so damn *close*! Within an hour or two of Turnabout when their luck ran out. They would've kept on driving if the rain hadn't come. Without wipers, Marcus couldn't see, so they'd decided to take a short nap till the weather cleared. Tiro had volunteered for guard duty. A little voice in her head had warned her to keep him company, but she had been too exhausted to do it. Tiro must've fallen asleep too. Or maybe they'd crept up so quietly he didn't hear them, what with the rain on the van's thin roof. Would she have heard them or seen them if she'd been on guard? Probably not. After saving the Stamos family, they saw themselves as rescuers, not victims. Forgot they were a bunch of former seeds driving through the militia-infested Madlands.

As they drove, Ji-ji watched the red taillights of the truck in front. Focusing on the lights helped her keep her eyes off their guns. She tried to follow where they were taking them. East. They were heading east. Or was it southeast? Either way, they seemed to be getting closer to the coast.

Maybe Charra would sense she was close by? Maybe she would arrive with her army of raiders and save them in the nick of time? She needed to keep a cool head and think things through, block out Ink's wails and focus. Ben and Germaine had taught her a lot about survival; so had Uncle Dreg, Zyla, and Lucky. Marcus had shared a few snippets along the way, and Tiro used to give her fighting lessons. She knew how to throw a man larger than she was, knew how to punch someone hard enough to break his nose. *And* she was the only person in the world with a pair of wings. Granted, she had no idea how to control them, but she would have to trust them to help her during a time of need. They'd been a liability; from now on, she'd turn them into an asset. But first things first. Was she sure they were militia? Could they be Clansmen? It made a difference. If they were part of a Clan, they would want to make a fast buck. If they were militia, they'd be more strategic. She went over what she knew about the two.

Some militias collaborated with plantings; others had their own agenda. Clansmen were more like the gold diggers in the Old West, not known for their discipline. Many Clans lacked resources and had crude weapons. Militias could be impoverished too, but their model was military. They often had a rigid hierarchy and strict codes of conduct. Their arsenals were handed down through the generations, and they'd accumulated more weapons over the years. Some militias traced their origins back to the late twentieth and early twenty-first centuries, when military-style weapons were available for purchase by anyone who could afford them. Didn't even need ID in some states, Zyla said. By the time people wised up to what was going on, it was too late.

Clansmen's roots were different. Some traced their history back to the original KKK of the South and the Margaret Mitchell book, but others were nothing like the old supremacists. Though many Clans in The Margins and the Madlands adhered to a supremacist doctrine, some didn't give a damn about the Color Wheel or the Territories. A few of them were multiracial, egalitarian communities, more like libertarian, self-governing communes than Clans. So which were these? So far, every indication was that their captors were trained militia. They had weapons, discipline, a hierarchy, and uniforms. The woman who'd searched her knew what she was doing and found the knife in a couple of seconds. Ji-ji was grateful she had cos afterward she only did a cursory search of her torso. If the woman had discovered her strange back, god knows what would have happened.

The militiawoman guarding her and Ink was the one weak link Ji-ji had detected. Though well trained, the woman seemed young, tentative. Her hesitation could be an opening. Maybe the peeing plan wasn't such a bad idea? Maybe she could sneak into the back of the truck, Free Laughing Tree and go from there?

Their captors wore emblems on their masks. In the dark, it took a while for Ji-ji to make out what they depicted. Eventually, when the headlights from the truck behind them lit up the mask the militiawoman wore, she recognized the image: a huge penal tree. Not just any penal tree either. This one had earrings and a gigantic canopy. Looked like it was inside a natural amphitheater too. It was Planting 437's Sylvie, the penal tree Coach Billy tended and spoke to, the hybrid tree viewed as sacred by steaders. The evidence was clear: this hardline militia was aligned with the Territories. The last vestige of hope that they could talk their way Free deserted her.

By the time they were pushed inside the barn, Ji-ji knew they had to act quickly before the three of them were separated. She was desperate to get them to take off Ink's hood and mouth tape, but she never expected them to unmask and untape her and Tiro. She was shocked when they did.

Quickly, she gauged the situation. There were horses in the barn—a means of escape. It wasn't clear how many armed guards were stationed outside. Two, at least. Her wrists were still cuffed, but luckily they were cuffed in front. Her wings weren't bound by anything except her clothing, a flimsy material she hoped she could rip. Tiro's hands were cuffed in the back, but he was an expert kickboxer. There was an outside chance they could still fight their way out if they only had to tackle a couple of guards.

It took awhile to calm Ink down. He said he wanted to see the ocean. Seemed like a crazy thing to say but she understood it. In a split second, she thought about how close the ocean was. They said you could look out over the ocean and not see anything but water for miles. No fences, no walls, no checkpoints, gates, or borders. They said you could go out in a boat and be totally alone for days, weeks, months even, with nothing chasing you but the wind and the weather. Maybe the militia had a rowboat they could steal? If they couldn't make it back to the van, or steal one of the trucks, or flee on horseback, they would steal a rowboat and escape that way. Before she had a chance to tell Tiro about her unfurling/rowboat plan, they heard footsteps outside.

The guards exchanged greetings with the new arrivals. One of them said, "We wear the mask," a quote from the famous poem. Ji-ji could've sworn she heard one of them say in reply, "Let the world dream otherwise." A firestorm of anger blazed inside her. The steaders had caged seeds and their symbols in the flying coop, and this militia had stolen the words of their poet and sewn the hybrid tree to their masks. The bastards had stolen everything. To hell with them all!

Ji-ji looked at Tiro. They would go down together. "You ready, Ji?" Yes, she was more than ready. "Ready for what?" Ink asked.

The door opened. "Here they are, Commander," someone said.

Masked guards, silhouetted against the light, and a young man, unmasked, his sunglasses twin panes of darkness. The man wore his hair in a style there was a name for, a name Ji-ji couldn't remember for the life of her, yet it struck her as a detail that could kill you if you lost sight of it. Hair braided on top, bald at the sides. Features in shadow. Was that a scar on his face or a tattoo?

Then the man spoke in a woman's voice. And Ji-ji knew.

"So it *is* you. Oh hell, Beany. Thought I'd gotten rid of you for good."

Too stunned to speak, Ji-ji held out her wrists as one of the two guards who'd been stationed at the barn door undid her handcuffs. He was young and nervous—sixteen perhaps, seventeen at the most, with a pleasant smile and cheeks healed after bouts with acne. The guard helped her stand. Another guard did the same for Tiro. Meanwhile, Charra turned to men standing nearby.

"Feral, Plate, meet Ji-ji, my little sister. I call her Beany, but I wouldn't advise any of you to try it. She's not near as laid-back as I am. That tall kid next to her is Tiro, grand-nephew of the famous Toteppi wizard." The taller of the two men began to speak, but Charra raised a hand before he had a chance. "Yeah, Feral. I know," she said. "We can talk about it later." She turned back to address their captives. "Both are devout Friends of Freedom. Isn't that right, Beany?"

Feral gave a mock salute. He had a head of curly gray hair and a body trim to the point of thinness. "Pleased to make your acquaintance, Friends Ji-ji and Tiro." The derision in his tone was unmistakable. "Name's Ferellis Shabberley Walkabout. People call me Feral or Shabby. I'm laid-back like the commander, so I'll answer to either. This fine specimen is Plato Youturn. Say hello, Plate."

"Hello, Plate," Plate parroted. Unlike Feral, whose skin was as dark as brown could be, Plato's complexion was a mid-brown. At least a decade younger than Feral, he looked to be in his late twenties or early thirties. One of his front teeth was missing. Tight braids adorned his head.

Feral laughed. "Always the comedian. Plate's more like you, Ji-ji. Don't wanna get on his prickly side. Call him Plato and he'll throttle you. Right, Plate?"

Plate, who barely looked up from the screen in his hand, settled for a nod in their direction.

In low tones, Charra conferred with Feral while he swiped a book-sized screen with his finger, occasionally turning the display toward Charra so she could see what was on it. They had the type of closeness you get from working side by side with someone for a long time. Feral must be her lieutenant.

A raider, a female, approached with news. The tree emblem was visible on her shirt where her seed symbol would have been if she'd lived on a planting.

Charra, much lighter-skinned than Ji-ji, was more tanned than she used to be, yet she would still be close to her original Raw Sienna Light arc on the steaders' Color Wheel, several arcs away from Ji-ji's Chestnut and many arcs from their mam's Burnt Sienna. Charra used to say, "I'm raw all right. No one's gonna smooth me out. Not Mam, not Lotter, not anyone." No other seed Ji-ji knew—apart from Uncle Dreg—spoke with the same conviction. Her boldness was contagious. It gave Ji-ji courage. Charra paid dearly for it, however. Her defiance resulted in beatings from Lotter, who was careful not to scar her face or inflict permanent damage on her body, mindful of the high price she could fetch when she was offered for mating. But it wasn't defiance Ji-ji saw in her sister now; it was something more compelling—power. In spite of everything, pride welled up inside Ji-ji. The stories were true. Charra really did lead an army of Freedom fighters.

After Ink's handcuffs were removed, Charra said, "Bring 'em to the house. They'll eat breakfast with us this morning."

"All three?" Plate asked, looking at Ink with scorn.

"All three," she commanded, in a voice that wouldn't countenance disobedience.

Feral wanted to know if the others should join them too.

"What others?" Charra asked.

It was Ink's cue: "Tree an' Marcus. They're good people—one is anyway. Friend of Freedom, like us. Tree is, not Marcus. Tree's a giant. Best battler ever."

For the first time, Charra smiled. It was so fleeting Ji-ji nearly missed it. "Tree's a strong name," Charra said. "What's your name, boy?"

"Ink . . . Ink Wrayseed."

Charra's temper flared. "You're no seed! Not here, not anywhere. Choose another name."

"Can I . . . can I choose anything?" he asked. Charra nodded. "Then . . . I'll be Ink Tree. Or somethin' else if Tree don't want me to use his name. Or Ink Laughing's good. Or Ink Trink. Catchy." Charra smiled again. A beautiful smile. Ji-ji ached to have it bestowed on her too. Ink, meantime, couldn't stop talking. "Tree's a seven-footer," he said.

By this time, Charra had lost interest. She conferred with her deputy again and pointed to something on the screen he held in his hand. Her caller rang. She answered it immediately and stepped away. It occurred to Ji-ji that her sister's indifference could be another mask. Maybe she didn't trust her followers and wanted to hide her true feelings? No. That wasn't wishful thinking, it was delusional. Charra was extremely irritated by their arrival, and her followers' loyalty appeared to be absolute, so she'd have no need to disguise her affection. Ji-ji didn't know what to make of her.

When the fighter who'd uncuffed him moved off, Tiro said, "Don't say much of anything, Ji. Let her take the lead. She sure as hell ain't the Charra we knew on the 437th." Ji-ji was especially fearful for Ink. Would her sister see the boy as a Damaged? Hard to believe she was asking herself that question. Charra used to get into trouble with their mam for bringing injured critters to the cabin so they could heal—frogs, ducks, snakes. When her wild pets died, Charra wept for hours.

The three of them were led out of the barn. Tiro carried Ink. The young raider who'd uncuffed her fell in beside them and offered to help. Tiro thanked him but said Ink wasn't heavy.

Charra forged ahead with Feral and Plate. Her sister had a limp, but it didn't slow her down. Ji-ji turned to the guard and asked where their friends were being held. All he would say was that the others were safe. Ink bombarded him with questions. Although he chose to ignore most of them, Ji-ji took comfort in the fact that he didn't tell the boy to shut up. A young recruit would take his cue from his commander, which meant Charra probably wouldn't be inclined to hurt Ink either.

The group walked up onto a sand dune. At the top, they got a fine view of the camp. Below them lay a cluster of tents and wooden buildings. Ji-ji could see now that the barn where they'd been held was located outside the limits of the fenced camp. The area was flat, for the most part, though dunes, most of which looked man-made, encircled it. The ocean lay straight ahead, though buildings obscured some of the view. Thick vegetation grew behind them. The camp was enclosed with a barricade cobbled together from salvaged materials—oil drums, corrugated aluminum, barbed wire and other types of fencing, and a few burnt-out vehicles. The size of a village, Charra's hideout wasn't a simple raider camp; it was a full-blown settlement. Smoke rose from chimneys and campfires; children ran around outside. Ji-ji spotted dogs, cats, and chickens, and goats.

They descended the dune and passed through a gate made from repurposed pipes and other tubing. Fastened to the top of the gate was a wrought-iron depiction of Sylvie. An armed guard held the gate open. It clanged shut behind them. They entered Turnabout.

The place was buzzing. A female raider trotted past them on horseback. A couple of errand boys on bicycles delivered packages. Three bikers, having conferred briefly with Charra and Feral, roared off in a flurry of sand and exhaust, exiting through Turnabout's main gates. Through the open double doors of a long wooden building, Ji-ji spied rows of bunks. Men leaned in the doorway smoking cigarettes. Some of the men shaved at a washstand erected nearby. Not far from the men's bunkhouses were similar structures for single females. It looked as though whole families lived in cabins and in some of the larger tents.

Unlike the Friends of Freedom, there appeared to be few White raiders. No surprise given their location. They walked past a farrier's, mechanics' sheds, a laundry, a tailor's, what looked like a computer repair shop, two bars, several other barns, a fortified building Ji-ji suspected was used for weapons storage, and an impressively large assembly hall with a pitched roof. The famous penal tree was again featured prominently, carved above the assembly hall's lintel. Ji-ji had been wrong to assume the tree was a tribute to the Territories. The reverse was true. The tribute to Sylvie was a way to reclaim what had been co-opted. Because the raiders were masked, goggled, and gloved, Sylvie's image must have often fooled Clans and militias into believing the raiders were allies. No doubt some of their foes learned too late they'd been suckered by a penal tree.

The young raider pointed out a one-room building with a rope-pull bell hanging from the front porch. Ji-ji caught a glimpse of small wooden desks through one of the window's open shutters. The raider, who said his name was Antonio, told them it was Turnabout's school. "Your sister shipped in a real teacher. A fairskin from Armistice. Taught me to read."

It made Ji-ji happy to hear that these Freedom fighters were a multiracial group after all. For all she knew, the teacher could be a rebellious Wife-Proper, like Alice.

Ji-ji noticed another large gate at the far end of the camp. Armed raiders stood guard. She asked where it led.

"To the pigpen," Antonio told her.

"You got pigs?" Tiro asked.

The young raider laughed. "Sure do," he said. "Couldn't manage without 'em."

Tiro sniffed the air. "Least they don't stink like the ones on the planting. Remember that, Ji? Petrus' pig farm stank." Yes, she remembered. She'd named Lua's wombling "Piglet" cos she hated Petrus so much. It still made her cringe to think about it. No wonder Lua Dimmered her. Not that she'd ever said the name out loud, but Dimmers probably sensed that kind of thing. If only Lua had lived to see this. If only Afarra could've seen it too. Charra would immediately realize that both brave females were worthy of living in her settlement.

Between the various buildings, at the end of sandy footpaths heading east, Ji-ji got glimpses of the waves. She felt the ocean breeze and tasted . . . was that salt? The ocean looked blue-gray in the morning light, laced with wisps of white. *Charra lives on the ocean,* she thought. *Amazing.* On the landlocked, fenced-in planting, Charra used to dream about living near a beach one day. Said she needed space to breathe. A place "without fences or in-your-face steaders." She used to tell Ji-ji stories about pirates and ocean liners, shipwrecks and battles at sea. Things she'd learned at the Planting legacy school, and things she'd invented.

Just then, several Whites clutching heavy baskets of laundry rushed past. Definitively a multiracial community. It pleased Ji-ji to know Zyla and Lucky would be welcome here.

They entered a two-story building. The simple entry with stairs straight ahead was flanked by a living room on the right and a fairly spacious dining room on the left. A long table was set for breakfast. Apparently, this house belonged to Charra, who was already seated at the head of the table in the dining room. Feral sat at the opposite end. Where they a couple? Plate had disappeared. The kitchen must be close by. Ji-ji smelled sausage and bacon and heard it spit in pans. The delicious aroma of fresh-baked bread wafted in. Charra beckoned to Ji-ji to take a seat on her left and instructed Tiro to place Ink in a seat to her right. Tiro took a seat beside Ink and opposite Ji-ji. Charra had an odd-looking caller glued to her ear. From what Ji-ji could deduce, there was a raid going on. Her sister ordered the person on the call—Heather?—to retreat.

While Charra spoke into the caller, Ji-ji studied her. On her strong, muscular frame, she wore a white shirt, an elaborately stitched black leather waistcoat, black jeans, and black military boots. A black bandana was tied loosely around her neck. The only ornamentation she wore was a silver brooch depicting Planting 437's penal tree. The long swath of hair she had on top was braided into three thick braids that ran from her forehead, over the top of her skull, and down her back. Ji-ji thought of the gorgeous black mane of the stallion who'd come to her rescue after she'd left Lucky, critically wounded, with the lynched boy under the live oak. The scar on the left side of Charra's face ran from her temple down the side of her face to her chin. Instead of trying to conceal it, she had highlighted the scar with a tattoo. The artist had surrounded it with tiny leaves and curlicues, as if the scar were the branch of a tree. Her sister's scar wasn't ugly, it was riveting; it certified her as a warrior. Charra had survived, and now her face served as a warning.

The left side of Charra's face told a different story from the right, as if two versions of the same person had merged. From the right side, apart from the shaved section of her head, she looked like she used to look. The effect was disconcerting and mesmerizing at the same time. Ji-ji found it hard to take her eyes off her. Her charismatic sister held sway in the room the way Lotter used to hold sway among steaders. One of her followers asked if they should switch on the generator so a large fan placed in the doorway could run. "What have I told you about saving gas?" she said. Chastened, they didn't ask again.

Ji-ji struggled to figure out what Charra knew about and what she didn't.

Could Man Cryday have lied about Charra's death not out of some crazy vindictiveness but to try to protect her? Or perhaps Charra herself initiated the lie? The thought flayed her, but she didn't have the luxury of indulging in self-pity. Another thing she felt clueless about was whether Charra knew about her transformation. And then there was this: Did she know their mam had been murdered trying to escape? God, she hoped so.

When Charra's call ended, Ji-ji overcame her apprehension and spoke up. "I got things to tell you," she said. "Important things. Can I tell you in private?"

Charra sat back in her chair. "Tell me now," she ordered.

Ji-ji hesitated. How could she speak openly while Feral glowered at one end of the table and raiders wandered in and out?

"Get on with it, for god's sake," Charra demanded. "I like to eat in peace."

"Okay," Ji-ji said. She took refuge in cliché: "A lot's changed since we saw each—"

Charra cut her off: "Course it's changed. For one, you're not where you're supposed to be."

"You didn't want me to come here." Ji-ji had stated it as fact, but it sounded like a child's question. It left her wide open to attack.

"Do you have any clue about the security risk you pose? S'pose you were followed? Well? What else you got to say, Beany? Something less whiny, I hope."

"Mam . . . I got some news."

To Ji-ji's relief, Charra said, "Yeah. Heard about it ages ago. The planting lieutenant you ran off with killed her." Of course! Charra thought she'd betrayed their mam. No wonder she hated her.

Tiro rushed to Ji-ji's defense, but Charra ordered him to speak only when spoken to.

Ji-ji spoke for herself: "Lucky—Matty Longsby—he didn't shoot Mam. Petrus shot her."

"Yeah. Heard that version too," Charra said, with only mild interest. "Sounds like something my father-mate would do. Danfrith Petrus always thirsted after murdering something. What else?"

Ji-ji realized that Charra only wanted to toy with her in public, to goad and mock and humiliate. She refused to participate any longer. "Can I speak with you in private?"

Charra glanced down the table at Feral. A look Ji-ji couldn't interpret passed between them.

"Fine," Charra said. "We'll go for a stroll after breakfast."

At that moment, Marcus and Tree, hooded and cuffed, were shoved into the room. Ink screamed in delight when he saw Tree, who blindly lunged toward Ink's voice and barged into the table, knocking off a plate and cutlery.

Feral rose, hurried over to them and removed their hoods and handcuffs before Tree did any more damage. The two of them squinted in the sudden light.

In the midst of the commotion, an older woman entered with loaves of bread and a platter of sausages and bacon. She placed the food on the table and hurried out.

Ink couldn't contain his elation: "*Tree!* We're in Turnabout! This is Ji-ji's *sister!*"

Tree slapped Marcus on the back. "Y'hear that, man?" Tree cried. "We made it!"

"Not through any skill of your own," Feral pointed out. "You're lucky we didn't shoot you."

"Wasn't luck," Ink crowed. "We were safe the whole time. We got *her*— the Existential. Ain't nothin' bad can happen with her on our side!"

"The Existential," Charra said. She looked at her sister. "My little sister, you mean?"

The room fell silent. Even Ink understood he'd said too much. Worried that Ink would keep talking, Ji-ji said, "I'll tell you all about it when we talk."

Marcus stepped in to alleviate the awkward silence. He reintroduced himself to Charra. Said they didn't know each other too well back on the planting, but he'd been a fan of hers for a while.

"I remember you," Charra said, icily. "The drug-sop. Diviner Shadowbrook's pet. Ran errands for her and smoked a shitload of weed."

Clearly stung by the characterization, Marcus said, "I remember you too. People change."

"Not usually," Charra said. "You boys hungry? Like to join us for breakfast?"

Ji-ji knew she wasn't the only one struck by the fact that Charra's invitation sounded more like a threat. But what choice did they have? Tiro gave up his chair to Laughing Tree so he could sit next to Ink. Tiro changed places and sat on Ji-ji's other side.

When Tree sat down, the chair groaned under his weight. Charra warned him if he broke the chair he'd have to mend it. "Of course," Tree said, respectfully. "I always mend stuff I break."

His response seemed to please her. Charra asked him if Ink was a relative.

"Not yet," he replied. "But we're working on it, right, son?"

Charra smiled. Not a fleeting smile this time. "We have a saying in Turnabout," she said. "'The tree is family, and the roots that bind us run deep.' I see the two of you live by that saying. Good. And now, I'm hungry, and Grunt's an exceptional cook. Chow down."

Grunt, the woman who'd brought in the meat platter and bread earlier, entered with a plate of eggs, along with two large bowls of fried potatoes and onions. She laid them on the table.

"You forgot the salt, Grunt," Feral said. She hurried out to fetch it.

Ink and Tree were soon locked in conversation. The two of them dug into the food, praising everything they ate and thanking their host. Marcus started up a conversation with Feral. Tiro, half starved from the look of things, focused on his food. Ji-ji took the opportunity to strategize. Although Turnabout was nothing like she'd expected, she felt more hopeful than she had when they'd sat down to breakfast. Charra's kindness toward Ink and Tree, and the discipline exhibited by her followers, boded well. Ji-ji had been encouraged too, when she'd heard the saying about the family tree. The two sisters were the only family either of them had that they knew of (apart from Lotter, who didn't count). Charra seemed to believe she'd run off with the man who'd murdered their mam. Of course she would be antagonistic toward her.

The serving woman brought in the salt. Feral mumbled something Ji-ji didn't catch. Tiro leaned over and whispered, "Be careful, Ji. Something's not right 'bout this place."

Ji-ji noticed that Charra was staring at her. Not at her face, her back. Ji-ji sat up straight in her chair and hoped her back's irregularities were less visible. Charra smiled, but it wasn't the warm, open smile she'd given Ink. This smile unnerved Ji-ji. Behind it lay a kind of menace. Ji-ji looked down at her food again. Plate entered and whispered to Feral, who stood up, walked to Charra's end of the table, dragged over a chair, and planted himself between her and Ji-ji, his back a wall between them. Soon, Feral and Charra were locked in conversation.

The woman serving them put a mug of milk down on Ji-ji's right. With her eyes, she urged her to taste it. Before Ji-ji could do so, the woman ran out again.

Ji-ji picked up the mug to take a sip. Something had been written on the inside rim of the mug. A one-word message in all caps.

Above the level of the milk someone had written a smudged but legible word: "HELP."

|||||||||||||

"Wow," Ji-ji murmured as she gazed at the ocean. She'd never seen a more powerful force than this. The waves flung themselves toward her and invited her to follow them back out if she dared. The loudness of the waves surprised her; she'd expected them to whisper. She felt an overwhelming connection to their rhythm. She'd have to come here again with her sketch pad. She decided that if Liberty painted its self-portrait, it would look like the ocean in Turnabout.

Ji-ji had seen bodies of water before, of course, but lakes, rivers, lagoons, inlets, and tidal basins were tame in comparison to the wildness of the ocean.

Though she and Afarra had dreamed about visiting what remained of Chincote-ague's barrier island and sailing out on the ocean, they never had. She wished Afarra could see this glorious sight. Ji-ji understood why her sister had settled on the coast, and why—assuming she'd christened the place herself—she'd chosen to call the place Turnabout. Charra had turned away from her old life of servitude and chosen this magnificent setting instead.

When Ji-ji was little, Charra used to tell her the tragic story of a mermaid called Mirabella who'd been granted her wish to replace her magnificent tail with legs so she could join the man she'd fallen in love with. For a while, they lived happily together. But Mermaid Mirabella tired of the man but never tired of the sea. She felt its pull and wept for its loss. In the end, unable to bear a life outside of her natural element, Mirabella rushed back into the sea during a storm. The next day her body washed up on the shore. Her tail had been re-stored, but it hadn't saved her. Ji-ji used to cry when Charra reached the end of the story, but Charra said the story wasn't sad cos Mirabella chose her own fate and died on her own terms. Ji-ji had never fully appreciated the story till now.

"First time you seen the ocean?" Charra asked.

"Seen rivers an' things. Nothing near as big as this. It's loud."

"Should hear it during a hurricane. Had two bad ones year before last. Dec-imated the place."

Ji-ji, shy of complimenting her sister in case it sounded fake, decided to com-pliment the community she'd built instead. "Turnabout's real impressive," she said. "Like a whole entire village."

"'Like a whole entire village,'" Charra chanted. Her mimicry was merci-less. Ji-ji felt like a fool.

"So," Charra said. "You got things to tell me."

"Can we sit?" Ji-ji asked. Charra shrugged as if she didn't give a damn one way or the other.

They walked back to one of the dunes and sat down facing the ocean. The dune afforded them privacy, but Ji-ji still felt exposed on the deserted beach. She sat on her sister's left side, the scar side. She got the feeling that Charra had maneuvered things to ensure that was the case.

"What did she tell you?" Ji-ji asked.

"Who? 'Bout what?"

"Man Cryday," Ji-ji said, in hopes of unearthing a few land mines before she stepped on them. "What did she tell you 'bout me?"

Charra's eyes narrowed. "You know she butchered me, right?"

"The wexcision, you mean?"

Charra, with a bitter laugh that belonged to their mam, said, "Surprised she still calls it that. A fancy word for butchery. The witch said my sproutings were infected. Ingrown, or some shit like that. Maybe they were, maybe they weren't. Guess I'll never know. Why'd you come here, Beany?"

"To see you, of course."

"Did Tree Witch send you?"

"No! She told me you were dead. No one knows we're here. Zyla an' Tiro told me you were dead too, but only cos they thought it was true. Then Marcus discovered the truth an' told Tiro. It's why we're here. . . . Man Cryday must've known the real truth all along. I see that now."

"Oh yeah, the bitch knew. We agreed that telling you I'd died was the best course of action. My idea to provide proof. That book of nursery rhymes. Knew you'd buy the lie if you saw that."

Ji-ji relinquished any lingering hope she had that her sister was glad to see her. She turned her face away, too proud to show her sister how much the lie wounded her.

After a moment or two, Ji-ji recovered sufficiently to ask, "Why didn't you want to see me?"

Charra sighed melodramatically, said, "Oh, Beany. You're such a . . . *bean.*"

The insult prompted Ji-ji to shed her timidity. "What the hell does that mean?"

"It means you were always beanlike—bland, uncomplicated, naïve. Always trusting people. Bought into that crap Dreg fed you. Guess the wizard's Seeing Eyes didn't help him much in the end. Guess you saw what Sylvie did?"

"When her limb broke off, you mean? I think Coach Billy may have had something to—"

Charra cut her off: "When the bullet ricocheted an' hit Herring. What did that tell you?"

"Some folks say it was Uncle Dreg getting revenge."

"What do you say?" Ironically, it was the type of question Man Cryday would ask.

"I don't know." She'd failed another test, though this time Charra had moved on.

As she spoke about the legendary tree, Charra became increasingly animated. "Maybe it had nothing to do with Dreg. Perhaps Sylvie had taken enough crap. Decided to fight back."

"Like you," Ji-ji said. "You fought back too, an' you won."

For once, something Ji-ji had said pleased Charra. "Guess I did, in a way. Thing is, you got to choose a side, Beany. If you don't, a side will choose you. Why'd you bring the others?"

"I guess . . . I mean . . . I can't drive."

Charra laughed for a second, then she cut the laughter off abruptly, like someone lopping off a finger. "That's the most honest thing you've said so far. Look, I know you must've expected me to fall all over myself when I saw you. But I'm not her, Beany. I'm not the sister you knew on the 437th. Haven't been her for years. This version of me is self-made. Doesn't belong to Lotter or Mam or the steaders or you or anyone. This Charra is mine, understand?"

"I think so," Ji-ji said.

"Good. So don't expect me to be like I was before. That Charra got butchered when the bitch excised the freak." Charra picked up a fistful of sand and let it run through her fingers.

Tentatively, Ji-ji asked, "Can I tell you what happened . . . after you left, I mean?"

"Fire away," Charra said.

Ji-ji told her how Lotter snatched Bonbon, Silapu's lastborn, and how it almost crushed her and their mam both. She described what happened at the fry-fence about fifteen months later. "I swear to you on Luvlydoll's grave, Lucky had nothing to do with Mam's death."

"That's the second time you've called him Lucky. Thought the bastard's name was Matty or Longsby or something."

"That was a phony name. He was sent to help me escape." Thinking fast, Ji-ji decided she shouldn't mention that Man Cryday had recruited him. Instead, she said, "Uncle Dreg knew him."

"Huh. The wizard works wonders again. I take it Lucky's a Friend of Freedom."

"Sort of . . . I mean . . . he's . . . an associate."

"What the hell's an associate?"

Damn. She sounded ridiculous. "He's, like, under contract," she said, feebly.

"A mercenary! Is that what you're saying? Huh. That's exactly what I'd expect from Wizard the Oz. Welcomes everyone into the tent, even the bastards who do it for money."

"You don't understand. Lucky's not like that. He saved my life. Sacrificed his own."

"He's dead then?"

"No . . . not exactly."

Charra's frustration level was rising fast. "What the fuck does *that* mean?"

"I *thought* he was dead, but he survived. He was . . . lucky, I guess." Ji-ji's voice trailed off.

"Lordy! This gets better and better. Okay, what else? C'mon, spit it out. Haven't got all day."

As Ji-ji explained how Petrus ambushed them at the fry-fence and shot Si-lapu, she could tell her sister believed her. "Mam saw each one of you at the end. Called you her lost babies. Wanted me to tell you how much she loved you."

Charra didn't say anything for a while. Then she said, "An' Lucky killed the sonuvabitch."

"No. Lotter killed Petrus."

Charra looked at her so intently it made Ji-ji squirm. "What the hell was *he* doing there?"

"Don't know how he found out we were running. Could be he followed her."

"Yeah," Charra said. "Couldn't bear it if his Mammy Tep was out of his sight for a second. Sick bastard. Think he knew how much she wanted to kill him? They call him the Twelfth now. Lotter's in thick with that snake the grand inquisitor. Birds of a feather."

Ji-ji wanted Charra to know how much she'd missed her. She explained how Silapu hadn't told her till a couple of weeks before they ran off that she wasn't dead. For all that time, Ji-ji said, till this latest news of her passing, she'd dreamed of finding her again. She took a chance and confessed she was hoping they could join up with her raiders and raid the 437th. "Williams won't let Zaini an' the boys go, even though he signed the kith-n-kin petition an' everything. Went back on it."

"What do you expect? Tiro was a total moron to believe him. Still can't figure out what you're doing with that loser. So what if he can flit around a cage. He's using big-time."

"What do you mean?"

"You didn't see his hands shake? Got that look drug-sops get when they need a pick-me-up. Had a few raiders like that. Sent 'em packing." Before Ji-ji could digest what she'd said, Charra spoke again. "So . . . you want us to raid the 437th?"

Rattled by what she'd said about Tiro, Ji-ji stammered a response. "Yes. I mean . . . I was hoping we could raid the 368th too. If there's time. Then search for Bonbon."

"Great idea, sis. Shouldn't lose more than three-quarters of my entire force doing that." Suddenly, Charra ditched the sarcasm and said, "I'm not some monster, in spite of how I look."

"You don't look like a monster. You're beautiful!"

Charra shook her head. "Should've known you'd show up one day an' complicate everything. . . . The 368th. You were leased to them, right?"

"Yes," Ji-ji replied, more hopefully. "During harvesting one year. Lotter wanted to teach me a lesson. Show me how good we had it on the 437th."

"Wasn't Lotter who leased you out, Beany. It was Mam persuaded Lotter to send you there to teach you a lesson. Thought you were getting uppity like me. Scared you'd up an' run one day."

"I don't believe you," Ji-ji declared.

"Course you don't. Why'd you think I was seedmated to Petrus for next to nothing? Silapu, that's why. Mam betrayed us at every turn. Raised us in captivity like the good seed she was."

Hurt and confused, Ji-ji grabbed on to something she knew for certain was true: "They do awful things there. On the 368th. . . . It was Ink's planting."

"Was it? Poor bugger. Was he a fly-boy too?"

"Yes. He was the flyer rep for the 368th. Got injured in the Jefferson Coop in Monticello during the Freedom Race. Laughing Tree blames himself."

"Should he?"

"No. Wasn't his fault."

Charra seemed impressed. "We treat the so-called Damaged with respect in Turnabout. It's the opposite of plantings here. Ink's got nothing to fear from us." Ji-ji felt ashamed. Of course Ink had nothing to fear from her. She might be a new version of Charra, but she wasn't a monster.

"The 437th," Charra mused. "Wouldn't mind blowing up Murder Mouth. S'where they screwed with Mam, remember? Carted her off to the arsenal all those times. She never would say what they did to her there, but could be that's how you an' me—an' Bonbon too, if what you say is true—got freaked. Wouldn't mind making the Twelfth squeal. You up for that, Beany?"

Ji-ji's heart flipped over. "You saying you'll raid the 437th?"

"No. I'm saying I'll think about it."

"Thank you!" Ji-ji reached out to hug her.

Charra put a hand up to stop her. "I told you. I'm not her anymore."

Ji-ji dropped her arms by her side. "Sorry."

Charra smiled at her. A real smile. "I guess it's not *all* bad you found me. Guess we got some crap in common. Man Cryday told me you're freaky too. Not that she used that term. You got 'em amputated, right?"

Ji-ji's mind began to race. *She doesn't know,* she thought. *Man Cryday lied to her. Why?*

"Not scars exactly," Ji-ji said. She needed to buy time. Charra was speaking.

". . . So count yourself lucky she didn't botch up your spine like she did mine. Takes everything I got to walk straight. You don't limp. Guess practice made her better at butchering."

Should I lie? Ji-ji thought. *No. Even if I do, she'll find out the truth soon enough. Ink's probably spilled the beans already.* She decided to treat Charra the way she wanted to be treated; she would tell her the truth, but she would strive not to implicate others.

Speaking fast, Ji-ji recounted more of what transpired after she escaped from the planting. She told Charra about entering the Freedom Race as a Wild Seed with Tiro and Afarra, the Serverseed Lotter gifted to Silapu in a futile effort to make up for snatching Bonbon. She told her about losing Afarra in the Dream, but she didn't mention Amadeus being her coach. She told her something amazing had happened, but didn't mention that Lucky had shown up when it did.

Charra glanced at her caller. "We need to head back."

Ji-ji took a deep breath. "Sorry. I'll be quick. For a while, my . . . appendages . . . they were paralyzed. I lost hope. Tried to kill myself, only I messed up."

"You botched your own suicide? Damn, Beany. That's pretty pathetic."

"I didn't really botch it. I fell from a Jim Crow's Nest where me an' Afarra've been hiding out. Only the fall was deliberate. An' then my back . . . took over on its own."

Charra, who'd been readying herself to leave, stopped dead. "What are you talking about?"

"They blossomed. Charra, I know it sounds crazy, but mine work. . . . I can fly. A little."

Charra began to laugh. The bitter, searing laugh their mam had. "You had me there for a second." Charra looked at her younger sister, saw she was serious. She lurched from denial to fury.

"*Liar!*" she screamed. She scrambled up from the dune, took a few steps toward the ocean, stumbled back. She grabbed Ji-ji's shoulders and shook her. "She cut 'em out! The witch *told* me!"

"She lied to you like she lied to me!" Ji-ji cried. "I don't think Man Cryday wanted to hurt us. I think she was trying to protect us both."

"You're *lying*! It's not physically possible . . . Show 'em to me! No one can see us here." Her trembling hand moved toward her holster. "Don't make me force you, Beany."

My sister's prepared to shoot me, Ji-ji thought. She remembered the word "HELP" painstakingly written on the inside of her mug of milk. She remembered the terror in the serving woman's eyes.

"I don't think they'll open. They got minds of their own. I don't control 'em."

Like a boiling kettle taken from the flame, Charra's fury stopped boiling as suddenly as it started. In an eerily quiet voice she ordered Ji-ji to stand up and take off her stupid cape.

Ji-ji looked at her sister's hand as it fingered the gun on her holster and did as she was told.

"Now take off your T-shirt an' show me your back."

Ji-ji did that too. Underneath she wore one of the special bras her friends had made for her.

"Turn around," Charra commanded.

Ji-ji turned around so her back faced her sister. Charra reached out and ran her hand over the ridges and wells that spanned out from her spine and up to her shoulders.

She gave a forced laugh. "You had me there for a minute! Back's as messed up as mine—"

In one swift motion, Ji-ji unfurled. Charra tumbled back into the dune.

Appalled, Ji-ji apologized. "I'm sorry! They got minds of their own!"

Charra had landed on her butt. She sat on the dune, astounded. "It's not possible!" she murmured. "*You're* . . . not . . . possible!" She tried to stand, but she was so disoriented she slid in the sand. Ji-ji bent to assist her. Charra pushed her away and buried her face in her hands.

Little by little, as Ji-ji stood over her wondering what to do, Charra composed herself. It was like watching a video Ji-ji had seen once of a building blown up during the Sequel, only this time it played out in reverse as the fragments of her sister came together, piece by piece.

She staggered up, commanded Ji-ji to turn around again. Ji-ji did as she was told.

Charra felt her sister's wings, asked what they were made of.

"I don't know," Ji-ji told. "No one does. They're just . . . weird."

"They don't feel *real*. These things like tiny windows . . . they open and close, react on both sides when I touch one side," she said.

"We don't know why that is. Guess they must be in sync or something."

"What are they?"

Ji-ji couldn't tell if Charra was fascinated or enraged. "Tiro calls 'em wing flaps," she said.

"He's seen you like this?" she said, as if she doubted it were true.

"Yeah, he's seen me."

"An' he didn't try to kill himself afterward?"

"No! Of course not!"

"Thought *he* was meant to be the famous flyer. Looks like you pissed on that dream. No wonder he's screwed up."

Ji-ji turned around, careful not to brush against her. "Tiro's happy for me," she insisted.

"You really are stupid. Why d'you think he uses? Cos of *this*, that's why."

Without her consciously controlling them, Ji-ji's wings furled in an instant. With a sound like an intake of breath and the whir of propellers, over so quickly you doubted you'd heard it, they tucked themselves back inside the ridges and hollows of Ji-ji's back.

Startled, Charra jumped back, demanded to know who gave her permission to do that. Ji-ji just looked at her.

"Is this why they call you the Existential?" Charra said. "The tree witch give you that name?"

"It's what the steaders thought I could be. Only now they think I'm either dead or . . ."

"Or maimed like me." Charra started to rail against Man Cryday. At times, her words were unintelligible. She seemed to forget Ji-ji was nearby, then her fury blossomed all over again when she caught sight of her. "She *LIED*! The bitch hated me. *I* was the one took after Mam. Bitch couldn't stand it so she maimed me!" Every so often, she placed her hand on her gun, as if Man Cryday were right there in front of her, as if target practice with a stand-in would suffice.

Desperately, Ji-ji searched for a way to calm her sister down. "I brought you a gift, Charra. I can give it to you, an' then we'll leave. We should've asked you first if we could come here."

Charra's mood reverted back to chumminess. She flung her arm around Ji-ji's shoulder, said, "You can't leave yet, Beany. Got to give you a tour." Either Charra was faking it to scare her, or her sister had a lot more in common with Silapu's erratic behavior than she used to. Not knowing how else to respond, Ji-ji nodded. Maybe she could humor her, then persuade her to let them leave?

Ji-ji got dressed again. Together, they walked back into the camp. Charra pointed out the same things Ji-ji had seen on her way to breakfast—the assembly hall, the bunkhouses, the school. . . .

"You seen our pigpen?" Charra pointed to the gates at the far end of the camp.

"That's okay," Ji-ji said. "I don't like pigs much."

"Me neither," Charra said. "C'mon, hurry up."

Roughly, she grabbed Ji-ji's elbow and walked toward the gate. Despite Charra's limp, Ji-ji had to jog to keep up with her.

Charra ordered the guards to unlock the gate and half dragged her sister through it. Four guards joined them as they walked up a sandy incline covered with sea oats and sawgrass. On the other side of the slope, two rows of about forty small sheds lined the path. The shoddy, windowless structures looked like giant dog kennels.

"Where are the pens?" Ji-ji asked.

"No pens," Charra said. "We got a kennel system here. It's kinder for the pigs."

Puzzled, Ji-ji said, "I thought pigs liked company."

"Some do, some don't."

A jolt of realization. The woman's plea in the dining room. Her name—
Grunt!

Ji-ji's knees gave way. Charra caught her arm before she fell and steadied her.

"What is this place?" Ji-ji murmured.

"Think of it as a POW camp."

"Prisoners? Is that what the woman is, the one called Grunt . . . served us breakfast? Is she a prisoner? Was she in a Clan?"

"A Clan? No. Her name was Sister Verity before she became Grunt-128. She used to be a member of the Sisters' Alliance. S'why we trust her with food. It would be a sin if she poisoned us."

A handful of pale, filthy faces appeared at the doors to the sheds on either side of the path. Dressed in rags, some wore chains around their ankles. All of them looked half starved.

"You're keeping them in kennels! They're *people* . . . men, women, children . . ."

Charra wagged a finger in Ji-ji's face. "Uh-uh. These aren't people. These are livestock."

"What . . . what do you do with them? At breakfast . . . we ate . . . You don't . . . you don't . . ."

"Oh for god's sake, Beany, we're not *insane*. We don't *eat* 'em."

She turned to the guards: "My sister thinks we're cannibals." The guards roared with laughter. "Don't worry, Beany. That was real bacon an' pork sausage Grunt served you this morning. The pigs are like our botanicals. But we're not monsters. We don't mate with pigs, or force them to mate with us, do we, raiders? They're unclean. They provide us with labor. In return, they get room an' board. To be honest, I thought you'd catch on sooner. The name? Turnabout? Turnabout is fair play. . . ." Charra prodded Ji-ji's temple with her index finger. "*Ah-ha!* The light goes on up there at last! You've always been slow on the uptake, Beany. Mark my words, it'll be your ruination."

Motionless, Ji-ji stared at the scene in front of her. "But . . . some of them are children!"

"Oh come on! You're telling me you never wanted to get even? Never dreamed about slitting Lotter's throat? Course you did. We rely on the livestock to help us. Couldn't have rebuilt so fast after the canes otherwise. Thing is, Ji-ji—an' I swear this is absolutely true—some of 'em wouldn't leave even if we begged 'em. In the beginning, we used to ransom most of the pigs we caught. Still do, occasionally. Mostly, we keep 'em. Snatched a teacher when we raided one of the plantings so my warriors can be educated. We even let her teach some of the grunts to read. We're progressive in Turnabout."

"I want to leave," Ji-ji said.

Charra tut-tutted and wagged a finger in her sister's face. "Now that's not very nice, is it? Hurts my feelings. You've only just arrived, sis. An' I've told the whole goddam camp you're my little sister. Told 'em you should be treated with respect. Don't make me change my mind."

"We're prisoners." It wasn't a question, but Charra took it as one.

"No you're not." Charra took Ji-ji's hand in hers and squeezed it. "You're my guests."

"Then let us leave. Please. We can go back to D.C. an' look for Afarra."

Charra let go of her hand and stepped away from her.

"From what you told me, Afarra's dead," Charra said. "You know it, I know it. Think old Chaff Man'll let her go? Think there'll be anything left after he does? No. You wanted to be useful. Well, Beany, now's your opportunity."

Ji-ji pleaded with her again to let them go.

"What is your problem, sis? I'm giving you what you wanted. A chance to fight by my side."

"But you don't want us here."

"I changed my mind. You've seen us now. No going back."

Charra pulled Ji-ji toward her and whispered in her ear so the guards couldn't hear her. "Besides, I've had an epiphany right there on the dune. Know how many we could recruit with the Existential on our side? Folks'll take one look at you and pledge allegiance to our cause. Way I see it, those things on your back are rightfully mine. You're the miracle I was meant to be."

Charra turned to head back. She called over her shoulder. She was laughing. "C'mon, Beany, move your ass! Thought you were s'posed to be the fastest runner the planting ever saw?"

Dazed, urged on by the guards, Ji-ji stumbled after her.

"We sisters are in this together now," Charra declared, jubilantly. "Time to wake the dream!"

21 DIMMERS WOULD DO THAT

At night, Afarra relives the executioner's plowing. She crashes into sleep with the stale smell of him and crashes into waking to get away. Sometimes she screams. She suppresses it, but silence is a habit you have to practice regularly if you want to be *Not Here, Not Now*. After she lied to the tribe of the Dimmer-dead, she should have seen it coming. Outcasts are not allowed to forget and survive. It's one or the other. Even in the Dream, those are the rules.

With Circus tucked under her arm or dozing in her lap, she camps at the feet of the Dreamer's statue with thousands of others. Risky. Even Papers have papers saying they have a grandfather right to camp there as Chronic Indigents. Afarra is hoping her luck will change soon and she'll get C-I status too, but she knows how unlikely that dream is. Without the residency documents she got after she completed the Freedom Race, she stays alert, especially at night. She keeps her bag tied to her body so no one can steal her treasures, and she keeps his Seeing Eyes hidden under her jacket. No problem. They still see in the dark.

Sometimes, she wants to gouge out the executioner's eyes for doing what he did. When Uncle Dreg's pleas about forgiveness fall short, she stares up at the bone-white statue, or she leans back against a section of the wall so the Dreamer's words engraved on the stone can lead her back from the dark. She hasn't looked in a mirror for ages, or into water (mirrors are hard to come by in the tent city of KingTown), afraid it will be *his* face she sees. If it's the Oz's whole face she'll be okay. If it's Uncle Dreg's shot-apart face, it's a problem.

She considers removing the necklace cos it's heavier than it used to be, and she suspects it's to blame for jumbling up time. You have to see the sequence of events *in sequence* (the wizard's phrase? hers?) the way others see them else people don't listen.

Every single night, D.C. patrollers search for people like her and drag them off to godknowswhere.

Godknowswhere is in the No Region or the Territories. Unpapered are traded on the Brown Market, Papers say. A death sentence, warns Peony, the female Paper who helps her read the words on the Dreamer's monument. Peony is very lucky. Her C-I papers and her three offspring's papers (not genuine residency papers but treasures nevertheless) are folded in a sealed plastic bag she carries in her skirt pocket or tucks into her bosom bra. Afarra has a pocket in her jacket where she used to keep her residency papers before Chaff Man and Sloppy snatched them.

Peony tended to her cut—the one she got on her thumb when she cut herself Free. She washed it with clean water from a charity bottle and put ointment on it. Peony's name sounds a lot like pee to Afarra but she doesn't bring it up. People are funny about their names.

When her thumb starts to throb again, Afarra wants to ask Peony for more ointment. But she only has a small jar, and Afarra knows she will give it to her if she asks, which is why she doesn't. Circus licks her wound better: *licklicklick.* "A little tickle of a lickle," she says to him. Elly, who's a word wizard like Uncle Dreg, would like that. Sloppy wouldn't. Sloppy only liked words she came up with herself. Got mad if anyone else did it.

Afarra trains Circus to answer to another name. It takes a long time, but eventually he answers to Monty. There's a good reason why she chooses that name. Zyla told them Coach Mack went on soup runs to feed the Papers—or was it the Maulers? Afarra's plan is that one day she'll be calling for Circus (*"Monty!Monty!Monty!"*) and who will come running? Coach Mack's Monty, that's who. (The coach's son, she hopes, not her python.) Coach Mack will be close behind. "Where have you been, my pet?" she'll say, all cozy. "We've been looking for you everywhere!" That whirring Scottish thing she does with her mouth—*rrrr,rrrr,rrrr*—will prove she's Coach Mack. Then they'll all go home to the Aerie and chase away intruders and live happy ever after like the Mirabella Mermaid Elly used to tell stories about on the planting when Afarra crept into her bed cos Silapu was knocked out with booze. Mirabella got herself a pair of legs but who wants legs when you can have a diamond-scaly fish tail? So Mirabella gave her friend a shimmershine tail too, and they swam off into the waves together happily ever after. *Elly, where are you? You forgotten me already? I am not forgetting you.*

The stone in the Dreamer's statue calls itself Hope. A good name for a stone and not one Afarra would've come up with herself. The Hope stone has been hacked from a mountain called Despair. Afarra's familiar with that mountain. She knows what it cost the Dreamer to wrench himself from it and step forward onto Fourth Hill in the Dream Revival District. Before journeying here, the Dreamer had been in another place near the water on flat land. People say they moved him out of the flood zone to man-made Fourth Hill not far from the Dream Coop for his own good. Jefferson will be moved to Founding Fathers Hill, surrounded by a lush garden. Lincoln will be relocated there too, one day. Peony says they moved the Dreamer away from the others—Jefferson especially—so he wouldn't keep pestering them. Says the Dreamer reminded them of things they'd just as soon forget.

You can tell how hard it was for the Dreamer King to break Free from Despair cos he dragged a whole section of the mountain along for the ride. Afarra *empathizes* with him. (A wizard word, for sure. Or a Zyla one. Or an Elly.) She wishes she could've been there when he did that. Must've been a sight for sore eyes when he broke clean away and heaved himself forward along with big fat chunks of stone.

The statue is very white. Afarra wonders if the Reverend Dreamer King was an albino. If so, she likes him even more. Two albino outcasts lived on Planting 437 and both were good to her. One was called Fuzzy and the other was called Merrywinkle. Fuzzy was an older female, Merrywinkle was a male about Afarra's age, whatever that is. The sun made their poor skins blister, but Doc Riff, who still worked on the planting back then, got them sun hats and sunglasses. Each time the hats and glasses were stolen, he or Uncle Dreg found new ones for them to wear. Their eyes were the best part of them, Afarra thinks. The prettiest colors. She loved their hair too. Pale as the moon. Fuzzy remembered her time in the Cradle before she was snatched. Said the butchery was bad in her village. Said it didn't matter where you were in the world, cruelty caught up with albinos. Afarra tried to tell her there was hope, but it's not easy to convince people if you don't have the right words or a stone nearby. Like trying to convince herself to forgive Chaff Man when she wants to gouge out his eyes. If they raid the 437th after she finds Elly (or Elly finds her), they'll Free Fuzzy and Merrywinkle along with Tiro's family. If Cloths got kith-n-kin petitions, she would've sent for them already. *I promise to save you,* Afarra tells Fuzzy and Merrywinkle, who should by rights be on the highest rung of the Great Ladder cos they're the whitest people she's ever seen. But it doesn't work like that in the Territories. They clout seeds with the Color Wheel every which way. The promise to Fuzzy and Merrywinkle reminds Afarra of the promise she made to the Dimmer-boy with the broken neck.

The Dimmer tribe appears when she has her guard down, the way Dimmers do. Sometimes, as she drifts off to sleep, she'll catch a whiff of them decomposing nearby. The tribe of Dimmer-dead don't like crowds. Their visitations are for her eyes only (and the wizard's eyes of course). They still think she's Uncle Dreg and she still hasn't told them they're wrong. If she hadn't made that stupid promise to save them, she would welcome the tribe's company. But now they're out to get her. Though she can't prove it, she suspects they had a lot to do with her being snatched by the Chaff and Sloppy. She suspects they had something to do with Elly leaving her as well.

Tiro's gone too. He's not in the Dream Coop. A few days ago, Afarra got up the courage to go ask. The whole time she was petrified Chaff Man or Sloppy would snatch her again. Marcus was not in the Dream Coop either. Neither was Laughing Tree or Ink, who always smiled at her. The custodian man was the one who told her they were out of town. But the fly-boys would be back soon, he said, cos it looked like there would be a fall season after all. Asked her if she had tickets. No, she said. Told her he could sneak her in to see the battle if she comes to the delivery back door like she did this time. Afarra wanted to believe him, but he was a man, and she'd had her fill of men, and there was no room for any more in her seed canal and that was that. So even though he probably wouldn't hurt her, she ran away while he was still speaking.

Next week, without letting the custodian man see her, she plans to sneak into the Dream Coop again. Maybe Master Amadeus, the famous coopmaster Tiro told her about, knows where they are? Or maybe he can work miracles and make Elly appear in an X Box? He's done similar things before, and he's very powerful, so it's not out of the question. He was an outcast too, Tiro said. But Master Amadeus probably doesn't even know who Elly is, so how could he help her?

When she gets lonely, the best thing of all is having Circus to hold on to. He appreciates it. Chaff Man loved his Pomeranian, but he stepped on him occasionally or dropped him when he was stagger-drunk. Circus was terrified of him. He's told her so. Not so often recently cos he's starting to forget him. Dogs are very lucky cos their memories are terrible.

Afarra surprises herself by how well she understands what Circus wants. He doesn't have to whimper to remind her he's hungry; she feels a pang in her stomach and she knows. He doesn't have to lick her face to wake her when the patrollers come around; when he tenses up she feels it in her gut. Often, she herself hardly understands what she's saying to him when she coos and clucks and uses words she barely recognizes. As per usual, words alight on her tongue then fly off before she has a chance to digest them. But it doesn't matter cos Circus understands every word she says. You can't often say that about anybody. Not even Elly understood her all the time.

Afarra knows now for certain the Oziadhee wizard was right: she isn't just an ant whisperer, she's an animal whisperer too.

Late at night, when she's scared to close her eyes and smell the executioner, Afarra wonders if the snarlcat is still trapped in his prison-cage. She hopes he burst through the bars and tore across the Mall. She hopes he leapt down into God's Furrow when the cops and the patrollers tried to shoot him. She hopes he made it all the way back to The Margins and is living Free with his own kind. If a man like the Dreamer King can drag a mountain to the Dream, nothing is impossible.

So far, Afarra's managed to evade capture. She listens out for Sloppy Delilah's rants, hears them in her dreams. Sometimes Chaff Man strangles Sloppy permanently. When this happens, Sloppy threatens to return as a Dimmer. Sometimes the executioner removes his hands from her throat just in time, like he did in real life. But one thing is always true. SloppyDelilahMoon is *angryangryangry*. In the dream and in real life, she wants to punish something so much it hurts. (Afarra is the "something," which is why she's lying low.)

Once in a blue moon, the Sloppy Delilah in Afarra's head doesn't shriek. Instead, she sings that song about suffering. The singing doesn't sound anything like Sloppy. It sounds like someone snatched her voice and inserted a tuneful of goodness into her mouth. (*Insert is an evil word. "Gruntgruntgrunt," Pokeprick said. Faster, faster, slurp-slurp, in and out. The end.*)

Twice, Afarra's found a safe space to lie in. Once behind a tent flap belonging to Peony (a mother), and her two male offspring—Wally, short for Wallaby, and Pangolin, called Pan. There's Ivy too, the girl, but she is very small. Their father was already dead when Ivy was born. Killed in a knife fight so he never got to meet her. There are a lot of fights in tent city. And even more knives.

Peony and her offspring weren't alarmed when they spotted Afarra crouching behind their tent flap. They let her stay there for days. Fed her and Circus what they could spare. After that, she moved to a corrugated aluminum lean-to, shoved up against the section of the wall where the Dreamer's words were written. She moved into the lean-to after a boy was hauled off by the patrollers for "further questioning." She hopes he doesn't come back. Then she feels bad cos she knows he will be shipped to godknowswhere. She feels safe in the lean-to, with the Dreamer's words carved into the wall behind her. She can read a few of them. Peony, who comes looking for her, helps her with the words she can't read, which is most of them. On Peony's planting—a progressive, like the 437th—some seeds were taught to read. Peony grew up there before the metaflu killed most of the steaders and seeds, which is how she escaped to Kingdom Come.

It was dangerous for Peony when Afarra slept behind the tent flap. If patrollers found her there, Peony and her little ones could be punished for harboring a non-Chronic. Peony doesn't mention this. Afarra only discovers it after Papers in the tent a few tents down are hauled away for harboring a non-C-I. That's when it hits Afarra that she has to find another place, which is how she finds the abandoned lean-to and the stone to lean up against.

Peony comes looking for her with the ointment. Afarra sees that the world is topsy-turvy in the Dream like it is on a planting. A lot of people who have a lot give a little, and a lot of people who have a little give a lot. That's the case with Peony, who walks all the way from the other side of Fourth Hill, through the hundreds of tents, through the mud, searching for her with little Ivy in her arms, who likes to cling, Peony says, so her name fits.

Peony walks past her at first. Says she didn't recognize her. Says, "How come you growed like that? Got boobs now and a butt coming in. Almost didn't recognize you, hon. Always thought you was little, but now I see you're a teen for sure."

Afarra says it happened overnight. Says her boobs surprised her too. One minute they weren't there, next minute they were. "Guess that's the way with puberty," Peony says. "Got a mind of its own. Victimizes the lot of us. Good job you got that jacket. Hides a lot." Peony must've seen the necklace she'd tried to keep hidden, and yet the mother still hadn't turned her away.

Peony digs her hand into her pocket and pulls out the precious ointment. "Here, it's yours."

Afarra doesn't want to take the jar, but Peony promises she's scooped out most of the contents for her little ones and what's left is for her friend. Afarra is her friend is what she's saying.

"You take care of little Monty," Peony says. "An' come see us if you want. I got some 'guana meat cooked up, an' some bread to stuff it in."

Afarra thinks of her iguana friend, Na-na, and hopes he's not a sandwich. "Thank you very much. I'll think about it," she says, politely. Something Elly used to say when she had no intention of thinking about a fuckin thing.

She tells Peony that sleeping by the stone is calming her down. Makes her hand feel better too, she says. That last part is a lie. Her thumb is messed up good from the knife cut. But Peony takes her word for it and is relieved to hear the news. Most lies don't count if they're told to make someone feel better. Now that she has an opportunity for reflection, Afarra sees that Elly lied to her sometimes for that same reason. One of the best reasons, if you think about it.

Then Peony says something that makes Afarra glad she didn't stay on the other side of the hill with Peony, Wally, Pan and Ivy.

"I almost forgot. A female come looking for you."

"Who?" Afarra says.

But Peony says she's got limited info. She was fetching clean water from the municipal tanker when the female stopped by. Wally and Pan spoke to her.

"The female is knowing my name?" Afarra asks.

"Yep," Peony tells her. "Said she knew you from the race an' was trying to find you again."

"What did she looks like?"

"Boys ain't good when it comes to noticing things like that," Peony says. "Sorry."

"She ask about the dog?"

"Not far as I know."

"The female—she is giving them her name?"

"Wally asked but she wouldn't give it. Got all cagey."

"Wally and Pan are telling her I'm here?"

"Hell no! Said they never seen you round here, like you asked us to say if someone come looking for you. My boys're pretty stupid on the whole cos they're boys, but they got potential."

Afarra asks Peony to thank Wally and Pan for keeping her a secret. She kisses Ivy on the cheek and gives a hug to Peony.

After Peony leaves, Afarra in her lean-to leans up against the stone behind her, more scared than she's been in ages. Sloppy's on her tail! Asked for her by name! Where do you hide when there's nowhere to go?

Tonight, Afarra's whole hand, her whole arm throbs. She's wrapped her thumb in a cloth she found. She unwraps it for the first time that day. Smells funky. She knows what she needs. Doc Riff taught her. Antibiotics. But Papers say patrollers are posted at the charity clinic. They demand to see your papers. She decides to risk it and go anyway. In the morning, when she feels stronger.

She hugs the dog closer and closes her eyes. She sees Elly unfurl. No trees nearby, only a *woosh-wooshing*. Is Elly standing on the sandy moon? Is the moon whispering to her? Did she fly there without her? Afarra's never seen a place like it before. *Windswept,* Uncle Dreg's eyes say.

Elly disappears. Replaced by the Dimmer-boy who digs down into his brain with his worn-away fingers so he can plant something. Is it a crown? No. It's a tree.

Yesterday, now, and tomorrow get jumbled up. Dream or waking, dead or alive it's the same.

Afarra leans back against the cool stone and says good night to the wizard and his eyes. She says good night to Monty-Circus, who's already snoring, and wishes she could be him and not remember things she wants to forget. Lastly, cos he's made another appearance in her peripheral, she says good night to the Dimmer-boy with the tree roots growing from his head like antlers. He yells in her face: "*COWARD!*" She would say anything to shut him up, which is why, recklessly, she promises again to save the entire tribe of the dead.

||||||||||||||||

Sloppy was mad as hell. Dog-tired too. Last night, she got about two hours of sleep. Been Dimmered by her mam again. The only female Sloppy knows who's angrier than she is.

Sloppy's never told anyone except Dip about the Dimmering. She used to tell Dip everything down to the last drop. Why? Cos she trusted her, that's why. Dipthong Spareseed adored her. Only person who ever did. Only person who ever really liked her after she got to know her.

Sloppy's mam, Trexie-Dim, was a bitch and a half. "How come you're still dithering about, Slop?" she said. "I'm your mam. You owe me," which was crap. Sloppy didn't owe anyone a fuckin thing (except maybe Dip). But luckily her own goals and Trexie's coincided: she hated Chaff Man with a passion, and her mam hated everyone, which made for a match made in heaven.

Sloppy knew exactly why her mam Dimmered her. For one, Trexie was spiteful as hell. Second, she wanted what most Dimmers wanted: revenge. Commanded Sloppy to kill her killer. Trouble was, till recently, Sloppy had assumed that Trexie's killer died years ago.

Sloppy had a few gaps when it came to her mam's history, but she always knew Trexie was a Commonseed (very common) on Planting 502 who got Pen-Penned for stealing and was confined in Planting 502's penitence penitentiary for months. Got executed along with other inmates when 502's cropmaster decided to spring-clean PenPen after a metaflu outbreak. Back then, Sloppy had already been exported to the 437th when she was eight and seedmated to Vanguard Casper at thirteen.

Sloppy had no intention of responding to Trexie-Dim's unreasonable request. What did her mam ever do for her? Didn't say a thing when her Last&Only was seedmated to a murderous bastard. Didn't petition to come see her in all those years, even though Planting 502 was less than a hundred miles from the 437th. Didn't write to her either. Not that she could have cos she was illiterate. But she could've done what others did and got someone to write it for her. Even if it was only the planting censors, it would've meant that, for once in her life, Sloppy received a letter.

A few nights ago, Sloppy happened to make a casual inquiry about Chaff Man's work history. He was rip-roaring drunk, so he was *garrulous* (the kind of word the ignorant lout wouldn't recognize if it spat in his face). Apparently, according to Chaff Man II, Chaff Man I, executioner for plantings in the 400s and 500s, poisoned his own liver with booze. Turns out, Chaff Man II took over the family execution business years earlier than she'd thought. Chaff Man II had no idea he was confessing to murdering Trexie when Sloppy inquired about executions he'd done over the years. Thought Sloppy was a sicko like him. Thought she wanted to hear the gruesome details cos she was living vicariously. Zyla Clobershay taught her that word—*vicarious*. There are times when she's sorry she parroted to the steaders about how her former teacher ignored the seed curriculum and taught her favorites whatever the hell she wanted. You ignore things at your peril on a planting. Bottom line: For years, Sloppy's told her dead mam she didn't know where her killer was. Then, lo and behold, she learned the killer fucked her too!

Chaff, a.k.a. Cherub, didn't remember anyone called Trexie. Why would he? Pyred her cos she was a Metafluer like the others and that was his profession. Besides, Trexie was a thief . . . and a liar, and a bully, and a whore. And she'd offed a couple of people in her time herself, one of whom was justified (Sloppy's father), so you could argue pyreing was called for in her case.

So now Sloppy knew it was definitely Chaff Man the Younger who did it. Now she knew he was guilty *for a fact*. Him. Not his father, or the substitute executioner who took over on the few occasions when Chaff Man II was away from the plantings. She'd confirmed the dates and they matched. Ever since then, she'd been torn about what to do. In her head, she was more powerful than she tended to be in real life, but she'd never let that fact deter her.

Problem was, Trexie had no patience. None whatsoever. Wanted the vengeance-kill done yesterday. Dimmered her half to death last night as she screamed, *"Kill the bastard!"* in her ear.

Sloppy has always invested in facts. Fact was, she was so tired she could barely crawl into bed next to Chaff Man, that great hump-lump of a chump. Fact was, sleeping next to him after she'd figured out he did indeed pyre her mam had become awkward. Fact was, Trexie used to beat her black and blue too. Bruises on top of bruises, cuts every which way. So how do you forgive your own mam for that *and* punish the man who killed her? It's a dilemma. And what should you do when she comes a-knocking from the grave, demanding you play vigilante, especially if the one she wants you to kill is your meal ticket and therefore your path to salvation in the earthly sense?

Sloppy thought about enlisting help. Chaff Man was a hefty bastard. Probably be difficult to kill him without a gun. Fat chance she could get hold of that. He slept with his Glock strapped in his shoulder holster. Van Casper did the same thing. But Casper, her father-mate, had a knife too, just in case slicing and dicing was preferable to blasting. She knew Sookie from the race and thought about enlisting her. But Sookie was unreliable. One day she was decent to you, the next day she was a bitch. Could easily rat her out to the authorities. And then there was another wrinkle.

Lotter was the one hired Chaff Man to track down his favorite seed, and so far all they'd managed to do was grab and then lose the Cloth, who'd refused to tell them where Jellybean was, however much they coaxed or tortured her. All they'd gotten so far was a measly advance on expenses. Strike that. All *he'd* gotten so far was a measly advance. *She* hadn't received a penny.

But there was a major payment coming down the pike if they nabbed Jellybean-Goody-Two-Shoes. Sloppy couldn't get rid of Chaff Man before then; she'd be cutting off her nose to spite her face. Lotter would never hand over all that lucre to her. Probably didn't even know she was involved cos Chaff Man wanted to snatch all the credit for himself.

Lotter had always looked down his snooty fairskin nose at her. Thought of her as his overseer's trashmate. Never once bothered to ask her why she was beaten to a pulp when she served him his food. Except for that one time when he noticed how exceptional her pronunciation was and said she was "articulate," the bastard never thought to notice her at all. Never thought to say, "Does my overseer beat you? Did he pry out that fingernail on your pinky and stomp on your foot till it's hard to tell where your foot ends and your toes begin? Did he pour hot coffee in your lap on purpose cos he damn well felt like it? And is that why you're clutching your bush cos that's where the scalding coffee hit?"

Due to the fact that Lotter was nauseatingly good-looking, it took Sloppy ages to see the truth staring her in the face: Arundale Lotter was a refined version of Vanguard Casper. Both fairskin steaders were savages, but one happened to look like a goddam angel and the other happened to look like a fuckin pig. A moral lesson, if ever there was one, about the danger of paying attention to appearances. Seemed like there was never a time when beauty didn't have a vicious side. It could doom you if you had it and doom you if you didn't. Look at the lovely Charra—seedmated to Petrus for next to nothing. Look at her own goddam self. The most intellectually gifted of all the seeds on Planting 437, given how much she had to contend with at home, and yet still she went unrecognized. Why wasn't intelligence as seductive as beauty? That's what she wanted to know.

Dip used to say "her Sloppy" was beautiful. Said she preferred her "a little worser for wear" cos then she could devote her life to "mending her till she got good as new." In spite of her grammatical faux pas and embarrassing accent, Dip was the best thing that ever happened to her. It wasn't fair that Dip hadn't made it to Freedom. Dip loved everything about Sloppy: her tits and her ass, her clit and her eyes, her nose, her mouth most of all. Dipthong Spareseed had loved Sloppy inside, on top of, and underneath. Kissed her with all kinds of devotion.

Sloppy had to hand it to the outcast. She would've sworn the Cloth would cave, 'specially after Cherub kept poking her. But she didn't. Thank god the Chaff was too dumb to figure out how the Cloth got away. Never realized she'd used the knife Sloppy had accidentally left behind on the shed floor. If he ever discovered the truth, he would throttle her without stopping this time. Instead, the dumb bastard bought Sloppy's ridiculous story about Circus betraying him and gnawing through the rope with his teeth. Sticking the executioner with the news about Circus' betrayal was dangerous. But it was enjoyable too, to see the executioner suffer. But she couldn't make her move. Not yet. Not before she discovered where the executioner hid her residency papers. And not when Lotter was in the background willing to pay for news.

Sloppy had spent days wandering the city looking for the Cloth. At night, she'd go back to Chaff Man. Not cos she wanted to but cos there was nowhere else to go.

Anger wasn't something Sloppy lived with; anger was who she was. It swilled around inside her. Anyone could tap into it. She hated that. Her lack of self-control made her vulnerable. Once, that bitch Sookie suggested she enroll in anger management classes. "They got classes for that?" Sloppy had said, genuinely shocked. Sookie had laughed in that mean way she had when she knew something Sloppy didn't. Said they had all kinds of classes in the E.S.S. and in the Western SuperState too. Said it was like paradise there. Said it was like the Age of Plenty when no one was angry cos they had everything handed to them on a silver platter. Gave Sloppy a lecture on self-control. One day, if that bitch Sookie wasn't careful, Sloppy would show her just how bad she was at anger fuckin management . . . show Chaff Man too. . . .

Ever since Circus had been snatched, Chaff Man had turned into a wimp. Sure, he smacked her around a bit, but he couldn't put his heart into it. Did it cos it was expected. Circus was Chaff Man's secret weapon, his superpower. Without the squealing little rat-mutt, Chaff Man was nothing. The Chaff had prostrated himself on the floor when he realized he'd lost his precious pet. Bawled like a baby. Put Sloppy in mind of the Bible story, the one Pastor Cam Gillyman (biggest ass-licker on the planting) liked to preach about. It was the tale of another mindless brute who got enfeebled. In this case, it was his hair that held his strength, not a little dog. All you had to do was cut it off. In the Bible story, God, a vigilante, returned Samson's strength to him so he could demolish a temple. If you extended the comparison, Circus became Chaff Man's hair, or Samson's hair became the Pomeranian. Either way, it was a useful analogy.

Now that his weakness had been made manifest, Sloppy wasn't scared of the executioner anymore. She was biding her time, playing it smart. All she needed to do was find the Cloth again, get her to lead her to Jellybean, score the reward from Lotter, and revenge-kill Chaff Man. Most girls would be overwhelmed by a list like that. Not her. She knew what she was capable of.

Each day, like clockwork, she went on a hunt for the Cloth.

Here she was doing it again.

On a trip to KingTown, she spotted her from a distance, flitting hither and thither among the Papers.

Sloppy thought about accosting her there and then. She liked accosting, but she changed her mind. Too crowded. Too much daylight left. Her target was pretty and fragile-looking in that fatuous feminine way. Someone would come to her rescue and fuck everything up.

Sloppy followed her around the tent city of KingTown, followed her around the Dream Revival District, the place Papers (idiots that they were) called Kingdom Come. Watched every move she made. Some people naturally get on your nerves, and everything about her was annoying. Like she never put a foot wrong. People took pity on her. Went out of their way to help her cos they thought (mistakenly) she was pretty. She wasn't. But that was the way the world worked. The so-called pretty ones got whatever the fuck they wanted, while the so-called ugly ones like herself got nothing but grief. And even if you were as plain as plain could be like Jellybean—mud-brown skin, ugly features, nappy hair—you still lived the good life if you had the right pedigree.

Night descended. Still Sloppy followed her unseen. Experience had taught her the only thing that paid off was persistence.

In the seediest part of Kingdom Come, an area where you never ran into cops or patrollers, Sloppy pounced. Got her in a headlock and dragged her down an alley.

Sloppy fought dirty and prevailed. Skin under her fingernails, flesh in her mouth when she gnawed on her victim's hand. She pulled out a knife and held it to her throat. A new knife to replace the one the Cloth stole.

"Now," Sloppy said, "tell me where she is."

"*I don't know!*" the girl squealed.

Sloppy pressed the blade of the knife harder against her victim's neck. "Want me to cut you?" she said. "I'm a gourmet when it comes to cutting. Wouldn't be pretty after that, would you?"

"*N-N-No!*"

"You scared?"

"*Yes!*"

"Good. I'll ask one more time. Where is she?"

"I don't know! I *swear* I don't! After the meeting, she took off with Tiro an' the others! Went down south, they say."

Sloppy was a gifted listener. Something had switchbacked on her. Her victim wasn't talking about who she thought she was talking about. She needed to tread carefully, say as little as possible.

"Go on," Sloppy urged.

"I heard . . . I heard she . . . w-went to search for her s-sister."

"Her sister?"

"She thought she was dead. But she's not."

"Yeah, I knew that," Sloppy said, deflated. "Now tell me something I don't know. Otherwise I gotta try out my new blade on your face."

"*Okay, okay! I'll tell you!*"

It was only when Tulip got to the part about Jellybean's back that Sloppy realized she'd found the Rosetta stone. No wonder Lotter was desperate to locate his seed; he had to get rid of his shame.

"Where's Afarra?" Tulip asked through a bloodied mouth.

"Chaff Man killed her," Sloppy said. "Cut her up in pieces an' buried her."

Tulip burst into tears. Sloppy punched her in the face to get her to shut up, and cos she'd been wanting to do it ever since the Freedom Race, then hauled herself up off the girl's body. Tulip had always been a preachy little bitch. Never listened to Sloppy when she warned her to steer clear of the Cloth cos she was a filthy outcast. Just cozied up to the Cloth even more. Sloppy kicked her in the stomach for old times' sake.

Funny how people change, Sloppy thought. The old Tulip from the Freedom Race would've struggled more, fought back. Something had happened to soften her up. Something nasty. A rape? Murder, perhaps?

All questions for another time. The only thing that was relevant was that Tulip Rogersseed had bleated like a little lamb and told her *everything.* She'd been chasing a Cloth and wound up snagging a much more valuable prize.

All of a sudden, life tasted sweet. Who cared about the Cloth anymore? This news was enough to buy her everything she wanted. Enough to buy Dip's Freedom too. "Hold on a tad bit longer, Dip," she whispered. "Soon, you an' me'll be together in the Dream."

Tonight, Sloppy would forgo the knife, let her cuts heal instead. The City of Dreams had turned into a dream come true. She pictured Lotter's face when she broke the news to him. He must suspect something was amiss. Must be why he hired the executioner. But Lotter didn't know the full extent of his seed's horrific mutancy. Chaff Man was lousy at secret keeping. If he'd known about Jellybean, been certain she was alive even, he would've spilled the beans. No way the moronic bastard could keep that to himself. Which meant Sloppy Casperseedmate, scorned and impoverished, was in possession of one of the most precious secrets in the world.

According to Tulip—who, with only a little nudging, had squawked like a parrot—Jellybean Lottermule was a mutant. A *winged* mutant . . . who could *fly!* All she needed to do now was get the executioner to disclose how she could get in touch with Lotter, then she'd leave him for good. (Or kill him when he was in a drunken stupor if her mam-Dim kept insisting.)

Her dreams resurfaced like a kraken, her favorite sea creature from the tales Miss Clobershay used to tell them. "Move over, freak!" the victor sang to herself. "Time for the world to make room for Delilah Moon."

22 A QUESTION OF TRUST

A s a seedling, in spite of her mam's warnings, Ji-ji secretly believed that Father-Man Lotter cared for her. Underneath a mask of indifference was the loving father she yearned for.

It was partly his fault. He could be charming, and there were occasions when Lotter didn't seem to view her as his property. When she was little and he took her into The Margins on hunting expeditions, he would hoist her up on a horse and place a loaded rifle in her arms as lovingly as any Father-Proper. On the way back to the planting, he'd let her ride in the front of his truck between him and Overseer Casper, and she'd know her father-man thought she was more special than any of his other seedlings by any of his other seedmates. In Silapu's cabin, Ji-ji would sit on Lotter's lap in front of a crackling fire and comb the blond hair on his arms, muss up the blond locks on his pretty head, run her small brown fingers over his blond beard. She'd even pull up his lip to check his teeth, something she'd seen him do when he inspected horses. Intimacy engendered trust.

On her part.

Even now, a decade later, it stung to think about how profoundly she'd misjudged Arundale Duke Lotter. From his point of view, seedling Jellybean and older Ji-ji were two different creatures. Although Lotter was impressed by the fact that she aced her lessons at the Planting legacy school, ran faster than any other seed on the 437th, and cooked like a dream, her other attributes ran counter to who she was supposed to be. Conflict was inevitable.

One day, while still a seedling, Ji-ji contradicted Lotter by asserting that the Territories' capital city of Armistice was known as the City of Cages. Lotter, tight-lipped, informed his seedling she was wrong.

"You're mistaken, Jellybean," he said. "The Territories' Father-City of Armistice has never been called the City of Cages. It's known as a City for the Ages. You confused two terms that sound alike."

Their dialogue was now concluded, but Ji-ji didn't know this was how the game was played. Her mam did, however. From across the seedmate cabin, Silapu had signaled frantically at her daughter to shut up. But Ji-ji was first in her class at the Planting legacy school for seeds, she always won the spelling bee, and no one sewed their seed symbol on faster or neater than she did. Jellybean

Lottermule was Lotter's favorite seedling by his favorite seedmate. How could she have known that her relationship with her handsome, authoritarian father-man, who paid attention to her when the whim took him, was rotten to the core? She'd missed the menacing uptick in his voice when he'd corrected her. Mistakenly, she'd thought they were having a conversation. "You're wrong, Father-Man," she'd declared. "Armistice *is* the City of Cages. Everyone knows that—right, Mam?"

Arundale Lotter had turned on his seedling with a viciousness that skinned her alive.

Years later, after Ji-ji read Maeve Exra's *An Abbreviated History of These Disunited States,* she began to comprehend why her comment had triggered Lotter's wrath. The planting system and its Territorial capital were inextricably bound. Founded by Swinburne Augustus, who'd led the Secessionist Surge, fractured the nation during the Civil War Sequel, and established the first crop of plantings in the Homestead Territories, Armistice could only be the City for the Ages, the shimmering Father-City on the great lake. The term City of Cages was heretical.

Sitting in the expensive rocker he'd had shipped from Armistice so he could relax before and after seedmating calls with her mam, Lotter impressed upon Ji-ji how ugly she was. "Skin the color of dung. Nothing like my ebony prize, my Mammy Tep." He'd grabbed her mam by the waist, jerked her toward him, and tilted her chin down so her lovely face could accuse Ji-ji of imperfection. "You're not like Charra either, your gorgeous sister. You're more Commonseed than Muleseed." He'd pushed Silapu to one side and grabbed Ji-ji by the scruff of her seed shift. He yanked her toward him till their noses nearly touched. "Hair like frizzy wire, a flat nose spread out all over your face, crooked teeth. How could my Mammy Tep seedbirth a dud like you?"

Lotter's attack was masterful, though its success wasn't due to the fact that Ji-ji put much stock in appearances. From childhood, she'd seen how much suffering was inflicted on female seeds who were forced to pay a steep price for their prettiness. Lotter's attack was masterful in that he knew his precocious Muleseed cared deeply about words. Even as a seedling, Ji-ji viewed the world through the prism of language. For Jellybean Lottermule, words didn't supplement or embellish experience, words were the essence of life itself. Lotter knew she would turn his insults on a spit in her head for years to come. Traumatized, Ji-ji realized she'd always been crap on the soles of his shoes, the animule he would slaughter without remorse when the beast had nothing more to give, the puppy he would toss into Blueglass Lake after it grew out of its cuteness.

Stupidly, Ji-ji didn't turn away from Father-Man Lotter all at once. She was naïve. She kept trying. But after the City of Cages incident, she wore extra armor in the vain hope it could prevent him from ever hurting her so deeply again.

No wonder Charra hated Lotter so much. What terrible things had he said to her elder sister over the years? What unspeakable things had he done to her?

||||||||||||||||

For the next few days, Ji-ji took comfort in the fact that Charra didn't appear to have disclosed her secret, though it was clear that Feral knew. (Ji-ji caught him staring at her back repeatedly.) Charra barely acknowledged her little sister's existence. Ji-ji was a "VIP guest," isolated from her travel companions but treated by the raiders with equal parts deference and suspicion. She slept in the storage shed behind Charra's house—close enough to keep tabs on and far enough away that she couldn't return the favor and keep tabs on the raiders.

On Ji-ji's second day in Turnabout, the raiding party Charra had ordered to retreat returned. From what Ji-ji could gather, the woman named Heather, who commanded the group, had attempted a raid on a planting in the 200s. Heather returned in battered, bullet-ridden trucks with two dozen raiders, roughly half her original contingent. Six of the returning raiders were severely injured, and Heather herself was wounded in the shoulder.

Ji-ji was nearby when Heather walked into Charra's house to announce her return. Charra rushed to embrace her. Before they kissed, Ji-ji already knew that Heather wasn't simply one of her lieutenants; Heather was the woman her sister loved. Charra fussed all over her, yelled frantically at the grunts to fetch one of the camp's nurses when she saw the blood on her shoulder. She led Heather inside. Amazed to see a version of her sister she recognized, Ji-ji ran to the window in hopes of catching a glimpse of her again. But Feral entered the house soon afterward, and Ji-ji heard Antonio return from a trip to the outhouse. She'd been forced to retreat before she was spotted.

In those first few days, Ji-ji observed the couple together on a handful of other occasions. It was easy to see why they cared so much for each other. A powerful-looking woman, Heather was a lot taller and broader than Charra, but she didn't use her physical size to intimidate. She wore her hair military-short, with elaborate patterns similar to the tattoo over her sister's facial scar shaved into it. Her complexion was a deep, honeyed brown. Heather didn't talk much, but she seemed curious when, later that day, Charra introduced her to Ji-ji. "I wanna know all Char's secrets," she said in a northern accent. Ji-ji immediately identified her as an African American from the Eastern SuperState—like Ben Turner, a Born-Free. Charra warned Heather she'd be disappointed. "Beany doesn't know a single one of my secrets," she said. The jab hurt. "Don't be mean, Char," Heather said. "Your kid sister's come a heckuva long way to find you. And I hear she's got a lot to offer us too. It's not wise to look a gift horse in the mouth. Am I right, Beany?" Normally, Ji-ji bristled when someone other than Charra called her that, but it sounded right coming from Heather's mouth.

After Heather's return, the camp shifted into high gear. The Turnabout community took care of the wounded, housing them in an infirmary at the opposite end of the camp from the Pig Pen. Ji-ji overheard raiders who said Heather's raiding party had been ambushed before they reached their target, which was why they had to abort the mission. Feral sent out scouts to make sure Territorial militia hadn't followed them. Extra guards were posted on the perimeter and at the gates. Rumors circulated that a parrot must've squawked to the enemy.

Ji-ji was ordered to help the camp's two nurses tend the wounded. Having volunteered in Doc Riff's seed clinic, she felt prepared to assist them. However, the assignment proved more difficult than she'd imagined. Two of the raiders, a male and a female, had sustained third-degree burns over much of their bodies. The young woman of eighteen died in agony within a day of their return; the man, only a few years older, soon followed. A pall descended on the camp. The idea that a parrot could be walking among them made the community more suspicious of strangers. As a consequence, the raiders eyed Ji-ji more warily than before.

The other injuries raiders had sustained were treatable: non-life-threatening bullet wounds, broken bones, cuts and mild concussions. Ji-ji hadn't noticed before how battle-weary many of the raiders were. Several were confined to rickety wheelchairs that had been cobbled together from bicycle parts and other salvaged material. Roughly a third of the raiders were female. Due to the fact that families were encouraged to settle in the camp, a significant number were pregnant. Impressive though the camp was, it didn't look as if Charra had the force necessary to attack the 437th.

As she tended to the wounded, Ji-ji learned more about the community. The raiders kept their precise location secret, but Ji-ji surmised they were close to where they'd thought they'd wind up—on the coastal plain in the former state of Florida, not far from the old state boundary with Georgia. Germaine had told her this region was lawless and sparsely populated. From what Ji-ji could gather, she was right. After the country was carved up following the Sequel, and coastal flooding and the Long Warming took their toll, much of the area now called the Madlands was abandoned. The population of the former United States, decimated by canes and metaflu, sought refuge elsewhere. Far from trade routes and lacking in technology, the region was so harsh people said you had to be mad to remain in the Madlands. Ji-ji heard the raiders refer to each other as "Motleys" and "Loonies." The tales of ferocious Clans and militias, hungry gators the size of trucks, hungrier stripers and snarlcats, and mosquitoes as long as your hand that carried a strain of malaria so lethal it could kill you within twenty-four hours, kept most folks away. You had to be looking for something in particular to risk venturing into the Madlands: a life without interference or accountability; a natural world that still looked—to some extent, at least—natural; or a sister you'd dreamed of reuniting with for years.

From the little Ji-ji had been able to discover, Turnabout sat in an area of salt marshes and coastal forest filled with red cedar, pine trees, palmettos and live oaks. Like other places along the coast, it was vulnerable to erosion. With its steady breezes, secluded beaches, and snarled mangroves, Turnabout was beautiful—all except the Pig Pen, which protruded from the camp's north end like an abscess. The faces of those held there haunted Ji-ji's dreams.

Turnabout wasn't simply out of the way, it took remoteness to a new level. Yet Ji-ji was drawn to the region's forgottenness and isolation. Instead of a road, a muddy trail led to the camp. Unless you knew where the camp was, it would be almost impossible to find it.

Every morning before breakfast, Ji-ji crept into Charra's kitchen to visit with Grunt-128 while she prepared breakfast for Charra and her entourage. Sister Verity's hands were cracked from constant labor. Ji-ji wanted to help her escape, but she had no idea how she would accomplish this while still a prisoner herself. In her fifties, Verity had a gentle aura about her and a generous nature. Originally from the Jurisdiction of Los Angeles in the Western SuperState, Verity said God called her to engage with the world, which was why she joined the most progressive sisterhood in the Sisters' Alliance, the Radical Sisterhood of the Renascent Beatitudes. The sisterhood eschewed the papacy, embraced poverty, and reported to a group called the Conclave of Activist Mothers Superior. Verity endeared herself to Ji-ji when she joked that all the sisters of the Renascent Beatitudes were known for having "impudent attitudes." (*Afarra would pee herself laughing at that joke,* Ji-ji thought.) Verity and the sisters had been on their way to the Rad Region to deliver medicine to a seed clinic when they'd been captured by a Clan near the Gulf. Last year Charra's raiders had attacked the Clan's settlement. At the time, the sisters, having taken note of the raiders' penal tree insignia, assumed they were being abducted by militia. But when Heather removed her hood and they saw she was a Black woman-warrior, the sisters thought they'd been liberated by the Friends of Freedom. One of the nuns, a former Commonseed, was set Free near the Liberty Independent of Tallahassee. The other four, all of them White, were transported to Turnabout. Only after they'd been shepherded into the Pig Pen did they have a true appreciation of their plight.

There were three of them left. Two months ago, one of the sisters, Sister Geraldine, "had gone to be with the Lord." It wasn't till Ji-ji's third visit to the kitchen that Verity disclosed the details of the sister's death. After the story was finished, Ji-ji tore back to the shed and almost tripped over the still-snoring Antonio. She entered the shed and shut the warped door behind her. Perched on the edge of the bed, she rocked back and forth in disbelief. "Charra," she whispered. "Charra, Charra . . . *why?*" In minutes, she pulled herself together. Rocking back and forth on her bed in a shed accomplished nothing, and Sister Verity had asked for her help.

In the beginning, each of the commander's VIP guests was accompanied by an armed raider. Antonio, the youngest and most inexperienced of the guard contingent, was assigned to Ji-ji, who didn't know whether to be grateful or insulted that her sister thought she could be effectively guarded by someone even greener than she was. A former seed from the 700s, liberated from his planting during a raid, Antonio was an ardent flyer-battler fan whose full name was Antonio Pineabout. He instructed Ji-ji to call him Tony. He told her that botanicals inducted into Charra's Liberty Raiders were ordered to jettison the name of their begetter, or, if they'd been classified as outcasts, the term *Cloth,* and ordered to dispense with suffixes like *seed, seedmate, spareseed,* and *mule.* They were invited to select a new name that honored their chosen community. Not being a poet, as he put it, Tony settled on Pine. Going from Cacklebumseed to Pineabout was a giant leap in the right direction, Tony said. Only problem, he got teased by other raiders, who'd say things like "What's Pineabout whining about now?"—which he didn't find funny.

The young raider felt deeply indebted to Charra, who had saved him from certain death at the hands of his begetter, Dusty Cacklebum, "a sonuvabitch overseer" originally from Boston, who'd immigrated to the Homestead Territories and sworn allegiance to the cropmaster so he could screw as many seedmates as he wanted, preferably all at once. "The commander says there's almost as many fairskin Northerners an' Westerners as there are Southerners an' Midwesterners in the Territories now, 'specially after the plantings introduced those big incentive bonuses." Tony didn't seem to know whether he should treat Ji-ji like a prisoner or a princess, so he vacillated between the two to a dizzying extent.

Ink wasn't as lucky as Ji-ji when it came to personal liberty. Without his usual mode of transportation, he was mostly confined to his bunk, while Laughing Tree was assigned to construction projects and vehicle repair. Tree's mechanical know-how put him in high demand, to say nothing of his superhuman strength, which impressed Charra and Feral so much they found multiple ways to exploit it. Left alone for hours at a stretch, Ink grew despondent. Ji-ji visited him as often as she could. Whenever he could get away, Tree took Ink for strolls along the beach.

Initially, Tiro and Marcus were watched like hawks. Plate was assigned to guard them round the clock. By the third day, however, Ji-ji noticed how friendly the three of them were getting. The next evening, she spotted them at a card table set up outside the men's bunkhouse, playing poker, drinking liquor, and smoking weed. None of that worried her. Maybe the soft stuff would help Tiro steer clear of the hard stuff. It was their coziness with Plate that concerned her.

On their sixth day in Turnabout, Ji-ji ran into Tiro in front of a laundry shed, where female "grunts," elbow deep in soapsuds, used washboards to scrub raiders' clothes and sheets clean. The two kept things casual, wary of revealing how happy they were to see each other. Tiro said he was on his way back from an errand for Plate.

"You allowed to wander round on your own now?" Ji-ji asked.

"Apparently," Tiro replied. "Turns out, Aurelius an' Plato are soul mates. Can't get enough of each other's company. Way back when, you think those dead guys hung out together in real life?"

Ji-ji shook her head. "One was Roman, the other was Greek. An' I think I'm right in saying they lived hundreds of years apart. But don't quote me on that."

"How'd you know shit like that, Ji?"

"I read. My head's full of shit."

"Fair enough. Guess I should try it sometime. . . . I see you still got your trusty bodyguard." Tiro waved at Antonio, who was issuing laundry advice to a female washerwoman with stringy brown hair and a black eye. He called her "Grunt Daisy" and told her if the collars didn't get cleaned up good this time she'd get a lashing, one he'd deliver personally.

Speaking softly so Tony couldn't hear him, Tiro said, "Your sister won't allow raiders to mate with fairskins."

"I know. She told me. Said they were unclean."

"Plate says Charra doesn't want half-breeds running round."

"That's insane. What's she think *we* are? Along with most of her followers, looks like."

"Marcus says that's how come she's against it. Thinks it screws people up."

A group of washerwomen hurried past them with piles of folded laundry. Tony ordered them to stop dawdling, though Ji-ji couldn't imagine how they could move any faster.

"Y'hear 'bout the four raiders she caught last year?" Tiro said, after he'd checked that Tony was occupied. Ji-ji said she hadn't and hoped he'd stop there. He didn't. "They dragged a female grunt to the beach an' raped her. Charra gets wind of it an' comes tearing out to the beach. Says as long as she's in charge there'll be no gang rapes." Ji-ji pictured her sister storming onto the beach, braids flying. She remembered the steaders' sickening term for gang rape: *all hands to the plow.* Tiro was still talking. "She has all four of 'em put in chains, then she casts 'em out to sea in a leaky boat."

Ji-ji shook her head in disbelief. "She drowned the raiders? All four?"

"According to Plate, who says it worked. Says no one's raped a grunt since. Marcus says Charra's a badass. Think the fly-boy's in love."

"What happened to the woman? The one who was raped?" Tiro shrugged to indicate ignorance. "Didn't you ask?"

Tiro held up his hands defensively. "Hey, Ji, give a man a break. Ask too many questions an' they know whose side you're on." Tiro glanced over at Tony again, said, "Still can't believe that Pig Pen and livestock crap's for real. . . . Listen, Ji, I got something to tell you."

Tiro put his arm on Ji-ji's elbow and guided her away from Tony, who called out a warning: "That's far enough!" Tiro complied at once. Tony, who didn't seem to have a clue how to respond to that kind of obedience from a famous flyer, resorted to a wave. "Least the kid's polite," Tiro said. "More'n I can say for some of these raiders."

Tiro's nervous rambling told Ji-ji to ready herself for bad news. He began haltingly: "Marcus told Plate . . . who told Feral . . . who told . . . Charra . . . what happened at breakfast."

"At breakfast?" Ji-ji asked, baffled. "This morning? Did something happen?"

"Not this morning. The day we arrived. Don't react to what I'm telling you, okay?" Tiro raised his voice to make sure Tony could hear him. "Got something in my shoe. Got a splinter in my big toe too. Hurts like hell." He bent down to take off his sneaker. As if to help him with his shoe, Ji-ji crouched down beside him, her back to Tony. Tiro glanced up to make sure Tony was still pestering the washerwoman.

"Marcus spilled the beans . . .'bout that woman. The one you told me is a nun. I mentioned it to Marcus, an' Marcus told 'em what she wrote in your mug of milk. . . . *Don't* react!" he whispered.

It took everything Ji-ji had not to scream at him. "What the hell's *wrong* with him?" she said.

"Not sure, but I got a theory. Think he may've wanted to get in good with Charra, prove he could be trusted. Marcus is angling for something. Don't know what it is yet, but I aim to find out."

Tiro removed his sneaker and snuck a peek at Tony, still sermonizing to the top of the washerwoman's head, while Ji-ji searched desperately for a silver lining.

"Think it's one of his Uncle Tom maneuvers? Think he's got a plan we can't figure out yet?"

"Honest, Ji, I wanna say yes but I don't know. I never figured Marcus for a traitor. Then again . . . I don't know . . . he's an enigma, if that's the right word. Asked me yesterday if I dreamed about turning the tables on steaders. Said, course I had. But it's different when you actually stuff fairskins into hovels whether they're guilty or not, an' call their children *piglets*. I mean, *Jesus!*"

Tiro examined his foot. "They brand some of 'em too, like they do on plantings." Ji-ji wanted to beg him to stop talking, but she didn't trust her own voice right now. "Got a pillory behind the assembly hall, an' a post for lashes. If the grunts disobey, they're lopped. It's tongues for back talking, hands for stealing, an' a half a foot for running off. The grunts're scared shitless."

In her distress, Ji-ji bit her lip too hard and tasted blood. She found it impossible to keep her voice from trembling. "So Verity could get lopped cos Marcus parroted."

"Don't call her by her real name, Ji. Not here. S'not safe."

Ji-ji's head hurt. What was Marcus thinking? "Doesn't make any sense. Why would he betray her like that? He doesn't even know her."

"Could be it's related to that shit went down at the museum. Marcus goes on an' on 'bout how the sisters should've known the planting replica would attract a swarm of steaders. Says dozens of Maulers were murdered that night by roving steader gangs, their bodies piled into trucks an' carted off. Says when the *Independent* tried to print a story about it, the mayor's office threatened Edelmann an' Lowenstein—the reporters who got that scoop last year 'bout Corker's son being held in Armistice. Threatened to prosecute 'em under the new Seditious Influencers Act."

Ji-ji recalled how angry Marcus was with the nun who'd apologized to them for mounting the exhibit. "I can't let her hurt Verity," Ji-ji stated. "She's gotta get through me first."

Tiro said loudly, "Told you there was a piece o' wood in there. Hurts like hell. You see a splinter in my big toe, Ji?" He held out his foot for inspection and whispered, "Ji, you're not thinking straight. You'll make things worse." She gave him a look that told him she'd made up her mind. "Shit," he said. "Wish I'd never told you. Listen, there's something else. Your sister's getting real chummy with Marcus. Came to see him today. They talked in private. Don't know what they said but—" He broke off. "Tony's lookin'. Look at my toe again."

Without missing a beat, Ji-ji peered at his big toe. "Yeah, it's a splinter," she confirmed.

As soon as Tony looked away Tiro whispered, "Just let it blow over, Ji. Could be Charra won't give a damn 'bout some nun writing 'Help me' on your mug of milk."

"Wasn't 'Help me,'" Ji-ji said. "It was 'HELP' in all caps."

"Damn, Ji. Anyone ever tell you you're way too nitpicky when it comes to details?"

His comment pissed her off even more. "Details can kill seeds if we forget 'em," she said. She forced herself to calm down and think rationally.

"We can't rely on Charra's mercy," she said. "She told me the things on my back belong to her. Said I was the miracle she was meant to be."

"She actually *said* that? Shit, Ji, that's not good." Tiro looked down. His voice tapped into fearfulness. "Marcus says the raid on the 437th's a done deal. I gotta trust he's right cos it's the only chance I got to Free 'em. If I wait for the Friends to make a move, it'll be too late. Little Yatho's real quiet but Bromadu talks back. He's sure to piss Williams off sooner or later."

He looked so stricken that Ji-ji placed her hand on his arm to comfort him.

He swallowed hard and said, "I'd mount a raid on my own, but I'd never make it out alive. Get 'em killed, more like. Marcus says the Friends spend months squabbling over every move they make cos they're paranoid about casualties. I don't got no choice but to hope Charra comes through. Can't risk making her mad. . . . I'm staying sober, Ji. Just a few joints here an' there, an' a whiskey or two if Plate's feeling generous. I want you to know that's all I done since we got here."

For a moment, Ji-ji had forgotten that Tiro carried different burdens than she did. She loved Zaini and the boys. She couldn't do anything rash.

"Don't say anything 'bout anything to Marcus," she said. "We can't trust him anymore."

"You watch your back too, pun intended. I seen the way Charra looks at you."

"Like she wants to kill me?"

"Like she loves you an' hates you at the same time. . . . Watch out! Tony's headed this way."

Tony told Ji-ji that Feral had ordered him to escort her to the infirmary so she could help the nurses. As Tony ushered her away, Tiro said, pointedly, "Don't go crying over spilled milk, Ji."

In response, she did the only thing she could think of. She pretended not to hear him.

〰〰〰〰〰〰

Ji-ji crept out of the small shed behind Charra's house. Charra and her raiders were at a meeting over in the assembly hall. All she had to do was tiptoe past Tony, who lay splayed out and snoring on a mat by her door. She didn't know how long her sister would be away, but her plan was to search for Verity and warn her she was in danger. She'd been excited when she'd learned that Charra, Heather, Feral and the rest of her sister's leadership council would be occupied for the evening. Forced to wait for more than an hour before Tony finally began to snore, Ji-ji was grateful his sinuses were shot, otherwise she'd never have known it was safe to leave. Given the delay, she wasn't surprised to find the kitchen deserted. Verity must be back at the Pig Pen. Damn.

Ji-ji turned to head back to the shed, then she changed her mind.

Ever since that first morning on the beach with Charra, she'd wanted to go back there. Seemed like the perfect place to find out what she could do with the Unknowables on her back. She didn't know how to bank into a turn, and her gliding skills were pathetic. She had to learn to ride currents of air so she could conserve energy. On this hot night in late summer, a robust breeze came off the ocean. Some part of her must've known she would try to fly again: she'd worn her libby bra underneath her T-shirt.

She crept out from behind Charra's house, reminding herself to avoid the wide-open space at the center of Turnabout where raiders hung out. She could hear voices coming to her over the breeze. Someone was playing a harmonica, someone else a guitar. She crept between the structures as fast as she could, skirted a barn, and ran past a cluster of tents. Soon, she was rushing down an alleyway between a mechanics' shop and a laundry.

A woman stepped out of a doorway directly into her path! Ji-ji gasped and stopped dead in her tracks. Grunt Daisy, the washerwoman with the black eye, cowered in front of her, hands raised to protect her face. Before Ji-ji could think of an excuse for why she was wandering around alone at night, the woman lowered her eyes, mumbled an apology, and ran back into the laundry shed.

Ji-ji had forgotten it wasn't her turn to be terrorized.

No time to lose! She heard the waves and kept running. Onto the sand, around the dune. . . . There it was. The ocean! She stood for a moment and drank it in. The stars were blazing; a halved moon-pie pinned to an inky sky, a moon she and Afarra had dreamed of flying to.

Afraid she'd lose her nerve, Ji-ji tore off her T-shirt and shorts, slipped off her shoes. . . . What should she do now? The answer echoed in her head: *Run!*

Without a moment's hesitation, she raced toward the black, roiling waves. She couldn't tell whether the tide was in or out. Didn't matter. Just like she used to as a seedling, she thrust out her arms, as if they alone could fly her to the moon. She turned right to gather speed and sprinted, ankle deep in the ocean, along the water's edge.

She didn't feel herself unfurl; she didn't know she'd started flapping. The first she knew that her feet had left the ground was when she noticed that the *slapslapslap* of her feet in the shallow water had been replaced by another sound. Not the waves. The sound of her wings pumping in the breeze! She banked to the left and traveled out over the water. She was rising, rising! The salt water lay beneath her. If she fell, the merciful ocean would catch her and she could swim back to shore. No better safety net in the world.

She rose higher. Didn't think about it. Didn't say to herself, "What you're doing is impossible." Didn't think about how to respond to the air till a stiff breeze caught her and shoved her backward. She couldn't fight against it. She had to let it take her before she could take herself back to where she wanted to be. So she rode the air like a sailboat rides the waves.

In the old days, when she used to run marathons, she would feel herself being propelled by something stronger than she was, as if the ground were thrusting her forward. But running paled in comparison to this. Her legs all but disappeared; her feet barely existed. She was heart and muscle, beat and wing. She banked right, then left. She stopped flapping and dived down into blackness. Unable to judge distances in the dark, she almost left it too late to pull up out of the dive. She laughed like a lunatic as her toes grazed the water. Nothing frightened her tonight.

She pulled up abruptly midair, switched from a horizontal to a vertical position. Behind her, she couldn't be sure, but she thought her wings re-formed themselves, allowing her to move them in an S shape so she could hover vertically like a painting of the Ascension. Gravity was a memory her wings gave her permission to forget. Strong force, weak force, Zyla had taught her about them. But now, *she* was the strong force, the Dark Who Mattered. She was the Dreamer *and* the Dream.

All of a sudden, exhaustion struck. She thought about flapping her way back to shore, but then she decided to see if she could coast back on the air currents. She could. Without expending much energy at all. Dream Master Amadeus Nelson had told her to listen to her wings; he'd said they would lead her in the right direction. In all her troubled years, she'd never felt so light. She'd left everything behind in Turnabout—her sister's rage, the grunts in their grotesque Pig Pen, Marcus' betrayal, guns, knives, fear, humiliation, disappointment, rejection. . . .

Movement in her peripheral vision drew Ji-ji's eyes to the beach. She saw the figure below and knew at once who it was. With the last of her energy, she banked to the left, flew straight, circled high above her sister's head once, twice, and alighted softly on the sand. The moment her feet touched the ground, her wings retracted. She was anchored to the earth again.

The sisters stood facing each other, Charra with a flashlight in one hand.

Her gun was holstered, but her grim expression told Ji-ji she hadn't forgotten it was there. *I should be scared,* Ji-ji said to herself, *but I'm not.*

An onslaught of resentment from her sister. "Marcus said you couldn't control those things. Said you couldn't fly worth a damn. He lied."

"No he didn't. I've never flown like that before. Didn't know I could. It was the ocean."

"Guess I'll have to bind you up in the future so you won't fly off. Or cage you maybe? Or clip your wings. You know why a caged bird sings, Beany? You learned the secret yet?"

"I know why she doesn't," Ji-ji replied.

Charra's mood shifted. She smiled, scarred and beautiful in the moonlight. "Yeah, Beany. Me too," she said, without rancor. Ji-ji didn't fool herself. This milder version of her sister wouldn't last.

"So what stopped you from flying off?" Charra asked.

Her sister must think she had a lot more strength than she did. She wouldn't disabuse her of that notion. "I promised Tiro I'd help get his family off the 437th."

"Ah, the drug-sop. Should've guessed. An' afterward? You'll come back to Turnabout with me? Join my noble army of raiders?"

I've just been handed a bargaining chip, Ji-ji thought. *An opening nuns can slip through.* "If I do," she said aloud, "will you agree to release the prisoners an' let my friends go?"

"The prisoners? The grunts, you mean?"

"An' my friends too, after the raid?"

Charra turned to face the ocean. "Marcus wants to stay. Claims he likes it here."

"He can stay for all I care. But Tiro, Tree, an' Ink—after the raid, you'll let 'em go?"

"Haven't decided what to do with you all yet," Charra said.

"You don't need prisoners anymore," Ji-ji argued. "You proved your point."

Charra stepped in closer: "You think you know what my point is? You got no idea."

Ji-ji stood her ground: "You wanted to prove to the world—to Lotter— you're as powerful as he is. You wanted to humiliate fairskins the way they humiliate us."

"Yeah, Beany, I'm an open book. This whole reversal exercise was cathartic. An' now you've shown up I can go back to being the sweet big sister I used to be. You're a *moron*! I could be a self-righteous bitch too if I had a back like yours. Take a look at Man Cryday's handiwork!" Charra thrust the flashlight into Ji-ji's hand. She struggled with the buttons on her shirt, tearing one of them off in her frenzy.

She turned around. Even in moonlight, Ji-ji could see how disfigured she was.

"Use the flashlight," Charra commanded. "I want you to see what that bitch did to me."

Ji-ji trained the flashlight on her sister's back. It was a mass of scars, the damage so extreme she couldn't fathom how her sister stayed upright.

"I shouldn't be able to walk. Know how I do it? A gifted surgeon who rectified some of the botched surgery the bitch gave me, willpower, an' pain meds. Strongest killers I can find."

Charra shoved her arms back into her shirt. In her frenzy, she misaligned the buttons.

"You buttoned it wrong," Ji-ji said. "Let me." Charra shied away initially, but Ji-ji persisted. It was the most intimate they'd been with each other. "There," Ji-ji said. "All done." She hadn't been shot down yet—literally or figuratively. Time to pose another question. "How come you haven't outed me yet as a mutant?"

"Is that what you are? Yeah, I guess you are. Maybe I'm saving it for a special occasion?"

"If you do out me, the steaders'll hunt me down an' kill me. They think I pose a threat."

"They're right. It's why I need to keep you by my side. Marcus says you were ready to let Alice and the Friends show you off to the Easterners in New York. Why is this any different?"

"You can't protect me like they can. There are thousands of Friends all over the world." Charra began to turn away. Ji-ji grabbed her shoulder. "If you out me an' we head back to the 437th, every Bounty Boy in the Territories'll be on our tails. Thought you wanted me as an asset."

"Maybe I want you as bait."

Bait. A word Marcus used when he'd spoken about Sidney. *Seed bait*, he'd said.

"You'll cut off your nose to spite your face," Ji-ji said. "An' another thing. You don't have near enough raiders to attack the 437th. Why draw attention to yourself?"

"That's where you're wrong, Beany. Thanks to you, I got a whole bunch of new recruits."

Taken aback, Ji-ji asked her what she was talking about.

"Marcus didn't bring you here for a sisterly reunion. He's an official envoy."

Ji-ji didn't believe her. Was this another test? "Marcus? An envoy for who?"

"Pretty sure that's meant to be *whom,* sis. But I'm not Lotter, so I'll let it slide. Marcus is an envoy for the Invisible Men. You heard of 'em?"

Something stirred in Ji-ji's memory. Where had she heard that phrase? At the Friends' meeting. Yes. Someone—Marcus—said it to who? (Should be to *whom.* Shit! When would Lotter get his crap out of her head?) Did Marcus say it to Tiro? No. He'd been speaking to Georgie-Porge at the museum. Wasn't the first time she'd heard it either. Years ago, Lotter had mentioned Invisible Men to Casper. She offered the latter up to her sister, a way to prove she wasn't as ignorant as Charra thought:

"Lotter mentioned the Invisible Men once," Ji-ji told her.

"Did he now? Guess I'm not surprised. I separated Marcus an' Tree from the rest of you in the beginning for a reason. I suspected the female was you, an' it was a no-brainer you'd bring that idiot drug-sop with you. Wanted to see if your stories jibed. Then Marcus tells Plate he's an envoy from the Invisible Men, an' the puzzle pieces start to fit together. Didn't it strike you as weird when Marcus volunteered to escort you to the Madlands? It was never about *you.* Well, to be fair, it was about those freaky things on your back, but that's the extent of it. Marcus realized you were the key we'd all been waiting for. Guess you could say you were the bait he needed to get me to the table."

Ji-ji refused to let Charra see how much her disclosure wounded her.

Charra moved over to the dune and sat down. She patted the place next to her. Ji-ji walked over cautiously and sat down beside her.

"I've always had a soft spot for the Men," Charra said. "I'm sick of do-gooder fairskins an' sanctimonious duskies. . . . The I-Ms have never partnered with a female before. It's against their religion, if you can call it that. They want to link up cos they know I can tap into raiding parties all along this coastline. Combined, we constitute a force to be reckoned with."

"An' you trust these Invisible Men? You trust Marcus?"

"Of course not. Haven't trusted anyone but Heather in years. But the Men need me. I can inspire a crowd. You'll see, Beany. I'm real good at inspirational. You an' me are sisters, seeded by one of the most famous steaders in the Territories—with a little help, quite possibly, from scientists in Murder Mouth. Yeah, Beany. The tree witch told me all about her theories.

"The I-Ms think they're using me," Charra went on, "when, in actual fact, it's the other way round. An' then who enters the scene? A giant battler named Laughing Tree who happens to carry a fly-boy round in a nest on his back! I mean, have you seen our logo? Took me a while to realize I'd hit the jackpot. Seeing you soar like that tonight confirmed it."

Ji-ji struggled to put the pieces together. "Is Tree an Invisible Man too?"

"Don't know, don't care. Either way, the giant will be worth his weight in gold. Add to that a pair of the best young flyer-battlers in the Disunited States. Tiro may be an idiot, an' that pretty sonuvabitch Marcus isn't nearly as smart as he thinks, but from what I hear, they fly the coop like a dream. How many do you think'll flock to Charra's Liberty Raiders when they hear their idols have joined up? Last but not least, the greatest prize of all. You, the Existential."

"S'pose Tree won't cooperate?" Ji-ji asked.

"He'll cooperate. He's got an Achilles' heel."

Ji-ji didn't need to ask what she meant. "You'd hurt Ink?"

"I'm not a monster. Tree will decide Ink's fate, not me. Same for you."

"For me?"

"The grunt. Verity. Your adopted sister, from what I hear. The naughty nun's been doing a little writing on the side. Words floating above the milk of human kindness."

"Don't hurt her, Charra! Please. I already agreed to go with you."

"You haven't agreed to stay after the raid, always assuming we go through with it. Well?"

Ji-ji needed to weigh her options. "What happens if I refuse?"

Charra opened her mouth, stuck out her tongue, and swiped her index finger across it. Before she could stop herself, Ji-ji drew back her hand to slap her. Charra caught Ji-ji's wrist and held on tight. "She's a *nun,* for god's sake!" Ji-ji cried.

Charra's eyes glittered. "That's more like it. Some raw, unfiltered honesty at last. Yeah, you hate me all right. Admit it! You've wanted to hit me ever since you saw the Pig Pen."

Ji-ji snatched her hand away. "This won't work! What if you can't control these Invisible Men? You don't even know them. There'll be a bloodbath!"

"You sound like Heather. For now, they need us an' we need them, so let *me* sweat the details. . . . Marcus heard from the diviner just before he took off from the city. Looks like the 437's ripe for the picking." Charra snatched up Ji-ji's hand again and pressed it against her own heart. It took Ji-ji a moment to realize her sister was making a vow.

"I swear to you, the raid on the 437th will be one for the ages. This isn't just for me. It's for both of us. For the others too, the innocents. It wasn't mere chance all this came together now. It was fate. I don't even believe in that crap, but it was. Every one of us have been on an intersecting path for years. The rebellion's about to begin. 'No more the seed, no more the plow!' Trust me, Beany, the Twelfth won't know what hit him."

23 GOOD SAMARITANS

Lucky Dyce, sweating in D.C.'s relentless humidity, stood debating with himself near the entrance to Uncle Tommy's Color Bar. The bar's name, on a hand-painted sign hung lopsidedly above the entrance, was some barkeep's poor attempt at humor. Lucky found that bars on this side of the pond were invariably seedy—residual guilt, he suspected, from the fractured country's puritanical roots. Whenever Lucky stepped into a bar in the Disunited States, he felt as if he were stepping into a brothel. Or, worse still, one of those vile *miscegenations* they had in the Monticello Protectorate.

Lucky hated this city, always had, though he had to admit it was a lot better than Planting 437. What kind of gormless sods built a city on a swamp and called it a Dream? Americans, that's who. Not that anyone used the term "American" outside of the SuperStates anymore. Even SuperStaters didn't usually refer to themselves by that name, in spite of the push by their governments to gin up enthusiasm for reunification. As far as Lucky was concerned, the whole damn lot of them would always be Americans—a peculiar breed of people with annoying traits, a scarcity of wit, and delusional tendencies. Who else would call themselves "exceptional" without irony? The only Americans he knew who could hold up their end when it came to a conversation were Ben, Germaine, Ji-ji, and Otto. . . . And Man Cryday, of course. . . . And Uncle Dreg, before he got killed. . . . And Doc Riff. But then he was an American Indian. No one appreciated irony better than indigenous people. So that was seven out of millions, and one of them dead. Pathetic.

Lucky had a critical decision to make: stop for a beer or keep going. The chalkboard sign out front was so tasteless it was almost funny: "*Cheap Beer!! All Hues & Skintones Welcome!!*" Next to it, someone without any artistic ability whatsoever had drawn a Black, minstrel-like face, and a White face with a nose so long and pointy it would give Cyrano de Bergerac a run for his money. Not for the first time, Lucky was struck with a pang of homesickness. What he'd do for a Boddingtons or any of the brews at the Wag the Royal Tail pub in London, where his parents used to take him and Rachel for a treat in the old days. They'd blow their ration cards on fish & chips, mushy peas, humungous slices of bread slathered with butter, and cider—real, honest-to-goodness British

cider served to anyone over twelve. A treat after the family had completed another soup run, or participated in another Quaker march, or finished handing
out flyers, or done one of the many selfless things they did till their good works
wound up killing the whole lot of them except him.

For the past two days, both before and after he finally received Ji-ji's letter,
Lucky had searched for Afarra in the blistering heat. Most of the time he'd
wandered from one miserable place to the next, with a printout of a photo of
Afarra in his hand and a description of her abductors. He'd wound up not far
from the Mall and spotted the sign for Uncle Tommy's. Friends of Freedom
had been combing the area for weeks to no avail. But each time Lucky thought
about giving up, he saw Ji-ji's face in his head. From her letter, he'd concluded
she'd gone to find her sister. To the Madlands, if the sentence in parentheses
was a clue. He'd learned from Germaine that Zyla had gone bonkers when
she'd learned Man Cryday had lied to her about Ji-ji's sister. Lucky couldn't
understand it. Man Cryday might be eccentric but she wasn't a liar. Mind you,
Zyla Clobershay could bring out the worst in anyone. Lucky was hurt that Ji-ji
hadn't asked him to accompany her. He had a knack for reading people and situations, could sniff out danger too. He'd learned to trust his instincts, which
rarely led him astray. Apparently, if what Ben surmised was true, she'd snuck
off with Tiro and the fly-boys instead. He didn't think much of Tiro, but at least
he seemed to care about Ji-ji.

Lucky glanced at the sign again. Screw it, he was going in. If he went in
with low expectations, he would only be mildly disappointed. He pushed open
the door, pulled a dirty beaded curtain to one side, and entered the establishment. Stepping from blazing sunshine into the bar's dim light momentarily
blinded him. His eyes adjusted. When he saw the scene in front of him, he
wished they hadn't.

Uncle Tommy's Color Bar was a one-room shack with four rickety barstools,
a soiled bar with a half-eaten, fly-encrusted burrito on a plate no one had bothered to clear away, and an antique oscillating fan in its death throes. The fan,
placed in front of the open back door near the rubbish bins, squeaked as it
churned heat from one corner of the poky bar to the other. The smell of rotten food was flung into the bar area with the kind of sullen indifference only
machines can muster.

To Lucky's surprise, given the name of the place, the man behind the bar
was White; his apron wasn't. He nodded at his new customer with the same
sullen indifference exhibited by his oscillating fan. Like his fan, the barman was
an antique.

Lucky sat down and discovered that his barstool was wobbly as hell. He was obliged to keep one foot on the ground to steady it. The seat felt sticky under his bum. He didn't want to think about why that could be. The barman asked him what he wanted to drink.

"What are the choices?" Lucky asked.

"Don't got choices," the barman replied. "This ain't New York City. Got beer an' whiskey. Whiskey's served in shot glasses. It's real strong, so go easy."

"I trust it's real whiskey from the Highlands," Lucky said, facetiously.

The man didn't look amused. "Beer comes in medium or small. Comes in extra-large too, if you feel like splurging. With them pretty blues, you look like the splurging type."

Oh, what the hell, Lucky thought. *In for a penny, in for a pound.* He ordered an extra-large.

"Extra-large is a ration card or five Statesers. No District dollars an' no Filthy Lucres."

"You take seedchips?" Lucky asked. Another stab at lightening the mood.

"Ha-de-ha-ha," the barman said, humorlessly. "What would a lily-white boy like you know 'bout seedchips? Only thing them splinters is good for is buying shit the steaders sell at those lousy planting stores. Another way to crap on seeds. You a steader? If so, take your ass somewhere else."

"Don't have steaders where I come from. Though we have our share of morons."

"Yep," the barman agreed. "Morons is everywhere. It's a contagion." He looked at Lucky as if to say he was staring at a moron right now. "You got Statesers or not? I don't got all day."

"Yes," Lucky said. "Sorry to delay you. I can see you're rushed off your feet."

Lucky handed over the money. The barman held the notes up to what little light there was to check they were genuine. Satisfied, he placed two glasses on the bar—one large glass and one medium-size. He turned away, bent over, and dug his forearm into a cooler contraption full of half-melted ice. His butt crack was clearly visible. And hairy.

"Don't got no extra-large glasses," he said. He pulled out a fat bottle and showed Lucky the label. A cheap brew Districters drank. "This do?" he asked, as though his customer had a choice. Lucky nodded. The barman picked up a bottle opener and flicked the bottle open with one hand, the only time he indulged in performance. "I take it you're not from round here?" he said, pushing the bottle toward Lucky and leaving him to pour his own drink.

Lucky was tempted to say, "Do I look or sound like a Mauler, punk?" But he didn't. First off, it would've made him sound racist and elitist, which he wasn't, even though he sometimes gave others that impression. Second, the barman had impressive biceps and a way of holding himself that indicated to Lucky he was a pugilist. Unlikely he'd take crap from a Brit less than half his age.

In an effort to keep the peace, Lucky punted: "I'm not from round here," meaning he came from about four thousand miles away.

"Thought so. You're from the Old Country, right? In with them Euros on the continent?"

Lucky was at a crossroads. Should he educate the ignoramus, let him know that Britain had abandoned the European Alliance yet again several decades ago to strike out on their own? Should he tell him England had shrunk into provincialism like almost every other once-powerful nation he could think of, and lecture him about the rise of feudal-like principalities and fascism in the wake of pandemics and climate horror? He glanced at the man's biceps again. Nah. No need.

"Yep," Lucky said. "I'm from the Old Country all right."

The man smiled. Or was that gas? It was gas.

Lucky was almost done with his extra-large beer (to which he added a whiskey chaser cos he rather liked the idea of being a splurger) when a man shuffled in and sat down on the barstool at the other end of the modest bar, leaving two empty barstools between them. In the afterglow of the chaser, Lucky appreciated the man's civility. Most Americans, not being genetically predisposed to good manners, would have planted their bums on the stool next to his, slapped him on the back as if they were old pals (the kind of American familiarity Lucky found intrusive) and commenced to spit-talk in his face.

At first glance, the new fella looked like the type with a story to tell. Lucky guessed he was slightly older than he himself was—early twenties probably. He smelled of lavender aftershave, though he didn't look like the aftershave type. Looked like someone who'd been through the wars—a pinky missing, to say nothing of the state of his teeth, the dent in his skull, or his smashed-up ear. But at least the guy had made an effort. His pants and shirt looked fairly clean, and his hair had been recently barbered. His smile made Lucky warm up to him. It lit up his face and invited you to see his scars and general imperfections as badges of honor. Lucky was almost certain he was an ex-seed. Poor bloke must've been through hell on his planting. Couldn't help but feel sorry for him.

More relaxed now after his beer and whiskey, and feeling somewhat empathetic for a change, Lucky smiled back. Bad move. Encouraged, the man got congenial. That was the trouble with Americans: give 'em an inch an' they took a mile.

The man started joking and laughing with him, even offered to buy him a drink. Lucky refused. He looked over at the barman. What if they'd spiked his drink? They could be working in tandem, hoping to rob the first moron who walked into the bar and looked like he had two pennies to rub together.

"Aw, c'mon," the Black man said. "I come into a little money recently via an inheritance. Be sweet to celebrate with someone. Get one for yourself too, Mr. Barman." He took out a bag filled with coins and a few notes and counted out the money meticulously.

"Don't want all them coins," the White man behind the bar said. "I'll take a few, not many."

The Black man made a face, then he exchanged some of the coins for a crumpled-up note.

"What you been doing?" the barman said. "Robbing a piggy bank?"

The man laughed. "S'my inheritance," he repeated. "Ain't much, but it's better'n nothing, right? Been a long time coming. Always been lucky."

"Me too," Lucky interjected.

"Starting over with a new leaf," the man announced. "Been scratching a living on the Mall. Boss is a bastard. A fairskin. No offense meant. Some fairskins're decent, some are pigs. This one'd rob his own mother if he could get away with it. Anyhow, after this, no more barflying. Decided this morning to go cold turkey. Today's my last day of indulgence. Need to stay sharp in my profession. Two more beers an' a coupla whiskey shots, an' I'm a teetotaler for good."

Lucky smiled. "'A Teetotaler for Good.' A spiffy title for your autobiography . . . life story."

"I know what a biography is," the man declared. Lucky thought the man had taken offense but he was wrong. He followed the comment with a disarming, broken-toothed smile.

The barman poured Lucky another whiskey. *What the hell,* Lucky thought.

He thanked the other patron and took a sip of the liquor. It burned his throat even worse than the first one. Tasted more like moonshine than whiskey but it did the trick. He was a lot mellower than he had been when he entered the place. *Uncle Tommy's Color Bar isn't so bad after all,* he thought. Smelled better, too, on account of the fact that soon-to-be Ex-Barfly was sitting directly in front of the fan. The scent of lavender (or was it musk?) wafted toward Lucky's end of the bar. Lucky couldn't put his finger on where he'd smelled the scent before.

Ex-Barfly's caller rang. "I should take this," he said, apologetically, as if Lucky had begged him not to. The call seemed to be from the boss he'd whinged about, if the man's obsequiousness was anything to go by. Lucky was grateful the bloke was occupied. Gave him a chance to think.

Lucky had been looking for Afarra that whole time, but he hadn't received Ji-ji's letter till the day before yesterday. He knew why too: Zyla hated him. The feeling was mutual. Lucky had assumed Ji-ji had taken off without saying anything. He'd complained to Otto about it, said if she didn't give a crap about her own safety or about finding Afarra, why should he? (Though of course he did care about Afarra, and it was Man Cryday who'd asked him to help, not Ji-ji.) The thing that irked him most—Ji-ji had no idea what he'd been through to get there, and no idea how bruised he was, literally, from his initial encounter with her. He'd planned to come and see her ages ago, bring her news about Bonbon. But he didn't have much news to share. None that was good anyway. In addition, if he was honest, there was another reason why he'd stayed away. Cowardice.

Last year, after Germaine told him Ji-ji's condition had deteriorated, he'd stayed away. Then, when it improved, he'd decided to visit. In the spring, he'd been about to set out for D.C. when he learned her condition had worsened again. Not that he was squeamish; he wasn't. Physical injuries didn't faze him much. Served for months on the 437th, and the shit he'd seen Lotter and the other father-men do . . . Yet the thought of watching another young girl he cared about die devastated him. He'd watched his sister disappear in that swirling water. He couldn't hang on to Rachel, and then she was gone. Didn't come up for air. You were supposed to come up at least once.

When Ben finally managed to get hold of him a few weeks ago, and he broke the news that Ji-ji was thriving, Lucky had moved heaven and earth to hurry down to the Dream so he could protect her like he'd promised Uncle Dreg he would. So although he hated Swamp City, as he called it, he came anyway, to keep a promise he'd made to an old man. Not that he'd necessarily believed all that stuff about an Existential, or the rumors about what steaders were doing in the arsenal on the 437th, the one seeds called Murder Mouth. And he certainly didn't believe the stuff the old wizard said about some bird tribe from the Cradle. He was an Englishman, for god's sake! Got more sense than to invest in outlandish stories. His grandfather, on the other hand, swallowed the wizard's tale without hesitation. His grandfather—and his dad and mum, for that matter—went gaga over Uncle Dreg. But then they loved everyone. No discrimination when it came to friendship. Jailbirds, police, preachers, believers, atheists, all colors, all sizes, it didn't matter. They saw what they wanted to see in people. He was still trying to decide whether they were blessed or gullible.

And then, back there in The Margins, when he thought he'd stopped believing in much of anything, things took an unexpected turn when Jellybean pulled out the same gun Petrus had used to kill her mum and started shooting

Bounty Boys, all to rescue some fake Muleseed kid she didn't even know. She was a rubbish marksman, but she was brave. She was willing to risk her life for the kid from the 368th in the ass's ears, a boy no one else gave a damn about. She'd left him with no choice. He was a couple of years older than she was and a mercenary who'd promised Man Cryday *and* Uncle Dreg he'd protect her, and there she was taking the initiative while he felt the buzz of a sunset and hoped to god the only one they'd kill that day was a no-name boy who was set to die anyway. Still shocked him to think about how he'd been willing to sacrifice himself like that.

A couple of days ago, before he got her letter, he'd assumed she'd just up and left. Ben presented him with the letter Zyla had failed to deliver promptly. Zyla's excuse was that she'd found it at the practice coop when they'd gone to clear out Ji-ji's and Afarra's stuff so there'd be no trace of them left behind. Alice had a hissy fit after Ji-ji ran off, but the Friends didn't own her any more than Lotter did. That was the problem. Everyone thought they had a right to a piece of you. Before long, you'd given away so much you didn't have anything left for yourself.

Otto told him the Friends had painted over the mural in Afarra's room. Made sense. Last thing they wanted was for steader spies to come upon a painting like that. But when Lucky heard the news, something came over him. He'd embarrassed Otto by choking up. Sobs had bounded up his throat and taken him by surprise. Not that the mural was some masterpiece, though it was a hundred times better than he could do. The thing was, when Ji-ji had shown it to him the first night he'd stayed at the Aerie, he'd seen the love in it. *Love* wasn't a word he used much, but in this case it fit. What got to him was Ji-ji powering up to the moon as if nothing could stop her from getting there. Reminded him of how she'd looked when she'd launched that insane attack against those Bounty Boys. Lucky reached into his pocket and took out her letter for the third time that day.

Dear Lucky,
I feel terrible leaving you after you've just arrived. (And saved me, again.) But I'm glad we had a few days to catch up. I got to go find someone I thought I'd lost. Someone as close to me as Rachel was to you. I know you'll understand. (Must be going Mad, I guess.) Please forgive me for taking off like this.
I have one favor to ask. A big one. <u>PLEASE keep searching for Afarra.</u> There is no one I trust more than you to find her. Afarra trusts you too. You gave her the orange. I told you she kept the peel. You're brave and you'll recognize the people who took her. Another reason why I can't think of anyone better to do this.

If she's gone for good, I want you to tell me. Then I can stop hoping. Hoping hurts too much when it's futile, so no sugarcoating, OK?

I know this is a lot to ask after everything you've done for her and me already, and I know I just took off without a word, so I'll understand if you say no. This is just "in the meantime." Soon I'll be back to look for her myself.

I can't pay you right now, but if all this strange business works out and I get some lucre someday, maybe I'll have something to give you? For now, all I got is an I.O.U. Here it is.

Ji-ji Silapu promises to pay her good friend Lucky Dyce whatever he needs to compensate him for searching for Afarra.

<u>Signed:</u> Ji-ji Silapu

I hope that's enough. If not, that's OK too. Whatever you decide, I'll always feel lucky to know you. I hope I didn't injure you too badly. Your annoying friend ☺——Ji-ji

"I see you got yourself a letter," Ex-Barfly said. "Me, I never liked 'em. I can read real good. Raised on a progressive. They taught the bright seeds to read. But I never trusted letters. Letters're traps. Evidence to use against you if you write the wrong thing or someone else writes it."

The barman had popped out back earlier—to smoke weed, smelled like. Lucky didn't fancy conversing with Barfly on his own. He stood up to leave.

"Where you off to, fairskin?"

Lucky tried not to show how much he despised that term. "Got things to do," he replied.

"Me too," the man said. "Got a job on the side. From another fairskin. Can't tolerate the sun cos he's pasty, so he can't look for it himself. Has me searching high an' low for his stupid—"

"Gotta go," Lucky said. He moved toward the exit.

"Yeah, we all got jobs to do!" the man called after him. "But if you see a squirmy little pedigree let me know. Never seen a grown man cut up like that over some fuckin dog. You call him, he'll come, the man says. I been calling all day. Dog goes by the name of—"

"*Circus!*" Lucky cried.

The man's eyes widened: "How'd you know that? You some kinda wizard?"

Lucky cursed himself. He should never have reacted like that. He had to come up with a story, quick. He strolled over, sat down on the stool next to the man, who looked at him suspiciously. "Just realized something, that's all," Lucky said. "A coincidence. Back there on the Mall, some fella asked me about a dog named Circus. Said someone was looking for it."

The man relaxed. "Yeah," he said. "I been asking around. You seen the little runt?"

Lucky shook his head. "Wish I had. Got a soft spot for dogs. I know what it's like to lose one. Lost my own dog last week. Had to euthanize him. Put him down, I mean."

"I know what that means," the man said, sourly. This time his irritation was clear. Lucky pretended not to notice.

"A black Lab," Lucky continued. "Sweetest dog you ever saw." Lucky pulled a name from his ass. "Euston, his name was."

"Houston, like the liberty city?" the man asked.

"No. Like the old railway station. In London." Lucky didn't let the man's puzzled look derail him. "I tell you what. You tell me where I can find Circus' owner an' I'll keep my eye out. Got to help a fellow dog lover. People don't understand what it's like to lose your best friend, your family."

"You gotta go through me," the man said, crabbily. "Owner's real private an' particular."

"Sure thing," Lucky said.

He'd been right to proceed with caution. This man was hiding something. Could be Chaff Man was offering a reward and he didn't want to split it, or it could be a lot more sinister than that.

Lucky gestured to the barman, who'd peered round the back door when he'd heard Lucky yell Circus' name. "Hey, man," Lucky said. "Next round's on me. It's still bloody hot outside, and this Good Samaritan here deserves another drink." Lucky turned back to his new friend and held out his hand, thought it best not to give his real name. "Where are my manners? Let me introduce myself. The name's John . . . John Compton. Time I repaid you for that drink."

The man grinned and shook Lucky's hand. The promise of booze softened him. "Candid Fish," he said. "Call me Can the Man. I guess one little drink won't defeat my teetotaling objective."

"That's my man, Can," Lucky said. They both chortled at that.

"Give me a double whiskey," Can said to the barman, who'd returned to his place behind the bar. "No. Scratch that. Make it a triple." The lucky man grinned at Lucky Dyce. A big old grin designed to make him feel all warm and cozy inside.

Lucky didn't let his face betray him; he played it cool. He was almost a hundred percent certain that either Ji-ji or Ben had told him Can was the name of the witness to Afarra's abduction. Had Can the Man been in league with Chaff Man all along? If so, why tell Tiro he'd witnessed it? Lucky needed to figure it out and fast. He hated loose ends. If you weren't careful, they turned into nooses. *I'm coming, Afarra,* he thought. *Hold on a little while longer, kid.*

As casually as he could, lucky John Compton began to reminisce about his undying love for the late Euston as he plied Can the Man with drinks.

|||||||||||||||

Lucky sat in the kitchen of Otto's modest apartment above the Friends' charity clinic in Adams Morgan with Otto, Ben, Germaine, and Zyla. He'd called Ben and Germaine and asked them to meet up with him and Otto. Seemed like as good a place to meet as any, and they could speak privately there. Lucky had been adamant that Ben and Germaine come alone. He'd been mad as hell when the two of them turned up with Zyla Clobershay, of all people. Germaine, always the peacemaker, had calmed him down. But now Lucky wished he'd insisted Zyla leave.

"Sorry to say, Lucky," Ben admitted, "I don't think much of your plan."

"Neither do I," Germaine agreed.

"It's risky all right," Otto added. "We make the wrong move an' the little one could pay."

Zyla weighed in to repeat the obvious: "If this Can guy's spooked, it could be disastrous."

"You think I don't know that?" Lucky shot back.

"Let's bury the hatchet for tonight, okay, Lucky?" Germaine said. "I still don't get it," she added. "Why would Can Fish tell Tiro what he'd seen if he was in on the kidnapping?"

"He could be playing both sides," Ben suggested. "Think he's capable of that?"

"Can the Man is out for himself," Lucky said. "Didn't get the sense loyalty's his thing."

Germaine said, "When you followed him, he led you straight back to the Mall?"

"Yep," Lucky replied. "Straight to a stall with some sleazy White drug dealer."

"Must be Lippy Verdi," Ben said. "The one Tiro told us about. Goes by Requiem. Fish's boss. Think Lippy's in on it too?"

"Don't think so," Lucky replied. "Can hates Lippy. Says he treats him like a dog. Didn't seem to hate Chaff Man. Seemed to pity him."

"Pity him!" Zyla exclaimed. "He's an executioner, for god's sake!"

"Probably doesn't know that, Zy," Germaine pointed out.

"Germaine's right," Lucky said. "Could be he's just sorry for the bloke cos he lost his dog. I hoped he'd lead me to Chaff Man. Easy-peasy. He'd drunk enough to drown a fish. But Fish the Man can hold his liquor. Couldn't persuade him to cough up Chaff Man's hideout."

Ben appeared to sense how bad Lucky felt for being unable to make more headway. "It's not your fault, man. If the executioner's as crazy about that Pomeranian as you say, there's a reward for sure. No way Candid would wanna share it."

Germaine looked worried. "S'pose Can's not the type to cave under pressure?"

On safer ground in that regard, Lucky reassured her. "Candid's no hero. Wouldn't say boo to a goose. All we've got to do is corner him. He'll cough up the address and lead us there. Would've done it there and then, but I needed backup to be safe. I was on foot. Didn't fancy dragging Can around if he was squirming like an eel."

Otto winked at Lucky. "Guess you could say you kicked the Can down the road," he joked.

Zyla brushed the joke aside and reminded everyone that Sloppy would probably be with Chaff Man. "All of us—except for you, Germ—should go with you to be on the safe side."

No way, Lucky thought. The last person he wanted on this raid was Zyla. "Don't need four," he insisted. "Fish'll swim away soon as we release him. That only leaves Chaff Man an' Sloppy."

Germaine still had doubts: "Candid may not be the wimp you think he is. He knows they took Afarra. He witnessed it. He may even have been in on it, yet he said nothing."

"Who would he report it to?" Otto countered. "Think the cops or patrollers give a damn 'bout some outcast being snatched? Not everyone's a hero like my good buddy—"

Zyla interrupted him: "Suppose Can's not with Lippy when you get back to the Mall?"

This latest note of caution from the schoolteacher, who'd failed to display any caution at all when she'd overstayed her welcome on the 437th and got a few Friends killed in the process, infuriated Lucky. "Candid won't be with Lippy if we spend the next hour arguing." Lucky glanced up at the clock on Otto's wall. "Enough talk. We should get going. Otto, Ben, you ready?"

A sharp rap on the door made them all jump. All except Zyla.

"Don't worry," Zyla said. "It's only Mackie."

Lucky glared at her. "Ji-ji's old coach? What's she doing here?"

Zyla hurried out of the kitchen without responding.

Otto took off after her, shouting, "Hey, wait up! Could be for me! It's *my* apartment!"

Lucky and the others heard Zyla and Otto argue as they descended the stairs and opened the front door. They heard another voice. Scottish.

Exasperated, Lucky turned to his friends: "I told you not to invite anyone else."

"We didn't know she'd invited Mackie," Ben insisted, "else I would've told you, man."

Germaine defended her friend: "You should take Zyla with you. There's no one cooler than she is in a crunch."

"Cooler'n me?" Ben asked.

Germaine reached up and stroked Ben's head, affectionately. "Way cooler, darlin'. Wish I could come." She rubbed her belly: "Not used to taking a back-seat."

"You got other fish to fry," Ben joked. He placed his hand on Germaine's belly. Lucky looked away. Pregnancy embarrassed him for some reason. And whenever the couple showed affection for each other, his anxiety was triggered—what with half-Mexican Germaine looking White and Ben being Black. He'd spent too much time in the Territories than was healthy. Had to keep reminding himself miscegenation was legal in D.C.

Zyla entered, with Otto, Coach Mack, and a girl Lucky didn't recognize at first. The girl, about Ji-ji's age, had a face so swollen on the left side that her eye was shut. She had bruises up and down her arms, and her hand was bandaged too. It was her hair that Lucky remembered. The one thing that looked the same as it had at the Friends' meeting when she'd been locked in conversation with Ji-ji. She wore it in braids piled on top of her skull like a crown.

Gently, Zyla took the girl's arm and eased her toward Lucky and the others. "You tell him what you told Coach Mack," she said. The girl looked petrified. "It's okay," Zyla urged. "Don't be scared. You know Ben and Germaine. This is Lucky. He was at the meeting. He's a decent guy. Pretends he's not, but Ji-ji thinks he hung the moon. Lucky, this is Tulip. She and her sisters, Rosemary and Thyme, are staying with Coach Mack and the two Montys for a while."

Coach Mack put her arm round Tulip. "Don't you worry, lass," she said. "You can trust them." She gave Lucky the evil eye. "Even that clootie over there. Cloven hooves and all. Tell them what happened with Sloppy."

Lucky leapt out of his chair. "You saw Sloppy?"

Tulip reared back in alarm. Mackie glared at Lucky as if he'd spat at the girl, then she shoved him unceremoniously to one side and eased Tulip into his chair. Scottish people aggravated Lucky almost as much as Americans.

"Tell them what you told me, dear," Mackie urged. "Don't be scared."

Tulip sat down and took a gulp of breath. She looked from one to the other.

In a voice so soft they had to lean forward to hear her, she said, "Friend Mack says you're Ji-ji's friends."

"We are," Germaine told her. "We love her. Even the clootie here. Whatever that means."

Tulip, who'd barely looked up since she'd entered the kitchen, met Germaine's eyes and seemed to trust them. "A few days ago," she said, timidly, "Sloppy . . . attacks me. . . . Tries to kill me!"

"Attacked you?" Lucky said. "Where? When?"

"*Haud yer wheesht!*" Coach Mack said. "Let her speak! Go on, dear."

Tulip half whispered, "I was in Kingdom Come, searching for Afarra like I promised Ji-ji I would. Don't know why but I kept thinking she was there. We're friends, the three of us. In the Freedom Race we was a team. Been through hell together, with pickers picking an' poking the runners, an' snarl-cats eating us, an' so on." Tulip paused for a moment to get a grip. "Ran into these boys called Wally an' Pan, an' a girl Ivy. It's their names, see? Wally says it's short for Wallaby, an' Pan is short for Pangolin. I'm thinking they're from my planting with names like that cos the female seeds were named after flowers an' plants an' herbs, and the males after animals. But it turns out Wally an' Pan're born Papers. But still, I decided to go back another day cos they lied about something. You can tell when boys lie. That shifty look they get behind the eyes."

Lucky, impatient, opened his mouth to speak, but Mack raised her hand to quiet him. "Tell them about Sloppy," Mack coaxed. "Tell them what she said. They need to head off soon."

"Okay. Sloppy—Delilah Moon's her chosen name—she comes at me 'fore I can defend myself. Takes a bite out of my hand, see?" As if she thought they wouldn't believe her without proof, Tulip pulled back the bandage to show some vicious teeth marks. "Scratched my neck up bad too. See?" She turned so they could see her scored neck. "She h-had a knife." Tulip started crying.

"Tell them what you told me," Mackie urged. "Tell them what Sloppy said."

Tulip could barely speak, but she managed to say, "She t-told me what happened to A-A-Afarra. She t-told me the man who snatched her c-cut her up in little p-pieces an' buried her!"

Lucky wanted to throw up. Germaine moaned in horror and clutched Ben's hand.

"Oh *no!*" Otto said, as he blinked back tears. "Poor kid!"

Zyla kept her head, said Sloppy could have lied to put everyone off the scent. "Sloppy Casperseedmate is a compulsive liar. The bastard she was mated to used to beat her nonstop." Zyla bent down so her face was closer to Tulip's. "You think she could've been lying, sweetie?"

Tulip looked up hopefully. "I g-guess. N-Never thought of that before. D-Don't know."

Zyla pressed her again: "Did she say anything about where Afarra was being held? Anything at all?" Tulip shook her head.

"Tell them the rest," Mack urged.

"There's more?" Germaine said, fearfully.

Coach Mack nodded. "Tell them the rest, Tulip. They won't be angry, will you?"

All of them except Lucky said they wouldn't. Mackie glared at him.

"How do I know?" Lucky said. "She hasn't told us yet. . . . Okay, okay. I won't be angry."

Tulip sniffed hard. Began to speak, faltered, then started over. "Sloppy said I had to tell her something she didn't know. So I couldn't think of nothing else cos of the knife . . . so I told her what I'd heard. Told her Ji-ji's g-gone to find her sister. That's what they're saying."

"Who told you that?" Lucky asked.

"Nymee. The runner who stayed back with Afarra during the Freedom Race to fight the snarlcats. She's a friend of mine an' a Friend of Freedom too, like me. Georgie-Porge told her, after Ink, the nice boy with the Tree, tells him they was going down south to find her sister."

Lucky was furious. "What's wrong with that stupid boy, blabbing like that?"

"Never mind about that now," Mackie said. "Tell them what you told me, lass."

"So I told Sloppy 'bout that, but she said she already knew her sister was alive. So I told her . . . something . . . else . . ." Tulip's voice got even softer. "I told her . . .'bout Ji-ji's back."

"You did *what?*" Lucky exclaimed.

"I'm *sorry!*" Tulip cried. "I was scared! She said she'd cut my face up!"

"If Sloppy and Chaff Man know," Lucky warned, "Lotter won't be far behind. I never could figure out why Lotter let him go after Chaff Man refused to lynch Uncle Dreg. Lotter should've had him shot or sent to the Rad Region. He just disappeared. Didn't make sense."

"So now what do we do?" Germaine asked.

Zyla said they needed to let the Friends know that Ji-ji's secret had almost certainly been compromised. "I'll never forgive Man Cryday for lying to us!" she said, angrily.

Ben reasoned it could be worse. "Charra's in the Madlands. Fly-boys are with her, so she's not alone. If Sloppy's parroted, we gotta hope the steaders didn't follow them down there. With any luck, we can intercept them on the way back to the city. They'll enter from the south. Then we whisk her off to the E.S.S. where she'll be safe."

"Ben's right," Germaine said. "We tell Alice and the Friends where Ji-ji and the fly-boys've gone and that her secret's out. We focus on Afarra for now. There's still a chance she's alive. We should go ahead with Lucky's plan. Zyla, Mack, Tulip an' me can tell Alice and Paul what's happened."

Ben concurred. "Otto, Lucky and I will head to the Mall. Get Can to take us to Chaff Man."

"Don't worry, Tulip," Germaine said. "If Afarra's alive, we'll find her."

"If not," Tulip said, dry-eyed at last, "I hope you kill Sloppy an' slice her up good." Tulip's animosity shocked them all into silence.

"Alrighty then," Lucky said, after a few moments. "I think that's our cue to head out."

"Lead the way, Lucky," Ben said. "Let's go can ourselves a little fish."

||||||||||||||||

It was almost too easy. Lucky had read Can the Man like a book. He was exactly where Lucky had said he'd be, sleeping it off behind Lippy Verdi's stall. The Maulers were starting to erect their night shelters. In all the commotion, it was easy for the three men to lift Can off his feet, drag him behind another stall nearby, and persuade him to tell them where Chaff Man lived. He begged them to leave him behind. Said Chaff Man would kill him if he saw he'd betrayed him. "It's the right address, I swear!" he cried. But none of the men were born yesterday. He was coming with them.

They loaded him into Otto's compact car. It was a tight squeeze.

Ben called Germaine to tell her where they were headed. Said it shouldn't take long to find out if the address was genuine. The place was in a dodgy area near the South Gate. The entire way there Fish kept telling them Chaff Man would cut off his balls if he discovered he'd betrayed him.

"No need to worry," Otto said. "It's obvious you ain't got none to speak of."

"It's okay," Ben said. "We don't want a little minnow like you. We're interested in the girl."

"What girl?" Can said.

Lucky warned him not to lie. Said they knew who he was, knew what he'd done.

"*Wasn't me!*" Can cried. "I wasn't even *there!*"

"You told him you were," Lucky said. "Said you saw the whole thing."

"Saw the whole thing?" Candid repeated, as if in a daze.

"On the Mall," Lucky said. "Saw her drag the girl away. Told Tiro you saw the necklace."

"Oh, *that*. Yeah . . . yeah. Now I see what you're referring to, John."

"Who's John?" Otto said.

"Shut up," Lucky told him.

Can Fish calmed down, which struck Lucky as odd. Clearly, he'd thought they were accusing him of something else. *Must have a few ghosts in his closet,* Lucky thought. His amnesia magically disappeared too. He remembered every detail. Admitted to speaking to the Pterodactyl. Said he'd told him the truth. Said he'd seen the evil eye beads peek out from the girl's jacket. Said he'd seen a necklace like that before. It belonged to a Toteppi witch on the planting where he was raised. "Necklace killed the witch," he said. "Told the Pterodactyl that story. Said it wasn't safe to strut around in them evil eye poppers cos it rubbed people the wrong way." He continued to vehemently deny having anything to do with the girl's abduction.

Ben was skeptical: "Yet you know all about his little dog, right?"

"Cos I run into him soon after," Can said. "It was synchronicity, that's what it was."

"Synchronicity?" Lucky said.

"Coincidence an' providence combined," Can told him. "Like me meeting up with you at the Color Bar. I could tell you was a good man soon as I saw you, Mr. Compton, or whatever your name is. I thought to myself, that's a good fairskin, full of righteousness an' mercy. You wouldn't hurt a poor Commonseed, would you? Let me out 'fore we get there, for pity's sake! Chaff Man's a bloodthirsty sonuvabitch! I swear to you on my mam's grave, I won't say a word! Not one word to the motherfuckin executioner!"

Lucky, sitting in the back with Can, perked up. "You know he's an executioner then?"

Fish looked flustered. "You said he was," he contended.

"No I didn't." At least, Lucky didn't think he did.

"Guess he must've mentioned it himself," Can said, evasively. Lucky didn't want to feel sorry for the wimp, but he did, a little.

"You knew he'd taken the girl," Ben said. "Yet you didn't do a thing to help her. I swear, man, if she's dead, I'll slit your throat myself."

Candid wailed: "What was I s'posed to do? He's a two-hundred-and-eighty-pound fairskin! Think some no-name seed could take on a fairskin like him an' get away with it?"

Otto sniffed the air. "What's that smell?" he asked.

"It's our friend here," Ben said. "Smells of lavender."

Otto sniffed the air again. "A bum like him an' lavender is an odd combo."

"It's Lippy's fault," Can said. "Sells it to sympathizers, those secessionists. They call it—"

"Dark Essenceial," Lucky said.

"*Christ Almighty!*" Candid exclaimed. "Why'd you keep doing that? You a mind reader?"

"It's the aftershave Lotter wore," Lucky said, forgetting Candid had ears too.

Candid stared at him in amazement. "You know Lord-Father Lotter?"

When Lucky, who could have kicked himself for giving too much away, didn't respond, Can kept talking. "He's the Twelfth. Special, the steaders say. Lippy's ordered a case o' the stuff. Can't keep it in stock. Makes me slather it on for marketing purposes."

A little later, Otto said, "We're getting close." He pulled over. "We can walk from here."

Lucky had no idea where they'd wound up, but he knew they shouldn't linger there for long. He heard gunshots echoing from a few blocks away. Garbage was strewn everywhere. No streetlights, of course. No working sewage system either, smelled like. Houses had smashed-in windows, and Lucky spotted plump rats scurrying along the gutters. Otto had a tight hold of Candid, threatened to throttle him if he made a peep.

Chaff Man and Sloppy's hideout was as run-down as Lucky expected. Looked like a flophouse or one of the drug-sop dens you found in the most wretched sections of the city.

"Where's he keeping her?" Lucky whispered, as they crouched in the yard. "Which room?"

"Don't know," Can said. "I swear I don't! Listen . . . I brought you here like I said I would. Let me go now." He appealed directly to Lucky. "Please! Be reasonable! A poor seed like me can't save all the ones need saving."

Candid's words touched a nerve. *He's right*, Lucky thought. *No one can save everyone*. Candid Fish was a pathetic former seed, scared of everything that wasn't nailed down.

Just then, Ben caught sight of a man in the window. "Is that him?" he asked.

Lucky's heart began to race. Had they got there in time? "Yeah," he replied, "that's him."

Candid Fish begged for mercy: "Let me go, *please*! Stomach's all messed up. Desperate to take a dump!"

"*Shut up!*" Lucky hissed. Suddenly he felt so damn sorry for the sniveling creature about to shit himself with fear that he had to let him go. "Okay, you held up your end. You can go."

Candid grabbed Lucky's hand in his and kissed it. "I'll find a way to pay you back, I *promise!*"

Otto didn't let go of Candid's arm. "You sure 'bout this, Lucky?" he said. Lucky nodded.

Otto relinquished his hold on Can Fish, who sped off into the dark like a rocket.

"Wow!" Ben said. "Look at him go! Thought the little weasel had a bum leg."

"Think Chaff Man's alone?" Otto asked. "Don't see anyone else, do you?"

"No," Lucky said, "but let's not take chances. Hey, look. He's sitting down."

"Is that a bottle of booze in his hand?" Otto said. "Sure is. He won't know what hit him."

They drew their weapons and crept through the dark as noiselessly as they could. The front door wasn't locked. They pushed it open onto a grimy hallway. On the left was a room with a kitchen in the back. Chaff Man sat in a rocker in the middle of the room with a whiskey bottle in one hand and a huge dirty handkerchief in another. This was too easy.

"Hands up!" Ben yelled, with the ease of a practiced fighter. "Stand up real slow."

Chaff Man turned to look at them. Seemed to have trouble understanding what Ben had said. Then, with hands raised—bottle in his right, handkerchief in his left—Chaff Man lumbered to his feet. "I ain't armed," he said, like someone who didn't care whether or not they believed him. *He looks the same as he looked on the planting,* Lucky thought. *Same red curly hair and mean mouth.*

At first, Lucky thought he was high or too drunk to understand what was happening. But it wasn't that. "Where is she?" Lucky said, hurrying up to the big man and patting him down.

"Who?" Chaff Man asked. Lucky saw then that the executioner had been crying.

"Who do you think?" Lucky said. "Afarra. The Cloth you snatched. Is she alive?"

"Yeah, she's alive. . . . Far as I know. My heart's broke. She snatched him. To get me back."

"What the hell's he talking about?" Ben asked. "Where's the other one? Where's Sloppy?"

"No clue," Chaff Man replied. "Slut up an' left. After all I did for her."

Lucky, afraid the executioner was about to bawl, demanded that he take them to her.

"Can't," Chaff Man told them. "She ain't here."

While Otto remained to guard the door, Ben stepped closer to the executioner.

"What the fuck do you mean?" Ben said.

"I mean, the stinking Cloth got away," Chaff Man said. "Ran off."

"She *escaped*?" Lucky said, incredulously.

Recognition spread across Chaff Man's tearstained face: "I know you! You're Lotter's lieutenant." Chaff Man started to panic. "He send you to kill me?"

"Is that who you're working for?" Lucky said. "Lotter?"

"Answer him," Ben said. He raised his gun and aimed for Chaff Man's broken heart.

Chaff Man looked completely befuddled. All of a sudden he caved. Seemed to be a relief to get it out. "Lotter's looking for his favorite Mule. Jellybean, her name is. Ran in the Big Race. Then we see the Cloth on the Mall. Sloppy tells me it's Jellybean's sidekick. Says if we snatch her, we won the lottery. So we grab her an' ask where Jellybean is. Turns out she's a fuckin witch!" He started to blubber. "Ran off an' took *Circus*! Selfish bitch took the only friend I ever had!" He sank back into the rocker. His shoulders heaved with sobs.

Shocked, Ben took a step back. "What the hell's wrong with you, man?" he said.

"Did you hurt her?" Lucky asked.

Chaff Man shook his head. "Never touched her! I swear to the Virgin! Not once! She had them wizard eye beads on! Then she starts sermonizing like he did. *Same voice!* How'd she *do* that?"

Ben lowered his gun. Lucky holstered his. Clearly, the blubbering executioner wasn't a threat. "Pathetic," he said. "Otto, look out back. Check and see if—"

"Drop your weapons or I blow this one's fuckin head off!"

Lucky and Ben turned. Can the Man, the former seed Lucky could read like a book, stood in the doorway with a gun to Otto's head. Lucky had never been more surprised to see anyone in his life. Fish had another gun too, aimed in their direction. Ben and Lucky looked at each other, looked at Otto, who shook his head at Ben in a desperate plea for him not to do it. Ben ignored him and dropped his gun. Lucky carefully removed his from his holster and dropped it too. Otto groaned.

Can ordered Chaff Man to pick up the guns. The executioner obeyed.

"Cherub," Can Fish said, "shut the fuck up! Keep your eyes on them two. 'Specially Blondie. He's a slippery cunt. But not near as slippery as he thinks."

"Why come back?" Lucky asked. "We let you go."

"I come back to save his ass cos I'm a Good Samaritan like you said. Wanted to do a friend a favor an' fuck with you boys at the same time. Can't exactly call Blubberman here a friend, but he's got his uses. Weren't expecting this, were you, John Compton, or whatever the fuck your name is? A switch in the power dynamic." He chuckled. "Bet you're thinking, how does an ignorant dusky know 'bout power dynamics? Cos I'm smart is why. Got a memory like a fuckin elephant."

"You were in on the kidnapping from the start," Lucky stated.

"Wrong again, Blondie. Told that fly-boy drug-sop the truth. Then I got to thinking 'bout it, an' I says to myself, 'How come some Cloth is being chased after by a famous fly-boy?' So I keep my eyes open, an' I spot Cherub one day an' follow him. Follow the money, they say. But *I* say, follow the mystery, look for clues. 'Fore you know it, the executioner an' me is best buddies. Had a few drinks together. Got to listen to his story. Chaff knew that Tribal wizard—you know that? Knows Lord-Father Lotter too, like you, Johnny, or Lucky, or what-ever the fuck your name is. Ol' Chaff Man here could write a decent biography if he wanted, which he don't. His writing sucks more than his reading. Then I get in good with his whore, Sloppy. Then she skedaddles, that's what Cherub says when I come across him, all weepy-weepy, searching for his pooch. Could be he killed her. I was moved by Cherub's predicament, so I—"

Lucky interrupted him. "Is she dead? Afarra. Is she dead?"

Can shrugged. "How the fuck should I know? I'm not some wizard. Don't know which slut he offed. Could be both, could be neither. You'll be dead real soon, so maybe you'll find out. Oh, an' by the by, Cherub here diddled the Cloth good 'fore she ran off—right, Cherub?"

Lucky took a step toward Chaff Man.

Can Fish's voice rang out clear and strong and lethal: "Don't try it, Blondie! Cherub's got a gun pointed at your head, an' Otto here's fucked if you make a move. You underestimated me, Johnny boy. Think I'll have a little fun with you. Store you in the shed where Cherub kept the Cloth tied up. What you say, Cherub? Let's have a little fun with Blondie here 'fore we—"

The bullet struck Candid in his side. A clean shot by Zyla, the first Good Samaritan.

Chaff Man reacted. Raised a gun and shot Ben. Hit him in the arm.

Zyla shot again, took out Fish's knee this time.

A split second later, Mary Macdonald, the second Good Samaritan, hit Chaff Man in the groin. The executioner dropped both guns and slammed to the floor.

The women stood in the doorway, their weapons pointed at Can and Chaff Man, who writhed in agony.

Otto hauled himself up, grabbed Fish's gun and his own. "How'd you know?" Otto cried.

"We didn't," Zyla said, keeping close watch on the wounded. "She did."

Tulip emerged from the hallway.

"Tulip heard us talking," Mackie said. "Wanted to know what Ben meant about canning fish. Put two and two together when she heard how Lucky described him." Candid Fish tried to haul himself up. "*Oy!* Fishface! You better stay down, otherwise I'll blast your stinking lavvy heid off! Don't think I won't either. Ask anyone. I don't like men much." With the barrel of her gun, Mackie pointed to Chaff Man's feet. "Would you look at that?" she observed. "Bastard's wearing sandals! What did I tell you, Zy? Can't trust a man in sandals. Bet he's got a wee pencil in his pocket too."

Chaff Man clutched his bloody groin. Can Fish, grasping his side, attempted to sit up. He looked like he'd seen a ghost.

"Ben, you okay?" Zyla asked.

"It's grazed, that's all," Ben said. "I'm okay."

"Is Afarra here?" Zyla said.

"They say she escaped," Lucky replied.

Tulip made her way over to Fish. "Soon as they said Fish, I knew," she told him.

"What the hell's going on?" Lucky said, as he helped a wounded Ben into the rocker.

"*Don't do it!*" Zyla cried.

Lucky turned and saw a gun in Tulip's hands. His! She must've grabbed it while he was helping Ben. She was standing over Can Fish.

"You killed her," Tulip stated.

"Afarra?" Lucky cried in dismay. "He killed Afarra?"

"Don't know," Tulip replied. "Did you kill Afarra, Clown? Better tell the truth. I can tell when you're lying."

"I swear to god I didn't do it, sis! Didn't even *see* the Cloth 'cept for that one time when they dragged her off! S'why we're all looking for the *fuckin dog*! She *stole* him! Ask Cherub!"

"But you killed Mam, didn't you, Clownfish? Bashed her face in."

Lucky didn't know what Tulip was talking about, but Fish did. He looked around wildly, desperate for an escape.

"It was self-defense," he cried. "*She* attacked *me*! You know how crazy Mam got!"

"You took the coins from her money jar. The one she hid under the floorboards. For Thyme, so she'd be okay when she got older. Scared Rosie half to death. Got blood all over little Thyme. Found her sitting in a pool mumbling herself. Mam's head all turned round the wrong way, eyes staring like glass. Mam was the only one of us loved you."

"C'mon, pet," Coach Mack said. "Let's get you home. The Friends will take care of—"

"*NO!*" Tulip shrieked. "Don't you see? They been killing us an' raping us an' beating us black an' blue *forever*! An' we been *taking* it! Shoulda killed you a hundred times over in your sleep! Shoulda killed you 'fore you did all them nasty things to me an' Rosie an' Thyme! You made me a bad big sister! I was scared of you for a long, long time. . . . But I ain't scared now."

Clownfish joined his hands in prayer and pleaded for his life: "*Don't shoot! I repent!* If a sinner repents, you gotta forgive him! Mam said that, remember?"

"I do forgive," Tulip said. Before Clownfish could thank her, she added, "I forgive myself, Lord Jesus, for what I'm about to do."

She pulled the trigger and blew her brother's face away.

Lucky tried to remember what Clownfish looked like before. He couldn't.

"Now," Tulip said, "you all can arrest me if you want. I'm done."

24 GIFTS FREELY GIVEN

Someone rapped loudly on the door of the shed out back where Ji-ji slept. She glanced at her watch: six A.M. Antonio's voice: "The commander requests your company at breakfast!" She leapt out of bed. Charra didn't countenance tardiness on anyone's part but her own.

Using the jug of water Tony filled for her each night, Ji-ji washed her face in the bowl, brushed her teeth, and dressed quickly while Tony paced around outside and implored her to hurry. After only a few minutes, she opened the shed door and stepped outside. Suddenly she remembered something. *"Wait!"* she cried and ran back inside.

Ji-ji grabbed her bag and pulled out the quilt. This might be the only chance she had to present it to Charra discreetly. If the gift pleased her sister, she could plead with her to release the three nuns or some of the fairskin children in the Pig Pen. After all, it was clear from the emblems the raiders wore and from things Charra said that they revered trees. Their mam's quilt had a tree on it. Not exactly foolproof logic but it would have to do. *Calm down,* Ji-ji told herself. *Breathe.* She hurried out with the folded quilt under her arm.

"What you got there?" Tony asked her.

"A gift. For the commander."

"She likes gifts, your sister," he said. He squinted at hers. "She likes useful ones best. Like the book of recipes Laughing Tree an' Ink give her, an' those weapons Marcus brought." Of course. That was why Marcus had brought along a crate of weapons. A gift from the Invisible Men.

Tony told her to get a move on. "Could be she'll flip over your ratty old blanket. Who knows?" He didn't sound optimistic. "Hurry up. The commander don't like to be kept waiting."

Charra and Heather, the only two at breakfast, were deep in conversation when Tony ushered Ji-ji into the dining room. In spite of the mismatched furnishings, most of which had obviously been lifted from plantings they'd raided, the room with its floral curtains and ornate rug had the warm, homey feel of a permanent dwelling rather than a makeshift camp. Momentarily, Ji-ji envied her sister. How wonderful to live in a setting as lovely as this.

Charra lowered her mug of coffee and looked Ji-ji up and down. "You're late," she said.

"Sorry. Didn't know you wanted me to join you for breakfast. If I had I—"

"What's that?" Charra asked.

Ji-ji placed the folded quilt on the table between Charra and Heather just as Verity hurried in with a plate of scrambled eggs. Afraid of antagonizing her sister, Ji-ji didn't look at the nun, who placed the plate on the table and rushed back to the kitchen.

"Unfold it," Charra ordered, in a voice that gave nothing away.

Ji-ji froze for a moment. Why hadn't she brought something useful? Even something as ordinary as socks would be in better taste than the old quilt their mam used to conceal her seedbed. Filled with trepidation, Ji-ji forced herself to unfold the gift. Its size made it unwieldy.

"Lay it on the floor," Charra commanded.

Ji-ji laid out the quilt beside the dining table. Charra rose to view it; Heather followed. They stood side by side gazing down at her gift. The wait was excruciating. Ji-ji braced herself.

Heather spoke first: "This is the quilt you told me about, Char. From your mam's cabin."

Charra bent down and touched it. From the tone of her voice, the gift caused her pain. "Mam called the tree Immaculate. Said trees like this were sacred to Toteppi. See the three birds perched on the branches? 'A trinity waiting to rise,' Mam called 'em. You remember, Beany?"

Ji-ji didn't remember. As far as she knew, their mam had never said anything like that to her.

"It's a beautiful quilt," Heather said. "Who made it?"

Charra answered her: "Aunt Zaini, Tiro's mam an' Dreg's niece. She's not our real aunt, but Mam used to be close to her. Remember I told you Zaini had to bury Amadee, Tiro's twin, after Williams accused him of Deviance an' hitched him to the penal tractor? Can't wait to find old Drexler Williams when we raid the planting. Me an' Tiro'll hitch him up an' take the tractor out for a spin. Tiro says he's up for that. What do you think, Beany?" Was she serious? Ji-ji didn't know. By the time she'd mumbled some incoherent response, Charra had moved on.

"The quilt was a grieving gift," Charra told Heather. "Zaini made it for Mam after we lost Luvlydoll." Ji-ji was all set to apologize when Charra added, "Sometimes you need something like this to remind you."

"Remind you of what?" Heather asked.

"How far you've come," Charra said. "Thank you, Beany."

To Ji-ji's amazement, Charra was sniffing back tears. Heather put her arm around Charra, who leaned her head on Heather's shoulder. She swiped her eyes dry with her sleeve and said, "Know why we respect the Tree, Beany?"

Oh crap! Another test she was unprepared for. Ji-ji took a stab at an answer: "Uncle Dreg used to say . . ." Her voice faded. She'd forgotten that Charra didn't think much of Uncle Dreg. Yet she couldn't come up with anything else. Hesitantly, she returned to the wizard and hoped Charra wouldn't explode. "He used to say the stories the trees told were ones we needed to hear. He said, like us, trees were rooted to the land, had kinship with the air, and were drawn skywards. Some folks said that Billy Brineseed spoke to Sylvie in her own language, but others said—"

Charra jumped in and explained to Heather that Billy was Planting 437's arborist and fly-coach, and Uncle Dreg's best friend. "He *could* speak to Sylvie," she declared. "I heard him. I used to hang out with Billy sometimes when I was little. He said I had a thumb as green as Uncle Dreg's. He spoke to Sylvie in this weird, guttural voice, kinda like snoring. Never heard anything like it before or since. It wasn't sentences, it was more like . . . angry humming or static. Billy would press his head up against Sylvie's massive trunk an' listen to what she had to say. Then he'd answer back."

Ji-ji was fascinated. "Did you hear Sylvie too?"

Charra looked at her as if she were as dumb as a brick. "Course not, Beany. Sylvie's a tree."

"Be nice, Char," Heather said.

"I am being nice," Charra argued.

"No you're not," Heather said.

Charra shrugged and continued reminiscing. "I asked Billy why he was angry when he talked to Sylvie. He said he took his cue from her. Said she was incensed on account of the perennial violations steaders inflicted upon her, meaning the lynching they did from her limbs, an' those disgusting metal tags they hung from her branches, etched with the names of executed seeds. . . . The steader pilgrims flock to the 437th nowadays. They gouge out hunks of Sylvie's bark an' pluck her leaves to take home as souvenirs. They got no idea who she really is."

Ji-ji thought it wiser not to admit that she had no idea who Sylvie really was either.

Charra went on: "Nothing's more sacred to steaders than Sylvie." Charra laughed bitterly. "Though I guess Lotter as the Twelfth is her main competition now. Crazy, huh, Beany? Grand Inquisitor Worthy issued a proclamation recently. He said Sylvie is—get this—'a manifestation of God's favor and evidence of Territorial exceptionalism.' Says it proves the steaders' Found Cause can never again be a lost one. See how they twist everything?"

"You think the tree on Zaini's quilt is Sylvie?" Ji-ji asked.

"Of course it is!" Charra replied, curtly. "Who else could it be?"

Silapu had said the tree was an Immaculate—it had never been violated by lynch ropes—but Ji-ji decided not to mention that. Besides, it made sense that Zaini would portray Sylvie. She decided to risk another observation.

"Uncle Dreg told me Sylvie was a hybrid. The offspring of a live oak and a kapok tree. Said she was an example of the unadulterated magnificence produced by unauthorized miscegenation."

"Wow," Heather said. "That's a mouthful."

"He could've been pulling my leg," Ji-ji admitted.

Charra seemed to appreciate Uncle Dreg's words. "Could be he was right," she said. "I asked Billy what Sylvie's voice sounded like. He told me it sounded like a chorus. As if all her leaves were tongues, an' every single one whispered an everlasting elegy."

"That's a beautiful description," Heather said.

Charra turned on her. "No it's not!" she cried, ripping herself from Heather's embrace. "It's depressing as hell. You grew up Free in a SuperState. How the hell would you know what Sylvie is?" Heather tried to explain herself, but Charra wouldn't listen. "Don't you see? She's in mourning . . . damaged. . . . All those purple tears they lash to her branches, the ones those bastards call *earrings*. Each one represents a lynched seed. She can't carry that much pain . . ."

Charra's anger abated as quickly as it had arisen. Her tone turned wistful: "When I was little, I used to think all we had to do was remove her tears, an' Sylvie would be herself again. But the way Billy said it, it sounded like she was ruined deep down into her heartwood, which meant she'd never recover. She was dying slowly from the *inside*. Her core was rotting. No way to save her."

Heather looked desperate to say something to dispel her lover's despair. "Billy was wrong," Heather said. "There's still time. We need to reclaim Sylvie before it's too late."

"Reclaim her?" Ji-ji said, hopefully.

"Oh, sorry," Heather said. "I assumed you knew it was settled."

Charra took over. "We're raiding the 437th," she announced. When Ji-ji didn't say anything, Charra grew angry. "Thought that's what you wanted. Or perhaps you're a coward like Mam."

Heather again attempted to intercede: "I'm sure Ji-ji's not a—"

Charra turned on her viciously: "Shut the fuck up, Heather! What the hell do you know?"

"Fine," Heather said, indignantly. "You don't need me here then, do you?"

Heather walked out of the dining room. Charra rushed after her. Ji-ji heard them arguing in the hallway. Soon, they returned arm in arm, Heather wrapped around Charra's little finger.

As if she'd never left off, Charra continued speaking. In an excited, almost frenzied voice, she laid out their plans. Ji-ji didn't know if the quilt had inspired her sister to trust her, but at least her gift didn't appear to have done any harm.

"The raid is only the first step," Charra outlined. "Long-term, conventional raids fail. We snatch a few dozen, then things revert right back to the status quo. We need *sustainability*. With the Invisible Men we can be ambitious. We snatch the planting like before, liberate as many seeds as we can transport. Only this time, we leave a contingent of Invisible Men on the 437th, along with a core group of raiders, an' the seeds we can't transport. They occupy the planting and keep it out of steader hands. Think about it, Beany. If the SuperStates and Liberty Independents ever get off their asses an' join with us to reunify the Disunited States, some plantings could already be under our control. The 437th is the biggest prize of all. Imagine how it would play if Lotter's Muleseed daughters, acting as one, toppled the Twelfth!"

Ji-ji stared at her sister, amazed by her audacity and terrified of her reckless-ness. A thousand reasons sprang to mind why a plan like this would fail. Raids succeeded cos they had an element of surprise; occupations couldn't draw on that. And what did "under our control" really mean? Would seeds be the new steaders and steaders be livestock? Planting 437 had become the Territories' crown jewel. Snatching it from under the steaders' noses would be a devastat-ing blow to the Found Cause; Armistice would fight to the death to get it back. But she could see that Charra had made up her mind. No one could stop her from going through with her daring plan.

In a move that Ji-ji found disconcerting, Charra approached and took her hand.

"I'm glad you're here, Beany," she said, with none of her customary sarcasm. "We were always meant to fight side by side." Charra looked over at Heather, who nodded. "We been talking. I won't out you to anyone. This needs to be your choice. I want you to offer yourself Freely, show yourself when you're ready, an' fight beside me cos you know it's the only righteous path to take."

Ji-ji struggled to find an adequate response. "Thank you" was all she came up with. She looked around to check that Verity wasn't nearby. She had to push her luck, however risky it was.

"If you mean that," Ji-ji said, "will you do something for me? Will you let the nuns go?"

Charra studied her sister intently. "You an' Heather have a lot in common. Heather's been pestering me to release the sisters for months. . . . If I say yes, will that make you happy, Beany?"

Ji-ji didn't hesitate. "It'll make me very happy."

Charra didn't seem to believe her. "Happy enough to stay an' never desert me?" she asked.

Heather warned Charra not to put pressure on her sister.

"I'm not," Charra insisted, then yelled suddenly, "*Grunt! Come here!*" Ji-ji jumped.

The sound of rushing footsteps. Verity's ashen face in the doorway.

"A new friend of mine told me about your indiscretion," Charra said. "*Help* is a loaded word. If you're not careful, you alert the enemy. You an' the other two will be blindfolded and—" Verity covered her mouth in horror. "No, not that," Charra said. "Lucky for you, my little sister, like Heather here, is filled with the milk of human kindness. They got you a reprieve. You'll be blindfolded and escorted to Jacksonville. You can find transport home from there."

Verity clutched the doorjamb. She turned even paler. Ji-ji was afraid she was going to faint.

"Free?" Verity said. "You mean, the other nuns too? All three of us? You're letting us go?" Charra nodded. Verity burst into tears. She begged to take the four orphans with them, all too sickly to work. The sisters had been caring for them, she said. They couldn't leave them behind.

Charra pondered her request for a few seconds then threw up her hands. "Fine," she said. "These two'll never shut up if I say no. You can take the four piglets. But don't you dare bad-mouth us. I got spies all over Jacksonville. Don't breathe a word about this place."

Charra yelled for Antonio, who came running, a half-eaten slice of toast in his hand. He attempted to swallow and almost choked. Charra ordered him to take Grunt-128 and the two other sister grunts to Jacksonville, and load up the four orphan piglets in the truck too. Take along a couple of armed guards for protection, she said.

Tony stood glued to the spot for several seconds, unable to comprehend the order. "*Free* 'em?" he said, as the remaining toast crumbs flew out of his mouth. "The pinks? I don't get it. . . . Who'll guard her?" he asked, pointing at Ji-ji.

Charra asked him why Ji-ji needed guarding when she was here of her own Free will. By this time, Tony didn't know which end was up. He didn't move again till Charra yelled at him.

"Look sharp, Pineabout! Or do I have to find someone else to do it who's not deaf?"

Ji-ji and Verity stole a glance at each other. The nun placed her hand on her heart in gratitude. Tony strode over to where Verity was standing, grabbed her roughly by the elbow, and propelled her out of the house. Before they exited through the front door, Charra had moved on.

"We'll take the quilt with us. Hang it over the great fireplace in the planting dining hall. What d'you think, Beany?" It was a rhetorical question. "So . . . you ready to write Dale Lotter's name onto one of Sylvie's purple tears? How 'bout I let you hang it there yourself? Pull the Culmination lever too. Not that there'll be much left of Lotter to lynch. My gift to you, little sister."

"Don't tease her, Char. It's not fair."

"Who says I'm teasing?" Charra replied, scornfully. She walked back to the table and sat down, gestured to Heather and Ji-ji to join her. "*Damn!*" Charra exclaimed. "Should've asked the grunt to finish serving breakfast 'fore she left."

Charra turned to Ji-ji and smiled sweetly. "Don't forget our motto, sis. Turnabout is fair play. From now on, *you'll* have to serve us instead."

||||||||||||||||

Charra's demotion of Ji-ji to a replacement kitchen grunt didn't last long. Like she tended to do with many of her spur-of-the-moment ideas, Charra lost interest in it. Yet no one knew how to play on people's emotions better than Charra. With a contemptuous laugh or a dismissive wave of her hand, she dissolved opposition. Her followers were on edge around her, and Charra made no secret of how much she reveled in their unease. Her power wasn't premised on her judicious temperament; it was built upon a capriciousness that took your breath away. Ji-ji didn't know whether one of the requirements of leadership was maniacal confidence, but Charra possessed it in abundance. Her sister's passionate hatred and menacing love, if you could call it that, acted upon Ji-ji like waves on a shoreline. It eroded her resistance, pulled her out into deep water then flung her back again. With each cycle, she felt herself become more compliant, swept up by an energy impossible to resist. In Turnabout, she was learning all over again that abuse had many faces. Charra's predilection for abusing others was implied in the way she tilted her head or looked at you sideways. Bullying sat at the end of a throwaway sentence or an ellipsis with a hook on the end. Violence could be detected in her footsteps, in the modulation of her breathing, or in a seemingly innocuous command. From Lotter, Charra had learned to use both the carrot *and* the stick simultaneously. The result was devastatingly effective. It endowed her with absolute control.

It hadn't taken long for Ji-ji to recognize that Heather Returnal wasn't an equal partner in the relationship, and the breakfast they'd shared confirmed it. Heather was Charra's cherished handmaiden and confidante. Charra could only be influenced when she allowed herself to be, and she held sway in all matters of significance. Heather paid meticulous attention to Charra's moods, susceptibilities, and preferences, accurately predicting when she needed her meds, when she should rest, and when she had to eat. She buoyed Charra's spirits and was skilled at suggesting alternative courses of action without antagonizing her. The lieutenant had learned to walk on eggshells around her lover-commander, and though Ji-ji envied their close connection, it also saddened her. A leader like Charra demanded sacrifice from her followers. Heather must have sacrificed almost everything to stand beside the volatile woman she loved.

An hour before a scheduled gathering of raiders in the assembly hall, Charra met with some of her lieutenants in an anteroom in that same building. Ji-ji and Marcus were invited to join them.

As it turned out, selecting Marcus as their envoy was a canny choice by the Invisible Men. In his role as Diviner Shadowbrook's unofficial errander, he had become exceptionally knowledgeable about Planting 437's layout and vulnerabilities. Marcus described the security around the arsenal and detailed how it could be successfully breached. Assuming Diviner Shadowbrook and her elderly sidekick, Silent Pete, shut off the fry-fence and disabled the planting's comm system, Marcus said, the raiding party could travel through the old Shot Tower tunnel without arousing suspicion or triggering the general alarm. They could Free the seeds in the planting's twelve seed quarters by splitting into twelve groups and advancing on the quarters all at once. Hundreds of steaders lived on the 437th at any one time. The raiders would need to swell their numbers by arming some of the seeds with weapons Marcus had supplied, and with arms the Invisible Men would bring with them.

Knowing the opposition they would face in the Doom Dell, the most forbidden area of the planting, Charra decided to liberate the prisoners inside Pen-Pen and breach Murder Mouth only after the other areas had been subdued and the seeds liberated. The various groups would need to be well coordinated. The raiders could transport about five hundred seeds, roughly a third of the planting's seed population. The other thousand or so would remain behind for the time being to help the Invisible Men hold the planting. Little was said about how they planned to convince hundreds of desperate seeds not to flee. Yet another thing to fret over.

Ji-ji remembered she had her map of the planting in her backpack. She ran to her sleep-shed and retrieved it. It felt good not to have Tony shadow her. Having run along all the planting's permissible paths and a few of the forbidden ones, she was able to fill in the significant gaps in her fanciful map and provide the raiders with accurate estimates of the distance between various points. Ji-ji pointed out the obvious: her rendition of the Planting 437 was subjective and not to scale.

Charra insisted it didn't matter. "My sister's map is priceless," she declared.

More useful than her map, in Ji-ji's opinion, was her knowledge of Lotter's security measures. Drawing upon her time observing him as security chief, Ji-ji identified the locations of numerous cameras, careful to remind them that her information was more than eighteen months old. She told them the story of how she and Afarra had taken a shortcut across the Doom Dell on Uncle Dreg's

Death Day and run into a hybrid whom she'd mistaken for an ape. (Given Charra's hostility toward Man Cryday, she didn't think it wise to mention that Drol had found refuge with the tree witch in Dimmers.) "He was held in the arsenal—Murder Mouth, seeds call it," Ji-ji told the leadership group. "There could be others. See it there on my map, near the fence in the restricted area? Looks like it's close to the Shot Tower, but it's a hike from one to the other."

"If there are more of these hybrid creatures we'll Free them," Charra promised.

During a break in their planning session, while Charra and Heather consulted with Feral and Plate, Ji-ji approached Marcus, who was helping himself to some whiskey in a fancy crystal decanter the raiders must have snatched from a father-house. He greeted her as if nothing had changed between them.

"How're your bites doing?" Ji-ji asked.

"Better. Put it down to that miracle ointment you gave me."

Ji-ji planned to ease into the conversation. No sense letting him know up front what an asshole she thought he was. But the cocky, patronizing way he had of speaking *at* her rather than *to* her made her fume. As soon as she was confident the others couldn't hear them from across the room, Ji-ji demanded to know why he'd parroted to Charra about the nun.

"It was for a higher cause," he said. "Had to prove I could be trusted."

"You put Verity an' the other nuns in great danger. Put me in danger too."

"From what I hear, she let the nuns go. Some of the Damaged too. The piglets."

Ji-ji's hackles rose: "Don't call 'em that."

"Lighten up, Ji-ji," Marcus said, as he sipped on the whiskey. "Think about it. She's only doing to fairskins what they've done to us for centuries."

Taking a chance that he wouldn't parrot to Charra again, Ji-ji told him the story Verity had shared with her about the other nun. He seemed shaken when she'd finished.

"You sure?" he said. "Your sister actually did that?" She nodded. It took him a few seconds to shrug it off. "Could be the nun deserved it," he said.

"No one deserves a death like that, an' you know it."

"Course they do," he argued. "Not the nun maybe, but fairskins've done worse. You think Drex Williams wouldn't benefit from having a few body parts lopped off after what he did to Amadee and dozens of others?" Marcus looked over at Charra. "Your sister's a force of nature. Won't take crap from anyone. Time to grow up, Ji-ji. The wizard's dead, the curtain's ripped away, an' we're not in Kansas anymore. Some of us never were." He leaned over her and spoke with an intensity she hadn't seen in him before. "Think of how seeds'll react when they see those things on your back. They'll go wild. For centuries we been waiting for a sign. All our stories, *all* of 'em, are about rising up. About flight. You an' Charra, allied with the Men, can turn everything on its head."

"You're full of crap, Marcus. You lied to all of us. Betrayed all of us."

"Haven't betrayed anyone," he told her. "Been true to the cause I believe in, that's all."

Ji-ji changed tactics. Convincing Marcus he was an asshole wasn't a top priority. "We could be walking into a trap," she said. "You sure Old Shadowy's info is accurate?"

"Who knows? Emmeline's always fancied she's got her finger on the pulse of the planting. Thinks she divines everything. She's never been in the inner circle. Females an' steaders don't mix."

"Females an' Invisible Men don't either, from what I hear."

Marcus smiled. "Can't argue with that. But with my help, the Men saw the light when it came to your sister." With evangelical fervor, he leaned in even closer and said, "We're not a bunch of idiots, Ji-ji. We're a brotherhood. The whole planting system's a way to humiliate an' debase us, to make sure we never feel like men. Throughout history that's what they've done, treated us like savages. We take a vow to live clean." Ji-ji just looked at him. "Okay, okay. I know I don't exactly practice what I preach. But I believe in what the I-Ms stand for. Black Manhood is about dignity an' self-respect, about making sure we're seen not as projections but as ourselves."

Ji-ji wondered if he'd ever been the drug-sop he'd played on the planting, or if all along he'd worn a mask. If so, it had certainly fooled her.

"Those things on your back are the most amazing things I've ever seen." He was a preacher again, a prophet. "We're on the brink of one of the greatest rebellions in history. We can soar or fizzle out. But if everyone plays their part, we got this."

"An' you know what part we need to play?" Ji-ji said, the derision in her tone unmistakable. "All of us?"

Marcus touched his neck. "Guess I forgot to bring my Seeing Eyes, otherwise I'd tell you. . . . All I'm saying is we don't stand a chance if don't put aside our differences an' stick together for the next few days. . . . An' for what it's worth, I asked Charra not to hurt the nun."

"Thought you hated nuns."

"Only the ones responsible for that shit in the museum. Don't give a crap either way 'bout nuns in general."

Ji-ji couldn't decide whether he was one of the most callous people she knew or the most honest. Marcus looked over at Charra again, deep in conversation with Feral and Plate.

"You admire her," Ji-ji observed, as he studied his face.

"Sure. Everyone does. Even Tiro. Even you. Your sister's fuckin fearless. Knows exactly what she wants. Knows how to inspire others who aren't nearly as brave as she is." Marcus, as Tiro would say, had defaulted to preaching mode again. He pushed each word a little too much till it felt like coercion, like he was shoving you up against a wall.

"You and Tiro got that Uncle Dreg mentality where you think everyone's a potential convert when it comes to enlightenment. Why d'you think the Dreamer's still revered in the Dream even though the city clings to its racist roots? Cos they made his vision palatable, that's why. Domesticated it. Even his goddam statue's white. You gotta admit, Ji-ji, Turnabout's got its upside. Can't have dumbos wielding power everywhere. We gotta upend that crap 'fore it upends us."

"Charra wields a lot of power too," Ji-ji pointed out. "So do the Invisible Men, apparently."

Marcus seemed annoyed that he hadn't been able to convert her yet. "That's a different type of power," he said, tersely. "That's antidote power."

Before she could stop herself, Ji-ji said, "What the hell's that?"

Marcus, who seemed happy to have another opportunity to persuade, said, "A power that resists domination. That's what your sister is. An antidote. S'what you could be if you loosened up an' stopped being a nun."

Why does everyone keep saying that? Ji-ji thought. "I'm *not* a nun. I'm just a girl with a freaky back. You sound like one of those propaganda leaflets they hand out in the Dream."

Her insult hit home. Up till then, Ji-ji assumed that Marcus didn't give a damn about her opinion of him. His hurt expression said differently, though he covered it up well.

"All beliefs are propaganda," he said. "But you're the only person alive who can preach with a pair of wings." He lowered his voice and leaned in closer again. "Guess that explains why you're the only person in the world your sister's intimidated by."

Ji-ji stifled a laugh. "You're nuts. She's not intimidated by me."

"Oh yes she is," Marcus said. Plate glanced over at them, curious. As smooth as silk, Marcus changed the subject. "You heard 'bout Wizard Dreg Dimmering the prisoners? Emmeline says the Oz wafts in an' out of PenPen regular as clockwork, ashy-kneed an' ghoulish."

Plate was still looking over at them. "Bettieann mentioned it ages ago, in a letter," Ji-ji said. "Guess Uncle Dreg has more power than some folks give him credit for."

"Seems to me there could be another interpretation," Marcus said, playing his old, easygoing self again. "Even in death, the Oz wound up in the penitence penitentiary, unable to fly the coop. Could be he's cooped up in PenPen cos he spent too long dreaming instead of doing."

"Or it could be they're the same thing when they're done right."

Marcus laughed. "You're smarter than your fly-boy looks, y'know that?"

Ji-ji didn't trust Marcus anymore. She didn't think she ever would again. Yet she couldn't hate him for long either, not when he reminded her so much of her brother Clay. Before he was shipped off to the auctionmart, Clay was smart as a whip. And like Clay, when Marcus laughed, he drew you into his circle. But he was more Charra than Clay . . . charismatic . . . fanatical . . .

Plate wasn't looking in their direction anymore. Ji-ji took a risk and said, "You came here for you. I was an excuse. All along, you knew what this place was."

Marcus shook his head. "I came here for all of us—me, you, Tiro. Black an' Brown gotta keep our Seeing Eyes open else someone'll open 'em for us permanently."

The weight of what they were about to do struck her. She blurted out a request: "Look out for Tiro. During the raid, I mean. If we don't get his family off the planting, it'll kill him."

"Sure I will," Marcus said, as if it were a given. "He's my fly partner. Saved his ass before, I'm sure I'll save it again. . . . You know he's not capable of being the person you need him to be, right?"

"I don't *need* him to be anything," Ji-ji said, offended.

"Sure you do."

"You're a patronizing idiot, Marcus."

"An' you're a pain in the ass, Jellybean," he said, more playfully than she expected. "Must be sweet up there on your high horse. Or better still, cruising along on those jet streams. You got a choice to make, angel. You gotta decide whose side you're on, an' how much you're willing to sacrifice for a cause you believe in. In the end, that's the only choice Invisibles like us get to make."

"I'm not an Invisible."

"You're the most Invisible one of us all. You just don't know it yet."

And then the former seed tipped his invisible hat at her and walked away.

IIIIIIIIIIIIII

Ink arrived at the assembly hall in his new transportation—a powered wheelchair. Breathless with excitement, he told Ji-ji the raiders had presented it to him earlier that day. Charra's raiders had snatched it from a cropmaster when they'd raided his planting. Originally, it had been purchased from the Western SuperState for the cropmaster's Son-Proper. "Your sister says I'm a Son-Proper of Turnabout," Ink boasted. "They powered it up using one o' them generators they got. Gotta leave it behind when we raid. No room. Get to come back for it though."

"You're coming with us on the raid?" Ji-ji asked, surprised.

"Tree wants me to. Gotta stay behind when you guys do the raid part. Then we head out together." *Head out where,* Ji-ji thought.

Laughing Tree was nearby, but she couldn't tell what he thought about the gift, or about anything else for that matter. Could be he knew that leaving Ink behind would create more problems than it solved. If, like her, he planned to escape after the raid, he'd want Ink close by. She valued Tree's opinion and was eager to speak with him in private to see if his reaction to Turnabout was similar to hers, but so far there'd been no opportunity. The same was true when it came to speaking with Tiro. She barely had time to greet the fly-boys before Charra, Feral, and Heather mounted the platform at the front of the assembly hall and the meeting got under way.

Ji-ji had met a few people in her life who could hold an audience captive for as long as they wanted. Arundale Lotter was one. He knew how to sow fear in his listeners. Uncle Dreg's rhetoric was the opposite of Lotter's. The Oz enthralled his listeners by telling them who they could be if they dreamed large enough. Tiro could hypnotize an audience by flying the coop with unparalleled ease and grace. When Charra gave a speech, she held you captive too, but it was a unique type of ensnarement. Unconventionally beautiful, with her scarred face and striking hairstyle, she *made* you listen by convincing you your courage was as boundless as hers. Charra didn't simply inspire, she sowed fear at the same time. A lethal combination.

Tonight, she began with an announcement. A parrot had been found in their midst. The man had betrayed Heather and her elite team of fighters to the steaders. His treachery had resulted in a bloody ambush. On cue, two raiders entered through a door behind the stage, a young raider between them. The raider had a tallness that apologized for itself by stooping over. Ji-ji spotted a planting brand on his calf. The boy looked to be around her age.

In a parody of planting ritual, Charra detailed his crimes. Her clear voice rang out through the hall where the raiders stood assembled in front of the platform.

"I, Charra Turnstone, Lord Commander of the Liberty Raiders of Turnabout, hereby sentence Desmond Roundabout, former raider, to a tongue lopping, and to servitude in the Pig Pen for the remainder of his days. From henceforth, this parrot will be known as Turncoat-34. All the rights and privileges afforded to members of this liberty camp will be denied him. He will never again set eyes on us as Desmond Roundabout. Blindfold the traitor, Lieutenant Plate. Take him from this hall, and see that his punishment is carried out forthwith."

Ji-ji understood why Verity had almost fainted when she'd heard she was to be blindfolded.

The raiders made a path for the traitor, who was led out between the two guards. As the group passed by, the raiders turned their backs on him. Desmond couldn't see them do it, but it didn't matter. He wasn't one of them anymore. A girl (his sister, someone said) collapsed and had to be carried out. Plato Youturn slammed the door behind them. Charra waited as Desmond's pleas for mercy died down. Ji-ji searched her sister's face for empathy or indecision and found neither.

Lord Commander Charra Turnstone and Lieutenant Commander Ferellis Shabberley Walkabout sketched out plans for the scheduled raid on the 437th. They reminded the raiders of their previous triumphs. They had systematically "brought the coastal plains, the inner banks, and the gator-ravaged swampland to heel," Feral said. Each day, more people flocked to the camp and to the three other satellite camps they'd established. Feral took a seat on the stage and Charra preached solo. Her rapt followers responded with a chorus of foot-stomping "Amen"s.

"The Friends of Freedom are yesterday's fighters," Charra told them. "Their strategy of avoiding collateral damage has made them weak. They have emboldened the enemy and liberated only a few dozen seeds this year. We, the Justice Seekers, who spring from the roots of the Tree, are a new generation of Freedom fighters. We remember the torment of the Middle Passengers, the fiasco of Reconstruction, the immorality of Jim Crow, the horror of the Sequel, and the barbarism of Swinburne Augustus, who cobbled together the steaders' *One True Text* to justify secessionist savagery. We remember who stood by while this country was torn limb from limb as a once-great nation was carved up into pieces! The SuperStates, where liberty still reigns, make trade deals with the devil. They hear us weeping, and do nothing. Who has the right not to see suffering? Who has the right to elevate peace over justice? We say to generations of fairskin founding fathers and fairskin father-men, you *do not own us*! You who sow seeds in bloody fields *cannot* defeat us!"

The crowd felt Charra's passion and echoed it with cries of "*Preach, Commander! Preach!*"

"We are the living Blossoms on the Tree of Truth, kin to the Birds of Benevolence. We are not Commonseeds or Muleseeds, Tribalseeds or Serverseeds, African-Indigenous, Native-Indigenous, Latins, Asians, Witches, Tainted, Heretics, Damaged, or Deviants! Our duskiness is our beauty; our scars are trophies! We have never been ground-bound. Not here." Charra pointed to her head. "An' not here." She placed her closed fist on her heart. "As Prophet Dreg reminded us, our ancestors dwell in the fault lines of this blind country; our people's spirits snake like roots under the earth! They will rise with us as all birdkin must! And now, we have new weapons in our arsenal."

Ji-ji stiffened. Would Charra go back on her promise not to reveal the truth about her?

Charra looked over at Ji-ji and said, "My sister and her flyer-battlers have made the perilous journey from the Dream to join us. They came seeking Justice and found Turnabout. We welcome them: Tiro the Pterodactyl, the warrior-philosopher Marcus Aurelius, Laughing Tree, whose name tells us who he is, and his adopted son, Ink Laughing Tree, who knows his father's name. These brave men are all here. Ink, too, is a warrior in his new chariot! Come stand with us, brothers all!"

To wild applause from the crowd, Charra opened her arms to welcome them. Tree lifted Ink out of his new chair and carried him up the stairs. The fly-boys lined up beside Charra.

"As you know, my beloved little sister Ji-ji is here too. She brings us a great gift."

Charra paused and looked down at Ji-ji, who was standing in the front row looking up at her.

Heather whispered something in Charra's ear. Tiro stepped forward, alarmed. Marcus grabbed Tiro's arm and said something to him. Ji-ji held her breath.

"The gifts my sister has brought us are the most precious gifts of all. . . . Her courage and her speed. She is one of the female winners of last year's Freedom Race. Tiro, Marcus, and Tree are three of the male winners. Some of you have seen them fly. Now, ALL of them fly for US!"

To deafening cheers, Charra invited Ji-ji to join them onstage. Ji-ji obeyed.

Charra raised her sister's fist in triumph. Her voice rang out to her cheering followers: "Ji-ji will march with me at the head of our righteous crusade as we reclaim what was ours!"

The Freedom fighters cheered and clapped and stomped their feet.

"Marcus, standing here beside me, did not come alone. He came bearing gifts. Weapons to use in our fight for justice! And he brought another gift too. The Invisible Men have petitioned to fight alongside us. Though we have seen things differently in the past, the fight we embark upon demands that all those who would die for Freedom *must* unite! For the first time in history, we will not simply raid a planting, we will *take* it! And after we take it, the Invisible Men, our allies, will occupy it in readiness for the coming reunification!"

The hall erupted. Charra pulled her little sister close and whispered in her ear: "You look nervous. You scared?"

"Terrified," Ji-ji replied, truthfully.

Charra put her arm around her. "Don't be," she said. "I got your back. They do too. See?"

Ji-ji looked out into a blur of faces, every one of them willing to die for her sister. She wasn't ready for what lay ahead. But looking at Charra's face as she drank in the adulation of her followers, she knew that her splendid, damaged, charismatic sister was ready for anything.

25 FOOLS RUSH IN

They set out for Planting 437 in the Dreamfleet van under cover of darkness. Ji-ji was relieved to be riding with the fly-boys. If she'd been riding with Charra, she would have to tiptoe around her sister's moods—an exhausting task when her nerves were already frayed.

Three veteran raiders accompanied them: Norton, Prayjon and Aisha. Norton, a small, wiry man with a wisp of a beard and an ironic smile, and Prayjon, who looked as if he were about to say something fascinating and never did, were in their forties or fifties. Aisha was a female raider in her late sixties or early seventies, who issued orders the way only Black women of a certain age can, with an authority honed by decades of suffering and an imperviousness to fear. She reminded Ji-ji of a younger, less acerbic version of Man Cryday—or so she thought when their journey began. Charra had asked Aisha to act as Ji-ji's bodyguard. It was a request rather than an order, and it demonstrated how much respect her sister had for the veteran fighter. Aisha had promised to remain by her side at all times, which explained why Ji-ji wasn't even allowed to go off on her own to pee.

The raiders wore civilian clothing. No tree emblems anywhere and no black uniforms or masks. They traveled in a variety of vehicles, from large truck transports to motorcycles. Weapons were hidden under crates of supplies. With any luck, none of the trucks would be searched, especially those with a dozen or more raiders in the back.

The only fly-boy not riding with them in the Dreamfleet van was Marcus, which meant they'd lost their principal driver. It wasn't a problem. Prayjon and Norton divided the driving duties between them. Their skillful dodging of potholes impressed Ji-ji. The van had been fitted with bigass rugged tires. She was thrilled when Laughing Tree informed her the raiders had not only attached new wipers, they'd also beefed up the suspension.

From the outset, the three raiders were in charge. When Tiro asked if he could drive, Aisha replied, "Over my dead body." Tiro assured her he'd never drive over her dead body. "What would be the point?" he joked. Aisha chuckled at that, but it was one of those old Black-person chuckles that said any young numbskull who messed with her did so at his own risk. Tiro didn't ask again.

Marcus rode with Charra and Heather several miles ahead in one of the all-terrain vehicles the Freedom fighters had seized during previous raids. Most of the raiders didn't realize till the night before they set out on the road that Feral had split them up into three separate contingents. Concerned Desmond might not be the only turncoat among them, Feral ordered each of the three groups to follow a different route so they would look as unlike a large convoy as possible. He advised them to avoid the toll roads where surveillance cameras monitored traffic and to stick to the minor roads, where possible.

The first contingent had set out several hours before the second group—the one Ji-ji and the fly-boys were in; the third group was due to set out several hours after them. The plan was simple enough. The three contingents would meet up in a densely forested location in The Margins, midway between the Salem Outpost and Planting 437, which put them only a few miles from their target. Plate commanded the first contingent; the second was commanded by Charra; and the third group, with Feral in command, would bring up the rear. Feral's contingent contained skilled hackers who would continuously monitor steader communications. For this raid, Heather served as Charra's second-in-command.

Charra's group was much smaller than the others by design. The second contingent would have room in their vehicles for the Invisible Men they would pick up at various points along the way. Though some of the Men had their own transportation, others needed to hitch a ride with the raiders. If things went according to plan, by the time they approached Planting 437, Charra's contingent would have swelled to three times its original size. Ji-ji told herself the plan sounded reasonable, but she would be the first to admit she knew almost nothing about military strategy and even less about raids.

The three raiders sat together at the front of the van. The mechanics at Turnabout had improvised a small seat between the driver's and front passenger's seats so Aisha, no bigger than Harriet Tubman, could ride in comfort and enjoy an unobstructed view. As they dodged potholes and the old van swayed less precariously than it used to, Prayjon and Norton checked repeatedly to see if she was comfortable. Norton, who refused to believe she was, stuffed a pillow behind her back and reminded her she could swap with him if she wanted. The men's affection for their auntie endeared them to Ji-ji from the start.

The seating arrangements worked out well: raiders up front and the four passengers in the middle and back rows, which allowed for several conversations to go on at the same time. Though it was unlikely they would be overheard, Tree shushed Ink when he mentioned Turnabout. For all they knew, the three raiders were on spy duty for Charra. They'd agreed not to say anything that could offend Ji-ji's sister—not till after the raid anyway. Marcus was another matter altogether. They all had a lot to say about the fly-boy who'd become invisible.

Ji-ji, Trink, and Tiro marveled at how much Marcus had changed. His flippancy was "turned off like a switch," Tiro said, replaced by a seriousness none of them were accustomed to, least of all Tiro. He complained that his fly partner had beefed up his sermonizing to a new level. Marcus had told him he didn't think he'd ever fly in the coop again. Said it didn't appeal to him anymore.

"Tell you what I think," Tiro said. "I think he only joined the fleet to spy for the Invisible Men. Says the Dreamfleet's as messed up as the planting system. Says he's sick of being someone's mule. Sick of circuses. He was always watching people, always griping 'bout Orlie, always taking notes in his head."

Ink, a devoted fan of the Pterodactyl and no fan of the Philosopher, agreed. "Them Invisibles is real note takers," the boy said. "Yep. They sure do like taking them goddam notes."

As the van rocked and swayed through the back roads of the Madlands, Tiro said mournfully: "Not one wisecrack from Marcus in days. Last night, he shaved off all his body hair." The others looked at him in surprise. "It's like a religious thing," Tiro added. "S'why he cut his head hair super short too. Shaved his body to symbolize cleanliness, or readiness . . . or something."

Tree reminded them that Marcus had a right to determine the fate of his own body hair.

Ink, not to be left out of the conversation, issued a grave warning about Lyme disease. "Ticks they love that pubic hair," he said. "'Specially them deer ticks. Found one there the other day."

"On Marcus?" Tiro asked.

"*No!* On *me!*" Ink protested.

"Ignore him, Ink," Ji-ji said. "He's trying to get a rise out of you."

Tiro reached back and swiped his hand across Ink's head good-naturedly, then continued his critique of his fly partner. Speaking more softly so only the four of them could hear him, Tiro said Marcus sounded even weirder than usual when he spoke about the Invisible Men. Ji-ji thought about the conversation she'd had with Marcus. Although zealots had always made her uncomfortable, there were times when Ji-ji wished she were one. It would make life a lot less complicated. Uncle Dreg had taught her to believe in the impossible, while Zyla taught her to question everything, especially her own assumptions. But believing in the impossible was burdensome, and questions beget more questions. Before you know it, nothing's reliable anymore. She wanted to trust her own body, yet that kept shifting on her too. Seemed like certainty was the least reliable thing of all.

The more miles they covered, the quieter everyone got. They all seemed to be reflecting on how much was on the line. The raid on the 437th, one Ji-ji had lobbied hard for originally, was more daring than any raid Charra and her followers had ever attempted. Planting 437, located in the far southwestern region of the Old Commonwealth of Virginia, was several days' journey from Turnabout. In theory, it was a straight shot north, but with so many crumbling, heat-buckled and flood-damaged roads in both the Madlands and The Margins, their journey would be a slow one. Feral was right: they had no choice but to avoid the toll roads. Ji-ji hoped that taking the roads less traveled wouldn't prove to be a huge mistake.

Soon after they set out, Aisha received a call. One of the vehicles in the first convoy had blown all four tires at once on a jagged pothole the driver hadn't seen in time to swerve. A voice on the other end said, "*All vehicles slow down! Repeat: all vehicles SLOW DOWN!*" Prayjon said there'd been several bouts of heavy rain recently; traveling at night would be treacherous, but stopping was more dangerous still. "Keep your seat belts fastened," he told them. Ji-ji was happy to see that Laughing Tree had a seat belt extension. He no longer had to ride with one hand grasping the strap above the window.

Lousy roads weren't the only problem. Ji-ji was on the lookout for the infamous roadblocks set up by Bounty Boys and Clansmen. The threat posed by such things as wild animals and malaria wasn't insignificant either. The raiders' advantage over the enemy was the element of surprise, so secrecy was essential. If the steaders got wind of an attack, the Supreme Council would dispatch a flotilla of buzzbuzz drones to pinpoint their location. Unlike the SuperStates, the Territories didn't have an air force, but these small, unmanned drones could be lethal. Not much bigger than one of Laughing Tree's shoes, the buzzbuzz drones, named for the steady buzz they emitted, could spy on targets from impressive heights with their long-range cameras and relay information to Armistice and to cohorts of cardinals, the army controlled by the inquisitors. During one of the strategy sessions, Heather reminded the leadership team that some of the new drones were armed and that her raiding party had been the target of a drone attack during the recent aborted raid. As Ji-ji understood it from her description, these high-tech, unmanned drones, larger than previous models, were capable of locking on to coordinates and neutralizing the enemy. Plate had insisted that buzzbuzz, unlike the sophisticated drones made in the SuperStates, were notoriously inaccurate. Hardly any of them ever hit their targets, he'd said, and those that did inflicted minimal damage. Heather, who didn't seem to think much of Plate, told him that those massacred in the drone attack "would take issue with your rosy fuckin assessment." Heather rarely swore. When she did, it carried weight. In the stunned silence that ensued, Plate had fallen all over himself apologizing, but Ji-ji could tell that Heather couldn't forgive him.

Originally, the Invisible Men were not assigned to ride in the van. A larger-than-expected cohort waiting for pickup not far from the old border between the Carolinas, just south of Charlotte, however, resulted in a change of plans. Heather, from several dozen miles farther on, called to ask if they could take two more passengers. Aisha told her that would be fine as long as they were closer in size to her than they were to the giant in the back. In addition to passengers, they were carrying a lot of gear, she explained, so space was limited. Heather promised to select the skinniest Men she could find.

A short while later, Prayjon pulled over in the middle of nowhere. It was getting dark and Ji-ji wished they hadn't stopped. She was relieved when Prayjon didn't cut the engine; at least they could escape quickly if this turned out to be an ambush. Two men—one tall and skinny and one short and skinnier—scurried out from the undergrowth. They were yelling something. Were they under attack? *"Life lived Free!"* one yelled. The other cried, *"I am invisible! You can't see me!"*

Norton wasn't impressed. "Dumbest passwords ever. If we can't see 'em, why let 'em in?"

Nevertheless, he slid the door open and both of the visible Invisibles climbed into the van. Once inside, the shorter man thanked him; the taller one seemed irritated that he hadn't opened the door sooner. Both looked a lot younger than Ji-ji had expected—not much older than she was. Their buzz cuts were almost identical. In spite of the heat and humidity, they wore several layers of clothing. Aisha advised them to take some of it off. They'd sweat themselves into an early grave otherwise, she warned. The shorter one obeyed; the taller one ignored her. The tall one looked mixed; the short one was darker. Ji-ji suspected the taller one was making up for past humiliation by carrying himself with an insolent indifference. She didn't like him. From what she could tell, neither did anyone else.

Norton attempted to introduce himself and his companions, but the taller of the Men waved him off. "We honestly don't give a flying fuck, man. Concentrate on the motherfuckin road." His unexpected rudeness triggered Ink's anxiety. The boy began to chatter the way he did when he was scared. Tree put a protective arm round his shoulder to quiet him. A look passed between the raiders. The Invisible Man had forgotten it was as easy to drop them off on the side of the road as it was to pick them up. But for now, the raiders let it go. The taller I-M's brashness was balanced by the shorter one's edginess. Ji-ji surmised that these two young men, like her, were virgins when it came to raids. The taller one's swagger was strained, and the shorter one's nerves soon manifested themselves in frequent pit stops.

"Seems like your buddy's got a waterworks problem," Aisha said, as the shorter man relieved himself yet again on the side of the road. "I got some medication for that." She grabbed a bag and started to rifle through it.

The tall I-M, who sat scrunched up on the floor behind the passenger seat, yelled at her: "Keep your fuckin nose out of our business, old wo—"

Two guns and a knife were out before the Invisible Man got to the "man" in "woman."

Aisha's knife was inches from the Invisible's throat. As if she were speaking to a child, Aisha explained that her nephews didn't take kindly to anyone insulting their auntie. She wasn't their blood relative, she explained, in a voice as sweet as a honeycomb with the bees still attached. She was a fake auntie, you could say. But it didn't matter cos Prayjon and Norton had adopted her and now they were family. Aisha called the Invisible Man "son," but Ji-ji noted that she didn't say it the way Tree did when he addressed Ink; she said it the way a pastor says it to a condemned man just before the lynch rope is slipped over his head.

The other Invisible Man nearly took off running when he slid open the van's side door and saw his comrade with a knife tickling his Adam's apple and two guns pointing at his pate, but Aisha told him to climb on in and not to worry. She said his friend's incontinence—oops, she meant impertinence—had subsided. "Right, son?" The tall Invisible, who hadn't needed to pee before but probably did now, nodded vigorously.

Aisha relayed to the shorter I-M how his buddy had told her to keep her fuckin nose out of their business and called her an old woman too. She found this offensive, she said, on account of the fact that her mother had taught her not to swear unless it was absolutely fuckin necessary. Her mother only swore when she had a knife at someone's throat, or the barrel of her gun stuck up their ass. "Your invisible friend here," she said, addressing the shorter man, "has been disrespectful."

"He ain't my friend!" the shorter man sputtered. "Don't know him! Just met the guy!"

"I see," Aisha said. "Thing is, you boys've forgotten you're not really invisible, not to us. We see you *real good,* don't we, nephews?"

"Yes, Auntie," Norton and Prayjon said in unison.

"Know what they say?" Aisha continued. "They say seeing is believing. And I for one believe that's true. So believe me, Seen One and Seen Two, when I say if either of you ever impertinence me again, I'll dice you up into teeny-weeny man nuggets, like my blessed mother—God rest her soul—taught me. Are we all on the same page now, motherfuckers?" Both men nodded vigorously.

Aisha smiled like a grandmother and slipped her knife back into its sheath. She urged the shorter visible man, who looked desperate to pay another visit to the undergrowth, to climb on up into the van. "Don't you be scared of an old woman," she said. "We'll be fighting alongside each other soon. Could be we'll turn out to be the best friends you two juvis ever had."

Prayjon holstered his weapon so he could drive, but Norton rested his hand on his gun "for consolation," as he phrased it.

"Well, folks," Aisha said to the passengers sitting toward the back, "we can only hope the others ain't as green as these two. Cos if these two are typical, we're screwed."

The same thought had occurred to Ji-ji. It was not a comforting one.

The mood in the van changed after that. The two new passengers were wise enough to keep their mouths shut. Ji-ji figured the shorter one wouldn't have said a word had it not been for the fact that, an hour later, he was desperate to pee again. The frequent stops made them fall behind. A series of carefully spaced raider vehicles in the second contingent passed them without acknowledgment. In an attempt to calm her nerves, Ji-ji used the time to prep herself for the attack.

If Tiro didn't need her help to rescue his mam and brothers, Ji-ji would head off to find Dip and Aunt Marcie, Lua's mam. If anyone deserved liberation from the 437th it was Aunt Marcie, whose nine offspring were either dead or exported to other parts of the Territories. Marcie had initially been included in the six kith-n-kin petitions Ji-ji was entitled to after her successful completion of the Freedom Race, but the selfless woman had given over her spot to one of the young kitchen-seeds. Claimed she wanted to stay close to where Lua, her Last&Only, was buried.

In addition to Dip and Marcie, Ji-ji dreamed of rescuing Afarra's outcast friends Fuzzy and Merrywinkle, as well as the outcast children. On the bottom rung of the steaders' Great Ladder, Serverseed outcasts lived in conditions worse than those found in Charra's Pig Pen. However much they tried to fortify the 437th against subsequent attacks, those who remained would be in great danger. There wasn't nearly enough room to transport the planting's entire seed population, even after some of Charra's raiders and most of the Invisible Men stayed behind, but maybe Ji-ji could persuade the raiders to squeeze in a few extra outcasts? Maybe Charra planned to do that already.

The nine of them ate and slept in the van. It wasn't long before it smelled funky. Funky turned fetid, and then putrid took over. Painstakingly, they

bounced along roads in desperate need of repair, through the night and through
the next day, then through the night again. Without any breaks to speak of, the
ride was rough, especially for Tree and Tiro whose long legs weren't a good
fit for the van's seats. Tree got painful cramps from sitting too long. He didn't
want to slow them down, so only at the others' insistence did he get out and
stretch every so often. No one gave him a hard time about it, however, and
even Seen Two, the Invisible with the nervous bladder, who went by the name
of Claudius Hamby, warmed up to the big man after a while.

The remainder of the journey was mind-numbingly tedious, but Ji-ji would
take monotony over terror any day. Rain was moving up from the southeast,
the remnants of a tropical storm, Norton said, so they had no choice but to
keep going if they wanted to outrun it. Skirting potholes required considerable
skill, even for the two experienced drivers; spotting and skirting flooded potholes in the dark was far worse. Seen One—the taller, ruder Invisible, whose
real name remained a mystery—battled nausea. Once, Claudius Hamby ran
back to the van screaming after he spotted the craggy head of a striper less than
twenty yards from where he was pissing. He said the ant was devouring something unidentifiable, which was why it only looked up for a second, its jaws
dripping blood, then went back to its feast. "Didn't wanna be dessert," Hamby
said. A chorus of voices reminded the shaken Invisible to zip himself up when
he clambered back into the van. From then on, all he wanted to talk about
was the mutant's weird antennae and its skunky stink. Ji-ji tried not to take
this reference to mutant odor personally. How was Hamby, or anyone other
than the fly-boys, to know that one of the passengers was a mutant too, whose
stench during her initial sprouting could make a striper swoon. (Thankfully,
Tree had impressed upon Ink how important it was to keep Ji-ji's secret. Whatever Tree had said to convince him to keep his mouth shut was working. So
far, Ink hadn't breathed a word. He had looked pointedly in Ji-ji's direction,
however, when Hamby said the word *mutant*. Ji-ji did the only thing a self-
respecting mutant could do and pretended not to notice.)

Hamby's close call with the striper helped cure him of his compulsive peeing for a while. When he was unable to hold it in any longer, he said if Tree
wanted to "step out an' stretch his legs" they could enter the wild together. Tiro
began calling the stops "Tree-pees," which made Ink laugh so hard he was in
danger of peeing himself. Seen One didn't much care for Ink, but he didn't
dare tell him to shut up—not with the granny from hell sitting up front and a
giant in the backseat.

The landscape changed dramatically when they took a winding, mountain-
ous road near a place called Mount Airy on the old North Carolina–Virginia
border. The road took them north through The Margins—"cats an' stripes

country, if ever there was one," Aisha said. If anyone had to pee (she looked at Hamby with an expression just this side of sympathy), they should go now or else pee later in one of the jelly jars she'd brought along.

"Ji-ji can't pee in a jar," Ink pointed out. "She's a girl. Got a wajina."

Tree corrected him. "It's vagina, son," he said. "An' that's not how she pees."

"Thought it was wajina."

"No, son," Tree assured him.

Aisha joined in: "You mean that one back there with you is *female?* Well I'll be. . . . That surprise you too, Seen One?" In full view of the passengers, the tall Invisible turned his face away from Aisha and glared out doggedly at the passing scenery.

Aisha was unperturbed. "Guess I should've taken Ji-ji's genitalia into account when I packed these jars. I'll need to accompany her if it turns out her bladder's half as messed up as yours, Hamby. Me being of the vagina variety myself, I'll take you along too, Tree, 'less you got an objection. Figure the cats an' stripes'll think twice when they see we got an outsized human on our side."

Utterly mortified, Ji-ji prayed for a strong bladder and strove to become invisible.

Ji-ji had expected it would be hard to return to the Territories. As it turned out, it was even more upsetting than she'd imagined it would be. It was hell for Tiro too. He took a couple of pills he said were for headaches and calmed down a little, but his knees still bobbed up and down nervously, and he kept squeezing his left hand with his right the way he did when he was anxious. Each time she looked over at Tiro as they sat side by side in the second row, Ji-ji found him staring out into the dark with a look of extreme anxiety on his face. She admired him for handling it as well as he did. If her mam, her siblings, or Afarra had been on the 437th, she would be a basket case. As it was, the prospect of confronting Lotter made her knees go weak.

Whenever she closed her eyes, Ji-ji saw her mam's cabin. Bettieann Plowman had told her Lotter had burned it down after Silapu was killed, but however often Ji-ji reminded herself of that she still expected to see it. She'd always hated the pokey dwelling Lotter had built, but knowing it wasn't there any longer pained her. Worried she'd have a nightmare and wake up screaming, she attempted to force herself to stay awake. . . .

She was digging up her mam with her bare hands. It should've been a nightmare but it wasn't. Silapu was unspoiled by death. Her only injury was the weeping hole in her chest where her seed symbol had been obliterated by the bullet wound. Dipthong Spareseed appeared then, looking the same as ever, her black contamination cross emblazoned across her chest. "My seed canal's clean as a whistle," Dip said. "Ask Doc Riff. He gave me a certificate 'fore he left." As Dip reached into the pocket of her striped regulation skirt in search of her certificate of cleanliness, she noticed that Ji-ji was digging up her mam. "You found her," Dip said, as if digging up your dead mam was an everyday occurrence. "I was coming to tell you where she was." The Tainted seed was carrying her four dead womblings; they balanced impossibly on her shoulders, two on each side, like parrots. "I knew you'd come back for us," someone said. "We knew you wouldn't forget . . ." Ji-ji spotted Auntie Zaini, Bromadu, and Eeyatho in the distance, on the far side of Execution Circle. She wondered why she was suddenly so far from the seed cemetery before the thought evaporated. Tiro appeared out of nowhere (or was he always there?) and ran toward them. She'd never seen him so joyful. His happiness was hers. "*I saved 'em!*" he cried. "*We got here in time!*" Ji-ji looked down at her mam again. "She's sleeping," a voice said. Her own? No. It was Afarra's. No. It was Sylvie's.

A pothole jerked her awake.

"You were dreaming," Tiro said. "Mumbling in your sleep. Everything okay?"

"What did I say?"

"Called out for your mam, my mother too. You okay?"

Embarrassed, Ji-ji assured him she was fine. "You think he'll be there? Lotter, I mean."

Tiro said he thought he would be. "According to Marcus, who got it from Old Shadowy, Lotter got back from a trip to Armistice a couple of days ago. So looks like he'll be there. Don't worry, Ji. I won't let him hurt you."

"I don't think he'll be doing the hurting. Not if Charra has anything to do with it. . . . Williams'll be there too. . . ." She checked that no one else could hear her before she asked the next question. "Charra said you plan to tractor-lynch him. That true?"

"Assuming there's a tractor handy, an' there's time to hitch the bastard up to it, yeah."

"Think you could?"

"After what he did to Amadee? For sure I could do it. Think you could kill Lotter?"

"Don't know. He's evil, but . . . it's hard to kill someone. You done it?"

"Hard to know." His answer puzzled her. She asked him why. "When Afarra an' Pheebs got separated from me an' Ben an' Germaine when we headed to Dimmers Wood, we got ambushed. I had to shoot someone. No choice. A Clanswoman. Don't know if she died."

Ji-ji knew how hard it could be to admit to a killing. "You never told me 'bout that."

"No. There's a lot to that story, an' some things are best forgotten." He changed the subject. "Crazy to think we'll be on the 437th again after we spent years plotting our escape."

"Think the raid'll be successful?" Ji-ji asked, praying he would say yes.

"It's gotta be." Tiro looked over at the newest passengers. "I hope the other Invisibles are more on the ball than that pair."

Ji-ji nodded in agreement, said, "Think all of 'em are that young?"

"Christ, I hope not. Guess we'll find out soon enough."

"You scared, Tiro?"

"Scared ain't the word for it. You?"

"Same."

He took her hand in his. They hadn't held hands for a while. She was grateful they were doing this impossibly hard thing together. She rested her head on his shoulder and fell asleep.

She woke to hear Aisha's announcement: they'd arrived at the rendezvous site.

Ji-ji sat bolt upright and looked around. It was dark. She peered through the van's mud-encrusted windows and struggled to make out how many fighters in the first two contingents had made it there safely. From the size of the camp it looked like a lot of them had. The forest was dense between the Salem Outpost and Planting 437. With luck, they hadn't be detected. Someone waved a flashlight and hurried toward them.

Plato. He poked his head through the front passenger-side window and said, "How come you're late? Trouble on the road?"

"Blame it on our Man Hamby here," Aisha said. "Got a leaky faucet. Had to pull over a hundred times. This other tall sliver of humanity made up for it with his scintillating conversation. Ain't that right, Seen One?"

Without uttering a word, the tall I-M shoved the door open, shouldered his bag, and stalked off into the night. Hamby dashed after his petulant comrade, throwing apologies over his shoulder.

Aisha called after them. "You're welcome!" She shook her head and turned back to Plate. "Please tell me they ain't typical of our new allies."

"We got a some good ones too, Miss Ai," Plate replied. "Some is green as grass, but most is seasoned. They know what they're doing. They brought a shitload o' weapons too. But it's a mixed bag. Most handle a gun as well as we do but some of 'em ain't never used one before."

Aisha shook her head. "I warned her not to put her trust in info she couldn't verify. Let's hope we don't all live to regret it. Or die regretting it more."

"Commander wants to see you," Plate said, indicating all of the passengers in the van. "She's at the far end of the camp. Park near the large tent. She's inside with Heather."

"Can we clean up first?" Ji-ji said from her seat toward the back.

"I wouldn't if I were you," Plate replied. "Your sister's not happy you're late. Not happy 'bout other things either." Plate slapped the side of the van as if it were a horse's rump. "Best get going," he said. "She'll have my hide if I hold you up."

A couple of minutes later, Ji-ji, Tiro, and Trink stood in Charra's tent with Aisha, Prayjon and Norton. Charra, Heather, Marcus, and a man Ji-ji didn't recognize were present.

Charra glanced up when they entered. She didn't look happy to be kept waiting, but she was obliged to turn her attention to other things. With two callers in her hand and several screens and maps laid out on a fold-out table in front of her, she and Heather issued orders and analyzed information coming at them thick and fast.

There was a snag. A big one. The third contingent was delayed. The storm had caught up with them a few hours north of Turnabout. The route they'd planned to take was flooded. The detour was likely to add hours to their journey. Charra was in the midst of a debate about whether or not to go ahead with the attack without them. Waiting was risky, Marcus said. If anyone had betrayed them, the steaders already knew an attack was planned. If they lost the element of surprise, that was it. Heather wasn't so sure. According to her, Feral's contingent included some of their most experienced fighters. But Charra seemed to be leaning toward Marcus' argument.

Without waiting for an invitation, Tiro joined them at the table. "Marcus is right," he insisted. "We shouldn't wait."

"Did I ask for your input, fly-boy?" Charra said. "Your mam an' brothers're on the 437th, so you're compromised. I need cooler heads than yours to weigh in."

While the debate heated up, the man Ji-ji hadn't recognized earlier approached her. He held out his hand to her and said, "Raphael the Fifth. Honored to make your acquaintance."

Of average height, with warm brown skin, inquisitive eyes, and close-cut salt-and-pepper hair, the man had an easy, outgoing manner, as if he'd launched perilous raids a hundred times before and all of them had been wildly successful. His grip was firm, his smile charming.

"I'm Ji-ji."

"Yes, I know. Ji-ji Silapu, Charra's remarkable sister."

Ji-ji immediately concluded she liked him. A split second later, she decided she'd been hasty. Raphael the Fifth didn't take his eyes off hers. His expression told her he knew what lay beneath the cape she wore. Ji-ji cursed Marcus, who'd once again shared her secret as if it belonged to him.

Aisha came up behind Ji-ji and slipped her arm into hers.

"Careful, Ji-ji," Aisha warned. "This fella here could model for one of the Seven Deadlies."

Raphael laughed good-naturedly: "Which one?" he asked.

Without any delay whatsoever, Aisha said, "Covetousness springs to mind."

Raphael didn't let his face stop smiling, but Ji-ji sensed how angry he was. "Do I know you, raider?" Raphael asked.

"We met a long time ago, Mr. Invisible," Aisha replied. "You weren't much more than a boy. I knew your daddy. Went by the ridiculous name of AyeAye Blottusrigg 'fore he elevated himself to Raphael the Fourth. Makes you think of angels that name. A bloody elevation, so I hear."

Raphael couldn't hide his ire anymore. His easy smile vanished as he looked down at the tiny woman in front of him. "I'm afraid you have me at a disadvantage," he said. "You seem to know a lot about me, while I know nothing about—"

Aisha interrupted: "Guess the organization's reinvented itself. God knows it needed a makeover after that fiasco in Mississip. Tricky to make a silk purse from a sow's ear, but if you're anything like AyeAye, you ain't the type to be deterred by details."

Raphael had clearly had enough. He ignored Aisha and turned his attention to Ji-ji. "I look forward to getting to know you better, Ji-ji. I've heard nothing but good things about you from your sister. I'm hopeful our historic partnership will be beneficial to all of us. Perhaps we can talk after the raid. I'm sorry you won't be joining us."

"What are you talking about?" Ji-ji asked.

Raphael looked as if he wished he'd kept his mouth shut. He didn't seem like the type of person who'd speak out of turn; Aisha's ambush must've thrown him. "Charra and I have agreed you're too important to the cause to risk damage. I'm sure your sister will go over the details with you. I should get back to her." Hurriedly, he moved off to rejoin Charra and Heather.

"What did I tell you?" Aisha said. "He's not a details man. Spitting image of his daddy too. Emphasis on spitting." She pulled Ji-ji closer and whispered in her ear. "He covets those wonders on your back. . . . Yeah, I know all about 'em. So does he, from the way he was gawking. Everyone wants a piece o' you, baby, your sister included. Make sure you keep the best part for yourself."

"I won't stay behind," Ji-ji said.

"You'll regret it if you don't. Stay behind with Ink. You can look out for the boy. He'll be scared without his daddy. You never been on a raid before. You got no idea how bad it can get."

"Why bring me here if I'm not gonna fight?"

"That's a question for her not me," Aisha said, as Charra approached them.

"Be careful, Beany," Charra warned. "Miss Ai could pull the wool over Dreg's Seeing Eyes if she set her mind to it. You're late, Ai."

"If you partner with fools, there's a penalty. We had to ferry an I-M with a bladder the size of a pea to match his brain, an' another who must've been raised by hyenas. No manners at all."

Ji-ji waited for Charra to lose her temper, but she only nodded. "Thought you an' Beany here would get on well together. Both equally annoying. So what do you think, Miss Ai? We wait, knowing there'll be at least a day or two's delay, or we strike now while the iron's hot?"

"Why ask us," Aisha replied, "when a blind man can see you've made up your mind?"

Charra shrugged before turning back to the others. "Listen up," she said. "I've made my decision. It's too risky to wait. We go. . . . Tonight, at midnight. Can your men be ready, Raffle?"

"They're ready," Raphael said.

"*Midnight!*" Heather exclaimed. "But that's even earlier than we'd—"

Discussion was over. "Midnight," Charra said. "We're sitting ducks if we stay here."

Heather couldn't believe it. "But no one's expecting to attack that early! Some aren't ready."

"Exactly," Charra told her. "Even if someone's parroted, steaders probably won't be ready either. Raffle, you sure your men know which of 'em'll stay an' hold the planting?"

Raphael looked insulted. "Of course they know. Do yours?"

"My men *and* my women know their assignments. Heather, tell Feral he's to drive on to the 437th when he gets here, meet up with us there. Probably run into some of us making our triumphant return."

Heather hesitated. With a sharp turn of her head, Charra let her know how unwise that was. After a second or two, Heather picked up a caller and contacted Feral. They could hear his cries of disbelief at the other end. He was being cut out of the raid altogether. Ji-ji knew exactly how he felt.

Charra turned back to Aisha: "So," she said. "You never told me whether you would stay or attack. Not that I give a damn, you understand. Well?"

Aisha's warning wasn't subtle: "You're rushing in where angels fear to tread."

"Is that so?" Charra said. Clearly, Aisha's response wasn't the one she'd wanted.

"Let's ask an angel what she thinks. Ji-ji, you know what's at stake." Charra raised her voice so everyone in the tent could hear. "Should we attack our planting now, Beany, or should we wait?"

Our planting. Ji-ji tried to wrap her mind around that idea. It had been

Lotter's planting, the steaders' planting, Uncle Dreg's planting, even their mam's planting. The place where Silapu and Uncle Dreg were shot dead, the place where Lua died in seedbirth, where she herself had been locked in a confessional by a man five times her age who had permission from Lotter to rape and "prune" her. The place where her sister had been repeatedly raped by the man she was mated to. The place where Zaini had rocked the torn-up remains of Tiro's twin brother in her arms. The place where the most famous penal tree in all the Homestead Territories stood. . . .

"Attack," Ji-ji said, her voice steady. "We should attack tonight." She reached out and grabbed hold of Charra's elbow. "I go with you. We fight together. Side by side. As sisters."

Charra looked at Ji-ji as if she were seeing her for the first time. She embraced her.

"That's my Beany," she murmured into her neck. "That's the sister I dreamed I'd find."

||||||||||||||||

Afarra knows it is a foolish thing to do. She tries to stop herself. But her thumb is bad now. Asking Peony to help her get to the clinic is the only option she has left. She still can't believe it. The devil is standing there talking to her friend! She sees his back and his scary-blond hair. He's chased her all the way from the 437th to Kingdom Come! First Sloppy chasing her, and now Father-Man Lotter leaning over Peony, talking to Wally and Pan too! She'd made her way over to Peony's tent to ask her friend to help her get to the clinic. That's when she sees the devil with his back to her. The last straw to break the camel hump in half. She, Afarra, is the camel. Without the hump but Broken.

Her thumb, her whole arm throbs. If Peony, Wally and Pan don't tell, he'll make them pay.

The practice coop isn't her first idea. The clinic is first. But when she creeps over there to watch from around the corner, a line of people, all like her, wind out from the door like a snake.

Patrollers! Moving up and down the line! *Show me your papers!* "*Show me your papers, duskies!*"

Patrollers snatch and snatch. Pile people into vans. Soon the line is shorter. Nowhere to go . . . nowhere to hide . . . except the practice coop. Where she lived almost happy ever after with Elly. *Rush! Rush!* to the nest!

Some things are too hard to keep doing over and over. Some things press on you like hands.

She is *hothothot* and more tired than she's been in her life. Monty-Circus has to walk. She can't carry him anymore. He doesn't mind. No leash, but he doesn't stray. This is what comforts her. This is why she makes it all the way to the practice coop. Burning up like a forest fire.

The doors to the practice coop are locked. But she knows a secret way in through a broken window. She picks up Monty-Circus, climbs through the back window with him in her arms.

Careful! Careful! No sound but tiptoe. "It's okay, the thieves have left."

She looks for Elly justincase. Not here. The thieves snatched everything . She sees the mural blacked over. Nothing but black ink for sky. The two of them painted over. No Afarra. No Elly. What did she expect, another miracle? Yes, she did.

It's hard to make it up Jacob and Harriet to Jim with Monty-Circus cradled in her sore arm. Halfway up she gets dizzy, almost takes a tumble. *Not yet. Too soon. Leap when you're ready. Not before.*

She makes it to the welkin platform at the top of the coop, makes it to the narrow walkway, makes it to the Jim Crow Nest where she and Elly used to happy-sleep.

She climbs in. It feels like home must feel. A small circle of peace—an eye to rest inside.

No blackbird quilt to cover them. No Elly to hold. No Na-na either. But Circus is here. Hungry but not scared. Neither is she. It's getting dark. No need to rush. She has all the time in the world. Was she a dumbass to come back here? Going back to a place can be a terrible thing. The worst thing if you're caught.

"I am being pressed down all the moments," Afarra says to Circus. "I miss her too much every day. You would too. If we jump, we jump together, okay?"

Afarra closes her eyes. If someone comes to snatch them she will jump. With Circus in her arms so the little dog is not alone. Clutch him tight to her body so they go together down. The worst thing is to be left behind. She knows.

The tribe of Dimmer-dead reach out to take her hand. They are ready to receive her.

She hears something rustle in her head. *Hot! Hot!* Something invisible moves through the night. A breeze on a thousand, thousand leaves. Wounds. No, not wounds. Jewels! Every single one a purple shimmershine, all sighing together. Wind chimes singing her story.

"Thank you," Afarra whispers, as his Seeing Eyes watch over her, and the Great Hybrid Tree of Trees sings her an ancient lullaby.

26 BIRD-WORD & TREE-CHAT: THE ONE TRUE TEXT

To tamper down the lonely for the far-off small one asleep in the strange nest, the Great Tree sets her tongues to singing. *Lulla-lulla-lullaby,* a ululating dialect of leaf and wind.

The Warden of Slow Things, though she is dying from the inside out, remembers. Most of her is buried alive. Her subterranean reflection spans out over generations.

The Birds who remain on the branches (*here* and *now* one moment, and *not-here* and *not-now* the next) watch for those who trespass against her.

She and her tribe of Trunks have chronicled the earth for thousands of years. Time-circles span out from the center. The One Tree is what the Three Birds are not: stationary, old. She is the Self she knows.

The Three are what the One is not: kinetic, dissimilar, which is why they love each other. Their question reveals how little they know her: "Are you lonely, Sylvie?"

She has forgotten what "lonely" is centuries ago, but she knows it is not the same as being rooted to the Earth and reaching for the Sky.

"Lonely is who we Three are without each other—bereft, like sleep without dreams."

Their type of lonely, real though it is to them, isn't hers. She knows age and repetition go hand in hand, which is why she feels the Flock ready itself for flight, the tension in their twig-legs and yearning in their wings. (If she had a yearning, it would be to experience that singular gift of elevation, a sacred communion the Bird tribe shares.) She feels their leaving, but the aftermath is not "lonely." She is the Keeper of Lost Things, the One they've been looking for. When Earth demands it, she becomes the roots that shake the shoulders of the world. When cut, she weeps like a Mother.

The Birds hear her voice: a cascade of red, a rush of blue, dark escalating to blackness as tears swing from her branches, poisoning her with rage, a contagion the color of mourning.

Blossoms clamor and clang in the breeze as seeds die in bloody refrains. In the afterburn of lost things, she weeps their names.

A shudder in the air and tremors underground. Her fury erupts over their perennial violations. Prying out her skin, ripping off her tongues, stringing up their dead in her branches. . . .

Seeds sown, graves full to blossoming! The Dimmer-dead riot under the earth!

But no blessed awakening—not here, not now. No heads of midnight, earth-light, moonlight. No bringing together the tribes of the world.

A girl's clear voice rises from the strange nest in the east: "*Our Mother, which art the Cradle, pray for us!*" The Flock takes off as the girl with the far-off name is drowned out by a chorus of voices that tongue a single word: *Massacre! Massacre! Massacre!*

|||||||||||||||||

A couple of miles from the fry-fence, they park the vehicles they piled inside to make the journey from the rendezvous site to the planting. They creep through the forest to the thirty-foot perimeter fry-fence, not far from the Main Gate, roughly the same spot where Ji-ji scaled the fence a year and a half ago. She holds her breath as Plate runs to it to see if it's dead or alive.

"Dead!" he confirms. Emmeline and Silent Pete have succeeded! So far so good. . . .

They're prepared. They mount the fence using a tarp to protect them from the barbed wire. They've brought flexible lightweight ladders too. Madness for a mutant to climb back into a planting, yet she's chosen this path. If things go south it's on her.

Ji-ji climbs alongside the other Freedom fighters, follows what they do. Can she fly over it? Leave them all dumbstruck and take off? Impossible. Her back's as petrified as she is.

It takes an age to climb the fence, but she's done it before with Lucky, Dip, and Mam, when she insisted the others go first cos she didn't trust Lucky would wait for them. Mam climbed to where Ji-ji is now. Petrus down below on the prison side, drunk, screamed at her to get down: "*GET DOWN NOW, BITCH, OR I SWEAR TO GOD I'LL SHOOT!*" Is that him shouting at them? Wrong. *Petrus is dead, remember? I carry his gun.*

Down below, on the prison side, Charra tosses up encouragement. (*How'd she get over so fast with a ravaged back and a limp?*) "That's it, Ji-ji," Charra calls up softly. "Almost there."

It occurs to Ji-ji that she isn't moving. Hasn't moved for a while. . . . Can't move. . . . Cos Lotter's about to switch the fence on again and fry them all! He'll do it too, even if he knows his daughters are among the Freedom warriors . . . *especially* if he knows they are.

Charra calls up again, coaxing her over to the prison side. "You can do it!"

Tiro starts to climb back up the fence to help her over. When she sees his face, she knows it's not a trap. All around them, Cropmaster Lotter's planting sleeps like a baby.

Ji-ji's hands are sweating. She rubs them against her cape to dry them off. She tries to picture her friend Dipthong Spareseed—her cry of disbelief when she sees the rescue party.

"Get your ass over the damn fence!" someone says. Her. She says it.

With Tiro's help, she makes it over the fence. She alights (wrong word) she *descends* onto the prison side, half expecting the ground to give way beneath her and bury her alive.

Marcus sets off with a couple of Invisible Men to the Main Gate's lookout tower to find Old Shadowy and Silent Pete. Together, they'll ensure the fence stays dead and the planting comm system stays down. One of the Men who accompanies Marcus is Seen One, the tall Invisible Man who rode in the van with them. Ji-ji wishes Marcus had selected weak-bladdered Claudius Hamby instead.

The raiding party splits up into twelve groups. Each group is ordered to make a beeline for one of the twelve seed quarters. The plan is simple. They will guide most of the seeds back to the fry-fence. Some will remain behind to occupy the planting, distract the steaders long enough for the escaping seeds and raiders to get a head start to the rendezvous camp. The Doom Dell is on the eastern side of the planting, near where they've scaled the fry-fence, which means they can retreat quickly, if necessary, as long as Emmeline and Marcus have control of the fry-fence, and the comm. It's doable, especially if, along the way, they steal the horses and wagons from the planting barns, and any steader vehicles they can lay their hands on.

As stealthily as they can, the twelve groups span out along the spokes that constitute the 437th's permissible and forbidden paths and backwoods trails. Ji-ji doesn't know who all is leading every group. But she knows that Laughing Tree leads a group heading southwest to Father-Man Petrus' former homestead while Norton and Prayjon lead groups heading to homesteads on the western side of the planting. Plate heads northeast for a homestead that lies on the other side of Murder Mouth. Ji-ji's in the group with Charra, Tiro, Heather, Aisha and Raphael. They'll be heading to Drexler Williams' homestead, where they'll find (*please, God!*) Zaini and the boys.

Ji-ji has trained herself to call on logic and reason during times like these. She begins where the raid began, with the fence. How did Emmeline, the oldest living drug-sop in the Territories, and so frail a gust of wind could knock her over, and Silent Pete, who lost half a foot, an ear, his voice, and three fingers when he served as a child soldier, overwhelm the planting guards and shut off the fence? How did Marcus convince them to do it? Did he pretend to be a Friend of Freedom, or did he tell them the truth about where his allegiance lies? Emmeline Shadowbrook is brave, but she can't change the fact that she isn't his mother and she is a fairskin. Ji-ji tells herself Marcus would never hurt the diviner after everything she's done for him. Then someone yells *"Grunt!"* in her head, and worry revs itself up again. Another word ricochets around her skull: *recaptured,* the cruelest verb in all of the Territories. If she's recaptured, the greatest threat to her own body will be her own body. Ji-ji looks back. Aisha jogs behind her like a shadow. *Stay there. Don't leave me.*

Ji-ji feels the planting push against her, wave after wave of resistance: the gloom of the Doom Dell and the pitilessness of PenPen, where "penitents" rot; Execution Circle, where seeds are locked inside viewing coops and forced to watch the steaders' parody of justice; the seed cemetery, where Lua's ghost scratched its way to the surface in search of her pretty deadborn. Is Silapu buried in that cemetery or did Lotter find another site for his Mammy Tep? Of course he did. He'd never house Silapu in a shared space with other seeds. In death, as in life, he'd want her all to himself. Ji-ji looks over at Charra, who's barking out orders to her raiders. If her sister, who's endured so many violations, can tough it out so can she.

Before they set out on this mission (*not a suicide mission—don't think it*) the two sisters shared a moment alone. They took a walk together in the forest surrounding the rendezvous camp. Heather accompanied them, stood at a respectful distance so the sisters could talk in private.

Charra, proud at last of her little sister, had slipped her arm through Ji-ji's the way she used to when they were seedlings. In the trees' quiet, Charra confided to her about her wexcision in Memoria and the deadborn she birthed. She remembered every detail: the little black body as helpless and exquisite as a baby bird's, the tiny, perfectly formed wings on his back "no bigger than a hummingbird's." Uncharacteristically devout, she'd called them "God's transparencies." Sheer and delicate, she said, and purple like his aunt's. "Like his aunt's." A remarkable phrase. A yearning took root inside of Ji-ji. Her deadborn nephew would always be someone she'd wish she'd known.

Charra said, "Man took from me the two greatest gifts any female's ever been given—wings and a Wingborn." Briefly, Ji-ji thought Charra was speaking about humanity as a whole before she figured out her sister was referring to Man Cryday. Or perhaps she meant both of them?

Some things once conjoined can never be separated without destroying them. Turnabout's perversions are as intertwined with Charra's suffering as Ji-ji's wings are with her back. The sisters are conjoined too, for better or worse, in sickness and in health. Tonight, the two of them are together at the No-Turning-Back Point, the same place Ji-ji was when she leapt from the Jim Crow Nest in the City of Dreams. Only this time, the last thing she wants to do is die.

She feels Charra beside her moving through the dark. Tiro is several yards ahead, but Ji-ji feels his apprehension. It spools back behind him like smoke. He's as terrified as she is.

"Don't worry, Ji-ji," Charra tells her, "we got this."

Charra has been calling her by her grown name ever since the meeting earlier that night when Ji-ji chose risk over caution. Ji-ji doesn't tell her sister how much she needs to be Beany, led by someone older who knows what the hell she's doing. For courage, Ji-ji pulls out her gun and grips it so tight it makes her fingers hurt.

"Put that damn thing away, Beany, 'fore you shoot yourself or me."

Beany again. Thank the good Lord! Ji-ji holsters the gun.

They enter the secret tunnel Ji-ji took with Lucky, Mam, and Dip, the one leading to and from the Shot Tower. She's reluctant to leave the night sky behind. It comforted her to think she could use it as a means of escape. If they ambush them in a tunnel, they're trapped. When she escaped before, Silapu told her the tunnels weren't made by seeds. "Sylvie made them," she said. "Rooted out every one." *Or did I make that part up?* she wonders.

Underground. Pitch-blackness. Ji-ji thinks of the long metal shaft flyers use to access the cage in the Dream Coop, the one flyers call Dreamblast Corridor. The nickname isn't comforting. Most of the raiders have flashlights that provide barely enough light to see by. If they're waylaid in the tunnel and the guards have hand grenades in their *bad kangaroos,* it's over. Every so often as they run, Ji-ji imagines she hears planting guards stampeding toward them. She wants to beg her companions to stop so they can listen out for an ambush, but she's too scared to admit how scared she is. Behind them to the east, assuming she's guessed right about where they are, sits Murder Mouth. According to Uncle Dreg, they may have experimented on her mam there. Could be they took Charra and Lua there too. Could be they took her as well, which would explain a lot. Or maybe neither she nor Charra has ever been inside Murder Mouth. If Silapu's first abduction happened long before the ones others recalled, maybe the sisters inherited their mutant genes from their mam? It's even possible Lotter's seed was tampered with. Not for the first time, Ji-ji wishes she'd spent less time researching flight and more time on genetic engineering.

Murder Mouth is where Uncle Dreg found Drol. After her own metamorphosis, Ji-ji pities the gorilla-man, who horrified her when she saw him in the

Doom Dell, and later in Dimmers Wood. Afarra, unafraid, had reached out to Drol from the start, just like she reached out to Muckmock on the Mall. When they lost Afarra, she and Tiro lost the best of themselves. Ji-ji vows again to Free every outcast she can find. She understands now that when someone you love is lost—someone truly good like Afarra, or Lua, or Uncle Dreg—a big chunk of you has to *become* them and live as they would have lived. The only meaningful way to honor them.

Maybe it's the feeling of claustrophobia produced by the tunnel, but Ji-ji can feel Lotter pressing his hand down on her head. Lotter will slaughter them efficiently, the way shanks on a chisel plow till the earth without regard for what's in their path.

In Turnabout one night, in the shed at the back of Charra's house when she couldn't sleep, Ji-ji remembered she'd brought her sketch pad. She pulled it out of her backpack, retrieved one of her lucky pencils (lucky cos she'd engraved Uncle Dreg's initials into the wood), and drew her father-man entirely from memory. The likeness was uncanny. Afterward, she took an eraser and removed the middle of his torso, leaving an empty circle. She repeated the process on his forehead, leaving another, much smaller circle. She couldn't explain why, but the white circles weren't added to Arundale Duke Lotter, they *were* him. The sketch disturbed her. The circles reminded her of Lua-Dim's eyes with their pulsing white irises. They possessed the same ghostly intensity Toteppi believe can blind you if you gaze into them. She hadn't consciously decided to blast holes through his torso and head. It happened instinctively.

Charra reaches out and takes her hand. "Almost there," she says.

Silapu took her hand on their last night together. The two nights are jumbled up in her head.

Just then, Charra stumbles, but Ji-ji, who has her sister's hand in hers, prevents her from crashing headfirst onto the tunnel's floor. Heather is at her lover's side in an instant.

"You okay, Char?" Heather says it quietly so no one but the three of them—and Aisha who's come up behind them—hears her. "Your back giving you fits?" Heather says. "Let me carry you."

She could too, Ji-ji thinks, *easy.* Heather's shoulders are almost as broad as Tiro's.

Charra gives Heather a withering look the darkness can't conceal, and Heather backs off. "Fine. Just thought I'd ask. You're not that big, y'know."

"You're not either," Charra asserts, even though Heather towers over all the other females.

Heather stations herself on Charra's weaker side and settles for jogging beside her. After Charra's stumble, Ji-ji no longer expects her elder sister to do the protecting; instead, they must protect each other. With a clearly defined task in front of her, Ji-ji feels less fearful.

At last, they emerge above ground. Not inside the Shot Tower as Ji-ji expected but somewhere completely different. The tunnel must have branches she knows nothing about. Of course it does. How could Lucky have carried her from the confessional in Stinky Brine's father-house to the Shot Tower otherwise? The tunnels must span out like the roots of a tree. Could be her mam was right about Sylvie excavating them.

Ji-ji thought she would prefer being out in the open again, but she's not sure where they are and it scares her not knowing. It's humid, sticky. There's drizzle on and off. In all the times she practiced for the Freedom Race, she never took this route. Tiro runs ahead. As the planting's runner champion, it wouldn't take much for her to pick up speed and join him, but she thinks better of it and remains by Charra's side.

They come upon the seed quarters before Ji-ji gets her bearings. She recognizes the error she's made. She thought they were on Homestead 2, Drexler Williams' old planting. But this isn't Homestead 2. It's Homestead 1, Lotter's former homestead. Father-Man Williams must've taken it over after Lotter became cropmaster. They're heading toward Lotter's former seed quarters, which lie north-northwest of the Commons. Homestead 1 forms the largest slice of the most arable land on the planting. Unless she's miscalculated again, the tunnel must pass beneath the steaders' residential area and the buildings on the Commons—the Gathering Place, the pray center, and the dining hall, where she used to work with her twelve kitchen-seeds. The path they're on winds through a sparsely populated section of the seed quarters.

Ji-ji lets go of Charra's hand and comes to a halt. This path winds its way in front of Silapu's cabin, the one she shared with her mam before Petrus murdered her, with little Luvlydoll before she came down with metaflu, with Clay before Lotter auctionmarted him, with Charra before Lotter seedmated her to Petrus, and with sweet Bonbon before Lotter declared that his infant son was a number 35 on the Midnight arc of the Color Wheel and therefore too dark to testify to the strength of the patriarchal seed. . . . The one place on the planting Ji-ji wanted to avoid.

They're passing the cabin now. Charra looks. Ji-ji doesn't.

"Nothing left," Charra says. "Bastard burned the place to the ground."

Ji-ji finds herself sprinting toward the burn site, little more than a pile of ash and a few blackened sticks. Someone pushes her to her knees. Memories again, that's who does it.

The cabin, set a ways off from the others in the seed quarters cos Lotter values his privacy, is gone. Nothing left, not even the outhouse. The stench of lost things scorches her nostrils.

Someone picks her up. Tiro. He runs with her in his arms till she begs him to put her down.

"It was the cabin," she says, as he plants her on her feet, steadies her. "Didn't know it would look dead like that. Didn't expect . . ."

"S'okay, Ji," Tiro says. "I woulda bawled too." *Oh crap,* she thinks. *I bawled.*

Charra and Heather come up to them. "You okay, Beany?" Charra asks.

Beany again, not Ji-ji. Makes sense. She's a beany baby sister. "I'm fine. Sorry."

"It's understandable," Heather says. "This was your home. Of course you were upset."

"It's not understandable," Charra says. "It's dumb. Place reeked of Lotter an' that revolting aftershave he wore. Mam would've burned it down herself if she could have."

"I'm better now," Ji-ji asserts.

"No you ain't," Tiro says, "but that's okay. Let's rescue 'em, Ji, an' get the hell outta here."

Fast forward revs itself up to super-fast forward. The raiders deal with the guardhouse in the seed quarters first. Easy to overpower. Only three guards inside. (Ji-ji dare not go inside to check.) "Slit the pigs' throats," Charra tells her special force, the ones she calls "my assassins." Barely a sound as the raiders and Invisibles silence the enemy.

Meanwhile, as fighters spread out all across the seed quarters, doling out near-coronaries as they wake the seeds, Tiro finds the cabin where Zaini and his brothers are held.

Zaini crying and laughing, the boys doing the same. Both of them grown so much Ji-ji barely recognizes them. At ten years old, Bromadu (the brave boy they call "Broma"), like all Zaini's boys, is tall. Eeyatho, at seven and a half (the sweet boy they call "Yatho"), is shy. He has the same gentle face as Amadee, the same way of furrowing his brow in concentration.

The cabin Zaini lives in is wretched—far worse than where they lived before. Zaini's face is bruised, her lip swollen. Tiro demands to know if Williams hit her. His mother insists she fell. No one believes her, but with Tiro in the mix, everyone pretends they do.

"How did you know to come now?" she asks her eldest living son.

"Now?" Tiro asks.

"Tomorrow—or today, I guess it is—Williams is shipping Bromadu off to the auctionmart."

Tiro can't believe it. "We didn't know. Luck, that's all."

Zaini shakes her head. "No. It wasn't luck. It was Uncle Dreg keeping his Eyes on us."

At that moment, Charra steps toward them. "*Charra!*" Zaini exclaims.

"Hi, Auntie Z," Charra says. "Glad to see you're still breathing."

"These your raiders?" Zaini asks. "Oh, your poor face!"

"Don't fuss, Auntie. You should see the other guy. He was sorry afterward. Gutted in fact."

"Yes," Zaini says, as she takes a long, hard look at Charra, "I bet he was."

Charra and Heather leave to join the others, who are releasing Williams' Muleseeds, Tribalseeds, Commonseeds, Serverseeds, Deviants, and Heretics from captivity. The raiders and Invisible Men are more disciplined than Ji-ji thought. Everyone except her seems to know what they're doing. She begins to believe there's a chance they'll make it out alive.

Eeyatho, who's been hiding behind his mother, works up the courage to throw himself at Tiro, who picks him up and swings him around. The boy clutches his brother's neck so fiercely that Tiro has to tell him to loosen his grip. "Are you out to choke me, Yatho? You don't know your own strength, kid." Ji-ji has never seen Tiro happier than he is tonight.

Zaini turns to Ji-ji and asks, "You okay, Ji-ji? Any changes I should know about?"

"A few," Ji-ji replies.

"Thought so," Zaini says. "Your sister know?" Ji-ji nods. "Damn," Zaini mutters. "Your sister ever tell you what she tried to do to Man Cryday?" Ji-ji stared at her. "Never mind," Zaini said. "Where's Afarra? I left his Eyes in her sleep-shed like he asked. He said she'd need protecting."

"It was *you* left 'em for her!" Ji-ji exclaims.

"Couldn't tell anyone. If the steaders thought there was something special about the little outcast, they'd be after her for sure. Guess she's not so little anymore. She with you?" Zaini sees their stricken faces and puts her hand to her mouth in consternation.

"Got snatched," Ji-ji says, "in the Dream."

Zaini shakes her head, sadly. "Guess his Eyes couldn't protect her after all."

Bromadu, who's hanging off Tiro's arm, doesn't believe it. "Can't get snatched in the Dream," he declares with the assurance of a ten-year-old. "Seeds is Free in the Dream."

Zaini takes Ji-ji's and Tiro's hands in hers and squeezes. "We're mighty glad you came back for us—right, Broma?"

Bromadu's glad all right. "You gonna teach me to fly in the Dream like you promised?"

Heather pokes her head around the door. "Reunion's over."

Zaini grabs a small sack she's stuffed with her few treasures, and slips jackets on herself and the boys. Tiro impresses upon his brothers that they have to stay very quiet and follow his orders.

Bromadu repeats Tiro's instructions for Eeyatho, as if his little brother won't take them seriously unless they come from his mouth. "You hear that, Yatho? No whimperin'. No nothin', no matter what, okay? We're headed for the Dream. Told you Tiro'd come back for us."

"Let's hope Lotter's sleeping like a baby," Ji-ji says, as they head for the door.

Tiro says, "Drex Williams too," adding ominously, "for his sake."

"Lotter's not here," Zaini tells them. "Ma Merrimac told me. Got back from Armistice then rushed off somewhere with Casper." Ji-ji's grateful. At least she won't have to watch Charra kill him. Or watch him kill the two of them, more like.

She asks if Dip was recaptured. Zaini says she was. "Search hounds found her in The Margins. Tore her arm up. Lotter branded her for escaping. She was locked up in PenPen last month for insolence. Hate to say it, but she's likely dead by now. No seed survives in PenPen for long."

As speedily as they can, the raiders usher Williams' dazed seeds to a small clearing at the edge of the quarters so they can address them all at once. Many of them call their rescuers Friends, thinking they're Friends of Freedom. No one corrects them. Some think their liberation is a hoax played on them by Cropmaster Lotter, a test of their fealty; others fear they'll be pilloried, lopped, lashed or lynched. They remind the raiders that no more than three seeds can assemble outside at night without permission. An old man wearing a Tribalseed symbol says the Twelfth has tripled his canine patrol, to which Raphael replies, "My men are taking care of the dogs. They won't trouble us." He speaks with such authority that some of the doubters begin to believe in Freedom.

The mood is on the upswing, particularly after Charra and Raphael order their followers to distribute weapons: knives for the juvis, guns for the grown seeds who can handle them, a grenade or two for the steady ones like Zaini, who can be trusted to hold off pulling the pin till they have to.

As the seeds adjust to the novelty of being armed, Charra steps up onto a rock so everyone can see her. Two-thirds of them will remain behind to hold the planting, she says. Disappointment ripples through the crowd. The seeds demand to know why.

"Not enough room for everyone," Raphael explains. "Got to do it in stages."

"The ones as stay'll die," someone calls out.

"No they won't," Charra pledges. "The ones who stay'll be armed. Many of these fighters will stay here with you so we can turn the tables on the pigs at last. You won't be seeds anymore."

While Charra and Raphael quickly work to convince the crowd that those who stay will be the lucky ones, Zaini pulls Ji-ji aside, says, "You know what she is, right?"

Instinctively, Ji-ji leaps to Charra's defense: "She's risking her life to save people."

"You're right. Your sister's brave and I'm very grateful. But she's changed, damaged."

"We're all damaged," Ji-ji says.

"True. But some are more damaged than others."

"'Sides," Ji-ji adds, in a move designed to end the argument, "Uncle Dreg wanted me to meet up with her. Man Cryday told me that. So did Mam."

"Uncle Dreg wanted a lot of things. Saw the best in everyone, but his See-ing Eyes had some blind spots." It shocks Ji-ji to hear how much she sounds like Man Cryday. Zaini isn't done yet: "Occupying this planting is a crazy idea, you know that. Unless you've got a whole army of Freedom fighters, it'll never work. Your sister's aiming to get us killed. She ferret you out or did you go looking for her?"

It's none of your damn business, Ji-ji wants to say. Then decides it's better to keep quiet. Zaini impresses upon her how crucial it is to get as many seeds as possible off the planting.

"I don't call the shots, Auntie Zaini."

"Well, you better start. You got more aces up your sleeve than the rest of us put together. Start using them, Ji-ji, 'fore it's too late."

|||||||||||||||

Tiro can't get his head around what's just happened. Things were going accord-ing to plan, then *BAM!* They made it to the fry-fence, to within feet of Free-dom, and everything went to hell!

He should've cottoned to it earlier. Only a few guards engaged them in the Doom Dell. They got all the way to the eastern section of the fence, the same place they'd scaled earlier. Fence was still down. Seeds, desperate to escape, started to climb. Then the sound of Marcus' voice coming through on Heather's caller, screaming out a warning: "The steaders've seized control of the power! The fence, the comm, *everything*! Planting guards're pouring out of Murder Mouth, heading in your direction! *It's a TRAP!*" Doesn't make sense. If Marcus and the others don't have control of the power, why's the fence still dead? And then it hits them. They start screaming, "*JUMP! Get down!*" A few leap, but most don't catch on till it's too late. About three dozen are still scaling the fence when the terrible buzz surges back. As long as he lives, he'll never forget that sound.

Tiro is closest to the fence carrying Yatho. He shoves his brother into Zaini's arms and catches one of the little ones as she falls, catches her clean. . . . It's no good! She's dead!

He turns back to the planting, looks down toward the Doom Dell, and sees the steaders' vehicles laboring toward them, surrounded by dozens of planting guards on foot and on horseback, many in riot gear. Marcus is right. They're trapped!

Tiro stands there frozen till Aisha rushes up, grabs the dead girl, and lays her on the ground. Terrified seeds fall on their knees, lay down their weapons. "*Don't surrender!*" Charra cries. "*Fight!*"

With a *schluff*, the floodlights near the fence come on. They're sitting ducks! Raphael bellows to his men, "*Shoot those goddam lights out!*" A volley of bullets, shattered glass. They can't shatter all of them from that angle, but the area near the fence reverts to semidarkness. In those few seconds of floodlight, Tiro sees who's orchestrating the attack. He draws his gun and keeps his eyes on the Jeep's headlights. On the passenger side, his head poking through the moon roof, is the gaunt, silhouetted figure of Drexler Williams, the bastard who seeded him.

Tiro bounds down the hill to get a better shot, takes cover behind an oak tree. He fires. Misses. Wants to fire again but there's no time! Some of the seeds are shooting wildly. A few steaders are hit, but most of the seeds are panic shooting. Thank god the raiders and Invisibles are more disciplined; they seek out cover and fire only when they have a chance of hitting their targets.

One of the I-Ms has a grenade launcher. An explosion decimates a section of the steaders' advancing line. It dissolves in disarray. Surprised by that level of resistance, the steaders fall back.

Tiro tears back up the hill to the fence. Heather calls him over to where she's taken cover with Charra. "We're backed up here!" she cries. "Take some of the seeds and head for the breach. See it? Down there below that line of trees. Hide in the Doom Dell. If we make it out, we'll come find you. Go on! We'll cover you!"

Tiro snatches Yatho from his mother's arms and tells her to grab Broma's hand. He shouts to Ji-ji and the others: "*Follow me!*" They run. *Pop!Pop!* coming at them through the dark. Screams. An explosion. Shrieks and yells in the darkness.

Why didn't they see this coming? The scant forces they encountered in the Doom Dell should've told them this was a trap. In the low-lying, swampy Doom Dell, the raiders and Men attacked guerrilla style, congratulated themselves on their success. One after another, small groups of steaders came looking for them only to be beaten back. "*Cowards!*" seeds yelled out as the steaders retreated. But the enemy was biding his time, luring them into danger, and they fell for it. Did the steaders know they were coming? Was there another turncoat?

The steaders pick off their targets, try not to shoot the seeds. It's the Freedom fighters they want to kill. As Yatho clings to his neck, Tiro and his ragged group of followers run parallel to the advancing steaders, search for a break in the line so they can slip through. A guard spots them, opens fire! Awkwardly, cradling Yatho in his arms, Tiro fires back. The guard falls.

They sneak through the line. Tiro leads them back in the direction of the Doom Dell. They take cover to catch their breath. "Stay real quiet," he tells them.

"They're rounding seeds up," Zaini whispers, "herding them to Execution Circle."

They'll lock seeds up in the viewing coops, surround the raiders, and slaughter them. Tiro is desperate to find out if Ji-ji's with them. But in the dark when he doesn't know if there are guards nearby, he dare not call out to her. Yatho's trembling in his arms. He wants to tell him everything'll be okay, but his throat's dry, and he keeps thinking about what the little dead girl looked like when he caught her in his arms. Keeps thinking he's still holding her, the dead girl. But he's not. He's holding Yatho. Tiro swallows hard and says, "It'll be okay, little man. Don't be scared."

His mother, who crouches next to him, looks up into his face. He sees the dread in her eyes; it terrifies him. He peers through the dark again, tries to find Ji-ji. He tells himself she'll fly to safety.

This was Williams' plan all along. Wait for them to congregate at the fence then pounce. Must've been watching them the whole time. Bet the surveillance cameras were working after all. So what if they had to sacrifice a few Homestead guards, a few suckers. Williams wouldn't give a shit. Bet they'd been watching Emmeline too. . . . More guards approaching. Tear gas! *Run! Run!*

They start running again, deeper into the Doom Dell. Twenty, thirty of them altogether, women and children mostly. Only a handful of men and women with guns, fewer who know how to use them. In the darkness, guards come at them from all sides. Nowhere to go! Yatho in his arms choking on his tears cos they've told him not to make a sound. Smoke, tear gas drifting toward them on the breeze. Their one remaining advantage—the steaders want to keep the seeds alive. They need them for labor. Maybe he can offer to surrender? Dumb idea. Williams would pyre Zaini and lynch the boys out of spite. Make him watch, then lynch him too, or worse.

Williams' voice off in the distance seeps down into the Doom Dell. He's yelling orders through a bullhorn. Tiro pictures Williams' gaunt shoulders and pale head poking out of the top of the Jeep and wishes to god he hadn't missed. Williams ducked down. A couple seconds later, he raised his head again and scanned the hill ferociously to see who'd done it. The bastard didn't spot Tiro. He has no idea his own Muleseed tried to kill him.

Tiro hasn't got a clue where he's running to. Steaders approach, order seeds to surrender. The search hounds bark excitedly. They've sniffed out another seed. So much for getting rid of the dogs. Raphael was full of shit. Where can they go? Where can they hide?

"PenPen!" Zaini cries. "*C'mon!*"

She takes off, dragging Bromadu after her. She's lost her mind! She's taking them to the planting prison! How will they even get in? Tiro's left with no choice: he rushes after her.

They reach the wall surrounding PenPen. Though he can't see it in the dark, Tiro remembers the shards of glass embedded in it. Affixed to the top are spirals of barbed wire. The smell of sewage accosts them in this morbid place where Uncle Dreg was held for fourteen days.

Just like he knew they would be, the gates are locked.

"This is crazy!" Tiro cries. "There's no place to hide! The seeds've got to surrender!"

"This is c-crazy, Mam!" Bromadu echoes, between sobs.

Zaini pulls out a key, slips it into the padlocked gate, undoes the padlock. Astonished, Tiro asks where she got the key. She doesn't reply. "The alarm," Tiro says frantically. "We'll set it off!"

"Maybe," Zaini says. She pushes the gate open and listens for a moment. "Alarm's down."

"What? . . . How?" he asks.

Zaini doesn't waste time answering him. She shoves everyone through the gate, locks it behind them, and takes off running through the prison compound. When she reaches the walls of the decaying, multistory prison, she veers to the right.

Tiro tries to reason with her: "We can't get inside! They'll see us when they come through the gate. They're on our tails. We can't fight 'em all!"

"We're not taking cover out here."

Zaini takes off yet again, leads them round to the back of the building to a door hidden behind a giant rhododendron bush. She knocks. Beyond the prison fence, the sound of dogs barking madly. Men shouting. *Pop! Pop! Pop!* His mother has gone mad! He tries to stop her from knocking again just as the door opens.

A man stands in deep shadow and grunts at them. Silent Pete, the child soldier grown old, who lost three of his fingers, half his foot, an ear, and his voice fighting for Freedom. He limps back into the shadows as Zaini pushes the group inside. Tiro can't believe it. *What's Silent Pete doing here? Thought he was at the lookout tower with Marcus.* A fixture on the planting, Silent Pete loads up the funeral wagon and drives the dead to the seed cemetery after harvesting ceremonies. He runs errands and drives Father-Man Brine's old jalopy. On the side, he turns off fry-fences, aids and abets rebels, turns prisons into sanctuaries, plans rebellions with Friend Emmeline, and smiles at Yatho, who is rigid with fear in Tiro's arms. He smiles at the other little ones too, and takes the hands of two of them. As if it's the most normal thing in the world, he leads them through the prison.

"How'd you know he'd be here?" Tiro asks his mother.

"A contingency plan your uncle and me drew up years ago," Zaini says. "Release the prisoners and use the place as a refuge of last resort. Didn't know if Pete could make it back to PenPen, but he managed it. We hide here and hope for rescue. Pete will let Charra and the others know where we are. All we got to do is hang tight."

They walk through dank corridors to the back of the prison. The cell doors are flung open and all the cells are empty. Silent Pete's been busy. He leads them up a small flight of stone steps to a large cell that's less filthy than the others. Fresh hay on the floor. Must've been prepping this place for a while. Pete shuffles to the corner of the cell and unlocks a wooden container. He takes out some bread, cheese, water, and wine. Tiro spots a piss bucket in the other corner. Beside it sits a roll of toilet paper. Pete's thought of everything.

The old soldier gives water and food to the little ones and invites Zaini to drink from the wine bottle. With hand gestures, he apologizes for not having cups. "No problemo," Tiro says cos he can't think of anything else to say. Pete insists Tiro drink some wine, then he offers it to the other growns in the group. He smiles like it gives him more satisfaction than anything else in the world to host them in PenPen. Two of the little ones are injured. Looks like one has a broken ankle, another's been grazed in the arm by a bullet. Everyone is traumatized. Tiro is too, but he can't show it, not when Bromadu is looking up at him like he can save them all if he puts his mind to it.

Twenty-eight of them, Tiro counts. Fourteen, including his brothers, are seedlings. Ji-ji's nowhere to be seen. The sound of battle is muted by PenPen's thick walls, but they hear the search hounds drawing close. *All we've done is bought a little time,* Tiro thinks, *drawn out the horror.*

After he's sure they've got what they need, Silent Pete talks to Zaini using hand gestures again. A minute later, he heads off to draw the hunting party off their scent.

"It's strange," Zaini says. "Pete says when he got here, PenPen was already empty."

"How'd the prisoners get out?" Tiro asks.

"He doesn't know," Zaini replies.

A short while later, they hear dogs yapping in the distance, followed by a single gunshot.

"He's okay," Zaini says, though she doesn't sound confident. "Pete's too wily to be caught."

Exhausted, most of them fall asleep quickly. Tiro tells his mother to sleep too. He'll take the first watch, he says. Not that he can do much of anything if they're discovered. He has a gun with a few bullets left in the mag. Some of the others have a few bullets left too. If the steaders storm the place it's over. The only chance they have is to escape under the cover of darkness, but it'll be dawn soon. No way they can escape in broad daylight. Tiro second-guesses himself. He should've gone with Pete, doubled their chances. "I'll never sleep, son," Zaini says, just before she does.

Bromadu snuggles between Zaini and Tiro and falls asleep too. Tiro looks around the cell, can't figure out how he wound up playing the Pied Piper with all these seedlings in tow. Could be some seedlings remembered him from before, or it could be they saw him with Broma and Yatho and felt safe. Several of the seedlings are outcasts. One of them is Merrywinkle, the albino boy Afarra befriended. The outcasts are handling this the best. It's like they know the worst is always on the horizon and they've trained themselves to function in spite of it.

In Tiro's lap, Yatho tries not to close his eyes but they grow heavy. Every so often, he jerks himself awake, lets out a little squeal of fear then goes back to sleep when Tiro hugs him.

Terrified he'll fall asleep on his watch like he did when they were surprised by Charra's raiders, Tiro asks one of the growns, a woman named Chrysalis, if she'll watch with him. "Sure," Chrysalis says. She looks terrible. Blood all over her shirt and pants. She has long wavy hair rolled up into a bun, and slightly protruding, pretty eyes. She's mixed, like him. Late twenties probably.

"Don't worry. Blood's not mine," she tells him. "Belongs to some kid. Some Invisible. Didn't know him. Short, skinny, scared. Never seen anyone scareder. He'd wet himself, smelled like, when he fell on top o' me after the steaders shot him. The rest of the blood's from a seed. An albino. Older. Jumped on a grenade. Saved my life. Saved a bunch of seedlings too. You grew up here, right? She sound familiar?"

"We only had two of 'em when I was here. That boy over there an' a female." Tiro figures the hero must've been Fuzzy, Afarra's other friend, but he also figures it's better not to share any details. What good does it do to put a name to a body blown to bits?

"You ever been in an ambush?" Chrys asks. It's obvious she's very frightened.

"Once. In The Margins. Nothin' like this. Half a dozen Clansmen . . . one Clanswoman."

"But you got out without a scratch in the end, right?"

"Yeah. I got out."

"There's hundreds of steaders out there, all armed. You seen the ones in riot gear?" He wants to smash his fist into the cell bars, kick the prison's moldy walls till his toes bleed. Chrys keeps talking: "And then I see one of them steaders shoot a raider point-blank in the chest like it's nothing. Never been on a planting before. . . . Grew up in Charlotte. Can't die here."

"You won't."

"You got a plan?"

Tiro almost laughs out loud. He strokes Yatho's pretty head and nods toward Zaini. "My mother's the one with the plans," he says. "She'll get us out. She's got a boatload o' contingencies."

"You're one of them fly-boys, right? The wizard's nephew. In the assembly hall in Turnabout, Commander Charra told us you joined up. Guess this ain't your first rodeo."

"You okay to take the first watch?" Tiro says, suddenly so tired the only thing he's capable of doing is falling asleep. He's out before he hears her reply. . . .

He hears him before he sees him, shuffling across the cell floor toward him, his whole body made of smoke. "How come you're made of smoke, Uncle Dreg?" Tiro says, before he realizes he's speaking to a Dimmer. "You a Dimmer?" he adds, like it's not obvious. Everything about his uncle looks the same except for a few details: his smokiness, his hair that's shedding a substance like flour (dandruff?), and his white-rimmed eyes that breathe in and out like a lung, the weirdest thing of all. Tiro knows he should be freaked out by the apparition, but of all the things he could've woken up to in that cell, Uncle Dreg's just about the best. Even in death, the old wizard would never hurt him.

Uncle Dreg doesn't say one word, yet somehow Tiro knows that Silent Pete is dead and they have to get out of there. Uncle Dreg doesn't say that, but he nods when Tiro thinks it.

Tiro wakes the others up to tell them they've got to leave.

"Why?" Zaini whispers.

"He's dead. Silent Pete."

"How'd you know?" Zaini asks him.

"Uncle Dreg."

She looks around. "Here? He told you to leave?" Tiro nods. "Then we leave," she says.

"S'pose I'm wrong?"

"If you're wrong, we do what's best for the boys." She pulls from her pocket the two grenades they gave her. "And we do what's best for each other."

He knows what she means, but he doesn't know how he'd ever bring himself to do it.

They wake the others and creep out through the dark prison corridors, past the empty cells. No sound but the drip-drip of condensation and the scurrying of rats. They unlatch the back door and are greeted by a miracle! Fog so dense it's hard to see more than ten feet ahead! It wasn't smokiness around Uncle Dreg, it was *this*! A shroud of fog to hide inside!

Tiro leads the way. Zaini unlocks PenPen's gate as quietly as she can and they creep back in the direction of the fry-fence. Tiro doesn't know what he'll do when he gets there. He heads up the hill anyway, propelled by something he can't explain. He tells the seedlings to stay very quiet.

In Tiro's arms, Yatho pulls his elder brother's head down to his lips and says, "You think the smoke man's coming with us, Tiro?"

"The smoke man? You saw him? Back there in the cell?"

Yatho nods. "Out here . . . Don't see him no more. Guess he's invisible, right?"

"Yeah, little man," Tiro says, "I guess he is."

||||||||||||||||

She thinks she's following Tiro. Thinks that's him up ahead. But it's dark and she's not sure. Afraid to call out, she tries not to be cowed by the volleys, the shrieks all around her. Aisha, who took the little dead girl from Tiro's hands and laid her gently down, jogs beside her.

"It's not Tiro," Aisha says. "We lost him." She grabs Ji-ji's arm, speaks to her firmly, calmly, as if there's no ambush, as if the fence hasn't fried twenty, thirty people, as if there's no swarm of bullets, no choking gas, no steaders: "We gotta head back to the fence! Head back to Charra."

No! She won't give up now!

Ji-ji breaks away and rushes into the darkness, runs like the wind. She can still catch up with him. . . . One stride, two strides, ten strides farther on. . . .

A steader guard in full riot gear steps out from behind a tree. For a split second, he's trying to figure out if she's a seed or a raider. It makes a difference. Seeds are for keeping, raiders are for killing. *My gun is in my hand,* she thinks. *Fire!*

He falls! But she didn't shoot him. The bullet whizzed past her ear and hit one of the few parts of the guard's body that was exposed. His neck opens like a flower . . . a fountain. A split second of hesitation killed him. The guard falls within kicking distance at her feet. She feels compelled to watch him choke on his own blood, but Aisha drags her back toward the fry-fence, swears and cusses, tells her she's a damn fool. Ji-ji can't argue. She's a damn fool if ever there was one.

She hears the men advancing up the hill, bearded steaders with their Found Cause. It takes her a while to figure out why she can hear Williams' voice in her head. Then she understands he's got a megaphone. That's why his mechanical voice slithers inside her ear: "*Seeds, surrender! Go to the Circle with your hands up! Peaceably gather in your viewing coops! SEEDS WILL BE SPARED!*"

Nearby, a woman with two small children raises her hands. Ji-ji doesn't need to see the brown Commonseed symbol on her shift or hear her voice to recognize her as Williams' third seedmate. Aisha rushes up to the woman, picks up the gun the woman has cast aside and tries to stuff it back into her hands. "Don't surrender! Defend these little ones!"

The woman tears herself from Aisha's grasp, leaving a scrap of her shift in Aisha's hand in the process. Crying out for mercy, she pushes her offspring forward. "*We surrender! We surrender!*"

"The hell we do," Aisha says. She flings down the scrap of fabric, grabs Ji-ji's hand.

Ji-ji doesn't know how Aisha keeps her bearings in the chaos, but soon the fence is directly ahead. They call out for Charra and Heather. They're nearby, not far from the carnage by the fence. They've taken cover behind a knot of trees and bushes, with Raphael and others.

Charra rushes up to them, drags Ji-ji behind a bush and slaps her hard across the jaw. It's a powerful slap but it barely registers. "Stupid *idiot!*" Charra cries. "Taking off like that almost got us killed!" Heather tries to calm Charra down. Ji-ji has no idea what Charra's talking about till Raphael explains they were reluctant to fire in case they hit her. *My sister loves me so much she wouldn't shoot,* Ji-ji thinks. Then she laughs out loud. "Cos of my back, right? That's why." Someone'll slap her again if she doesn't shut up, but she can't help it. A laughter fountain spews from her mouth.

"Oh my god!" Raphael says. "She's bleeding!" Ji-ji looks where he's looking. He's right. A dark wet shadow on her shirt. Who knew?

Without asking, Raphael grabs Ji-ji's shirt, pulls it up, and trains a flashlight on the wound in her side. "Looks like it's not real deep, but it sheared off some flesh. Don't worry," he adds, "I'll take care of it." Aisha berates herself for not seeing Ji-ji was hit. She takes Ji-ji's hand.

"Bet it was that guard," Aisha says, adding, "If you hurt her, Raphael, you'll answer to me."

Ji-ji plans to tell Aisha it's unnecessary to make threats or take her hand, but the very next moment her concentration deserts her. Raphael (she knows an archangel by that name) pulls out a syringe contraption, administers a shot near the wound. Hurts like hell before it doesn't. He sprays the wound with something that tickles. Next, working fast, he pulls out an instrument Ji-ji's never seen before. Fiddles with it like he knows what he's doing. Takes out a small clamp thingy and applies a gooey paste to it like it's a toothbrush. In the light from the flashlight he tells Aisha to hold steady. The goo sparkles. He applies the clamp thing to her wound. The bleeding stops. "Thank god for the E.S.S.," he says. She'll decide later if she's grateful.

Charra and Heather have heard from Marcus again. He's made it to Murder Mouth. Says it's the one place on the planting they can gather to mount a defense. Aisha points out the obvious: there's an army of steaders between them and the arsenal. Raphael, who's packed up his miracle gear, suggests they split in two. One group can head to the right, the other to the left. With any luck, at least one group will make it through the line of steaders. He asks Ji-ji if she feels strong enough to stand. Scared of being left behind, she says she feels fine. "Can't feel a thing," she assures him.

Charra pulls her sister close. "Don't mess things up again, Beany, and keep your goddam mouth shut, or I swear I'll shut you up myself." Ji-ji's hand takes the initiative and salutes. Charra raises her eyes to heaven.

Ji-ji is in Charra's group with Aisha, Heather and Raphael, along with about a dozen raiders, half a dozen Invisible Men and a bunch of seeds. The group heads to the right. Anyone can see that the group going left drew the short straw; most of the ones in that group are seeds and seedlings. *They're left behind,* she thinks. She knows her thoughts are screwy. Must be the shot he gave her or the shot someone else gave her earlier when they shot her. "Aisha," she says, "you the one who shot me?" If looks could kill, she'd be dead right now. She stifles a giggle.

They're running in the Right group. A good sign. But she's lost Tiro, lost Zaini and the boys. A steader ambush. Seeds got fried. She got shot. Charra slapped her. Normally, that would make for a lousy day. Each time she tries to focus, a giggle scrambles up her throat. She suspects she's in shock. She likes being there, doesn't want to come out again. They run, shoot, take cover, run again. Her sister limp-runs like a champion, even though Ji-ji was faster than her by the time she was seven (Yatho's age) and Charra was eleven (around Broma's age). Pissed Charra off. Accused her of being a freak. The first person to call her that.

Before she knows it, they've made it to Murder Mouth. Dawn is fast approaching. How come the gates are unguarded and wide open? Then she sees the reason for it.

Marcus is there to greet them, so is Emmeline, whose long gray hair flows like a silver river. She hugs Ji-ji to her breast as if she's her long-lost granddaughter. Calls her the Freedom Race champion. The tall I-M who rode with them in the van is there too. (*Shame he made it out alive,* Ji-ji thinks, *when lots of good ones didn't.*) His name isn't Seen One, even though that's what Aisha calls him. His name is Meaty Bustall (goes by "Meat"). *Name doesn't suit him,* Ji-ji thinks, *not skinny enough.* Silent Pete isn't with them. She wants to ask them where he is but she forgets.

As dawn inches closer, Marcus guides some of them back into the building, says you should see what those pigs did back there. Marcus and Emmeline insist they leave most of the seeds in the main building with some of the raiders to protect them while they take a look. "It's not something you can forget after you've seen it," the diviner says. She looks like she's seen a ghost.

There are surveillance cameras in the compound, and though Marcus and Meat have smashed all the cameras they could find, the group is advised to keep to the shadows and hug the buildings just in case. There are no windows in the evil-looking building at the back of the compound, so it's safe to switch on the lights. Marcus flicks them on.

Slaughter! The concrete floor is slick with it.

What the steaders have left behind is so shocking it forces Ji-ji into lucidity all at once. In a rush of remembrance, she knows where she is, what happened, and what's at stake. To protect herself, she doesn't look at the pitiful freaks. Being one herself, she tries not to see them. Though none of the dead look like her, some remind her of Drol. Most look like nothing she's ever seen.

Marcus tells them they counted about five dozen corpses, but there are many more empty cells and cages than that. He doesn't know where the rest are, but he suspects they could've been hauled off somewhere. They go from room to room, lab to lab, in horrified silence.

Charra and Ji-ji find something else shocking too. Something Marcus, Meat and Emmeline didn't find earlier. Attracted by the hum of what sounds like a generator, the sisters enter the strange room alone, as if they know this space belongs to them. It looks like a giant shipping container, but inside they find a temperature-controlled, state-of-the-art morgue. The light in there is so glaringly artificial, so unlike the light in the rest of the arsenal, Ji-ji thinks it's not real. Hanging on a wall is a glassed-in display case. Inside is a copy of the steaders' *One True Text.* Charra and Ji-ji slide out the drawers together, grab each other's hands when they see who's inside one of them. Charra has to drag Ji-ji away, otherwise she would never have left.

They enter a lab and find Heather taking photos. She isn't trusting anything to memory. She takes photo after photo with her caller, documenting what they've found. She moves from one lab to the next, gazes at the victims without speaking. Some are unrecognizable as human. In front of a cage that contains a mutilated toddler with its dead mam (impossible to tell whether it was a boy or a girl) Heather throws up. She's can't take another photo. Tenderly, Charra removes the caller from Heather's hands, takes over as photographer. Marcus records the devastation, his hand remarkably steady. They need video too, to go along with the still photos. They need everything so politicians in the SuperStates and Liberty Independents can't plead ignorance anymore.

They know how futile this effort is. There's no way to get the images off the planting, and there's an excellent chance they'll all be dead soon. The callers work over short distances as two-way radios, but they're locked out of the main network. They'll trigger an alarm and alert the steaders to their position if they try to access it. Their only option is to smuggle the footage out the old-fashioned way, get it to the only people who can distribute it widely— Abbyjill Edelmann and E. K. Lowenstein at the D.C. *Independent*. The reporters have come through for them before, been jailed for it too. "Abby and Ezra understand suffering," Emmeline says. "They'll know this is real. They won't cheapen it or sensationalize it. I'll take it to them."

"Don't be a fool," Marcus says. "Think they'll allow you to drive through the Main Gate? I keep telling you, they know you're a traitor."

Raphael offers to take it. Orders Marcus to accompany him.

Marcus shakes his head. "Rafe, you know I'd go along with that idea if it stood a chance of working. I pull off some of the trickiest vaulting maneuvers in the Dream Coop. But even if I had the right pole, no one can leap over a thirty-foot electric—" He breaks off, looks over at Ji-ji.

Charra interposes herself between Marcus and her sister. "No," Charra says. "We defend this place and wait for reinforcements. Feral will be here soon. Beany stays with us."

Raphael tries to reason with her: "How long before they catch on and blast their way through the arsenal gates? Ji-ji's the only one can make it over the fence. She's a mutant. A living, breathing example of this whole enterprise. The combination of her and that footage is all we need to get them to listen, all we need to jump-start a revolution. How many more have to die before—"

"*No!*" Charra insists. "The others, they're not like her. How's she gonna persuade anyone what the steaders're doing is obscene when she looks like a goddam angel? She stays with us."

Ji-ji's barely there. She's thinking about what she saw with her sister in the morgue, trying to figure out how they preserved the bodies so well in those strange, coffinlike drawers. SuperState technology for sure, though there was only one among the twelve corpses that wasn't mutilated or autopsied. "Mam!" the sisters had exclaimed in unison. Over her beautiful corpse, they'd recited the Toteppi prayer Auntie Zaini taught them as seedlings: "Our Mother, which art the Cradle, hallowed be Thy name." On the way out, Charra smashed the glass and snatched the *One True Text* from its shrine. In one of the labs, she dropped the open book into a pool of blood in one of the cages so the sisters could witness its ruination.

Ji-ji takes hold of Charra's shoulders and eases her to one side. She takes up a position between Charra and Raphael. "I don't think my back can take me far," Ji-ji says.

"See," Charra says. "I told you she couldn't—"

Ji-ji interrupts her: "The things on my back don't work well if I'm scared. But I can run fast, an' get there on foot. An' there's a chance, a *good* chance, I can make it over the fence. But I'll need cover from people I can trust." Ji-ji takes her sister's hand and says, "Know anyone?"

'm sure she's up in that wobbly nest," Mackie said, having returned from her investigation to join them in the locker room underneath the Aerie and adjacent to the coop. "Caught the two of them sleeping there. Cautioned them it wasn't safe."

A tip had brought the rescue party of six to the abandoned practice coop. One of the Friends of Freedom, who checked on the place regularly, thought he'd heard someone moving around there.

After his fruitless days of searching and the shocking turn of events at Chaff Man's hideout, Lucky was skeptical. "Did you actually see her?" he asked Mackie.

"How could I see her, you dunderheid? She's in the nest a hundred feet up! You want me to call up there in the middle of the night and scare the lass half to death?"

"What's she doing up there?" Ben, the third member of the party, asked.

"Sleeping, I suppose," Mackie said. "Crept up there with Ji-ji and lied about it afterward. Terrible liars they were, her most of all. Worst I've ever seen." Mackie turned to her son Monty, the fourth group member, who stood beside her. "Even you lie better than they did, son."

Lucky had never seen a mother and son who looked more alike than Mary Macdonald and her son, Monty. The resemblance made no sense, given that Monty was adopted. A burly man in his thirties with a full head of mussed-up brown hair (his ma mussed it up whenever she ran her hand playfully through his curls), Monty had his mother's unapologetic eyebrows, bright eyes, canny smile, and perfectly round face. Monty's hair curled around his ears like his ma's did. And though he lacked her Scottish accent and was a lot more easygoing than she was, his voice had the same register, hers being low for a woman, his being high for a man. On a call, it was hard to tell the difference between them. Lucky was more envious of their mutual affection than he liked to admit. It was the kind of intuitive connection mothers had with their infant children, as if Mackie knew when Monty needed to burp before he did.

Every time Lucky saw them together and felt the intensity of Mackie's mother-love for her lumbering, good-natured son, it depressed him. He used to have a mother who idolized him and a sister who did the same. Afarra had given him that same adoring look when, as a planting guard, he'd placed an orange in her hand, even though it was against every planting regulation in the book to "bestow gifts" on an outcast. When Ji-ji had told him Afarra had kept the peel, he knew he'd got something right. It was the kind of thing a mother or sister would do—hang on to the worthless crap you gave them as though it were the most valuable thing in the world.

Lucky needed to know someone needed him, that someone still gave a damn if he lived or died. He'd thought Ji-ji cared about him that way, but the girl he'd dropped everything to come and help was living it up at the seaside with her sister. Lucky knew that was a gross exaggeration, especially after what he'd learned about Charra's dodgy state of mind in a recent call with Man Cryday. But he couldn't do anything to help Ji-ji right now except complete the mission she and Man Cryday had asked him to undertake, which so far had led to the partial decapitation of a fish and the probable castration of an executioner. Hardly a win-win. Afarra *had* to be hiding out in that nest. He'd failed to save Rachel, failed to save or even find Bonbon. As if lugging those failures around weren't enough, he was hounded by the idea that, if he'd tried harder, he could've found out more about what was really going on when he served as a guard on the 437th. Lotter had promised to loop him into the circle, as he called it, and Lucky suspected the "circle" had a lot to do with the notorious arsenal. But he'd had to get Ji-ji out of there in a hurry and never got looped in. He couldn't help feeling he'd let everyone down, particularly after he saw her doing the impossible in this very coop, which proved that Man Cryday's suspicions about the arsenal could've been right.

"The doors are locked," Zyla, the fifth member of the party, pointed out. "How'd she get in?" At that moment, Otto hurried into the locker room. There were six of them now. Zyla called out to him: "You found out how she got in, Otto?"

"Yep," he said, breathlessly, "if it's her. The transom window in the basement. Could be burglars. Hard to say."

"So what the hell are we waiting for?" Lucky asked, exasperated.

He was snapping at everyone. After the fiasco with Tulip the other night, he couldn't find his equilibrium, as Germ would call it. From the get-go, he'd misread everything about that situation and almost got everyone killed. If D.C. law enforcement had given a shit about that neighborhood, they'd have been dragged into the precinct to answer a whole host of questions. As it was, they'd left Clownfish's body to the rats, confident cops would see it as another drug deal gone bad.

The episode had left all of them—except Tulip, ironically—in a state of shock. As often happens after an incident like that, a residual antagonism sloshed around in the group. Otto wasn't fussy about who came to his rescue, but Lucky and Ben, though grateful, weren't thrilled about having to be saved by Zyla and Mackie. All of them had misjudged Tulip. The only person who'd misjudged her more than they had was Clownfish. Lucky still couldn't believe how calm Tulip was when she pulled the trigger. The only other people he'd seen with that same level of homicidal intensity were steaders and executioners.

Lucky had lobbied hard to leave the wounded executioner there where he lay. Argued he could keep Clownfish company. He'd seen Chaff Man at work on the 437th, and they didn't owe that son of a bitch a thing. To his surprise, seeing as how Mackie thought most males were scum, the coach had sided with Zyla and voted to save him. Mackie, relying on platitudes, said you never knew what someone would do with their lives after a close call with death. Neither Ben nor Otto mounted a vigorous defense of his idea to let the executioner bleed out, so that was that.

Getting Chaff Man to a doctor who'd keep his mouth shut hadn't been easy. He bled like a stuck pig all over Otto's backseat. As Zyla worked to stanch the bleeding, Lucky, who'd volunteered to ride with them and put the bastard out of his misery if necessary, wanted to smother the wailing executioner. "Circus! Bitch took my Circus!" No mention of the fact that Fish, his partner in crime, had just had his face blown off by his sister. No begging for forgiveness for all the people he'd murdered, raped, and robbed. Lucky took comfort in the fact that it didn't look like Chaff Man would make it, or so Sleaze-Doc said as he counted out the cash Zyla handed over. Sleaze-Doc's real name was Doc Wheelright, though Lucky suspected he'd made it up so he could sound professional and vaguely cowboyish. The doc insisted payment be in Supers, wouldn't save the Chaff otherwise. The man had the grimiest fingernails Lucky had ever seen. Those filthy digits told you sepsis was in the executioner's future.

Lucky hoped Chaff's groin injury was a game changer. Hoped his willy shriveled up and dropped off so he could never rape anyone else. Lucky couldn't stand the idea of Afarra being brutalized by a savage like Chaff Man. He'd wanted to leave him to rot so fiercely his throat ached. He would have gone through with it if Bleeding-Heart Zyla and Mary Queen of Scots hadn't intervened. By the time they'd finished saving evildoers, decent people were screwed. What do-gooders like them failed to understand was that mercy wasn't necessarily merciful in the end.

The full weight of what they would or wouldn't find up in that nest hit Lucky all at once. Afarra *had* to be there. If she wasn't, what was the point? She'd made her way to the Dream only to be violated by the same bastard who'd terrorized everyone on the planting. That couldn't be the end of her story.

Zyla seemed to know how scared he was. She reached around Ben and rested her hand lightly on Lucky's arm. "I think she's up there in the nest," she said simply. "Let's go get her."

He didn't know what to do with Zyla's kindness. It stung him, felt patronizing. He jerked his arm away and hated himself all over again. Zyla's face fell. With her haircut she looked younger than he did. He wanted to apologize, but where do you start if you've made a habit of demonizing someone you blame for your dad's death?

They headed out into the corridor and strategized along the way, reminding each other that Afarra was so traumatized she'd probably panic as soon as she realized she wasn't alone.

When Lucky visited Kingdom Come to follow up on Tulip's questioning of Peony and her kids, Peony said she still had the little dog. In a crisis situation, the Pomeranian could turn out to be another wild card. Took ages to get any info out of Peony cos she didn't want to betray her friend and didn't trust him at first. But then he'd told her some of the history between them, including the stuff about the orange, and how close she was to a friend of his, a girl called Ji-ji. Then he remembered Germaine had told him Afarra called her Elly. "Elly" turned out to be the secret password. Peony warmed up to him after that. She wouldn't take money for the info, so Lucky pretended he needed an errand run and jammed Supers in Wallaby's hand so he didn't feel like crap about the fact that they lived next to an open sewer in a tent city of paperless refugees.

They finally agreed upon a course of action. Ben, Zyla and Lucky would climb up to the nest while Mackie, Monty and Otto stayed down below. It was Mackie's idea to string up the safety net just in case. Because it was already fastened in place above the center ring it wouldn't take long. The net was slack right now, but all they needed to do was tighten it. They had to be careful, Ben warned, drawing on his experience as a veteran flyer. The net wasn't foolproof. If Afarra fell, she could bounce out of it like Ink had at the Jefferson Coop, or miss it altogether cos it only covered the central area of the fly cage.

Zyla had another suggestion, one she was reluctant to make till Mackie told her to spit it out. She addressed Lucky: "I don't mean anything bad by it," Zyla said, "but you're the spitting image of Lotter. If she sees you, she'll freak out. Think he's come to get her."

Inwardly, Lucky cursed himself for not thinking of that. He grabbed a knitted cap from his pocket and stuffed his blond hair under it. Zyla smiled at him. Such a pretty smile. Without consciously making it happen, he found himself smiling back. Then he went a step further and thanked her. "Thanks for the other stuff too. We wouldn't be here if you and Mackie hadn't shown up." He could tell she was touched by what he'd said.

"Just glad we got there in time," she told him.

"See?" Ben whispered, as they stood at the bottom of the wonky metal spirals of the Harriet's Stairs leading up to the Jacob's Ladders. "That wasn't so tough, was it? Germ'll be thrilled you and Zy are friends at last. Could be we'll name the kid after you after all."

"Shut up and climb," Lucky said.

After they'd climbed the first of the Harriets, Zyla whispered a hasty reminder to them. "She's been traumatized, and she could be sick too. We don't want to wake her till we're in the nest with her and Circus. Till then, don't make a sound."

Stealthily they made their way up to the dome of the coop.

The closer they got to the nest, the more nervous Lucky got. In spite of the recent gunshot wound he'd sustained, Ben moved like a flyer. Lucky was athletic himself, a trained fighter, but Ben had the kind of agility only flyer-battlers possess. If Germaine had been there, she'd be giving him a run for his money too. Lucky was grateful the three of them were ascending together. Nothing would go wrong if they worked as a team, he told himself. He wouldn't even care if Zyla saved the day again, as long as Afarra was okay.

Ben stood waiting at the start of the narrow walkway that led from the welkin platform to the Jim Crow Nest. He'd warned Lucky that it was high up in the dome, but Lucky hadn't thought it would bother him as much as it did. The coop was falling apart. Rust and mold everywhere. The walkway was just about shot. Ben decided it wasn't safe for more than one of them to use the walkway at a time. Zyla, by far the lightest of the three, offered to go first, see if Afarra was in the nest. "Kid's been attacked," she told them. "She could be scared of men."

Lucky agreed. He'd take his cue from her this time.

Before they could make a move, however, a loud clatter reverberated up from below. They peered over the railing into the well of the coop. One of the anchors holding the net had given way as they tried to adjust the tension.

"Shit!" Ben muttered. A dog began to yap. The sound came from the nest. *Circus!*

Zyla called out to Afarra. No answer. She stepped onto the walkway and edged herself forward, called out Afarra's name again. Silence. Then, when Lucky had almost given up hope, they saw the top of Afarra's head. It disappeared again behind the rim of the nest.

Zyla rushed forward. Ben and Lucky did too, forgetting Ben's warning about their weight on the walkway. Mackie yelled up at them to be careful. The men retreated back to the welkin platform.

Afarra stood up again in the nest, looked around, swayed as if she were on a sailing ship. She was taller than Lucky remembered and bone thin. She wore Uncle Dreg's Seeing Eyes. In her arms she cradled Circus. Lucky could tell she was disoriented.

"*No!*" she cried, thrusting out her arm to stop them from coming any farther. "I am . . . not being taken! I am *jumping!*" She shuffled to the edge of the basket. Lucky's heart stopped.

From down below, Mackie cried, "Be careful, my pet!"

Zyla eased herself across the walkway, talking as she went. "It's just me, Afarra. Zyla. Your friend. Ji-ji's teacher, remember? I'm here with your other friends. We've been looking for you."

Afarra stared at them with glazed eyes as Circus squirmed and bucked in her arm. "I am *hearing* her!" Afarra cried. "I am hearing her singing. I am hearing them *buzz!*"

She tottered unsteadily in the nest and batted at something invisible.

"What's she talking about?" Ben cried.

"I think she's delirious," Lucky told him. A sense of dread gripped him. He felt certain she was about to tumble out of the nest. He heard his own voice telling him he couldn't save her. He listened. Then he didn't as Afarra threw a leg over the rim. She was going to jump! It was now or never!

Lucky dashed along the walkway, lunged past Zyla, and flung himself forward as Afarra tumbled over the rim! Circus shot out of her grasp and into the air. In the nick of time, Lucky grabbed Afarra's arm as she tumbled. He wouldn't let go.

"*CIRCUS!*" Afarra screamed as she thrashed about. Lucky dragged her back inside the nest. Afarra knocked off his cap. His blond hair tumbled around his shoulders. "*Devil!*" she screamed as she tried to pull away and leap after the little dog. Zyla and Ben rushed into the nest to help him.

"Afarra! It's *me*! It's Lucky! Matty Longsby! I gave you an orange, remember?" She wasn't looking at him. She gazed down at Circus, who'd fallen into the net *before* Otto had managed to reattach one side of it to the anchor. So Otto improvised. He held the unanchored end up above his head so the net was taut. Not taut enough for a human, but taut enough for a little dog.

Circus fell into the net with a yelp. Bounced high. Bounced a second time a little lower. If he'd been heavier, the net would have been too low off the ground. But Circus was a Pomeranian, and tonight that detail was significant. Each bounce was more modest until, eventually, the little dog lay in the center of the net. The dog with nine lives had escaped death yet again.

Triumphantly, Circus stood up on all fours, fell down in the wobbly net, got his paw tangled up in one of the holes, stood up again. He barked at Afarra high up in the nest.

"She's burning up," Lucky said.

"Let's get her to Doc Riff," Zyla said. "He'll take care of her."

A few minutes later, Afarra lay in the backseat of an SUV Otto had borrowed from a friend so everyone could ride together, his car being too small and alarmingly bloodstained. Zyla had already administered an antibiotic, Doc Riff having advised her to do so if Afarra had an infection. Zyla crouched on the floor between the seats and examined Afarra's swollen hand.

Mackie, overcome with emotion when Afarra was carried down safely from the nest, rode in the front passenger seat. Occasionally, she took out a scrunched-up tissue and dabbed her eyes.

Monty rode in the back with Ben. Both Friends of Freedom were cramped but neither complained. Monty cradled Circus in his hairy arms.

"Think she'll be okay?" Lucky asked.

"Yeah, I think so," Zyla replied. "Doc Riff'll need to take a look at her hand, but he'll take care of her."

Lucky hadn't felt this happy since he'd learned Ji-ji wasn't going to die after all. He wanted to laugh like a fool; he wanted to blubber like Chaff Man.

Circus began to bark frantically. "What is it, little fella?" Ben asked, adding, "Hey, guys, smells funky back here. It's making the dog antsy."

"Must be Monty," Mackie said.

"That's not very nice," Zyla said.

"Not Son Monty," Mackie informed them. "The other one."

"What do you mean?" Ben asked, his voice rising in panic.

"We brought Monty along," Mackie said. "Pythons are human too; they get lonely. He's in that crate behind you, Ben. The one with the big holes. Don't worry. Monty wouldn't hurt a fly, would he, Monty? A mouse maybe, or a nice juicy rat, or a bird or pig, if the fancy takes him. . . ."

Ben leapt up and crashed the top of his head into the roof of the vehicle. Circus went crazy, yapping so hard he almost jumped out of Monty's arms.

"*Hey!*" Otto yelled. "Watch it back there!"

Ben was beside himself. "Are you telling me there's a goddam *python* back here? I *hate* snakes! Hate 'em worse than anything!" Frantic, he attempted to climb over into the seat in front.

The commotion made Afarra stir. She called out for Circus.

Sheepishly, Ben came to his senses. He apologized to her and sat back down in the back, as far from Serpent Monty as he could manage. Meanwhile, Son Monty leaned over and placed the Pomeranian gently on Afarra's chest. Instantly, the dog stopped yapping. Afarra calmed down too as he nestled into a sleeping position in the crook of her arm.

"Guess we'll have a lot of news for Ji-ji when she gets back," Zyla said.

"Ji-ji," Afarra murmured. "Elly. . . . . *Fly!*"

"She'll fly, Afarra," Zyla said. "Right back here to D.C. when she hears we've found you."

"Well," Lucky said, "looks like we've got ourselves a story with a happy ending for once."

"We should call it 'Lucky Saves the Day,'" Ben said.

Mackie objected. Lucky prepared for the worst, but he soon realized he shouldn't have worried when Mackie said, "We should call it 'Lucky *and* Otto Save the Day.'" Otto beamed.

"Not bad," Lucky said. "But I think we should call it 'Monty's Python and the Flying Circus.'" He waited for them to applaud. Instead, they looked at him blankly.

"Don't tell me you've never heard of *Monty Python?*"

Ben and Otto shrugged. Zyla shook her head. Monty uttered something resembling a syllable. Lucky couldn't believe it.

"How's that even possible? It's a *classic,* for god's sake! Coach Mackie, tell me you've seen it."

"Are you talking about that silly English show from the Age of Plenty?" Mackie asked. "They're not my cup of tea. Mindless pranksters arguing over a dead parrot, singing about ham and lumberjacks when they should be counting their lucky stars that they don't have to live in the poor excuse of a world we live in now. Perhaps if they hadn't wasted so much time singing about ham and claiming dead parrots were alive, we wouldn't be in this bloody mess today."

"Spam," Lucky corrected her. "It's Spam. That's the whole point. It's a commentary on—"

"That's what I said, dear," Mackie insisted. "Not my cup of tea."

Otto demanded to know what was wrong with Spam.

Lucky moaned. "You're a lost cause. Every one of you. Not you, Afarra," he added. "You're the exception that proves the rule." She smiled at him and cuddled Circus, who slept soundly.

A short while later, after they'd hurried Afarra into Doc Riff's clinic, Zyla pulled Lucky aside and said, "You were wonderful back there. You really did save the day. I never would've been able to hold on to her. No one deserves more luck than Afarra does. Thank you for giving it to her."

Lucky, who didn't trust himself to say anything coherent in response, settled for a nod.

||||||||||||||

Having assigned raiders and Invisible Men who would remain behind at the arsenal with the seeds they'd attempted to liberate, Charra, Heather and Raphael, with a small group of six handpicked followers, assembled near one of the entrances to the arsenal, well aware of the danger ahead. Ji-ji's side hurt. Whatever Raphael had used to numb it had worn off. A short while ago, she'd pleaded with him for another shot. He'd given it to her against his better judgment. She hoped it worked fast.

Charra hadn't ordered the diviner to accompany them, but Emmeline had lobbied hard to be included. "Dregulahmo would want me to go with Ji-ji," the diviner said. "He was my friend, you see. Not simply a fellow Friend of Freedom, my *friend*." Though Marcus didn't make his position known either way, Aisha had spoken up for Emmeline. Said there weren't many females of any color who had the kind of guts Emmeline had. "Would be disrespectful to leave her behind," she asserted. Charra didn't argue. Ji-ji, still reeling from the horrors she'd seen but remembering her manners, thanked Diviner Shadowbrook for her courage.

When they opened the door, an eerie fog greeted them.

Raphael chuckled and said, "Guess God's on our side this morning, Marcus. Looks like the steaders've got themselves a problem."

Charra wasn't nearly as sanguine about the fog as her ally was. "They can't see us, but we can't see them either."

Aisha was leery too: "We could lose each other in this fog, or whatever this is."

"What you saying, Ai?" Charra asked. "You don't think it's natural?"

"Beats me," Aisha replied. "Ain't seen much that's natural today. Could be it's another trap. You ever seen fog this thick on the coast, Charra? I ain't. They burn a lot o' coal round here?"

Charra said they used to. The arsenal sometimes spewed out black smoke too . . . and ash. Ji-ji didn't want to think about what that could mean.

Heather asked Charra if she thought the fog would be as thick up by the fry-fence.

"Could be. Or it could be ditch fog. It's low-lying an' damp here. Guess we'll find out."

"Weapons drawn," Raphael ordered, his voice steady. "Let's try not to shoot each other."

Ji-ji shivered. The thick fog spooked her. She remembered what her mam used to say about the area of the planting near Execution Circle—that Toteppi believed the roaming spirits of the Dimmer-dead manifested themselves as fog. She said this was why the seeds' name for Execution Circle was Dimmers Ditch, and the Dell was known as the Doom Dell. "There are not many Toteppi left in this world," Silapu used to say, "yet our stories and our spirits are too stubborn to die." As her offspring were snatched from her one by one,

Silapu's hope waned and she stopped telling the old stories. "The planting system was a fatal uprooting," she'd mutter into her mug of whiskey. "Without roots to feed them, bodies die."

Charra ordered everyone to stay alert. "The bastards can't see us, but they sure as hell can hear us," she warned. "You ready, Beany?" she asked. Ji-ji nodded. "Okay then. Stay close together. Ji-ji, Marcus, Emmeline, an' me know this planting, so we'll lead the way. Don't make a sound."

The fog didn't disappear as they climbed out of the low-lying section of the Dell. If anything, it got thicker, so thick Ji-ji imagined she could grab a handful and devour it like cotton candy.

They walked forward together. Charra glanced at her compass, but Ji-ji didn't need one. She overlaid the terrain onto what she recalled of Lotter's security maps. Although they were traversing the restricted zone and following forbidden paths, she felt confident of her location and the distance to the fry-fence. Marcus walked on her left side, Charra on her right. Emmeline was on Marcus' other side. Aisha, determined not to lose sight of her charge, stepped on Ji-ji's heels several times.

"You think you can do it?" Marcus asked her.

"Do what?" Ji-ji asked.

"Fly in this."

It hadn't occurred to her how much trickier it would be than flying in clear weather. "I think so," she said, reluctant to admit his question had thrown her. "Just gotta get over the fence is all. I can travel on foot after that."

Problem was, the fog robbed her of her takeoff capability. No way she could sprint and flap if she couldn't see what was ahead, which meant she would have no choice but to elevate from a standstill, something she'd done once only at the Friends' meeting, and not deliberately either. This was never going to be easy; now it looked close to impossible. She just had to hope the fog wasn't as dense up by the fry-fence.

Raphael had taken off one of the cross-body leather satchels he carried. He'd put Heather's caller and the camera's flash drive in there. Ji-ji had added Petrus' gun to the mix, and Aisha had undone the sheathed knife strapped to her thigh and slipped it in with the rest, warning her it was sharp enough to slice her fingers off. "Curved, for gutting." Ji-ji had wanted to tell the veteran raider she wasn't good at gutting, not even fish. Instead she said, "Thank you, Miss Ai," and left it at that.

By Ji-ji's calculation, they were only a couple of hundred yards from the fry-fence when they heard the screams in the distance.

"It's coming from the Circle!" Emmeline cried. "What are they doing down there?"

The screams turned into shrieks of terror. Agonized cries came at them through the fog.

"We should go help!" Ji-ji cried.

"We will," Charra promised. "*After* we see you over the fence."

The shrieks got louder as they forged ahead. Pretty soon, Emmeline couldn't keep up.

"The diviner's fallen behind," Ji-ji said to Marcus. "You gonna help her?" Marcus didn't answer. Didn't need to. He hadn't slowed down one bit. Ji-ji tried again: "If they catch her, they'll pyre her. They know she's a traitor now."

"It was her choice to help us," Marcus said. "No one made her do it." As far as Ji-ji could tell, he didn't look back once, not that he would have been able to see the diviner if he did.

When they were no more than a few yards away from it, they spied the vague outline of the fence. Ji-ji tripped. Fell flat on her face. Aisha and Marcus bent down to help her, but not before she caught sight of what she'd stumbled over: one of the fallen seeds. Must've been thrown several yards from the fence when he was electrocuted, or maybe he was still alive and tried to crawl to safety in the dark. The seed's one remaining eye was open. *He must've fallen forward into the fence before falling backward,* she thought, with surprising clarity. *That's why his face is burned up.* She tried to feel sorry for him, but after what she'd seen in the arsenal, she couldn't make room for more pity.

Marcus picked her up and planted her on her feet. Her back was to the thirty-foot fence. She heard its lethal buzz behind her. To her relief, the fog had lifted a little up here. She looked around for steaders, but they must all have gone down to Execution Circle, where Sylvie and the viewing coops were. More shrieks and screams came from there. Men yelling. Gunshots. More yelling.

Someone was racing up the hill toward them! They heard huffing and puffing and drew their weapons as a huge, dark, misshapen figure emerged from the fog!

Ji-ji ran toward him, crying out as loudly as she dared, "*Don't shoot!*"

Laughing Tree—a boy in one arm and a girl in the other, and a third seedling clinging to his massive back—pulled up when he saw her. "Thought you were dead!" he cried. Ji-ji scooped the seedling off his back and they hurried up the hill together. Tree looked around and saw faces he recognized, Marcus and Aisha among them. "Thought you were all dead!"

Ji-ji wrapped her arms around him. "I'm so glad to see you!" she said.

Marcus ran up, took the girl from Tree's arms and slapped him on the back. "You seen Tiro or his family?" Ji-ji asked.

"'Fraid not," Tree replied, as he struggled to catch his breath. "Is the fence dead?"

"No," Charra said. "It's very much alive. Ji-ji's about to fly over it. Deliver a message for us."

"What message?" Tree asked. But there was no time to explain.

Raphael approached them, said to Tree, "Think the tide's turning back there?"

Tree, still breathing hard, said he doubted it. "We took cover in the Dell. Steaders appeared out of nowhere. Couldn't hold 'em off. Me and my group got herded into that amphitheater."

"How'd you escape?" Ji-ji asked.

"Wouldn't have, but then the man with the megaphone—"

"Williams," Ji-ji said. "Tiro's father-man."

"That's who the bastard was? Williams figures there's more seeds hiding under the penal tree, beneath the platform. They can't shoot at Sylvie to extract them cos she's sacred, so Williams orders his men to bang on the trunk. They were picking off the raiders and Invisibles when—" Tree broke off and looked around. "Weird," Tree said. "Fog's cleared up in the Circle. It's why we saw it when it fell. Hey, those aren't bodies, are they?"

"The fence went live earlier," Ji-ji told him, adding, "When what fell?"

"The biggest damn nest you ever saw! Thought it was a boulder. Thousands of killer bees! Huge to match the tree. In the melee, I tackled the guards, grabbed some seedlings an' ran."

Still breathing hard, Tree bent over to catch his breath. "Saw Plate back there. Warned me the fence was still buzzing. But I wasn't about to hang around with those killers—the bees or the steaders. Think they ambushed the rendezvous camp? Ink's there an' he—"

"*Ji-ji!*" Charra called. "There's not much time. Quick! They're *coming!*"

Her sister was right. Ji-ji heard it too. A vehicle roaring up the hill!

She'd taken her shirt off earlier and stuffed it into the bag. All she had under her cape was her flight bra and shorts so she could move Freely. Her wings would push the cape up round her neck when she flew, assuming they unfurled. She knew it wouldn't be safe on the Freedom side of the fence either. The steaders might be scouring the area in a hunt for raiders' vehicles. If she made it over the fence without getting fried like the other poor people all around them, she would be on her own in The Margins with snarlcats and stripers.

She focused, tried to unfurl. Nothing! Behind her, the vehicle roared up the hill, closer and closer. *It's only thirty feet, for god's sake,* she told herself. *You can do this!*

"What's wrong?" Charra asked her.

"I can't do it!" Ji-ji cried.

Charra stood with her back to the fence, facing Ji-ji and urging her on, so when she raised her gun, Ji-ji thought for a second she planned to make her elevate by force. But Charra wasn't aiming at her. Ji-ji turned to see that the truck had crested the hill. They'd run out of time!

The vehicle stopped. A creature got out of the passenger side and stumbled toward them. The driver was screaming bloody murder from inside the truck, flailing his arms around, but it was not him they were concerned about. The unnatural passenger staggered through the fog. His grotesque head, moving, pulsing! What was that? A Dimmer? A mutant? Buzzing! What the hell?

In a flash, Ji-ji knew what they were looking at. It wasn't a Dimmer. It wasn't a mutant. Drexler Williams, his head a nest for the outsized killer bees, lurched toward them!

Ji-ji stood beside Charra and raised Petrus' gun. "For Tiro and Uncle Dreg," she murmured.

"For Amadee and all the rest," Charra murmured back.

The sisters fired at the same time. Multiple shots to the head. Some of the killer bees took off; most didn't give a damn. Williams keeled over.

Shooting him was an act of mercy, but that wasn't why they did it. "We should've let the motherfucker writhe some more," Charra said.

Gingerly, so as not to disturb too many bees, Marcus and Raphael kicked the corpse away from where they were standing. It entered the fog and rolled down the hill.

Shrieks, screams! A frenzy of others rushing up the hill toward them!

Charra turned to Ji-ji and screamed, "Fly, Beany! *FLY!*"

Her sister's words surged through Ji-ji's body like ignition. She saw the word "*FLY!*" spiral out from Charra's mouth, heard it come back to her like a boomerang in another person's voice—Afarra's?—then spiral up and out. Not a single voice anymore, a chorus of voices urged her to soar!

A surge across her back as the twin impossibilities unfurled. She turned her legs into a spring and leapt into the air! Up, up, until the buzz was gone and all she could hear was chorus!

She flew over the fence with ease, rose some more, and emerged suddenly above the fog. The clarity of the world she entered up above the fog stunned her.

Without looking back, she beat a path east toward the risen sun.

|||||||||||||||

She was heading in the wrong direction. They'd told her to deliver the evidence. She'd done what they asked her to do, sort of. Handed it over to Petra and

Boston, two raiders Feral swore he would trust with his life. Along with an armed guard Feral assigned them, the raiders would travel up to D.C. and hand the evidence over to Edelmann and Lowenstein.

"She wouldn't want you to do this," Feral told her again. "She'll be mad as hell. At me."

He poked his hand out of the rolled-down window of the truck and flicked a column of ash off his cigarette. His truck reeked of smoke. His curly salt-and-pepper hair ruffled only slightly in the stiff breeze their speed created. Ji-ji couldn't decide if he was always a terrible driver or if today was the exception. He shifted in his seat, complained again about his bony butt.

"Forgot my donut," he said. "A buttless guy like me needs a donut. . . . This is madness."

"I need to go back," Ji-ji told him for the umpteenth time. "Tiro an' his family, Charra, Tree—they're all trapped there. I couldn't live with myself if I didn't try an' help them."

"You did already," Feral insisted. "Those images could change everything for us."

"Only if they survive to see it make a difference. Besides, I can fly over the fence."

"Get shot at like a clay pigeon while you're doing it too."

Feral launched a spit wad out of the window, a gesture of disgust to make his objection more emphatic. He gave her the side-eye as he sucked on his cigarette. She looked away.

She hadn't liked the lieutenant much when she first met him, but he'd grown on her. Increasingly, she'd understood that, like Heather, Feral tried to guide Charra away from recklessness. He'd asked her several times how Plato You-turn had fared. The two men were much closer than she realized, like brothers almost. All she could relay was what Laughing Tree had told her. It wasn't much. Feral had shaken his head, said, "Plato's been hanging out with that Marcus Aurelius too much for my liking. Fuckin Invisible Men . . . Jury's out on 'em far as I'm concerned. Led us into a fuckin trap, sounds like."

Ji-ji didn't point out that Charra was the one who'd insisted they leave early, nor did she mention that she herself was equally responsible. Charra's refusal to wait for him had hurt Feral deeply, but he placed all the blame on their new allies.

Feral reserved the brunt of his ire for Raphael. "Man's a con artist," he said. "Smoke an' mirrors." It was time, once again, to remind Ji-ji she was heading in the wrong direction. "You're injured. We need to get you to the Dream. I can transfer you to one of the trucks so you can head east. She wouldn't want you risking—"

She cut in: "You trust 'em, right? The ones we gave the footage an' photos to?"

"How many times you plan to ask me that?" Feral saw how upset she was and relented. "Don't worry. They'll deliver it safely. But no man can predict the future, not even that wizard of yours, so I made two copies for insurance." He reached into his shirt pocket and handed her a thumb drive. "Which means we got two insurance policies. I got one, you got one. We're fuckin golden."

Golden, Ji-ji thought. Only they weren't. The only person Ji-ji knew was safe was Ink. After Ji-ji made it to the rendezvous camp, Ink had been loaded into a van heading back to D.C. He would wait for Tree at Ben and Germaine's. Ji-ji consoled herself with the idea that if Tree hadn't made it, at least his adopted son would be among friends.

She still couldn't believe she'd pulled off her escape. Less than a mile from the planting the fog below her had ended abruptly, as if it had crashed into some invisible wall. As she anticipated, she hadn't had the strength to fly for long. Being able to land quickly saved her.

She'd run the rest of the way and come across the escape vehicles Charra had ordered to lie in wait for their return a few miles from the planting. Exhausted and giddy with relief that her sister had left trucks and raiders close by, Ji-ji had hitched a ride back to the rendezvous camp, where a handful of raiders stayed behind to guard the remaining vehicles. From there, Ji-ji had climbed into another vehicle and headed back to D.C. She was shocked when, after some time on the road, she'd encountered Feral, leading his contingent on a roundabout route to Planting 437 to avoid the floodwaters. In an expletive-laden rant, Feral had told her he'd made it up from the Madlands to Mount Airy in record time by breaking every speed limit there was and driving like a man on fire, only to be forced to deviate from his route again to avoid washed-out secondary roads and head for a while in the wrong fuckin direction before being able to loop around and get back on track. Which explained why, for this last part of the worst fuckin journey he'd made in his entire life, he was on a road heading southwest to the planting instead of the more direct route heading northwest.

As fast as she could, Ji-ji had described the ambush and the horrific scenes in Murder Mouth. And then she'd said something that surprised her as much as it surprised him. She wasn't heading up to D.C.; she was heading back to Planting 437 with him. Utterly exasperated, Feral told her she could do whatever she wanted as long as she kept her trap shut and didn't delay them anymore. Said he didn't give a fuck if she really had flown over some fuckin fence or if she wanted to fly back over it for that matter. All he cared about was getting to the planting they never would've raided in the first place if she hadn't shown up to torment her sister and make Charra feel guilty as shit, cos that's what sisters did to each other. Ji-ji had handed off the evidence to the two raiders Feral said were trustworthy and climbed into Feral's truck. They'd been arguing about her crazyass decision ever since.

The closer they got to the planting, the more taciturn Feral became. He swore under his breath, and sucked down one cigarette after another.

They were about twenty-five miles from the planting on one of the backwoods trails when a convoy approached. Feral recognized them at once: trucks from Charra's second contingent.

Feral, and the handful of drivers who'd managed to keep up with him, pulled over.

Ji-ji thrust open the door and jumped out before the truck stopped. Feral cussed her out and ran after her. Terrified, Ji-ji sprinted from vehicle to vehicle calling Tiro's name, Charra's, Zaini's and Laughing Tree's. Many in the trucks were badly wounded.

Marcus jumped down from the bed of a truck and strode toward her. "What the hell?" he yelled. "She ordered you to get that evidence to the Dream!"

If he hadn't looked as if he'd walked through a firestorm, Ji-ji would have lit into him. As it was, she hurriedly explained that Feral had handed off the evidence to trusted raiders Petra and Boston. Feral came up behind her and assured Marcus the footage would reach D.C.

"Is Tiro with you?" Ji-ji asked. She could barely get the words out. "What about Charra?"

"Tiro's way back at the end of the convoy," Marcus said.

"No fuckin way this is everyone," Feral said. Marcus couldn't look at him.

Ji-ji asked again: "You seen Charra?"

"She's injured." Marcus gestured to a van a couple of vehicles down, grabbed hold of Ji-ji's arm before she could rush over there. "It's bad," he warned her.

Ji-ji raced to the vehicle with Feral and Marcus. "Make way for the commander's sister!" Feral cried, as they pushed through a group of raiders who'd gathered there. She clambered up into the back of the van, which was set up like an ambulance. Feral climbed in after her. A covered corpse occupied the stretcher on the right. On the left, Charra. Heather and a medic bent over her.

Heather looked up. "I'm sorry, Feral," she said. "Plate didn't make it." Ji-ji understood then that Plate was under the sheet on the right side of the van.

Feral made a sound in the back of his throat like someone choking and sank down next to his brother-friend's corpse.

Charra was barely conscious. Ji-ji took her hand. It was clammy. When she saw Ji-ji, Charra tried to sit up. Heather placed a hand on her shoulder to stop her. "The . . . footage," Charra said. Ji-ji tried to explain, but Charra drifted in and out of consciousness. Ji-ji asked Heather how bad it was.

"Bad," Heather said. "She got shot in the side and the back. She didn't stop fighting, Ji-ji. We're headed for Richmond. There's a surgeon there I trust."

"It's not safe in Richmond," Feral told her.

Heather turned on him: "And what do you suggest? She won't make it to the Dream. And she sure as hell won't make it to Turnabout."

"All right," Feral said. Ji-ji saw how much it cost him not to break down. "I'll accompany you. An' I'll bring some raiders with me to keep you safe."

Marcus stood at the open back door of the van. He looked dazed, lost. "It was a massacre," he said. "Emmeline found a way into the lookout tower when the chaos hit with the bees. Rerouted the comm and opened the Main Gate. We got out by the skin of our teeth. We'd all be dead otherwise."

"Is Emmeline with you?" Ji-ji asked.

Meat walked up and stood beside Marcus. "Old lady didn't make it," he said.

"Sounds like you don't give a damn," Ji-ji shot back.

"Looks like you don't either," he said. "Thought they loaded the homing pigeon up with all kinds o' shit and told you to head to D.C. And yet, here you are, Mutant."

Marcus took hold of Meat by the collar and lifted him off his feet. He slammed him up against the vehicle. "Shut the fuck up!" Marcus said. "That's the commander's sister you're bad-mouthing!"

Heather pleaded from the vehicle: "We got to get Charra to a doctor!"

Marcus flung Meat to the ground.

Feral offered to lead the van to Richmond. "You'll have to step on it to keep up. You wanna ride with me, Ji-ji?"

She shook her head. "I gotta get to D.C. Be a witness like she asked me. I'll ride with Tiro."

"*Charra!*" Heather cried. Charra coughed up so much blood it spilled over Heather's cupped hands. Heather looked at the medic. He shook his head.

Charra gestured to Ji-ji, whispered to her to come closer. Ji-ji leaned in close.

"I got a gift for you, Beany," Charra said, in a voice so much like her old one it burned Ji-ji to the bone. "Show her, Heather."

Heather reached into a bag and pulled out an envelope. "It's signed," Charra said. "Heather an' Feral are witnesses. It's yours now. Trust this one," she looked at Heather, "she's a good woman. Better than I deserved. An' trust Feral too. . . . Open it." Ji-ji opened the envelope. Inside was a letter. "I bequeathed it to you," Charra whispered. "Signed it before we left, just in case."

Ji-ji began to tell Charra she didn't want it, but Heather touched her arm to stop her.

"Turnabout is yours now," Charra said. "They'll follow you like they followed me. . . . Give her back the quilt, Heather. She needs to . . . hang on to that."

Heather couldn't speak, so she simply nodded.

Charra tried to say something else. Her voice was so faint Ji-ji had to close the gap between them to a few inches. "Remember . . . remember what I told you after Luvlydoll died?"

"I remember," Ji-ji said. "Every word."

"I meant it." Charra sucked in some breath. "An' I would never . . . have outed you to those bastards," she said. "One more thing you . . . gotta promise me." Ji-ji nodded. "Kill him. Kill Lotter. You see what he is now. Back there at . . . Murder Mouth . . . that was all *him*. Promise me."

"I promise," Ji-ji said, without hesitation.

Charra stared into her eyes. Ji-ji waited for her to blink. When she didn't, Ji-ji kissed first one eye, then the other. A wail went up from those assembled near the van. Raiders wept like children. Heather pulled Charra toward her and let out a yell of rage and anguish. Feral fell to his knees and began to pray. Dazed, Ji-ji stumbled out of the vehicle. Charra's grieving followers stepped aside for her. She heard some of them address her as "Commander." Marcus was waiting for her.

"Listen," he said. "I'm sorry, Ji-ji. I need to tell you something 'bout Tiro an' his—"

Ji-ji shoved Marcus aside and sprinted toward the back of the convoy. Tiro had to be okay. He *had* to be. She passed Tree, who sat in a truck bed with the seedlings he'd saved, his arm in a makeshift sling. He'd made it out. "You seen the little guy?" Tree called out. Her mind wouldn't work. She didn't know who he meant at first. Then she understood. "Ink's fine," she called back. "Headed to the Dream. He'll be at Ben an' Germaine's. Gotta find Tiro." She didn't tell him her sister was dead. If she didn't say it, it hadn't happened.

Up ahead, almost at the end of the convoy, she saw Tiro step out of a van. He was okay!

She ran to him and flung herself into his arms. He buried his head in her shoulder. After a few seconds, without saying a word, he walked her over to the van he was riding in. Bromadu was fast asleep in the front passenger seat, his mouth covered in chocolate. Ji-ji smiled with relief when she saw him. Tiro slid the van's side door open. In the back, Zaini held Eeyatho in her lap. She rocked him like a cradle. If you didn't look closely, you'd never know he wasn't sleeping.

Zaini looked up and saw Ji-ji. "Yatho stayed quiet," she said, "like we told him to—right, Tiro? Even at the end, he didn't make a sound."

She rocked her offspring in her arms and sang him to sleep, as if all he had ever been and all he would ever be was her baby.

28 UNDER THE COVER OF PLAIN SIGHT

On the journey back to D.C. in the raider van with Tiro and his family, no one spoke much. The driver of the van, a wiry African American/Asian American raider named Richard Upturn, had a compassionate smile and reticent manner. Feral had taken care to assign a driver who would handle the situation with sensitivity, one who could also handle the treacherous back roads to D.C. Ji-ji had no idea how Richard stayed awake. He pulled over once about halfway through the journey, took a two-hour nap, then floored it again. Apart from the nap, he stopped only to pee.

Tiro offered to drive, but everyone, including Tiro, knew it was a bad idea. Behind them, Marcus and Laughing Tree struggled to keep up in the Dreamfleet's spluttering van.

Before they set out, Ji-ji had asked Zaini's permission to ride with them. Zaini had said yes, though Ji-ji suspected she'd barely heard her. Tiro rode in the first row of passenger seats with Bromadu, who wouldn't let go of his hand. Ji-ji rode in the row behind them, and Zaini rode in the last row of seats. Said she wanted to reach behind her to make sure Yatho wasn't afraid.

In the back of the van, the boy lay in his makeshift shroud. It had taken a while to convince Zaini to let them wrap him in an improvised body bag, which consisted of an old blanket and some tarp. Twice during the first hour, Zaini insisted Tiro check to see if his little brother's breathing had spontaneously started up again. "Dregulahmo wouldn't let me lose another of my boys," she insisted. "He'll wake up. You'll see."

Of all the dead she'd seen from the raid, the three Ji-ji thought about most were Eeyatho, Charra, and her mam. The idea that Lotter had hoarded Silapu away in a drawer so he could slide her in and out whenever he wanted repulsed her. Even in death, her mam couldn't escape Arundale Lotter's need to possess her.

Ji-ji realized too late that she and Charra should have removed their mother from the drawer and burned her body to ash. She can't imagine why they didn't.

To keep herself from listening to the way a boy's corpse sounded each time they hit a pothole (*thump, thump*), Ji-ji tried to figure out what to do with the grief rampaging through her body. Too tired to wage war with it, she soon gave up and let it run amok.

At one point, Marcus came up to their van while Richard was taking a piss. Marcus poked his head through the window and avoided looking at the passengers. Directed his comments at the steering wheel instead. He said that Raphael, who had survived the attack, had ordered him to return to the Dream and rejoin the fleet, so that's what he planned to do. Tiro didn't react to the news. "Don't say a word to the Dreamfleet or anyone else about the Invisible Men," Marcus instructed, as if they were all planning to turn parrot.

The next thing Ji-ji knew, Richard Upturn was back in the driver's seat and they were hurtling through the rain. She didn't know if she'd fallen asleep or if she'd been awake the whole time. A short time later, as she climbed back into the van following a pit stop, Richard asked if she was in pain. Thinking he meant the purple pain of grief, she nodded. But he meant the ugly pain of a wound. She was bleeding. He tended to her, gave her a killer. In spite of the bumpy ride, she slept a lot after that.

They reached the city, took the toll road for the last few miles. First time she'd seen Dream Corridor, the main artery leading from the west into the city, since they ran along it during the Freedom Race. Both vehicles were waved through the Main Gate after the guard recognized the fly-boys. Ji-ji could have sworn she saw one of the gate operators give Richard an odd handshake. It made sense that the raiders would have some friends (without the capital letter) on the inside. Though Ji-ji half expected him to, the guards didn't ask them why they all looked like zombies.

When the two vehicles pulled up outside a drab-looking building, the Friends of Freedom hurried out to greet them. Roughly a year and a half ago, Zyla had escorted Ji-ji and Afarra back to her apartment after their victory in the Freedom Race and welcomed them into the ramshackle edifice that served as the Friends' unofficial headquarters. And now, here Ji-ji was back here again, without Afarra and with so many others gone.

Marcus or Tree must've thought to call ahead, cos the Friends already knew how disastrous the raid had been. Ben, outside in the rain, rapped on the window to get Tiro's attention. Ji-ji had been eager for the trip to end, but now she discovered she'd forgotten how to exit the van. Someone had tipped her up and poured out the contents—that's what it felt like anyway.

Tiro climbed out and rushed round to the back of the van. He opened the doors and reached for the small bagged body. Monty and Otto told him not to worry, they would take care of everything. Otto lifted the corpse from the van while Monty went ahead to clear a path for him. Ben put his arm around Tiro's shoulders, and Bromadu rushed up to his elder brother and held on to him like someone drowning. Absentmindedly, Tiro patted Broma's head. Ben led them both inside.

Germaine and Mackie helped Zaini out of the van, while Lucky climbed in beside Ji-ji and took her hand. Instinctively, her friend seemed to know she was scared to move, afraid she would shatter like glass. Lucky helped her out of the van. Once outside, he slipped her hand into the crook of his arm and grasped it firmly. In the lobby of the building, at the foot of the stairs, they passed Tiro, Bromadu and Ben, who'd been joined by Marcus and Tree. Tiro yelled at his fly partner. Ji-ji wished she could yell at someone too, but she lacked the energy to do it.

Lucky probably broke the news about Afarra before they ascended the stairs to the second floor, but it didn't register. Ji-ji screamed when Afarra dashed out of Zyla's apartment and flung her arms around her. More than anything, Ji-ji wanted to hug her. But her arms refused to comply, so she simply stood there like a statue and let Afarra hold her.

Tiro came up the stairs with Bromadu's arms still tight around his waist. He didn't recognize Afarra for a moment, then he did. "I'm sorry!" Tiro sobbed into Afarra's shoulder.

"No sorrys," Afarra said, as she patted his back with a heavily bandaged hand.

After Tiro promised to catch up with Afarra later tomorrow—or, rather, later today—he accompanied Zaini and Bromadu across the hall into Ben and Germaine's apartment.

Ji-ji panicked. She couldn't figure out where Otto and Monty had taken the corpse. She hadn't kept her eye on him! Why hadn't she done that one small favor? "We've lost him!" she cried.

"It's okay," Lucky said, guessing what she meant. "Otto and Monty will take care of him."

Ink's ecstatic cries came to them as Laughing Tree entered Ben and Germaine's apartment. "I knew you'd come back!" Ji-ji pictured the big man as he charged up to the fry-fence through the fog with seedlings in both arms and another hanging on to his back. Like Uncle Dreg taught her, she'd conjured up "a moment of translation," a way to translate suffering into something bearable.

Afarra took Ji-ji's head in her hands and read her face. She seemed to see all the terrible things Ji-ji had seen. Ji-ji saw Afarra's pain too, sensed what the executioner had done to her, noticed her bandaged hand. Someone (Zyla? Germaine?) must have braided her hair. Not one braid was undone. Finding Afarra alive was so far beyond what she'd imagined would await her in the Dream that Ji-ji couldn't process it.

As Zyla ushered them into the apartment, Ji-ji said, "Chaff Man and Sloppy didn't kill you."

"I escaped with Circus. He is my rescue." Sometimes Afarra's voice sounded like Afarra's old voice; at other times, it sounded older. *Pain is a bully,* Ji-ji thought. *It grows girls up by force.*

Afarra continued: "Then I live beside the Dreamer, who is very pale like the moon. I am thinking they are forgetting he was Black. But Zyla says no. They knew all along. Did you find Fuzzy and Merrywinkle? I hope they are fine in the Dream like us. The python is very big and that is a problem for Ben but not for me cos animals are my favorite. Lucky an' Ben an' Zyla are finding me in the nest. Circus is falling down and down but Otto is holding the net an' he bounces up and up."

"Circus, she means," Lucky said. "He did the bouncing. Not Otto."

"We are locking him in the bathroom," Afarra said. "Listen."

"Circus, not Otto," Lucky said.

Ji-ji could hear whimpers as the dog tried to scratch his way out of prison. *It's futile,* Ji-ji thought. *Nothing an' no one escapes. May as well give up.*

"You are very tired," Afarra said. "Me too. Time for sleep."

"The photos!" Ji-ji exclaimed. She grabbed Lucky's arm. "The video!"

"It's okay, Ji-ji," Zyla said. "The raiders delivered those to Abby and Ezra. They're working on a story. They need to verify the evidence. They've asked to speak with you, but we can talk about that later. You look exhausted."

"They slaughtered us," Ji-ji told them. "Fried us like meat. Turned on the fence while folks were climbing. Lotter kept her in Murder Mouth. Frozen or something."

"Who?" Zyla asked.

"Mam," Ji-ji said. "My mam . . . Charra's too. Charra's dead. It's not a lie this time. I saw it."

Zyla said, "We know. Marcus called ahead."

Afarra led her into her old room, which Zyla had prepared for her. The same lumpy double bed, minus Silapu's quilt. The same chair Tiro sat in when he kept vigil during her transformation. There were flowers on a side table. Daisies. Ji-ji loved daisies, but tonight their freshness hurt her.

Doc Riff appeared out of nowhere. He wore his black hair loose around his shoulders. It had streaks of gray in it. When did that happen? Like Afarra, he'd speed-aged. If she had a mirror, she would probably see that she had too. Time was running a marathon, dragging them all along by the hair. In the van, on one of the few occasions she got up the guts to say something, she told them about Father-Man Williams. "Me and Charra killed him," she'd said, bluntly. Either they hadn't heard her, or they hadn't been able to absorb the information cos they were up to their eyes in misery, or everything paled in comparison to the indisputable truth of the body in the back.

Outside in the hallway, through the paper-thin walls, Ji-ji heard Germaine call down to Marcus. *"Marcus!* We need to speak with you."

Marcus shouted up: "Gotta deliver the fleet van."

"It's four A.M.," Germaine said. "Get your ass back up here! You've got a shitload of explaining to do." Then Zyla must've closed the door to her apartment cos the voices disappeared.

Doc Riff was speaking. Ji-ji tried to pay attention. Doctors expected you to do that.

"Marcus said you were injured." Ji-ji couldn't immediately recall if that was true, but the doc told her not to worry. She was safe now, he said. A lie of course, but she liked the way he said it.

"You left the 437th," she said to him, in an accusatory tone. An odd thing to say cos he'd left at roughly the same time she had many months ago and it had never bothered her till tonight.

Doc Riff gave an answer she wasn't expecting. "I had to leave. I'd seen too much. It began to make me impervious to suffering. Fatal for a physician. I would've killed someone if I'd stayed. I like to think it would've been a father-man, but I suspect I would've killed myself in the end."

Ji-ji understood. "We killed Drexler Williams. Charra an' me. Together."

"Good," Doc Riff said. "He was a sadistic sonuvabitch who had it coming."

"Yeah," Ji-ji agreed. "Sylvie's killers got to him first. Me an' Charra finished him off. I flew over the fence where the bodies were lying. Think you can revive Eeyatho? Think it's too late?"

"I need to examine you, Ji-ji," Riff said. "It's okay. I won't hurt you."

"You can't hurt me. It's excised."

"What is?" Zyla asked her.

"Everything," she replied.

Afarra acted as interpreter: "She's being *Not Here, Not Now,* but she'll be back."

Ji-ji looked around for Tiro. She, Afarra, and Tiro had been together in this room when the miracle happened. Urgently, she wanted them to be together again in case another miracle was on the horizon (namely, Eeyatho's resurrection). It couldn't come to pass unless the three of them were present. All seeds knew wishes didn't come true in real life hardly ever. But Afarra was here beside her, and that was a miracle. And the Purple Tears on her back worked, and that was a miracle too.

After Doc Riff left and they'd climbed into bed together, Ji-ji and Afarra heard the friends arguing across the hallway in Ben and Germaine's apartment, Tree's voice so deep it would be jet-black if she drew it. They heard Zyla go across the hall and join them. Had she left them alone?

They heard a noise! They called out. A tap on the door. "It's only me," Lucky said. "Zyla asked me to keep an eye on things while they put Marcus through the wringer. You need anything?"

No, they replied. They didn't need anything.

Ji-ji heard Lucky return to the kitchen, heard him pour what sounded like liquor into a glass, heard the thump of something being laid down on the table. His gun?

"Chaff Man hurt you," Ji-ji stated. "I'll find him an' kill him. Sloppy too."

"I got good news," Afarra said. "Lucky says they got Chaff Man good in the goolies. He says Sloppy is gone. Could be Cherub killed her already."

Though Ji-ji didn't think Chaff Man's punishment was sufficient, she let it slide. "Zaini was the one left Uncle Dreg's Seeing Eyes for you. The Oz asked her to do it."

"Zaini?" Afarra thought for a moment. "I'm glad it was Zaini. She is a brave-good one."

"Yatho, Tiro's little brother, got killed."

"I know. He told me."

"Who? Zyla? Lucky? Eeyatho?"

"No. . . . Yes. After. But first *he* is telling me." She touched the necklace. "We see you fly, Elly. Fly up into the high cloudy. I tell you to do it."

Some of the battle fog lifted: "I heard your voice with Charra's," Ji-ji said, "telling me to fly."

"Oh yes, Elly. It was me saying it, over and over." Afarra's voice changed. Got old again. "I have bad news too. At the Aerie they scrubbed us away from your painting on the wall of my room. Before we get to the moon they did it."

Ji-ji couldn't be certain if it was the first time she'd ever heard Afarra weep, but she thought it might be. She cast her own sorrow aside and hugged the former outcast, a veteran when it came to calamity. Ji-ji told her not to worry. She would paint another mural, a better one. Then, before they could say another word to console each other, Sleep tiptoed in and kidnapped them both.

|||||||||||||||

The studio was little more than a warehouse in one of the older sections of the city not far from the Dream Revival District. They'd been there since late afternoon. The place was almost bare, apart from a few chairs arranged around a glass coffee table, some harsh studio lights, and a few cameras. Ji-ji had been mic'ed—what they called it when they attached a mic to your shirt.

"You don't have to speak into it like that," Chuck the producer said, when they asked her to do a mic test. "People don't want to see the top of your head." No, they didn't. They wanted to see the freakishness of her back. Chuck had a wisp of red hair on the top of his head and thickets of red hair elsewhere. Hair peeked out from his open shirt and sprouted from his arms and fingers. His hair was a real nice copper color, so she tried not to let it remind her of Chaff Man. Chuck was tense, which made her more nervous than ever.

Utilizing connections they had with producers in D.C. and the SuperStates, Alice and the Friends of Freedom had set this up. The show would be taped this afternoon and simulcast tomorrow evening to multiple media outlets in the SuperStates and Liberty Independents. It would coincide with the publication of an in-depth investigative piece in the *D.C. Independent*. All over the Disunited States, the lucky people with access to technology would watch the interview on their homescreens and on the fancy callers some people had in the SuperStates. The footage and photos would appear in what Chuck described as "a sickening montage of horror." Chuck took pains to assure her she wasn't part of the montage. She was "the frosting on the cake," he said.

Less than a month after her return to the City of Dreams, everything was happening at once. The reporters at the *Independent* had gathered supporting evidence, and the Friends had revealed to some trusted members of the Dreamer Coalition in the D.C. Congress what they'd discovered on the 437th. As a result, the investigation into the Dreamfleet had concluded faster than expected. The fleet's hiatus was over. Rumor had it that Redipp had been given his notice and would be stepping down within the next few days. Sean Corcoran was to be reinstated as wing commander. Mayor Yardley's hold on power was severely, if not fatally, diminished. He'd been forced to announce a mayoral election before the end of the year, way ahead of schedule.

To make up for the delayed season, an extra battle against the fleet's archrivals had been added to the schedule for tonight. The match sold out as soon as it was announced. The flyers' intensive training schedule had resumed two weeks ago. She hadn't seen Tiro since then, but Ben had promised to look out for him.

Today signaled the last time Ji-ji would be like everyone else. After the show aired and the story was published, she would forfeit her anonymity and privacy for the rest of her life and become public property. Her "reveal" would come toward the end of the show, after they'd discussed what went on in Murder Mouth. Only she couldn't call the arsenal by that name. "Better if viewers feel like they've reached their own conclusions," Chuck said. Ji-ji couldn't figure out how there could be more than one conclusion after people viewed the footage. "Video can be tampered with," Chuck told her, "which is why we need you. So people see the travesty for themselves."

According to the sheet they'd given her, toward the end of the show, after they'd spoken with her and the two famous journalists from the *Independent*, they would ask her (the Travesty) to go behind a huge screen and slip off her shirt. The lighting ensured that her silhouette would be visible so there'd be no cheating, Chuck said, a statement that struck her as ridiculous. She was supposed to emerge unfurled. They would ask her to elevate a few feet. After that, they would examine her back, panning over it slowly (she didn't know why they called it panning) from the roots to the tips of her Purple Tears. Only she couldn't call them that, Chuck said, cos it would be very confusing. "Not to seeds," she said. Chuck reminded her that seeds wouldn't be watching. She couldn't think of an argument to counter that. After she'd elevated, they would ask her to furl and unfurl and open and close her wing flaps. They hadn't rehearsed it cos it was a recording, and they could always do another "take."

They'd brought in a physician, a Dr. Oliver Bristol, who would talk about avian biology. They had a recording of Dr. Bristol explaining why it was impossible for humans to have functional wings. Ji-ji had seen it. He was utterly convincing. She had no idea why she could fly either. The doctor would join them "on set" and do an on-the-spot examination. Currently, he was in "a holding pattern" in the "green room," which wasn't green. The physician was meant to seal the deal, which was why it was critical he not see her beforehand. His shock had to be authentic. Ji-ji's level of discomfort had increased tenfold after she learned he was there. Finally, they would all "chat" some more in a "roundtable" (the coffee table was oblong) and then the "credits would roll." Ji-ji suspected the saying was similar to the phrase "heads will roll," and that some participants would be scolded (her? Dr. Bristol? the reporters?) for not performing as anticipated.

The woman interviewing her was called Maisy Millingford. Chuck said Maisy was a fixture in the Independent and SuperState markets, who polled extremely well when it came to trust. Ji-ji was to call her by her first name. Maisy was from the state of California in the Western SuperState. She had a very tanned skin, shiny legs, shinier lips, and hair that shone in the studio lights like thick strands of molten plastic. She tilted her head to the side compassionately and seemed to mean it—although she did that with everyone, so Ji-ji didn't put much faith in it.

Like Ji-ji, the reporters were decidedly uncomfortable in the studio. "We've got to do this shit," Abbyjill Edelmann said, "otherwise they won't believe us. And they've got to believe us, Ji-ji. If they don't, this shit'll continue for decades." Though she was a writer, Abby substituted the word "shit" for many other words, which made Ji-ji think about how much Lotter would detest her foul mouth, a trait he found especially loathsome in females.

Zyla had told her she didn't need to do anything she didn't want to do. "It's your choice," she said. "No one else's." Traumatized and guilt-ridden, Ji-ji knew her grasp on the rational world was impaired. Therefore, before she came to a final decision, she mulled it over with her hastily appointed Council of Confidants—Afarra, Lucky and Germaine. She would have talked it over with Tiro too, but he was back in the fleet with Marcus and Tree, who'd been persuaded by soon-to-be-reinstated Wing Commander Corcoran to return. The conclusion reached by the majority of her council members was the same as hers: she had no choice but to do it. "It'll drive you crazy," Germaine said, "if you thought there was something you could do to help and you didn't do it." *Maybe,* Ji-ji thought, worried it would drive her crazy either way. "Besides," Germaine added, "too many people know your secret, including Sloppy. Which means Lotter probably knows. Safer to be out in the open. If you're famous, the steaders will think twice before they come after you." Lucky told Ji-ji he also thought she should do the interview, though he insisted on accompanying her if she did, which was why he and Afarra were sitting in the shadows prepared to "storm to the rescue," as Lucky put it, if necessary. Their presence gave her courage, even though Afarra had advised against doing the show. She claimed that Uncle Dreg thought it was a bad idea too. After some mild interrogation, however, she admitted she'd lied. Uncle Dreg hadn't said a word about it.

They'd made Ji-ji up. She looked so unlike herself when they'd finished that she understood why they called it that, and why Camilla, the friendly African American woman who made you up, was called a makeup artist. The picture she'd painted on Ji-ji's face bore little resemblance to her everyday appearance. Not a portrait exactly but close. More like how Camilla wished Ji-ji could have looked if she were prettier. In the bathroom, Ji-ji wiped a lot of the crap off. When she returned, Camilla eyed her suspiciously.

There were only a few minutes to go before they were set to begin recording. No one had seen Ji-ji's back yet, and she got the sense that Maisy didn't believe it would amount to much.

They did a quick run-through of the video on the big screen behind them to check it was working. Camilla, pregnant, was in the throes of applying another layer to Maisy when the caged mother and child Ji-ji and the others had seen in Murder Mouth appeared on screen. Camilla screamed and dropped her magic tricks. She made it to one of the cameras and threw up. Chuck called in someone to clean up the mess and apply another coat to Miss Millingford, whose eyes were also glued to the big screen overhead. "Fuck me," Maisy murmured. "This shit's for real!" *Another female to drive Lotter crazy,* Ji-ji thought, buoyed by the idea.

In the time they had left before they began recording, Ji-ji asked Ezra and Abby the question that had tumbled around in her head for years: "Why don't the SuperStates help us? Do they know how bad it is in the Territories? I mean, before the Sequel an' the Secessionist Surge, this was one nation indivisible. Don't they want us to be unified again?"

Ezra rubbed his short beard. She could tell he took her question seriously. "Some of them know how bad it is in the Territories," Ezra said, "but if they acknowledge it, they need to do something about it, and doing something about it is risky."

Abby took over: "The SuperStates aren't nearly as stable or as technologically advanced as we think they are. It was chaos after the Sequel. The Second Dark Ages, some call it. The world's been devastated by climate catastrophes and pandemics. The secessionists were clever. They established plantings in the light of day, emphasized the fact that they employed White indentured labor along with imported labor from the Cradle. Every shitty colorist measure they introduced was couched in reasonable terms. The despicable agreement a handful of the Liberty Independents made with the Territories to truck their refugees to plantings tells you all you need to know about moral cowardice."

Ji-ji's frustration boiled over: "I'm *sick* of cowards! People've got to understand. It's *hell* on plantings. . . . How they treat us, it's . . ." She searched for a word. ". . . it's a cataclysm!"

"Yes," Abby agreed. "But sometimes it takes a shocking revelation to jerk people awake."

Abby leaned toward her. She looked to be in her late forties, with short hair that reminded Ji-ji of Zyla's. Her eyes were kind and very tired, another reason why Ji-ji trusted her. She didn't trust people who looked too rested. "Ezra and I have been working to help bring about a moment like this for twenty years. After they see these sickening pictures, no one can deny the evil of the planting system. From what we've heard, seeing your amazing back could make the truth undeniable. Remember, Ji-ji, you're not alone. We're sitting right here beside you with our swords at the ready." She took out a pen. "See?"

Ji-ji was about to ask another question when a Black man in a black fedora, an expensive black suit, and a shirt so white it made you want to bow, came tearing into the studio. He leapt onto the small platform and ripped the mic off Ji-ji's shirt. Lucky tore up behind him and shoved him aside.

"It's okay, Lucky!" Ji-ji cried. "I know him! He's my friend!"

Abby jumped up from her chair. "Amadeus!" she exclaimed. "What are you doing here?"

"It's a trap!" the Dream Master told them.

"What the hell are you talking about, man?" Chuck cried. "Thought this was airtight."

Amadeus spoke fast: "Within the hour, this place will be swarming with patrollers. They'll confiscate the footage and arrest everyone."

"That's absurd!" Chuck cried. "You've got your wires crossed, man. D.C.'s a Liberty—"

The Dream Master yelled at him: "You're not *listening*! They'll confiscate the video and—"

"Won't make a damn bit of difference," Ezra told him. "The editors made copies. Our story's due out tomorrow tonight. We ditch plan A and go for our plan to show it tonight instead."

Amadeus Nelson said, "The *Independent*'s being shut down as we speak. Computers and servers seized, editors and reporters close to the story placed under house arrest. Someone at the paper must be working on the inside. For Yardley probably."

"That's *impossible*!" Ezra said, punching numbers into his caller.

"Comm's down too in some places," Amadeus said. "Bastards have got something special planned for tonight."

Ezra looked up from his caller. His ashen face confirmed Amadeus' story. "We've got to get out of here," he said.

Maisy pelted them with objections: "No way! You're not leaving! It's the story of the *decade,* for fuck's sake! We can still broadcast the show live to—" At that moment, the power went out and the studio plunged into darkness.

Amadeus Nelson and Lucky wasted no time. They grabbed Ji-ji and Afarra and hustled them out through a side door to where Zyla waited in a getaway car. They bundled Ji-ji and Afarra into the back seat. Lucky climbed in next to Zyla, who asked Amadeus if he needed a ride.

"Wish I could take you up on that," he said. "Got a coop to fly and a car waiting to take me back there." He winked at her. "Flyers can't fly the coop without me, Zy."

"You think the match'll still be on?" Lucky asked him.

"I think that's the whole point," the Dream Master replied. "Be careful. Patrollers are out in force, sweeping up Papers and Maulers by the hundreds. Something else is going down tonight too. Looks like the Dream Coop battle is the bull's-eye."

"Tiro!" Ji-ji cried.

Amadeus bent down to see the girls in the backseat. "Don't worry, Just Jellybean. I'll do my damndest to get him out in one piece. Take care of the Wingchild, Miss Clobershay. Afarra, I'm glad they found you. Now, get going." Amadeus leaned inside the car and kissed Zyla on the cheek.

"Be careful," Zyla warned. "They'll be coming for you too."

"They'd never dare hurt the Dream Master. I'll give 'em nightmares if they try."

With one last glance in his direction, Zyla stepped on the gas and drove off.

"Where are we going?" Ji-ji asked, as they sped through dark streets.

"We're heading out of the city," Zyla replied. "We'll team up with our allies in the E.S.S. I've packed your possessions. Alice and Paul are waiting to meet up with us at the North Gate."

"We can't leave yet!" Ji-ji cried. "We gotta get Tiro first! And Tree an' Ink! An' Zaini an' Bromadu! Tulip too! An' Rosemary an' Thyme!"

Lucky gestured in frustration: "And Uncle Tom Cobley and all, right?"

"What's that even mean?" Ji-ji said. "Why don't you speak English?"

Lucky sighed. "I won't even begin to explain why that comment is so fucked up."

"I am the same like Elly," Afarra said, fearfully. "We get Tree too. With Ink."

"*Perfect!*" Lucky said, as he saw what lay up ahead. "So much for a hasty retreat."

A traffic jam of vehicles stretched for what seemed like miles. "Looks like everyone's heading to the coop. This road's all one-way too. Shit."

"What's that buzzing sound?" Ji-ji asked.

Lucky rolled down his window and peered up into the sky. "Buzzbuzz drones," he said. "Bet they've got that recognition protocol. Keep your heads inside the car."

"Let's try this side street," Zyla said. "You strapped in, girls?"

She took the turn at a clip and tried to find a new route. Every road in the area appeared to be one-way, and every one of them headed toward the Dream Revival District and the Dream Coop.

"You see this, Zy?" Lucky said.

"Oh yes," Zyla replied. "I see it."

Snaking along the city streets were pedestrians. Many were Districters, many more weren't. In the midst of the locals, bearded steaders chanted for their team. "*AR-MIS-TICE!*" they yelled, as they raised clenched fists in the night air. Seemingly, just for the hell of it, a steader with a stick banged on vehicles' hoods as he strolled by dressed in his team's red and white colors. "*Hell's Yells Forever!*" he yelled. As he approached, Ji-ji saw Lucky reach for his gun.

"Keep the windows rolled up," Zyla instructed. "Ji-ji, Afarra, scoot down in the back so this moron up ahead can't see you. Whether we like it or not, we're headed to the coop."

||||||||||||||

Zyla, Lucky, Ji-ji and Afarra abandoned the car on one of the side streets near the arena and traversed the final quarter mile on foot. Walking among thousands of jostling fans, many of whom were steaders, was unnerving. Yet raucous though they were, the steaders kept themselves to themselves. No jeering at the Districters and former seeds, no attempt to start a fight, relatively little open carry. Ji-ji wanted to feel reassured, but the size and scale of this invasion dwarfed the one at the museum. Their discipline unnerved her; they were saving themselves for something greater than skirmishes. Worthy's words in his letter to his brother accosted her. The sentences in obsessively neat handwriting had bounced around in her head since she'd read them: *If you keep up the good work, all should be ready soon after the season begins in the fall. We will move under the cover of plain sight.* All along, the Territories had been telling the city they were coming. And now, they were living up to their promise to reclaim the Dream.

In the arena's parking lot, the lights were on. Must be power going to the coop. The crowd fanned out as spectators headed to their designated entrance. Briefly, the comm system was up again. Zyla learned that Ben and Germaine were at one of the service entrances. The four friends left the crowd and hurried down a ramp leading to a service entrance where, sure enough, they found Ben and Germaine. The couple led the group through a maze of corridors, pushed open a creaking door Ji-ji would have missed if she'd been on her own, and led them down a dark, musty tunnel. Directly above them, tens of thousands of fans made their way into the arena.

In a transparent attempt to defuse the tension, Germaine told them how the tunnels had been dug during construction by workers reluctant to place their trust in the city's commitment to liberty. The tunnel they were in led to a hidden door that led to a narrow corridor. At the end of the corridor, Ben pushed open a door to reveal a tight storage room filled with crates. The group of six stepped into the windowless room, which reminded Ji-ji of the storeroom she and Afarra had hidden in with Tree and Georgie-Porge. Ben located a battery-powered lantern and switched it on. They wouldn't have to be here for long, Ben said. As soon as the streets were clear, Friends would come pick them up. Ji-ji looked around for exits and couldn't find any. If steaders found them, they had no escape route.

A minute later, they heard footsteps. One person . . . two!

Lucky, Ben, Germaine and Zyla drew their guns. Ji-ji had neglected to bring her gun. It would be in the car in the bag Zyla packed. Ji-ji wished she'd thought to bring it. Afarra surprised them all when she pulled out a knife.

"It's only me," a voice hissed on the other side of the door.

"Zaini?" Zyla exclaimed.

"You alone?" Ben asked.

"Got Tree with me," Zaini replied. "Ran into him in the tunnel." Ben drew back the heavy bolt on the door and let them in. The two squeezed inside and Ben bolted the door again.

The room was cramped before; now they could barely stand. Ji-ji clambered onto a crate so there would be more floor space. Afarra did the same.

Tree spoke first: "Alice says the vehicles'll be here in an hour, tops. Came to tell you. Callers don't work down here."

Ben addressed Zaini: "You shouldn't be here," he said. "You got enough to deal with."

"Think I'll let those bastards murder another of my boys?" Zaini asked him, in a voice that wouldn't tolerate contradiction. Ben stuttered out an apology.

"Where is Ink?" Afarra asked. "And Circus?"

Tree assured her they were safe. "Ink, Bromadu, and Circus too, they're on the way to the E.S.S. Coach Mack and the Montys are escorting them there."

"There's something else, isn't there?" Zyla said. "Spit it out, Tree."

Tree looked more agitated than Ji-ji could recall seeing him. "You know that plan the fleet had to fill the pit with cats an' stripers then open up the center of the cage? It's on again."

Germaine gasped. "The flyers'll all be killed!" she said.

"I'm sorry," Tree said. "Hate to be the bearer of bad news, but there's another thing. Amadeus told me to come in behind the rigging guys an' check the equipment. So far, I've found a harness they screwed with, and an X Box that detaches from its anchor when it spins clockwise."

"Where's Tiro an' the other flyers?" Ji-ji asked. "Do they know?"

"That's another wrinkle," Tree told them. "The flyers are confined to the locker rooms. Redipp says he's heard reports of drug-sopping, so he's administering drug tests. Searching them all too. It's a ruse of course. I'm only roaming round cos Amadeus gave me errands to do before he took off somewhere. But soon as they catch me they'll confine me to the locker rooms too."

"Amadeus went to the studio to warn us," Zyla said. "Should be back soon."

Ben echoed Ji-ji's earlier question: "Do the flyers know about the mutants?"

"They will after I spread the word," Tree assured him. "They've posted armed guards at the doors. Looks like the spectators will be trapped too."

Ben moaned. "Thousands of armed steaders among the spectators. Armed guards at the exits, paperless fans loaded into trucks and hauled away. It's a co-ordinated attack."

"Yep," Tree said, "which is why, when Amadeus started to get suspicious this was a trap, he made sure some of the tickets went to Friends of Freedom. Marcus says other tickets were routed to Invisible Men. A few raiders are here too, the ones that made it through the raid. No one's checking for weapons at the entrances, so that works both ways. Some of our people are armed, but I wish there were a lot more of them."

Barely suppressed anger permeated Lucky's voice: "Why the hell do

Americans always expect people to play by the rules? You could've seen this coming a mile off."

Ben got defensive. "I don't see your country doing much better. It's as fucked up as we are."

Zyla told them both to shut up. "We don't have time for this," she said.

Zaini asked how many Friends, Invisibles, and raiders Tree thought would be in the arena.

"Not enough, I'm afraid," he told her, as if he himself were to blame. "Alice an' Paul thought the Dreamer Coalition in Congress had things under control, so did the Coalition. Got overconfident. Thought they'd stomped the fire out before, but they forgot about the embers."

Ji-ji's stomach turned over. "The Dream Master'll be a sitting duck when the battle begins."

"Maybe not, angel," Tree said, kindly "Redipp's not the only one with tricks up his sleeve."

Zaini said they had to try to get the flyers out before the battle began, but Tree said they were too heavily guarded for a rescue attempt, with soldiers stationed throughout the nearby corridors.

"So if we can't get them out," Ben said, "we'll need to tilt things back in their favor." He took Germaine's hand. She snatched it away as if he'd burned her.

"I know what you're gonna say, Ben! I'm begging you, please don't!"

Ben pushed back her hair and kissed her tenderly on the cheek. "You know I gotta do this, Germ. I'm not as good as you in coop—there, I admit it. But I've still got a few good moves. Arm's healed up nicely, an' those young flyers'll need all the help they can get from us veterans. Zy, keep an eye on my beautiful wife here and the baby-to-be too, okay?"

Zyla seemed touched by the unexpected request. "Sure thing, Ben," she said.

A pall fell over all of them. Everyone knew what Ben had just volunteered to do.

Zaini turned to Ji-ji. "Did they record the interview?" Ji-ji shook her head and quickly described what happened. Zaini's face fell. "What about the folks at the *Independent*? Ezra? Abby?"

Lucky broke the bad news about the newspaper.

The news hit Tree hard. He said Amadeus had it all planned out. His crew in the control booth were loyal to him, not Redipp. They'd been coordinating with this guy at the media studio—a backup plan in case things went south faster than expected. If things went haywire, the guy was set to deliver the recording to the control booth tonight, a day ahead of the official broadcast, so it could be livestreamed to the SuperStates and some of the Liberty Independents during the battle in the coop. "Not many people in the Independents'll have access to the livestream of course, but some will. An' most of the folks in the SuperStates could've seen it. But now that plan is shot to pieces. Don't even know if the power will stay on."

"Okay then," Zaini announced. "Looks like all the other plans have gone up in smoke. We need to go to plan F."

Lucky asked if that was the We're-Fucked Plan.

"No," Zaini said, with remarkable steadiness. "It's the Freedom-at-All-Costs Emergency Plan. Ben, Germaine, hurry on out so you can get a signal on your callers, assuming the comm's up, an' call every veteran flyer you know who's on the side of Freedom. Get them over here. Tell them what's at stake. Tell them to hurry. I have a job to do myself that may take a while."

The grieving mother had stunned the other occupants of the room into silence.

"Dregulahmo shared a few contingency plans with me," Zaini said, by way of explanation. "My uncle was sneaky. People forget that about him. . . . Stop staring at me like a bunch of idiots. We need to save my son, an' a lot of others too. We're not dead yet, an' I'll be damned if I'll surrender."

"*Wait!*" Ji-ji cried. She pushed aside her cape and slipped her hand into a purse she carried on a belt at her waist. She took out small object no bigger than her thumb. "The cats an' stripers aren't the only mutants here tonight," she said. "An' if I'm not enough, we've got this too."

"What is it?" Zyla asked.

Ji-ji placed the flash drive in Tree's huge hand and said, "It's the video from the planting. I brought it along just in case. Give it to the Dream Master and tell him it's from Just Jellybean." Before anyone could interrupt her, she added, "An' tell him something else. I'll be flying the Dream with him tonight."

The storeroom erupted in protest. Afarra leaned over and whispered in Ji-ji's ear: "We are saying it is a good plan, Elly. I like the flying part. You carry me on your back so we can battle together." It was one of the best, most generous, most ridiculous offers Ji-ji had ever had.

Above them the arena shuddered in anticipation of a reckoning, while far away from where the dream was dreamed, three birds perched on a giant, stricken tree refused to fly away.

29 PROMISES TO KEEP

From where Tiro sat in the Dream Coop's locker room, it looked like things were going downhill fast. He tried to give a damn and couldn't.

Some time ago, half a dozen heavily armed D.C. patrollers in riot gear had barged in to the locker room. The lead patroller, his face obscured by a visor, barked out orders to the forty-odd flyer-battlers assembled there. By order of Drayborn Redipp and Mayor Adolphus Yardley, some of them were Free to go. He reeled off the names of the fortunate on the Free-To-Go list. Tiro, sitting next to Marcus on a bench near the showers, noticed what all the flyers noticed: the only ones whose names were called were those steaders would categorize as fairskins, certified African Indigenous, Native Indigenous, or Hispanic. If they categorized you as Hispanic, it was dicey: two Latin flyers were on the list, two weren't. If you were a female, or if you could possibly be categorized as a so-called Deviant or Heretic, your name wasn't on the list either.

Some of the "fairskins" and "A-Is" on the Free-To-Go list were reluctant to leave the other fleeters to their fate, and one of the Hispanics, a veteran flyer named Alonso, adamantly refused to abandon them. "Fine," the lead patroller said. "Stay. We don't give a fuck, do we boys?" When the patroller, a jokester, finished reeling off the names, he said, "Looks to me like duskies, bitches, an' perverts need not apply." The other patrollers showed their appreciation for his wit with uproarious laughter.

Re-Router took the omission of her name better than any of them. Said she didn't want steaders determining her fate; she would determine it her own damn self in the Dream Coop. Her fly partner had a different reaction. In his sequined, skintight leotard and crested headdress, X-Clamation, Bird of Paradise, routinely demonized in the Territories for his "dandification," was outraged. Aware that his skills drew thousands of fans to the Dream Coop, X prided himself on how often he shocked spectators and pushed the owners' buttons. "They owe me, Ree," he told Re-Router, his fly partner of fifteen years. "They owe me big-time. I've done favors you wouldn't believe for that mayor. Favors for the cowardly cocksuckers in the D.C. Congress too." He added loudly, "I'll write a book about it. Expose them all for the dickheads they are!"

A patroller entered the locker room and handed a slip of paper to the lead patroller, who nodded and read out what was on it: "Orlie Mallorymule, reservist, you will accompany this patroller. Georgie-Porge Snellingseed, you are promoted to the first team. Congratulations."

Marcus tore over to Orlie, who raised his arms defensively. "Motherfuckin *traitor!*" Marcus said. "Who'd you betray this time?"

Tiro and Georgie-Porge pulled Marcus away while the patrollers relished the entertainment. Since they'd returned to the city, Tiro had noticed (when he noticed anything at all) that Georgie-Porge and Orlie had resolved their differences. The other day, Marcus had accused Georgie of being an Uncle Tom, demanded he teach Orlie a lesson. "You think your black ass is safe if you play nice," Marcus had said. "Cos if you do, you're as dumb as that little bitch you fly with." Marcus had always bullied Orlie, but Tiro had to agree with Georgie-Porge when he said there was a murderous edge to his harassment now, as if Orlie were to blame for everything that went down on the 437th.

Orlie looked back desperately at Georgie as the patroller led him away. Marcus could barely contain his fury: "Told you Orlie was a parrot. Bet he's off squawking to Red Droopy, reporting every word of our conversation."

"Orlie ain't no parrot," Georgie asserted. He slumped down on a bench and put his head in his hands. Marcus plopped down on one side, Tiro on the other. The three friends, who'd spent years together under Coach Billy's watchful eye, didn't speak till Georgie broke the silence. He kept his voice low so only his close buddies could hear him.

"Redipp took a . . ." He hunted for the right word. ". . . *fancy* to Orlie when we got here. Been doing stuff to him. Red Droopy's preference is for fair an' young, only his preference is illegal in D.C., so he settles for substitutes. Done things I won't go into."

Marcus looked like Georgie had punched him. "I didn't know, man. How was I to know?"

Georgie-Porge agreed. "No one knew. Orlie was embarrassed so he didn't tell no one. Made me swear I wouldn't say nothing. I used to be shitty to him too."

Out of the blue Tiro said, "Orlie tried to kill himself. On the planting. I visited him afterward in the clinic." None of the fly-boys dared look at each other.

Georgie kneaded his hands nervously and stared at his feet. "I saw Orlie come outta Redipp's office months ago. Figured he was parroting. Learned later what was really going on. Promise me one thing. If you come across that sonuvabitch Redipp an' you happen to have a gun in your hand, blast the fucker's head off, okay?"

Just then, Laughing Tree entered the locker room. He spoke briefly to the patrollers. Said he'd been doing errands for Coopmaster Nelson. The patrollers shrugged and ordered him to go sit with the others. Tree walked over and joined his friends on the bench.

Flabbergasted, Georgie asked, "What you come back for? You could've escaped, man."

"Only in the physical sense," Tree replied.

Georgie lost patience: "What the fuck does that mean, man?"

"Means we're a team," Tree told him. "*Damn!*" Tree said suddenly. "Forgot to give Mackie the stash of weed for Ink's leg pain. Only thing that helps. Poor little guy'll suffer without it. Well, I guess it's too late now. I've got a few messages to deliver from the coopmaster. Listen up."

As inconspicuously as he could, Tree huddled with the three of them. Marcus, incensed when he heard about the aborted media broadcast and the newspaper closure, took some solace in the idea that the video and photos from the 437th might see the light of day after all. But Tree had to warn him that they might not be able to get away with showing much of the evidence before Redipp stormed the control box. The sting came for Tiro when Tree disclosed that Zaini hadn't left the city. He was furious at first. She was a mother, for god's sake, and Bromadu needed her now more than ever. He railed at Tree, demanded to know why he hadn't slung her over his shoulder and carted her to safety. Marcus pointed out that a giant Black man with a part-Toteppi woman slung over his shoulder could attract attention from the city's steader guests. The news about Ji-ji was even crazier. The last place she needed to be was inside the coop tonight. Tree, however, insisted they owed Ji-ji a debt of gratitude.

"Let's not count our chickens 'fore they're hatched," Marcus said. "Unless the control box crew is on our side, we're all screwed. We'll be Inked off that equipment for sure."

Tree put his hand on Philosopher Phil's knee. "Listen up, Marcus. I've had enough of this Ink business. I'll be his daddy soon, assuming we make it out, so no more of this Inked crap." Marcus was about to object but Tree placed his index finger on the flyer's lips. Tiro couldn't help noticing how big Tree's index finger was, the size of a bratwurst sausage. "I warned you in the van coming back from the raid," Tree said. "Now I'm warning you again. Shut up about Ink. If you don't, I'll knock your teeth out. Which would be a shame cos they're exceptionally white an' pretty."

Tree stood up and moved off to share Amadeus' plan, having instructed the others to do the same. Tiro couldn't tell how Marcus took Tree's threat till he heard him mutter "patronizing sonuvabitch" under his breath. Then he got a pretty good idea how it had been received.

Soon, all the flyers on the Not-Free-To-Go category, plus Wild Man Alonso, knew the Dream Master's plan. Not exactly foolproof, they all agreed, but at least it might prevent some of them from getting slaughtered. The news about the ravenous ants had the most sobering effect on everyone. The flyer-battlers in the Dreamfleet were accustomed to danger. They all knew luck was tilted in favor of the coop. The net, for example, didn't extend beyond the center of the cage, which was why the flyers had a saying: *The net nets the smart fish, tosses out the dumbfish.* The worst insult you could give a flyer was to call him a *dumbfish.* The miserliness of the net had nothing to do with cost or engineering and everything to do with the fact that spectators got a rise out of what Marcus called "vicarious risk." But tonight the risk would be less vicarious than usual for the non-steader fans.

For the past two weeks, while preparing for the season, Tiro hadn't experienced PS—not even once. He'd figured out you needed fear for PS to work, and fear for his own safety had flown away. Georgie's words about Orlie, however, and Tree's words about Ink had stirred something inside him. Pity maybe, or compassion. No. It was a word Zyla had taught them in the legacy school: *empathy.* He thought about what else Tree had told him. Bromadu was safely on his way to the E.S.S. with Ink, Coach Mack, and the Montys. Circus hadn't been forgotten either. Tree had also learned, from the runner called Big Pike, that Tulip and her sisters were with them.

Ever since the Devastation Raid (the name he'd given the debacle in his head), all Tiro could think about was one thing: When had Yatho gotten hit? He'd narrowed it down to the moments when they were exiting through the Main Gate after Emmeline managed to release the locking mechanism and turn off the fence. He was pretty certain the little man had smiled up at him through the fog as they passed through the gate. Bullets whizzed past. He'd assumed they'd missed. Everyone screaming, yelling, scrambling to get out, the din in his ears so loud he couldn't have heard even if Yatho cried out. Tiro had yelled at his mother to run. She'd sprinted ahead dragging Bromadu after her. Broma had lost his footing. They'd picked him up. Bullets still whizzing around them. . . . Maybe it was then, when they were just beyond the gate before the convoy pulled up to rescue them? He had to figure out when Yatho got hit cos then he'd know how long his little brother had stayed silent. Like they told him to, like *he* told him to. *But not if you're shot, buddy, not then.* He'd forgotten to add that part.

Automatically, like Billy and Amadeus had trained him to do, Tiro found himself going over the moves he'd make after they entered the cage. When the Hell's Yells entered (an all-male, all-White team, of course), the steader fans would stomp and scream like they wanted to set the world afire and watch it burn. The hostile fans would do everything they could to distract the Dreamfleet flyers.

Since their return to the Dream, Tiro had been going through the motions. Now, he was getting switched on again like one of those fancy lights on a dimmer switch . . . which made him think of his uncle Dreg-Dim. Why hadn't he warned him to protect Yatho better? In a rush of sorrow that almost made him choke, he was sorry beyond sorry for his mother, for Bromadu, and for Ji. Afarra too. And Ben and Germaine. He looked around at the flyers, all of them quiet now as they thought about what awaited them. He didn't want to lose any of them, not even Marcus.

Without consciously intending to do so, Tiro stood up. The startled guards raised their weapons in readiness. "Easy, guys," Tiro said to the patrollers. "This ain't about you. It's about us."

The patrollers looked at each other nervously. Seemed to think they should shut him up. Tiro gambled they wouldn't, not before the show. The wizard's great-nephew needed to suffer tonight in front of a packed arena. If they'd executed him already, how could that happen?

Tiro looked around at the two dozen or so flyers held in the locker room at gunpoint. "They think they can cage us, think they can kill us. They think we'll be too scared to fly."

"They're *wrong*!" Laughing Tree thundered. He walked over and stood beside Tiro.

"I, Tiro Dregulahmo, will *not* be told this is not my land, or that my own body does *not* belong to me! I am a man! With pride, I claim my body! With pride, I claim my own blood! I fly in the cage tonight like a goddam bird of prey!"

Marcus stood up beside him, crossed his arms over his chest, and said, "My brother is right. We do not fly alone. Oz Dregulahmo flies with us! Invisible forces swarm at our backs!"

Re-Router stood then: "A vast swarm of females is ready to conquer the goddam *world*!"

X-Clamation came and stood beside her. "They may kill us," X cried, "but we'll refuse to die! Tonight we fly the dream like we've never flown it before!"

All the flyers were standing and cheering now. Nothing had changed; they knew they were as vulnerable and as doomed as they'd been before they'd found their voices. But they also knew they'd seen each other and heard each other as they most wanted to be.

Tiro spoke again: "My great-aunt, the Gardener of Tears, says the Freedom Race ain't a runners' or a flyers' race. She says the Freedom Race is *us*! An' I, for one, believe her!"

"The Freedom Race is *us*!" the flyers cried together.

The guards yelled at them to shut up and sit down, but they ignored them.

Instead, they lifted up their voices and yelled, "*Long live the Dreamers! The Free-dom Race is us!*"

And just like that, Tiro woke up completely. And just like that, he realized he was a dumbfish, if ever there was one. Cos there's a penalty if you turn up the dimmer switch all the way so it sheds light on everything. A big penalty. Just like that, he'd forgotten how *not* to be afraid.

||||||||||||||||

The bar was packed. Sloppy had paid good money for this seat and the one next to it. She'd haggled. Tried to get the table for less, but the bitch said she was doing her a favor letting her in (as if she was scum and this shitty bar was a palace). All she would take were SuperStates, so Sloppy had to fork them over. And then of course there was a man with a fat head who sat himself down at the table in front of hers as though he owned the place, and now they'd have to peer around him to see the match. What kind of moron puts a screen down low like that and then puts a man with a fat head in front of it and charges you a cover charge to not see it? A Mule who owns a bar, that's who. Muleseeds all over the place in this city. Give her a Commonseed any day. Or a Tainted even.

Sloppy turned and looked toward the door again. Nothing. A part of her wished she hadn't offered to forfeit some of the lucre in exchange for a Tainted. Lotter had been greedy for the info she had, and whatever else you said about Lotter, he was a man of his word. Not like Casper, who was ignorant as dog dung. Lotter had agreed to the deal with that superior Lottery glint in his eyes. Who has eyes that blue anyway? Martians, that's who. It was unnatural.

Sloppy didn't know which part of the story she liked best. The fact that Jel-lybean Lottermule was a freak, or the fact that she'd wrung the truth out of Tulip "Ain't-My-Hair-a-Fuckin-Marvel" Rogersseed by scaring the bitch—another Mule—half to death. Taken both bitches down a peg or two. Lotter would kill Jellybean for absolute certain cos she was a freak. Bitch wouldn't even let her twelve downtrodden kitchen-seeds get a tiny bit of joy from a pin-ball machine. *What cropmaster in his right mind wants a mutant for a seedling? Not Lotter, that's for sure. He'll puke when he sees her. He's had the info for a while now, which could mean Ji-ji is dead already.*

Chaff Man must be dead too. He'd never abandon their hideout like that. Didn't take any of his lucre or papers. No nothing. She'd found the bastard he hung out with—that Candid Fish—when she'd gone back there to see if there was anything she could steal out from under Chaff's nose. Found Candid's worm-ridden, rat-nibbled-on, maggoty corpse. *Yuk!* Took ages to drag him out and burn the motherfucker. She hadn't gone back to get her papers cos she didn't need them anymore. Cropmaster Lotter had seen to that. She had new ones folded in a neat square in a plastic bag inside her bra. Her first genuine, honest-to-goodness bra with elastic that was still elastic. Two perfect pockets for her tits and her treasures. She hadn't had a proper bra during the Freedom Race so her tits bounced up and down like meatballs when she ran.

And now here she was, sitting in a bar in the part of town that wasn't the dregs, with a beer and a gin chaser, and a plate of homemade potato chips and a pickle, waiting for the Dreamfleet-Armistice opening battle of the season cos her fortunes had changed. The jerk on the screen promised it would be the "Game of the Century." Swooned over Tiro and Marcus. "I know those two flyers," Sloppy told a nearby customer. "They're personal friends of mine." The man laughed in her face. "Why would a ugly cunt like you be buddies with them?" he said, then turned back to his beer. He had no idea how close he'd come to having a broken glass jammed down his gullet.

A woman limped up to the table. Sloppy didn't recognize her. "It's me," the woman said.

"Sit down," Sloppy hissed. "Can't you see 'em looking at you? This is a classy establishment, for fuck's sake. Sit *down*!"

The woman sat down. "Guess I ain't much to look at," the woman said.

Sloppy snuck a look at her. "This side's okay. Can't see the shit they did on the other side."

"It's a chisel plow an' a sheaf of—"

"I'm not *blind*, Dip. Knew it was the planting seal soon as I saw it. . . . Who did it?"

"Williams."

"Fucker. Figures. You still see out your right eye?"

"Some. . . . Williams is dead. They say an angel killed him. Or Wizard Dreg come back as a Dimmer. Dimmer Dreg Freed the prisoners from PenPen. S'how I got out. Cell door was wide open. Only they caught me again. Wanted to cut the other toes off for running. Would have if . . ."

"Guess I plucked you off that planting in the nick of time. . . . You actually see the wizard?"

"Well, no . . . but—"

"Thought not. Gullibility runs rampant among botanicals. That means you believe all kinds of crap without the proper evidence. It'll be your downfall."

They didn't speak for a while as Sloppy let that observation settle.

"Guess you may not want me now you seen me," Dip said, tremulously. "I'm a mess."

Sloppy shrugged. "Are you still all about adopting four seedlings to make up for the ones you did away with? I'm not good around seedlings. If you're still about that, you an' me are history."

"Couldn't take care of 'em after what they done to me," Dip said. "Not even one. . . . How'd you get the lucre to buy me out, Slop? Delilah, I mean."

"Did a gentleman a favor. Coop battle starts soon. You drink beer, or whiskey, or gin?"

Sloppy knew what Dip was thinking. She'd never been asked a question as classy as that in her life. The question revealed that Sloppy had made it big in the big city, with lucre to spare for things like booze and chips and a pickle. Dip had been the leader before cos she was ten years older, but Dip wasn't the woman she used to be. Sloppy would take the lead now. She thought of how much reward she'd forfeited to get Dip off the 437th, and how much more she'd have if she hadn't done it. She felt something rise in her as she looked across the table at the woman who'd been branded and lopped and dragged by hounds and whose foot was half gone and whose arm was half useless and whose face was just about the most messed-up face she'd ever seen. She couldn't stop herself. She swallowed hard and blurted out the truth.

"I missed you, Dipthong Spareseed. Missed you like crazy. Guess you can live with me if you want. Got my own place. Two rooms to ourselves, plus an indoor kitchen with a window with glass, an' a shed out back for tools an' such. It's a nice shed. Nothing like the crappy lean-to Casper stuck me in on the planting. It's over in a part of town where we can mind our own damn business. No one'll care how bad you look. Neighbors keep to themselves. S'my place now. The other person moved out. Took a shine to me an' bequeathed it. But we can share it if you want."

Sloppy despised blubberers. But when Dip started blubbering, she didn't mind.

"Oh Sloppy! Delilah, I mean. This is . . . a dream come true!"

"You can call me Sloppy if you like. Not here, not in public. At home. . . . Right. I'll order you a gin with a real lemon slice. An' now stop crying. I saved you like I promised. The shitty part's over." Sloppy reached over and patted her best friend's hand, then swiped her own hand away real fast so no one would see her do it.

"It's okay," Sloppy said, "I got you, Dip. You're safe in the Dream with me. Now let's get drunk as skunks an' watch those fly-boys make asses of themselves in the coop."

|||||||||||||

She knows what Ji-ji is planning without waiting to hear her say it. Ever since Lotter gifted her to Silapu, she's always known. Like she's inside Elly's head and her own head (and his, the wizard's) at the same time. It's a dangerous place, so it takes a while for Ji-ji to convince them.

Tree leaves first, then Zyla, Ben, and Elly. Lucky promises to get Afarra to safety. No one asks her opinion about it, so even though she doesn't want to do it, she kicks Lucky in the shin when he tries to stop her and dashes off after Elly. She hears Lucky groan and she is *sorrysorrysorry,* but not sorry enough to stop running. She knows more than they do sometimes. For example, she told everyone there were pickers in the Dream and they didn't listen and she got picked.

Lucky runs after her like the little wooden people on the clock Cropmaster Herring had in his study who are running round in a circle to catch up on the hour time. She liked to watch them when the old man poked her cos they always wind up in the beginning and start up again like nothing happens in between.

She isn't fast enough and Elly is gone! She turns to look behind her and Lucky is gone too! Where are they? She doesn't know. She's *lost*! She hears the sound from the cages. Faint roars and snuffles and snarls. She follows their cry of anguish to its conclusion. (The wizard's words, not hers.) She finds them in cages in a circle beneath the center ring. They saw this place before when Tree and Georgie-Porge led them out of the coop.

There are guards around with whips and guns, but she is very good at hiding and they don't see her. After the guards leave, she greets the snarlcat she met on the Mall and tells him how sorry she is she couldn't Free him. He is pissed off with her. He will not say a word. Not even his name. So she reminds him it is Lonesome. He can take it or leave it is his attitude.

And then she sees her friend Muckmock. She is very glad indeed to see him, but not there in the Coop Pit, which is more like what she imagines penitence penitentiaries on plantings must be like—dark and dingy and blaring with sorrowfulness. She tries to cheer the ants up. She can't blame them when they don't listen. Some sadness is too loud for listening. It yells in your ear like Cropmaster Herring and blasts your eardrum to smithereens.

The creatures in the cages tell her their sad stories. She tries to Free them but the cages are locked and she can't find a key and then some guards come back and she hides. The stripers dart around the cages crazy with hunger. The striped fur on their backs stands upright on their sloped shoulders, the flesh on their antennae is a sad, pus-blister yellow. The snarlcats are hungry too, but they show it differently. They splay themselves out on the floor of the cages and rest their maned heads on their paws. They are sadder than Blueglass Lake when it swallowed Mbeke's mam, not only cos they are *ravenous* (the wizard's word) but also cos they don't like noise and there's noise all around. Creaking, cranking noises, metal noises, men shouting.

A man sees her! She tries to run. She's *caught*! He likes the look of her, drags her off to a room with empty in it, tears at the zipper on her jacket and out pop the Eyes. The man's eyes bulge out like the ones on the necklace, and she knows she is being saved again by the wizard.

"You're that Cloth the Pterodactyl was looking for! The one Fish saw! Get *away* from me! What you do to him? You been following me?"

Afarra looks at him, says in her wizardy voice, "I come to find you! I come to eat you *alive*!"

The guard backs away. "What are you? Some kinda witch?"

"Free the ants!" Afarra says. "Free *every single one*!"

"Leave me alone!" he pleads. "I'm sorry, okay? I know it's not right to cage the apey one. I told 'em. He's almost like a real person. But the market's dried up. Can't find a fuckin sunset anywhere. Only brokered the deal cos—"

Afarra sees them again. "I am seeing them!" she cries. "They are *falling*!"

The man crosses himself and rushes out.

Afarra exits the Pit, heads up to the arena's big belly. In one of the hallways, she spots a friend in the crowd whose head sticks up above the rest. She calls to her. "*Big Pike!*" Big Pike comes lolloping. "You seen Elly? Ji-ji?" Afarra asks. "Nope, sorry," Big Pike says. She pulls Afarra off to the side, warns her to be careful-careful. Says she thinks the steaders are planning something. Says she ran into Laughing Tree who told her to get out of there. She's been trying, but the crush of people has made it impossible and some of the exits are locked. The battle will start soon, she says. God only knows what will happen then.

Then she spies Afarra's necklace under her wide-open jacket and says Tulip told her Clownfish killed a woman for wearing a necklace like that. He told people the necklace killed her but it was him. Used the necklace to do it, so, technically, it was the necklace. According to Tulip, when he was a seedling, Clownfish buried the bones of animals he'd tortured all over the planting, like a damn dog. Big Pike says she feels bad cos she'd told Tulip to forgive people but "scum like that you gotta exterminate." Afarra taps the knife she's got strapped to her thigh. "I know," she says. Pike begs her to stay with her. "I'll protect you," she says. "Get you out safely, I promise." Afarra thanks her but she sees the flyers *fallingfallingfalling* in her head, and who will protect Elly if she's not there to do it? She takes off again while Big Pike is telling her not to, zips up her jacket just in case.

The next person she bumps into is the broken-neck boy in mule ears. He wisps right on through her like smoke, the way Dimmers do, so she almost misses him. "You promised you would save us," he shrieks. "I know!" she replies, as she keeps on going. "I'm *doing* it!"

Afarra is on the verge of giving up when she spies Lucky running down a corridor away from the crowd. She follows him up the stairs cos she's lost an' could be he's chasing after Elly, only she is way behind so she loses him at the top. Then she hears voices. Heads down another corridor.

Lucky is crouched behind a big door that's open just enough for him to see what's going on inside. Lucky sees her coming and puts his finger to his lips for quiet. Afarra sees through the crack in the door too. Lucky's gun is pointed at his target, but he can't fire cos that would mean blasting through Elly! Then she sees who he's really aiming for, sees the other gun pointed at Elly. Lucky slaps his hand over her mouth just in time so she doesn't scream.

Afarra feels her eyes weep, all of them, in advance. *Hush now, hush,* she thinks to the necklace. *Don't look!* But the eyes have slithered out of her jacket and they are stuck on open. She tries not to be scared and pulls out her knife. She waits with Lucky for the end to begin.

IIIIIIIIIIIIIII

Ji-ji obeyed the order and started to remove her shirt. She didn't have to look again in Zyla's direction to see that Lotter's longtime overseer had a gun pointed at her teacher's head.

The four of them—her, Lotter, Zyla, and Vanguard Casper—stood in a high-ceilinged room off one of the coop's side corridors. Looked like they used the room for physical therapy sessions. It was filled with exam tables and bulky training equipment. At one end, a line of massage tables. A few lights were turned on, but the room was dimly lit, full of shadows. Ji-ji could hear the sound of the steader fans—their steps, their aggressive cheers—coming to them from somewhere in the vast complex. She had to keep telling herself this wasn't a dream, that Lotter really stood there in front of her with a gun pointing at her chest.

Once again, Casper had come through for Lotter. He'd spotted Ji-ji and Zyla as they made their way down a deserted hallway en route to the top of the coop. Ji-ji planned to descend from the dome, catch them all unawares. Instead, she'd been caught unawares herself.

Ben had taken off a few minutes earlier to find another way into the fly cage. Ji-ji's method for entering the coop was fine for a bird, Ben said, but not too good for a wingless Born-Free battler from New England. If Ben had been there too, this might not have happened.

Ironically, the sheer number of steaders roaming around the building tricked her into a false sense of security. Normally, the smell of Lotter's lavender-citrusy aftershave, Dark Essenceial, that he had shipped to him from Armistice in a fancy box the same shade as her mam's skin, would have alerted her to danger. That evening, however, the scent permeated everything. So when she caught a whiff of it just before Casper came up behind them, she didn't pay enough attention to this one detail cos she'd smelled the bootlegged version on the steaders. She wondered why she was thinking of garbage like this in what could be her last moments on this Earth, as if Casper had stomped into her brain and occupied it like a squatter. Lotter too. He was the worst squatter of all.

Lotter, a gun in his right hand, looked exactly the same and totally different. The same thick blond locks, the same unnaturally blue eyes, the same way of holding himself bolt upright as if he had a rod in his back, and the same clipped way of speaking where he pronounced each consonant with unnerving precision. Yet in his olive-green cropmaster robe, with the heavy cropmaster chain slung around his neck, he seemed changed. When Ji-ji knew him before, there'd been a frenzied excitement in him, especially when he was around her mam. Now, in its place, there was . . . nothing. Almost like he was a projection.

He spoke at her in a voice devoid of emotion: "You're ugly. Anyone ever tell you that?"

"Yes," she said, "you did."

"*Ha!*" he exclaimed, joylessly. "Well, I was right. Plain as mud. Darker than most Commonseeds. Not stunningly dark like she was or like Oletto either. Can't see a drop of me or a drop of her in you. Just a common, everyday, run-of-the-mill brown. And you, Miss Clobershay," he said, "you look like a boy with your hair shorn off. If you'd shown up at the planting like that, we'd have pyred you as unnatural."

"I'm not the unnatural one," Zyla said. "That's what torments you. You're not blind to the horror of what you're doing. Are you still trying to numb yourself with drugs and booze?"

At first, Ji-ji thought Zyla wanted to prove she wasn't intimidated. Then she realized her teacher was stalling for time. As Casper steered them down corridors at gunpoint, having forced Zyla to give up her gun if she wanted to see Ji-ji's head remain on her shoulders, Zyla had whispered to Ji-ji that she'd caught sight of Lucky. They needed to draw this out for as long as possible.

Lotter told Zyla to keep her mouth shut and turned his attention back to Ji-ji. "You tried to take her from me," he said. "But I kept her. In a safe place."

Ji-ji said the next words slowly so they would sink in. "Charra an' me saw her at the arsenal."

Lotter's head jerked in surprise. "So. . . . You were there with the raiders. A couple of my men said they spotted you, but I didn't believe you'd be stupid enough to come looking for trouble. You've got blood on your hands now too, Jellybean. Hurry. I'm getting impatient."

Ji-ji undid the second-to-last button on her shirt.

"I hear they function. Rumor has it you can elevate with the things."

"I wish," she said. She had to gamble that he didn't know everything. "I'd fly the fuck out of here if I could do that."

"Don't swear," he said, predictably. "Nothing worse than foul language in a female."

She made herself laugh. "Nothing worse! *Ha-ha!* You must be *joking!* What about rape, lynching, lashing, and lopping? What about those?"

In a soft, measured voice, every syllable clear, Arundale Duke Lotter, Twelfth Cropmaster of the 437th, said, "After I finish speaking, you have ten seconds before Casper blasts a hole in Miss Clobershay's head. Casper favors big guns. Likes to feel the weight of them banging up against him. So it will be a very big hole. Irreparable."

Ji-ji hated him more than anyone else in the world. Her fingers trembled, but she managed to undo the last button. She slipped off her shirt to reveal her flight bra.

Lotter's eyes scanned her body. Off to the side, she felt Casper's eyes on her too.

Lotter ordered her to turn around. She did as she was told. He walked up to her, ran his long, pianist fingers over her back.

"Christ!" he murmured. "You're ugly. I don't think Casper could mutilate you more severely if he tried."

"Don't blaspheme," Ji-ji said, unable to stop herself. "It's unbecoming."

Several seconds of silence was followed by Lotter's laughter, dry as a bone. "*Ha!* Maybe you are mine after all. All right then. Let's see what you've got here. The slut says you can fly. Show me."

He must mean Sloppy, Ji-ji thought, and put her plan into action. It was risky. She'd only managed it once, and that was by accident and in private. She saw Zyla try to smile at her through her terror. She had to get this right. Casper had a gun at the head of her other mother.

Ji-ji tightened the muscles in her back and released her shoulders like a spring, and *voilà!* there they were—a tiny pair of semitransparent wings not much longer than her forearm. Though she couldn't see them, she could feel that she'd pulled it off.

"Is that it?" Lotter said, contemptuously. "*That's* the existential threat? I should have known it was only a story. Go on then," he added, "fly."

Outside the room in some distant part of the coop, a ruckus kicked up. Shouts, a fistfight. No one would hear him shoot her. She turned to face him. She needed to keep her eye on him, gauge his reaction. She made a half turn so he could see her mini wings and she could see his face. She jumped into the air and fell back down again. She repeated the process.

"I'm not very good at it yet. But . . . if I . . . push myself, I can leap three or . . . four feet."

Lotter's laughter ricocheted around the room. "You're a chicken," he said, disgusted. "I've been chasing a goddam chicken!" He ordered her to stop jumping. "And now, because you've wasted my time, I'm going to ask my loyal overseer to shoot Miss Clober—"

A shot rang out before he'd finished the sentence. "*Zyla!*" Ji-ji screamed and ran toward her. She pulled up. Zyla wasn't hit! It wasn't Casper who'd pulled the trigger!

Lucky burst through the door! Afarra ran in after him wielding a knife!

"*Lucky! Afarra!*" Ji-ji cried.

Casper, wounded, took cover behind a massage table. Lucky fired again. A hail of bullets. Lotter dove behind some training equipment.

"*Afarra!*" Ji-ji called out and ran to protect her. Behind her, another shot! Ji-ji turned in time to see the fat barrel of Casper's gun poking out from behind the table.

Afarra's voice rang out, "He is shooting! *He is shooting her!*"

The blast hit Zyla in the side, turned her around like a ballet dancer on a music box.

"*Zyla!*" Ji-ji screamed again.

Lucky fired at Casper. Once, twice. *Got him!*

They'd taken their eyes off Lotter. He leapt up, ran to Ji-ji, and grabbed her round the waist. He jabbed the barrel of his gun into her neck.

"Drop it," he ordered. "Drop it, Longsby, or I'll blast your whore's throat out."

"I'll kill you before you do," Lucky told him.

"Yes, you probably will. But I'm betting you think chicken-girl's worth saving, otherwise you'd never have risked your life to run off with the slut. So . . . on the count of three, if you don't drop it, the bitch is dead. One . . . two . . ." Lucky dropped his gun. It clattered to the floor.

Lotter kept his gun on Ji-ji's throat. "Cloth," he said, "come here and pick his gun up by the barrel, not by the heel. Pick it up by the shaft, the long part, so it's safe. Then bring it over to me."

By this time Afarra had reached Zyla, who lay on her side in a pool of blood. Afarra didn't move.

"You want me to kill her?" Lotter asked. "Is that what you want?" Afarra shook her head. "Good. Do as I say and I won't hurt her. Take three steps back, Lieutenant, away from the gun. I said, take three steps back! That's one . . . two . . . three. Good."

"Let me tend to Zyla," Lucky pleaded. "Please, man."

Lotter shook his head. "You move, Longsby or Lucky or whatever your name is, and Jellybean dies."

Afarra still hadn't moved. Lotter told her to get up and do as she was damn well told.

Trembling, Afarra stood up and crept forward. She grasped Lucky's gun by the barrel and picked it up. She had her knife in the other hand. With her eyes, Ji-ji told Afarra to shoot, but Afarra gave a barely perceptible shake of her head. "That's good, Cloth. Now lay it on the floor. That's it."

As soon as she did, Lotter flung Ji-ji away and scooped up Lucky's weapon. He stepped back a few paces. With a gun in either hand, he could murder two people at once. He pointed one gun at Ji-ji and the other at Lucky. He didn't bother with Afarra or her knife.

Afarra rushed to help Zyla. "You're wasting your time, Cloth," Lotter called out. "She's dead already. I told you. He doesn't mess around when it comes to caliber. I can see her guts from here."

Lotter addressed Lucky. "You know how often I've dreamed about blasting your head off?"

Lotter ordered Ji-ji to stay on the ground, told Afarra to check and see if Casper was dead.

Afarra looked at Zyla, then Lucky, then Ji-ji. Ji-ji could see her agonize over what to do, before she scrambled up and ran over to Casper. "Dead," she called back.

"Shame," Lotter said. "He was the best overseer I ever had. Crass but dedicated."

In a rush of clarity, Ji-ji realized that Casper's gun must be in arm's reach of Afarra. She wanted to tell her to pick it up and shoot. But as far as she knew, Afarra had never held a gun. She'd never be able to control a gun like that— probably shoot herself or one of them by mistake. But Zyla was bleeding to death! They had to get help for her!

Lotter addressed Ji-ji again: "You look nothing like my Mammy Tep. Charra did. She led the raid, I hear. She still a beauty?"

"Her face got scarred up in a fight, but it made her even more beautiful."

Desperate to hurt him, Ji-ji added, "Charra died on the way back from the raid."

Lotter looked as though he doubted her, then his expression changed, and it looked as though he didn't give a damn. "You two took my Mammy Tep from me," he told Ji-ji and Lucky. "You both deserve to die."

"*No!*" Afarra cried. She stood up. At the other end of the room, she had Casper's gun in her two hands! "*I kill you if you do it!*" she cried.

Lotter glanced over at Afarra and let out that parched laugh again. "Looks like the Cloth's a fan of chickens," he said. "Bet she's a lousy shot." He sounded to Ji-ji like he was talking to himself when he added, "I promised I wouldn't hurt you . . . her seedlings. . . . I promised. . . ."

They all heard it at the same time. Voices raised together in song. The Freedom Anthem. The Dreamfleet fans were in the minority but it sounded as if the entire arena was singing.

A knock on the door startled them. A young inquisitor dressed in the customary bloodred robes of Territorial clerics entered, took one look at the scene before him, and nearly ran out again.

"What is it, Napperton?" Lotter growled.

The young inquisitor, leery of the two guns in Lotter's hands, crept up to him timidly. Lotter wouldn't bend, so the cleric had to stand on tiptoe to whisper in his ear.

Lotter didn't bother to whisper his response: "Tell him it turns out the earlier call was premature. She's a dud. Flies like a goddam chicken." He nodded over at Casper's body. "Get someone to clean up. And before you go, take the gun from the Cloth over there." Napperton looked horrified. "Go take the gun from the Cloth," Lotter repeated, "or I'll shoot you myself."

Lotter still had one gun pointed at Ji-ji and the other at Lucky. Ji-ji could tell he wanted an excuse to fire. Unable to think of anything more important to say, she told Afarra she loved her.

Inquisitor Napperton walked gingerly toward Afarra. "Give me the gun, Cloth," he stammered. "*Please!* He won't hurt you if you give me the gun, I promise."

Up to the last moment, it looked as though Afarra would shoot. She didn't. She handed the gun to the inquisitor, who threw up when he saw Casper's corpse up close.

Lotter ordered Napperton to take the gun and get out. The man tore from the room.

For several seconds, Lotter stood without moving. Ji-ji waited for him to kill them.

Lord-Father Lotter made a dismissive sound with his mouth. He'd lost interest. He removed the mag from Lucky's gun and tossed the weapon down on the floor. Without looking back, he walked out.

Ji-ji jumped up off the floor and dashed over to Zyla. Afarra joined them. Lucky had gotten there first. His hands were bloodied up to the elbow. Casper had blown Zyla's torso to shreds.

Lucky looked down at his bloody arms, looked up at Ji-ji's face.

"She's gone," Ji-ji said. "C'mon, Lucky. *Come on!*" she said again. Afarra grabbed one of Lucky's hands, slippery with blood. Ji-ji grabbed another. On the way out, Ji-ji picked up Lucky's empty gun. Her beloved teacher was dead, and she'd broken her promise to Charra. But the evening wasn't over yet. "*C'mon!*" Ji-ji cried again. Covered in blood, the three of them fled the scene like criminals.

||||||||||||||

Down the hallway, up two flights of stairs, down another hallway, up more flights . . .

Lucky struggled to keep his thoughts under control. He couldn't think about the small body they'd left behind. He had blood on his pants leg at the knee. His pants were dark, so the stain looked like water, but he knew what it was. It slapped up against his flesh, wet but not warm anymore. He hadn't been quick enough. He'd winged Casper the first time, not killed him. Missed Lotter altogether. He'd tried to save Zyla, but he knew when he knelt down she was gone. He went to press down on the wound and the heel of his hands slipped through her guts to the floor. He nearly puked like the inquisitor. He'd wiped his hands on his jacket, which was also dark. He'd need to toss that too. He couldn't take Zy's body. Had to get the girls out of there. That's what he'd tell Germaine, whose heart would be broken. But it was the other way around. The girls had got him out of there.

They came to a deserted corridor. The noise from inside the arena shook the building. The shaft must be on the other side of an access panel on the wall, like Laughing Tree had told them.

"She's dead," Ji-ji said. "Zyla's dead." Like him, she was in shock. He tried to tell her to forget about her plan, but she only repeated, "I can do this, I know I can do this."

Lucky suppressed his emotions the way he'd trained himself to do and called upon logic. "Zyla wouldn't want you to try that ridiculous stunt. Not now. She'd want you to get to safety. Right, Afarra?" Lucky turned to solicit support. She'd gone! "Oh shit! Where did she go?"

"Go after her!" Ji-ji told him. She shoved his gun in his hand. "You got more ammo?"

"Yes," Lucky said. "I'll stay here and pick off anyone who tries to stop you. If Tree is right, there's a shaft on the other side of this panel. You can enter the dome of the cage from here."

"No," Ji-ji insisted. "The threat won't come from out here. It'll come in the arena."

"They'll kill you soon as they see you," he said.

"They'll kill all of us eventually. It's another massacre. We just gotta send a message first."

Lucky felt as if they'd swapped places. Back in The Margins, after they'd battled the Bounty Boys, he'd been the steady one with the logical options.

He reminded her about meeting up in the parking lot by the back entrance. Said the vehicles would be waiting, even though he didn't believe any of them would make it out of the Dream Coop. "I'm sorry I couldn't save Zyla," he said. "I know how close you were."

"You can't save everyone," Ji-ji told him, sounding old again. "You found Afarra once already. Find her again, for my sake. You know what they'll do to her if you don't. If it comes to it, make sure you're the last person she sees. Promise me you'll make sure she's lucky at the end."

"I promise," he told her. "Lotter'll have a heart attack when he realizes what he let go."

Ji-ji looked very small as she climbed into the access shaft that led to the dome of the coop and began to crawl through it.

After she disappeared into the darkness, Lucky affixed the panel again. He leaned against it for a second, took a deep breath, and headed off to find Afarra one last time.

||||||||||||||

Amadeus Nelson stood at the coopmaster's podium, a.k.a. "the hutch," a.k.a. the Master's Controls. Everything boiled down to the first fifteen minutes of the battle. Tree had delivered the evidence to the control booth. Thank god Just Jellybean was thinking ahead. He should have made a copy of the video himself. He'd overplayed his hand. Hadn't done that in years. Problem was, as soon as the video started playing, all hell would break loose. Redipp's men would smash down the door to the control booth and cut off the power. With that in mind, he'd decided to leave the video until the fifteen minutes was almost up. He had to hold the coop till then, make sure they thought he was playing *their* game on *their* terms. He hoped Tree had gotten word to the flyers about their new routine, and he hoped that, for the ex-seeds among the fans and for others watching the battle all over the once-United States, it would mean something.

What the hell was Ji-ji planning to do? Flit around like some mad bird in the cage? They'd shoot her down in a second. To make matters worse, they couldn't coordinate. If he'd known she'd wind up in the Dream Coop (Zyla hadn't come through—it wasn't like her), he would've at least thought to give her one of three earpieces he'd given Tree. Told Tree to keep one for himself and give the others to Marcus and Tiro. He himself wouldn't be able to communicate with them cos he was mic'ed and monitored. But he could hear what they said to each other, and "speak" in code to his engineers via his coopmaster's console. Ji-ji was the wild card. Could be anywhere, do anything, screw the whole thing up. *Zyla,* he thought, *why didn't you get her to safety like you promised?* It was the only time he'd ever known Zyla to fall short.

If they somehow got out of this alive, he'd ask Zyla to try again, for real this time. The first time around, she'd married him out of generosity. (He hoped it was that and not pity.) She knew the noose was tightening around him and that the murders of Burke Gowler and Ezekiel Etcher could easily be pinned on him if the authorities figured out he had a major grudge against them both. It took years for the rights of former outcasts to be fully ratified in D.C. But if he was married to a fairskin Districter, he'd be entitled to due process and a public hearing. So he'd appealed to Zyla, asked if she'd be willing to marry him in secret. No need to publicize it unless the law came after him. Zyla had never asked him if he was guilty, but he'd told her the truth later, on the one night they slept together—that night in the No Region when it looked, like it did tonight, as though none of them would make it out alive. Afterward, she said if she ever got permanently attached to any man in the world it would be him. It had shocked him how much that night had affected him—how he kept coming back to it, as if their story wasn't over. And now he knew why.

Tonight, as the small woman, fearless as a snarlcat, sat there in the car, ready to drive the Existential and Afarra to safety, he realized he loved Zyla, had always loved her. And she loved him too, he could tell. Maybe not in the way he loved her. He knew she preferred women, and he knew she'd probably say no if he asked her again to be with him. But if they survived, he planned to ask her. And if she said no, he would settle for friendship and try to be the best friend she ever had.

What the hell was he doing? He'd spent the past three minutes daydreaming while all around him tier upon tier of menace rained down in the thirty-thousand-seat arena. Spectators stomped their feet in a countdown from twelve to one to mark the entrance of the twelve black-robed judges, who sat outside the cage at ring level at a special table in front of the spectator section. Usually, after they were seated, they removed their hoods so you could see their faces. Not tonight. To boos from Districters and former seeds, the Jury of Their Tears, as they were colloquially known, chose not to reveal their faces.

From his raised platform in the center ring, I'm-a-God watched them all. He was dressed in his customary top hat and tails but he'd substituted his multicolored sequined waistcoat and his rainbowed top hat with a demure black waistcoat and a top hat and black tailcoat so black they looked purple under the lights. The crew of twelve engineers, all of whom had been with him for years, sat ready in the control booth. His crew was scheduled to be swapped out when he was, after the first fifteen minutes. No reason had been given for what Redipp called "the switcheroo." Amadeus had wanted to stuff Redipp's smirk down his throat when he'd said that.

A half hour ago, Redipp had informed him what was at stake if he didn't comply with the new rules of the game. "Play your cards right, and you can retire in comfort. You've been flying the coop for a long time, Amadeus. You must be tired." Redipp was right. Like most Black men and even more Black women he knew, he was very tired.

Inside the gigantic flight cage, the floor of the center ring would soon be the most dangerous place in the coop. When the center ring's jaws opened and the mutants rose, his Dreamfleet battlers would be sitting ducks. But first things first. He had fifteen minutes to prevent catastrophe. Through his earpiece, he heard Marcus tell the engineers they'd been frisked before they entered the coop; the team from Armistice hadn't. Flyers were meant to use regulation weapons in the arena—blunt-edged swords, wooden staffs, and the like. It was obvious some of the Armistice players had brought their own weapons. Amadeus turned his mic from "open" to "Redipp" and demanded to know why the team from Armistice weren't being searched. Redipp's sleazy voice came back. The transgression was brazen: "We found weapons on some of the fleeters. The Armistice battlers decided to take precautions. Keep off this channel. I need to keep it clear for emergencies."

A man's nasal whine echoed through the arena. The announcement came from someone he'd never heard before, one of Redipp's lackeys, for sure. Redipp had warned him they'd be rerouting some of the comm up to the VIP box, where Redipp sat with Mayor Adolphus Yardley, a handful of the most reactionary Dreamfleet owners, and other VIP guests. "Tonight," the announcer said, "we welcome you to the Dream Coop for the Battle of the Century." He ran quickly through the roster of flyers. As each of them appeared on the giant screens dotted around the arena, shouts of approval rose up from the fans. The Dreamfleet team was introduced first. The flyers entered through Dreamblast Corridor to the frenzied beat of drums. The loudest cheers were reserved for Mudmudoom the Quadroon, Laughing Tree the Giant, Georgie-Porge the Forge, Philosopher Phil (Marcus would hate that), X-Clamation, Re-Router, and Tiro the Pterodactyl. When Tiro's face appeared on the big screens, Dreamfleet fans chanted, "*DRE-GU-LAH-MO!*" Tiro's face was taken down hastily to a chorus of boos from aggrieved fans.

The deafening roars for the team from Armistice told Amadeus the Dreamfleet fans were badly outnumbered. The adversary's team included Sledgehammer Sid, Manfred the Mighty Mouse, A Part I'd Rather Be, and the White Night. The huge men appeared on the screen stroking their beards like bad actors in a horror movie. The Dreamfleet had been matched up against

Armistice before, but they'd never seen most of these flyer-battlers. Their gargantuan size made almost all of them, apart from Manfred, nearly as impressive in size and strength as Laughing Tree. Obviously, the Hell's Yells hadn't come here to fly; they'd come here to battle. They would avoid the equipment. Not only had it been tampered with, they weren't agile enough to cope with the curveballs the high-tech equipment would throw at them. They'd stick to static platform battles, for the most part, in the cage's lower tiers. Tonight, the façade of the game would be ripped off.

A final drumroll. Nasal Whine came on again: "Mayor Yardley would like to welcome a distinguished guest to the Dream Coop tonight, the champion of law and order, the wise counselor and friend to the city, who has reached out in friendship and forged new alliances that will last far into the future. Districters and steader guests, I ask you to put your hands together for Grand Inquisitor Fightgood Worthy!"

The steaders rose on cue. They stomped their feet and screamed up at the West Wing entrance to the wing commander's VIP box as Worthy entered with his entourage. The inquisitor's face was thrown up on the screen. In his bright red robes and magnificent chain of office, he stepped forward onto the balcony. Worthy moved to the front of the balcony with Yardley. They smiled down at the steaders and waved like kings. The uneasy silence from local fans was mirrored by some of the reactions in neighboring boxes. Some guests got up and left. Among them, Amadeus spotted Corcoran, whose face turned almost as red as Worthy's robe.

Amadeus didn't recognize all of those who'd entered with the inquisitor, but he did notice the man in an olive robe who stood slightly behind him and to his right. When his face was shown on the screen, Amadeus knew he'd identified him correctly as Arundale Lotter. The coopmaster wondered if Ji-ji could see her father-man. After all the terrible things he'd surely done to her, how strange it must be for her if she could. Amadeus was glad his daughter looked nothing like him. The ingrained cruelty in his chiseled face and its mannequin-like absence of expression were chilling.

The Dream Master had been told three things just before he'd stepped into the cage. First, the safety net would be down tonight. Second, the team of twenty-four flyer-battlers would remain in the cage throughout; there would be no subs. He knew what that meant. As the team tired, they would be picked off one by one. Third, there were snipers positioned all around the coop. If he did "anything untoward," as Redipp put it, he would be "taken out." Amadeus understood the ominous nature of the threat. "If you take me out," he'd told Redipp, "fans will riot." "If so," Redipp had countered, "we'll need to institute law and order. Shame if fans got injured or killed in the fracas."

The Dream Master looked around at the equipment. If (when?) Redipp opened the floor up and the ants invaded the cage, the flyers mustn't be on the cage floor. Their safest bet was to stay on the upper levels, or at least stay within arm's length of one of the dozen hope-ropes. The Jim Crow's Nest was the refuge of last resort. The Armistice team wouldn't want to battle in the highest piece of equipment in the coop, but it could be a trap if the fleet sought refuge there, especially if Redipp's men had tampered with it, or if they'd seized the controls.

Redipp had given him fifteen minutes for one main reason: to fulfill the terms of the sponsorship agreements. The sponsors, particularly those in the SuperStates, specified that Amadeus Nelson fly the coop for at least that long. Fans loved him. If Redipp swapped him out too early and inserted himself into the mix, it would violate the terms of the agreements. No one paid to watch Drayborn Redipp conduct the coop—like paying to watch a drain unclog. As one sportscaster wrote in the *Independent* after Redipp took over during one of the practices, "As soon as I'm-a-God handed the baton to Drayborn Redipp, magic flew out of the coop." Redipp had seethed about the critique for weeks. Funny thing was, in spite of the unprecedented success he enjoyed, Amadeus always felt there was something big he still had to do, as if being the first outcast to conduct a major coop wasn't big enough. He'd been reminded of the fact that he needed to do more after he'd seen Ji-ji's back. Man Cryday had told him he'd understand why she'd asked him to coach the girl after he saw what had taken root there. As usual, the Gardener of Tears was right. If he survived tonight, he'd find another calling. Maybe Zyla and he could do something together. . . .

The Dream Master didn't fool himself. Odds weren't in his favor that he'd make it. He'd put it at ten-to-one, tops. Yet it didn't make him sad, didn't frighten him either. He had one more story to tell. The one he'd always wanted to tell in the Dream Coop. And he had a flight to witness. A Toteppi saying came to him: "Dreams are promises your imagination makes to itself." Tonight, in a coop where some fans yearned for the dream to continue, and most fans wanted to exterminate it, he'd been given one final chance to master the dream.

He switched his mic to "arena" and spoke to the crowd.

J i-j sat hunched over in the sloping entry shaft to the fly cage. Something primal had risen up inside her when Lotter ordered Zyla's execution. He'd done it on a whim, as if her life had no worth to speak of. He'd disposed of Zyla like a paper cup. He would probably never think of her again. Ji-ji had no illusions. Her wings were unreliable at best. She had to make whatever time she had left count for something. In her perch up above the seating area known as the gods, she could take in the entire coop. The shaft made the dome accessible to maintenance workers. She was grateful for the ladderlike struts inside it. She braced herself against them so she didn't tumble into the cage.

Two stories or more below her, the high welkin, the metal platform that enabled flyers to get within thirty feet of the Jim Crow's Nest, hugged the cage's circumference. Due to the fact that the Dream Coop didn't have a walkway connecting the nest to the rest of the cage, flyers usually climbed to the high welkin and swung to the nest on a hope-rope.

She resolved to fly for her murdered teacher, who'd taught her how to escape the planting by seeking refuge inside books. She would fly for the mother who'd taught her it was never too late to find courage. She would fly for Cloths and Muleseeds, Commonseeds and Tribalseeds raised in captivity on plantings. She would fly for the heroic "Tainted," the courageous "Deviants," and the persecuted everywhere. She would fly for the lynched boy in mule ears she'd been unable to save in The Margins, and for the others who'd been lynched by Bounty Boys, picked by pickers, or sold like chattel. Tonight, in the Disunited States, she would fly for all mutants and all caged creatures who yearned to be Free.

She remembered her teacher's words as Zyla read from the play she loved that had touched Ji-ji so deeply she'd had to lay her head down on the wooden desk so no one would see how affected she was. *"We are such stuff / As dreams are made on,"* Zyla had told them. Ji-ji believed her.

"I will never forget you, Zyla," she murmured. "Help me become the stuff of dreams."

||||||||||||||

Ji-ji's clarity of mind reflected her intensity of purpose. In the Dream Coop's variegated light, which ranged from night-dark to multicolored day, courtesy of the lighting engineers in the control booth, she saw the cage in piercing detail. On the twelve huge screens that lined the arena, she saw a close-up of Tiro's face as he stood with Marcus on the donut, the only midlevel platform that ran round the entire circumference of the cage. She saw Laughing Tree, side by side with Mudmudoom the Quadroon, on one of the rotating King-spins. She spied Ben, who'd found a way to enter one of the cage's upper levels. She saw him slip into a glittering X Box and prayed that it hadn't been tampered with. Ben-in-the-Box would be the Easter egg they didn't see coming. "Don't take too many chances, Ben," she whispered. He had to live for the sake of Germaine, who had already lost her best friend tonight.

To exultant cheers from the home crowd and jeers from the visitors, X-Clamation stalked into the coop, resplendent in his ankle-length, feathered bird-of-paradise cape, his dark skin shining like Christmas. Re-Router strode beside him in a train of glittering sequins, prompting the women among the crowd of thirty thousand to rise as one and perform a call-and-response: "*Rout out the Louts, Re-Router!*" women on the north side of the arena cried; female fans on the south side responded with, "*Reign supreme in the Dream, Ree!*"

Ji-ji saw Orlie, a reservist, rush in late, a few seconds before the Chief Justice of the Jury of Judges stood and brought down his gavel to signal that scoring would begin. Orlie joined Georgie-Porge on the raft of Douglass Pipes that hung by four thick cables at one end of the cage. They'd chosen a good spot. The Pipes and could be "played"—raised and lowered—to give them access to multiple levels of the cage. She hadn't expected the two feuding flyers to hug each other; she rejoiced when she saw it. Though not a strong battler, Orlie was as agile as any of them and small enough to get into the countless nooks and crannies inside the cage.

If Ji-ji were to drop a plumb line from the shaft it would land in the Jim Crow's Nest. Drop a hope-rope from the underside of the Jim Crow and eventually, way down in the well of the coop, it would land in the center of the cage's center ring, a stone's throw from the Dream Master's platform. She wished the Dream Master would look up and see her way above him, but she was in shadow. He would never see her even if he looked up at the dome. Amadeus Nelson was the most vulnerable person in the coop, with a spotlight trained on him at all times. He would have to sprint halfway across the enormous cage to take cover.

She pulled off her shirt. Heat rose in the coop like it did everywhere, and she'd begun to sweat. She must've left her cape behind in the room where Zyla . . . *Don't think about that.* She wished she knew more about the Dreamfleet's plan of attack. She'd have to play it by ear. She had no idea if Tree had got the evidence to the control box, and no idea when (or if) they would be able to run it.

The announcer—a man with a whiny voice—came on to introduce a special guest. Ji-ji scooted forward to get a view of the entire cage and the massive screens. Worthy and Lotter appeared in Wing Box 1, the VIP balcony to her left, midway up the arena—the balcony Afarra had begged to sit in when they'd snuck in to watch Tiro and Marcus. The banner below the balcony that featured D.C.'s seal had been replaced by a banner divided in half: on the left, the familiar Justitia Omnibus seal of D.C.; on the right, the Territorial seal—a steader straddling a planting, an ear of corn in one hand and a rifle in the other. The black and gold colors of the Dreamfleet were featured on the D.C. side; the red and white colors of Armistice's Hell's Yells on the other. Standing behind bulletproof glass, Lotter looked as haughty as ever. His manner told her he didn't give a damn that Vanguard Casper, the ignorant brute who'd served him as loyally as a search hound for decades, had just been shot dead. She could tell from the way the Grand Inquisitor inclined his head to confer with Lotter they were close. Steaders chanted, *"The Twelfth! The Twelfth! The Twelfth!"* Worthy encouraged the chant, taking it up himself and clapping in an awkward, unrhythmic way, as if he'd watched someone clap but never attempted it himself. *Worthy manufactured this adulation,* Ji-ji thought. *The cult following, the knockoff aftershave.*

She turned her attention to the cage again. Usually, the flyer-battlers selected weapons from an approved cache. Not this time. Weapons had been stuffed into their hands as soon as they entered the cage. Looked like lousy weapons too. Their long staffs were short, their clubs looked too light to be useful, and their swords—always blunt so no one would be sliced unintentionally—looked hopelessly warped and rusty. The contrast between what they were given and what the Hell's Yells received drew virulent protests from Dreamfleet fans. Ji-ji was alarmed to see that many members of the Armistice team had brought their own weapons. Complaints from fleet fans to the Jury of Judges went unheeded. She'd never seen the judges remain masked before. They sat at the Judges' Bench in their black hoods like a row of executioners.

To Ji-ji's dismay, none of the Dreamfleet wore safety harnesses, and they were several flyers short. More disturbingly, the subbing benches sat empty. Not a single flyer-battler for either side.

Then she spotted something worse—something she should have noticed immediately. There was no net! There was *always* a net! Didn't they know the Armistice flyers could be killed if . . . The truth smacked her in the face. The Armistice battlers had no intention of flying the coop, which was why all of them were harnessed to the hilt. No somersaults off trampolines or leaps onto the expanding and contracting Ellison Wheel. They would not be swinging on the high trapezes or balancing on Lincoln Logs. The huge brawny men weren't artists, they were assassins.

Something winked on the other side of the dome. Ji-ji leaned forward and peered across the expanse. There, in another one of the access shafts in the dome, a figure dressed in black lay on his stomach. A *sniper*! The light bouncing off his scope caught her eye. It hit her how close she'd come to choosing the wrong shaft. Even now, she could be joined by a sharpshooter. She looked around the dome and spotted three other snipers—two in maintenance shafts, one behind a steel beam. Looked like every one of them had their weapons trained onto the parts of the cage where the fleet's flyer-battlers waited to perform.

The Dream Master gave his opening spiel. Afterward, Ji-ji felt horribly disappointed. In a tone so obsequious he received applause from steaders, Amadeus praised Redipp and the owners of the fleet. His ass-licking elicited a rumble of discontent from local fans who, though they clearly hadn't realized the danger the flyers and they themselves were in, could see this battle was rigged. Had I'm-a-God chickened out? Maybe Marcus had been right about him all along?

The Dream Coop Orchestra readied itself to play. A singer (a generously-sized African American with a queenly hairstyle that reminded Ji-ji of Tulip's) rose to sing the D.C. Independence Anthem, an uninspiring song full of clichés. To the shock of the crowd, after the first bar she abandoned it, as did the coop's multiracial orchestra. She sang the Freedom Anthem instead.

Spectators sympathetic to the cause were too stunned to join in at first. Gradually, however, one by one, they stood with the hair-crowned singer and sang. To cries of "*Shame!*" from steaders and cries of encouragement from the locals, a huge chorus of voices rose inside the arena:

> *No more the seed, no more the plow*
> *Seeds are the victors now!*
> *Hear the wind whisper*
> *the dream's holy name*
> *"Freedom," it whispers, again and again.*

Before they got to the next verse, the music stopped abruptly. The conductor and singer were hauled off. Amadeus Nelson had not joined in with the singing.

Neither Redipp's patrollers nor the battlers from Armistice knew what to do next. If they reacted too aggressively at this stage, their spectacle of violence might not occur. They didn't seem eager to blow things up at the beginning of the broadcast. The tactic was all too familiar. Like cropmasters on hundreds of plantings throughout the Territories, they wanted violence to function like a fireworks display and be spectacular enough to extinguish opposition.

Another conductor, a very small, very pale White man in a very large, ill-fitting tuxedo which they'd obviously ripped from the previous conductor's back, was led to the podium. The man appeared on the twelve jumbo screens, a look of abject terror on his face. He tapped his baton on the music stand and looked over at the Dream Master for his cue. Occasionally, rather than begin with a series of dueling maneuvers that allowed each team to demonstrate their prowess, another "set piece" opened the show. Such was the case this time. The Dream Master nodded to the orchestra, who played a few bars of insipid music.

"*Long ago,*" the Dream Master began, in a voice smooth and dark, "*before we kept time with Time, there was One Being in the world.*"

Laughing Tree, who'd been standing on the edge of the middle platform, grabbed a hope-rope and swung himself onto a center perch. He stood there alone, surveying the coop. The Dream Master was telling the First Story. A Toteppi story. The story Uncle Dreg had told her and Tiro as they'd gazed at the ancient story-cloths all those years ago. The same story Man Cryday had told her when she'd sought refuge in Dimmers Wood. Would Redipp and the steaders know it was Toteppi? Maybe not. But everyone would know a story like this would be classified as heretical in the Territories, where genesis stories not from Genesis were banned. Ji-ji felt the tension rise in the arena. Some of the former seeds recognized the words. A few jumped up from their seats to recite them with I'm-a-God. The story was a masterstroke. In a Liberty Independent like D.C., it couldn't be classified as treasonous, yet everyone in the arena sensed its artful defiance. The guests in the VIP box conferred madly with each other; the Armistice team shuffled uneasily on the staging platforms as the Dream Master continued his tale.

"*The One Being was lonely beyond lonely. It therefore made of Itself Two.*"

Tiro and Marcus grabbed trapezes and swung from one side of the coop to the other. Then they began to perform. A series of daring moves on the 'Bama's Drama trampolines, the King-spins and Douglass Pipes, the Ali Stingers, Baldwin Beams, Owens Jumps, and Biles Trials. They steered clear of the Ellison Wheel, but they used the much smaller Wheatley Wheel to full advantage. Tree must have told them which equipment had been tampered with and which hadn't. A trick they did on DuBois Toys (a projection booth that made them look like two pairs of twins) so confused a pair of Armistice battlers that they attacked the projections and wound up languishing in pain on their harnesses. The Dreamfleet fans went wild. Ji-ji whooped in triumph. She scooted back inside her shaft as a bullet whizzed past her ear and pinged off the dome! She'd given herself away. She had to fly, *now*!

She was about to launch herself from the shaft when she looked over and saw another person in black grab hold of the sniper's head in the shaft across from hers. A second later, the sniper lay still. The replacement pushed the man over to one side of the shaft, settled on his belly, and aimed his rifle on the team from Armistice. She thought she saw him nod at her. At least they had one sniper on their side. Ji-ji, her heart hammering in her chest, scooted closer to the front of the shaft again. She reminded herself to keep quiet from now on.

She breathed a sigh of relief when Tiro and Marcus finished their routine. After the Jury of Their Tears awarded them a pitiful handful of points, all semblance of fairness was jettisoned.

Ji-ji thought she might have figured out the Dream Master's strategy. It wasn't about scoring points; it was about winning over fans in the SuperStates and the Unaligned Territories, the Liberty Independents, the Madlands, and even a few fans around the world who would probably be watching. The more appealing Tiro and Marcus were, the harder it would be to kill them in cold blood. Hadn't Tiro also told her that Amadeus had the "sweet fifteen" all to himself— the first fifteen minutes of the game? It was in the Dream Master's contract that no one could substitute for him before then.

The Dream Master's voice again: "*The breaking of the One was terrible. A rupture so powerful we find echoes of it now when the earth erupts or shakes, and when the sky rumbles across our heads like a herd of buffalo.*"

Spectators shrieked as the arena plunged into darkness! Thunder shook the roof and lightning blazed across the dome! The sound came from speakers so close to Ji-ji's ears she screamed. Luckily, the storm was too loud for anyone to hear her this time.

Under the cover of darkness, Mudmudoom, Orlie, and Georgie-Porge must have crept up to three of the Armistice battlers who stood on a lower ring, jeering with the rest. As the lights came up, they engaged them with their wooden battle staffs. Mudmudoom knocked his opponent out in seconds; Georgie-Porge shoved his man off the platform, then rushed to help Orlie, who dodged the knife thrusts of a battler twice his size. Georgie came up behind the Armistice battler and smacked him so hard with his staff that the man toppled from the platform to join the other Yellers who dangled helplessly from their harnesses. "*Out! Out!*" the Dreamfleet fans yelled. The Jury of Judges had no choice but to disqualify the vanquished battlers, who were winched down to safety. To the cheers of local fans, the three knockouts appeared on the scoreboard.

I'm-a-God's voice rang out again: "*But because It was Two instead of One It was less lonely than before, though there were still times when Two yearned for more. So They made a Third—like Them, only smaller.*"

Re-Router, X-Clamation, and Ben leapt from X Boxes onto two battlers. Like the spectators, the Hell's Yells had no idea they were hiding in there. X bested his opponent in seconds. Ji-ji looked over at Ben and Re-Router, who'd managed to grab her opponent's sword and was beating him with it. The other Armistice battlers, terrified of the equipment, refused to come to his aid. The big man clutched his head and fell from the platform. Re-Router held up the sword, which glinted in the light. She yelled to the crowd as her triumphant face was projected onto the screens.

"This was *his* weapon, not mine! A little nick and he thinks he's *dying!*" Thousands of Dreamfleet fans roared their approval. "They're cheating! All of them! They've come here armed with their own weapons. Why? Because they're scared of us! Won't come down off the platforms! Too chicken to fly! *Cowards!*"

This challenge from a female would force some of the Armistice battlers to respond. The Dream Master was playing the coop all right, and so were his flyers.

Amadeus had more to share with them: "*After many ages, there were countless others, each smaller than before, until tribes resided all over the world. The Earth tribe grew arms and legs and walked on land; the Fish tribe grew gills to breathe in the water; and the Bird tribe grew wings and took to the air.*"

All at once, to evocative strains from the orchestra, in a flock of black and gold, the Dreamfleet flyers took to the air. Some leapt onto zip lines and flew across the cage, pumping their legs back and forth as they "ran"; some leapt onto King-spins, Lincoln Logs, and trampolines in the well of the coop, lit in such a way that it looked as though they were underwater; and some, including Tiro, Marcus, X-Clamation, and Re-Router, climbed to the Sojourner's Sill and Parks Perches and performed on the high trapezes. Their somersaults brought fans to their feet. No battles, just beauty. In spite of the obvious disapproval of the new conductor, the Dream Coop Orchestra played their hearts out. They didn't need a conductor; they knew what was coming next. The music changed, shifted to something sinister.

"*But the tribes tethered to the earth were sick with envy. For why should some rise while others were unable to do so?*"

Semidarkness descended. The home team knew the coop, the visitors didn't. In the dim light, the Dreamfleet attacked. Armistice battlers rushed around in confusion.

The Dream Master kept speaking: "*Their chief was a skinny man with fat ambitions.*"

A spotlight aimed at the Wing Box ferreted out Worthy's face. The Dream-fleet fans roared with laughter. The lights dimmed further.

"*The chief ordered his warriors to make war on the Bird tribe. The slaughter was immense. Such wailing! Such purple tears!*"

The arena was plunged into pitch-darkness as the twelve screens lit up around the arena.

And there they were: the victims Ji-ji saw in Murder Mouth.

The video elicited horrified gasps from the spectators—images of experimentation so disturbing that fans shrieked when they saw them. People wept openly when the mother appeared with the mutilated child in the cage.

The orchestra took over. One horrific image after another lit up all twelve screens. Violins screeched, cellos wailed, and drums beat out a torturous rhythm.

A voice rang out, "*It's the Twelfth's planting!*"

As if surprised by the outburst, Amadeus Nelson scanned the cage for the disembodied voice that came from speakers all over the coop.

"*It's Planting 437! See the seeds Cropmaster Lotter has sown!*"

Steaders bellowed at the Dream Master to shut his mouth, assuming the voice belonged to him. Amadeus raised his hands in denial. "Noble guests, good people of the District, and visitors," he said. "Someone has breached the system. The unauthorized broadcast will cease momentarily."

A SWAT team must have been dispatched to the control booth. Ji-ji heard them bang on the door and demand entry. Mayor Yardley stumbled forward onto the Wing Box balcony. Sweating profusely, he wiped his brow with a white handkerchief. He glanced over his shoulder, looked back, cleared his throat, and spoke. "We've learned," he said, "that these disgusting images were doctored. We believe the system has been hacked by a . . . by foreigners. A foreign government . . . from another country. I and the D.C. Congress pledge to track down the perpetrators and bring them to justice."

Some of the steaders in the crowd stood up and pumped their fists at the screen and cried, "*Fake! Fake!*" Their outrage elicited laughter from locals because it looked as if they were condemning Yardley rather than the screen. Crestfallen, the mayor retreated into the box.

Undaunted, the Dream Master took up the story where he'd left off, as if the images were part of the same narrative: "*The chief's wives knew that without the birds there would be a great wound in the world. A few of the Bird tribe escaped up into the mountains, where the clipped ones took root and the chained ones dreamed of a New Breaking.*"

While the photos continued in their accusatory loop on the screens, Tiro appeared in the Jim Crow's Nest beneath her. "*Tiro!*" Ji-ji cried, forgetting to stay quiet. He didn't hear her. A spotlight shone onto the nest. Would he be picked off by snipers? No. Not yet.

The remaining Armistice battlers started to engage with the Dreamfleet. They moved all at once, weapons drawn. The special forces entered the control booth. Through the glass paneling, she saw them line up the engineers and march them out of the booth. Others quickly took their places.

Suddenly, above the nest, snow! A virtual blizzard! No snow anywhere else. It didn't deter Tiro, who leapt up, sure-footed, onto the rim of the nest a mere fifteen feet or so beneath where she crouched. Spectators cried out. There was no net beneath him and he was not wearing a harness.

The orchestra, ignoring their ineffectual conductor, faded into a decrescendo. Within seconds, the only instruments playing were a flute and an oboe, one instrument calling to the other to respond. Tiro, defiant, shouted the words Dregulahmo the Oziadhee had uttered on his Death Day. A declaration of war right there in the coop.

Tiro began on his own, but soon a swell of voices from seeds below joined in. "*Heads of midnight, heads of earthlight, heads of moonlight! Faith and Hope will nourish you, but only Love can dream you Free! My beautiful birds of paradise, you are destined to fly the coop and bring together the tribes of the world!*"

While the spotlight was on Tiro and eyes were turned toward the nest, Ji-ji looked down at the Dream Master's platform. He was gone! I'm-a-God was invisible, yet still his voice echoed through the coop. No longer trained on Tiro, the spotlight darted round the cage in search of him.

"*We are the Freedom Race,*" the Dream Master cried, "*a spontaneous, wingless flock of ripened need! In Totepp, to means 'bird,' and teppi means 'to remember.'*"

"*We remember!*" the former seeds roared.

This must be her cue! Ji-ji said a desperate prayer and flung herself out of the shaft.

Before she started falling, she already knew she was doomed. She tumbled through the dark, unable to unfurl. Her last thoughts before she surrendered to death were how Lotter would never see her for what she really was, and how much that pissed her off.

If Tiro hadn't looked up, he would have missed it. Missed *her*. Careening toward the nest uncontrollably, she would have bounced off the rim and tumbled to the center ring below. His flyer's reflexes saved her. He caught her flailing body as she struck the rim of the nest.

"*Jesus!*" he cried. He had her. He drew her down inside the nest. "What the hell are you doing, Ji? You almost *died!*"

"I'm flying," she cried. "Okay, not flying exactly. But that was the idea. The Freedom Race . . . a wingless flock of ripened—"

"You were wingless all right. *Jesus, Ji!*"

"There are snipers, Tiro. See? Up there."

He looked up to where she was pointing. It was too dark to see much. "That's all we need."

"But I think at least one of 'em is ours." She couldn't hold it in: "Tiro . . . Zyla's dead."

"What?" He pulled out an earpiece and shoved it into a pocket in his flight suit. "Goddam thing is screeching in my ear. Guess we've lost the comm for good." He hadn't heard her. Too much of a din in the coop. *Don't make me say it again,* Ji-ji thought.

She was forced to say it again: "Zyla's dead. Casper killed her. Lotter told him to do it."

"Oh Ji! Oh *shit!*" He pulled her toward him and embraced her. It was still snowing above them. The nest was filling up. They broke away and sat in the nest helplessly.

Ji-ji looked at the cables supporting the nest. No way to climb those. Even if you could, you'd wind up in the dead end of the dome. "How do you plan to get out of here?" she asked him.

"Hope-rope," he said. "Soon as we get the all clear, you climb up on my back. We'll ride down together." He peered over the side. "It's not that far to—" He broke off and dropped back inside the nest. "The bastards must've cut the rope!"

At that moment, the nest began to sway. It was almost imperceptible at first. But soon, the rocking became more pronounced, like a sailing ship on the ocean. They clung to the nest as it tilted first one way then the other. A scraping sound rose up from below. They both looked at each other.

"The *ants!*" they cried.

Far below, the ring slid open to reveal an oblong gash of darkness, what flyers called the Maw. A platform rose up from the pit beneath the center ring. They couldn't see the ants yet, but they could hear them roar. The Dream Master's voice came over the speaker system. "Look at them! Those cowards in the Wing Box! Fight for the District! *Fight for Freedom!*"

Ji-ji spotted him. The Dream Master was running up a Harriet's Stair, up a Jacob's Ladder.

The twelve screens went dead and then the lights came up. The arena was as bright as day. A moment later, it was plunged into semidarkness. One circuit blew, then another.

Somehow, Coopmaster Nelson's voice still echoed throughout the arena: *"And though there has not been a full-fledged Wingchild in so long that even our elders' elders' elders do not recall exactly what they look like, the story has not lost its power!"*

She'd been wrong. That other line wasn't her cue. *This* was. "That's me! My cue!"

"What the hell are you talking about, Ji? No way you're trying that stunt again." He grabbed her, wouldn't let go. "We just gotta hold on here. Hope this thing stops swinging."

"Tiro! It's okay! The nest won't hurt me!" She didn't know why she said that. But when she stood up, the nest came to rest as suddenly as it had begun to sway. A spotlight found her. The spectators looked up. To the roar of the crowd and the mutants, Ji-ji relaxed the muscles in her strange back. The steaders wouldn't kill her, not yet. They'd want their caged bird to fly for them.

No room in the nest anymore. Her sudden unfurling knocked Tiro to the floor. No time to apologize before she was rising and flapping, up and up and up to the dome of the Dream! The air held her like a hammock. The floor of the cage became the ocean, the top of the cage was sky, as if she were out over the waves in Turnabout. The spotlight stayed with her. Somehow, the camera followed her too. Her image was flung up onto the big screens. The Dreamfleet fans went wild.

She swooped down low to grab the rope, which lay coiled on the center ring floor beneath the nest. Before the mutants, all of them unchained, could attack, she plucked it up.

Pumping her wings, she flew up to the Jim Crow and handed one end to Tiro. "Tie it off in the nest!" she cried. She took the other end to the high welkin platform.

As if he knew this would be her plan, the Dream Master was waiting. He caught the other end of the rope and tied it off. Tiro gripped it in his hands, wrapped his legs securely around it, and began his dangerous journey over the chasm to where Amadeus stood.

Meanwhile, Ji-ji swooped over to the part of the cage that faced the Wing Box. As she tilted back into a vertical position, she felt each wing re-form itself into an *S* so she could hover like a hummingbird. She heard the sweet whir of them behind her, heard Zyla's soothing voice read Emily: "*A Route of Evanescence . . . A Rush of Cochineal.*" Lotter tore to the balcony with Worthy, Redipp, and the rest of the fools. "*Don't shoot!*" Worthy yelled. "Hold your fire! *Don't shoot!*"

She hovered in front of them, turned in a circle so they could see how glorious and strange she was. Worthy stood transfixed. Lotter reached out to touch her wings. He'd forgotten the bulletproof glass was there. His hand smashed up against it. He'd reached out with such force it looked as though he'd broken his fingers. He swore, then cradled his injured hand under his arm. He didn't take his eyes off her for a second.

Ji-ji, however, had seen enough. She swooped away and didn't look back.

The spectators who'd seen her on the jumbo screens and in the cage too, were ecstatic. The ex-seeds stood up with the Districters and cheered. She saw them from above.

The wizard's words came back to her: "*Heads of midnight, heads of earthlight, heads of moonlight!*" His voice joined with that of the Dream Master, who said: "*Stories are the wings of dreamers, and that is why some of the Passengers found their way back home to the tribe of lost birds whose songs filled their dreams.*"

She stopped in midair and hovered vertically again. She'd spotted something! She dived down to the center ring like a bird of prey as the entire arena plummeted back into darkness.

|||||||||||||||

Dip recognized Ji-ji. She jumped up and clapped her hands together. Her childish delight offended Sloppy. Why had she paid all that money to purchase an ignoramus? The minute before, Dip had been wailing like a seedling. Said the pictures were shocking and asked if they were genuine. Sloppy had snapped at her: "How the hell would I know?" Trouble was, Dip was right. The video and pictures *were* horrifying. Sloppy had seen photos of the mountain of bodies after the chemical attacks during the Sequel, and photos of victims in the Rad Region. These pictures and video, like those, made you want to kill someone. Worse still, this was her planting, hers and Dip's.

Chaff Man had seen some shit too. He'd said as much on the wizard's Death Day. Sloppy had tried to wheedle it out of him. Felt like she was getting somewhere, but then the ungrateful Cloth stole Circus, and she couldn't get the Chaff to focus on anything except that stupid dog.

The corpse mother in the cage with her dead . . . her dead what? Son? Daughter? Child? She didn't know what that was. The bodies with pieces missing; the bodies with pieces that looked like they'd been grafted on. . . . The pile of corpses in that lab, where it looked like they'd been gassed. . . . You almost forgot these were people. *Your* people.

Not that Sloppy was squeamish. Hell, she'd dug out a two-inch splinter from her foot, drained the pus from her own sores, had her wombling beaten out of her by Casper, to say nothing of what she'd witnessed him do to seeds for fun. But this changed how she saw everything. She felt unsteady, like someone in a rowboat during a storm.

In the rank-smelling, smoke-filled bar, excitement bubbled all around her. Some of the fairskin patrons jeered at the screen; some of the duskies (*We're in the minority,* she thought) cheered. Sloppy looked over in disgust at Dip, who was still jumping up and down like a loon. "She's *flying!*" Dip cried. "You see the snow? You see her grab that rope? How'd they do that?"

"Sit your ass down, you stupid idiot," Sloppy said.

The angry fairskin at the next table who'd insulted Sloppy earlier said, "It's a cheap trick. You can see the mechanics of it if you look close. It's, like, projectors and pulleys. Wings aren't purple and shimmery like that. Wings've got feathers. Those she's got are glass or plastic, I bet."

The Dream Master's voice sounded out again: "*Fans of Freedom, I give you, the Existential!*"

The man nodded smugly. "Got a fuckin ridiculous name too!"

Sloppy agreed: "Mule flies like a chicken. Always was a snotty bitch."

The fairskin turned to her. In his pudgy eyes, she was scum again. "Don't tell me you know that one too, dusky?" He laughed mockingly, took a slurp of beer, and turned to his buddy at the table. "I'm thinking of growing a beard, Vlad. We need a few more steader types round here. It's an invasion, if you ask me. Maulers and Papers clogging up the works. Who needs 'em?"

Sloppy was reaching for her knife when Dip caught hold of her wrist before the man caught on to the fact that he was about to have his throat slit.

"You'll miss it, Delilah!" Dip cried. "You'll miss the *good* part!" Dip stared into the eyes of the woman she loved and pleaded, "Don't miss the good part. We been waiting *so long* for this."

Sloppy snatched her hand away. "I can do whatever the fuck I want," she mumbled, though she no longer reached for the knife in her belt. "Bet she thinks she's the bee's knees now."

"Bet she'll be glad to see us," Dip said, while oohs, aahs, and denials accompanied Ji-ji's flight around the cage. "We should go find her. City's real big. Think we'll find her?"

"Oh, we'll find her all right. I guarantee it."

It happened when Ji-ji hovered like a hummingbird in front of the balcony and Lotter stepped out of the Wing Box to see it. Sloppy suddenly realized she could turn this in her favor. He'd smashed his fist up against the glass for all the world to see. Looked like he'd broken something. When she'd told Lotter about his freaky Mule, he'd only half believed her. Not anymore, not now he'd witnessed his seed's freakiness with his own eyes. He'd conclude that Delilah Moon was completely trustworthy, someone who could ingratiate herself back into the snooty mutant's good graces. Which meant he'd almost certainly want to utilize her services again. Sloppy picked up her glass of gin and put it to her lips. She watched Ji-ji perform her witchy tricks, which were guaranteed to get her pyred in the end.

Yet something squirmed like a maggot at the pit of Sloppy's stomach. She saw the dead mother with the pitiful seedling-thing in the cage. She used the edge of her sleeve to wipe her eyes and swipe mucus from the nose Casper had broken. "What you looking at?" Sloppy said.

"Nothing," Dip replied.

Sloppy hissed at her: "I ain't nothing. I'm *something*. . . . So are you. Don't you forget it."

Over the years, Sloppy had trained herself to be keenly aware of her surroundings, but living in a Liberty Independent had dulled her warning system. The savage energy of the men in the bar, who sympathized with the steaders' Found Cause and were always up for a little fun, struck her like a fist. She saw the men's shifty eyes swing over to where they and other duskies sat. The hostility grew as Existential Bitch flitted around the Dream Coop.

Sloppy eased her gutting knife out of its sheath. At the moment when she was trying to decide how she could get Dip to safety, the lights in the bar went out. Sloppy knew how to take advantage of an unexpected turn of events—a deus ex fuckin machina. That blond bitch Zyla Clobershay had told them all about that. She grabbed hold of Dip and fled out into the night.

Outside, it was dark as pitch. Power out all over the city, looked like.

Sloppy pulled out a flashlight from her pants pocket and dragged Dip down the nearest alley. She switched off the flashlight, took Dip's persecuted face in her hands, and kissed her long and hard and meaningfully. "I'm so goddam glad to see you, Dipthong Spareseed, you ugly bitch," she said, more grateful than she'd ever been in her life. "C'mon, hon. Let's you an' me head home."

||||||||||||||||

On account of the fact that she broke her promise, the tribe of the Dimmer-dead have come for her. Afarra, on the floor of the arena near one of the entrances to the cage, tries to yell up at Ji-ji to let her know what's going on and why the nest is tilting. Ji-ji can't hear her. Too much *kerfuffle*. (Whose word is that? Not her word, that's for sure.) She sees the Dimmers, mad as hell, swarm onto the nest where it's snowing even though it's fall not winter. The cause is her. She is the One. The Dimmer-dead hang there like right-side-up bats, smoky-gray and throbbing. She can tell they are not liking snow cos they are cold enough already. The agile ones leap from one side of the nest to the other so it tilts and swings, yet Dimmers don't weigh a thing. *Except if they want to,* a voice says. Whose? The Dimmers who lack limbs hang on for mere life.

Elly is in the nest! Afarra screams up, "*GET OUT!*" As usual, everyone is not hearing her.

It wasn't all her fault. The pictures on the screen summoned them too. The tribe of Dimmer-dead heard the Dream Master's story and began to congregate after he said "*a spontaneous, wingless flock of ripened need.*" She knows why too. Spontaneous is *how* they are. Wingless is *what* they are. Ripened is *who* they are. Need is *why* they are.

They are Rememberers too. That is all Dimmers can do. Remember *overandover* and be mad about it. (Like she will remember Zyla *overandover*.) She wonders if Vanguard Casper-Dim is among them. She peers up at the nest to see if he's there. She can't see him among the horde of Dimmers. She smells him though, all around her. Probably takes a while for the dead to *translate* themselves (the wizard's phrase) into Dimming. The Dream Master doesn't know the Dimmers are on the wrong team. He doesn't know that Dimmers are only being on their *own* side *always*.

She sees the boy in the donkey ears again, the ringleader who led them to the center ring and up to the nest. Afarra calls up to him. Maybe she can persuade him to come and attack her instead?

"Boy in the ears! Elly is in there! And Tiro too! Do not rock the boat! *Please!*"

The lynched boy looks down at her, his head lolling off to one side, his eyes twin balls of white, cartwheel fireworks. Without him leaping down from the nest, his eyes come closer. (*How?*) His eyes *spinspinspin*. He is madder than ever this time. He cannot forgive them. But he's attacking the wrong ones. She tries to tell him she's not up there in the nest anymore. "This is a different coop!" she cries. "I'm not *there* an' *then*! I'm *here* an' *now*!" He doesn't listen.

All those Weepings on the planting! All those Purple Tears! She is never hearing them when they are screaming. Why not? Murder was close by, eating.

The boy's eyes zip back up to the nest. All of him is on the rim again, swinging on it so he can un-nest the birds. "Stop, Dimmer-Boy! *Stop!*" Like the others, he doesn't listen.

Afarra saw all this *fallingfallingfalling* in her private eyes (and his Eyes too) for a long time. She tried to tell them the flyers are falling when she was here before. She tried to tell them at Monticello too. They didn't understand it will happen *here* and *now*. She needs to get the Dimmers' attention. *Havoc* (the wizard's word) in the Dream Coop means no one will see her.

She is close to one of the gates to the fly cage. She sees a patroller forget to lock it behind him. He runs off somewhere, weapon drawn. In the shadows, she opens it, steps inside, closes it again. She stands beneath the nest and calls up to them. They do not see her but the boy does. He spits at her like an angry snarlcat. "You promised to save us!" he shrieks without a sound.

And then she sees Elly the Secret. Unfurled. Ah! So beautiful! The tribe of Dimmers see Elly too. They stop their tilting business to look. Elly, mostly bird now, becomes the air. *Fly!Fly!*

Afarra has been waiting all their lives for this.

Too busy to see the mutants rise through the Dream Coop's Murder Mouth, Afarra doesn't know they've joined her. The Dimmers do. Afraid of mutants, they shriek like torment and vanish.

Elly swoops down. Picks up a white snake and drops one end in the nest. She flies the other end over to Amadeus-One. Tiro escapes on a lynch rope! The nest is empty now.

Afarra gazes upward. Sees Elly like a hover-cross in front of the balcony where Murderer Lotter stares at her. *Elly flies the coop! Elly flies the coop!*

At last Afarra stops tilting her head up and looks straight ahead. She sees the ants. Uncaged and unchained. When did that happen? The roar of ravenous mutants. Lights out! Afarra screams.

|||||||||||||

As soon as Tiro made it over from the nest to the high welkin, he and the Dream Master took cover behind a pair of wide metal struts. Tiro couldn't stop himself from swaying. The nest had been tilting so much before Ji unfurled, he knew it was over.

"Why the hell did it tilt like that?" Tiro demanded.

"Don't know," Amadeus replied. "Safety mechanisms should've kicked in. Perhaps the steaders tampered with it? I don't know." Tiro had never heard the Dream Master sound shaky before. Felt weird to hear it, like I'm-a-God was just a man.

Tiro leaned round the strut and peered over the edge to see what was going on. Ji was giving them a show. Christ, he wished he could see Lotter's face, but the angle was wrong. "The bastard killed her," Tiro said. "Lotter. He killed her. Ji told me."

Amadeus couldn't figure out what he meant. "What do you mean? She's flying."

"No, not Ji. Zyla. Ji told me just now. Said he had his overseer shoot her. Hey. You okay?"

Amadeus sank to the floor. Tiro didn't know what to do. Then he vaguely remembered something about him knowing Zyla from way back. Why did he blurt out that shit now?

"I'm sorry, man," he said. "I really am. Forgot you knew Zyla. You did, right?"

"Yes," the Dream Master said. "I knew her."

Tiro saw something down in the cage. The dim lighting made it difficult to say for sure, but then he made her out. Afarra on the floor of the cage with the mutants! *Jesus Christ!*

He moved away from his hiding place and tried to call over to Ji, let her know about Afarra. He'd forgotten about the swaying. A hand reached out in the nick of time as he was about to tumble over into the well of the coop.

"She's down there with the ants!" Tiro cried. "Afarra!"

Darkness! Tiro almost lost his balance again. Amadeus reached out again and steadied him.

"Ji can't fly in the dark!" Tiro cried.

"Redipp cut the power," Amadeus said, just as a shot rang out, followed by another.

Down below them the spectators panicked. A terrified wave of fans, Districters and former seeds, swarmed toward the exits, only to discover they were trapped.

Mayor Yardley stepped forward again onto the VIP balcony. On cue, a spotlight lit him up. Tiro searched frantically for Ji and Afarra, but the center ring was a swirl of shadows.

"The seeds are rioting!" Yardley announced. "Patrollers, get them under control!"

Like someone only half there, Amadeus said, "That's their cue. Patrollers and steaders both."

The lights inched up a little more, enough for snipers to take aim. More shots rang out. A volley this time, followed by another lie from Yardley: "The duskies are armed!"

Tiro saw them fall.

Georgie-Porge, exposed on the Sojourner's Sill, had rushed to Orlie's aid again. They were battling an unharnessed Armistice battler and winning. And just like that they weren't.

A bullet struck Orlie in the head, then another struck Georgie in the back. They fell there on the midlevel platform. The Armistice battler began to roll them off into the center ring when a bullet took him out. Foolishly, he'd removed his harness. He tumbled into the center ring below. The half-starved ants heard the thud and the frenzy began.

"Orlie . . . Georgie-Porge . . ." Tiro whispered, horrified.

A voice rang out again. Not Yardley's this time. In the shadows, Tiro managed to make out the crimson skullcap on top of the speaker's head. "Do *not* shoot the mutant girl!" Fightgood Worthy ordered. "Get her out of that cage and bring her to me, understand? Bring her to *me!*"

The Dream Master grabbed Tiro's arm again to steady him. "Stay close," he said. "Think you can make it down? Want me to carry you?"

"I can make it down. Think they're both dead? Georgie's pappy thought he hung the moon is the thing. Snelling's a Liberty Laborer. A fairskin. Saving up to buy Georgie's mam her Freedom. It's like they got shot too."

"Saving a friend's a good way to go," the Dream Master told him. "The best way. You're a mess, son. Let me know if I need to carry you."

Guided by the Dream Master, Tiro began to descend.

|||||||||||||||

More than a dozen men trained their guns on Lucky. One of them told him to drop his weapon. Without viable options, he obeyed. Coming to them from all over the coop, the screams of terrified fans as they pounded on exits. The roars of mutants mixed with fans' desperate cries. Gunshots reverberated through the building. If the smell of smoke was anything to go by, part of the coop was on fire. A huge explosion had rocked the Dream Coop a few minutes ago. Lucky had no idea what the result had been or where exactly the explosion had occurred. Some areas were flooded with tear gas. When the power went out and all hell broke loose, the steaders in the crowd began shooting indiscriminately. Desperate for a way out, fans who managed to escape the arena stampeded down corridors. Lucky managed to evade a cohort of steaders by hiding in a utility shaft, but now the only thing he wanted to do was get back inside the cage and find Ji-ji and Afarra. He was almost certain he'd seen Ji-ji swoop down toward Afarra just before the lights went out. But what the hell was Afarra doing in the cage in the first place?

He'd been pushed out of the arena when fans had overwhelmed patrollers at one of the locked doors and tumbled out into the corridor. Been trying to find a way back in ever since, but the emergency lighting in the vast perimeter corridor that encircled the coop turned it into a murky tunnel, and every door he tried was locked.

A small band of armed men came upon him in a tight hallway before Lucky had a chance to raise his weapon. He breathed a sigh of relief when he saw they were all Black or Brown. Must be Friends of Freedom, or Districters. Only problem, he didn't look to them like a friend. He tried the Friends' password. "*Alis volat propriis*," he said, passionately. Nothing doing.

"You a steader?" one of them said. The speaker sounded very young. "You got a beard."

"I'm no steader," Lucky insisted. "I'm a Friend of Freedom. Who are you?"

"Some folks call us one thing, some folks call us another," another said, annoyingly. Yes, they were all boys. Most looked to be no more than thirteen or fourteen.

"Let's shoot him and get on with it," another boy suggested.

"*No!*" Lucky cried. Maybe they were members of the group Marcus belonged to? He took a chance and said, "You're Invisible Men. We're on the same side.

I'm a friend of Charra's Liberty Raiders." Not completely accurate, but close enough. "You've got to help me rescue her."

"Rescue who?" one of the boys asked. Another said, "Who's Charra?"

"Ji-ji's sister. Jellybean. You know. The Existential. The girl who flew!"

"Didn't see no flying girl," the taller boy said. "We been out here patrolling the perimeter."

"Whitey's a fly-girl groupie!" one of the boys sneered. "Why you talking so fucked up?"

"Oh bloody hell!" Lucky said. "I'm Lucky Dyce, Friend of Freedom." Another white lie. "Your leader is Ralph or Ruffle or some such name. My friends are your Friends. They were at the raid on the 437th. If we don't get back in there and save her, we're toast."

"Think he's telling the truth?" one said.

"How the fuck should I know?" the other answered. "What you doing here?" he added.

"Fighting for Freedom," Lucky said. "What are you doing?"

"We answered the call."

"What call?"

"Don't tell him nothing, Dom. We don't know who this dickhead is."

Just then, they heard the sound of feet. Many feet. Steaders or patrollers. Must be.

"Someone's coming!" the boys' leader cried. "Take his gun, Dom." Dom snatched Lucky's gun from his hand. Lucky had no choice but to let him. "Everyone, take cover! Not you," he added, waving his gun at Lucky. "This'll be a test. If the fuckers shoot you, we'll know you're for real!"

"That will certainly be a comfort," Lucky told them.

"Sarcastic sonuvabitch," the tall boy said. "How 'bout we shoot you either way?"

Their weapons trained on his head and chest, the boys ordered him to stand in the middle of the hallway while they took cover in a nearby alcove. Lucky almost laughed out loud. If the Invisible Boys didn't kill him, the Visible Men rushing down the corridor would. Lucky had time for three last thoughts before he met his maker: he wished he'd shaved off his sodding beard and worn a mask; he wished he'd found Afarra—for her sake; and he wished he'd been able to save Zyla Clobershay.

The group tearing along in the dark pulled up a few feet before they reached him. *"No more the seed, no more the plow!"* a man said.

"Alis volat propriis!" Lucky declared.

"Is that you, Lucky?" Tiro's voice. *"Don't shoot!* He's Lucky Dyce. A friend!"

Two men rushed up. Tiro embraced Lucky.

"This is the Dream Master," Tiro said. "And these are the men and women who answered the call. Blew up the main doors."

"*I am myself! Nobody else!*" a boy cried, as he rushed out of the alcove. If Lucky hadn't stepped between them and the others, the Invisible boys would have gotten killed when they visibled themselves. Yells of greeting came back from a spattering of other men.

"What kind of idiotic password is that?" Lucky muttered.

"Sorry we nearly blew your head off," one of the boys said. "You look like the enemy."

"Only to morons," Lucky replied. "Now give me my bloody gun, you little shits." Begrudgingly, they handed it over.

"Did you send out the second call?" Tiro asked.

"Second call?" Lucky said.

"The call the people responded to. The beacon?"

Lucky had no idea what he meant, but there wasn't time to discuss it. He looked at the people behind them and what he saw made him believe that maybe, just maybe, humanity wasn't crap after all. Dozens—no, *hundreds* of Districters of all races, women and men, along with D.C. cops, Friends of Freedom, Papers, Maulers, and even a handful of nuns willing to fight and die for the city's independence—all of them had answered the call to arms. Though some had guns, others had knives or wooden staffs. He saw women armed with pepper spray and a girl of no more than ten with a slingshot. Tiro asked where he was headed. Lucky told him he was headed to the cage to find Ji-ji and Afarra. He thought they were still in there.

"Great," Tiro said. "S'where we're headed. You can come with us. We need all the help we can get."

Before he set off with a group of Friends, the Dream Master yelled out instructions to the others: "Don't forget, if we can hack into the controls, we'll use the hazers—the smoke machines—and fill the arena with smoke. Should disorient the ants and make it harder to pick you off." A second group set out to open up the exits to the arena. The third contingent, the one Lucky joined, headed for the cage.

They found an exit guarded by a handful of patrollers, who took off running as soon as they saw them coming. The group attempted to push their way inside the arena through the door. Hopeless. A tsunami of fans overwhelmed them. They were swept back and away from the entrance.

With a small group of fighters, Lucky and Tiro broke off from the rest and worked their way round the coop's circular corridor, found a hidden side exit, smashed it open and plunged inside.

The arena was even darker than the perimeter corridor. Snipers could be anywhere. Lucky warned against the use of flashlights. If they gave away their location, they would be picked off like flies. The small group felt their way forward as quietly as they could. They followed the roars and growls of the mutants through Dreamblast Corridor into the cage. In the cavernous coop, it was impossible to tell where the greatest danger came from.

"We're surrounded," Tiro said. "Ants everywhere! Keep your eyes peeled."

Lucky could hear the creatures roaming around in the cage. Smell them too. The sound of something big-jawed tearing into flesh.

"Think Ji escaped?" Lucky whispered. "Flew off somewhere with Afarra?"

"No, man," Tiro whispered back. "Don't think she could lift 'em both, an' she wouldn't leave Afarra in the cage alone, that's for sure."

"Think Lotter took her?"

"No. She'd kill herself first."

Yes, Lucky thought. *She would.*

With their guns drawn, ears peeled for an attack from cats and stripers, they crept down Dreamblast Corridor and entered the cage proper. At that moment, a single floodlight came up. Amadeus must have wrested control of the lights from Redipp. The sole floodlight only lit up a small part of the cage. Lucky was grateful that most of the cage, including where they were, remained in shadow.

"What the . . . ?" Lucky said, as he gazed ahead.

He thought it might be a trick of the light at first. It wasn't. Ji-ji and Afarra were partly submerged in a hole! A black hole . . . that moved! Only it wasn't a black hole. It was a creature! The hole-man squatted on a ledge about eight feet up from the floor of the center ring. Ji-ji clung to him on one side, Afarra on the other.

They were alive! If Lucky hadn't known how insane it would be to do it, he would have danced with joy. Tiro and he signaled to each other and the rest of the group to advance slowly.

The creature spotted them. He shoved the girls behind him, protectively. From what Lucky could tell, most of the cats and stripers were occupied. They feasted on the fallen. But a snarlcat and a striper hadn't given up. They leapt at the ledge. Each time they did so, the creature swiped at them with a staff he had in his huge hand.

Afarra saw the rescuers approach with their weapons drawn. She stood up and screamed at them. "Don't *kill* them! They are *starving!* Don't *hurt* them!"

She spoke to the ape-man then. Some funny, ridiculous language Lucky couldn't understand. It was full of clicks and clucks, lisps and what sounded to Lucky like yodels.

"She a witch?" one of the fighters asked him.

"No," Lucky replied. "She's a girl."

Lucky trained his weapon on the largest of the snarlcats. One shot would never kill it. He'd need three or four at least.

"Let go of the . . . the . . ." Lucky gave up finding a word. "Let go of your friend and walk towards us, okay?"

"Elly is hurting," Afarra said. "She is crashing onto the floor."

"I'm fine," Ji-ji said, though she sounded weak. "Couldn't judge distance. Lights went out."

"Muckmock is protecting us," Afarra said.

"Muckmock," Lucky said. "Is that . . ." He hesitated. For all he knew the ape-man was the only creature in D.C. who understood proper English. "Is that your friend's name?"

"Yeah," Afarra said. "It means Whole."

Makes sense, Lucky thought, thinking of holes.

One of the quick-thinking Friends in the group had found some food for the ants. She tossed it a few yards away. To Lucky's profound relief, the animals took the bait. He tried not to think about what exactly she'd tossed to them.

"Follow me," Tiro said, hurriedly. "I know the best way out."

"Muckmock comes with us," Afarra insisted.

Lucky whispered to Tiro: "I'll cover you. Shoot the ants if I have to." Afarra began to berate him. "How'd she hear me?" Lucky asked.

Smoke began to fill the coop. The cats and stripers became disoriented.

They hurried out of the cage in single file. Tiro snatched Ji-ji from Hole-Man and carried her, but Afarra wouldn't let go when Lucky tried to grab her, so he fell to the rear. Looked as though the ant was a hell of a lot scarier than he was, so odds were good she'd be safer with him anyway.

Afarra rattled off her ant-talk to the mutants already disoriented by the smoke. Lucky couldn't say if it was the smoke, Muckmock, Afarra's chatter, or simply the fact that the bodies in the cage provided them with sufficient food, but none of the ants attacked.

On the way out through the smoke, Lucky saw the shapes of mutilated seeds. They looked like the poor seeds on the Murder Mouth video. They mistook him for a steader and told him he would never be Free of them. He covered his ears. They weren't real.

Lucky ran behind Hole-Man while, all around him, smoke shrieked like ghosts.

|||||||||||||

By the time they reached the North Gate, along the Main Toll Road leading up to the Eastern SuperState, one thing was clear: the city had fallen. Parts of D.C. were engulfed in flames. Steaders marched through the streets draped in

Territorial flags. Residents cowered in homes and places of worship as a river of rage tore through their neighborhoods. The sound of gunshots and explosions ripped the night to shreds.

Mayor Yardley's voice on the radio announced the successful disruption of a coup coordinated by Papers, Maulers, and their sympathizers, who'd attempted to usurp the Dream Coop and assassinate visitors from the Territories. The audacity of the claim made it more credible. In the chaos that erupted in the coop, everyone would have different versions of what occurred.

In a convoy of trucks, and cars, and pedestrians fleeing the city, Ji-ji sat inside one of the armored vehicles the Friends had sent to pick her and others up. They were all refugees now. She and Afarra sat with Tiro, Lucky, and some of the others who'd fought alongside them. Afarra had wanted Muckmock to ride with them too. But Ben (who had survived, thank god) had convinced her to let Muckmock ride with some of the fighters Man Cryday sent up from Dimmers Wood to help the Friends. They would escort him safely to the tree witch, he said. The notion that he would be with Drol, the only other person who looked like him, sealed the deal for Afarra, especially after Lucky insisted that New Yorkers, being unreasonably fastidious, weren't big on mutants.

The Friends had set up a staging area for a retreat near one of the parking lots. They'd surrounded it with a cordon of armed guards. There, the Dream Master caught up with them.

"Thank you for coaching me," Ji-ji said, as he helped her into the back of the vehicle.

"Don't forget," he told her, "you have a duty to teach someone else to fly."

"You think there are others like me?" she asked him.

"I wouldn't be surprised, Existential," he said.

Laughing Tree climbed into the vehicle a minute before they drove off. They cheered when they saw him, but the mood shifted quickly when he described how he and Marcus had carried the corpses of Georgie-Porge and Orlie from the cage and brought them out safely so they wouldn't be tossed to the mutants. Ji-ji and Afarra, who hadn't known that the fly partners had been killed, were shocked to learn about it.

Everyone assumed both Tree and Marcus would ride with them, but Marcus declined. Said he planned to head south to Turnabout. When he hugged Ji-ji goodbye, he whispered, "We'll be waiting for you to join us, kid. You got a duty to honor your sister. Don't let the side down." She didn't have a chance to respond before he exited the vehicle.

On the way out of the city, Tree told them Amadeus was headed back into the Dream Coop to retrieve Zyla's body. "But they'll kill him," Ji-ji said. "Zyla wouldn't want that."

Zaini, who was riding with them too, and who was tending to the injuries
Ji-ji sustained, argued he did the right thing. "It's a gift to have a body to care
for at the end," she said. "You need something to hold on to, so you can say
goodbye." Zaini looked over at the son who'd survived. "You gave that gift to
me," she said to him. "You held on to Yatho and didn't let go."

Ji-ji wondered why it hadn't been obvious to her from the very beginning
that Zaini was the strongest of them all.

They readied themselves for a battle on the road that never materialized.
When they reached the North Gate, it had already been abandoned. The bodies
of patrollers lay in a sad pile near the open gate—two dozen corpses at least.
Ji-ji hoped that the Latin patroller who'd given them the orange at the South
Gate wasn't among them. They drove through the gates without incident.

On unofficial channels, they heard reports of battles breaking out all over
the city, stories of steader militiamen marching through the streets, and fire-
bombing residents' homes. They'd already laid waste to the Mall and Kingdom
Come. Buzzbuzz drones had dropped bombs on the tent city in the Dream Revival District. The Papers and Maulers who hadn't been carted off or killed
had scattered. Some said the Dreamer's statue had been smashed to pieces,
but Laughing Tree told them Districters were defending it. Mudmudoom, X-
Clamation, and Re-Router had gone to join the hundreds who had swarmed to
the Dreamer's defense.

"It was the story," Tiro said. "That was the first call to arms, the Toteppi
Origin Story. The old-timers and some of the Friends recognized it and flocked
to the coop. But it was the other call, the second one, that galvanized the rest
into action."

"What was the second one?" Ji-ji asked.

Tree answered her. "The beacon at the top of the coop. Amadeus says it was
on for twenty minutes before patrollers cottoned to it an' shot the lights out."

"What are you talking about?" Lucky asked.

While Zaini, who'd been waiting for them in the truck, made a sling for
Ji-ji's arm, Tiro explained that the beacon featured the Freedom Race logo, a
bird about to escape through the open door of its cage, and some other sign.
One of the fighters had mentioned what it was, but he couldn't remember what
he'd said. "When they were constructing the new coop," Tiro went on, "Districters mounted the beacon on the dome. The Dream Master asked ex-seeds
among the construction workers to put it there. The beacon has its own power
source."

"Did they turn it on from the control booth?" Tree asked.

"No," Tiro replied. "That's the strange thing. According to Amadeus, you gotta climb up past the gods to get to the beacon, then go up all these fire ladders on the outside of the dome to turn it on. Gotta be a real athlete to do it. Only a handful of people know where the controls are or how to activate it."

"Who did it then?" Lucky asked.

"It's a mystery," Tiro said. "Couldn't've been the Dream Master. He was in the cage."

"Think it was Ben or one of the flyers?" Lucky suggested.

"There," Zaini said to Ji-ji. "I've immobilized it. When we get to New York, we'll get a doctor to look at it. But it should be okay for now." Zaini gave Ji-ji killers to alleviate the pain.

"Guess we'll never know who it was then," Lucky said.

"Could've been Uncle Dreg," Tiro suggested.

Lucky looked at him. "Could be," Lucky said. "He probably had some time on his hands."

One of the passengers in the truck, a former Commonseed named Hayley, who'd thought to distract the cats and stripers by throwing them a bone in the coop, said she and her mam had responded when the beacon lit up the night sky. She hadn't known what it was, but her mother had identified it as an emergency signal. They'd arrived together but got separated. She was still back there in all that horror, Hayley said. "The other sign on the beacon was Sylvie," she added. "A flock of birds flew off her branches."

"Some of the birds are staying," Afarra said. "I see them do it."

Hayley shrugged. "If they stayed, I never saw it. Looked to me like they all flew off." Afarra looked very disappointed, so Hayley added, "But what do I know?"

Softly, so only Zaini and Ji-ji could hear him, Tiro, as if he only half believed it, said, "It was you, Mother! You were the one turned on the beacon."

Zaini addressed them in a voice just loud enough for the two of them to hear. "Uncle Dreg raised me. You think I don't have a few tricks up my sleeve? I'm done with waiting and weeping. No one will take a goddam thing from me anymore without a fight to the death."

Much later, when he thought Ji-ji was sleeping, Lucky said, "Lotter knows her secret now. Worthy too. She's not safe."

"She'll be safe in the Eastern SuperState," Tiro assured him. "Nowhere else like it in the Disunited States. They got all kinds of techno-wizardry there. All kinds of surveillance."

"Maybe," Lucky said. He didn't sound convinced.

Ji-ji attempted to force herself back to sleep. If she managed it, this was what she wanted to dream about: a small, fair-haired woman with hair like a boy and a book in her hand; a lonely holy man who fought off attackers with a big stick; and a mother—no, an army of warrior-mothers cradling their not-lost children.

Sleep came again. Inside its loamy furrows, she sowed another dream—not the same as the one she'd pictured for herself, but a good one nevertheless.

She flew through a cage's open mouth and ascended a mast of light. She glided over forests, mountains, deserts, and oceans. For a long time, she was afraid, till the roots on her back reminded her she was flying a way home.

In the seam of consolation between dreams and waking, she spotted her kith and kin in the distance. The Lost and Found were all there, eager to welcome her home. A tribe of birds nesting among the quilted stars.

ACKNOWLEDGMENTS

In the Acknowledgments for *The Freedom Race,* the first book in this series, I thanked the family members, friends, colleagues, and fellow writers who have supported and inspired me. They deserve my thanks again, as do my students, past and present, who remind me why teaching is a privilege.

With thanks, as always, to my agent, Jennifer Weltz, who has seen the Dreambird Chronicles trilogy from its inception to now, when it is nearing completion. To Jennifer and the staff at the Jean V. Naggar Literary Agency—your staunch advocacy gives me the time to write. How lucky I am to work with an agent and an agency I trust.

To Dr. Jen Gunnels, my editor at Tor, whose astute feedback I treasure—sincere thanks for helping me, a writer of literary fiction and poetry, to chart a course through this narrative, even though it doesn't play by the usual SFF conventions. Working with you has been one of the highlights of my writing career.

To those I've worked with at Tor/Macmillan, who have handled everything from publicity to copy editing, especially Saraciea Fennell, Rachel Taylor, Jamie Stafford-Hill, Oliver Dougherty, and Terry McGarry, I offer my sincere thanks. Thanks also to cover artist Eli Minaya, whose stunning work is again featured on the cover.

As always, my friends and colleagues at Virginia Tech have inspired me. Special thanks to Professors Erika Meitner, Carmen Giménez Smith, and Matthew Vollmer in Creative Writing, whose friendship and writing inspire my own. To Dr. Menah Pratt-Clarke, whose note arrived when I was most in need of it. Thank you for knowing what it would mean to me when you wrote: "scared to pick it up, scared to put it down . . . GIRL GIRL GIRL."

To the Wintergreen sister-writers, especially Joanne Gabbin of the Furious Flower Poetry Center, Opal Moore, Ethel Morgan Smith, Daryl Cumber Dance, Karla Holloway, Trudler Harris, Gena Chandler-Smith, DaMaris Hill and, of course, Nikki Giovanni and Virginia Fowler—thank you for welcoming me into this truly gifted group of women writers.

And to the four to whom this book is dedicated. My thanks to Paula Robinson, writer, interior designer, and fierce advocate for writing. The pivotal scenes in this book at D.C.'s Museum of African American History and Culture are partly inspired by the time I spent there with you and Michael. I see in you what I see in Afarra—a contagious, unquenchable delight in the world.

My thanks to my brother Tamba, whose eloquent comments nurtured me when I needed it the most. You are the inspiration for Ji-ji's quest for Bonbon, the brother she cherishes. Some of the conversations I've had with you and Gail about race, global politics, and biracial identity are reflected in this story.

My thanks to Joseph for being the child I dreamed about and somehow managed to wind up with. The love and respect I have for you is boundless. When you were about five years old, you turned to me and asked, out of the blue, "What is the meaning of life, Mama?" I wrote my first novel as a kind of lengthy response to your question. In my subsequent books, I realize I have addressed the same thorny issue. What I should have said in response is this: "You are the meaning of life, Joseph." And now, because I am more fortunate than I have a right to be, your beautiful son gives life its most cherished meaning too.

My thanks, most of all, to Larry, who has often stayed up into the wee hours so he can provide me with his first impressions of the latest chapter. In the process, he continually reminds me that the most important spell Middle Passengers, Civil Righters, and all those oppressed by injustice can invoke is encapsulated in a simple, necessary word: *Onward*.

Lucinda Roy, January 2022